Praise for Stieg Larsson's

THE GIRL WHO PLAYED WITH FIRE

"Lisbeth Salander could be the female Jason Bourne. . . . It's an intelligent, fascinating story that draws readers in, and keeps them turning the pages."　　　　—Associated Press

"Boasts an intricate, puzzlelike story line . . . even as it accelerates toward its startling and violent conclusion."
　　　　—Michiko Kakutani, *The New York Times*

"I couldn't put down *The Girl Who Played with Fire* and eagerly await book three. . . . You must find out what happens next."　　　　—Erica Marcus, *Newsday*

"Larsson has bottled lightning. . . . *The Girl Who Played with Fire* buzzes with ideas [and] fizzes with fury."
　　　　—*Los Angeles Times*

"A combustible new thriller. . . . Extremely well-written— Larsson's minimalist prose is frosted with Scandinavian cool. . . . Burns with blue-flame intensity. . . . Larsson keeps a tight rein on the bullet-train plot."　　　—*San Antonio Express-News*

"A dynamite thriller."　　　　　　　　　　　　—*Variety*

"Fantastic. . . . Like all the great stories of just avengers that populate literature, this trilogy is secretly comforting, making us think that maybe all is not lost in this imperfect and deceitful world of ours. . . . Welcome to the immortality of fiction, Lisbeth Salander!"   —Mario Vargas Llosa, *El País*

"Enthralling. . . . Confirms the impression left by *Dragon Tattoo*."   —*The Washington Post*

"Will likely confirm Larsson's position as the most successful crime novelist in the world."   —*Slate*

Stieg Larsson

THE GIRL WHO
PLAYED WITH FIRE

Stieg Larsson, who lived in Sweden, was the editor in chief of the magazine *Expo* and a leading expert on antidemocratic, right-wing extremist, and Nazi organizations. He died in 2004, shortly after delivering the manuscripts for *The Girl with the Dragon Tattoo*, *The Girl Who Played with Fire*, and *The Girl Who Kicked the Hornet's Nest*.

THE GIRL WHO PLAYED WITH FIRE

THE GIRL WHO PLAYED WITH FIRE

Stieg Larsson

Translated from the Swedish by Reg Keeland

VINTAGE CRIME/BLACK LIZARD
Vintage Books
A Division of Random House, Inc.
New York

THE GIRL WHO PLAYED WITH FIRE

PROLOGUE

She lay on her back fastened by leather straps to a narrow bed with a steel frame. The harness was tight across her rib cage. Her hands were manacled to the sides of the bed.

She had long since given up trying to free herself. She was awake, but her eyes were closed. If she opened her eyes she would find herself in darkness; the only light was a faint strip that seeped in above the door. She had a bad taste in her mouth and longed to be able to brush her teeth.

She was listening for the sound of footsteps, which would mean he was coming. She had no idea how late at night it was, but she sensed that it was getting too late for him to visit her. A sudden vibration in the bed made her open her eyes. It was as if a machine of some sort had started up somewhere in the building. After a few seconds she was no longer sure whether she was imagining it.

She marked off another day in her head.

It was the forty-third day of her imprisonment.

Her nose itched and she turned her head so that she could rub it against the pillow. She was sweating. It was airless and hot in the room. She had on a simple nightdress that was bunching up beneath her. If she moved her hips she could just hold the cloth with her first two fingers and pull the nightdress down on one side, an inch or so at a time. She did the same on the other side. But there was still a fold under the small of her back. The mattress was lumpy. Her isolation sharply amplified all the tiny sensations that she would not otherwise have noticed. The harness was loose enough that she could change position and lie on her side, but that was uncomfortable because then she had to keep one hand behind her, which made her arm keep going to sleep.

She was not afraid. But she did feel a great pent-up rage.

At the same time she was troubled by unpleasant fantasies about what was going to happen to her. She detested this helplessness. No matter how hard she tried to concentrate on something else—to pass the time and to distract her from the situation she was in—the fear came trickling out. It hovered like a cloud of gas around her, threatening to penetrate her pores and poison her. She had discovered that the most effective method of keeping the fear at bay was to fantasize about something that gave her a feeling of strength. She closed her eyes and conjured up the smell of gasoline.

He was sitting in a car with the window rolled down. She ran to the car, poured the gasoline through the window, and lit a match. It took only a moment. The flames blazed up. He writhed in agony and she heard his screams of terror and pain. She could smell burned flesh and a more acrid stench of plastic and upholstery turning to carbon in the seats.

She must have dozed off, because she did not hear the footsteps, but she was wide awake when the door opened. The light from the doorway blinded her.

He had come, at any rate.

He was tall. She did not know how old he was, but he had reddish-brown, tangled hair and a sparse goatee, and he wore glasses with black frames. He smelled of aftershave.

She hated the smell of him.

He stood at the foot of the bed and observed her for a long time.

She hated his silence.

She could see him only in silhouette from the light in the doorway. Then he spoke to her. He had a dark, clear voice that stressed, pedantically, each word.

She hated his voice.

He told her that it was her birthday and he wanted to wish her happy birthday. His tone was not unfriendly or ironical. It was neutral. She thought that he was smiling.

She hated him.

He came closer and went around to the head of the bed. He laid the back of a moist hand on her forehead and ran his fingers along her hairline in a gesture that was probably intended to be friendly. It was his birthday present to her.

She hated his touch.

She saw his mouth move, but she shut out the sound of his voice. She did not want to listen. She did not want to answer. She heard him raise his voice. A hint of irritation at her failure to respond. He talked about mutual trust. After a few minutes he stopped. She ignored his gaze. Then he shrugged and began adjusting her leather straps. He tightened the harness across her chest a bit and leaned over her.

She twisted suddenly to the left, away from him, as abruptly as she could and as far as the straps would allow. She pulled up her knees to her chin and kicked hard at his head. She aimed at his Adam's apple and the tip of her toe hit him somewhere below his jaw, but he was ready for that and turned away so it was only a light blow. She tried to kick again, but he was out of reach.

She let her legs sink back down onto the bed.

The sheet slid down onto the floor. Her nightdress had slid up above her hips.

He stood still for a long time without saying a word. Then he walked around the bed and tightened the foot restraint. She tried to pull her legs up, but he grabbed hold of one ankle, forced her knee down with his other hand, and fastened her foot with a leather strap. He went around the bed and tied down her other foot.

Now she was utterly helpless.

He picked up the sheet from the floor and covered her. He watched her in silence for two minutes. She could sense his excitement in the dark, even though he did not show it. He undoubtedly had an erection. She knew that he would reach out and touch her.

Then he turned and left, closing the door behind him. She heard him bolt it, which was totally unnecessary because she had no way of getting free from the bed.

She lay for several minutes looking at the narrow strip of light over the door. Then she moved and tried to feel how tight the straps were. She could pull her knees up a bit, but the harness and the foot restraints grew taut immediately. She relaxed. She lay still, staring at nothing.

She waited. She thought about a gasoline can and a match.

She saw him drenched with gasoline. She could actually feel the box of matches in her hand. She shook it. It rattled. She opened the box and selected a match. She heard him say something, but she shut her ears, did not listen to the words. She saw the expression on his face as she moved the match towards the striking surface. She heard the scraping sound of sulphur. It sounded like a drawn-out thunderclap. She saw the match burst into flame.

She smiled a hard smile and steeled herself.

It was her thirteenth birthday.

PART 1

Irregular Equations

Equations are classified by the highest power (value of the exponent) of their unknowns. If this is one, the equation is of first degree. If this is two, the equation is of second degree, and so on. Equations of higher degree than one yield multiple possible values for their unknown quantities. These values are known as roots.

The first-degree equation (the linear equation):

$$3x - 9 = 0 \text{ (root: } x = 3)$$

CHAPTER 1

Thursday, December 16– Friday, December 17

Lisbeth Salander pulled her sunglasses down to the tip of her nose and squinted from beneath the brim of her sun hat. She saw the woman from room 32 come out of the hotel side entrance and walk to one of the green-and-white-striped chaises longues beside the pool. Her gaze was fixed on the ground and her progress seemed unsteady.

Salander had seen her only at a distance. She reckoned the woman was around thirty-five, but she looked as though she could be anything from twenty-five to fifty. She had shoulder-length brown hair, an oval face, and a body that was straight out of a mail-order catalogue for lingerie. She had a black bikini, sandals, and purple-tinted sunglasses. She was American and spoke with a southern accent. She dropped a yellow sun hat next to the chaise longue and signalled to the bartender at Ella Carmichael's bar.

Salander put her book down on her lap and sipped her iced coffee before reaching for a pack of cigarettes. Without turning her head she shifted her gaze to the horizon. She could just see the Caribbean through a group of palm trees and the rhododendrons in front of the hotel. A yacht was on its way north towards St. Lucia or Dominica. Further out, she could see the outline of a grey freighter heading south in the direction of Guyana. A breeze made the morning heat bearable, but she felt a drop of sweat trickling into her eyebrow. Salander did not care for sunbathing. She had spent her days as far as possible in shade, and even now was under the awning on the terrace. And yet she was as brown as a nut. She had on khaki shorts and a black top.

She listened to the strange music from steel drums flowing out of the speakers at the bar. She could not tell the difference between Sven-Ingvars and Nick Cave, but steel drums fascinated her. It seemed hardly feasible that anyone could tune an oil barrel, and even less credible that the barrel could make music like nothing else in the world. She thought those sounds were like magic.

She suddenly felt irritated and looked again at the woman, who had just been handed a glass of some orange-coloured drink.

It was not Lisbeth Salander's problem, but she could not comprehend why the woman stayed. For four nights, ever since the couple had arrived, Salander had listened to the muted terror being played out in the room next door to hers. She had heard crying and low, excitable voices, and sometimes the unmistakable sound of slaps. The man responsible for the blows—Salander assumed he was the woman's husband—had straight dark hair parted down the middle in an old-fashioned style, and he seemed to be in Grenada on business. What kind of business, Salander had no idea, but every morning the man appeared with his briefcase, in a jacket and tie, and had coffee in the hotel bar before he went outside to look for a taxi.

He would come back to the hotel in the late afternoon, when he took a swim and sat with his wife by the pool. They had dinner together in what on the surface seemed to be a quiet and loving way. The woman may have had a few too many drinks, but her intoxication was not obnoxious.

Each night the commotion in the next-door room had started just as Salander was going to bed with a book about the mysteries of mathematics. It did not sound like a full-on assault. As far as Salander could tell through the wall, it was one repetitive, tedious argument. The night before, Salander had not been able to contain her curiosity. She had gone out to the balcony to listen through the couple's open balcony door. For more than an hour the man had paced back and forth in the room, declaring that he was a jerk who didn't deserve her. Again and again he said that she must think he was a fraud. No, she would answer, she didn't, and she tried to calm him. He became more intense, and seemed to give her a shake. So at last she gave him the answer he wanted . . . *Yes, you are a fraud.* And he immediately took this as a pretext to berate her. He called her a whore, which was an accusation that Salander would have taken measures to combat if it had been directed at her. It had not been, but nevertheless she thought for a long time about whether she ought to take some sort of action.

Salander had listened in astonishment to this rancorous bickering, which all of a sudden ended with something that sounded like a slap in the face. She had been on the point of going into the hotel corridor to kick in her neighbours' door when silence descended over the room.

Now, as she scrutinized the woman by the pool, she could see a faint bruise on her shoulder and a scrape on her hip, but no other injury.

Some months earlier Salander had read an article in a *Popular Science* that someone had left behind at Leonardo da Vinci Airport in Rome, and she developed a vague fascination with the obscure topic of spherical astronomy. On impulse she had made her way to the university bookshop in Rome to buy some of the key works on the subject. To be able to get a grasp of spherical astronomy, however, she had had to immerse herself in the deeper mysteries of mathematics. In the course of her travels in recent months she had been to other university bookshops to seek out more books.

Her studies had been unsystematic and without any real objective, at least until she wandered into the university bookshop in Miami and came out with *Dimensions in Mathematics,* by Dr. L. C. Parnault (Harvard University Press, 1999). That was just before she went down to the Florida Keys and began island-hopping through the Caribbean.

She had been to Guadeloupe (two nights in a hideous dump), Dominica (fun and relaxed, five nights), Barbados (one night at an American hotel where she felt terribly unwelcome), and St. Lucia (nine nights). She would have considered staying longer had she not made an enemy of a slow-witted young hoodlum who haunted the bar of her backstreet hotel. Finally she lost patience and whacked him on the head with a brick, checked out of the hotel, and took a ferry to St. George's, the capital of Grenada. This was a country she had never heard of before she bought her ticket for the boat.

She had come ashore on Grenada in a tropical rainstorm at 10:00 one November morning. From the *Caribbean Traveller* she learned that Grenada was known as Spice Island and was one of the world's leading producers of nutmeg. The island had a population of 120,000, but another 200,000 Grenadians lived in the United States, Canada, or Britain, which gave some indication of the employment market in their homeland. The terrain was mountainous around a dormant volcano, Grand Etang.

Grenada was one of many small, former-British colonies. In 1795, Julian Fedon, a black planter of mixed French ancestry, led an uprising inspired by the French Revolution. Troops were sent to shoot, hang, or maim the rebels. What had shaken the colonial regime was that even poor whites, so-called *petits blancs,* had joined Fedon's rebellion without the least regard for racial boundaries. The uprising was crushed, but Fedon was never captured; he vanished into the mountainous Grand Etang and became a Robin Hood–like legend.

Some two hundred years later, in 1979, a lawyer called Maurice Bishop started a new revolution, which the guidebook said was inspired by the Communist dictatorships in Cuba and Nicaragua. But Salander was given a different picture of things when she met Philip Campbell—teacher, librarian, and Baptist preacher. She had taken a room in his guesthouse for the first few days. The gist of the story was that Bishop was a popular folk leader who had deposed an insane dictator, a UFO nutcase who had devoted part of the meagre national budget to chasing flying saucers. Bishop had lobbied for economic democracy and introduced the country's first legislation for sexual equality. And then in 1983 he was assassinated.

There followed a massacre of more than a hundred people, including the foreign minister, the minister for women's affairs, and some senior trade union leaders. Then the United States invaded the country and set up a democracy. As far as Grenada was concerned, this meant that unemployment rose from around 6 percent to almost 50 percent and the cocaine trade once more became the largest single source of income. Campbell shook his head in dismay at the description in Salander's guidebook and gave her some tips on the kinds of people and neighbourhoods she should avoid after dark.

In Salander's case, such advice normally fell on deaf ears. However, she had avoided making the acquaintance of the criminal element on Grenada by falling in love with Grand Anse Beach, just south of St. George's, a sparsely populated beach that went on for miles. There she could walk for hours without having to talk to or even encounter another living soul. She moved to the Keys, one of the few American hotels on Grand Anse, and stayed for seven weeks, doing little more than walking on the beach and eating the local fruit, called chinups, which reminded her of sour Swedish gooseberries—she found them delightful.

It was the off season, and barely a third of the rooms at the Keys Hotel were occupied. The only problem was that both her peace and quiet and her preoccupation with mathematical studies had been disturbed by the subdued terror in the room next door.

Mikael Blomkvist rang the doorbell of Salander's apartment on Lundagatan. He did not expect her to open the door, but he had fallen into the habit of calling at her apartment every week or so to see whether anything had changed. He lifted the flap on the mailbox and could see the same heap of junk mail. It was late, and too dark to make out how much the pile might have grown since his last visit.

He stood on the landing for a moment before turning on his heel in frustration. He strolled leisurely to his own apartment on Bellmansgatan, put on some coffee, and looked through the evening papers before the late TV news *Rapport* came on. He was irritated and depressed not to know where Salander was. He felt stirrings of unease and wondered for the thousandth time what had happened.

He had invited Salander to his cabin in Sandhamn for the Christmas holidays. They had gone for long walks and calmly discussed the repercussions of the dramatic events in which they had both been involved over the past year, when Blomkvist went through what he came to think of as an early midlife crisis. He had been convicted of libel and spent two months in prison, his professional career as a journalist had been in the gutter, and he had resigned from his position as publisher of the magazine *Millennium* more or less in disgrace. But at that point everything had turned around. A commission to write a biography of the industrialist Henrik Vanger—which he had regarded as an absurdly well-paid form of therapy—had turned into a terrifying hunt for a serial killer.

During this manhunt he had met Salander. Blomkvist

unconsciously stroked the faint scar that the noose had left beneath his left ear. Salander had not only helped him to track down the killer—she had saved his life.

Time and again she had amazed him with her odd talents—she had a photographic memory and phenomenal computer skills. Blomkvist considered himself virtually computer illiterate, but Salander handled computers as if she had made a pact with the Devil. He had come to realize that she was a world-class hacker, and within an exclusive international community devoted to computer crime at the highest level—and not only to combatting it—she was a legend. She was known online only as *Wasp*.

It was her ability to pass freely into other people's computers that had given him the material which transformed his professional humiliation into what was to be "the Wennerström affair"—a scoop that a year later was still the subject of international police investigations into unsolved financial crimes. And Blomkvist was still being invited to appear on TV talk shows.

At the time, a year ago, he had thought of the scoop with colossal satisfaction—as vengeance and as rehabilitation. But the satisfaction had soon ebbed. Within a few weeks he was sick and tired of answering the same questions from journalists and the financial police. *I'm sorry, but I can't reveal my sources.* When a reporter from the English-language *Azerbaijan Times* had come all the way to Stockholm to ask him the same questions, it was the last straw. Blomkvist cut the interviews to a minimum, and in recent months he had relented only when the woman from *She* on TV4 talked him into it, and that had happened only because the investigation had apparently moved into a new phase.

Blomkvist's cooperation with the woman from TV4 had another dimension. She had been the first journalist to pounce on the story, and without her programme on the evening that *Millennium* released the scoop, it might not have made the impact it did. Only later did Blomkvist find out that she had had to fight tooth and nail to convince her editor to run it. There had been massive resistance to giving any prominence to "that clown" at *Millennium,* and right up to the moment she went on air, it was far from certain that the battery of company lawyers would give the story the all clear. Several of her more senior colleagues had given it a thumbs-down and told her that if she was wrong, her career was over. She stood her ground, and it became the story of the year.

She had covered the story herself that first week—after all, she was the only reporter who had thoroughly researched the subject—but some time before Christmas Blomkvist noticed that all the new angles in the story had been handed over to male colleagues. Around New Year's Blomkvist heard through the grapevine that she had been elbowed out, with the excuse that such an important story should be handled by experienced financial reporters, and not some little girl from Gotland or Bergslagen or wherever the hell she was from. The next time TV4 called, Blomkvist explained frankly that he would talk to them only if "she" asked the questions. Days of sullen silence went by before the boys at TV4 capitulated.

Blomkvist's waning interest in the Wennerström affair coincided with Salander's disappearance from his life. He still could not understand what had happened.

They had parted two days after Christmas, and he had not seen her for the rest of the week. On the day before New Year's Eve he telephoned her, but there was no answer.

On New Year's Eve he went to her apartment twice and rang the bell. The first time there had been lights on, but she had not answered the door. The second time there were no lights. On New Year's Day he called her again, and still there was no answer, but he did get a message from the telephone company saying that the subscriber could not be reached.

He had seen her twice in the next few days. When he could not get hold of her on the phone, he went to her apartment and sat down to wait on the steps beside her front door. He had brought a book with him, and he waited stubbornly for four hours before she appeared through the main entrance, just before 11:00 at night. She was carrying a brown box and stopped short when she saw him.

"Hello, Lisbeth," he said, closing his book.

She looked at him without expression, no sign of warmth or even friendship in her gaze. Then she walked past him and stuck her key in the door.

"Aren't you going to offer me a cup of coffee?" he said.

She turned and said in a low voice: "Get out of here. I don't want to see you ever again."

Then she shut the door in his face, and he heard her lock it from the inside. He was bewildered.

Three days later, he had taken the tunnelbana from Slussen to T-Centralen, and when the train stopped in Gamla Stan he looked out the window and she was standing on the platform less than two yards away. He caught sight of her at the exact moment the doors closed. For five seconds she stared right through him, as though he were nothing but air, before she turned and walked out of his field of vision as the train began to move.

The implication was unmistakable. She wanted nothing to do with him. She had cut him out of her life as surgically and decisively as she deleted files from her computer, and without explanation. She had changed her mobile phone number and did not answer her email.

Blomkvist sighed, switched off the TV, and went to the window to gaze out at City Hall.

Perhaps he was making a mistake in going to her apartment from time to time. His attitude had always been that if a woman clearly indicated that she did not want anything more to do with him, he would go on his way. Not respecting such a message would, in his eyes, show a lack of respect for her.

Blomkvist and Salander had slept together. It had been at

her initiative, and the relationship had lasted for half a year. If it was her decision to end the affair—as surprisingly as she had started it—then that was OK with Blomkvist. He had no difficulty with the role of *ex*-boyfriend—if that was what he was—but Salander's total repudiation of him was astonishing.

He was not in love with her—they were about as unlike as two people could possibly be—but he was very fond of her and really missed her, as exasperating as she sometimes was. He had thought their liking was mutual. In short, he felt like an idiot.

He stood at the window a long time.

Finally he made a decision. If Salander thought so little of him that she could not even bring herself to greet him when they saw each other in the tunnelbana, then their friendship was apparently over and the damage irreparable. He would make no attempt to contact her again.

Salander looked at her watch and realized that although she was sitting, perfectly still, in the shade, she was drenched with sweat. It was 10:30. She memorized a mathematical formula three lines long and closed her book, *Dimensions in Mathematics.* Then she picked up her key and the pack of cigarettes on the table.

Her room was on the third floor, which was also the top floor of the hotel. She stripped off her clothes and got into the shower.

A green lizard eight inches long was staring at her from the wall just below the ceiling. Salander stared back but made no move to shoo it away. There were lizards everywhere on the island. They came through the blinds at the open window, under the door, or through the vent in the bathroom. She liked having company that left her alone. The water was almost ice cold, and she stayed under the shower for five minutes to cool off.

When she came back into the room she stood naked in front of the mirror on the wardrobe door and examined her body with amazement. She still weighed less than ninety pounds and stood four foot eleven. Well, there was not much she could do about that. She had doll-like, almost delicate limbs, small hands, and hardly any hips.

But now she had breasts.

All her life she had been flat-chested, as if she had never reached puberty. She thought it had looked ridiculous, and she was always uncomfortable showing herself naked.

Now, all of a sudden, she had breasts. They were by no means gigantic—that was not what she had wanted, and they would have looked ridiculous on her otherwise skinny body—but they were two solid, round breasts of medium size. The enlargement had been well done, and the proportions were reasonable. But the difference was dramatic, both for her looks and for her self-confidence.

She had spent five weeks in a clinic outside Genoa getting the implants that formed the structure of her new breasts. The clinic and the doctors there had absolutely the best reputation in all of Europe. Her own doctor, a charmingly hard-boiled woman named Alessandra Perrini, had told her that her breasts were abnormally underdeveloped, and that the enlargement could therefore be performed for medical reasons.

Recovery from the operation had not been painless, but her breasts looked and felt completely natural, and by now the scars were almost invisible. She had not regretted her decision for a second. She was pleased. Even six months later she could not walk past a mirror with her top off without stopping and feeling glad that she had improved her quality of life.

During her time at the clinic in Genoa she had also had one of her nine tattoos removed—a one-inch-long wasp—from the right side of her neck. She liked her tattoos, especially the dragon on her left shoulder blade. But the wasp was conspicuous and it made her too easy to remember and identify. Salander did not want to be remembered or identified. The tattoo had been removed by laser treatment, and when she ran her index finger over her neck she could feel the slight scarring. Closer inspection would reveal that her suntanned skin was a shade lighter where the tattoo had been, but at a glance nothing was noticeable. Altogether her stay in Genoa had cost 190,000 kronor.

Which she could afford.

She stopped dreaming in front of the mirror and put on her panties and bra. Two days after she had left the clinic in Genoa she had for the first time in her twenty-five years gone to a lingerie boutique and bought the garments she had never needed before. Since then she had turned twenty-six, and now she wore a bra with a certain amount of satisfaction.

She put on jeans and a black T-shirt with the slogan CONSIDER THIS A FAIR WARNING. She found her sandals and sun hat and slung a black bag over her shoulder.

Crossing the lobby, she heard a murmur from a small group of hotel guests at the front desk. She slowed down and pricked up her ears.

"Just how dangerous is she?" said a black woman with a loud voice and a European accent. Salander recognized her as one of a charter group from London who had been there for ten days.

Freddy McBain, the greying reception manager who always greeted Salander with a friendly smile, looked worried. He was telling them that instructions would be issued to all guests and that there was no reason to worry as long as they followed all the instructions to the letter. He was met by a hail of questions.

Salander frowned and went out to the bar, where she found Ella Carmichael behind the counter.

"What's all that about?" she said, motioning with her thumb towards the front desk.

"Matilda is threatening to visit us."

"Matilda?"

"Matilda is a hurricane that formed off Brazil a few weeks ago and yesterday tore straight through Paramaribo, the capital of Surinam. No-one's quite sure what direction it's going to take—probably further north towards the States. But if it goes on following the coast to the west, then Trinidad and Grenada will be smack in its path. So it might get a bit windy."

"I thought the hurricane season was over."

"It is. It's usually September and October. But these days you never can tell, because there's so much trouble with the climate and the greenhouse effect and all that."

"OK. But when's Matilda supposed to arrive?"

"Soon."

"Is there something I should do?"

"Lisbeth, hurricanes are not for playing around with. We had one in the seventies that caused a lot of destruction here on Grenada. I was eleven years old and lived in a town up in the Grand Etang on the way to Grenville, and I will never forget that night."

"Hmm."

"But you don't need to worry. Stay close to the hotel on Saturday. Pack a bag with things you wouldn't want to lose—like that computer you're always playing with—and be prepared to take it along if we get instructions to go down to the storm cellar. That's all."

"Right."

"Would you like something to drink?"

"No thanks."

Salander left without saying goodbye. Ella Carmichael smiled, resigned. It had taken her a couple of weeks to get used to this odd girl's peculiar ways and to realize that she was not being snooty—she was just very different. But she paid for her drinks without any fuss, stayed relatively sober, kept to herself, and never caused any trouble.

The traffic on Grenada consisted mainly of imaginatively decorated minibuses that operated with no particular timetable or other formalities. The shuttle ran during the daylight hours. After dark it was pretty much impossible to get around without your own car.

Salander had to wait only a few minutes on the road to St. George's before one of the buses pulled up. The driver was a Rasta, and the bus's sound system was playing "No Woman No Cry" full blast. She closed her ears, paid her dollar, and squeezed in next to a substantial woman with grey hair and two boys in school uniforms.

St. George's was located on a U-shaped bay that formed the Carenage, the inner harbour. Around the harbour rose steep hills dotted with houses and old colonial buildings, with Fort Rupert perched all the way out on the tip of a precipitous cliff.

St. George's was a compact and tight-knit town with narrow streets and many alleyways. The houses climbed up every hillside, and there was hardly a flat surface larger than the combined cricket field and racetrack on the northern edge of the town.

She got off at the harbour and walked to MacIntyre's Electronics at the top of a short, steep slope. Almost all the products sold on Grenada were imported from the United States or Britain, so they cost twice as much as they did elsewhere, but at least the shop had air-conditioning.

The extra batteries she had ordered for her Apple Power-Book (G4 titanium with a seventeen-inch screen) had finally arrived. In Miami she had bought a Palm PDA with a folding keyboard that she could use for email and easily take with her in her shoulder bag instead of dragging around her Power-Book, but it was a miserable substitute for the seventeen-inch screen. The original batteries had deteriorated and would run for only half an hour before they had to be recharged, which was a curse when she wanted to sit out on the terrace by the pool, and the electrical supply on Grenada left a lot to be desired. During the weeks she had been there, she had experienced two long blackouts. She paid with a credit card in the name of Wasp Enterprises, stuffed the batteries in her shoulder bag, and headed back out into the midday heat.

She paid a visit to Barclays Bank and withdrew $300, then went down to the market and bought a bunch of carrots, half a dozen mangoes, and a big bottle of mineral water. Her bag was much heavier now, and by the time she got back to the harbour she was hungry and thirsty. She considered the Nutmeg first, but the entrance to the restaurant was jammed with people already waiting. She went on to the quieter Turtleback at the other end of the harbour. There she sat on the veranda and ordered a plate of calamari and chips with a bottle of Carib, the local beer. She picked up a discarded copy of the *Grenadian Voice* and looked through it for two minutes. The only thing of interest was a dramatic article warning about the possible arrival of Matilda. The text was illustrated with a photograph showing a demolished house, a reminder of the devastation wrought by the last big hurricane to hit the island.

She folded the paper, took a swig from the bottle of Carib, and then she saw the man from room 32 come out on the veranda from the bar. He had his brown briefcase in one hand and a glass of Coca-Cola in the other. His eyes swept over her without recognition before he sat on a bench at the other end of the veranda and fixed his gaze on the water beyond.

He seemed utterly preoccupied and sat there motionless for seven minutes, Salander observed, before he raised his glass and took three deep swallows. Then he put down the glass and resumed staring out to sea. After a while she opened her bag and took out *Dimensions in Mathematics*.

All her life Salander had loved puzzles and riddles. When she was nine her mother gave her a Rubik's Cube. It had put her abilities to the test for barely forty frustrating minutes before she understood how it worked. After that she never had any difficulty solving the puzzle. She had never missed the daily newspapers' intelligence tests; five strangely shaped figures and the puzzle was how the sixth one should look. To her, the answer was always obvious.

In elementary school she had learned to add and subtract. Multiplication, division, and geometry were a natural extension. She could add up the bill in a restaurant, create an invoice, and calculate the path of an artillery shell fired at a certain speed and angle. That was easy. But before she read the article in *Popular Science* she had never been intrigued by mathematics or even thought about the fact that the multiplication table was math. It was something she memorized one afternoon at school, and she never understood why the teacher kept going on about it for the whole year.

Then, suddenly, she sensed the inexorable logic that must reside behind the reasoning and the formulas, and that led her to the mathematics section of the university bookshop. But it was not until she started on *Dimensions in Mathematics* that a whole new world opened to her. Mathematics was actually a logical puzzle with endless variations—riddles that could be solved. The trick was not to solve arithmetical problems. Five times five would always be twenty-five. The trick was to understand combinations of the various rules that made it possible to solve any mathematical problem whatsoever.

Dimensions in Mathematics was not strictly a textbook but rather a 1,200-page brick about the history of mathematics from the ancient Greeks to modern-day attempts to understand spherical astronomy. It was considered the bible of math, in a class with what the *Arithmetica* of Diophantus had meant (and still did mean) to serious mathematicians. When she opened *Dimensions in Mathematics* for the first time on the terrace of the hotel on Grand Anse Beach, she was enticed into an enchanted world of figures. This was a book written by an author who was both pedagogical and able to entertain the reader with anecdotes and astonishing problems. She could follow mathematics from Archimedes to today's Jet Propulsion

Laboratory in California. She had taken in the methods they used to solve problems.

Pythagoras' equation $(x^2 + y^2 = z^2)$, formulated five centuries before Christ, was an epiphany. At that moment Salander understood the significance of what she had memorized in secondary school from some of the few classes she had attended. *In a right triangle, the square of the hypotenuse is equal to the sum of the squares of the other two sides.* She was fascinated by Euclid's discovery in about 300 BC that a perfect number is always *a multiple of two numbers, in which one number is a power of 2 and the second consists of the difference between the next power of 2 and 1.* This was a refinement of Pythagoras' equation, and she could see the endless combinations.

$$6 = 2^1 x \, (2^2 - 1)$$
$$28 = 2^2 x \, (2^3 - 1)$$
$$496 = 2^4 x \, (2^5 - 1)$$
$$8,128 = 2^6 x \, (2^7 - 1)$$

She could go on indefinitely without finding any number that would break the rule. This was a logic that appealed to her sense of the absolute. She advanced through Archimedes, Newton, Martin Gardner, and a dozen other classical mathematicians with unmitigated pleasure.

Then she came to the chapter on Pierre de Fermat, whose mathematical enigma, "Fermat's Last Theorem," had dumbfounded her for seven weeks. And that was a trifling length of time, considering that Fermat had driven mathematicians crazy for almost four hundred years before an Englishman named Andrew Wiles succeeded in unravelling the puzzle, as recently as 1993.

Fermat's theorem was a beguilingly simple task.

Pierre de Fermat was born in 1601 in Beaumont-de-Lomagne in southwestern France. He was not even a mathematician; he was a civil servant who devoted himself to mathematics as a hobby. He was regarded as one of the most gifted self-taught mathematicians who ever lived. Like Salander, he enjoyed solving puzzles and riddles. He found it particularly amusing to tease other mathematicians by devising problems without supplying the solutions. The philosopher Descartes referred to Fermat by many derogatory epithets, and his English colleague John Wallis called him "that damned Frenchman."

In 1621 a Latin translation was published of Diophantus' *Arithmetica* which contained a complete compilation of the number theories that Pythagoras, Euclid, and other ancient mathematicians had formulated. It was when Fermat was studying Pythagoras' equation that in a burst of pure genius he created his immortal problem. He formulated a variant of Pythagoras' equation. Instead of $(x^2 + y^2 = z^2)$, Fermat converted the square to a cube, $(x^3 + y^3 = z^3)$.

The problem was that the new equation did not seem to have any solution with whole numbers. What Fermat had thus done, by an academic tweak, was to transform a formula which had an infinite number of perfect solutions into a blind alley that had no solution at all. His theorem was just that—Fermat claimed that nowhere in the infinite universe of numbers was there any whole number in which a cube could be expressed as the sum of two cubes, and that this was general for all numbers having a power of more than 2, that is, precisely Pythagoras' equation.

Other mathematicians swiftly agreed that this was correct. Through trial and error they were able to confirm that they could not find a number that disproved Fermat's theorem. The problem was simply that even if they counted until the end of time, they would never be able to test all existing numbers—they are infinite, after all—and consequently the mathematicians could not be 100 percent certain that the next number would not disprove Fermat's theorem. Within mathematics, assertions must always be proven mathematically and expressed in a valid and scientifically correct formula. The mathematician must be able to stand on a podium and say the words *This is so because* . . .

Fermat, true to form, sorely tested his colleagues. In the margin of his copy of *Arithmetica,* the genius penned the problem and concluded with the lines *Cuius rei demonstrationem mirabilem sane detexi hanc marginis exiguitas non caperet.* These lines became immortalized in the history of mathematics: *I have a truly marvellous demonstration of this proposition which this margin is too narrow to contain.*

If his intention had been to madden his peers, then he succeeded. Since 1637 almost every self-respecting mathematician has spent time, sometimes a great deal of time, trying to find Fermat's proof. Generations of thinkers had failed until finally Andrew Wiles came up with the proof everyone had been waiting for. By then he had pondered the riddle for twenty-five years, the last ten of which he worked almost full-time on the problem.

Salander was at a loss.

She was actually not interested in the answer. It was the process of solution that was the point. When someone put a riddle in front of her, she solved it. Before she understood the principles of reasoning, the number mysteries took a long time to solve, but she always arrived at the correct answer before she looked it up.

So she took out a piece of paper and began scribbling figures when she read Fermat's theorem. But she failed to find a proof for it.

She disdained the idea of looking at the answer key, so she bypassed the section that gave Wiles' solution. Instead she finished her reading of *Dimensions* and confirmed that none of the other problems formulated in the book presented any overwhelming difficulties for her. Then she returned to Fermat's riddle day after day with increasing irritation, wondering what was Fermat's "marvellous proof." She went from one dead end to another.

She looked up when the man from room 32 stood and

walked towards the exit. He had been sitting there for two hours and ten minutes.

Ella Carmichael set the glass on the bar. She had long since realized that crappy pink drinks with stupid umbrellas were not Salander's style. She always ordered the same drink, rum and Coke. Except for one evening when she had been in an odd mood and got so drunk that Ella had to call the porter to carry her to her room, her normal consumption consisted of caffè latte and a few drinks. Or Carib beer. As always, she sat at the far right end of the bar and opened a book that looked to have complicated lines of numbers in it, which in Ella's eyes was a funny choice of reading for a girl of her age.

She also noticed that Salander did not appear to have the least interest in being picked up. The few lonely men who had made advances had been rebuffed kindly but firmly, and in one case not very kindly. Chris MacAllen, the man dispatched so brusquely, was a local wastrel who could have used a good thrashing. So Ella was not too bothered when he somehow stumbled and fell into the pool after bothering Miss Salander for an entire evening. To MacAllen's credit, he did not hold a grudge. He came back the following night, all sobered up, and offered to buy Salander a beer, which, after a brief hesitation, she accepted. From then on they greeted each other politely when they saw each other in the bar.

"Everything OK?"

Salander nodded and took the glass. "Any news about Matilda?"

"Still headed our way. It could be a real bad weekend."

"When will we know?"

"Actually not before she's passed by. She could head straight for Grenada and then decide to swing north at the last moment."

Then they heard a laugh that was a little too loud and

turned to see the lady from room 32, apparently amused by something her husband had said.

"Who are they?"

"Dr. Forbes? They're Americans from Austin, Texas." Ella Carmichael said the word *Americans* with a certain distaste.

"I could tell they're Americans, but what are they doing here? Is he a GP?"

"No, not that kind of doctor. He's here for the Santa Maria Foundation."

"What's that?"

"They support education for talented children. He's a fine man. He's discussing a proposal for a new high school in St. George's with the Ministry of Education."

"He's a fine man who beats his wife," Salander said.

Ella gave Salander a sharp look and went to the other end of the bar to serve some local customers.

Salander stayed for ten minutes with her nose in *Dimensions*. She had known that she had a photographic memory since before she reached puberty, and because of it she was very different from her classmates. She had never revealed this to anyone—except to Blomkvist in a moment of weakness. She already knew the text of *Dimensions in Mathematics* by heart and was dragging the book around mainly because it represented a physical link to Fermat, as if the book had become some kind of talisman.

But this evening she could not concentrate on Fermat or his theorem. Instead she saw in her mind Dr. Forbes sitting motionless, gazing at the same distant point in the sea at the Carenage.

She could not have explained why she knew that something was not right.

Finally she closed the book, went back to her room, and booted up her PowerBook. Surfing the Internet did not call for any thinking. The hotel did not have broadband, but she had a built-in modem that she could hook up to her Panasonic mobile phone and with that setup she could send and receive email. She typed a message to <Plague_xyz_666@hotmail.com>:

> No broadband here. Need info on a Dr. Forbes with the Santa Maria Foundation, and his wife, living in Austin, Texas. $500 to whoever does the research. Wasp.

She attached her public PGP key, encrypted the message with Plague's PGP key, and sent it. Then she looked at the clock and saw that it was just past 7:30 p.m.

She turned off her computer, locked her door, and walked four hundred yards along the beach, past the road to St. George's, and knocked on the door of a shack behind the Coconut.

George Bland was sixteen and a student. He intended to become a lawyer or a doctor or possibly an astronaut, and he was just as skinny as Salander and only a little taller. Salander had met him on the beach the day after she moved to Grand Anse. She had sat down in the shade under some palms to watch the children playing football by the water. She was engrossed in *Dimensions* when the boy came and sat in the sand a few yards away from her, apparently without noticing she was there. She observed him in silence. A thin black boy in sandals, black jeans, and a white shirt.

He too had opened a book and immersed himself in it. Like her, he was reading a mathematics book—*Basics 4*. He began to scribble in an exercise book. Five minutes later, when Salander cleared her throat, he jumped up with a start. He apologized for bothering her and was on the brink of being gone when she asked him if what he was working on were complicated formulas.

Algebra. After a minute she had shown him an error in his calculation. After half an hour they had finished his homework. After an hour they had gone through the whole of the next chapter in his textbook and she had explained the trick behind the arithmetical operations as though she were his tutor. He had looked at her awestruck. After two hours he told her that his mother lived in Toronto, that his father lived in Grenville on the other side of the island, and that he himself lived in a shack a little way along the beach. He was the youngest in the family, with three older sisters.

Salander found his company surprisingly relaxing. The situation was unusual. She hardly ever began conversations with strangers just to talk. It was not a matter of shyness. For her, a conversation had a straightforward function. *How do I get to the pharmacy?* or *How much does the hotel room cost?* Conversation also had a professional function. When she worked as a researcher for Dragan Armansky at Milton Security, she had never minded having a long conversation if it was to ferret out facts.

On the other hand, she disliked personal discussions, which always led to snooping around in areas she considered private. *How old are you? Guess. Do you like Britney Spears? Who? What do you think of Carl Larsson's paintings? I've never given them a thought. Are you a lesbian? Piss off.*

This boy was gawky and self-conscious, but he was polite and tried to have an intelligent conversation without competing with her or poking his nose into her life. Like her, he seemed lonely. He appeared to accept without puzzlement that a goddess of mathematics had descended onto Grand Anse Beach, and with pleasure that she would keep him company. They got up as the sun sank to the horizon. They walked together towards her hotel, and he pointed out the shack that was his student quarters. Shyly he asked if he might invite her to tea.

The shack contained a table that was cobbled together, two chairs, a bed, and a wooden cabinet for clothes. The only lighting was a desk lamp with a cable that ran to the Coconut. He had a camp stove. He offered her a meal of rice and vegetables, which he served on plastic plates. Boldly he even offered her a smoke of the local forbidden substance, which she also accepted.

Salander could not help noticing that he was affected by her presence and did not know how he should treat her. She, on a whim, decided to let him seduce her. It developed into a painfully roundabout procedure in which he certainly understood her signals but had no idea how to react to them. Finally she lost patience, pushed him roughly onto the bed, and took off her shirt and jeans.

It was the first time she had shown herself naked to anyone since the operation in Italy. She had left the clinic with a feeling of panic. It took her a long while to realize that no-one was staring at her. Normally she didn't give a damn what other people thought, and she did not worry about why she felt nervous now.

Young Bland had been a perfect initiation for her new self. When at last (after some encouragement) he managed to unfasten her bra, he immediately switched off the lamp before undressing himself. Salander could tell that he was shy, and she turned the lamp back on. She watched his reactions closely as he began to touch her clumsily. Only much later did she relax, certain that he thought her breasts were natural. On the other hand, it was unlikely he had much to compare them to.

She had not planned to get herself a teenage lover on Grenada. It had been an impulse, and when she left him late that night she didn't consider going back. But the next day she ran into him on the beach and realized that the clumsy boy was pleasant company. For the seven weeks she lived on Grenada, George Bland became a regular part of her life. They did not spend time together during the day, but they spent the hours before sundown on the beach and the evenings alone in his shack.

She was aware that when they walked together they looked like two teenagers. Sweet sixteen.

He evidently thought that life had become much more interesting. He had met a woman who was teaching him about mathematics and eroticism.

He opened the door and smiled delightedly at her.

"Would you like company?" she said.

Salander left the shack just after two in the morning. She had a warm feeling in her body and strolled along the beach instead of taking the road to the Keys Hotel. She walked alone in the dark, knowing that Bland would be a hundred yards behind.

He always did that. She had never slept over at his place, and he often protested that she, a woman all alone, should not be walking back to her hotel at night. He insisted it was his duty to accompany her back to the hotel. Especially when it was very late, as it often was. Salander would listen to his objections and then cut the discussion off with a firm no. *I'll walk where I want, when I want. And no, I don't want an escort.* The first time she caught him following her she was really annoyed. But now she thought his wanting to protect her was rather sweet, so she pretended that she did not know he was there behind her or that he would turn back when he saw her go in the door of the hotel.

She wondered what he would do if she were attacked.

She would make use of the hammer she had bought at a hardware store and kept in the outside pocket of her shoulder bag. There were not so many physical threats that could not be countered with a decent hammer, Salander thought.

There was a full moon and the stars were sparkling. Salander looked up and identified Regulus in Leo near the horizon. She was almost at the hotel terrace when she stopped short. She had caught sight of someone near the waterline below the hotel. It was the first time she had seen a living soul on the beach after dark. He was almost a hundred yards off, but Salander knew at once who it was there in the moonlight.

It was the fine Dr. Forbes from room 32.

She took three quick steps into the shadow of a tree. When she turned her head, Bland was invisible too. The figure at the water's edge was walking slowly back and forth. He was smoking a cigarette. Every so often he would stop and bend down as if to examine the sand. This pantomime continued for twenty minutes before he turned and with rapid steps walked to the hotel's beach entrance and vanished.

Salander waited for a few minutes before she went down to where Dr. Forbes had been. She made a slow semicircle, inspecting the sand. All she could make out was pebbles and some shells. After a few minutes she broke off her search and went back to the hotel.

On her balcony, she leaned over the railing and peered in her neighbours' door. All was quiet. The evening's argument was obviously over. After a while she took from her shoulder bag some papers to roll a joint from the supply that Bland had given her. She sat down on a balcony chair and gazed out at the dark water of the Caribbean as she smoked and thought.

She felt like a radar installation on high alert.

CHAPTER 2

Friday, December 17

Advokat Nils Erik Bjurman set down his coffee cup and watched the flow of people outside the window of Café Hedon on Stureplan. He saw everyone passing in an unbroken stream, but observed none of them.

He was thinking of Lisbeth Salander. He thought often about Salander.

What he was thinking made him boil with rage.

Salander had crushed him. He was never going to forget it. She had taken command and humiliated him. She had abused him in a way that had left indelible marks on his body. On an area the size of a book below his navel. She had handcuffed him to his bed, abused him, and tattooed him with I AM A SADISTIC PIG, A PERVERT, AND A RAPIST.

Stockholm's district court had declared Salander legally incompetent. He had been assigned to be her guardian, which made her inescapably dependent on him. From the first time he met her he had fantasized about her. He could not explain it, but she seemed to invite that response.

. . .

What he had done—he, a fifty-five-year-old lawyer—was reprehensible, indefensible by any standard. He knew that, of course. But from the moment he'd laid eyes on Salander in December two years earlier, he had not been able to resist her. The laws, the most basic moral code, and his responsibility as her guardian—none of it mattered at all.

She was a strange girl—fully grown but with an appearance that made her easily mistaken for a child. He had control over her life; she was his to command.

She had a record that robbed her of credibility if she ever had a mind to protest. Nor was it a rape of some innocent— her file confirmed that she had had many sexual encounters, could even be regarded as promiscuous. One social worker's report had raised the possibility that Salander had solicited sexual services for payment when she was seventeen. A police patrol had observed a drunken older man sitting with a young girl on a park bench in Tantolunden. The police had confronted the pair; the girl had refused to answer their questions, and the man was too intoxicated to give them any sensible information.

In Bjurman's eyes the conclusion was straightforward: Salander was a whore at the bottom of the social scale. It was risk-free. If she dared to protest to the Guardianship Agency, no-one was going to believe her word against his.

She was the ideal plaything—grown-up, promiscuous, socially incompetent, and at his mercy.

It was the first time he had exploited one of his clients. Previously it had never occurred to him to make advances to anyone with whom he had a professional relationship. To satisfy his sexual needs, he had always turned to prostitutes. He had been discreet and he paid well; the problem was that prostitutes were not serious, they were only pretending. It was a service he bought from a woman who moaned and rolled her eyes; she played her part, but it was as phony as street theatre.

He had tried to dominate his wife in the years that he was

married, but she had merely gone along with it, and that too was a game.

Salander had been the perfect solution. She was defenceless. She had no family, no friends: a true victim, ripe for plundering. The opportunity makes the thief.

And then out of the blue she had destroyed him. She had struck back with a power and determination that he had not dreamed she possessed. She had humiliated him. She had tortured him. She had all but demolished him.

During the almost two years since then, Bjurman's life had changed dramatically. After Salander's nighttime visit to his apartment he had felt paralyzed—virtually incapable of clear thought or decisive action. He had locked himself in, did not answer the telephone, and was unable even to keep up contact with his regular clients. After two weeks he went on sick leave. His secretary was deputized to deal with his correspondence at the office, cancelling all his meetings and trying to keep irritated clients at bay.

Every day he was confronted by the tattoo on his body. Finally he took down the mirror from the bathroom door.

He returned to his office at the beginning of summer. He had handed over most of his clients to his colleagues. The only ones he kept for himself were companies for whom he dealt with legal business correspondence without being involved in meetings. His only active client now was Salander—each month he wrote up a balance sheet and a report for the Guardianship Agency. He did very precisely what she had demanded: the reports had not a grain of truth in them and made plain that she no longer needed a guardian. Each report was an excruciating reminder of her existence, but he had no choice.

Bjurman had spent the summer and the autumn in helpless, furious brooding. And then, in December, he pulled himself together and went on a vacation to France. While there, he consulted a specialist at a clinic for cosmetic surgery outside Marseilles about how best to remove the tattoo.

The specialist had examined his abdomen with ill-concealed astonishment. At last he recommended a course of action. One way would be laser treatment, he said, but the tattoo was so extensive and the needle had penetrated so deeply that he was afraid the only realistic solution was a series of skin grafts. It would be expensive and would take time.

In the past two years Bjurman had seen Salander on only one occasion.

On the night she attacked him and established control over his life, she had taken the spare set of keys to his office and apartment. She would be watching him, she had told him, and when he least expected it she would drop in. He had almost begun to believe it was an empty threat, but he had not dared to change the locks. Her warning had been unmistakable—if she ever found him in bed with a woman, Salander would make public the ninety-minute video that documented how he had raped her.

In January a year ago he had woken at 3:00 a.m., not sure why. He turned on his bedside light and almost howled in fright when he saw her standing at the foot of his bed. She was like a ghost suddenly there. Her face was pale and expression-less. In her hand she held her fucking Taser.

"Good morning, Mr. Advokat Bjurman," she said. "So sorry for waking you this time."

Good God, has she been here before? While I slept?

He could not tell whether she was bluffing. Bjurman cleared his throat and was about to speak. She cut him off with a gesture.

"I woke you for one reason only. I'm going to be away for a long time quite soon. Keep writing your reports every month, but don't post copies to me. Send them to this hotmail address."

She took a folded paper from her jacket pocket and dropped it on the bed.

"If the Guardianship Agency wants to get in touch with me, or anything else comes up that might require my being here, write me an email at this address. Is that understood?"

He nodded. "I understand . . ."

"Don't speak. I don't want to hear your voice."

He clenched his teeth. He had not dared to try to reach her, since she had threatened to send the video to the authorities if he did. Instead he had thought for months what he would say to her when eventually she contacted him. He really had nothing he could say in his defence. All he could do was appeal to her humanity. He would try to convince her—if she would only give him a chance to speak—that he had done it in a fit of insanity, that he was utterly sorry for it and wanted to make amends. He would grovel if that would convince her, if he could only somehow defuse the threat that she posed.

"I have something to say," he said in a pitiful voice. "I want to ask your forgiveness . . ."

She listened in silence to his plea. Then she put one foot on the bottom of the bed and stared at him in disgust.

"Now you listen, Bjurman: you're a pervert. I have no reason to forgive you. But if you keep yourself clean, I'll let you off the hook the day my declaration of incompetence is rescinded."

She waited until he lowered his gaze. *She's going to make me crawl.*

"There's no change to what I said a year ago. You fail, and the video goes to the agency. You contact me in any way other than I tell you to, then I make the video public. I die in an accident, the video will be made public. You ever touch me again, I will kill you."

He believed her.

"One more thing. The day I set you free, you can do as you like. But until that day you will not set foot again in that clinic in Marseilles. If you begin treatment, I will tattoo you again, and this time I'll do it on your forehead."

How the fucking hell did she find out about the clinic?

The next moment she was gone. He heard a faint click as she turned the front-door key. It was as if a ghost had paid him a visit.

At that instant he began to loathe Lisbeth Salander with an intensity that blazed like red-hot steel in his brain and transformed his life into an obsession to crush her. He fantasized about killing her. He toyed with fantasies of having her crawl at his feet and beg him for mercy. But he would be merciless. He would put his hands around her throat and strangle her until she gasped for air. He wanted to tear her eyes from their sockets and her heart from her chest. He wanted to erase her from the earth.

Paradoxically, it was at this same moment that he felt as though he had begun to function again, and he discovered in himself a surprising emotional balance. He was obsessed with the woman and she was on his mind every waking minute. But he had begun to think rationally again. If he was going to find a way of destroying her, he would have to get his head in order. His life settled on a new objective.

He stopped fantasizing about her death and began planning for it.

Blomkvist passed less than six feet behind Advokat Bjurman's back as he navigated with two scalding glasses of caffè latte to editor in chief Erika Berger's table at Café Hedon. Neither he nor Berger had ever heard of Nils Bjurman, so neither was aware of his being there.

Berger frowned and moved an ashtray aside to make room for her glass. Blomkvist hung his jacket over the back of his chair, slid the ashtray over to his side of the table, and lit a cigarette. Berger detested cigarette smoke and gave him a furious look. He turned his head to blow the smoke away from her.

"I thought you gave up."

"Temporary backsliding."

"I'm going to stop having sex with guys who smell of smoke," she said, smiling sweetly.

"No problem. There are plenty of girls who aren't so particular," Blomkvist said, smiling back.

Berger rolled her eyes. "So what's the problem? I'm meeting Charlie at the theatre in twenty minutes." Charlie was Charlotta Rosenberg, a childhood friend.

"Our intern bothers me," Blomkvist said. "I don't mind her being the daughter of one of your girlfriends, but she's supposed to be in editorial for another eight weeks and I don't think I can put up with her that long."

"I've noticed the hungry glances she's been casting your way. Naturally I expect you to behave like a gentleman."

"Erika, the girl's seventeen and has a mental age of ten, and I may be erring on the generous side."

"She's just impressed. Probably a little hero worship."

"At 10:30 last night she rang the entry phone on my building and wanted to come up with a bottle of wine."

"Oops," Berger said.

"Oops is right. If I were twenty years younger I might not have even hesitated. I'm going to be forty-five any day now."

"Don't remind me. We're the same age."

The Wennerström affair had given Blomkvist a certain celebrity. Over the past year he had received invitations to the most improbable places, parties, and events. He was greeted with air kisses from all sorts of people he had hardly shaken hands with before. They were not primarily media people—he knew all of them already and was on either good or bad terms with them—but so-called cultural figures and B-list celebrities now wanted to appear as though they were his close friends. Now it was the thing to have Mikael Blomkvist as your guest at a launch party or a private dinner. "Sounds lovely, but unfortunately I'm already booked up," was becoming a routine response.

One downside of his star status was an increasing rash of rumours. An acquaintance had mentioned with concern that he heard a rumour claiming that Blomkvist had been seen at a rehab clinic. In fact Blomkvist's total drug intake since his teens consisted of half a dozen joints and one experiment with cocaine fifteen years earlier with a female singer in a Dutch rock band. As to alcohol, he was only ever seriously intoxicated at private dinners or parties. In a bar he would seldom have more than one large, strong beer. He also liked to drink medium-strong beer. His drinks cabinet at home had vodka and a few bottles of single malt Scotch, all presents. It was absurd how rarely he indulged in them.

Blomkvist was single. The fact that he had occasional affairs was known both inside and outside his circle of friends, and that had led to further rumours. His long-lasting affair with Erika Berger was frequently the subject of speculation. Lately it had been bandied about that he picked up any number of women, and was exploiting his new celebrity status to screw his way through the clientele of Stockholm's nightspots. An obscure journalist had once even urged him to seek help for his sex addiction.

Blomkvist had indeed had many brief relationships. He knew he was reasonably good-looking, but he had never considered himself exceptionally attractive. But he had often been told that he had something that made women interested in him. Berger had told him that he radiated self-confidence and security at the same time, that he had an ability to make women feel at ease. Going to bed with him was not threatening or complicated, but it might be erotically enjoyable. And that, according to Blomkvist, was as it should be.

Blomkvist's best relationships had been with women he knew well and whom he liked a lot, so it was no accident that he had begun an affair with Berger twenty years earlier, when she was a young journalist.

His present renown, however, had increased women's interest in him to a point that he found bizarre. Most astonishing were the young women who made impulsive advances in unexpected circumstances.

But Blomkvist was not turned on by teenagers with miniskirts and perfect bodies. When he was younger his women friends had often been older than he—in some cases considerably older—and more experienced. Over time the age difference had evened out. Salander had definitely been a step in the other direction.

And this was the reason for his hastily called meeting with Berger.

Millennium had taken on a media school graduate for work experience, as a favour to one of Berger's friends. This was nothing unusual; they had several interns each year. Blomkvist had said a polite hello to the girl and rapidly discovered that she had only the vaguest interest in journalism beyond that she "wanted to be seen on TV" and that—Blomkvist suspected—at present it was quite a coup to work at *Millennium*.

She did not miss an opportunity to be in close contact with him. He pretended not to notice her blatant advances, but that only induced her to redouble her efforts. Quite simply, it was becoming tiresome.

Berger burst out laughing. "Good Lord, you're being sexually harassed at work."

"Ricky, this is a drag. There's no way I want to hurt or embarrass her. But she's no more subtle than a mare in heat. I'm worried what she might come up with next."

"She's got a crush on you and she's too young to know how to express herself."

"You're wrong. She knows damned well how to express herself. There's something warped about how far she goes, and she's getting annoyed that I'm not taking the bait. I don't need a new wave of rumours making me out to be some lecherous rock-star type on the hunt for a nice lay."

"OK, but let me get to the nub of the problem. She rang your doorbell last night—is that the extent of it?"

"With a bottle of wine. She said she'd been to a party at a friend's house close by and tried to make it look like pure chance that she found herself in my building."

"What did you tell her?"

"I didn't let her in, obviously. I said that she'd come at an awkward time, that I had a friend there."

"How did she take that?"

"She was really upset, but she did leave."

"What do you want me to do?"

"Get her off my back. I'm thinking of having a serious talk with her on Monday. Either she lays off or I'll kick her out of the office."

Berger thought for a moment. "Let me have a talk with her. She's looking for a friend, not a lover."

"I don't know what she's looking for, but . . ."

"Mikael. I've been through what she's going through. I'll talk to her."

Like everyone else who had watched TV or read an evening paper in the past year, Bjurman had heard of Mikael Blomkvist. But he did not recognize him in Café Hedon, and in any case he had no idea that there was a connection between Salander and *Millennium*.

Besides, he was too wrapped up in his own thoughts to pay attention to his surroundings.

Ever since the lifting of his mental paralysis, he had been continuously circling round and round the same conundrum.

Salander had in her possession a video of his assault on her which she had recorded with a hidden camera. She had made him watch the video. There was no room for favourable inter-pretations. If it ever got to the Guardianship Agency, or, God for-bid, if it ended up in the hands of the media, his career, his freedom, and his life would be over. He knew the penalties for aggravated rape, exploitation of a person in a subordinate position, abuse and aggravated abuse; he reckoned he would get at least six years in prison. A zealous prosecutor might use one section of the video as the basis for a charge of attempted murder.

He had all but asphyxiated her during the rape when he had excitedly pressed a pillow over her face. He devoutly wished he had finished the job.

They would not accept that she was the whole time playing a game. She had enticed him with her cute little-girl eyes, had seduced him with a body that looked like a twelve-year-old's. She had provoked him to rape her. They would never see that she had in fact put on a performance. She had planned . . .

The first thing he would have to do was to gain possession of the video and make sure somehow that there were no copies. That was the crux of the problem.

There was no doubt in his mind that a witch like Salander would have made enemies over the years. Here Bjurman had an advantage. Unlike anyone else who might try to get at her, he had access to all her medical records, welfare reports, and psychiatric assessments. He was one of the very few people in Sweden who knew her secrets.

The personal file that the agency had copied to him when he agreed to serve as her guardian had been a mere fifteen pages that mainly presented a picture of her adult life, a summary of the assessment made by the court-appointed psychiatrists, the district court's ruling to place her under guardianship, and her bank statements for the preceding year.

He had read the file over and over. Then he had begun systematically to gather information on Salander's life.

As a lawyer he was well practiced in extracting information from the records of public authorities. As her guardian he was able to penetrate the layers of confidentiality surrounding her medical records. He could get hold of every document he wanted that dealt with Salander.

It had nevertheless taken months to put together her life, detail by detail, from her first elementary school reports to social workers' reports to police reports and transcripts from the district court. He had discussed her condition with Dr. Jesper H. Löderman, the psychiatrist who on her eighteenth birthday had recommended that she be institutionalized. Löderman gave him a rundown of the case. Everyone was helpful. A woman at the welfare agency had even praised him for showing such determination to understand every aspect of Salander's life.

He found a real gold mine of information in the form of two notebooks in a box gathering dust in the archive of the Guardianship Agency. The notebooks had been compiled by Bjurman's predecessor, the lawyer Holger Palmgren, who had apparently come to know Salander as well as or better than anyone. Palmgren had conscientiously submitted a report each year to the agency, and Bjurman supposed Salander had probably not known that Palmgren also made meticulous notes for himself. Palmgren's notebooks had ended up with the Guardianship Agency, where it seemed no-one had read their contents since he had suffered a stroke two years earlier.

They were the originals. There was no indication that copies had ever been made. Perfect.

Palmgren's picture of Salander was completely different from what could be deduced from the welfare agency's report. He had been able to follow her laborious progress from unruly teenager to young woman to employee at Milton Security—a job she had obtained through Palmgren's own contacts. Bjurman learned from these notes that Salander was by no means a slow-witted office junior who did the photocopying and made coffee. On the contrary, she had a real job, carrying out real investigations for Dragan Armansky, Milton's CEO. Palmgren and Armansky obviously knew each other well and exchanged information about their protégée from time to time.

. . .

Salander seemed to have only two friends in her life. Palmgren was out of the picture now. Armansky remained, and could possibly be a threat. Bjurman decided to steer clear of Armansky.

The notebooks had explained a lot. Bjurman understood how Salander had discovered so much about him. He could not for the life of him see how she had found out about his visit to the plastic surgery clinic in France, but much of the mystery surrounding her had vanished. She made her living burrowing into other people's lives. He at once took fresh precautions with his own investigations and decided that since Salander had access to his apartment, it was not a good idea to keep any papers there that dealt with her case. He gathered all the documentation and filled a cardboard box to take to his summer cabin near Stallarholmen, where he was spending more and more of his time in solitary brooding.

The more he read about Salander, the more convinced he became that she was pathologically unwell. He shuddered to remember how she had handcuffed him to his bed. He had been totally under her control then, and he did not doubt that she would make good her threat to kill him if he provoked her.

She lacked social inhibitions, one of her reports stated. Well, he could conclude a stage or two further: *she was a sick, murderous, insane fucking person. A loose cannon. A whore.*

Palmgren's notebooks had provided Bjurman with the final key. On several occasions he had recorded very personal diary-type accounts of conversations that he had had with Salander. A crazy old man. In two of these conversations he had used the expression "when 'All The Evil' happened." Presumably Palmgren had borrowed the expression directly from Salander, but it was not clear what event it referred to.

Bjurman wrote down the words *All The Evil*. The years in foster homes? Some particular attack? The explanation ought to be there in the documentation to which he already had access.

He opened the psychiatric assessment of Salander as an eighteen-year-old and read it through for the fifth or sixth time. There had to be a gap in his knowledge.

He had excerpts from journal entries from elementary school, an affidavit to the effect that Salander's mother was incapable of taking care of her, and reports from various foster homes during her teens.

Something had set off the madness when she was twelve.

There were other gaps in her biography.

He discovered to his great surprise that Salander had a twin sister who had not been referred to in any of the material to which he had previously had access. *My God, there are two of them.* But he could not find any reference to what had happened to the sister.

The father was unknown, and there was no explanation as to why her mother could not take care of her. Bjurman had supposed that she had become ill and that as a result the whole process had begun, including the spells in the children's psychiatric unit. But now he was sure that something had happened to Salander when she was twelve or thirteen. *All The Evil.* A trauma of some kind. But there was no indication in Palmgren's notes as to what "All The Evil" could have been.

In the psychiatric assessment he finally found a reference to an attachment that was missing—the number of a police report dated March 12, 1991. It was handwritten in the margin of the copy from the social welfare agency archive. When he put in a request for the report he was told that it was stamped "TOP SECRET by Order of His Royal Highness," but that he could file an appeal with the relevant government department.

Bjurman was stymied. The fact that a police report dealing with a twelve-year-old girl was classified was not in itself surprising—there could be all manner of reasons for the protection of privacy. But he was Salander's guardian and had the right to study any document at all which concerned her. He could not understand why gaining access to such a report should require an appeal to a government department.

He submitted his application. Two months passed before he was informed that his request had been denied. What could there be in a police report almost fourteen years old about so young a girl to classify it as top secret? What possible threat could it contain to Sweden's government?

He returned to Palmgren's diary, trying to tease out what might be meant by "All The Evil." But he found no clue. It had to have been discussed between Palmgren and his ward but never written down. The references to "All The Evil" came at the end of the second notebook. Perhaps Palmgren had never had time to write up his own conclusions about this apparently crucial series of events before he had his stroke.

Palmgren had been Salander's trustee from her thirteenth birthday and her guardian from the day she turned eighteen. So he had been involved shortly after "All The Evil" had taken place and Salander was put away in the children's psychiatric unit. Chances were that he knew about everything that had happened.

Bjurman went back to the archive of the Guardianship Agency, this time to find the detailed brief of Palmgren's assignment, drawn up by the social welfare agency. At first glance the description was disappointing: two pages of background information. Salander's mother was now incapable of bringing up her daughter; the two children had to be separated; Camilla Salander was placed through the social welfare agency in a foster family; Lisbeth Salander was confined at St. Stefan's children's psychiatric clinic. No alternative was discussed.

Why? Only a cryptic formulation: "In view of the events of 3/12/91 the social welfare agency has determined that . . ." Then again a reference to the classified police report. But here there was the name of the policeman who wrote the report.

Bjurman registered the name with shock. He knew it well. Indeed he knew it very well, and this discovery put matters in a wholly new light. It still took him two more months to get the report, this time via completely different methods. It consisted of forty-seven pages of A4, with a dozen or so pages of notes that were added over a six-year period. And finally the photographs. And the name.

My God . . . it can't be possible.

Now he realized why the report had been stamped top secret.

There was one other person who had reason to hate Salander with the same passion as he did.

He had an ally, the most improbable ally he could have imagined.

Bjurman was roused from his reverie by a shadow falling across the table at Café Hedon. He looked up and saw a blond . . . *giant* was the only word for him. For a few seconds he recoiled before he regained his composure.

The man looking down at him stood more than six foot six and had an exceptionally powerful build. A bodybuilder without a doubt. Bjurman could not see a hint of fat. The man made a terrifying impression. His blond hair was cropped close at the sides with a short shock left on top. He had an oval, oddly soft, almost childlike face. His ice-blue eyes, however, were not remotely gentle. He was dressed in a midlength black leather jacket, blue shirt, black tie, and black trousers. The last thing Bjurman noticed was his hands. If all of the rest of him was large, his hands were enormous.

"Advokat Bjurman?"

He spoke with some European accent, but his voice was so peculiarly high-pitched that Bjurman was tempted to smile. With difficulty he kept his expression neutral and nodded.

"We got your letter."

"Who are you? I wanted to meet . . ."

The man with the enormous hands was already sitting opposite Bjurman and cut him off.

"You'll have to meet me instead. Tell me what you want."

Bjurman hesitated. He disliked intensely the idea of having to be at the mercy of a stranger. But it was a necessity. He reminded himself that he was not alone in having a grudge against Salander. It was a question of recruiting allies. In a low voice he explained his business.

CHAPTER 3

Friday, December 17– Saturday, December 18

Salander woke at 7:00 a.m., showered, and went down to see Freddy McBain at the front desk to ask if there was a dune buggy she could rent for the day. Ten minutes later she had paid the deposit, adjusted the seat and rearview mirror, test-started it, and checked that there was fuel in the tank. She went into the bar and ordered a caffè latte and a cheese sandwich for breakfast, and a bottle of mineral water to take with her. She spent breakfast scribbling figures on a paper napkin and pondering Pierre de Fermat's ($x^3 + y^3 = z^3$).

Just after 8:00 Dr. Forbes came into the bar. He was freshly shaven and dressed in a dark suit, white shirt, and blue tie. He ordered eggs, toast, orange juice, and black coffee. At 8:30 he got up and walked out to a waiting taxi.

Salander followed at a suitable distance. Forbes left the taxi below Seascape at the start of the Carenage and strolled along the water's edge. She drove past him, parked near the centre of the harbour promenade, and waited patiently until he passed her before she followed him again.

By 1:00 p.m. Salander was drenched with sweat and her feet were swollen. For four hours she had walked up one street in St. George's and down another. Her pace had been leisurely, but she never stopped. The steep hills began to strain her muscles. She was astonished at Forbes' energy as she drank the last drops of her mineral water. She had begun to think of giving up the project when suddenly he turned towards the Turtleback. She gave him ten minutes before she too entered the restaurant and sat outside on the veranda. They both sat in the same places as the day before, and just as he had done then, he drank a Coca-Cola as he stared at the harbour.

Forbes was one of very few people on Grenada in a suit and tie. He seemed untroubled by the heat.

At 3:00 he disturbed Salander's train of thought by paying and leaving the restaurant. He walked unhurriedly along the Carenage and hopped on one of the minibuses heading out to Grand Anse.

Salander parked outside the Keys Hotel five minutes before the bus dropped him off. She went to her room, ran a bath with cold water, and stretched out in it, frowning deeply.

The day's exertions—her feet were still aching—had given her a clear message. Every morning Forbes left the hotel dressed for battle with his briefcase, yet he spent the day doing absolutely nothing except killing time. Whatever he was doing on Grenada, he was not planning the building of a new school, and yet he wanted to give the impression that he was on the island for business.

Then why all this theatre?

The only person he might want to hide something from in this connection was his wife, who presumably thought that he was extremely busy during the day. But why? Had the deal fallen through and he was too proud to admit it? Did he have another objective on this visit to the island? Was he waiting for something, or someone?

Salander had four email messages. The first was from Plague and had been sent only an hour after she had written to him. The message was encrypted and posed the question: "Are you really alive?" Plague had never been much for writing rambling, sentimental emails. Nor, for that matter, had Salander.

Two further emails had been sent around 2:00 a.m. One was from Plague, also encrypted, telling her that an Internet acquaintance who went by the name of Bilbo, who apparently lived in Texas, had snapped up her enquiry. Plague attached Bilbo's address and PGP key. Minutes later Bilbo emailed her from a hotmail address. The message said only that Bilbo would send the data on Dr. Forbes and his wife within twenty-four hours.

The fourth email was also from Bilbo, sent late that afternoon. It contained an encrypted bank account number and an FTP address. Salander opened the URL and found a Zip file of 390 KB, which she extracted and saved. It was a folder containing four low-resolution photographs and five Word documents.

Two of the pictures were of Dr. Forbes alone; one of them had been taken at the première of a play and showed Forbes with his wife. The fourth photograph was of Forbes in a church pulpit.

The first document contained eleven pages of text, which was Bilbo's report. The second document contained eighty-four pages of text downloaded from the Internet. The next two documents were OCR-scanned newspaper clippings from the *Austin American-Statesman,* and the final document was an overview of Dr. Forbes' congregation, the Presbyterian Church of Austin South.

Apart from the fact that Salander knew the Book of Leviticus by heart—the year before, she had had occasion to study biblical references to punishment—she had little more than a sketchy grasp of religious history. She had only a vague sense of the differences between Jewish, Presbyterian, and Catholic churches, apart from the fact that the Jewish ones were called synagogues. For a moment she was afraid that she would have to immerse herself in the theological details. But on reflection she didn't give a flying fuck what sort of congregation Dr. Forbes belonged to.

Dr. Richard Forbes, aka Reverend Richard Forbes, was forty-two. The home page of the Church of Austin South showed that the church had seven employees. Reverend Duncan Clegg was at the top of the list. The photograph showed a powerful man with bushy grey hair and a well-groomed grey beard.

Forbes was the third name on the list, responsible for educational matters. Next to his name it also said "Holy Water Foundation" in parentheses.

Salander read the introduction to the church's mission statement.

> *Through prayer and thanksgiving we shall serve the people of Austin South by offering the stability, theology, and hopeful ideology as defended by the Presbyterian Church of America. As Christ's servants we offer a refuge for people in need and a promise of atonement through prayer and the sacrament of baptism. Let us be joyful in God's love. Our duty is to remove the barriers between people and to erase the obstacles to an understanding of God's message of love.*

Below the introduction was the church's bank account number and an appeal to convert one's love of God into action. From Bilbo's succinct biography Salander learned that Forbes was born in Pine Bluff, Nevada, and had worked as a farmer, businessman, school administrator, local correspondent for a newspaper in New Mexico, and manager of a Christian rock band before joining the Church of Austin South at the age of thirty-one. He was a certified public accountant and had also studied archaeology. Bilbo had not been able to find the source of his doctorate.

Forbes had met Geraldine Knight in the congregation, the

only daughter of rancher William F. Knight, also a member of Austin South. The couple had married in 1997, and subsequently Forbes' star in the church had risen. He became the head of the Santa Maria Foundation, the aim of which was to "invest God's funds in educational projects for the needy."

Forbes had been arrested twice. At the age of twenty-five, in 1987, he had been charged with aggravated bodily harm following a car accident. He was acquitted by the court. As far as Salander could tell from the press clippings, he was indeed innocent. In 1995 he was charged with embezzling money from the Christian rock band he managed. He was acquitted that time too.

In Austin he had become a prominent public figure and a member of the city's board of education. He was a member of the Democratic Party, participated diligently in charity work, and collected money to fund schooling for children in less fortunate families. The Church of Austin South concentrated its work among Spanish-speaking families.

In 2001, allegations had been made against Forbes for financial irregularities in his work with the Santa Maria Foundation. According to one newspaper article, Forbes was suspected of having placed a larger portion of the assets into investment funds than was stipulated in the statutes. The accusations were denied by the church, and the Reverend Clegg stood firmly on Forbes' side in the controversy. No charges were filed, and an audit turned up nothing untoward.

Salander studied Bilbo's summary of Forbes' own finances. He had an annual income of $60,000, which was considered a decent salary, but he himself had no assets. Geraldine Forbes was responsible for their financial stability. Her father had died in 2002. The daughter was sole heir to a fortune worth at least $40 million. The couple had no children.

Forbes was therefore dependent on his wife. Salander thought that this was not a good position to be in if you were in the habit of abusing your wife.

She logged on to the Internet and sent an encrypted message to Bilbo thanking him for his report, and then she transferred $500 to his account.

She went out on the balcony and leaned against the railing. The sun was about to set. A breeze was rustling the crowns of the palm trees along the seawall. Grenada was feeling the outer bands of Matilda. She followed Ella Carmichael's advice and packed her computer, *Dimensions in Mathematics,* some personal effects, and a change of clothes into her shoulder bag and set it on the floor next to the bed. Then she went down to the bar and ordered fish for dinner and a bottle of Carib.

The only event of interest was when Dr. Forbes, who had changed into a light-coloured tennis shirt, shorts, and tennis shoes, approached the bar to ask Ella about Matilda's movements. He did not seem particularly anxious. He wore a cross on a gold chain around his neck and looked vigorous, even attractive.

Salander was worn out after the day's fruitless wandering in St. George's. She took a short walk after dinner, but the wind was blowing hard and the temperature had dropped sharply. She went back to her room and crept into bed by 9:00. The wind was rattling the windows. She had intended to read for a while but fell fast asleep almost immediately.

She was awakened all of a sudden by a loud banging. She looked at her watch: 11:15. She lurched out of bed and opened the door to the balcony. Gusts of wind made her take a step back. She braced herself on the doorjamb, took a cautious step onto the balcony, and looked around.

Some hanging lamps around the pool were swinging back and forth, creating a dramatic shadow play in the garden. She noticed that several hotel guests were standing by the opening in the wall, looking out at the beach. Others were grouped near the bar. To the north she could see the lights of St. George's.

The sky was overcast, but it was not raining. She could not see the ocean in the dark, but the roar of the waves was much louder than usual. The temperature had dropped even further. For the first time since she had arrived in the Caribbean she shivered with cold.

As she stood on the balcony there was a loud knock on her door. She wrapped a sheet around her and opened the door. Freddy McBain looked resolute.

"Pardon me for bothering you, but there seems to be a storm."

"Matilda."

"Matilda," McBain said. "She struck outside Tobago earlier this evening and we've received reports of substantial destruction."

Salander went through her knowledge of geography and meteorology. Trinidad and Tobago lay about 125 miles southeast of Grenada. A tropical storm could spread to a radius of 60 miles, and its eye could move at a speed of 20 to 25 miles an hour. Which meant that Matilda might be knocking at Grenada's door any time now. It all depended on which direction it was heading.

"There's no immediate danger," McBain said, "but we're not taking any chances. I want you to pack your valuables in a bag and come down to the lobby. The hotel will provide coffee and sandwiches."

Salander washed her face to wake up, pulled on some jeans, shoes, and a flannel shirt, and picked up her shoulder bag. Before she left the room she went and opened the bathroom door and turned on the light. The green lizard wasn't there; it must have crept into some hole. Smart girl.

In the bar she settled in her usual spot and watched Ella Carmichael directing her staff and filling thermoses with hot drinks. After a while she came over to Lisbeth's corner.

"Hi. You look like you just woke up."

"I did sleep a little. What happens now?"

"We wait. Out at sea there's a heavy storm, and we got a

hurricane warning from Trinidad. If it gets worse and Matilda comes this way, we'll go into the cellar. Can you lend us a hand?"

"What do you want me to do?"

"We have a hundred and sixty blankets in the lobby to be carried down. And we have a lot of things that need to be stowed."

Salander helped carry the blankets downstairs and brought in flower vases, tables, chaises longues, and other unfixed items from around the pool. When Ella was satisfied and told her that was enough, Salander went over to the opening in the wall that faced the beach and took a few steps out into the darkness. The sea was booming menacingly and the wind tore at her so strongly that she had to brace herself to stay upright. The palm trees along the wall were swaying.

She went back inside, ordered a caffè latte, and sat with it at the bar. It was past midnight. The atmosphere among the guests and staff was anxious. People were having subdued conversations, looking towards the horizon from time to time, and waiting. There were thirty-two guests and a staff of ten at the Keys Hotel. Salander noticed Geraldine Forbes at a table by the front desk. She looked tense and was nursing a drink. Her husband was nowhere to be seen.

Salander drank her coffee and had once more started in on Fermat's theorem when McBain came out of the office and stood in the middle of the lobby.

"May I have your attention, please? I have been informed that a hurricane-force storm has just hit Petite Martinique. I have to ask everyone to go down to the cellar at once."

McBain stonewalled the many questions and directed his guests to the cellar stairs behind the front desk. Petite Martinique, a small island belonging to Grenada, was only a few sea miles north of the main island. Salander glanced at Ella Carmichael and pricked up her ears when the bartender went over to McBain.

"How bad is it?"

"No way of knowing. The telephone lines are down," McBain said in a low voice.

Salander went down to the cellar and put her bag on a blanket in the corner. She thought for a moment and then headed back up against the flow to the lobby. She found Ella and asked her if there was anything else she could do to help. Ella shook her head, looking worried.

"Matilda is a bitch. We'll just have to see what happens."

Salander watched a group of five adults and about ten children hurrying in through the hotel entrance. McBain took charge of them too and directed them to the cellar stairs.

Salander was suddenly struck by a worrisome thought.

"I suppose everybody will be going down into their cellars about now," she said quietly.

Ella watched the family going down the stairs.

"Unfortunately ours is one of the few cellars on Grand Anse. More people will probably be coming to seek shelter here."

Salander gave her a sharp look.

"What will the rest do?"

"The ones who don't have cellars?" She gave a bitter laugh. "They'll huddle in their houses or look for shelter in a shed. They have to trust in God."

Salander turned and ran through the lobby and out of the entrance.

George Bland.

She heard Ella call after her, but she did not stop to explain.

He lives in a fucking shack that will collapse with the first gust of wind.

As she reached the road to St. George's she staggered in the wind that tore at her body, and then she began to jog. She was heading stubbornly into a heavy headwind that made her reel. It took almost ten minutes to cover the four hundred yards to the shack. She did not see a living soul the whole way there.

The rain came out of nowhere like an ice-cold shower from a fire hose. At the same instant, she turned in towards the shack and saw the light from his kerosene lamp swinging in the window. She was drenched in a second, and she could hardly see two yards in front of her. She hammered on his door. George Bland opened it with eyes wide.

"What are you doing here?" He shouted to be heard above the wind.

"Come on. You have to come to the hotel. They have a cellar."

The boy looked shocked. The wind slammed the door shut and it was several seconds before he could force it open again. Salander grabbed hold of his T-shirt and dragged him out. She wiped the water from her face, then gripped his hand and began to run. He ran with her.

They took the beach path, which was about a hundred yards shorter than the main road, which looped inland. When they had gone halfway, Salander realized that this might have been a mistake. On the beach they had no protection at all. Wind and rain tore at them so hard that they had to stop several times. Sand and branches were flying through the air. There was a terrible roar. After what seemed an eternity Salander finally spied the hotel walls and picked up the pace. Just as they made it to the entrance and the promise of safety, she looked over her shoulder at the beach. She stopped short.

Through a rain squall she spotted two figures about fifty yards down the beach. Bland pulled her arm to drag her through the door. She let go of his hand and braced herself against the wall as she tried to focus on the water's edge. For a second or two she lost sight of the figures in the rain, but then the entire sky was lit up by a flash of lightning.

She knew already that it was Richard and Geraldine Forbes. They were at about the same place where she had seen Forbes wandering back and forth the night before.

When the next flash came, Forbes appeared to be dragging his wife, who was struggling with him.

All the pieces of the puzzle fell into place. The financial

dependence. The allegations of chicanery in Austin. His restless wandering and motionless hours at the Turtleback.

He's planning to murder her. Forty million in the pot. The storm is his camouflage. This is his chance.

Salander turned and shoved Bland through the door. She looked around and found the rickety wooden chair the night watchman usually sat on, which had not been cleared away before the storm. She smashed it as hard as she could against the wall and armed herself with one of its legs. Bland screamed after her in horror as she ran towards the beach.

She was almost bowled over by the furious gusts, but she clenched her teeth and worked her way forward, step by step, into the storm. She had almost reached the couple when one more flash of lightning lit up the beach and she saw Geraldine Forbes sink to her knees by the water's edge. Forbes stood over her, his arm raised to strike with what looked like an iron pipe in his hand. She saw his arm move in an arc towards his wife's head. Geraldine stopped struggling.

Forbes never saw Salander coming.

She cracked the chair leg over the back of his head and he fell forward on his face.

Salander bent and took hold of Geraldine Forbes. As the rain whipped across them, she turned the body over. Her hands were suddenly bloody. Geraldine Forbes had a wound on her scalp. She was as heavy as lead, and Salander looked around desperately, wondering how she was going to pull her up to the hotel wall. Then Bland appeared at her side. He shouted something that Salander could not make out in the storm.

She glanced at Forbes. He had his back to her, but he was up on all fours. She took Geraldine's left arm and put it around her neck and motioned to Bland to take the other arm. They began laboriously dragging her up the beach.

Halfway to the hotel wall Salander felt completely drained, as if all strength had left her body. Her heart skipped a beat when she felt a hand grab her shoulder. She let go of Geraldine and spun around to kick Forbes in the crotch. He stumbled to his knees. Then she kicked him in the face. She saw Bland's horrified expression. Salander gave him half a second of attention before she again took hold of Geraldine Forbes and resumed dragging her.

After a few seconds she turned her head. Forbes was tottering ten paces behind them, but he was swaying like a drunk in the gusting winds.

Another bolt of lightning cleaved the sky and Salander opened her eyes wide.

She felt a paralyzing terror.

Behind Forbes, a hundred yards out to sea, she saw the finger of God.

A frozen image in the sudden flash, a coal black pillar that towered up and vanished from sight into space.

Matilda.

It's not possible.

A hurricane—yes.

A tornado—impossible.

Grenada is not in a tornado zone.

A freak storm in a region where tornadoes can't happen.

Tornadoes cannot form over water.

This is scientifically wrong.

This is something unique.

It has come to take me.

Bland had seen the tornado too. They yelled at each other to hurry, not able to hear what the other was saying.

Twenty yards more to the wall. Ten. Salander tripped and fell to her knees. Five. At the gate she took one last look over her shoulder. She caught a glimpse of Forbes just as he was tugged into the sea as if by an invisible hand and disappeared. She and Bland heaved their burden through the gate. As they staggered across the back courtyard, over the storm Salander heard the crash of windowpanes shattering and the screeching whine of twisting sheet metal. A plank flew through the air right past her nose. The next second she felt pain as something solid struck her in the back. The violence of the wind diminished when they reached the lobby.

Salander stopped Bland and grabbed his collar. She pulled his head to her mouth and yelled in his ear.

"We found her on the beach. We didn't see the husband. Understood?"

He nodded.

They carried Geraldine Forbes down the cellar stairs and Salander kicked at the door. McBain opened it and stared at them. Then he pulled them in and shut the door again.

The noise from the storm dropped in a second from an intolerable roar to a creaking and rumbling in the background. Salander took a deep breath.

Ella poured hot coffee into a mug. Salander was so shattered she could scarcely raise her arm to take it. She sat passively on the floor, leaning against the wall. Someone had wrapped blankets around both her and the boy. She was soaked through and bleeding badly from a gash below her kneecap. There was a rip about four inches long in her jeans and she had no memory of it happening. She watched numbly as McBain and two hotel guests worked on Geraldine Forbes, wrapping bandages around her head. She caught words here and there and understood that someone in the group was a doctor. She noticed that the cellar was packed and that the hotel guests had been joined by people from outside who had come looking for shelter.

After a while McBain came over to Salander and squatted down.

"She'll live."

Salander said nothing.

"What happened?"

"We found her beyond the wall on the beach."

"I was missing three people when I counted the guests

down here in the cellar. You and the Forbes couple. Ella said that you ran off like a crazy person just as the storm got here."

"I went to get my friend George." Salander nodded at Bland. "He lives down the road in a shack that can't possibly still be standing."

"That was very brave but awfully stupid," McBain said, glancing at Bland. "Did either of you two see the husband?"

"No," Salander said with a neutral expression. Bland glanced at her and shook his head.

Ella tilted her head and gave Salander a sharp look. Salander looked back at her with expressionless eyes.

Geraldine Forbes came to at around 3:00 a.m. By that time Salander had fallen asleep with her head on Bland's shoulder.

In some miraculous way, Grenada survived the night. McBain allowed the guests out of the cellar, and when dawn broke the storm had died away, replaced by the most torrential rain Salander had ever seen.

The Keys Hotel would be needing a major overhaul. The devastation at the hotel, and all along the coast, was extensive. Ella's bar beside the pool was gone altogether, and one veranda had been demolished. Windows had peeled off along the facade, and the roof of a projecting section of the hotel had bent in two. The lobby was a chaos of debris.

Salander took Bland with her and staggered up to her room. She hung a blanket over the empty window frame to keep out the rain. Bland met her gaze.

"There'll be less to explain if we didn't see her husband," Salander said before he could ask any questions.

He nodded. She pulled off her clothes, dropped them on the floor, and patted the edge of the bed next to her. He nodded again and undressed and crawled in beside her. They were asleep almost at once.

When she awoke at midday, the sun was shining through

cracks in the clouds. Every muscle in her body ached, and her knee was so swollen that she could hardly bend it. She slipped out of bed and got into the shower. The green lizard was back on the wall. She put on shorts and a top and stumbled out of the room without waking Bland.

Ella was still on her feet. She looked dog-tired, but she had gotten the bar in the lobby up and running. Salander ordered coffee and a sandwich. Through the blown-out windows by the entrance she saw a police car. Just as her coffee arrived, McBain came out of his office by the front desk, followed by a uniformed policeman. McBain caught sight of her and said something to the policeman before they came over to Salander's table.

"This is Constable Ferguson. He'd like to ask you some questions."

Salander greeted him politely. Constable Ferguson had obviously had a long night, too. He took out a notebook and pen and wrote down Salander's name.

"Ms. Salander, I understand that you and a friend discovered Mrs. Richard Forbes during the hurricane last night."

Salander nodded.

"Where did you find her?"

"On the beach just below the gate," Salander said. "We almost tripped over her."

Ferguson wrote that down.

"Did she say anything?"

Salander shook her head.

"She was unconscious?"

Salander nodded sensibly.

"She had a nasty wound on her head."

Salander nodded again.

"You don't know how she was injured?"

Salander shook her head. Ferguson muttered in irritation at her lack of response.

"There was a lot of stuff flying through the air," she said helpfully. "I was almost hit in the head by a plank."

"You injured your leg?" Ferguson pointed at her bandage. "What happened?"

"I didn't notice it until I got down to the cellar."

"You were with a young man."

"George Bland."

"Where does he live?"

"In a shack behind the Coconut, on the road to the airport. If the shack is still standing, that is."

Salander did not add that Bland was at that moment asleep in her bed three floors above them.

"Did either of you see her husband, Richard Forbes?"

Salander shook her head.

Constable Ferguson could not, it seemed, think of any other questions to ask, and he closed his notebook.

"Thank you, Ms. Salander. I'll have to write up a report on the death."

"Did she *die*?"

"Mrs. Forbes? No, she's in hospital in St. George's. Apparently she has you and your friend to thank for the fact that she's alive. But her husband is dead. His body was found in a parking lot at the airport two hours ago."

Six hundred yards further south.

"He was pretty badly knocked about," Ferguson said.

"How unfortunate," Salander said without any great sign of shock.

When McBain and Constable Ferguson had gone, Ella came and sat at Salander's table. She set down two shot glasses of rum. Salander gave her a quizzical look.

"After a night like that you need something to rebuild your strength. I'm buying. I'm buying the whole breakfast."

The two women looked at each other. Then they clinked glasses and said, "Cheers."

For a long time to come, Matilda would be the object of scientific studies and discussions at meteorological institutes in the Caribbean and across the United States. Tornadoes of Matilda's scale were almost unknown in the region. Gradually the experts agreed that a particularly rare constellation of weather fronts had combined to create a "pseudo-tornado"— something that was not actually a tornado but looked like one.

Salander did not care about the theoretical discussion. She knew what she had seen, and she decided to try to avoid getting in the way of any of Matilda's siblings in the future.

Many people on the island had been injured during the night. Only one person died.

No-one would ever know what had induced Richard Forbes to go out in the midst of a full-fledged hurricane, save possibly that sheer ignorance which seemed common to American tourists. Geraldine Forbes was not able to offer any explanation. She had suffered a severe concussion and had only incoherent memories of the events of that night.

On the other hand, she was inconsolable to have been left a widow.

PART 2

From Russia with Love

An equation commonly contains one or more so-called unknowns, often represented by x, y, z, etc. Values given to the unknowns which yield equality between both sides of the equation are said to satisfy the equation and constitute a solution.

Example: $3x + 4 = 6x - 2$ $(x = 2)$

CHAPTER 4

Monday, January 10– Tuesday, January 11

Salander landed at Stockholm's Arlanda Airport at noon. In addition to the flying time, she had spent nine hours at Grantley Adams Airport on Barbados. British Airways had refused to let the aircraft take off until a passenger who looked vaguely Arabic had been taken away for questioning and a possible terrorist threat had been snuffed out. By the time she landed at Gatwick in London, she had missed her connecting flight to Sweden and had had to wait overnight before she could be rebooked.

Salander felt like a bag of bananas that had been left too long in the sun. All she had with her was a carry-on bag containing her PowerBook, *Dimensions,* and a change of clothes. She passed unchecked through the green gate at Customs. When she got outside to the airport shuttle buses she was welcomed home by a blast of freezing sleet.

She hesitated. All her life she had had to choose the cheapest option, and she was not yet used to the idea that she had more than three billion kronor, which she had stolen by means of an Internet coup combined with good old-fashioned fraud. After a few moments of getting cold and wet, she said to hell with the rule book and waved for a taxi. She gave the driver her address on Lundagatan and fell asleep in the backseat.

It was not until the taxi drew up on Lundagatan and the driver shook her awake that she realized she had given him her old address. She told him she had changed her mind and asked him to continue on to Götgatsbacken. She gave him a big tip in dollars and swore as she stepped into a puddle in the gutter. She was dressed in jeans, T-shirt, and a thin cloth jacket. She wore sandals and short cotton socks. She walked gingerly over to the 7-Eleven, where she bought some shampoo, toothpaste, soap, kefir, milk, cheese, eggs, bread, frozen cinnamon rolls, coffee, Lipton's tea bags, a jar of pickles, apples, a large package of Billy's Pan Pizza, and a pack of Marlboro Lights. She paid with a Visa card.

When she came back out on the street she hesitated about which way to go. She could walk up Svartensgatan or down Hökens Gata towards Slussen. The drawback with Hökens Gata was that then she would have to walk right past the door of the *Millennium* offices, running the risk of bumping into Blomkvist. In the end she decided not to go out of her way to avoid him. She walked towards Slussen, although it was a bit longer that way, and turned off to the right by way of Hökens Gata up to Mosebacke Torg. She cut across the square past the statue of the Sisters in front of Södra Theatre and took the steps up the hill to Fiskargatan. She stopped and looked up at the apartment building pensively. It did not really feel like "home."

She looked around. It was an out-of-the-way spot in the middle of Södermalm Island. There was no through traffic, which was fine with her. It was easy to observe who was moving about the area. It was apparently popular with walkers in the summertime, but in the winter the only ones there were those who had business in the neighbourhood. There was hardly a soul to be seen now—certainly not anyone she recognized, or who might reasonably be expected to recognize her. Salander set down her shopping bag in the slush to dig out her keys. She took the elevator to the top floor and unlocked the door with the nameplate V. KULLA.

One of the first things Salander had done after she came into a very large sum of money and thereby became financially independent for the rest of her life (or for as long as three billion kronor could be expected to last) was to look around for an apartment. The property market had been a new experience for her. She had never before invested money in anything more substantial than occasional useful items which she could either pay for with cash or buy on a reasonable payment plan. The biggest outlays had previously been various computers and her lightweight Kawasaki motorcycle. She had bought the bike for 7,000 kronor—a real bargain. She had spent about as much on spare parts and devoted several months to taking the motorcycle apart and overhauling it. She had wanted a car, but she had been wary of buying one, since she did not know how she would have fit it into her budget.

Buying an apartment, she realized, was a deal of a different order. She had started by reading the classified ads in the online edition of *Dagens Nyheter,* which was a science all to itself, she discovered:

1 bdrm + living/dining, fantastic loc. nr Södra Station, 2.7m kr or highest bid. S/ch 5510 p/m.

3 rms + kitchen, park view, Högalid, 2.9m kr.

2? rms, 47 sq. m., renov. bath, new plumbing 1998. Gotlandsgat. 1.8m kr. S/ch 2200 p/m.

She had telephoned some of the numbers haphazardly, but she had no idea what questions to ask. Soon she felt so idiotic that she stopped even trying. Instead she went out on the first Sunday in January and visited two apartment open houses.

One was on Vindragarvägen way out on Reimersholme, and
the other on Heleneborgsgatan near Hornstull. The apartment
on Reimers was a bright four-room place in a tower block with
a view of Långholmen and Essingen. There she could be content. The apartment on Heleneborgsgatan was a dump with a
view of the building next door.

The problem was that she could not decide which part of
town she wanted to live in, how her apartment should look, or
what sort of questions she should be asking of her new home.
She had never thought about an alternative to the 500 square
feet on Lundagatan, where she had spent her childhood.
Through her trustee at the time, the lawyer Holger Palmgren,
she had been granted possession of the apartment when she
turned eighteen. She plopped down on the lumpy sofa in her
combination office/living room and began to think.

The apartment on Lundagatan looked into a courtyard. It
was cramped and not the least bit comfortable. The view from
her bedroom was a firewall on a gable facade. The view from
the kitchen was of the back of the building facing the street
and the entrance to the basement storage area. She could see a
streetlight from her living room, and a few branches of a birch
tree.

The first requirement of her new home was that it should
have some sort of view.

She did not have a balcony, and had always envied well-to-
do neighbours higher up in the building who spent warm days
with a cold beer under an awning on theirs. The second
requirement was that her new home would have to have a balcony.

What should the apartment look like? She thought about
Blomkvist's apartment—700 square feet in one open space in
a converted loft on Bellmansgatan with views of City Hall and
the locks at Slussen. She had liked it there. She wanted to have
a pleasant, sparsely furnished apartment that was easy to take
care of. That was a third point on her list of requirements.

For years she had lived in cramped spaces. Her kitchen was

a mere 100 square feet, with room for only a tiny table and two chairs. Her living room was 200 square feet. The bedroom was a 120. Her fourth requirement was that the new apartment should have plenty of space and closets. She wanted to have a proper office and a big bedroom where she could spread herself out.

Her bathroom was a windowless cubbyhole with square cement slabs on the floor, an awkward half bath, and plastic wallpaper that never got really clean no matter how hard she scrubbed it. She wanted to have tiles and a big bath. She wanted a washing machine in the apartment and not down in some basement. She wanted the bathroom to smell fresh, and she wanted to be able to open a window.

Then she studied the offerings of estate agents online. The next morning she got up early to visit Nobel Estates, the company that, according to some, had the best reputation in Stockholm. She was dressed in old black jeans, boots, and her black leather jacket. She stood at a counter and watched a blond woman of about thirty-five, who had just logged on to the Nobel Estates website and was uploading photographs of apartments. At length a short, plump, middle-aged man with thin red hair came over. She asked him what sort of apartments he had available. He looked up at her in surprise and then assumed an avuncular tone:

"Well, young lady, do your parents know that you're thinking of moving away from home?"

Salander gave him a stone-cold glare until he stopped chuckling.

"I want an apartment," she said.

He cleared his throat and glanced appealingly at his colleague on the computer.

"I see. And what kind of apartment did you have in mind?"

"I think I'd like an apartment in Söder, with a balcony and a view of the water, at least four rooms, a bathroom with a window, and a utility room. And there has to be a lockable area where I can keep a motorcycle."

The woman at the computer looked up and stared at Salander.

"A motorcycle?" the thin-haired man said.

Salander nodded.

"May I know . . . uh, your name?"

Salander told him. She asked him for his name and he introduced himself as Joakim Persson.

"The thing is, it's rather expensive to purchase a cooperative apartment here in Stockholm . . ."

Salander did not reply. She had asked him what sort of apartments he had to offer; the information that it cost money was irrelevant.

"What line of work are you in?"

Salander thought for a moment. Technically she was a freelancer; in practice she worked only for Armansky and Milton Security, but that had been somewhat irregular over the past year. She had not done any work for him in three months.

"I'm not working at anything at the moment," she said.

"Well then . . . I presume you're still at school."

"No, I'm not at school."

Persson came around the counter and put his arm kindly around Salander's shoulders, escorting her towards the door.

"Well, you see, Ms. Salander, we'd be happy to welcome you back in a few years' time, but you'd have to bring along a little more money than what's in your piggy bank. The fact is that a weekly allowance won't really cover this." He pinched her good-naturedly on the cheek. "So drop in again, and we'll see about finding you a little pad."

Salander stood on the street outside Nobel Estates for several minutes. She wondered absentmindedly what little Master Persson would think if a Molotov cocktail came flying through his display window. Then she went home and booted up her PowerBook.

It took her ten minutes to hack into Nobel Estates' internal computer network using the passwords she happened to notice the woman behind the counter type in before she started uploading photographs. It took three minutes to find out that the computer the woman was working on was in fact also the company's Net server—*how dim can you get?*—and another three minutes to gain access to all fourteen computers on the network. After about two hours she had gone through Persson's records and discovered that there were some 750,000 kronor in under-the-table income that he had not reported to the tax authorities over the past two years.

She downloaded all the necessary files and emailed them to the tax authorities from an anonymous email account on a server in the USA. Then she put Master Persson out of her mind.

She spent the rest of the day going through Nobel Estates' listed properties. The most expensive one was a small palace outside Mariefred, where she had no desire to live. Out of sheer perversity she chose the next most expensive, a huge apartment just off Mosebacke Torg.

She scrutinized the photographs and floor plan, and in the end decided that it more than fulfilled her requirements. It had previously been owned by a director of the Asea Brown Boveri power company, who slipped into obscurity after he got himself a much-discussed and much-criticized golden parachute of several billion kronor.

That evening she telephoned Jeremy MacMillan, partner in the law firm MacMillan & Marks in Gibraltar. She had done business with MacMillan before. For a fee even he thought generous he had set up P.O. box companies to be owners of the accounts that administered the fortune she had stolen a year ago from the corrupt financier Hans-Erik Wennerström.

She engaged MacMillan's services again, instructing him to open negotiations with Nobel Estates on behalf of Wasp Enterprises to buy the apartment on Fiskargatan near Mosebacke Torg. It took four days, and the figure finally arrived at made her raise her eyebrows. Plus the 5 percent commission to

MacMillan. Before the week was out she had moved in with
two boxes of clothes and bed linens, a mattress, and some
kitchen utensils. She slept on the mattress in the apartment for
three weeks while she investigated clinics for plastic surgery,
straightened out a number of unresolved bureaucratic details
(including a nighttime talk with a certain lawyer, Nils Bjurman), and paid in advance for the rent at her old place, as well
as the electricity bills and other monthly expenses.

Then she had booked her journey to the clinic in Italy. When
the treatments were done and she was discharged, she sat in a
hotel room in Rome and thought about what to do next. She
should have returned to Sweden to get on with her life, but for
various reasons she could not bear to think about Stockholm.

She had no real profession. She could see for herself no
future at Milton Security. It was not Armansky's fault. In all
probability, he would have liked her to work full-time and turn
herself into an efficient cog in the company machine, but at
the age of twenty-five she lacked the education, and she had
no wish to find herself pushing fifty and still plodding away
doing investigations of crooks in the corporate world. It was
an amusing hobby—not a lifetime career.

Another reason she was reluctant to return to Stockholm
was Blomkvist. In Stockholm she would risk running into *Kalle
Fucking Blomkvist,* and at the moment that was just about the
last thing she wanted to do. He had hurt her. She acknowledged
that this had not been his intention. He had behaved rather
decently. It was her own fault that she had fallen "in love" with
him. The very phrase was a contradiction when it came to *Lisbeth Fucking Bitch Salander.*

Blomkvist was known for being a ladies' man. At best she
had been an amusing diversion, someone on whom he had
taken pity at a moment when he needed her and there was no-
one better available. But he had quickly moved on to yet more
amusing company. She cursed herself for lowering her guard
and letting him into her life.

When she came to her senses again she cut off all contact

with him. It had not been easy, but she had steeled herself. The last time she saw him she was standing on a platform in the tunnelbana at Gamla Stan and he was sitting in the train on his way downtown. She had stared at him for a whole minute and decided that she did not have a grain of feeling left, because it would have been the same as bleeding to death. *Fuck you.* He had noticed her just as the doors closed and looked at her with searching eyes before she turned and walked away as the train pulled out.

She didn't understand why he had so stubbornly tried to stay in contact with her, as if she were some fucking welfare project he had taken on. It annoyed her that he was so clueless. Every time he sent her an email she had to force herself to delete the message without reading it.

Stockholm did not seem in the least attractive. Apart from the freelance work for Milton Security, a few discarded bed partners, and the girls in the old rock group Evil Fingers, she hardly knew anyone in her hometown.

The only person she had any respect for now was Armansky. It was not easy to define her feelings for him. She had always felt a mild surprise that she was attracted to him. If he had not been quite so married, or quite so old, or quite so conservative, she might have considered making an advance.

So she took out her diary and turned to the atlas section. She had never been to Australia or Africa. She had read about but never seen the Pyramids or Angkor Wat. She had never ridden on the Star Ferry between Kowloon and Victoria in Hong Kong, and she had never gone snorkelling in the Caribbean or sat on a beach in Thailand. Apart from some quick business trips when she had visited the Baltics and neighbouring Nordic countries, as well as Zurich and London, of course, she had hardly ever left Sweden. As a matter of fact, she had seldom been outside Stockholm.

In the past she could never afford it.

She stood at the window of her hotel room overlooking Via Garibaldi in Rome. The city was like a pile of ruins. Then she made up her mind. She put on her jacket and went down to the lobby and asked if there was a travel agent in the vicinity. She booked a one-way ticket to Tel Aviv and spent the following days walking through the Old City in Jerusalem and visiting the al-Aqsa Mosque and the Wailing Wall. She viewed the armed soldiers on street corners with distrust, and then she flew to Bangkok and kept on travelling for the rest of the year.

There was only one thing she really had to do. She went to Gibraltar twice. The first time to do an in-depth investigation of the man she had chosen to look after her money. The second time to see to it that he was doing it properly.

It felt quite odd to turn the key to her own apartment on Fiskargatan after such a long time.

She set down her groceries and her shoulder bag in the hall and tapped in the four-digit code that turned off the electronic burglar alarm. Then she stripped off her damp clothes and dropped them on the hall floor. She walked into the kitchen naked, plugged in the refrigerator, and put the food away before she headed for the bathroom and spent the next ten minutes in the shower. She ate a meal consisting of a Billy's Pan Pizza, which she heated in the microwave, and a sliced apple. She opened one of her moving boxes and found a pillow, some sheets, and a blanket that smelled a little suspect after having been packed away for a year. She made up her bed on the mattress in a room next to the kitchen.

She fell asleep within ten seconds of her head hitting the pillow and slept for almost twelve hours. Then she got up, turned on the coffeemaker, wrapped a blanket around herself, and sat in the dark on a window seat, smoking a cigarette and looking out towards Djurgården and Saltsjön, fascinated by the lights.

· · ·

The day after Salander came home was a full day. She locked the door of her apartment at 7:00 in the morning. Before she left her floor she opened a ventilation window in the stairwell and fastened a spare key to a thin copper wire that she had tied to the wall side of a drainpipe clamp. Experience had taught her the wisdom of always having a spare key readily accessible.

The air outside was icy. Salander was dressed in a pair of thin, worn jeans that had a rip beneath one back pocket where her blue panties showed through. She had on a T-shirt and a warm polo sweater with a seam that had started to fray at the neck. She had also rediscovered her scuffed leather jacket with the rivets on the shoulders, and decided she should ask a tailor to repair the almost nonexistent lining in the pockets. She was wearing heavy socks and boots. Overall, she was nice and warm.

She walked down St. Paulsgatan to Zinkensdamm and over to her old apartment on Lundagatan. She checked first of all that her Kawasaki was still safe in the basement. She patted the seat before she went up to the apartment and had to push the front door open against a mountain of junk mail.

She hadn't been sure what to do with the apartment, so when she'd left Sweden a year ago, the simplest solution had been to arrange an automatic bank account to pay her regular bills. She still had furniture in the apartment, laboriously collected over time from various trash containers, along with some chipped mugs, two older computers, and a lot of paper. But nothing of value.

She took a black trash bag from the kitchen and spent five minutes sorting the junk from the real mail. Most of the heap went straight into the plastic bag. There were a few letters for her, mainly bank statements and tax forms from Milton Security. One advantage of being under guardianship was that she never had to deal with tax matters—communications of that sort were conspicuous by their absence. Otherwise, in a whole year she had accumulated only three personal letters.

The first was from a lawyer, Greta Molander, who had
served as executor for Salander's mother. The letter stated that
her mother's estate had been settled and that Lisbeth Salander
and her sister Camilla had inherited 9,312 kronor each. A
deposit of said amount had been made to Ms. Salander's bank
account. Would she please confirm receipt? Salander stuffed
the letter in the inside pocket of her jacket.

The second was from Director Mikaelsson of Äppelviken
Nursing Home, a friendly reminder that they were storing a
box of her mother's personal effects. Would she please contact Äppelviken with instructions as to what she would like
done with these items? The letter ended with the warning that
if they did not hear from Salander or her sister (for whom they
had no address) before the end of the year, they would have no
alternative—space being at a premium—but to discard the
items. She saw that the letter was dated June, and she took out
her mobile telephone. The box was still there. She apologized
for not responding sooner and promised to pick it up the next
day.

The last letter was from Blomkvist. She thought for a
moment before deciding not to open it, and threw it into the
bag.

She filled another box with various items and knickknacks
that she wanted to keep, then took a taxi back to Mosebacke.
She put on makeup, a pair of glasses, and a blond shoulder-
length wig and tucked a Norwegian passport in the name of
Irene Nesser into her bag. She studied herself in the mirror and
decided that Irene Nesser looked a little bit like Lisbeth Salander, but was still a completely different person.

After a quick lunch of a Brie baguette and a latte at Café
Eden on Götgatan, she walked down to the car rental agency on
Ringvägen, where Irene Nesser rented a Nissan Micra. She
drove to IKEA at Kungens Kurva and spent three hours brows-
ing through the merchandise, writing down the item numbers
she needed. She made a few quick decisions.

She bought two Karlanda sofas with sand-coloured upholstery, five Poäng armchairs, two round side tables of clear-
lacquered birch, a Svansbo coffee table, and several Lack
occasional tables. From the storage department she ordered two
Ivar combination storage units and two Bonde bookshelves, a
TV stand, and a Magiker unit with doors. She settled on a Pax
Nexus three-door wardrobe and two small Malm bureaus.

She spent a long time selecting a bed, and decided on a
Hemnes bed frame with mattress and bedside tables. To be on
the safe side, she also bought a Lillehammer bed to put in the
spare room. She didn't plan on having any guests, but since she
had a guest room she might as well furnish it.

The bathroom in her new apartment was already equipped
with a medicine cabinet, towel storage, and a washing machine
the previous owners had left behind. All she had to buy was a
cheap laundry basket.

What she did need, though, was kitchen furniture. After
some thought she decided on a Rosfors kitchen table of solid
beechwood with a tabletop of tempered glass and four colourful kitchen chairs.

She also needed furniture for her office. She looked at some
improbable "work stations" with ingenious cabinets for storing
computers and keyboards. In the end she shook her head and
ordered an ordinary desk, the Galant, in beech veneer with an
angled top and rounded corners, and a large filing cabinet. She
took a long time choosing an office chair—in which she would
no doubt spend many hours—and chose one of the most
expensive options, the Verksam.

She made her way through the entire warehouse and
bought a good supply of sheets, pillowcases, hand towels,
duvets, blankets, pillows, a starter pack of stainless steel cutlery, some crockery, pots and pans, cutting boards, three big
rugs, several work lamps, and a huge quantity of office sup-
plies—folders, file boxes, wastepaper baskets, storage boxes,
and the like.

She paid with a card in the name of Wasp Enterprises and showed her Irene Nesser ID. She also paid to have the items delivered and assembled. The bill came to a little over 90,000 kronor.

She was back in Söder by 5:00 p.m. and had time for a quick visit to Axelsson's Home Electronics, where she bought a nineteen-inch TV and a radio. Just before closing time she slipped into a store on Hornsgatan and bought a vacuum cleaner. At Mariahallen market she bought a mop, dishwashing liquid, a bucket, some detergent, hand soap, toothbrushes, and a giant package of toilet paper.

She was tired but pleased after her shopping frenzy. She stowed all her purchases in her rented Nissan Micra and then collapsed in Café Java on Hornsgatan. She borrowed an evening paper from the next table and learned that the Social Democrats were still the ruling party and that nothing of great significance seemed to have occurred in Sweden while she had been away.

She was home by 8:00. Under cover of darkness she unloaded her car and carried the items up to V. Kulla's apartment. She left everything in a big pile in the hall and spent half an hour trying to find somewhere to park. Then she ran water in the Jacuzzi, which was easily big enough for three people. She thought about Blomkvist for a moment. Until she saw the letter from him that morning, she had not thought about him for several months. She wondered whether he was home, and whether the Berger woman was there now in his apartment.

After a while she took a deep breath, turned over on her stomach, and sank beneath the surface of the water. She put her hands on her breasts and pinched her nipples hard, holding her breath for far too long, until her lungs began to ache.

Erika Berger, editor in chief, checked her clock when Blomkvist arrived. He was almost fifteen minutes late for the planning meeting that was held on the second Tuesday of each month at 10:00 a.m. sharp. Tentative plans for the next issue were outlined, and decisions about the content of the magazine were made for several months in advance.

Blomkvist apologized for his late arrival and muttered an explanation that nobody heard or at least bothered to acknowledge. Apart from Berger, the meeting included the managing editor, Malin Eriksson, partner and art director Christer Malm, the reporter Monika Nilsson, and part-timers Lotta Karim and Henry Cortez. Blomkvist saw at once that the intern was absent, but that the group had been augmented by a new face at the small conference table in Berger's office. It was very unusual for her to let an outsider in on *Millennium*'s planning sessions.

"This is Dag Svensson," said Erika. "Freelancer. We're going to buy an article from him."

Blomkvist shook hands with the man. Svensson was blond and blue-eyed, with a crew cut and a three-day growth of beard. He was around thirty and looked shamelessly fit.

"We usually run one or two themed issues each year." Berger went on where she had left off. "I want to use this story in the May issue. The printer is booked for April 27th. That gives us a good three months to produce the articles."

"So what's the theme?" Blomkvist wondered aloud as he poured coffee from the thermos.

"Dag came to me last week with the outline for a story. That's why I asked him to join us today. Will you take it from here, Dag?" Berger said.

"Trafficking," Svensson said. "That is, the sex trade. In this case primarily of girls from the Baltic countries and Eastern Europe. If you'll allow me to start at the beginning—I'm writing a book on the subject and that's why I contacted *Millennium*—since you now have a book-publishing operation."

Everyone looked amused. Millennium Publishing had so far issued exactly one book, Blomkvist's year-old brick about the billionaire Wennerström's financial empire. The book was in its sixth printing in Sweden, had been published in Norwegian, German, and English, and was soon to be translated into French too. The sales success was remarkable given that the story was by now so well known and had been reported in every newspaper.

"Our book-publishing ventures are not very extensive," Blomkvist said cautiously.

Even Svensson gave a slight smile. "I understand that. But you do have the means to publish a book."

"There are plenty of larger companies," Blomkvist said. "Well-established ones."

"Without a doubt," Berger said. "But for a year now we've been discussing the possibility of starting a niche publication list in addition to our regular activities. We've brought it up at two board meetings, and everyone has been positive. We're thinking of a very small list—three or four books a year—of reportage on various topics. Typical journalistic publications, in other words. This would be a good book to start with."

"Trafficking," Blomkvist said. "Tell us about it."

"I've been digging around in the subject of trafficking for four years now. I got into the topic through my girlfriend—her name is Mia Johansson and she's a criminologist and gender studies scholar. She previously worked at the Crime Prevention Centre and wrote a report on the sex trade."

"I've met her," Eriksson said suddenly. "I did an interview with her two years ago when she published a report comparing the way men and women were treated by the courts."

Svensson smiled. "That did create a stir. But she's been researching trafficking for five or six years. That's how we met. I was working on a story about the sex trade on the Internet and got a tip that she knew something about it. And she did. To make a long story short: she and I began working together, I as a journalist and she as a researcher. In the process we started dating, and a year ago we moved in together. She's working on her doctorate and she'll be defending her dissertation this year."

"So she's writing a doctoral thesis while you . . . ?"

"I'm writing a popular version of her dissertation and adding my own research. As well as a shorter version in the form of the article that I outlined for Erika."

"OK, you're working as a team. What's the story?"

"We have a government that introduced a tough sex-trade law, we have police who are supposed to see to it that the law is obeyed, and we have courts that are supposed to convict sex criminals—we call the johns sex criminals since it has become a crime to buy sexual services—and we have the media, which write indignant articles about the subject, et cetera. At the same time, Sweden is one of the countries that imports the most prostitutes per capita from Russia and the Baltics."

"And you can substantiate this?"

"It's no secret. It's not even news. What's new is that we have met and talked with a dozen girls. Most of them are fifteen to twenty years old. They come from social misery in Eastern Europe and are lured to Sweden with a promise of some kind of job but end up in the clutches of an unscrupulous sex mafia. Those girls have experienced things that you couldn't even show in a movie."

"OK."

"It's the focus of Mia's dissertation, so to speak. But not of the book."

Everyone was listening intently.

"Mia interviewed the girls. What I did was to chart the suppliers and the client base."

Blomkvist smiled. He had never met Svensson before, but he felt at once that Svensson was the kind of journalist he liked—someone who got right to the heart of the story. For Blomkvist the golden rule of journalism was that there were always people who were responsible. The bad guys.

"And you found some interesting facts?"

"I can document, for instance, that a civil servant in the Ministry of Justice who was involved with the drafting of the sex-trade law has exploited at least two girls who came to Sweden through the agency of the sex mafia. One of them was fifteen."

"Whoa."

"I've been working on this story off and on for three years. The book will contain case studies of the johns. There are three policemen, one of whom works for the Security Police, another on the vice squad. There are five lawyers, one prosecutor, and one judge. There are also three journalists, one of whom has written articles on the sex trade. In his private life he's into rape fantasies with a teenage whore from Tallinn—and in this case it's not consensual sex play. I'm thinking of naming names. I've got watertight documentation."

Blomkvist whistled. "Since I've become publisher again, I'll want to go over the documentation with a fine-tooth comb," he said. "The last time I was sloppy about checking sources I ended up spending two months in prison."

"If you want to publish the story I can give you all the documentation you want. But I have one condition for selling the story to *Millennium*."

"Dag wants us to publish the book too," Berger said.

"Precisely. I want it to be dropped like a bomb, and right now *Millennium* is the most credible and outspoken magazine in the country. I don't believe any other publisher would dare publish a book of this type."

"So, no book, no article?" said Blomkvist.

"I think it sounds seriously good," Eriksson said. There was a murmur of agreement from Cortez.

"The article and the book are two different things," Berger said. "For the magazine, Mikael is the publisher and responsible for the content. With regard to the book publication, the author is responsible for the content."

"I know," Svensson said. "That doesn't bother me. The moment the book is published, Mia will file a police report against everyone I name."

"That'll stir up a hell of a fuss," Cortez said.

"That's only half the story," said Svensson. "I've also been analyzing some of the networks that make money off the sex trade. We're talking about organized crime."

"And who's involved?"

"That's what's so tragic. The sex mafia is a sleazy bunch of nobodies. I don't really know what I expected when I started this research, but somehow we—at least I—had the idea that the 'mafia' was a gang in the upper echelon of society. A number of American movies on the subject have probably contributed to that image. Your story about Wennerström"—Svensson turned to Blomkvist—"also showed that sometimes this is actually the case. But Wennerström was an exception in a sense. What I've turned up is a gang of brutal and sadistic losers who can hardly read or write; they're total morons when it comes to organization and strategic thinking. There are connections to bikers and somewhat more organized groups, but in general it's a bunch of assholes who run the sex business."

"This is all made clear in your article," Berger said. "We have laws and a police force and a judicial system that we finance with millions of kronor in taxes each year to deal with the sex trade . . . and they can't even nail a bunch of morons."

"It's a tremendous assault on human rights, and the girls involved are so far down society's ladder that they're of no interest to the legal system. They don't vote. They can hardly speak Swedish except for the vocabulary they need to set up a trick. Of all crimes involving the sex trade, 99.99 percent are not reported to the police, and those that are hardly ever lead to a charge. This has got to be the biggest iceberg of all in the Swedish criminal world. Imagine if bank robberies were handled with the same nonchalance. It's unthinkable. Unfortunately I've come to the conclusion that this method of handling the problem would not survive for a single day if it weren't for the fact that the criminal justice system simply does not want to deal with it. Attacks on teenage girls from Tallinn and Riga are not a priority. A whore is a whore. It's part of the system."

"And everyone knows it," Nilsson said.

"So what do you all think?" Berger said.

"I like it," Blomkvist said. "We'll be sticking our necks out with that story, and that was the whole point of starting *Millennium* in the first place."

"That's why I'm still working at the magazine. The publisher has to jump off a cliff every now and then," Nilsson said.

Everyone laughed except Blomkvist.

"He was the only one crazy enough to take on the job of publisher," Berger said. "We're going to run this in May. And your book will come out at the same time."

"Is the book done?" Blomkvist said.

"No. I have the whole outline but only half the text. If you agree to publish the book and give me an advance, then I can work on it full-time. Almost all the research is done. All that's left are some supplementary details—actually just checking stuff I already know—and confronting the johns I'm going to hang out to dry."

"We'll produce it just like the Wennerström book. It'll take a week to do the layout"—Malm nodded—"and two weeks to print. We'll complete the confrontations in March and April and sum it all up in a final fifteen-page section. We'll have the manuscript ready by April 15 so we'll have time to go over all the sources."

"How will we work things with the contract and so on?"

"I've drawn up a book contract once before, but I'll probably have to have a talk with our lawyer." Berger frowned. "But I propose a short-term contract from February to May. We don't pay over the odds."

"That's fine with me. I just need a basic salary."

"Otherwise the rule of thumb is fifty-fifty on the earnings from the book after the costs are paid. How does that sound?"

"That sounds damn good," Svensson said.

"Work assignments," Berger said. "Malin, I want you to plan the themed issue. It will be your primary responsibility starting next month; you'll work with Dag and edit the manuscript. Lotta, that means I want you here as temporary editorial assistant for the magazine from March through May. You'll have to go full-time, and Malin or Mikael will back you up as time permits."

Eriksson nodded.

"Mikael, I want you to be the editor of the book." Berger looked at Svensson. "Mikael doesn't let on, but he's actually one hell of a good editor, and he knows research. He'll put each syllable of your book under the microscope. He's going to come down like a hawk on every detail. I'm flattered that you want us to publish your book, but we have special problems at *Millennium.* We have one or two enemies who want nothing more than for us to go under. If we stick out our necks to publish something like this, it has to be 100 percent accurate. We can't afford anything less."

"And I wouldn't want it any other way."

"Good. But can you put up with having somebody looking over your shoulder and criticizing you every which way all spring?"

Svensson grinned and looked at Blomkvist. "Bring it on."

"If it's going to be a themed issue, we'll need more articles. Mikael—I want you to write about the finances of the sex trade. How much money are we talking about annually? Who makes the money from the sex trade and where does it go? Can we find evidence that some of the money ends up in government coffers? Monika—I want you to check out sexual attacks in general. Talk to the women's shelters and researchers and doctors and welfare people. You two plus Dag will write the supporting articles. Henry—I want an interview with Mia Johansson—Dag can't do it himself. Portrait: Who is she, what is she researching, and what are her conclusions? Then I want you to go in and do case studies from police reports. Christer—pictures. I don't know how we're going to illustrate this. Think about it."

"This is probably the simplest theme of all to illustrate. Arty. No problem."

"Let me add one thing," Svensson said. "There's a small minority on the police force who are doing a hell of a fine job. It might be an idea to interview some of them."

"Have you got any names?" Cortez said.

"Phone numbers too," Svensson said.

"Great," Berger said. "The theme of the May issue is the sex trade. The point we have to make is that trafficking is a crime against human rights and that these criminals must be exposed and treated like war criminals or death squads or torturers anywhere in the world. Now let's get going."

CHAPTER 5

Wednesday, January 12–
Friday, January 14

Äppelviken felt unfamiliar, even foreign, when for the first time in eighteen months Salander turned into the drive in her rented Nissan Micra. From the age of fifteen she had come twice a year to the nursing home where her mother had been since "All The Evil" had happened. Her mother had spent ten years at Äppelviken, and it was where she finally died at only forty-six, after one last annihilating cerebral haemorrhage.

The last fourteen years of Agneta Sofia Salander's life had been punctuated by small cerebral haemorrhages which left her unable to take care of herself. Sometimes she had not even been able to recognize her daughter.

Thinking about her mother always pitched Salander into a mood of helplessness and darkness black as night. As a teenager she had cherished the fantasy that her mother would get well and that they would be able to form some sort of relationship. That was her heart thinking. Her head knew that it would never happen.

Her mother had been short and thin, but nowhere near as anorexic-looking as Salander. In fact, her mother had been downright beautiful, and had a lovely figure. Just like Salander's sister, Camilla.

Salander did not want to think about her sister.

For Salander it was an irony of fate that she and her sister were so dramatically dissimilar. They were twins, born within twenty minutes of each other.

Lisbeth was first. Camilla was beautiful.

They were so different that it seemed grossly unlikely that they could have come from the same womb. If something hadn't gone wrong with her genetic code, Lisbeth would have been as radiantly beautiful as her sister. And probably as crazy.

From the time they were little girls Camilla had been outgoing, popular, and successful at school, while Lisbeth had been ungiving and introverted, rarely responding to the teachers' questions. Camilla's grades were very good; Lisbeth's never were. Already in elementary school Camilla had distanced herself from her sister to the point that she would not even take the same route to school that Lisbeth took. Teachers and friends noticed that the two girls never had anything to do with each other, never sat next to each other. From the age of eight they had been in separate classes. When they were twelve and "All The Evil" happened, they had been sent to different foster homes. They had not seen each other since their seventeenth birthday, and that meeting had ended with Lisbeth getting a black eye and Camilla a fat lip. Lisbeth did not know where Camilla was living now, and she hadn't made any attempt to find out.

In Lisbeth's eyes Camilla was insincere, corrupt, and manipulative. But it was Lisbeth whom society had declared incompetent.

She zipped up her leather jacket before she walked through the rain to the main entrance. She stopped at a garden bench and looked around. On this very spot eighteen months ago, she had seen her mother for the last time. She had paid an unscheduled visit to the nursing home when she was on her way north to help Blomkvist in his attempt to track down a serial killer. Her mother had been restless and didn't seem to recognize Salander. She held on tight to her hand and looked at her with a bewildered expression. Salander was in a hurry. She loosened her mother's grip, gave her a hug, and rode away on her motorcycle.

The director of Äppelviken, Agnes Mikaelsson, greeted her warmly and took her to a storeroom where they found the cardboard box. Salander hefted it. Only five or six pounds. Not much in the way of an inheritance.

"I had a feeling you'd come back someday," Mikaelsson said.

"I've been out of the country," Salander said.

She thanked her for saving the box, carried it back to the car, and left Äppelviken for the last time.

Salander was back in Mosebacke just after noon. She put her mother's box unopened in a hall closet and left the apartment again.

As she opened the front door a police car drove slowly past. Salander warily observed the presence of the authorities outside her building, but when they showed no sign of interest in her she put them out of her mind.

She went shopping at H&M and KappAhl department stores and bought herself a new wardrobe. She picked up a large assortment of basic clothes in the form of pants, jeans, tops, and socks. She had no interest in expensive designer clothing, but she did enjoy being able to buy half a dozen pairs of jeans at one time without a second thought. Her most extravagant purchases were from Twilfit, where she chose a drawerful of panties and bras. This was basic clothing again, but after half an hour of embarrassed searching she also settled on a set that she thought was sexy, even erotic, and which she would never have dreamed of buying before. When she tried them on that night she felt incredibly foolish. What she saw in the mirror was a thin, tattooed girl in grotesque underwear. She took them off and threw them in the trash.

She also bought herself some winter shoes and two pairs of
lighter indoor shoes. Then she bought a pair of black boots
with high heels that made her a couple of inches taller. She also
found a good winter jacket in brown suede.

She made coffee and a sandwich before she drove the rental
car back to its garage near Ringen. She walked home and sat in
the dark all evening on her window seat, watching the water in
Saltsjön.

Mia Johansson cut the cheesecake and decorated each slice
with a scoop of raspberry ice cream. She served Berger and
Blomkvist first before she put down plates for Svensson
and herself. Eriksson had resolutely resisted dessert and was
content with black coffee in an old-fashioned flowered porce-
lain cup.

"It was my grandmother's china service," said Mia when she
saw Eriksson examining the cup.

"She's scared to death that a cup is going to break," Svensson said. "She takes it out only when we have really important
guests."

Johansson smiled. "I spent several years with my grandmother when I was a child, and the china is almost all I have
left of her."

"They're really beautiful," Eriksson said. "My kitchen is one
hundred percent IKEA."

Blomkvist didn't give a damn about flowered coffee cups
and instead cast an appraising eye on the plate with the cheesecake. He pondered letting his belt out a notch. Berger apparently shared his feelings.

"Good God, I should have said no to dessert too," she said,
glancing ruefully at Eriksson before taking up her spoon with
a firm grip.

It was supposed to be a simple working dinner, in part to
cement the cooperation they had agreed on and in part to con-

tinue to discuss plans for the themed issue. Svensson had suggested that they meet at his place for a bite to eat, and Johansson had served the best sweet-and-sour chicken Blomkvist had ever tasted. Over dinner they put away two bottles of robust Spanish red, and Svensson asked if anyone would like a glass of Tullamore Dew with their dessert. Only Berger was foolish enough to decline, and Svensson got out the glasses.

It was a one-bedroom apartment in Enskede. Svensson and Johansson had been going out for a few years, but had taken the plunge and moved in together a year ago.

The group gathered at around 6:00 p.m., and by the time dessert was served at 8:30 not a word had been said about the ostensible reason for the dinner. But Blomkvist did discover that he liked his hosts and enjoyed their company.

It was Berger who finally steered the conversation to the topic they had all come to discuss. Johansson produced a print-out of her thesis and placed it on the table in front of Berger. It had a surprisingly ironic title—"From Russia with Love"—an homage, of course, to Ian Fleming's classic novel. The subtitle was "Trafficking, Organized Crime, and Society's Response."

"You have to recognize the difference between my thesis and the book Dag is writing," she said. "Dag's book is a polemic aimed at the people who are making money from trafficking. My thesis is statistics, field studies, law texts, and a study of how society and the courts treat the victims."

"The girls, you mean."

"Young girls, usually fifteen to twenty years old, working class, poorly educated. They often have unstable home lives, and many of them are subjected to some form of abuse even in childhood. One reason they come to Sweden is that they have been fed a pack of lies."

"By the sex traders."

"In this sense there is a sort of gender perspective to my thesis. It's not often that a researcher can establish roles along gender lines so clearly. Girls—victims; boys—perpetrators. Apart from a handful of women working on their own who profit from the sex trade, there is no other form of criminality in which the sex roles themselves are a precondition for the crime. Nor is there any other form of criminality in which social acceptance is so great, or which society does so little to prevent."

"And yet Sweden does have tough laws against trafficking and the sex trade," Berger said. "Is that not the case?"

"Don't make me laugh. Several hundred girls—there are no published statistics, obviously—are transported to Sweden every year to work as prostitutes, which in this case means making their bodies available for systematic rape. After the law against trafficking went into effect, it was tested in the courts a few times. The first time was in April 2003, the case against that crazy brothel madam who had a sex change. And she was acquitted, of course."

"I thought she was convicted."

"Of running a brothel, yes. But she was acquitted of trafficking charges. The thing was, the girls who were the victims were also the witnesses against her, and they vanished back to the Baltics. Interpol tried to track them down, but after months of searching it was decided that they were not going to be found."

"What had become of them?"

"Nothing. The TV show *Insider* did a follow-up and went over to Tallinn. It took the reporters exactly one afternoon to find two of the girls, who were living with their parents. The third girl had moved to Italy."

"The police in Tallinn, in other words, weren't very effective."

"Since then we have actually won a couple of convictions, but in each case they were men who had been arrested for other crimes, or who were so conspicuously stupid that they couldn't help but be caught. The law is pure window dressing. It isn't enforced. And the problem here," Svensson said, "is that the crime is aggravated rape, often in conjunction with abuse, aggravated abuse, and death threats, and in some instances, illegal imprisonment as well. That's everyday life for many of the girls who are brought, wearing miniskirts and heavy makeup, to some villa in the suburbs. The thing is that a girl like that doesn't have any choice. Either she goes out and fucks dirty old men or she risks being abused and tortured by her pimp. The girls can't run away—they don't know the language, they don't know the law, and they don't know where they could turn. They can't go home because their passports have been taken away, and in the case of the brothel madam the girls were locked in an apartment."

"It sounds like slave labour camps. Do the girls make any money at all?"

"Oh yeah," Johansson said. "They usually work for several months before they're allowed to go back home. They're given between 20,000 and 30,000 kronor, which in Russian money is a small fortune. Unfortunately they've often picked up heavy alcohol or drug habits and a lifestyle that means the money will run out very quickly. This makes the system self-sustaining: after a while they're back again and return voluntarily, so to speak, to their torturers."

"How much money is this business turning over annually?" Blomkvist asked.

Mia glanced at Svensson and thought for a moment before she responded.

"It's very hard to give an accurate answer. We've calculated back and forth, but most of our figures are necessarily estimates."

"Give us a broad brush."

"OK, we know, for example, that the madam, the one convicted of procuring but acquitted of trafficking, brought thirty-five women from the East over a two-year period. They were all here for anything from a few weeks to several months. In the course of the trial it emerged that over those two years they took in two million kronor. I have worked out that a girl can bring in an estimated 60,000 kronor a month. Of this about

15,000, say, is costs—travel, clothing, full board, etc. It's no life of luxury; they may have to crash with a bunch of other girls in some apartment the gang provides for them. Of the remaining 45,000 kronor, the gang takes between 20,000 and 30,000. The gang leader stuffs half into his own pocket, say 15,000, and divides the rest among his employees—drivers, muscle, others. The girl gets to keep 10,000 to 12,000 kronor."

"And per month?"

"Suppose a gang has two or three girls grinding away for them, and they take in around 150,000 a month. A gang consists of two or three people, and that's their living. That's about how the finances of rape look."

"And how many of them are we talking about . . . if you extrapolate?"

"At any given time there are about a hundred active girls who are in some way victims of trafficking. That means the total income in Sweden each month would be around six million kronor, around seventy million per year. And that's only the girls who are victims of trafficking."

"That sounds like small change."

"It is small change. And to bring in these relatively modest sums, around a hundred girls have to be raped. It drives me mad."

"That sounds like an objective researcher! But how many creeps are living off these girls?"

"I reckon about three hundred."

"That doesn't sound like an insurmountable problem," Berger said.

"We pass laws and the media gets outraged, but hardly anyone has actually talked to one of these girls from the East or has any idea how they live."

"How does it work? I mean, in practice. It's probably fairly difficult to bring a sixteen-year-old over here from Tallinn without anyone noticing. How does it work once they arrive?" Blomkvist asked.

"When I started researching this, I thought we were talking about an incredibly well-run organization with some form of professional mafia spiriting girls unnoticed across the borders."

"But it's not?" Eriksson said.

"The business is organized, but I came to the conclusion that we're talking about many small and badly organized gangs. Forget the Armani suits and the sports cars—the average gang is half Russians or Balts and half Swedes. The gang leader is typically forty, has very little education, and has had problems all his life. His view of women is pure stone age. There's a clear pecking order in the gang and his associates are often afraid of him. He's violent, frequently high, and he beats the shit out of anyone who steps out of line."

Salander's furniture from IKEA was delivered at 9:30 in the morning three days later. Two extremely robust citizens shook hands with blond Irene Nesser, who spoke with a sprightly Norwegian accent. They began at once, shuttling the boxes up to the apartment in the undersized elevator, and spent the day assembling tables, cabinets, and beds. Irene Nesser went down to Söderhallarna market to buy Greek takeout for their lunch.

The men from IKEA were gone by midafternoon. Salander took off her wig and strolled around her apartment wondering how she was going to like living in her new home. The kitchen table looked too elegant to be true. The room next to the kitchen, with doors from both the hall and the kitchen, was her new living room, with modern sofas and armchairs around a coffee table by the window. She was pleased with the bedroom and sat down tentatively on the Hemnes bedstead to test the mattress.

She sat at the desk in her office, enjoying the view of Salt-sjön. *Yes, this is a good setup. I can work here.*

What she was going to work on, though, she didn't know.

. . .

Salander spent the rest of the evening unpacking and arranging her belongings. She made the bed and put the towels, sheets, and pillowcases in the linen closet. She opened the bags of new clothes and hung them in the closets. In spite of all she had bought, it filled only a fraction of the space. She put the lamps in place and arranged the pots and pans, the crockery, and the cutlery in the kitchen cupboards and drawers.

She looked critically at the empty walls and realized that she was going to have to find some posters or pictures. A vase for flowers wouldn't hurt either.

Then she opened her cardboard boxes from Lundagatan and put away books, magazines, clippings, and old research papers that she probably should have thrown away. Without any regret, she discarded her old T-shirts and socks with holes in them. Suddenly she found a dildo, still in its original box. She smiled wryly. It had been one of those freaky birthday presents from Mimmi. She had entirely forgotten that she had it and had never even tried it. She decided to rectify that situation and set the dildo on her bedside table.

Then she became serious. *Mimmi.* She felt a pang of guilt. She had been with Mimmi fairly regularly for a year and then left her for Blomkvist without a word of explanation. She had not said goodbye or told her she was thinking of leaving the country. Nor had she said goodbye to Armansky or told the girls in Evil Fingers anything at all. They must think she was dead, or else they had simply forgotten about her—she had never been a central figure in the group.

She realized at that moment that she had not said goodbye to George Bland on Grenada either, and she wondered whether he was walking on the beach looking for her. She remembered what Blomkvist had told her about friendship being based on respect and trust. *I keep squandering my friends.* She wondered whether Mimmi was still around, whether she should try to get in touch with her.

She spent most of the evening and a good part of the night sorting papers in her office, installing her computers, and surfing the Net. She did a swift check of her investments and found that she was better off than she had been a year earlier.

She did a routine check of Bjurman's computer but found nothing in his correspondence that gave her reason to think that he was not toeing the line. He seemed to have scaled back his professional and private activities to a semi-vegetative state. He seldom used email, and when he surfed the Internet he mostly went on porn sites.

She did not log off until around 2:00 in the morning. She went into the bedroom and undressed, flinging her clothes over a chair. In the bathroom mirror she looked at herself for a long time, examining her angular, asymmetrical face, her new breasts. And the tattoo on her back—it was beautiful, a curving dragon in red, green, and black. During the year of her travels she had let her hair grow to shoulder length, but at the end of her stay on Grenada she had taken a pair of scissors to it. It still stuck out in all directions.

She felt that some fundamental change had taken place or was taking place in her life. Maybe it was having access to billions of kronor and not having to think about every krona she spent. Maybe it was the adult world which was belatedly pushing its way into her life. Maybe it was the realization that, with her mother's death, her childhood had come to an end.

During the operation on her breasts at the clinic in Genoa, a ring in her nipple had to be removed. Then she had done away with a ring from her lower lip, and on Grenada she had taken the ring out of her left labium—it had chafed, and she had no idea why she had let herself be pierced there in the first place.

She yawned and unscrewed the stud she had had through her tongue for seven years. She put it in a bowl on the shelf next to the sink. Her mouth felt empty. Apart from the rings in her earlobes, she had now only two piercings left: a ring in her left eyebrow and a jewel in her navel.

At last she crept under her new duvet. The bed she had bought was gigantic; she felt as if she were lying on the edge of a soccer field. She pulled the duvet around her and thought for a long time.

CHAPTER 6

Sunday, January 23–
Saturday, January 29

Salander took the elevator from the garage to the third floor, the uppermost floor occupied by Milton Security in the office building near Slussen. She opened the elevator door with a card key that she had pirated several years earlier. She automatically glanced at her watch as she stepped into the unlit corridor. Sunday, 3:10 a.m. The night watchman would be sitting at the alarm station on the second floor, a long way from the elevator shaft, and she knew that she would almost certainly have this floor to herself.

She was, as always, astonished that a security company had such basic lapses in its own operations.

Not much had changed on the third floor in the year that had passed. She began by visiting her old office, a cubicle behind a glass wall in the corridor where Armansky had installed her. The door was unlocked. Absolutely nothing had changed, except that someone had set a cardboard box of wastepaper inside the door: the desk, the office chair, the wastepaper basket, one (empty) bookshelf, and an obsolete Dell PC with a pitifully small hard drive.

Salander could see nothing to suggest that Armansky had

turned the room over to anyone else. She took this to be a good sign, but she knew that it did not mean much. It was space that could hardly be put to any sensible use.

Salander closed the door and strolled the length of the corridor, making sure that there was no night owl in any of the offices. She stopped at the coffee machine and pressed the button for a cup of cappuccino, then opened the door to Armansky's office with her pirated card key.

His office was, as always, irritatingly tidy. She made a brisk tour of inspection and studied the bookshelf before sitting down at his desk and switching on his computer.

She fished out a CD from the inside pocket of her jacket and pushed it into the hard drive, then started a programme called Asphyxia 1.3. She had written it herself, and its only function was to upgrade Internet Explorer on Armansky's computer to a more modern version. The procedure took about five minutes.

When she was done, she ejected the CD and rebooted the computer with the new version of Internet Explorer. The programme looked and behaved exactly like the original version, but it was a tiny bit larger and a microsecond slower. All installations were identical to the original, including the install date. There would be no trace of the new file.

She typed in an FTP address for a server in Holland and got a command screen. She clicked *copy,* wrote the name *Armansky/MiltSec* and clicked OK. The computer instantly began copying Armansky's hard drive to the server in Holland. A clock indicated that the process would take thirty-four minutes.

While the transfer was in progress, she took the spare key to Armansky's desk from a pot on the bookshelf and spent the next half hour bringing herself up to date on the files Armansky kept in his top right-hand desk drawer: his crucial, current jobs. When the computer dinged as a sign that the transfer was complete, she put the files back in the order that she had found them.

Then she shut down the computer and switched off the

desk lamp, taking the empty cappuccino cup with her. She left the Milton Security building the same way she had come. It was 4:12 a.m.

She walked home and sat down at her PowerBook and logged on to the server in Holland, where she started a copy of Asphyxia 1.3. A window opened asking for the name of the hard drive. She had forty different options and scrolled down. She passed the hard drive for *NilsEBjurman,* which she usually glanced through every other month. She paused for a second at *MikBlom/laptop* and *MikBlom/office.* She had not clicked on those icons for more than a year, and she wondered vaguely whether to delete them. But she then decided as a matter of principle to hang on to them—since she had gone to the trouble of hacking into a computer it would be stupid to delete the information and maybe one day have to do the whole procedure all over again. The same was true for an icon called *Wennerström* which she had not opened in a long time. The man of that name was dead. The icon *Armansky/MiltSec,* the last one created, was at the bottom of the list.

She could have cloned his hard drive earlier, but she had never bothered to because she worked at Milton and could easily retrieve any information that Armansky wanted to keep hidden from the rest of the world. Her trespassing in his computer was not malicious: she just wanted to know what the company was working on, to see the lay of the land. She clicked and a folder immediately opened with a new icon called *ArmanskyHD.* She tried out whether she could access the hard drive and checked that all the files were in place.

She read through Armansky's reports, financial statements, and email until 7:00 a.m. Finally she crawled into bed and slept until 12:30 in the afternoon.

On the last Friday in January, *Millennium*'s annual board meeting took place in the presence of the company's bookkeeper, an outside auditor, and the four partners: Berger (30 percent),

Blomkvist (20 percent), Malm (20 percent), and Harriet Vanger (30 percent). Eriksson was there as the representative of the staff and the staff committee, and the chair of the union at the magazine. The union consisted of Eriksson, Lotta Karim, Cortez, Nilsson, and marketing chief Sonny Magnusson. It was Eriksson's first board meeting.

The meeting began at 4:00 and lasted an hour. Much of the time was spent on the financials and the audit report. Clearly *Millennium* was on a solid footing, very different from the crisis in which the company had been mired two years earlier. The auditors reported a profit of 2.1 million kronor, of which roughly 1 million was down to Blomkvist's book about the Wennerström affair.

Berger proposed, and it was agreed, that 1 million be set aside as a fund against future crises; that 250,000 kronor be reserved for capital investments, such as new computers and other equipment, and repairs at the editorial offices; and that 300,000 kronor be earmarked for salary increases and to allow them to offer Cortez a full-time contract. Of the balance, a dividend of 50,000 kronor was proposed for each partner, and 100,000 kronor to be divided equally among the four employees regardless of whether they worked full- or part-time. Magnusson was to receive no bonus. His contract gave him a commission on the ads he sold, and periodically these made him the highest paid of all the staff. These proposals were adopted unanimously.

Blomkvist proposed that the freelance budget be reduced in favour of an additional part-time reporter. Blomkvist had Svensson in mind; he would then be able to use *Millennium* as a base for his freelance writing and later, if it all worked out, be hired full-time. The proposal met with resistance from Berger on the grounds that the magazine could not thrive without access to a large number of freelance articles. She was supported by Harriet Vanger; Malm abstained. It was decided that the freelance budget would not be touched, but it would be investigated whether adjustments of other expenses might be made. Everyone wanted Svensson on the staff, at the very least as a part-time contributor.

There followed a brief discussion about future direction and development plans; Berger was reelected as chair of the board for the coming year; and then the meeting was adjourned.

Eriksson had said not a word. She was content at the prospect that she and her colleagues would get a bonus of 25,000 kronor, more than a month's salary.

At the close of the board meeting, Berger called for a part-ners' meeting. Berger, Blomkvist, Malm, and Harriet Vanger remained while the others left the conference room. Berger declared the meeting open. "There is only one item on the agenda," she said. "Harriet, according to the agreement we made with Henrik, his part ownership was to last for two years. The agreement is about to expire. We have to decide what is going to happen with your—or rather, Henrik's—interest in *Millennium*."

"We all know that my uncle's investment was an impulsive gesture triggered by a most unusual situation," Harriet said. "That situation no longer exists. What do you propose?"

Malm squirmed with annoyance. He was the only one in the room who did not know what that "unusual situation" was. Blomkvist and Berger had to keep the story from him. Berger had told him only that it was a matter so personal involving Blomkvist that he would never under any circumstances dis-cuss it. Malm was smart enough to realize that Blomkvist's silence had something to do with Hedestad and Harriet Vanger. He also knew that he didn't need all the details to be able to make a decision, and he had enough respect for Blomkvist not to make an issue of it.

"The three of us have discussed the matter and we have arrived at a decision," Berger said. She looked Harriet in the eye. "But before we explain our reasoning we would like to know what you think."

Harriet Vanger glanced at them in turn. Her gaze lingered on Blomkvist, but she could not read anything from their expressions.

"If you want to buy the family out it will cost around three million kronor plus interest. Can you afford to buy us out?" she asked mildly.

"Yes, we can," Blomkvist said with a smile.

He had been paid five million kronor by Henrik Vanger for the work he had done for the old industrial tycoon. Part of that work, ironically, had been to find out what had happened to Harriet, his niece.

"In that case, the decision is in your hands," Harriet said. "The agreement stipulates that you can cancel the Vanger shareholding as of today. I would never have written a contract as sloppy as the one Henrik signed."

"We can buy you out if we have to," Berger said. "But the real question is what you want to do. You're the CEO of a substantial industrial concern—two concerns, actually. Our annual budget might correspond to what you turn over during a coffee break. Why would you give your time to a business as marginal as *Millennium*?"

Harriet Vanger looked calmly at the chair of the board, saying nothing for a long moment. Then she turned to Blomkvist and replied:

"I've been the owner of something or other since the day I was born. And I spend my days running a corporation that has more intrigues than a four-hundred-page romance novel. When I first joined your board it was to fulfil obligations that I could not neglect. But you know what? During the past eighteen months I've realized that I'm having more fun on this board than on all the others put together."

Blomkvist absorbed this thoughtfully. Vanger now turned to Malm.

"The problems you face at *Millennium* are small and manageable. Naturally the company wants to operate at a profit—

that's a given. But all of you have another goal—you want to achieve something."

She took a sip from her glass of water and fixed her eyes on Berger.

"Exactly what that something is remains a bit unclear to me. The objective is hazy. You aren't a political party or a special-interest group. You have no loyalties to consider except your own. But you pinpoint flaws in society, and you don't mind entering into battles with public figures. Often you want to change things and make a real difference. You all pretend to be cynics and nihilists, but it's your own morality that steers the magazine, and several times I've noticed that it's quite a special sort of morality. I don't know what to call it, except to say that *Millennium* has a soul. This is the only board I'm proud to be a part of."

She fell silent for so long that Berger had to laugh.

"That sounds good. But you still haven't answered the question."

"This has been some of the wackiest, most absurd stuff I've ever been involved with, but I enjoy your company and I've had a great time. If you want me to stay on I gladly will."

"OK," Malm said. "We've been back and forth and we're all agreed. We'll buy you out."

Vanger's eyes widened. "You want to get rid of me?"

"When we signed the contract we had our heads on the block waiting for the axe. We had no choice. From the start we were counting the days until we could buy out your uncle."

Berger opened a file, laid some papers on the table, and pushed them over to Vanger, together with a cheque for exactly the sum due. Vanger read through the papers and without a word she signed them.

"All right, then," Berger said. "That was fairly painless. I want to put on record our gratitude to Henrik Vanger for all he did for *Millennium*. I hope you will convey this to him."

"I will," Harriet Vanger said in a neutral tone, betraying

nothing of what she felt. She was both hurt and deeply disappointed that they had let her say that she wanted to stay and then had simply kicked her out.

"And now let me see if I can interest you in a completely different contract," Berger said.

She took out another set of papers and slid them across the table.

"We were wondering if you personally had any interest in being a partner at *Millennium*. The price would be the same as the sum you've just received. The agreement has no time limits or exception clauses. You would be a full partner with the same responsibilities as the rest of us."

Vanger raised her eyebrows. "Why this roundabout process?"

"It had to be done sooner or later," Malm said. "We could have renewed the old agreement a year at a time or until the board had an argument and put you out. But it was always a contract that would have to be dissolved."

Harriet leaned on her elbow and gave him a searching glance. She looked at Blomkvist and then at Berger.

"We signed our agreement with Henrik when we were in financial straits," Berger said. "We're offering you this agreement because we want to. And unlike the old one, it won't let us boot you out so easily in the future."

"That's a very big difference for us," Blomkvist said in a low voice, and that was his only contribution to the discussion.

"The fact is that we believe you add something to *Millennium* besides the financial underpinning implied by the name of Vanger," Berger said. "You're smart and sensible and you come up with constructive solutions. Until now you've kept a low profile, almost like a guest visiting us once a quarter, but you represent for this board a stability and direction that we've never had before. You know business. Once you asked if you could trust me, and I wondered the same thing about you. By now we both know the answer. I like you and I trust you—we all do. We don't want you to be a part of us by way of some complicated legal mumbo jumbo. We want you as a partner and a real shareholder."

Harriet reached for the contract and spent five minutes reading through it. Finally she looked up.

"And all three of you are agreed?" she said.

Three heads nodded. Vanger lifted her pen and signed. She shoved the cheque back across the table, and Blomkvist tore it up.

The partners of *Millennium* had dinner together at Samir's Cauldron on Tavastgatan. It was a quiet party—to celebrate the new arrangement—with good wine and couscous with lamb. The conversation was relaxed, and Vanger was noticeably dazed. It felt a little like an uncomfortable first date: something is going to happen, but no-one knows exactly what it might be.

Vanger had to leave at 7:30. She excused herself by saying that she had to go to her hotel and get an early night. Berger was heading home to her husband and walked with her some of the way. They parted at Slussen. Blomkvist and Malm stayed on for a while before Malm excused himself and said that he too had to get home.

Vanger took a taxi to the Sheraton and went straight to her room on the eighth floor. She got undressed and had a bath and put on the hotel's robe. Then she sat at the window and looked out towards Riddarholmen. She took a pack of Dunhills from her bag. She smoked three or four cigarettes a day, so few that she could consider herself a nonsmoker and still enjoy it without a guilty conscience.

At 9:00 there was a knock at the door. She opened it and let Blomkvist in.

"You scoundrel," she said.

He smiled and gave her a kiss on the cheek.

"I really thought you guys were going to kick me out."

"We never would have done it like that. Do you understand why we wanted to rewrite the contract?"

"Of course. It makes perfect sense."

Blomkvist opened her robe and put a hand on her breast, caressing it cautiously.

"You scoundrel," she said again.

Salander stopped at the door with a nameplate that said WU. She had seen a light from the street, and now she could hear music coming from inside. So Miriam Wu still lived here in the studio apartment on Tomtebogatan near St. Eriksplan. It was Friday evening, and Salander had half hoped that Mimmi would be out having fun somewhere. The only questions that remained to be answered were whether Mimmi still wanted to have anything to do with her and whether she was alone and available.

She rang the bell.

Mimmi opened the door and her eyebrows lifted in surprise. Then she leaned against the doorjamb and put her hand on her hip.

"Salander. I thought you were dead or something."

"Or something."

"What do you want?"

"There are many answers to that question."

Miriam Wu looked around the stairwell before she again fixed her eyes on Salander.

"Try one."

"Well, I just wanted to see whether you're still single and might want some company tonight."

Mimmi looked astonished for a few seconds and then laughed out loud.

"I know only one person who would even dream of ringing my bell after a year and a half's silence to ask me if I wanted to fuck."

"Do you want me to leave?"

Mimmi stopped laughing. She was quiet for a few seconds. "Lisbeth . . . Jesus, you're serious."

Salander waited.

Finally Mimmi sighed and opened the door wide.

"Come on, then. I can at least offer you a coffee."

Salander followed her in and sat on one of two stools by a small table in the hall. The apartment was about 250 square feet: one cramped room and a hall. The kitchen was little more than a niche for cooking in a corner of the hall. Mimmi had fixed a hose to the sink from the bathroom.

Mimmi's mother was from Hong Kong, her father from Boden. Salander knew that her parents lived in Paris. Mimmi was studying sociology in Stockholm, and she had an older sister studying anthropology in the States. Her mother's genes were visible in Mimmi's raven black hair, cut short, and her slightly Asian features. Her father had given her the clear blue eyes. She had a wide mouth and dimples that did not come from either of her parents.

Mimmi was thirty-one. She liked to dress up in leather and go to clubs where they did performance art—sometimes she appeared in the shows. Salander had not been to a club since she was sixteen.

Besides her studies, Mimmi had a job one day a week as a sales clerk at Domino Fashion on a street off Sveavägen. Customers desperate for outfits such as a rubber nurse's uniform or black leather witch's garb frequented Domino, which both designed and manufactured the clothes. Mimmi was part owner of the boutique with some girlfriends, and the shop provided a modest supplement to her student loan of a few thousand kronor each month. Salander had first seen Mimmi when she performed in a show at the Gay Pride Festival a couple of years before and then ran into her in a beer tent later that night. Mimmi had been dressed in an odd lemon yellow plastic dress that revealed more than it concealed. Salander saw nothing erotic about the outfit, but she had been drunk enough to suddenly want to pick up a girl dressed like a lemon. To Salander's great surprise the citrus fruit had taken one look at her, laughed out loud, kissed her without embarrassment, and said *You're the one I want.* They had gone back to Salander's place and had sex all night long.

"I am what I am," Salander said. "I ran away from everything and everybody. I should have said goodbye."

"I thought something had happened to you. Not that we had been in touch that much in the last months you were here."

"I was busy."

"You're such a mystery. You never talk about yourself. I don't even know where you work or who I could have called when you didn't answer your mobile."

"I'm not working anywhere right now, and besides, you're just like me. You wanted sex but you weren't particularly interested in a relationship. Or were you?"

"That's true," Mimmi said at last.

"And it was the same with me. I never made any promises."

"You've changed," Mimmi said.

"Not a lot."

"You look older. More mature. You have different clothes. And you've stuffed your bra with something."

Salander said nothing. Mimmi had seen her naked—of course she would notice the change. In the end she lowered her eyes and mumbled, "I had a boob job."

"What did you say?"

Salander looked up and raised her voice, unaware that it had taken on a defiant tone.

"I went to a clinic in Italy and had breast implants. That's why I disappeared. Then I just kept on travelling. Now I'm back."

"Are you joking?"

Salander looked at Mimmi, expressionless.

"Stupid of me. You never joke about anything, Mr. Spock."

"I'm not going to apologize. I'm just being honest. If you want me to leave, just say the word."

Mimmi laughed out loud. "Well, I certainly don't want you to leave without letting me see how they look. Please."

"I've always liked having sex with you, Mimmi. You didn't give a damn what sort of work I did, and if I was busy you found somebody else."

Mimmi nodded. When she was seventeen, after a number of fumbling attempts, she was finally initiated into the mysteries of sex at a party organized in Göteborg by the Swedish Federation for Lesbian, Gay, Bisexual, and Transgender Rights. She had never considered any other lifestyle after that. Once when she was twenty-three she had tried having sex with a man. She mechanically did everything she was expected to do, but it was not enjoyable. She also belonged to the minority within the minority who were not interested in marriage or fidelity or cosy evenings at home.

"I've been home for a few weeks. I needed to know if I had to go out and pick somebody up or if you're still interested."

Mimmi bent down and kissed her lightly on the lips.

"I was thinking of studying tonight."

She unbuttoned the top button of Lisbeth's blouse.

"But what the hell . . ."

She kissed her again and kept unbuttoning.

"I just have to see this."

She kissed her again.

"Welcome back."

Harriet Vanger fell asleep around 2:00 a.m. Blomkvist lay awake listening to her breathing. After a while he got up and filched a Dunhill from the pack in her handbag. He sat in a chair next to the bed and looked at her.

He had not planned to become Harriet Vanger's lover. Far

from it. After his time in Hedestad he wanted more than anything to keep the whole Vanger family at arm's length. He had
seen Harriet at board meetings and kept his distance. They
knew each other's secrets, but apart from Harriet Vanger's role
on *Millennium*'s board, their dealings were at an end.

During the Whitsuntide vacation the year before, Blomkvist
had gone to his cabin in Sandhamn for the first time in several
months, to have some peace and quiet and sit on the porch and
read crime novels. On the Friday afternoon, he was on his way
to the kiosk to buy some cigarettes when he ran into Harriet.
She had apparently felt a need to get away from Hedestad herself and had booked a weekend at the hotel in Sandhamn. She
had not been there since she was a child. She had been sixteen
when she left Sweden and fifty-three when she came back. It
was Blomkvist who had tracked her down.

After their surprised greetings, Harriet had lapsed into an
awkward silence. Blomkvist knew her history, and she was
aware that he had compromised his principles in order to cover
up the Vanger family's horrific secrets. And in part he had done
it for her.

Blomkvist invited her to his cabin. He made coffee and they
sat on the porch outside for several hours, talking. It was the
first time they had talked at length since her return.

Blomkvist could not resist asking: "What did you do with
the stuff in Martin's basement?"

"Do you really want to know?"

"Yes."

"I cleaned it up myself. I burned everything that would
burn. I had the house torn down. I couldn't live there, and I
couldn't sell it and let someone else live there. For me all its
associations were with evil. I'm planning another house to take
its place, a small cabin."

"Didn't people raise their eyebrows when you had the
house torn down? It was quite luxurious and modern."

She smiled. "Dirch Frode put about the story that there was

so much damp in the foundation that it would be more expensive to rebuild than to take it down." Frode was the family's lawyer.

"How is Frode getting on?"

"He's going to be seventy soon. I'm keeping him busy."

They had lunch together, and Blomkvist realized that Harriet Vanger was sitting there telling him the most intimate and private details about her life. When he asked her why, she thought for a moment and said that there really was no-one else in the whole world with whom she could be so open. Besides, it was hard not to open her heart to a kid she had babysat all of forty years ago.

She had had sex with three men in her life. First her father and then her brother. She had killed her father and run away from her brother. Somehow she had survived and met a man with whom she had created a new life for herself.

"He was tender and loving. Dependable and honest. I was happy with him. We had a wonderful twenty years together before he became ill."

"You never remarried? Why not?"

She shrugged. "I was the mother of two children in Australia and the owner of a big agricultural business. I could never get away for a romantic weekend. And I've never missed sex." They sat quiet for a while. "It's late. I should be getting back to the hotel."

Blomkvist made no move to get up.

"Do you want to seduce me?"

"I do," he said.

He stood up and took her hand, leading her into the cabin and up to the sleeping loft. Suddenly she stopped him. "I don't really know how. This is not something I do every day."

They spent the whole weekend together and then one night every three months after the magazine's board meetings. It was not a relationship that could be sustained. She worked around the clock and was very often travelling, and every other month she was in Australia. But she had come to value her occasional rendezvous with Blomkvist.

Mimmi made coffee two hours later as Salander lay naked and sweaty on top of the bedclothes. She smoked a cigarette and watched Mimmi through the doorway. She envied Mimmi's body. She was impressively muscled. She worked out at a gym three evenings a week, one of them doing Thai boxing or some sort of karate shit, and this had given her body an awesome shape.

She was just delicious. Not beautiful like a model, but genuinely attractive. She loved to provoke and flirt. When she dressed up for a party she could get anyone whatsoever interested in her. Salander did not understand why Mimmi cared about a goose like her. But she was glad she did. Sex with Mimmi was so dramatically liberating that Salander just relaxed and enjoyed it, taking what she wanted for herself and giving in return.

Mimmi came back and put two mugs on a stool beside the bed. She crawled onto the bed and leaned over to nibble at one of Salander's nipples.

"They'll do," she said.

Salander said nothing. She looked at Mimmi's breasts. Mimmi's breasts were small too, but they looked completely natural on her body.

"If I'm going to be honest, Lisbeth, you look fantastic."

"That's silly. My breasts don't really make any difference one way or the other, but at least I've got some now."

"You're so hung up about your body."

"You're one to talk, working out like an idiot."

"I work out like an idiot because I like to work out. It's a kick, almost as good as sex. You ought to try it."

"I do some boxing."

"Bullshit—you boxed once a month max. And mostly

because you got a buzz out of smacking those snotty guys around. That's not the same as working out to feel good."

Salander shrugged. Mimmi sat straddling her.

"Lisbeth, you're so obsessed. You should know by now that I like having you in bed not because of how you look but because of the way you act. I think you're sexy as hell."

"You too. That's why I kept coming back."

"Not for love?" Mimmi said, pretending to be hurt.

Salander shook her head.

"Are you seeing somebody?"

Mimmi hesitated a moment before she nodded.

"Maybe. In a way. Possibly. It's a little complicated."

"I'm not snooping."

"I know, but I don't mind telling you. It's someone at the university who's a little older than me. She's been married twenty years, but her husband travels a lot, so we get together when he's not around. Suburbs, villa, all that. She's a closet dyke. It's been going on since last autumn and it's getting a bit boring. But she's really luscious. And then I hang out with the usual gang, of course."

"I was just wondering whether I could come and see you again."

"I'd really like to hear from you."

"Even if I disappear for another six months?"

"Just keep in touch. I'd like to know if you're dead or alive. And in any case I'll remember your birthday."

"No strings?"

Mimmi sighed and smiled.

"You know, you're a dyke I could imagine living with. You'd leave me alone when I wanted to be left alone."

Salander said nothing.

"Apart from the fact that you're not really a dyke. You're probably bisexual. But most of all you're sexual—you like sex and you don't care about what gender. You're an entropic chaos factor."

"I don't know what I am," Salander said. "But I'm in Stockholm now and pretty bad at relationships. In fact, I don't know one single person here. You're the first person I've talked to since I got home."

Mimmi studied her with a serious expression.

"Do you really want to know people? You're the most secretive and unapproachable person I know. But your breasts really are luscious." She put her fingers under one nipple and stretched the skin. "They fit you. Not too big and not too small."

Salander sighed with relief that the reviews were satisfactory.

"And they feel real."

She squeezed the breast so hard that Salander gasped. They looked at each other. Then Mimmi bent and gave Salander a deep kiss. Salander responded and threw her arms around Mimmi. The coffee was left to get cold.

CHAPTER 7

Saturday, January 29– Sunday, February 13

At around 11:00 on Saturday morning, a car drove into Svavelsjö between Järna and Vagnhärad—the community consisted of no more than fifteen buildings—and stopped in front of the last building, about 500 feet outside the village proper. It was a tumbledown industrial structure that had once been a printing factory but now had a sign over the main door identifying it as Svavelsjö Motorcycle Club. There was no other car in sight. Nevertheless the driver looked around carefully before he got out of his car. He was huge and blond. The air was cold. He put on brown leather gloves and took a black sports bag from the trunk.

He was not worried about being observed. It would be impossible to park close to the old printing factory without being seen. If any police or government unit wanted to keep the building under surveillance, they would have to equip their people with camouflage and telescopes and dig them in at the far end of a field. Inevitably that would be talked about by the villagers, and three of the houses were owned by Svavelsjö MC members.

On the other hand, he did not want to go inside the building. The police had raided the clubhouse on several occasions, and no-one could be sure whether or not bugging equipment had been hidden there. This meant that conversation inside was pretty much about cars, girls, and beer, and sometimes about which stocks were good to invest in.

So the man waited until Carl-Magnus Lundin came out to the yard. Magge Lundin was club president. He was tall with a slim build, but over time he had acquired a hefty beer belly. He was only thirty-six. He had dark blond hair in a ponytail and wore black jeans, boots, and a heavy winter jacket. He had five counts on his police record. Two of them were for minor drug offences, one for receiving stolen goods, and one for stealing a car and drunk driving. The fifth charge, the most serious, had sent him to prison for a year: it was for grievous bodily harm when, several years ago, he had gone berserk in a bar in Stockholm.

Lundin and his huge visitor shook hands and walked slowly along the fence around the yard.

"It's been a few months," Lundin said.

The man said: "We've got a deal going down. 3,060 grams of methamphetamine."

"Same terms as last time?"

"Fifty-fifty."

Lundin pulled a pack of cigarettes out of his breast pocket. He liked doing business with the giant. Meth brought a street price of between 160 and 230 kronor per gram, depending on availability. So 3,060 grams would yield a cut value of about 600,000 kronor. Svavelsjö MC would distribute the three kilos in batches of about 250 grams each to known dealers. At that stage the price would drop to somewhere between 120 and 130 kronor per gram.

It was an exceptionally attractive deal for Svavelsjö MC. Unlike deals with other suppliers, there was never any crap about advance payment or fixed prices. The blond giant supplied the goods and demanded 50 percent, an entirely reasonable share of the revenue. They knew more or less what a kilo of meth would bring in. The exact amount depended on to what extent Lundin could get away with cutting the stuff. It could vary by a few thousand one way or the other, but when the deal was done the giant would collect around 190,000 kronor.

They had done a lot of business together over the years, always using the same system. Lundin knew that the giant could have doubled his take by handling the distribution himself. He also knew why the man accepted a lower profit: he could stay in the background and let Svavelsjö MC have all the risk. He made a smaller but a safer income. And unlike with all other suppliers he had ever come across, it was a relationship that was based on sound business principles, credit, and goodwill. No hassle, no bullshit, and no threats.

The giant had also swallowed a loss of almost 100,000 kronor over a weapons delivery that went bust. Lundin knew no-one else in the business who could absorb a loss like that. He was terrified when he'd had to tell him. Lundin explained how the deal had gone sour and how a policeman at the Crime Prevention Centre might be about to make a big score off a member of the Aryan Brotherhood in Värmland. But the giant had not so much as raised an eyebrow. He was almost sympathetic. Shit happens. The whole delivery had to be written off.

Lundin was not without talents. He understood that a smaller, less risky profit was good business.

He had never once considered double-crossing the giant. That would be bad form. The giant and his associates settled for a lower profit so long as the accounting was honest. If he cheated the blond, he would come calling, and Lundin was convinced that he would not survive such a visit.

"When can you deliver?"

The giant dropped his sports bag to the ground.

"Delivery has been made."

Lundin did not feel like opening the bag to check the contents. Instead he reached out his hand as a sign that they had a deal and he intended to do his part.

"There's one more thing," the giant said.

"What's that?"

"We'd like to put a special job your way."

"Let's hear it."

He pulled an envelope out of his inside jacket pocket and gave it to Lundin, who opened it and took out a passport photograph and a sheet of A4 containing personal data. He raised his eyebrows inquiringly.

"Her name is Lisbeth Salander and she lives in Stockholm, on Lundagatan in Södermalm."

"Right."

"She's probably out of the country at present, but she'll turn up sooner or later."

"OK."

"My employer would like to have a quiet talk with her. She has to be delivered alive. We suggest that warehouse near Yngern. And we need someone to clean up afterwards. She has to disappear without a trace."

"We should be able to handle that. How will we know when she's home?"

"I'll tell you."

"And the price?"

"What do you say to ten thousand for the whole job? It's pretty straightforward. Drive to Stockholm, pick her up, deliver her to me."

They shook hands again.

On her second visit to Lundagatan, Salander flopped down on the lumpy sofa to think. She had to make a number of decisions, and one of these was whether or not she should keep the apartment.

She lit a cigarette, blew smoke up towards the ceiling, and tapped the ash into an empty Coke can.

She had no reason to love this apartment. She had moved in with her mother and her sister when she was four. Her mother had slept in the living room, and she and Camilla shared the tiny bedroom. When she was twelve and "All The Evil" happened, she was moved to a children's clinic and then, when she was fifteen, to the first in a series of foster families. The apartment had been rented out by her trustee, Holger Palmgren, who had also seen to it that it was returned to her when she turned eighteen and needed a place to live.

The apartment had been a fixed point for almost all of her life. Although she no longer needed it, she did not like the idea of selling it. That would mean strangers in her space.

The logistical problem was that all her mail—insofar as she received any at all—came to Lundagatan. If she got rid of the apartment she would have to find another address to use. Salander did not want to be an official entry in all the databases. In this regard she was almost paranoid. She had no reason to trust the authorities, or anyone else for that matter.

She looked out at the firewall of the back courtyard, as she had done her whole life. She was suddenly glad of her decision to leave the apartment. She had never felt safe there. Every time she turned onto Lundagatan and approached the street door—sober or not—she had been acutely aware of her surroundings, of parked cars and passersby. She felt sure that somewhere out there were people who wished her harm, and they would most probably attack her as she came or went from the apartment.

There had been no attack. But that did not mean that she could relax. The address on Lundagatan was on every public register and database, and in all those years she had never had the means to improve her security; she could only stay on her guard. Now the situation was different. She did not want anyone to know her new address in Mosebacke. Instinct warned her to remain as anonymous as possible.

But that did not solve the problem of what to do with the old apartment. She brooded about it for a while and then took out her mobile and called Mimmi.

"Hi, it's me."

"Hi, Lisbeth. So you make contact after only a week this time?"

"I'm at Lundagatan."

"OK."

"I was wondering if you'd like to take over the apartment."

"What do you mean?"

"You live in a shoebox."

"I like my shoebox. Are you moving?"

"It's empty here."

Mimmi seemed to hesitate at the other end of the line.

"Lisbeth, I can't afford it."

"It's a housing association apartment and it's all paid off. The rent is 1,480 a month, which must be less than you're pay-ing for the shoebox. And the rent has been paid for a year."

"But are you thinking of selling it? I mean, it must be worth quite a bit."

"About one and a half million, if you can believe the estate agents' ads."

"I can't afford that."

"I'm not selling. You could move in here tonight, you can live here as long as you like, and you won't have to pay any-thing for a year. I'm not allowed to rent it out, but I can write you into my agreement as my roommate. That way you won't have any hassle with the housing association."

"But Lisbeth—are you proposing to me?" Mimmi laughed.

"I'm not using the apartment and I don't want to sell it."

"You mean I could live there for free, girl? Are you serious?"

"Yes."

"For how long?"

"As long as you like. Are you interested?"

"Of course I am. I don't get offered a free apartment in the middle of Söder every day of the week."

"There's a catch."

"I thought as much."

"You can live here as long as you like, but I'll still be listed as resident and I'll get my mail here. All you have to do is take in the mail and let me know if anything interesting turns up."

"Lisbeth, you're the freakiest. Where are you going to live?"

"We'll talk about that later," Salander said.

They agreed to meet that afternoon so that Mimmi could have a proper look at the apartment. Salander was already in a much better mood. She walked down to Handelsbanken on Hornsgatan, where she took a number and waited her turn.

She showed her ID and explained that she had been abroad for some time and wanted to know the balance of her savings account. The sum was 82,670 kronor. The account had been dormant for more than a year, and one deposit of 9,312 kronor had been made the previous autumn. That was the inheritance from her mother.

Salander withdrew 9,312 kronor. She wanted to spend the money on something that would have made her mother happy. She walked to the post office on Rosenlundsgatan and sent an anonymous deposit to one of Stockholm's crisis centres for women.

It was 8:00 on Friday evening when Berger shut down her computer and stretched. She had spent nine hours solid putting the finishing touches on the March issue of *Millennium,* and since Eriksson was working full-time on Svensson's themed issue she had had to do a good part of the editing herself. Cortez and Karim had helped out, but they were primarily writers and researchers, and not used to editing.

So she was tired and her back ached, but she was satisfied both with the day and with life in general. The accountant's graphs were pointing in the right direction, articles were coming in on time, or at least not unmanageably late, and the staff was happy. After more than a year, they were still on a high from the adrenaline rush of the Wennerström affair.

After trying for a while to massage her neck, Berger decided she needed a shower and thought about using the one in the office bathroom. But she felt too lazy and put her feet up on the desk instead. She was going to turn forty-five in three months, and that famous future she had longed for was starting to be a thing of the past. She had developed a network of tiny wrinkles and lines around her eyes and mouth, but she knew that she still looked good. She worked out at the gym twice a week, but she had noticed it was getting more difficult to climb the mast during her long sailing trips. And she was the one who always had to do the climbing—her husband had terrible vertigo.

Berger reflected that her first forty-five years, despite a number of ups and downs, had been by and large successful. She had money, status, a home which gave her great pleasure, and a job she enjoyed. She had a tenderhearted husband who loved her and with whom she was still in love after fifteen years of marriage. And on the side she had a pleasant and seemingly inexhaustible lover, who might not satisfy her soul but who did satisfy her body when she needed it.

She smiled as she thought of Blomkvist. She wondered when he was going to come clean and tell her that he was sleeping with Harriet Vanger. Neither of them had breathed a word about their relationship, but Berger wasn't born yesterday. At the board meeting in August she had noticed a glance that passed between them. Out of sheer cussedness she had tried both of their mobile numbers later that evening, and both were turned off. That was hardly watertight evidence, of course, but after subsequent board meetings Blomkvist was always unavailable in the evening. It was almost comical to watch the way Vanger would leave after dinner with the same excuse—that she had to go to bed early. Berger did not pry, and she was not jealous. On the other hand, she would certainly tease them both about it at some suitable occasion.

She never got involved in Blomkvist's affairs with other women, but she hoped that his affair with Vanger would not give rise to problems on the board. Yet she was not really worried. Blomkvist had all manner of terminated relationships behind him, and he was still on friendly terms with most of the women involved.

Berger was incredibly happy to be Blomkvist's friend and confidante. In certain ways he was a fool, and in others so insightful that he seemed like an oracle. But he had never understood her love for her husband, had never been able to grasp why she considered Greger Beckman such an enchanting person: warm, exciting, generous, and above all without many of the traits that she so detested in most men. Beckman was the man she wanted to grow old with. She had wanted to have children with him, but it had not been possible and now it was too late. But in her choice of a life partner she could not imagine a better or more stable person—someone she could so completely and wholeheartedly trust and who was always there for her when she needed him.

Blomkvist was very different. He was a man with such shifting traits that he sometimes appeared to have multiple personalities. As a professional he was obstinate and almost pathologically focused on the job at hand. He took hold of a story and worked his way forward to the point where it approached perfection, and then he tied up all the loose ends. When he was at his best he was brilliant, and when he was not at his best he was still far better than the average. He seemed to have an almost intuitive gift for deciding which story was hiding a skeleton in the closet and which story would turn into a dull, run-of-the-mill piece. She had never regretted working with him.

Nor had she ever regretted becoming his lover.

The only person who understood Berger's passion for sex with Blomkvist was her husband, and he understood it because she dared to discuss her needs with him. It was not a matter of infidelity, but of desire. Sex with Blomkvist gave her a kick that no other man was able to give her, including her husband.

Sex was important to her. She had lost her virginity when

she was fourteen and spent a great part of her teenage years in a frustrated search for fulfilment. She had tried everything, from heavy petting with classmates and an awkward affair with a teacher to phone sex and fetishism. She had experimented with most of what interested her in eroticism. She had toyed with bondage and been a member of Club Xtreme, which arranged parties of the kind that were not socially acceptable. On several occasions she had tried sex with other women and, disappointed, admitted that it simply was not her thing and that women could not excite her even a fraction as much as a man could. Or two. With Beckman she had explored sex with two men—one of them a famous gallery owner—and discovered both that her mate had a strong bisexual inclination and that she herself was almost paralyzed with pleasure at feeling two men simultaneously caressing and satisfying her, just as she experienced a sense of pleasure that was difficult to define when she watched her husband being caressed by another man. She and Beckman had repeated that excitement with the same success with a couple of regular partners.

It was not that her sex life with her husband was boring or unsatisfying. It was just that Blomkvist gave her a completely different experience.

He had talent. He was quite simply so good that it felt as if she had achieved the optimal balance with Beckman as husband and Blomkvist as lover-when-needed. She could not do without either of them, and she had no intention of choosing between them.

And this was what her husband had understood, that she had a need beyond what he could offer her, even in the form of his most imaginative acrobatic exercises in the Jacuzzi.

What Berger liked best about her relationship with Blomkvist was the fact that he had no desire whatsoever to control her. He was not the least bit jealous, and even though she herself had had several attacks of jealousy when they first began to go out together twenty years ago, she had discovered that in his case she did not need to be jealous. Their relationship was built on friendship, and in matters of friendship he was boundlessly loyal. It was a relationship that would survive the harshest tests.

But it bothered her that so many of her acquaintances still whispered about her relationship with Blomkvist, and always behind her back.

Blomkvist was a man. He could go from bed to bed without anyone raising their eyebrows. She was a woman, and the fact that she had a lover, and with her husband's consent—coupled with the fact that she had also been true to her lover for twenty years—resulted in the most interesting dinner conversations.

She thought for a moment and then picked up the phone to call her husband.

"Hi, darling. What are you doing?"

"Writing."

Beckman was not just an artist; he was most of all a professor of art history and the author of several books. He often participated in public debate, and he acted as consultant to several large architecture firms. For the past year he had been working on a book about the artistic decoration of buildings and its influence, and why people prospered in some buildings but not in others. The book had begun to develop into an attack on functionalism which (Berger suspected) would cause a furor.

"How's it going?"

"Good. It's flowing. How about you?"

"I just finished the latest issue. It's going to the printer on Thursday."

"Well done."

"I'm wiped out."

"It sounds like you've got something in mind."

"Have you planned anything for tonight? Would you be terribly upset if I didn't come home?"

"Say hello to Blomkvist and tell him he's tempting fate," said Beckman.

"He might like that."

"OK. Then tell him that you're a witch who's impossible to satisfy and he'll end up aging prematurely."

"He knows that."

"In that case all that's left for me is to commit suicide. I'm going to keep writing until I pass out. Have a good time."

Blomkvist was at Svensson and Johansson's place in Enskede, wrapping up a discussion about some details in Svensson's manuscript. She wondered if he was busy tonight, or would he consider giving a massage to an aching back.

"You've got the keys," he said. "Make yourself at home."

"I will. See you in an hour or so."

It took her ten minutes to walk to Bellmansgatan. She undressed and showered and made espresso. Then she crawled into bed and waited naked and full of anticipation.

The optimum gratification for her would probably be a threesome with her husband and Blomkvist, and that would never happen. Blomkvist was so straight that she liked to tease him about being a homophobe. He had zero interest in men. Apparently you could not get everything you wanted in this world.

The blond giant frowned in irritation as he manoeuvred the car at ten miles an hour along a forest road in such bad repair that for a while he thought he must have taken a wrong turn. It was just beginning to get dark when the road finally widened and he caught sight of the cabin. He stopped, turned off the engine, and took a look around. He had about fifty yards to go.

He was in the region of Stallarholmen, not far from the town of Mariefred. It was a simple 1950s cabin in the middle of the woods. Through a line of trees he could see a strip of ice on Lake Mälaren.

He could not imagine why anyone would want to spend

their free time in such an isolated place. He felt suddenly uncomfortable when he shut the car door behind him. The forest seemed threatening, as if it were closing in around him. He sensed that he was being watched. He started towards the cabin, but he heard a rustling that made him stop short.

He stared into the woods. It was dusk, silent with no wind. He stood there for two minutes with his nerves on full alert before, seeing it out of the corner of his eye, he realized that a figure was silently, slowly moving in the trees. When his eyes focused, he saw that the figure was standing perfectly still about thirty yards into the forest, staring at him.

He felt a vague panic. He tried to make out details. He saw a dark, bony face. It appeared to be a dwarf, no more than half his own size, and dressed in something that looked like a tunic of pine branches and moss. A forest troll? A leprechaun?

He held his breath. He felt the hairs rise on the back of his neck.

Then he blinked six times and shook his head. When he looked again the creature had moved about ten yards to the right. *There was nobody there.* He knew that he was imagining things. And yet he could so clearly make out the figure in the trees. Suddenly it moved and came closer. It seemed to be lurching in a semicircle to get into a position to attack him.

The blond giant hurried to the cabin. He knocked a little too hard on the door. As soon as he heard voices within, his panic subsided. He looked over his shoulder. *There was nothing there.*

But he did not breathe out until the door opened. Bjurman greeted him courteously and invited him in.

Miriam Wu was panting when she arrived back upstairs after dragging the last trash bag of Salander's possessions down to the recycling room in the cellar. The apartment was clinically clean and smelled of soap, paint, and freshly brewed coffee made by Salander. She was sitting on a stool, gazing thoughtfully at the bare rooms from which curtains, rugs, discount coupons on the refrigerator, and her usual junk in the hall had vanished as if by magic. She was amazed at how much bigger the apartment seemed.

Mimmi and Salander did not have the same taste in clothes, furniture, or intellectual stimulation. Correction: Mimmi had taste and definite views on how she wanted her living quarters to look, what kind of furniture she wanted, and what sort of clothes one should wear. Salander had no taste whatsoever, Mimmi realized.

After she had inspected the apartment on Lundagatan as closely as an estate agent might, they had discussed things and Mimmi had decided that most of the stuff had to go. Especially the disgusting dirt-brown sofa in the living room. Did Salander want to keep any of the things? No. Then Mimmi had spent a few long days as well as several hours each evening for two weeks throwing out bits of old furniture, cleaning cupboards, scrubbing the floor, scouring the bathtub, and repainting the walls in the kitchen, living room, bedroom, and hall. She also varnished the parquet floor in the living room.

Salander had no interest in such tasks, but she came several times to watch Mimmi at work, fascinated. Eventually the apartment was empty of everything except for a kitchen table of solid wood, much the worse for wear, that Mimmi intended to sand down and refinish, two stools that Salander had pounced on when an attic in the building was cleared, and a set of sturdy shelves in the living room that Mimmi thought she could repaint.

"I'm moving in this weekend, unless you're going to change your mind."

"I don't need the apartment."

"But it's a great apartment. I mean, there are bigger and better apartments, but it's slap in the middle of Söder and the rent is nothing. Lisbeth, you're passing up a fortune by not selling it."

"I have enough to get by."

Mimmi shut up, not sure how to interpret Salander's brusque dismissal.

"Where are you living now?"

Salander did not reply.

"Could a person come and visit you?"

"Not right now."

Salander opened her shoulder bag, took out some papers, and passed them over to Mimmi.

"I've fixed the agreement with the housing association. The simplest thing is to register you as my roommate and say I'm selling half of the apartment to you. The price is one krona. You have to sign the contract."

Mimmi took the pen and signed the contract, adding her date of birth.

"Is that all?"

"That's it."

"Lisbeth, I've always thought that you were a little weird. Do you realize that you just gave away half of this apartment to me? I'd love to have the apartment, but I don't want to end up in a situation where you suddenly regret it or it causes bad feelings between us."

"There will never be any bad feelings. I want you to live here. It feels right to me."

"But with nothing in return? You're nuts."

"You're taking care of my mail. That's the deal."

"That'll take me an average of four seconds a week. Do you intend to come over once in a while to have sex?"

Salander fixed her eyes on Mimmi. She was quiet for a moment.

"I'd like to very much, but it's not part of the contract. You can say no whenever you want."

Mimmi sighed. "And here I was just beginning to enjoy being a kept woman. You know, having somebody who gives me an apartment and pays my rent and comes over now and then to wrestle around in bed."

They sat in silence for a while. Then Mimmi stood up resolutely and went into the living room to turn off the bare bulb
in the ceiling fixture.

"Come here."

Salander followed her.

"I've never had sex on the floor of a newly painted apartment with almost no furniture. I saw a movie with Marlon
Brando once about a couple in Paris who did it."

Salander glanced at the floor.

"I feel like playing. Are you up for it?" Mimmi said.

"I'm almost always up for it."

"Tonight I think I'll be a dominating bitch. I get to make
the decisions. Take off your clothes."

Salander smiled a crooked smile. She took off her clothes.
It took at least ten seconds.

"Lie down on the floor. On your stomach."

Salander did as Mimmi commanded. The parquet floor was
cool and her skin got goose bumps immediately. Mimmi used
Salander's T-shirt with the slogan YOU HAVE THE RIGHT TO
REMAIN SILENT to tie her hands behind her back.

Salander could not help thinking that this was similar to
the way Nils Fucking Slimebag Bjurman had tied her up two
years ago.

The similarities ended there.

With Mimmi, Salander felt only lustful anticipation. She
was compliant when Mimmi rolled her over on her back and
spread her legs. Salander watched her in the dim room as she
pulled off her own T-shirt, and was fascinated by her soft
breasts. Then Mimmi tied her T-shirt as a blindfold over Salander's eyes. She could hear the rustle of clothes. A few seconds
later she felt Mimmi's tongue on her belly and her fingers on
the inside of her thighs. She was more excited than she had
been in a long time. She shut her eyes tight beneath the blindfold and let Mimmi set the pace.

CHAPTER 8

Monday, February 14– Saturday, February 19

Armansky looked up when he heard the light knock on the doorjamb and saw Salander in the doorway. She was balancing two cups from the espresso machine. He put down his pen and pushed the report away.

"Hi," she said.

"Hi."

"This is a social call," she said. "May I come in?"

Armansky closed his eyes for a second. Then he pointed at the visitor's chair. He glanced at the clock. It was 6:30 in the evening. Salander gave him one of the cups and sat down. They took stock of each other for a moment.

"More than a year," Armansky said.

Salander nodded.

"Are you mad?"

"Should I be?"

"I didn't say goodbye."

Armansky pursed his lips. He was shocked to see her, but at the same time relieved to discover that at least she wasn't dead. He suddenly felt a strong sense of irritation and weariness.

"I don't know what to say," he said. "You don't have any

obligation to tell me what you're working on. What do you want?"

His voice sounded cooler than he had intended.

"I'm not sure. I mostly just wanted to say hello."

"Do you need a job? I'm not going to employ you again."

She shook her head.

"Are you working somewhere else?"

She shook her head again. She seemed to be trying to formulate her words. Armansky waited.

"I've been travelling," she said at last. "I'm only recently back."

Armansky studied her. There was a new kind of . . . maturity in her choice of clothes and her bearing. And she had stuffed her bra with something.

"You've changed. Where have you been?"

"Here and there . . ." she said, but when she saw his annoyance she added, "I went to Italy and kept going, to the Middle East, to Hong Kong via Bangkok. I was in Australia for a while and New Zealand, and I island-hopped my way across the Pacific. I was in Tahiti for a month. Then I travelled through the U.S. and I spent the last few months in the Caribbean. I don't know why I didn't say goodbye."

"I'll tell you why: because you don't give a shit about other people," Armansky said matter-of-factly.

Salander bit her lower lip. "Usually it's other people who don't give a shit about me."

"Bullshit," Armansky said. "You've got an attitude problem and you treat people like dirt when they're trying to be your friends. It's that simple."

Silence.

"Do you want me to leave?"

"You do as you like. You always have. But if you leave now I never want to see you again."

Salander was suddenly afraid. Someone she respected was about to reject her. She did not know what to say.

"It's been two years since Holger Palmgren had his stroke. You haven't once visited him," Armansky went on relentlessly.

Salander stared at Armansky, shocked. "Palmgren is alive?"

"You don't even know if he's alive or dead."

"The doctors said that he—"

"The doctors said a lot about him," Armansky interrupted. "He was in a very bad way and couldn't communicate with anyone. But in the last year he's recovered quite a bit. He doesn't articulate too well—you have to listen carefully to understand what he's saying. He needs help with a lot of things, but he can go to the toilet by himself. People who care about him call in to spend time with him."

Salander sat dumbfounded. She was the one who had found Palmgren after he had his stroke two years earlier. She had called the ambulance and the doctors had shaken their heads and said that the prognosis was not encouraging. She had lived at the hospital for three days until a doctor told her that Palmgren was in a coma and it was extremely unlikely that he would come out of it. She had stood up and left the hospital without looking back. And obviously without checking to find out what had happened.

She frowned. She had had Nils Bjurman foisted on her at the same time, and he had absorbed a lot of her attention. But nobody, not even Armansky, had told her that Palmgren was still alive, or that he was getting better. She had never considered that possibility.

Her eyes filled with tears. Never in her life had she felt like such a selfish shit. And never had she been savaged in such a furious manner. She bowed her head.

They sat in silence until Armansky said, "How are you doing?"

Salander shrugged.

"How are you making a living? Do you have work?"

"No, I don't, and I don't know what kind of work I want. But I've got a certain amount of money, so I'm getting by."

Armansky scrutinized her with searching eyes.

"I just came by to say hello . . . I'm not looking for a job. I don't know . . . maybe I'd do a job for you if you need me sometime, but it would have to be something that interests me."

"I don't suppose you want to tell me what happened up in Hedestad last year."

Salander did not answer.

"Well, something happened. Martin Vanger drove his car into a truck after you'd been back here to borrow surveillance gear, and somebody threatened you. And his sister came back from the dead. It was a sensation, to put it mildly."

"I've given my word I wouldn't talk about it."

"And you don't want to tell me what role you played in the Wennerström affair either."

"I helped Kalle Blomkvist with research." Her voice was suddenly much cooler. "That was all. I didn't want to get involved."

"Blomkvist has been looking for you high and low. He's called here once a month to ask if I've heard anything from you."

Salander remained silent, but Armansky saw that her lips were now pressed into a tight line.

"I can't say that I like him," Armansky said. "But he cares about you too. I met him once last autumn. He didn't want to talk about Hedestad either."

Salander did not want to discuss Blomkvist. "I just came to say hello and tell you that I'm back. I don't know if I'll be staying. This is my mobile number and my new email address if you need to get hold of me."

She handed Armansky a piece of paper and stood up. She was already at the door when he called after her.

"Wait a second. What are you going to do?"

"I'm going to say hello to Holger Palmgren."

"OK. But I mean . . . what kind of work will you be doing?"

"I don't know."

"But you have to make a living."

"I told you, I have enough to get by."

Armansky leaned back in his chair. He was never quite sure how to interpret her words.

"I've been so fucking angry that you vanished without a word that I almost decided never to trust you again." He made a face. "You're so unreliable. But you're a damned good researcher. I might have a job coming up that would be a good fit for you."

She shook her head, but she came back to his desk.

"I don't want a job from you. I mean, I don't need one. I'm serious. I'm financially independent."

Armansky frowned.

"OK, you're financially independent, whatever that means. I'll take your word for it. But when you need a job . . ."

"Dragan, you're the second person I've visited since I got home. I don't need your work. But for several years now you've been one of the few people that I respect."

"Everybody has to make a living."

"Sorry, but I'm no longer interested in doing personal investigations. Let me know if you run into a really interesting problem."

"What sort of problem?"

"The kind you can't make heads or tails of. If you get stuck and don't know what to do. If I'm going to do a job for you, you'll have to come up with something special. Maybe on the operations side."

"Operations side? *You?* But you disappear without a trace whenever you feel like it."

"I've never skipped out on a job that I agreed to do."

Armansky looked at her helplessly. The term *operations* was jargon, but it meant field work. It could be anything from bodyguard duty to surveillance assignments for art exhibitions. His operations personnel were confident, stable veterans, many of them with a police background, and 90 percent of them were men. Salander was the polar opposite of all the criteria he had set out for personnel in the operations unit of Milton Security.

"Well . . ." he said dubiously, but she had vanished out the door. Armansky shook his head. *She's weird. She's really weird.*

The next second Salander was back in the doorway.

"Oh, by the way . . . You've had two guys spending a month protecting that actress Christine Rutherford from the nutcase who writes her threatening letters. You think it's an inside job because the letter writer knows so many details about her."

Armansky stared at Salander. An electric shock went through him. *She's done it again. She's flung out a line about a case she absolutely cannot know a thing about.*

"So . . . ?"

"It's a fake. She and her boyfriend have been writing the letters as a publicity stunt. She's going to get another letter in the next few days, and they'll leak it to the media next week. They'll probably accuse Milton of leaking it. Cross her off your client list now."

Before Armansky could say anything she was gone. He stared at the empty doorway. She could not possibly have known a single detail of the case. She must have an insider at Milton who kept her updated. But only four or five people apart from himself knew about it—the operations chief and the few people who reported on the threats—and they were all stable pros. Armansky rubbed his chin.

He looked down at his desk. The Rutherford file was locked inside it. The office had a burglar alarm. He glanced at the clock again and realized that Harry Fransson, chief of the technical department, would have finished for the day. He started up his email and sent a message asking Fransson to come to his office the following morning to install a surveillance camera.

. . .

Salander walked straight home to Mosebacke. She hurried because she had a feeling it was urgent.

She called the hospital in Söder and after some stalling from the switchboard managed to find out Palmgren's whereabouts. For the past fourteen months he had been in a rehabilitation home in Ersta. All of a sudden she had a vision of Äppelviken. When she called she was told that he was asleep, but that she was welcome to visit him the next day.

Salander spent the evening pacing back and forth in her apartment. She was in a foul mood. She went to bed early and fell asleep almost at once. She woke at 7:00 a.m., showered, and had breakfast at the 7-Eleven. At 8:00 she walked to the car rental agency on Ringvägen. *I've got to get my own car.* She rented the same Nissan Micra she had driven to Äppelviken a few weeks earlier.

She was unaccountably nervous when she parked near the rehabilitation centre, but she gathered up her courage and went inside.

The woman at the front desk consulted her papers and explained that Holger Palmgren was in the gym for therapy just then and would not be available until after 11:00. Salander was welcome to take a seat in the waiting room or come back later. She went and sat in the car and smoked three cigarettes while she waited. At 11:00 she went back to the front desk. She was told to go to the dining hall, down the corridor to the right and then to the left.

She stopped in the doorway and recognized Palmgren in the half-empty dining room. He sat facing her, but was focusing all his attention on his plate. He held his fork in an awkward grip and steered the food to his mouth with great concentration. Every third time or so he missed and the food fell off the fork.

He looked shrunken; he might be a hundred years old. His

face seemed strangely immobile. He was sitting in a wheelchair. Only then did Salander take it in that he was alive, that Armansky had not just been punishing her.

Palmgren swore silently as he tried for the third time to spear a bite of macaroni and cheese onto his fork. He was resigned to being unable to walk properly, and he accepted that there was a great deal he would be unable to do. But he hated not being able to eat properly and the fact that sometimes he drooled like a baby.

He knew exactly what it was he should do: lower the fork at the right angle, push it forward, lift it, and guide it to his mouth. The problem was with the coordination. His hand had a life of its own. When he instructed it to lift, it would slide slowly to the side of the plate. If he did manage to steer it towards his mouth, it would often change direction at the last moment and land on his cheek or his chin.

But the rehabilitation was producing results. Six months earlier his hand would shake so much that he could not get a single spoonful into his mouth. His meals might still be taking a long time, but at least he was eating by himself, and he was going to go on working at it until he once again had full control over his limbs.

As he lowered his fork to collect another mouthful, a hand appeared from behind him and gently took it from him. He watched as the fork shovelled up some of the macaroni and cheese and raised it. He thought he knew the thin, doll-like hand and turned his head to meet Salander's eyes. Her gaze was expectant. She seemed anxious.

For a long moment Palmgren stared at her face. His heart was suddenly pounding in a most unreasonable way. Then he opened his mouth and accepted the food.

She fed him one bite at a time. Normally Palmgren hated being spoon-fed, but he understood Salander's need. It was not because he was a helpless piece of baggage. She was feeding him as a gesture of humility—in her case an extraordinarily rare occurrence. She put the right-size portions on the fork and waited until he was finished chewing. When he pointed at the glass of milk with the straw, she held it up so he could drink.

When he had swallowed the last mouthful, she put the fork down and gave him a questioning look. He shook his head. They had not said a word to each other during the entire meal.

Palmgren leaned back in his wheelchair and took a deep breath. Salander picked up the napkin and wiped around his mouth. He felt like a Mafia boss in an American movie where a *capo di tutti capi* was showing respect. He imagined how she would kiss his hand and smiled at the absurdity of this fantasy.

"Do you think it would be possible to get a cup of coffee in this place?" she said.

He slurred his words. His lips and tongue could not shape the sounds.

"Srvg tab rond corn." *The serving table is around the corner,* she worked it out.

"You want a cup? Milk, no sugar, as always?"

He signalled yes with a hand. She carried his tray away and came back a minute later with two cups of coffee. He noticed that she drank hers black, which was unusual. He smiled when he saw that she had saved the straw from his milk for the coffee cup. Palmgren had a thousand things to say but he could not formulate a single syllable. But their eyes kept meeting, time after time. Salander looked terribly guilty. Finally she broke the silence.

"I thought you'd died," she said. "If I'd known you were alive I would never have . . . I would have come to see you a long time ago. Forgive me."

He bowed his head. He smiled, a twist of the lips.

"You were in a coma when I left you and the doctors told me you were going to die. They said you would be dead within a few days and I just walked away. I'm so sorry."

He lifted his hand and laid it on her little fist. She took his hand in a firm grip.

"Ju dsperd." *You disappeared.*

"Dragan Armansky told you?"

He nodded.

"I was off travelling. I needed to get away. I didn't say good-bye to anybody, just left. Were you worried?"

He shook his head from side to side, slowly.

"You don't ever have to worry about me."

"I nv word bow ju. Ju alws get ba. Bt Armshy's word." *I never worried about you. You always get by. But Armansky was worried.*

She smiled her usual crooked smile at him and Palmgren relaxed. He studied her, comparing his memory of her with the woman he saw before him. She had changed. She was whole and clean and rather well dressed. She had taken out the ring that was in her lip and . . . hmm . . . the wasp tattoo on her neck was gone too. She looked grown up. He laughed for the first time in many weeks. It sounded like a coughing fit.

Salander's smile grew bigger and she suddenly felt a warmth that she had not felt in a long time filling her heart.

"Ju dd gd." *You did good.* He aimed a hand at her clothes. She nodded.

"I'm doing fine."

"Howz z noo gardn?" *How is the new guardian?*

Palmgren noticed Salander's face darken. Her mouth tightened. She looked at him frankly.

"He's OK . . . I can handle him."

Palmgren's eyebrows questioned her. Salander looked around the dining room and changed the subject.

"How long have you been here?"

Palmgren may have had a stroke and he still had difficulty speaking and coordinating his movements, but his mind was intact and his radar instantly picked up a false tone in Salander's voice. In all the years he had known her, he had come to realize that she never lied to him directly, but neither was she totally candid. Her way of not telling him the truth was to distract his attention. There was obviously some problem with her new guardian. Which did not surprise Palmgren.

He felt a deep sense of remorse. How many times had he thought about calling his colleague Nils Bjurman—a fellow lawyer after all, if not a friend—to ask how Salander was doing, but then neglected to do so? And why had he not contested her declaration of incompetence while he still had the power? He knew why—he had wanted, selfishly, to keep his contact with her alive. He loved this damned difficult child like the daughter he never had, and he wanted to have an excuse to maintain the relationship. Besides, it was physically too difficult. He had enough trouble just opening his fly when he tottered to the toilet. He felt as if he were the one who had let Lisbeth Salander down. *But she'll always survive . . . She's the most competent person I've ever met.*

"Dscrt."

"I didn't understand."

"Dstrc crt."

"The district court? What do you mean?"

"Gtta cancl yr d . . . dc . . . dclrash incmp . . ."

Palmgren's face turned red and he grimaced when he could not pronounce the words. Salander put a hand on his arm and pressed gently.

"Holger . . . don't worry about me. I have plans to take on my declaration of incompetence soon. It's not your worry any longer, but I may need your help eventually. Is that OK? Will you be my lawyer if I need you?"

He shook his head.

"Tu old." He rapped his knuckle on the arm of his wheelchair. "Dum ld man."

"Yeah, you're a dumb old man if you have that attitude. I need a legal advisor and I want you. You may not be able to give a statement in court, but you can give me advice when the time comes. Would you?"

He shook his head again, and then he nodded.

"Wrk?"

"I don't understand."

"Wut ju work on? Not Armshi." *What are you working on? Not Armansky.*

Salander hesitated while she debated how to explain her situation. It was complicated.

"I'm not working for Armansky anymore. I don't need to work for him to make a living. I have my own money and I'm doing fine."

Palmgren's eyebrows knitted together again.

"I'll come and visit you a lot, starting today. I'll tell you all about . . . but let's not get stressed about things. Right now there's something else I want to do."

She bent down and lifted a bag to the table and took out a chessboard.

"I haven't had the chance to sweep the floor with you for two whole years."

He gave up. She was up to some mischief that she did not want to talk about. He was quite sure he would have severe reservations, but he trusted her enough still to know that whatever she was up to might be dubious in the eyes of the law but not a crime against God's laws. Unlike most other people who knew her, Palmgren was sure that Salander was a genuinely moral person. The problem was that her notion of morality did not always coincide with that of the justice system.

She set out the chessmen in front of him and he recognized with shock that it was his own board. *She must have pinched it from the apartment after he fell ill.* As a keepsake? She gave him white. All of a sudden he was as happy as a child.

Salander stayed with Palmgren for two hours. She had crushed him three times before a nurse interrupted their bickering over the board, announcing that it was time for his afternoon physical therapy. Salander collected the chessmen and folded up the board.

"Can you tell me what kind of physical therapy he's getting?" she said.

"It's strength and coordination training. And we're making progress, aren't we?"

Palmgren nodded grimly.

"You can already walk several steps. By summer you'll be able to walk by yourself in the park. Is this your daughter?"

Salander's and Palmgren's eyes met.

"Ster dotr." *Foster daughter.*

"How nice that you came to visit." *Where the hell have you been all this time?* Salander ignored the unmistakable meaning. She leaned forward and kissed Palmgren on the cheek.

"I'll come again on Friday."

Palmgren stood up laboriously from his wheelchair. She walked with him to an elevator. As soon as the elevator doors had closed she went to the front desk and asked to speak to whoever was responsible for the patients. She was referred to a Dr. A. Sivarnandan, whom she found in an office further down a corridor. She introduced herself, explaining that she was Palmgren's foster daughter.

"I'd like to know how he's doing and what's going to happen with him."

Dr. Sivarnandan looked up Palmgren's casebook and read the introductory pages. His skin was pitted by smallpox and he had a thin moustache which Salander found absurd. Finally he sat back. To her surprise he spoke with a Finnish accent.

"I have no record of Herr Palmgren having a daughter or foster daughter. In fact, his nearest relative would seem to be an eighty-six-year-old cousin in Jämtland."

"He took care of me from when I was thirteen until he had his stroke. I was twenty-four at the time."

She dug into the inside pocket of her jacket and threw a pen onto the desk in front of the doctor.

"My name is Lisbeth Salander. Write my name in his casebook. I'm the closest relation he has in the world."

"That may be," replied Dr. Sivarnandan firmly. "But if you are his closest relation you certainly took a long time letting us know. As far as I know, he has only had a few visits from a person who, while not related to him, is to be notified in case the state of his health worsens or if he should pass away."

"That would be Dragan Armansky."

Dr. Sivarnandan raised his eyebrows.

"That's correct. You know him?"

"You can call him and verify that I am who I say I am."

"That won't be necessary. I believe you. I was told that you sat and played chess with Herr Palmgren for two hours. But I cannot discuss the state of his health with you without his permission."

"And you'll never get it from that stubborn devil. You see, he suffers from the delusion that he shouldn't burden me with his troubles and that he is still responsible for me, and not the other way around. This is how it is: for two years I thought he was dead. Yesterday I discovered that he was alive. If I'd known that he . . . it's complicated to explain, but I'd like to know what sort of prognosis he has and whether he will recover."

Dr. Sivarnandan picked up the pen and wrote Salander's name neatly into Palmgren's casebook. He asked for her social security number and telephone number.

"OK, now you're formally his foster daughter. This may not be completely by the book, but considering that you're the first person to visit him since last Christmas when Herr Armansky stopped by . . . You saw him today—you can see for yourself that he has problems with coordination and speech. He had a stroke."

"I know. I was the one who found him and called the ambulance."

"Aha. Then you should know that he was in intensive care for three months. He was in a coma for a long time. Most patients never wake up from a coma like that, but it does happen. Obviously he wasn't ready to die. First he was put in the dementia ward for chronic long-term patients who are completely unable to take care of themselves. Against all the odds he showed signs of improvement and was moved here for rehabilitation nine months ago."

"Tell me what chances he has of getting his mobility and speech back."

Dr. Sivarnandan threw out his hands. "Have you got a crystal ball that's better than mine? The truthful answer is that I have no idea. He could die from a cerebral haemorrhage tonight. Or he could live a relatively normal life for another twenty years. I have no way of knowing. You might say it's God who decides."

"And if he lives another twenty years?"

"It's been a laborious rehabilitation for him, and it's only in the past few months that we have been able to see improvements. Six months ago he couldn't eat without assistance. One month ago he could hardly get out of his chair, which is partly due to muscle atrophy from being in bed for so long. Now at least he can walk by himself for short distances."

"Can he get better?"

"Yes. Even a lot better. The first threshold was hard, but now we're seeing progress every day. He has lost almost two years of his life. In a few months, by the summer, I hope he'll be able to walk in the park."

"And his speech?"

"His problem is that both his speech centre and his ability to move were knocked out. He was helpless for a long time. Since then he has been forced to learn how to control his body and talk again. He doesn't always remember which words to use, and he has to learn some words again. But it's not like teaching a child to talk—he knows the meaning of the word, he just can't articulate it. Give him a couple of months and you'll see how his speech has improved compared with today. The same is true of his ability to get around. Nine months ago he couldn't tell left from right, or up from down in the elevator."

Salander thought about this for a minute. She discovered that she liked this Dr. A. Sivarnandan with the Indian looks and the Finnish accent.

"What does the *A* stand for?" she asked.

He gave her an amused look. "Anders."

"Anders?"

"I was born in Sri Lanka but then adopted by a couple in Åbo when I was three months old."

"OK, Anders, how can I help?"

"Visit him. Give him intellectual stimulation."

"I can come every day."

"I don't want you to be here every day. If he likes you, I want him to look forward to your visits, not get bored with them."

"Could any type of special care improve his odds? I can pay whatever it costs."

He smiled at Salander. "I'm afraid that we're all the special care there is. Of course I wish we had more resources and that the cutbacks didn't affect us, but I assure you that he's getting very competent care."

"And if you didn't have to worry about the cutbacks, what else could you offer him?"

"The ideal for patients like Holger Palmgren, of course, would be if I could offer him a full-time personal trainer. But it's been quite a while since we had resources like that in Sweden."

"Hire one."

"Excuse me?"

"Hire him a personal trainer. Find the best you can. Please do it first thing tomorrow. And make sure he has everything he needs in the way of technical equipment. I'll see to it that the funds are available by the end of the week to pay for it."

"Are you pulling my leg, young lady?"

Salander gave Dr. Anders Sivarnandan her hard, steady look.

. . .

Johansson braked and pulled her Fiat over to the curb outside Gamla Stan tunnelbana station. Svensson opened the door and slipped into the passenger seat. He leaned over and gave her a kiss on the cheek as she drew away behind a bus.

"Hello, you," she said without taking her eyes off the traffic. "You look so serious. Has something happened?"

Svensson sighed as he fastened his seat belt.

"No, nothing major. A little problem with the manuscript is all."

"What problem?"

"Two months till the deadline. I've done only nine of the twenty-two confrontations we planned. I'm having trouble with Björck at the Security Police. The bastard is on long-term sick leave and he's not answering his home telephone."

"Is he in hospital?"

"Don't know. Have you ever tried getting information out of Säpo? They won't even admit that he works there."

"Did you try his parents?"

"Both dead. He's not married. He has a brother who lives in Spain. I just have no idea how to get hold of him."

Johansson glanced at her partner as she navigated across Slussen to the tunnel leading to Nynäsvägen.

"Worst-case scenario, we jettison the section on Björck. Blomkvist insists that everyone we're planning to expose must have a chance to comment before being hung out to dry."

"But it would be a shame to miss out on a representative of the Security Police who runs around with prostitutes. What are you going to do?"

"Find him, of course. How are you doing? Nervous?"

He poked her carefully in the side.

"Actually, no. In two months I have to defend my dissertation and become a full-fledged doctor, and I feel as cool as a cucumber."

"You know the subject backwards. Why be nervous?"

"Look behind you."

Svensson turned and saw an open box on the backseat.

"Mia—it's printed!" he said in delight. He held up a copy of the bound thesis.

From Russia with Love
Trafficking, Organized Crime, and Society's Response
by Mia Johansson

"It wasn't going to be ready until next week. Damn . . . we're going to have to crack open a bottle when we get home. Congratulations, Doctor!"

He leaned over and kissed her again.

"Calm down. I won't be a doctor for another two months. And keep your hands under control while I'm driving."

Svensson laughed. Then he turned serious.

"By the way, fly in the ointment and all that . . . you interviewed a girl named Irina P. about a year ago."

"Irina P., twenty-two, from St. Petersburg. She first came here in 1999 and has made some return trips. What about her?"

"I ran into Gulbrandsen today. The policeman involved in the Södertälje brothel investigation. Did you read last week that they'd found a girl floating in the canal there? There were headlines in the evening papers. It was Irina P."

"Oh no. That's horrible."

They drove in silence past Skanstull.

"She's in my thesis," Johansson said at last. "I gave her the pseudonym Tamara."

Svensson turned to the interview section of "From Russia with Love" and leafed through it to find "Tamara." He read with concentration as Mia passed Gullmarsplan and the Globe Arena.

"She was brought here by somebody you call Anton."

"I can't use real names. I might get criticism for it during my oral exams, but I cannot name the girls. It would put them in real, mortal danger. And obviously I can't identify the johns either, since they could work out which of the girls I had talked to. So in all the case studies I only use pseudonyms."

"Who's Anton?"

"His name is probably Zala. I've never been able to pin down who he is, but I think he's a Pole or a Yugoslav and that's not his real name. I talked with Irina P. four or five times, and it wasn't until our last meeting that she told me his name. She was trying to straighten out her life and get out of the business, but she was certainly really afraid of him."

"I'm just wondering . . . I ran into the name Zala a week or so ago."

"Where was that?"

"I confronted Sandström—the john who's a journalist. A complete bastard."

"In what way?"

"He's not a real journalist. He does advertising newsletters for various companies. And he has sick fantasies about rape that he'd get off on with that girl . . ."

"I know. I was the one who interviewed her."

"But did you know that he did the text for a brochure about sexually transmitted diseases for the Public Health Institute?"

"I didn't know that."

"I confronted him last week. He totally lost it when I laid out all the evidence and asked why he uses teenage prostitutes from the East to live out his rape fantasies. Gradually I got some sort of explanation out of him."

"And what was it?"

"Sandström had gotten into a situation where he wasn't just another customer. He also ran errands for the sex mafia. He gave me the names he knew, including this Zala. He didn't say anything specific about him, but it's not a common name."

Johansson glanced at him.

"Do you know who he is?" Svensson said.

"No. I've never been able to identify him. He's just a name that crops up now and then. The girls all seem terrified of him, and none of them was willing to tell me anything else."

CHAPTER 9

Sunday, March 6– Friday, March 11

Dr. Sivarnandan stopped in his tracks on his way into the dining room when he caught sight of Palmgren and Salander. They were bent over their chessboard. She came once a week now, usually on Sundays. She always arrived at around 3:00 and spent a couple of hours playing chess with Palmgren. She left around 8:00 in the evening, when it was time for him to go to bed. The doctor had observed that she did not treat him as you would an invalid—on the contrary, it looked like they were squabbling all the time, and she did not mind Palmgren waiting on her, fetching her coffee.

Dr. Sivarnandan could not make her out, this peculiar young woman who took herself for Palmgren's foster daughter. She had a very striking look about her and she seemed to treat everything around her with suspicion. She appeared to have no sense of humour at all. Or the ability to carry on a normal conversation. And when he asked what kind of work she did, she somehow contrived not to give him an answer.

A few days after her first visit she had come back with a bundle of documents which declared that a nonprofit foundation had been established with the sole purpose of assisting the care centre with Palmgren's rehabilitation. The chair of the trustees of the foundation was a lawyer in Gibraltar. There was another lawyer mentioned, also with an address in Gibraltar, and an accountant by the name of Hugo Svensson with an address in Stockholm. The foundation was to make available funds of up to 2.5 million kronor, which Dr. Sivarnandan could dispose of as he wished, but with the exclusive object of giving the patient Holger Palmgren every possible care and facility towards full recovery. Sivarnandan had only to request the necessary funds from the accountant.

It was an unusual, if not unique, arrangement. Sivarnandan had thought hard for several days about whether there was anything unethical about the situation. He decided that there was not and accordingly hired Johanna Karolina Oskarsson as Holger Palmgren's personal assistant and trainer. She was thirty-nine, a certified physical therapist with a degree in psychology and with extensive experience in rehabilitation care. To Sivarnandan's surprise her first month's salary was paid to the hospital in advance, as soon as her employment contract was signed. Until then he had vaguely worried that this might be some sort of hoax.

Within a month Palmgren's coordination and overall condition had markedly improved. This could be seen from the tests he underwent every week. How much the improvement was due to the training and how much was thanks to Salander, Sivarnandan could only wonder. There was no doubt that Palmgren was making great efforts and looked forward to her visits with the enthusiasm of a child. It even seemed to amuse him that he was regularly pummelled at the chessboard.

Dr. Sivarnandan had kept them company on one occasion. Palmgren was playing white and had opened the Sicilian quite correctly. He had pondered each move long and hard. Whatever his physical handicap as a result of the stroke, there was nothing wrong now with his intellectual acuity.

Salander sat there reading a book on the frequency calibration of radio telescopes in a weightless state. She was sitting on a cushion, the better to be level with the table. When Palmgren made his move she glanced up and moved her piece, apparently without studying the board, and went back to her book. Palmgren resigned after the twenty-seventh move. Salander looked up and with a frown inspected the board for perhaps fifteen seconds.

"No," she said. "You have a chance for a stalemate."

Palmgren sighed and spent five minutes studying the board. At last he narrowed his gaze at Salander.

"Prove it."

She turned the board around and took over his pieces. She forced a stalemate on the thirty-ninth move.

"Good Lord," Sivarnandan said.

"That's the way she is. Don't ever play with her for money," Palmgren said.

Sivarnandan had played chess himself since he was a boy, and as a teenager he was in the school tournament in Åbo, and came in second. He regarded himself as a competent amateur. Salander, he could see, was an uncanny chess player. She had obviously never played for a club, and when he mentioned that the game seemed to have been a variant of a classic game by Lasker, she gave him an uncomprehending look. She had never heard of Emanuel Lasker. He could not help wondering whether her talent was innate, and if so, whether she had other talents that might interest a psychologist.

But he did not say a word. He could see that his patient was feeling better than he ever had since coming to Ersta.

Bjurman arrived home late in the evening. He had spent four whole weeks at his summer cabin outside Stallarholmen, but he was dispirited. Nothing had happened to change his situation except that the giant had informed him that his people were interested in the proposal and that it would cost him 100,000 kronor.

Mail was piled up on the doormat. He put it all on the

kitchen table. He was less and less interested in everything to do with work and the outside world, and he did not look at the letters until later in the evening. Then he shuffled through them absentmindedly.

One was from Handelsbanken. It was a statement for the withdrawal of 9,312 kronor from Lisbeth Salander's savings account.

She was back.

He went into his office and put the document on his desk. He looked at it with hate-filled eyes for more than a minute as he collected his thoughts. He was forced to look up the telephone number. Then he lifted the receiver and dialled the number of a mobile with a prepaid calling card.

The blond giant answered with a slight accent: "Yes?"

"It's Nils Bjurman."

"What do you want?"

"She's back in Sweden."

There was a brief silence at the other end.

"That's good. Don't call this number again."

"But—"

"You will be notified shortly."

Then, to his considerable irritation, the connection was cut. Bjurman swore to himself. He went over to the drinks cabinet and poured himself a triple measure of Kentucky bourbon. He swallowed the drink in two gulps. *I've got to go easy on the booze,* he thought. Then he poured one more measure and took the glass back to his desk, where he looked at the statement from Handelsbanken again.

Mimmi was massaging Salander's back and neck. She had been kneading intently for twenty minutes while Salander mainly enjoyed herself and uttered an occasional groan of pleasure. A massage from Mimmi was a fantastic experience, and she felt like a kitten who just wanted to purr and wave its paws around.

She stifled a sigh of disappointment when Mimmi slapped her on the backside and said that should do it. For a while she lay still in the vain hope that Mimmi would go on, but when she heard her pick up her wineglass, Salander rolled onto her back.

"Thank you," she said.

"You're sitting in front of your computer all day. That's why your back hurts."

"I just pulled a muscle."

They were lying naked in Mimmi's bed on Lundagatan, drinking red wine and feeling silly. Since Salander had resumed her friendship with Mimmi, it was as if she couldn't get enough of her. It had become a bad habit to call her every day—much too often. She looked at Mimmi and reminded herself not to get too close to anyone again. It might end with someone getting hurt.

Mimmi leaned over the edge of the bed and opened the drawer of her bedside table. She took out a small flat package wrapped in flowered paper with a gold bow and tossed it into Lisbeth's lap.

"What's this?"

"Your birthday present."

"My birthday's more than a month away."

"It's your present from last year, but I couldn't find you."

"Should I open it?"

"If you feel like it."

She put down her wineglass, shook the package, and opened it carefully. She drew out a beautiful cigarette case with a lid of blue and black enamel and some tiny Chinese characters as decoration.

"You really should stop smoking," Mimmi said. "But if you won't, at least you can keep your cigarettes in a pretty box."

"Thank you," Salander said. "You're the only person who ever gives me birthday presents. What do the characters mean?"

"How on earth would I know that? I don't understand Chinese. I just found it at the flea market."

"It's beautiful."

"It's just some cheap nothing, but it looked as if it was made for you. We've run out of wine. You want to go out and get a beer?"

"Does that mean we have to leave the bed and get dressed?"

"I'm afraid so. But what's the point of living in Söder if you can't go to a bar now and then?"

Salander sighed.

"Come on," Mimmi said, pointing at the jewel in Salander's navel. "We can come back here afterwards."

Salander sighed again, but she put one foot on the floor and reached for her underwear.

Svensson was working late at the desk he had been assigned in a corner of the *Millennium* offices when he heard the rattle of a key in the door. He looked at the clock and saw that it was past 9:00 p.m. Blomkvist seemed surprised to find someone still working there.

"The lamp of diligence and all that, Mikael. I'm fine-tuning the book and I lost track of time. What are you doing here?"

"Just stopped by to pick up a file I forgot. Is everything going well?"

"Sure . . . Well, actually no . . . I've spent three weeks trying to track down Björck from Säpo. He seems to have vanished without a trace. Perhaps he's been kidnapped by some enemy secret service."

Blomkvist pulled up a chair and sat thinking for a moment.

"Have you tried the old lottery trick?"

"What's that?"

"Think of a name, write a letter saying that he's won a mobile telephone with a GPS navigator, or whatever. Print it out so it looks official and post it to his address—in this case that P.O.

box he has. He's already won the mobile, a brand-new Nokia. But more than that, he's one of twenty people who can go on to win 100,000 kronor. All he has to do is take part in a marketing study for various products. The session will take about an hour and be done by a professional interviewer. And then . . . well."

Svensson stared at Blomkvist, openmouthed. "Are you serious?"

"Why not? You've tried everything else, and even a spook from Säpo should be able to figure out that the odds of winning a hundred grand are pretty good if he's one of only twenty people on the list."

Svensson laughed out loud. "You're nuts. Is that legal?"

"I can't imagine it's illegal to give away a mobile telephone."

"You really are out of your mind."

Svensson kept laughing. Blomkvist hesitated a moment. He was actually on his way home and seldom went to bars, but he liked Svensson's company.

"Do you feel like going out for a beer?" he said.

Svensson looked again at the clock.

"Why not?" he said. "Gladly. A quick one. Let me leave a message for Mia. She's out with the girls and was going to pick me up on her way home."

They went to Kvarnen, mostly because it was comfortable and close by. Svensson chuckled as he composed the letter to Björck at Security Police HQ. Blomkvist looked dubiously at his easily amused colleague. They were lucky enough to get a table near the door. Each of them ordered a large glass of strong beer, and with their heads together they began to drink and discuss Svensson's book.

Blomkvist did not see Salander standing at the bar with Miriam Wu. Salander took a step back to put Mimmi between her and Blomkvist. She looked at him from behind Mimmi's shoulder.

She had not been in a bar since she came back and—just her luck—she had to run into him. Kalle Fucking Blomkvist. It was the first time she had seen him in more than a year.

"What's wrong?" Mimmi said.

"Nothing."

They kept talking. Or rather, Mimmi went on with her story about a dyke she had met on a trip to London a few years back. She had been visiting an art gallery and the situation had gotten funnier and funnier as Mimmi tried to pick her up. Salander nodded now and then, but as usual missed the point of the story.

Blomkvist had not changed much, she decided. He looked absurdly well—approachable and relaxed, but with a grave expression. He was listening to what his companion was saying, nodding now and then. It seemed to be a serious discussion.

Salander looked at Blomkvist's friend. A man with a blond crew cut several years younger than Blomkvist, who was talking intently. She had no idea who he was.

All of a sudden a whole group came up to Blomkvist's table and shook hands with him. Blomkvist got a pat on the cheek from a woman who said something everyone else laughed at. Blomkvist looked self-conscious, but he laughed too.

Salander scowled.

"You're not listening to what I'm saying," Mimmi said.

"Of course I am."

"You're terrible company in a bar. I give up. Should we go home and fuck instead?"

"In a bit," Salander said.

She moved a little closer to Mimmi and put a hand on her hip.

Mimmi looked down at her partner and said, "I feel like kissing you on the mouth."

"Don't do it."

"Are you afraid people will think you're a dyke?"

"I don't want to attract attention right now."

"Let's go home then."

"Not yet. Wait a while."

They did not have long to wait. Twenty minutes after they arrived, the man Blomkvist was with got a call on his mobile. They drained their glasses and stood up simultaneously.

"Check it out," Mimmi said. "That guy over there is Mikael Blomkvist. He was more famous than a rock star after the Wennerström affair."

"You don't say."

"Did you miss all that? It was about the time when you left the country."

"I've heard it mentioned."

Salander waited for another five minutes before she looked at Mimmi.

"You wanted to kiss me on the mouth."

Mimmi looked at her in surprise. "I was just teasing."

Salander stood on tiptoe and pulled Mimmi's face down to her level and gave her a long, deep kiss. When they separated there was applause.

"You're nuts, you know that?" Mimmi said.

Salander did not get home until 7:00 in the morning. She pulled out the neck of her T-shirt and sniffed. She thought about taking a shower but decided the hell with it, and instead left her clothes on the floor and went to bed. She slept till 4:00 in the afternoon, then got up and went down to Söderhallarna market and had breakfast.

She thought about Blomkvist, and about her reaction to suddenly finding herself in the same room as him. She had been annoyed at his presence, but she also discovered that it no longer hurt to see him. He had been transformed to a little

blip on the horizon, a minor perturbation factor in her existence. There were worse disturbances in life.

But she wished she had had the guts to go up to him and say
hello. Or possibly break his legs. She wasn't sure which.

Anyway, she was curious about what he was up to. She ran
a few errands in the afternoon and came home around 7:00
p.m. She booted up her PowerBook and started Asphyxia 1.3.
The icon *MikBlom/laptop* was still on the server in Holland.
She double-clicked and opened a copy of Blomkvist's hard
drive. It was her first visit to his computer since she had
left Sweden more than a year before. She noticed with satisfaction that he still had not upgraded to the latest MacOS,
which would have meant that Asphyxia would have crashed
and the hacking would have been terminated. She realized that
she would have to rewrite the programme so that an upgrade
would not interfere with it.

The volume on the hard drive had increased by almost 6.9
gigabytes since her previous visit. A large part of the increase
was due to PDF files and Quark documents. The documents
did not take up much room but the bitmaps did, despite the
fact that the images were compressed. Since he had returned as
publisher he had apparently archived every issue of *Millennium*.

She sorted the files on the hard disk by date with the oldest
at the top and noticed that Blomkvist had spent a great deal of
time over the past few months on a folder named <Dag Svens-
son>, apparently a book project. Then she opened Blomkvist's
email and read carefully through the address list in his correspondence.

One address made Salander jump. On January 26 Blomkvist
had got an email from Harriet Fucking Vanger. She opened the
message and read a few concise lines about a board meeting to
take place at the *Millennium* offices. The message ended with
the information that Vanger had booked the same hotel room
as last time.

Salander digested the information. Then she shrugged and

downloaded Blomkvist's mail, Svensson's book manuscript with the working title *The Leeches* and the subtitle *Society's Support for the Prostitution Industry.* She also found a copy of a thesis entitled "From Russia with Love" written by a woman named Mia Johansson.

She disconnected and went into the kitchen to put on some coffee. Then she sat on her new sofa in the living room with her PowerBook. She opened Mimmi's cigarette case and lit a Marlboro Light. The rest of the evening she spent reading.

By 9:00 she had finished Johansson's thesis. She bit her lower lip.

By 10:30 she had finished Svensson's book. *Millennium* would soon be making headlines again.

At 11:30 she was reading the last of Blomkvist's emails when she suddenly sat up and opened her eyes wide.

She felt a cold shiver go down her spine.

It was a message from Svensson to Blomkvist.

In an aside Svensson mentioned that he had some tentative ideas about an Eastern European gangster named Zala who might get a chapter all to himself—but acknowledged that there was not much time till the deadline. Blomkvist hadn't answered the email.

Zala.

Salander sat motionless until the screen saver went on.

Svensson put aside his notebook and scratched his head. He gazed at the single word at the top of the page in his notebook. Four letters.

Zala.

He spent three minutes deep in thought, drawing labyrinthine rings around the name. Then he went and got a cup of coffee from the kitchenette. It was time to go home to bed, but he had discovered that he enjoyed working late at the *Millennium* offices when it was quiet in the building.

He had all the material under control, but for the first time since he started the project he felt uneasy that he might have missed an important detail.

Zala.

Until that point he had been impatient to finish the writing and get the book published, but now he wished he had more time.

He thought about the autopsy report that Inspector Gulbrandsen had let him read. Irina P.'s body had been found in Södertälje canal. She had devastating injuries to her face and chest. The cause of death was a broken neck, but two of her other injuries had been judged fatal. Six ribs had been broken and her left lung punctured. She had a ruptured spleen. The injuries were hard to interpret. The pathologist had offered the suggestion that a wooden club wrapped in cloth had been the weapon used. Why a killer would wrap a murder weapon in cloth could not be explained, but the scale of the injuries was not characteristic of an ordinary assault.

The murder remained unsolved, and Gulbrandsen had said that the prospect of their solving the case was slender.

The name Zala had come up on four occasions in the material that Mia had gathered over the last two years, but always on the periphery, always eerily elusive. Nobody knew who he was and nobody could provide proof that he even existed. Some of the girls had referred to his name being used as a threat, a terrifying warning to those who did not toe the line. He had spent a whole week hunting for more concrete information about Zala, asking questions of police, journalists, and several recently developed sources with contacts in the sex trade.

He had been in touch with the journalist Sandström, whom he had every intention of exposing in the book. Sandström had begged and pleaded for Svensson to have mercy. He had offered a bribe. Svensson was not going to change his mind, but he did use his advantage to pressure Sandström for information about Zala.

Sandström claimed he had never met Zala, but he had talked to him on the telephone. No, he did not have the number. No, he could not say who had set up the contact.

Svensson had been struck by the realization that Sandström was terrified. It was a terror beyond the threat of exposure. He was afraid for his life. *Why?*

CHAPTER 10

Monday, March 14– Sunday, March 20

The journeys to and from Ersta were time-consuming and a hassle. In the middle of March Salander decided to buy a car. She started by acquiring a parking place, a much greater problem than buying the car itself.

She had a space in the garage beneath the building in Mosebacke, but she did not want anyone to be able to connect the car to where she lived on Fiskargatan. On the other hand, several years before she had put herself on a waiting list for a space in the garage of her old housing association apartment on Lundagatan. She called to find out where on the list she was now and was told that she was at the top. And not only that— at the end of the month there would be a spot free. Sweet. She called Mimmi and asked her to make a contract with the association right away. The next day she started hunting for a car.

She had the money to buy whatever Rolls-Royce or Ferrari she wanted, but she was not remotely interested in anything ostentatious. Instead she went to two dealers in Nacka and came away with a four-year-old burgundy Honda automatic. She spent an hour going over every detail, including the engine, to the salesman's exasperation. On principle she talked the price down a couple of thousand and paid in cash.

Then she drove to Lundagatan, where she knocked on Mimmi's door and gave her a set of keys. Sure, Mimmi could use the car if she asked in advance. Since the garage space would not be free until the end of the month, they parked on the street.

Mimmi was on her way to a date and a movie with a girl-friend Salander had never heard of. Since she was made up outrageously and dressed in something awful with what looked like a dog's collar round her neck, Salander assumed it was one of Mimmi's flames, and when Mimmi asked if she wanted to come along she said no thanks. She had no desire to end up in a threesome with one of Mimmi's long-legged girlfriends who was no doubt unfathomably sexy but would make her feel like an idiot. Anyway, Salander had something to do in town, so they took the tunnelbana together to Hötorget, and there they parted.

Salander walked to OnOff on Sveavägen and made it with two minutes to spare before closing time. She bought a toner cartridge for her laser printer and asked them to take it out of the box so that it would fit in her backpack.

When she came out of the shop, she was thirsty and hungry. She walked to Stureplan, where she decided on Café Hedon, a place she had never been to before or even heard about. She instantly recognized Nils Bjurman from behind and turned right around in the doorway. She stood by the picture window facing the pavement and craned her neck so that she could observe her guardian from behind a serving counter.

The sight of Bjurman aroused no dramatic feelings in Salander, not anger, nor hatred, nor fear. As far as she was concerned, the world would assuredly be a better place without him, but he was alive only because she had decided that he would be more useful to her that way. She looked across at the man opposite Bjurman, and her eyes widened when he stood up. *Click.*

He was an exceptionally big man, at least six foot six and well built. Exceptionally well built, as a matter of fact. He had a weak face and short blond hair, but overall he made a very powerful impression.

Salander saw the man lean forward and say something quietly to Bjurman, who nodded. They shook hands and Salander noticed that Bjurman quickly drew his hand back.

What sort of guy are you and what business do you have with Bjurman?

Salander walked briskly down the street and stood under the awning of a tobacconist shop. She was looking at a newspaper headline when the blond man came out of Café Hedon and without looking around turned left. He passed less than a foot behind Salander. She gave him a good head start before she followed him.

It was not a long walk. The man went straight down into the tunnelbana station at Birger Jarlsgatan and bought a ticket at the gate. He waited on the southbound platform—the direction Salander was going anyway—and got on the Norsborg train. He got off at Slussen, changed to the green line towards Farsta, and got off again at Skanstull. From there he walked to Blomberg's Café on Götgatan.

Salander stopped outside. She studied the man the blond hulk had come to meet. *Click.* Salander saw immediately that something sinister was going on. The man was overweight and had a narrow, untrustworthy face. His hair was pulled back into a ponytail and he had a mousy moustache. He wore a denim jacket, black jeans, and high-heeled boots. On the back of his right hand he had a tattoo, but Salander could not make out the design. He wore a gold chain around his wrist and was smoking Lucky Strikes. His gaze was glassy-eyed, like someone who got high too often. Salander also noticed that he had a leather vest on under his jacket. She could tell he was a biker.

The giant did not order anything. He seemed to be giving instructions. The man in the denim jacket paid close attention but did not contribute to the conversation. Salander reminded herself that one day soon she should buy herself a shotgun mike.

After only five minutes the giant left Blomberg's Café. Salander retreated a few paces, but he did not even look in her direction. He walked forty yards to the steps to Allhelgona-gatan, where he got into a white Volvo. Salander managed to read his licence plate number before he turned at the next corner.

Salander hurried back to Blomberg's, but the table was empty. She looked up and down the street but could not see the man with the ponytail. Then she caught a glimpse of him across the street as he pushed open the door to McDonald's.

She had to go inside to find him again. He was sitting with another man who was wearing his vest outside his denim jacket. Salander read the words SVAVELSJÖ MC. The logo was a stylized motorcycle wheel that looked like a Celtic cross with an axe.

She stood on Götgatan for a minute before heading north. Her internal warning system had suddenly gone on high alert.

Salander stopped at the 7-Eleven and bought a week's worth of food: a jumbo pack of Billy's Pan Pizza, three frozen fish casseroles, three bacon pies, two pounds of apples, two loaves of bread, a pound of cheese, milk, coffee, a carton of Marlboro Lights, and the evening papers. She walked up Svartensgatan to Mosebacke and looked all around before she punched in the door code of her building. She put one of the bacon pies in the microwave and drank milk straight from the carton. She switched on the coffee machine and then booted up her

computer, clicking on Asphyxia 1.3 and logging in to the mirrored copy of Bjurman's hard drive. She spent the next half
hour going through the contents of his computer.

She found absolutely nothing of interest. He seemed to use
his email rarely; she discovered only a dozen brief personal
messages to or from acquaintances. None of the emails had any
connection to her.

She found a newly created folder with porn photos that
made clear that he was still interested in the sadistic humiliation of women. Technically it wasn't a violation of her rule that
he couldn't have anything to do with women.

She opened the folder of documents dealing with Bjurman's role as Salander's guardian and read through each of his
monthly reports. They corresponded precisely to the copies he
had sent to one of her hotmail addresses.

Everything normal.

Maybe a small discrepancy . . . When she opened the file
properties in Word for the various monthly reports, she could
see that he usually wrote them in the first few days of each
month, that he spent about four hours editing each report, and
sent them punctually to the Guardianship Agency on the twen-
tieth of every month. It was now the middle of March and he
had not yet begun work on the current month's report. *Lazy?
Out too late? Busy with something else? Up to some tricks?* Salander frowned.

She shut down the computer and sat on her window seat
and opened her cigarette case. She lit a cigarette and looked
out at the darkness. She had been sloppy about keeping track
of him. *He's as slippery as an eel.*

She was genuinely worried. *First Kalle Fucking Blomkvist,
then the name Zala, and now Nils Fucking Slimebag Bjurman
together with an alpha male on steroids with contacts in some
gang of ex-con bikers.* Within a few days, several ripples of dis-
quiet had materialized in the orderly life Salander was trying to
create for herself.

. . .

At 2:30 the following morning Salander put a key in the front door of the building on Upplandsgatan near Odenplan, where Bjurman lived. She stopped outside his door, carefully lifted up the mail slot cover, and shoved in an extremely sensitive microphone she had bought at Counterspy in Mayfair in London. She had never heard of Ebbe Carlsson, but that was the shop where he had bought the famous eavesdropping equipment that caused Sweden's minister of justice to resign suddenly in the late 1980s. Salander inserted her earpiece and adjusted the volume.

She could hear the dull humming of the refrigerator and the sharp ticking of at least two clocks, one of which was the wall clock in the living room to the left of the front door. She turned up the volume and listened, holding her breath. She heard all sorts of creaks and rumbles from the apartment, but no evidence of human activity. It took her a minute to notice and decipher the faint sounds of heavy, regular breathing.

Bjurman was asleep.

She withdrew the microphone and stuffed it in the pocket of her leather jacket. She was wearing dark jeans and sneakers with crepe soles. She inserted the key in the lock without a sound and pushed the door open a crack. Before she opened it all the way she took the Taser out of her pocket. She had brought no other weapon. She did not think she would need anything more powerful for dealing with Bjurman.

She closed the door behind her and padded on soundless feet towards the corridor outside his bedroom. She stopped when she saw the light from a lamp, but from where she stood she could already hear his snoring. She slipped into his bedroom. The lamp stood in the window. *What's wrong, Bjurman? A little scared of the dark?*

She stood next to his bed and watched him for several minutes. He had aged and seemed unkempt. The room smelled of a man who was not taking good care of his hygiene.

She did not feel a grain of sympathy. For a second a hint of merciless hatred flashed in her eyes. She noticed a glass on the nightstand and leaned over to sniff it. Whiskey.

After a while she left the bedroom. She took a short tour through the kitchen, found nothing unusual, continued through the living room, and stopped at the door of Bjurman's office. From her jacket pocket she took a handful of small bits of crispbread, which she placed carefully on the parquet floor in the dark. If anyone tried to follow her through the living room, the crunching noise would alert her.

She sat down at Bjurman's desk and placed the Taser in front of her. Methodically she searched the drawers and went through correspondence dealing with Bjurman's private accounts. She noticed that he had become sloppier and more sporadic with balancing his accounts.

The bottom drawer of the desk was locked. Salander frowned. When she had visited a year before, all the drawers had been unlocked. Her eyes remained unfocused as she visualized the drawer's contents. It had contained a camera, a telephoto lens, a small Olympus pocket tape recorder, a leather-bound photograph album, and a little box with a necklace and a gold ring inscribed TILDA AND JACOB BJURMAN • APRIL 23, 1951. Salander knew that these were the names of his parents and that both of them were dead. Presumably it was a wedding ring, now a keepsake.

So, he locks up stuff he thinks is valuable.

She inspected the rolltop cabinet behind the desk and took out the two binders containing his reports of her guardianship. For fifteen minutes she read each one. Salander was a pleasant and conscientious young woman. Four months earlier he had written that she seemed so rational and competent that there was good reason to discuss at the next annual review whether or not she required further guardianship. It was elegantly phrased and amounted to the first building block in the revocation of her declaration of incompetence.

The binder also contained handwritten notes that showed Bjurman had been contacted by one Ulrika von Liebenstaahl at the Guardianship Agency for a general discussion of Salander's condition. The words *necessity for psychiatric assessment* had been underlined.

Salander pouted, replaced the binders, and looked around. She could not find anything of note. Bjurman seemed to be behaving in accordance with her instructions. She bit her lower lip. She still had a feeling that something was not right.

She got up from the chair and was about to turn off the desk lamp when she stopped. She took out the binders and looked through them again. She was perplexed. The binders should have contained more. A year ago there had been a summary of her development since childhood from the Guardianship Agency. That was missing. *Why would Bjurman remove papers from an active case?* She frowned. She could not think of any good reason. Unless he was filing additional documentation somewhere else. Her eyes swept across the shelves of the rolltop cabinet and the bottom desk drawer.

She did not have a picklock with her, so she padded back to Bjurman's bedroom and fished his key ring out of his suit jacket, which was hanging over a wooden valet stand. The same objects were in the drawer as a year ago. But the collection had been supplemented with a flat box whose printed illustration showed a Colt .45 Magnum.

She thought through the research that she had done about Bjurman two years ago. He liked to shoot and was a member of a shooting club. According to the public weapons registry he had a licence for a Colt .45 Magnum.

Reluctantly she came to the conclusion that it was no surprise he kept the drawer locked.

She did not like the situation, but she could not think of any immediate pretext for waking him and scaring the shit out of him.

. . .

Johansson woke at 6:30 a.m. She heard the morning TV on low volume from the living room and smelled freshly brewed coffee. She also heard the clacking of keys from Svensson's iBook. She smiled.

She had never seen him work so hard on a story before. *Millennium* had been a good move. He was often afflicted with writer's block, and it seemed as though hanging out with Blomkvist and Berger and the others was having a beneficial effect on him. He would come home gloomy after Blomkvist had pointed out shortcomings or shot down some of his reasoning, but then he'd work twice as hard.

She wondered whether it was the right moment to interrupt his concentration. Her period was three weeks late. She had not yet taken a pregnancy test. Perhaps it was time.

She would soon turn thirty. In less than a month she had to defend her dissertation. Dr. Johansson. She smiled again and decided not to say anything to Svensson before she was sure. Maybe she would wait until he was finished with his book and she was giving a party after she got her doctorate.

She dozed for ten more minutes before she got up and went into the living room with a sheet wrapped around her. He looked up.

"It's not 7:00 yet," she said.

"Blomkvist is acting superior again."

"Has he been mean to you? Serves you right. You like him, don't you?"

Svensson leaned back in the living-room sofa and met her eyes. After a moment he nodded.

"*Millennium* is a great place to work. I talked to Mikael at Kvarnen before you picked me up last night. He was wondering what I was going to be doing after this project was finished."

"Aha. And what did you say?"

"That I didn't know. I've hung around as a freelancer for so many years now. I'd be glad of something more steady."

"*Millennium.*"

He nodded.

"Mikael has tested the waters, and wanted to know if I'd be interested in a part-time job. Same contract as Henry Cortez and Lotta Karim are on. I'd get a desk and a retainer from *Millennium* and could take in the rest on the side."

"Do you want to do that?"

"If they come up with a concrete offer, I'll say yes."

"OK, but it's not 7:00 yet and it's Saturday."

"I know. I just thought I'd polish it up a bit here and there."

"I think you should come back to bed and polish something else."

She smiled at him and turned up a corner of the sheet. He put the computer on standby.

Salander spent a good deal of time over the next few days doing research on her PowerBook. Her search extended in many different directions, and she was not always sure what she was looking for.

Some of the fact collecting was simple. From the Media Archive she put together a history of Svavelsjö MC. The club appeared in newspaper stories going by the name Tälje Hog Riders. Police had raided the clubhouse, at that time located in an abandoned schoolhouse outside Södertälje, when neighbours reported shots fired. The police turned up in astonishing force and broke up a beer-drenched party that had degenerated into a shooting contest with an AK-4, which later turned out to have been stolen from the disbanded I20 regiment in Västerbotten in the early 1980s.

According to one evening paper, Svavelsjö MC had six or seven members and a dozen hangers-on. All the full members had been in jail. Two stood out. The club leader was

Carl-Magnus "Magge" Lundin, who was pictured in *Afton-bladet* when the police raided the premises in 2001. He had been convicted on five charges of theft, receiving stolen goods, and for drug offences in the late 1980s and early 1990s. One of the sentences—for a crime which involved grievous bodily harm—put him away for eighteen months. He was released in 1995 and soon afterwards became president of Tälje Hog Riders, now Svavelsjö MC.

According to the police gang unit, the club's number two was Sonny Nieminen, now thirty-seven years old, who had run up no fewer than twenty-three convictions. He had started his career at the age of sixteen when he was put on probation and in institutional care for assault and battery and theft. Over the next ten years he was convicted on five counts of theft, one of aggravated theft, two of unlawful intimidation, two narcotics offences, extortion, assault on a civil servant, two counts of possessing an illegal weapon, one criminal weapons charge, driving under the influence, and six counts of assault. He had been sentenced according to a scale that was incomprehensible to Salander: probation, fines, and repeated stints of thirty to sixty days in jail, until 1989, when he was put away for ten months for aggravated assault and robbery. He was out a few months later and kept his nose clean until October 1990. Then he got into a fight in a bar in Södertälje and ended up with a conviction for manslaughter and a six-year prison sentence. He was out by 1995.

In 1996 he was arrested as an accessory to an armed robbery. He had provided three of the robbers with weapons. He was sentenced to four years and released in 1999. According to a newspaper article from 2001 in which Nieminen was not named—but where the details of the suspect were such that he was effectively identified—he looked more than likely to have played his part in the murder of a member of a rival gang.

Salander downloaded the mug shots of Nieminen and Lundin. Nieminen had a photogenic face with dark curly hair and dangerous eyes. Lundin just looked like a complete idiot, and was without doubt the man who had met the giant at Blomberg's Café. Nieminen was the man waiting in McDonald's.

Via the national vehicle register she traced the white Volvo to the car rental firm Auto-Expert in Eskilstuna. She dialled their number and spoke to a Refik Alba:

"My name is Gunilla Hansson. My dog was run over yesterday by someone who just drove off. The bastard was driving a car from your firm—I could tell from the licence plate. A white Volvo." She gave the number.

"I'm so sorry."

"That's not enough, I'm afraid. I want the name of the driver so that I can sue him."

"Have you reported the matter to the police?"

"No, I'd like to settle it directly."

"I'm sorry, but I can't give out the names of our clients unless a police report has been filed."

Salander's voice darkened. She asked whether it was good practice to oblige her to report the company's clients to the police force instead of resolving matters with much less trouble. Refik Alba apologized once more and repeated that he was powerless to circumvent company rules.

The name Zala was another dead end. With two breaks for Billy's Pan Pizza, Salander spent most of the day at her computer with only a big bottle of Coca-Cola for company.

She found hundreds of Zalas—from an Italian athlete to a composer in Argentina. But she did not find the one she was looking for.

She tried Zalachenko, but that was a dead end too.

Frustrated, she stumbled into bed and slept for twelve hours straight. When she woke it was 11:00 a.m. She put on some coffee and ran a bath in the Jacuzzi. She poured in bubble bath and brought coffee and sandwiches for breakfast. She wished that she had Mimmi to keep her company, but she still had not even told her where she lived.

At noon she got out of the bath, towelled herself dry, and put on a bathrobe. She turned on the computer again.

The names Dag Svensson and Mia Johansson yielded better results. Via Google's search engine she was able to quickly put together a brief summary of what they had been up to in recent years. She downloaded copies of some of Svensson's articles and found a photographic byline of him. No great surprise that he was the man she had seen with Blomkvist at Kvarnen. The name had been given a face, and vice versa.

She found several texts about or by Mia Johansson. She had first come to the media's attention with a report on the different treatment received by men and women at the hands of the law. There had been a number of editorials and articles in women's organizations' newsletters. Johansson herself had written several more articles. Salander read attentively. Some feminists found Johansson's conclusions significant, others criticized her for "spreading bourgeois illusions."

At 2:00 in the afternoon she went into Asphyxia 1.3, but instead of *MikBlom/laptop* she selected *MikBlom/office*, Blomkvist's desktop computer at *Millennium*. She knew from experience that his office computer contained hardly anything of interest. Apart from the fact that he sometimes used it to surf the Net, he worked almost exclusively on his iBook. But he did have administrator rights for the whole *Millennium* office. She quickly found what she was looking for: the password for *Millennium*'s internal network.

To get into other computers at *Millennium*, the mirrored hard drive on the server in Holland was not sufficient. The original of *MikBlom/office* also had to be on and connected to the internal computer network. She was in luck. Blomkvist was apparently at work and had his desktop on. She waited ten minutes but could not see any sign of activity, which she took to indicate that he had turned on the computer when he came into the office and had possibly used it to surf the Net, then left it on while he did something else or used his laptop.

This had to be done carefully. During the next hour Salander hacked cautiously from one computer to another and downloaded email from Berger, Malm, and an employee whose name she did not recognize, Malin Eriksson. Finally she located Svensson's desktop. According to the system information it was an older Macintosh PowerPC with a hard disk of only 750 MB, so it must be a leftover that was probably only used for word processing by occasional freelancers. It was linked to the computer network, which meant that Svensson was in *Millennium*'s editorial offices right now. She downloaded his email and searched his hard drive. She found a folder with the short but sweet name <Zala>.

The blond giant had just picked up 203,000 kronor in cash, which was an unexpectedly large sum for the three kilos of methamphetamine he had delivered to Lundin in late January. It was a tidy profit for a few hours of practical work—collecting the meth from the courier, storing it for a while, making delivery to Lundin, and then taking 50 percent of the profit. Svavelsjö MC could turn over that amount every month, and Lundin's gang was only one of three such operations—the other two were around Göteborg and Malmö. Together the gangs brought him roughly half a million kronor in profit every month.

And yet he was in such a bad mood that he pulled over to the side of the road and turned off the engine. He had not slept for thirty hours and was feeling fuzzy. He got out to stretch his legs and take a piss. The night was cool and the stars were bright. He was not far from Järna.

The conflict he was having was almost ideological in nature. The potential supply of methamphetamine was limitless within a radius of 250 miles from Stockholm. The demand was indisputably huge. The rest was logistics—how to transport the product from point A to point B, or to be more precise, from a cellar workshop in Tallinn to the Free Port in Stockholm.

This was a recurring problem—how to guarantee regular transport from Estonia to Sweden? In fact it was the main problem and the weak link, since after several years he was still improvising every time. And fuckups had been all too frequent lately. He was proud of his ability to organize. He had built up a well-oiled network cultivated with equal portions of carrot and stick. He was the one who had done the legwork, cemented partnerships, negotiated deals, and made sure that the deliveries got to the right place.

The carrot was the incentive offered to subcontractors like Lundin—a solid and relatively risk-free profit. The system was a good one. Lundin did not have to lift a finger to get the goods—no stressful buying trips or dealings with people who could be anyone from the drug squad to the Russian mafia. Lundin knew that the giant would deliver and then collect his 50 percent.

The stick was for when complications arose. A gabby street dealer who had found out far too much about the supply chain had almost implicated Svavelsjö MC. He had been forced to get involved and punish the guy.

He was good at dealing out punishment.

But the operation was becoming too burdensome to oversee.

He lit a cigarette and stretched his legs against a gate into a field.

Methamphetamine was a discreet and easy-to-manage source of income—big profits, small risks. Weapons were risky, and considering the risks they were simply not good business.

Occasionally industrial espionage or smuggling electronic components to Eastern Europe—even though the market had dropped off in recent years—was justifiable.

Whores from the Baltics, on the other hand, were an entirely unsatisfactory investment. The business was small change, and liable at any time to set off hypocritical screeds in the media and debates in that strange political entity called the Swedish parliament. The one advantage was that everybody likes a whore—prosecutors, judges, policemen, even an occasional member of parliament. Nobody was going to dig too deep to bring that business down.

Even a dead whore would not necessarily cause a political uproar. If the police could catch a suspect within a few hours who still had bloodstains on his clothes, then a conviction would follow and the murderer would spend several years in prison or some other obscure institution. But if no suspect was found within forty-eight hours, the police would soon enough find more important things to investigate, as he knew from experience.

He did not like the trade in whores, though. He did not like them at all, their makeup-plastered faces and shrill, drunken laughter. They were unclean. And there was always the risk that one of them would get the idea she could seek asylum or start blabbing to the police or to reporters. Then he would have to take matters into his own hands and mete out punishment. And if the revelation was blatant enough, prosecutors and police would be forced to act—otherwise parliament really would wake up and pay attention. The whore business sucked.

The brothers Atho and Harry Ranta were typical: two useless parasites who had found out way too much about the business. Most of all he would like to tie them up with chains and dump them in the harbour. Instead he had driven them to the Estonia ferry and patiently waited until it sailed. Their little vacation was the result of some fucking reporter sticking his nose into their business, and it was decided that they had better make themselves scarce.

He sighed.

Above all he did not appreciate diversions like that Salander girl. She was utterly without interest as far as he was concerned. She represented no profit whatsoever.

He did not like Bjurman, and he could not imagine why they had decided to do what he wanted. But now the ball was rolling. Instructions had been issued, the contract had been awarded to a freelancer from Svavelsjö MC, and he did not like the situation one bit.

He looked out across the dark field, tossing his cigarette butt into the gravel by the gate. He thought he saw movement out of the corner of his eye and froze. He focused his gaze. There was no light except from a faint crescent moon and the stars, but he could still make out the contours of a black figure creeping towards him about a hundred feet away. The figure advanced, making short pauses.

The man felt a cold sweat on his brow. He hated the creature in the field. For a minute he stared spellbound at its steady approach. When it was close enough that he could see its eyes glimmer in the darkness he spun round and ran to the car. He tore open the door. He felt his panic growing until he got the engine started and turned on the headlights. The creature had come out to the road and at last he could make out features in the beam. It looked like an enormous sting ray slithering along. It had a stinger like a scorpion.

The creature was not of this world. It was a monster from the underworld.

He put the car in gear and screeched off. As he passed the creature he saw it strike, but it did not touch the car. He did not stop shaking until several miles later.

Salander spent the night going over the research that Svensson and *Millennium* had compiled about trafficking. Gradually she was getting a good overview, even though it was based on cryptic fragments that she had to piece together from their various documents.

Berger sent an email to Blomkvist asking how the confrontations were going; he replied briefly that they could not run the man from the Cheka to earth. Salander took this to mean that one of the people who was going to be hung out to dry worked at Säpo, the Security Police. Eriksson sent a summary of a supplementary research assignment to Svensson with copies to Blomkvist and Berger. Svensson and Blomkvist replied with comments and suggestions. Blomkvist and Svensson exchanged emails a few times each day. Svensson described a confrontation he had had with a journalist, Per-Åke Sandström.

From Svensson's emails she also saw that he was communicating with a person by the name of Gulbrandsen at a Yahoo address. It took her a while to realize that Gulbrandsen was a policeman and that their exchange was off the record, using a private email address instead of Gulbrandsen's police address. So Gulbrandsen was a source.

The folder named <Zala> was disappointingly brief, only three Word documents. The longest of them, just 128 KB, was called [Irina P] and gave a sketch of a prostitute's life, followed by Svensson's summary of the autopsy report, his curt outline of her appalling wounds.

She recognized a phrase in the text that was a word-for-word quotation from Johansson's dissertation. There the woman had been called Tamara, but Irina P. and Tamara had to be one and the same, so she read the interview section of the thesis with great interest.

The second document, [Sandström], contained the summary that Svensson had emailed to Blomkvist, showing that the journalist was one of several johns who had abused a girl from the Baltics, and also that he ran errands for the sex mafia in exchange for drugs and sex. Sandström, besides producing company newsletters, had written freelance articles for a daily newspaper indignantly condemning the sex trade. One of his revelations was that an unnamed Swedish businessman had visited a brothel in Tallinn.

Zala was not mentioned in either document, but Salander assumed that since both were in a folder named <Zala> there must be a connection. The last document was, however, named [Zala]. It was short and only in note form.

According to Svensson, the name Zala had turned up in nine cases related to drugs, weapons, or prostitution since the mid-nineties. Nobody knew who Zala was, but sources had variously indicated that he was a Serb, a Pole, or perhaps a Czech. All the information was secondhand.

Svensson had discussed Zala exhaustively with *source G.* (Gulbrandsen?) and suggested that Zala may have been responsible for the murder of Irina P. There was no saying what G. thought about this theory, but there was a note to the effect that Zala had been on the agenda a year earlier at a meeting with "the special investigative group on organized crime." The name had cropped up so many times that the police had started asking questions, trying to establish whether Zala was a real person, and whether he was still alive.

As far as Svensson could discover, the name Zala had first appeared in connection with the holdup of a security van in Örkelljunga in 1996. The robbers had gotten away with more than 3.3 million kronor, but they had so dramatically botched their getaway that after only twenty-four hours the police were able to identify and arrest the gang members. The following day another arrest was made. It was Nieminen, a member of Svavelsjö MC, whose role had been to supply the weapons used in the holdup.

A week after the robbery in 1996, three more people were arrested. The ring thus included eight people, of whom seven had refused to talk to the police. The eighth, a boy of nineteen named Birger Nordman, had broken down and confessed everything he knew during questioning. The trial turned into a runaway victory for the prosecution. One consequence was (Svensson's police source suspected) that Nordman was found two years later buried in a sandpit in Värmland after running away during temporary leave from prison.

According to G., the police believed that Nieminen had been the catalyst behind the whole gang. They also believed that Nordman had been killed on contract by Nieminen, who was regarded as dangerous and ruthless, but there was no evidence. While in prison he had apparently had dealings with the Aryan Brotherhood, a Nazi prison organization that in turn was linked to the Wolfpack Brotherhood and to ex-con Hell's Angels clubs around the world, as well as to other cretinous violent Nazi organizations such as the Swedish Resistance Movement.

What interested Salander, however, was something else entirely. Nordman had admitted to police that the weapons used in the robbery had come from Nieminen, and that he in turn had got them from a Serb not known to Nordman whom he named as "Sala."

Svensson had taken him for an anonymous figure in the criminal scene and reckoned that "Zala" was a nickname. But he warned that they might be dealing with a particularly cunning criminal who operated under an alias.

The last section contained Sandström's information on Zala, such as it was. Sandström had once talked on the telephone to someone using that name. The notes did not say what the conversation had been about.

At around 4:00 in the morning Salander shut down her PowerBook and sat on her window seat looking out at Saltsjön. She sat quietly for two hours, smoking one cigarette after another, thinking. She had a number of strategic decisions to make—and she had to do a risk assessment.

She had to find Zala and settle their accounts once and for all.

On Saturday evening the week before Easter, Blomkvist visited an old girlfriend on Slipgatan in the Hornstull neighbourhood. He had, for once, accepted an invitation to a party. She was

married now and not remotely interested in Blomkvist as anything more than a friend, but she worked in the media and had
just finished a book that had been in gestation for ten years,
which dealt with the image of women in the mass media.
Blomkvist had contributed to the book, which was why he was
invited.

His role had been to do research on one question. He had
chosen to examine the equal opportunity policies which the
TT wire service, *Dagens Nyheter,* the TV show *Rapport,* and a
number of other media ostentatiously promoted. Then he
checked off how many men and women were in each company's management above the level of editorial assistant. The
results were embarrassing: CEO—man; chairman of the
board—man; editor in chief—man; foreign editor—man;
managing editor—man . . . et cetera, until eventually the first
woman turned up.

The party was at the author's house and the people there
were mostly those who had helped her with the book. It was a
high-spirited evening with good food and relaxed conversation.
Blomkvist had meant to go home reasonably early, but many
of the guests were old acquaintances he seldom saw. Besides,
no-one jabbered on too much about the Wennerström affair.
The party went on until around 2:00 on Sunday morning.

Blomkvist saw the night bus drive past before he could
make it to the bus stop, but the air was mild and he decided to
walk home instead of waiting for the next one. He followed
Högalidsgatan to the church and turned up Lundagatan, which
instantly awakened old memories.

Blomkvist had kept the promise he'd made in December to
stop visiting Lundagatan in the vain hope that Salander might
appear. Tonight he stopped on the other side of the street from
her building. He longed to ring the doorbell, but he knew how
unlikely it was that she would want to see him, let alone at this
time of night with no warning.

He shrugged and kept walking towards Zinkensdamm. He

had gone about sixty yards when he heard a door open and turned, and then his heart skipped a beat. It was impossible to mistake that skinny body. Salander had just walked out to the street and away from him. She stopped at a parked car.

Blomkvist opened his mouth to call to her when his voice caught in his throat. He saw a man get out of another of the cars parked along the curb. He moved rapidly up behind Salander. Blomkvist could see that he was tall and had a ponytail.

Salander heard a sound and saw a movement out of the corner of her eye just as she was putting the key in the door of the Honda. He was approaching at an angle behind her, and she spun around two seconds before he reached her. She identified him instantly as Carl-Magnus Lundin of Svavelsjö MC, who several days ago had met the blond hulk at Blomberg's Café.

She gauged him as aggressive and weighing over 265 pounds. She used her keys as brass knuckles and didn't hesitate a millisecond before, with a movement as swift as a lizard, she slashed a deep wound in his cheek, from the bottom of his nose to his ear. He was flailing at the air as Salander then seemed to sink through the ground.

Blomkvist saw Salander lash out with her fist. At the instant she struck her attacker she dropped to the ground and rolled beneath the car.

Seconds later Salander was up on the other side of the car, ready for fight or flight. She met the enemy's gaze across the hood and decided on the latter option. Blood was pouring from his cheek. Before he even managed to focus on her she was away across Lundagatan, running towards Högalid Church.

Blomkvist stood paralyzed, his mouth agape, when the attacker suddenly dashed after Salander. He looked like a tank chasing a toy car.

Salander took the steps to upper Lundagatan two at a time. At the top of the stairs she glanced over her shoulder and saw her pursuer reaching the first step. He was fast. She noticed the piles of boards and sand where the local authority had dug up the street.

Lundin was almost up the steps when Salander came into view again. He had time to register that she was throwing something, but he did not have time to react before the sharp-edged cobblestone hit him on the temple. The stone was thrown with considerable force, and it ripped another wound on his face. He could feel himself losing his footing and then the world spun as he fell backwards down the stairs. He managed to break his fall by grabbing the railing, but he had lost several seconds.

Blomkvist's paralysis dissolved when the man disappeared up the stairs. He started yelling for him to fuck off.

Salander was halfway across the churchyard when she heard Blomkvist's voice. *What the hell?* She switched directions and looked over the railing of the terrace. She saw Blomkvist ten feet below her. She hesitated a tenth of a second before she took off again.

At the same time as Blomkvist began to run towards the steps he noticed that a Dodge van was starting up outside Salander's front door, behind the car she had tried to get into. The vehicle swung out from the curb and passed Blomkvist, going in the direction of Zinkensdamm. He caught a glimpse of a face as it passed. It was too dark to read the licence plate.

Blomkvist caught up with Salander's pursuer at the top of

the steps. The man had stopped and stood motionless, looking around.

Just as Blomkvist got to him he turned and gave him a powerful backhand across the face. Blomkvist was completely unprepared. He tumbled headlong down the steps.

Salander heard Blomkvist's stifled cry and almost stopped. *What the hell is going on?* But when she turned she saw Lundin only a hundred feet from her. *He's faster. Shit, he's going to catch me.*

She turned left and ran up several steps to the terrace between two buildings. She reached a courtyard that did not present the least cover and ran as fast as she could to the next corner. She turned right and realized just in time that she would be heading into a blind alley. As she reached the end of the next building she saw Lundin arrive at the top of the steps to the courtyard. She kept running—out of his sight—for another few yards and dived headfirst into a rhododendron bush alongside the building.

She heard Lundin's heavy footsteps, but she could not see him. She held her breath, pressing herself into the soil beneath the bush.

Lundin passed her hiding place and stopped. He hesitated for ten seconds before jogging around the courtyard. A minute later he came back. He stopped at the same place as before. This time he stood still for thirty seconds. Salander tensed her muscles, poised for instant flight if she were discovered. Then he moved again, passing less than six feet from her. She listened to his steps fade away across the courtyard.

Blomkvist felt pain in his neck and jaw as he got laboriously to his feet, feeling dizzy. He tasted blood from a split lip.

He made his way unsteadily to the top of the steps and

looked around. He saw the man with the ponytail running a hundred yards further down the street. The man stopped and peered between the buildings, and then ran across Lundagatan and climbed into the Dodge van. The vehicle sped off towards Zinkensdamm.

Blomkvist walked slowly along the upper part of Lundagatan, looking for Salander. He could not see her anywhere. There was not a living soul. He was astonished how desolate a street in Stockholm can be at 3:00 a.m. on a Sunday morning in March. After a while he went back to the front door of Salander's apartment building on lower Lundagatan. As he passed the car where the attack had taken place he stepped on a key ring. He bent to pick it up and saw a shoulder bag under the car.

Blomkvist stood there a long time, waiting, unsure what to do. At last he tried the keys in her door. They did not fit.

Salander stayed under the bush for fifteen minutes, moving only to look at her watch. Just after 3:00 she heard a door open and close and footsteps making for the bicycle shed in the courtyard.

When the sound died away she raised herself slowly to her knees and peered out of the bush. She looked steadily at every nook and cranny in the courtyard, but she saw no sign of Lundin. She walked back to the street, prepared to turn tail at any moment. She stopped at the top of the wall and looked out over Lundagatan, where she saw Blomkvist outside her apartment building. He was holding her bag in his hand.

She stood perfectly still, hidden behind a lamppost when Blomkvist's gaze swept over the stairs and the wall. He did not see her.

Blomkvist stood outside her door for almost half an hour. She watched him patiently, without moving, until finally he gave up and headed down the hill towards Zinkensdamm.

When he was gone she began to think about what had happened.

Kalle Blomkvist.

She could not for the life of her imagine how he had sprung up out of nowhere. Apart from that, the attack was not difficult to account for.

Carl Fucking Magnus Lundin.

Lundin had met the hulk she had seen talking to Bjurman.

Nils Fucking Slimebag Bjurman.

That piece of shit has hired some diabolical alpha male to get me out of the way. And I made it crystal clear to him what the consequences would be.

Salander was seething inside. She was so enraged that she tasted blood in her mouth. Now she was going to have to punish him.

PART 3

Absurd Equations

MARCH 23–APRIL 3

Those pointless equations, to which no solution exists, are called absurdities.

$$(a + b)(a - b) = a^2 - b^2 + 1$$

CHAPTER 11

Wednesday, March 23– Maundy Thursday, March 24

Blomkvist took his red pen and in the margin of Svensson's manuscript drew a question mark with a circle around it and wrote "footnote." He wanted a source reference inserted.

It was Wednesday, the evening before Maundy Thursday, and *Millennium* was more or less closed down for Easter week. Nilsson was out of the country. Karim had gone to the mountains with her husband. Cortez had come in to deal with telephone messages for a few hours, but Blomkvist sent him home since nobody was calling. Cortez left smiling happily, on his way to see a new girlfriend.

Svensson had not been around. Blomkvist sat in the office alone, plodding through his manuscript. The book was going to be twelve chapters and 288 pages long. Svensson had delivered the final text of nine of the twelve chapters, and Blomkvist had been over every word and given the hard copy back with requests for clarification and suggestions for reworking.

Svensson was a talented writer, and Blomkvist confined his editing for the most part to marginal notes. During the weeks when the manuscript had been growing on his desk they had disagreed about only one paragraph, which Blomkvist wanted to delete and Svensson fought tooth and nail to keep. It stayed in.

In short, *Millennium* had an excellent book that would very soon be off to the printer. There was no doubt that it would make dramatic headlines. Svensson was merciless in his exposure of the johns, and he told the story in such a way that nobody could fail to understand that there was something wrong with the system itself. It was journalistic work of the type that should be on the endangered species list.

Blomkvist had learned that Svensson was an exacting journalist who left very few loose ends. He did not employ the heavy-handed rhetoric typical of so much other social reporting, which turned texts into pretentious trash. His book was more than an exposé—it was a declaration of war. Blomkvist smiled to himself. Svensson was about fifteen years younger, but he recognized the passion that he himself had once had when he took up the lance against second-rate financial reporters and put together a scandalous book. Certain newsrooms had not forgiven him.

The problem with Svensson's book was that it had to be watertight. A reporter who sticks out his neck like that has to either stand behind his story 100 percent or refrain from publishing it. Right now Svensson was at 98 percent. There were still a few weak points that needed more work and one or two assertions that he had not adequately documented.

At 5:30 p.m. Blomkvist opened his desk drawer and took out a cigarette. Berger had decreed a total ban in the office, but he was alone and nobody else was going to be there that weekend. He worked for another forty minutes before he gathered up the pages and put the chapter on Berger's desk. Svensson had promised to email the final text of the remaining three chapters the following morning, which would give Blomkvist a chance to go through them over the weekend. A summit meeting was planned for the Tuesday after Easter when they would all sign off on the final version of the book and the *Millennium* articles.

After that only the layout remained, which was Malm's headache alone, and then it would go to the printer. Blomkvist had not sought bids from different printers; he would entrust the job to Hallvigs Reklam in Morgongåva. They had printed his book about the Wennerström affair and had given him a damn good price and first-rate service.

Blomkvist looked at the clock and decided to reward himself with another cigarette. He sat at the window and stared down on Götgatan. He ran his tongue over the cut on the inside of his lip. It was beginning to heal.

He wondered for the thousandth time what really had happened outside Salander's building early on Sunday morning.

All he knew for certain was that Salander was alive and back in Stockholm.

He had tried to reach her every day since then. He had sent emails to the address she had used more than a year ago. He had walked up and down Lundagatan. He was beginning to despair.

The nameplate on the door now read SALANDER-WU. There were 230 people with the surname Wu on the electoral roll, of whom about 140 lived in and around Stockholm, none of them on Lundagatan. Blomkvist had no idea whether she had a boyfriend or had rented out the apartment. No-one came to the door when he knocked.

Finally he went back to his desk and wrote her a good old-fashioned letter:

Hello, Sally,
I don't know what happened a year ago, but by now even a numbskull like me has worked out that you've cut off all contact. It's for you to decide who you hang around with, and I don't mean to nag. I just want to tell you that I still think of you as my friend, that I miss your company and would love to have a cup of coffee with you—if you felt like it.

I don't know what kind of a mess you've got yourself into, but the ruckus on Lundagatan was alarming. If you need help you can call me anytime. As you know, I am deeply in your debt.

Plus, I have your shoulder bag. When you want it back, just let me know. If you don't want to see me, just give me an address to mail it to. I promise not to bother you, since you've indicated clearly enough that you don't want anything to do with me.

Mikael

As anticipated he never heard a word from her.

When he had got home the morning after the attack on Lundagatan, he opened the shoulder bag and spread the contents on the kitchen table. There was a wallet with an ID card, about 600 kronor, 200 American dollars, and a monthly travel card. There was a pack of Marlboro Lights, three Bic lighters, a box of throat lozenges, a packet of tissues, a toothbrush, toothpaste, three tampons in a side pocket, an unopened pack of condoms with a price sticker that showed they were bought at Gatwick Airport in London, a bound notebook with stiff black A4 dividers, five ballpoint pens, a can of Mace, a small bag with makeup, an FM radio with an earphone but no batteries, and Saturday's *Aftonbladet*.

The most intriguing item was a hammer, easily accessible in an outside pocket. However, the attack had come so suddenly that she had not been able to make use of it or the Mace. She had evidently used her keys as brass knuckles—there were still traces of blood and skin on them.

Of the six keys on the ring, three of them were typical apartment keys—front door, apartment door, and the key to a padlock. But none of them fit the door of the building on Lundagatan.

Blomkvist opened the notebook and went through it page

by page. He recognized Salander's neat hand and could see at once that this was not a girl's secret diary. Three-quarters of the pages were filled with what looked like mathematical notations. At the top of the first page was an equation that even Blomkvist recognized.

$$(x^3 + y^3 = z^3)$$

Blomkvist had never had trouble doing calculations. He had left secondary school with the highest marks in math, which in no way meant, of course, that he was a mathematician, only that he had been able to absorb the content of the school's curriculum. But Salander's pages contained formulas of a type that Blomkvist neither understood nor could even begin to understand. One equation stretched across an entire double page and ended with things crossed out and changed. He could not even tell whether they were real mathematical formulas and calculations, but since he knew Salander's peculiarities he assumed that the equations were genuine and no doubt had some esoteric meaning.

He leafed back and forth for a long time. He might as well have come upon a notebook full of Chinese characters. But he grasped the essentials of what she was trying to do. She had become fascinated by Fermat's Last Theorem, a classic riddle. He let out a deep sigh.

The last page in the book contained some very brief and cryptic notes which had absolutely nothing to do with math, but nevertheless still looked like a formula:

$$(\text{Blond Hulk} + \text{Magge}) = \text{NEB}$$

They were underlined and circled and meant nothing to him. At the bottom of the page was a telephone number and the name of a car rental company in Eskilstuna, Auto-Expert.

STIEG LARSSON

. . .

Blomkvist made no attempt to interpret the notes. He stubbed out his cigarette and put on his jacket, set the alarm in the office, and walked to the terminal at Slussen, where he took the bus out to the yuppie reserve in Stäket, near Lännersta Sound. He had been invited to dinner with his sister, Annika Blomkvist Giannini, who was turning forty-two.

Berger began her long Easter weekend with a furious and anxiety-filled two-mile jog that ended at the steamboat wharf in Saltsjöbaden. She had been lazy about her hours at the gym and felt stiff and out of shape. She walked home. Her husband was giving a lecture at the Modern Museum and it would be at least 8:00 before he got home. Berger thought she would open a bottle of good wine, switch on the sauna, and seduce him. At least it would stop her thinking about the problem that was worrying her.

A week earlier she had had lunch with the CEO of the biggest media company in Sweden. Over salad he had set forth in all seriousness his intention to recruit her as editor in chief of the company's largest daily newspaper, the *Svenska Morgon-Posten. The board has discussed several possibilities, but we are agreed that you would be a great asset to the paper. You're the one we want.* Attached to the offer was a salary that made her income at *Millennium* look ridiculous.

The offer had come like a bolt of lightning out of a clear blue sky, and it left her speechless. *Why me?*

He had been oddly vague, but gradually the explanation emerged that she was known, respected, and a certifiably talented editor. They were impressed by the way she had dragged *Millennium* out of the quicksand it had been in two years earlier. The *Svenska Morgon-Posten* needed to be revitalized in the same way. There was an old-man atmosphere about the newspaper that was causing a steady decline in the new-subscriber rate. Berger was a powerful journalist. She had clout. Putting a woman—a feminist no less—in charge of one of Sweden's most conservative and male-dominated institutions was a provocative and bold idea. Everyone was agreed. Well, almost everyone. The ones who counted were all on his side.

"But I don't share the basic political views of the news-paper."

"Who cares? You're not an outspoken opponent either. You're going to be the boss—not an apparatchik—and the edi-torial page will take care of itself."

He hadn't said it in so many words, but it was also a matter of class. Berger came from the right background.

She had told him that she was certainly attracted by the proposal but that she could not give him an answer immedi-ately. She was going to have to think the matter through. But they agreed that she would give them her decision sooner rather than later. The CEO had explained that if the salary offer was the reason for her hesitation, she was probably in a posi-tion to negotiate an even higher figure. A strikingly generous golden parachute would also be included. *It's time for you to start thinking about your pension plan.*

Her forty-fifth birthday was coming up. She had done her apprenticeship as a trainee and a temp. She had put together *Millennium* and become its editor in chief on her own merits. The moment when she would have to pick up the telephone and say yes or no was fast approaching, and she did not know what she was going to do. During the past week she had con-sidered time and again discussing the matter with Blomkvist, but she had not been able to summon up the nerve. Instead she had been hiding the offer from him, which gave her a pang of guilt.

There were some obvious disadvantages. A yes would mean breaking up the partnership with Blomkvist. He would never follow her to the *Svenska Morgon-Posten,* no matter how sweet a deal she or they could offer him. He did not need the money now, and he was getting on fine writing articles at his own pace.

Berger liked being editor in chief of *Millennium*. It had given her a status within the world of journalism that she considered almost undeserved. She had never been the producer of the news. That was not her thing—she regarded herself as a mediocre writer. On the other hand, she was first-rate on radio or TV, and above all she was a brilliant editor. Besides, she enjoyed the hands-on work of editing, which was a prerequisite for the post of editor in chief at *Millennium*.

Nevertheless, she was tempted. Not so much by the salary as by the fact that the job meant that she would become without question one of Sweden's big-time media players. *This is a once-in-a-lifetime offer,* the CEO had said.

Somewhere near the Grand Hotel in Saltsjöbaden she realized to her dismay that she was not going to be able to turn the offer down. And she shuddered at the thought of having to tell Blomkvist.

Dinner at the Gianninis' was, as always, mildly chaotic. Annika had two children: Monica, thirteen, and Jennie, ten. Her husband, Enrico, who was the head of the Scandinavian arm of an international biotech firm, had custody of Antonio, his sixteen-year-old son from his first marriage. Also at dinner were Enrico's mother Antonia, his brother Pietro, his sister-in-law Eva-Lotta, and their children Peter and Nicola. Plus Enrico's sister Marcella and her four kids, who lived in the same neighbourhood. Enrico's aunt Angelina, who was regarded by the family as stark raving mad, or on good days just extremely eccentric, had also been invited, along with her new boyfriend.

At the dining-room table, abundant with food, the conversation went on in a rattling mixture of Swedish and Italian, sometimes simultaneously. The situation was made more annoying because Angelina spent the evening wondering out loud—to anyone who would listen—why Annika's brother was still a bachelor. She also proposed a number of suitable solutions to his problem from among the daughters of her friends. Exasperated, Blomkvist finally explained that he would be happy to get married but that unfortunately his lover was already married. That shut up even Angelina for a while.

At 7:30 Blomkvist's mobile beeped. He'd thought he had shut it off and he almost missed the call as he dug it out of the inside pocket of his jacket, which someone had hung on the coatrack in the hall. It was Svensson.

"Am I interrupting something?"

"Not particularly. I'm at dinner with my sister and a platoon of people from her husband's family. What's up?"

"Two things. I've tried to get hold of Christer, but he's not answering."

"He's at the theatre with his boyfriend."

"Damn. I'd promised to meet him at the office tomorrow morning with the photographs and graphics for the book. Christer was going to look at them over the weekend. But Mia has suddenly decided to drive up to see her parents in Dalarna for Easter to show them her thesis. We'll have to leave early in the morning and some of the pictures I can't email. Could I messenger them over to you tonight?"

"You could . . . but look, I'm out in Lännersta. I'll be here for a while, but I'm coming back into town later. Enskede wouldn't be that far out of my way. I could drop by and pick them up. Would around 11:00 be OK?"

"That's fine. The second thing . . . I don't think you're going to like this."

"Shoot."

"I stumbled across something I think I had better check out before the book goes to the printer."

"OK—what is it?"

"Zala, spelled with a Z."

"Ah. Zala the gangster. The one people seem to be terrified of and nobody wants to talk about."

"That's him. A couple of days ago I came across him again.

I believe he's in Sweden now and that he ought to be in the list of johns in chapter seven."

"Dag—you can't start digging up new material three weeks before we go to press."

"I know. But this is a bit special. I talked to a policeman who had heard some talk about Zala. Anyway, I think it would make sense to spend a couple of days next week checking up on him."

"Why him? You've got plenty of other assholes in the book."

"This one seems to be an Olympian asshole. Nobody really knows who he is. I've got a gut feeling that it would be worth our while to poke around one more time."

"Don't ever discount your gut feelings," Blomkvist said. "But honestly . . . we can't push back the deadline. The printer is booked, and the book has to come out simultaneously with the *Millennium* issue."

"I know," Svensson said, sounding dejected.

"I'll call you later," Blomkvist said.

Johansson had just brewed a pot of coffee and poured it into the table thermos when the doorbell rang. It was just before 9:00 p.m. Svensson was closer to the door and, thinking it was Blomkvist coming earlier than he had said he would, he opened it without first looking through the peephole. Not Blomkvist. Instead he was confronted by a short, doll-like girl in her late teens.

"I'm looking for Dag Svensson and Mia Johansson," the girl said.

"I'm Dag Svensson."

"I'd like to speak with both of you."

Svensson automatically looked at the clock. Johansson was curious and came into the hall to stand behind her boyfriend.

"It's a bit late for a visit," Svensson said.

"I'd like to talk about the book you're planning on publishing at *Millennium*."

Svensson and Johansson looked at each other.

"And who are you?"

"I'm interested in the subject. May I come in, or shall we discuss it here on the landing?"

Svensson hesitated for a second. The girl was a total stranger, and the time of her visit was odd, but she seemed harmless enough, so he held the door open. He showed her to the table in the living room.

"Would you like some coffee?" Johansson said.

"How about first telling us who you are," Svensson said.

"Yes, please. To the coffee, I mean. My name is Lisbeth Salander."

Johansson shrugged and opened the table thermos. She had already set out cups in anticipation of Blomkvist's visit. "And what makes you think I'm publishing a book at *Millennium*?" Svensson said.

He was suddenly deeply suspicious, but the girl ignored him and turned instead to Johansson. She made a face that could have been a crooked smile.

"Interesting thesis," she said.

Johansson looked shocked.

"How could you know anything about my thesis?"

"I happened to get hold of a copy," the girl said cryptically.

Svensson's annoyance grew. "Now you're really going to have to explain who you are and what you want."

The girl's eyes met his. He suddenly noticed that her irises were so dark that in this light her eyes might be raven black. And perhaps he had underestimated her age.

"I'd like to know why you're going around asking questions about Zala. Alexander Zala," Salander said. "And above all I'd like to know exactly what you know about him already."

Alexander Zala, Svensson thought in shock. He had never known the first name.

The girl lifted her coffee cup and took a sip without releasing him from her gaze. Her eyes had no warmth at all. He suddenly felt vaguely uneasy.

. . .

Unlike Blomkvist and the other adults at the dinner party (and despite the fact that she was the birthday girl), Annika Giannini had drunk only light beer and refrained from any wine or aquavit with the meal. So at 10:30 she was stone-cold sober. Since in some respects she took her big brother for a complete idiot who needed to be looked after, she generously offered to drive him home via Enskede. She had already planned to drive him to the bus stop on Värmdövägen, and it wouldn't take that much longer to go into the city.

"Why don't you get your own car?" she complained anyway as Blomkvist fastened his seat belt.

"Because unlike you I live within walking distance of my work and need a car about once a year. Besides, I wouldn't have been able to drive anyway after your husband started serving spirits from Skåne."

"He's becoming Swedish. Ten years ago it would have been grappa."

They spent the ride talking as brothers and sisters do. Apart from a persistent paternal aunt, two less persistent maternal aunts, two distant cousins, and one second cousin, Mikael and Annika had only each other for family. The three-year age difference meant that they had not had much in common during their teens. But they had become closer as adults.

Annika had studied law, and Blomkvist thought of her as a great deal more talented than he was. She sailed through university, spent a few years in the district courts, and then became the assistant to one of the better-known lawyers in Sweden. Then she started her own practice. She had specialized in family law, which gradually developed into work on equal rights. She became an advocate for abused women, wrote a book on the subject, and became a respected name. To top it off, she had become involved politically for the Social Democrats, which prompted Blomkvist to tease her about being an apparatchik. Blomkvist himself had decided early on that he could not combine party membership with journalistic credibility. He never willingly voted, and on the occasions when he felt absolutely obliged to vote he refused to talk about his choices, even with Berger.

"How are you doing?" Annika said as they crossed Skur-ubron.

"Oh, I'm doing fine."

"So what's the problem?"

"What problem?"

"I know you, Micke. You've been preoccupied all evening."

Blomkvist sat in silence for a moment.

"It's a complicated story. I've got two problems right now. One is about a girl I met two years ago who helped me on the Wennerström affair and then just disappeared from my life with no explanation. I haven't seen hide nor hair of her in more than a year, except for last week."

Blomkvist told her about the attack on Lundagatan.

"Did you report it to the police?"

"No."

"Why not?"

"This girl is manically private. She was the one who was attacked. She'll have to make the report."

Which Blomkvist expected would not be high on Salander's list of priorities.

"Bullheaded as usual," Annika said, patting Blomkvist on the cheek. "What's the second problem?"

"We're working on a story at *Millennium* that's going to make headlines. I've been sitting all evening wondering whether I should consult you. As a lawyer, I mean."

Annika glanced in surprise at her brother. "Consult me?" she exclaimed. "That'd be something new."

"The story's about trafficking and violence against women. You deal with violence against women and you're a lawyer. You probably don't work with cases of freedom of the press, but I would be really grateful if you could read through the manuscript before we send it to the printer. There are magazine articles and a book, so there's quite a bit to read."

Annika was silent as she turned down the Hammarby industrial road and passed Sickla lock. She wound her way down side streets parallel to Nynäsvägen until she could turn up Enskedevägen.

"You know, Mikael, I've been really mad at you only once in my whole life."

"Is that so?" he said, surprised.

"It was when you were taken to court by Wennerström and sent to prison for libel. I was so furious with you that I thought I would explode."

"Why? I only made a fool of myself."

"You've made a fool of yourself many times before. But this time you needed a lawyer, and the only person you didn't turn to was me. Instead you sat there taking shit in both the media and the courtroom. You didn't even defend yourself. I thought I was going to die."

"There were special circumstances. There wasn't a thing you could have done."

"All right, but I didn't understand that until later, when *Millennium* got back on its feet and mopped the floor with Wennerström. Until that happened I was so damn disappointed in you."

"There was no way we could have won that trial."

"You're not getting the point, big brother. I understand that it was a hopeless case. I've read the judgment. The point was that you didn't come to me and ask for help. As in, hey, little sister, I need a lawyer. That's why I never turned up in court."

Blomkvist thought it over.

"I'm sorry. I admit it, I should have done that."

"Yes, you should have."

"I wasn't functioning at all that year. I couldn't face talking to anybody. I just wanted to lie down and die."

"Which you didn't do, exactly."

"Forgive me."

Annika Giannini gave him a big smile.

"Beautiful. An apology two years later. OK. I'll happily read through the text. Are you in a rush?"

"Yes. We're going to press very soon. Turn left here."

Annika parked across the street from the building on Björneborgsvägen where Svensson and Johansson lived. "This'll just take a minute," Blomkvist said. He jogged across the street to punch in the door code. As soon as he was inside he could tell that something was wrong. He heard excited voices echoing in the stairwell and ran up the three flights to the apartment. Not until he reached their floor did he realize that the commotion was all around their apartment. Five neighbours were standing on the landing. The apartment door was ajar.

"What's going on?" Blomkvist said, more out of curiosity than concern.

They all fell silent and looked at him. Three women, two men, all in their seventies it seemed. One of the women was wearing a nightgown.

"It sounded like shots," said a man in a brown dressing gown, who seemed to know what he was talking about.

"Shots?"

"Just now. There was shooting in the apartment about a minute ago. The door was open."

Blomkvist pushed forward and rang the doorbell as he walked into the apartment.

"Dag? Mia?" he called.

No answer.

Suddenly he felt an icy shiver run down his neck. He recognized the smell: cordite. Then he approached the living-room door. The first thing he saw was *HolyMotherofGod*

Svensson slumped beside the dining-room chairs in a pool of blood a yard across.

Blomkvist hurried over. At the same time he pulled out his mobile and dialled 112 for emergency services. They answered right away.

"My name is Mikael Blomkvist. I need an ambulance and police."

He gave the address.

"What is this regarding?"

"A man. He seems to have been shot in the head and is unconscious."

Blomkvist bent down and tried to find a pulse on Svensson's neck. Then he saw the enormous crater in the back of his head and realized that he must be standing in Svensson's brain matter. Slowly he withdrew his hand.

No ambulance crew in the world would be able to save Dag Svensson now.

Then he noticed shards from one of the coffee cups that Johansson had inherited from her grandmother and that she was so afraid would get broken. He straightened up quickly and looked all around.

"Mia," he yelled.

The neighbour in the brown dressing gown had come into the hall behind him. Blomkvist turned at the living-room door and held his hand up.

"Stop there," he said. "Back out to the stairs."

The neighbour at first looked as if he wanted to protest, but he obeyed the order. Blomkvist stood still for fifteen seconds. Then he stepped around the pool of blood and proceeded warily past Svensson's body to the bedroom door.

Johansson lay on her back on the floor at the foot of the bed. *NonononotMiatooforGodssake*. She had been shot in the face. The bullet had entered below her jaw by her left ear. The exit wound in her temple was as big as an orange and her right eye socket gaped empty. The flow of blood was if possible even greater than that from her partner. The force of the bullet had been such that the wall above the head of the bed, several yards away, was covered with blood splatter.

Blomkvist became aware that he was clutching his mobile in a death grip with the line to the emergency centre still open and that he had been holding his breath. He took air into his lungs and raised the telephone.

"We need the police. Two people have been shot. I think they're dead. Please hurry."

He heard the voice from emergency services say something but did not catch the words. He felt as if there was something wrong with his hearing. It was utterly silent around him. He did not hear the sound of his own voice when he tried to say something. He backed out of the apartment. When he got out to the landing he realized that his whole body was shaking and that his heart was pounding painfully. Without a word he squeezed through the petrified crowd of neighbours and sat down on the stairs. From far away he could hear the neighbours asking him questions. *What happened? Are they hurt? Did something happen?* The sound of their voices echoed as if coming through a tunnel.

Blomkvist felt numb. He knew that he was in shock. He leaned his head down between his knees. Then he began to think. *Good God—they've been murdered. They were shot just a few minutes ago. The killer could still be in the apartment . . . no, I would have seen him.* He couldn't stop shaking. The sight of Johansson's shattered face could not be erased from his retina.

Suddenly his hearing came back, as if someone had turned up a volume control. He got up quickly and looked at the neighbour in the dressing gown.

"You," he said. "Stay here and make sure nobody goes inside the apartment. The police and an ambulance are on their way. I'll go down and let them in."

Blomkvist took the stairs three at a time. On the ground floor he glanced at the cellar stairs and stopped short. He took a step towards the cellar. Halfway down the stairs lay a revolver in plain sight. Blomkvist thought it looked like a Colt .45 Magnum—the kind of weapon used to murder Olof Palme.*

He suppressed the impulse to pick up the weapon. Instead he went and opened the front door and stood in the night air. It was not until he heard the brief honk of a car horn that he remembered his sister was waiting for him. He walked across the street.

Annika opened her mouth to say something sarcastic about her brother's tardiness. Then she saw the expression on his face.

"Did you see anyone while you were waiting?" Blomkvist asked. His voice sounded hoarse and unnatural.

"No. Who would that be? What happened?"

Blomkvist was silent for a few seconds while he looked left and right. Everything was quiet on the street. He reached into his jacket pocket and found a crumpled pack with one cigarette left. As he lit it he could hear sirens approaching in the distance. He looked at his watch. It was 11:17 p.m.

"Annika—this is going to be a long night," he said without looking at her as the police car turned up the street.

The first to arrive were officers Magnusson and Ohlsson. They had been on Nynäsvägen responding to what turned out to be a false alarm. Magnusson and Ohlsson were followed by a staff car with the field superintendent, Oswald Mårtensson, who had been at Skanstull when the central switchboard had sent out a call for all cars in the area. They arrived at almost the same time from different directions and saw a man in jeans and a dark jacket standing in the middle of the street raising his hand for them to stop. At the same time a woman got out of a car parked a few yards away.

All three policemen froze. The central switchboard had

*Olof Palme was the prime minister of Sweden from 1969 to 1976 and 1982 to 1986. He was assassinated in 1986, shot twice in a street ambush in central Stockholm. His murder remains unsolved.

reported that two people had been shot, and the man was holding something in his left hand. It took a couple of seconds to be sure that it was a mobile telephone. They got out of their cars at the same time and adjusted their belts. Mårtensson assumed command.

"Are you the one who called about a shooting?"

The man nodded. He seemed badly shaken. He was smoking a cigarette and his hand was trembling when he put it in his mouth.

"What's your name?"

"Mikael Blomkvist. Two people were just shot in this building a very short time ago. Their names are Dag Svensson and Mia Johansson. Three floors up. Their neighbours are standing outside the door."

"Good Lord," the woman said.

"And who are you?" Mårtensson asked Annika.

"Annika Giannini. I'm his sister," she said, pointing at Blomkvist.

"Do you live here?"

"No," Blomkvist said. "I was going to visit the couple who were shot. My sister gave me a ride from a dinner party."

"You say that two people were shot. Did you see what happened?"

"No. I found them."

"Let's go up and have a look," Mårtensson said.

"Wait," Blomkvist said. "According to the neighbours the shots were fired only a minute or so before I arrived. I dialled 112 within a minute of getting here. Since then less than five minutes have passed. That means the person who killed them must still be in the area."

"Do you have a description?"

"We haven't seen anyone, but it's possible that some of the neighbours saw something."

Mårtensson motioned to Magnusson, who raised his radio and talked into it in a low voice. He turned to Blomkvist.

"Can you show us the way?" he said.

When they got inside the front door Blomkvist stopped and pointed to the cellar stairs. Mårtensson bent down and looked at the weapon. He went all the way down the stairs and tried the cellar door. It was locked.

"Ohlsson, stay here and keep an eye on this," Mårtensson said.

Outside the apartment the crowd of neighbours had thinned out. Two had gone back to their own apartments, but the man in the dressing gown was still at his post. He seemed relieved when he saw the uniformed officers.

"I didn't let anyone in," he said.

"That's good," Blomkvist and Mårtensson said together.

"There seem to be bloody tracks on the stairs," Officer Magnusson said.

Everyone looked at the footprints. Blomkvist looked at his Italian loafers.

"Those are probably from my shoes," he said. "I was inside the apartment. There's quite a bit of blood."

Mårtensson gave Blomkvist a searching look. He used a pen to push open the apartment door and found more bloody footprints in the hall.

"To the right. Dag Svensson's in the living room and Mia Johansson's in the bedroom."

Mårtensson did a quick inspection of the apartment and came out after only a few seconds. He radioed to ask for backup from the criminal duty officer. As he finished talking, the ambulance crew arrived. Mårtensson stopped them as they were going in.

"Two victims. As far as I can see, they're beyond help. Can one of you look in without messing up the crime scene?"

It did not take long to confirm. A paramedic decided that the bodies would not be taken to hospital for resuscitation. They were beyond help. Blomkvist suddenly felt sick to his stomach and turned to Mårtensson.

"I'm going outside. I need some air."

"Unfortunately I can't let you go just yet."

"I'll just sit on the porch outside the door."

"May I see your ID, please?"

Blomkvist took out his wallet and put it in Mårtensson's hand. Then he turned without a word and went outside, where Annika was still waiting with Officer Ohlsson. She sat down next to him.

"Micke, what happened?"

"Two people I liked a lot have been murdered. Dag Svensson and Mia Johansson. It was his manuscript I wanted you to read."

Annika realized that this was no time to ply him with questions. Instead she put her arm around her brother's shoulders and hugged him. More police cars arrived. A handful of curious nighttime onlookers had stopped on the pavement across the street. Blomkvist watched them while the police started to set up a cordon. A murder investigation was beginning.

It was past 3:00 a.m. by the time Blomkvist and his sister were allowed to leave the police station. They had spent an hour in Annika's car outside the apartment building in Enskede, waiting for a duty prosecutor to arrive to initiate the pre-investigative stage. Then, since Blomkvist was a good friend of the two victims and since he was the one who had found them, they were asked to follow along to Kungsholmen to assist the investigation.

There they'd had to wait a long time before they were interviewed by an Inspector Nyberg at the station. She had light blond hair and looked like a teenager.

I'm getting old, Blomkvist thought.

By 2:30 he had drunk so many cups of police canteen coffee that he was sober and feeling unwell. He had to interrupt the interview and run to the toilet, where he was violently sick. He still had the image of Johansson's face swimming in his head. He drank three cups of water and rinsed his face over and over before returning to the interview. He tried to pull himself together to answer all of Inspector Nyberg's questions.

"Did Dag Svensson or Mia Johansson have enemies?"

"No, not that I know of."

"Had they received any threats?"

"Not that I know of."

"How would you describe their relationship?"

"They gave every appearance of loving each other. Dag told me that they were thinking of having a baby after Mia got her doctorate."

"Did they use drugs?"

"I don't know for sure, but I don't think so, and if they did it would be nothing more than a joint at a party when they had something to celebrate."

"Why were you visiting them so late at night?"

Blomkvist explained that they were doing last-minute work on a book, without identifying the subject.

"Wasn't it unusual to call on people so late at night?"

"That was the first time it had ever happened."

"How did you know them?"

"Through work."

The questions were relentless as they tried to establish the time frame.

The shots had been heard all over the building. They had been fired less than five seconds apart. The seventy-year-old man in the dressing gown, a retired major from the coastal artillery, as it turned out, was their nearest neighbour. He was watching TV. After the second shot, he went out to the stair-well. He had a hip problem and so getting up from the sofa was a slow process. He estimated that it had taken him thirty seconds to reach the landing. Neither he nor any other neighbour had seen anybody on the stairs.

According to the neighbours, Blomkvist had arrived at the apartment less than two minutes after the second shot was fired.

Calculating that he and Annika had had a view of the street

for half a minute while she found the right building, parked, and exchanged a few words before he crossed the street and went up the stairs, Blomkvist figured there was a window of thirty to forty seconds. During which time the killer had left the apartment, gone down three flights of stairs—dropping the weapon on the way—left the building, and disappeared before Annika turned into the street. They had just missed him.

For a dizzying moment Blomkvist realized that Inspector Nyberg was toying with the possibility that he himself could have been the killer, that he had only run down one flight and pretended to arrive on the scene after the neighbours had gathered. But he had an alibi in the form of his sister. His whole evening, including the telephone conversation with Svensson, could be vouched for by a dozen members of the Giannini family.

Eventually Annika put her foot down. Blomkvist had given all reasonable and conceivable help. He was visibly tired and he was not feeling well. She told the inspector that she was not only Blomkvist's sister but also his lawyer. It was time to bring all this to a close and let him go home.

When they got out to the street they stood for a time next to Annika's car.

"Go home and get some sleep," she said.

Blomkvist shook his head.

"I have to go to Erika's," he said. "She knew them too. I can't just call and tell her, and I don't want her to wake up and hear it on the news."

Annika hesitated, but she knew that her brother was right.

"So, off to Saltsjöbaden," she said.

"Can you take me?"

"What are little sisters for?"

"If you give me a lift out to Nacka I can take a taxi from there or wait for a bus."

"Nonsense. Jump in and I'll drive you."

CHAPTER 12

Maundy Thursday, March 24

Annika Giannini was exhausted too, and Blomkvist managed to persuade her to save herself the hour-long detour round the Lännersta Sound and drop him off in Nacka. He kissed her on the cheek, thanked her for all her help, and waited until she had turned the car and driven off before he called a taxi.

It was two years since Blomkvist had been to Saltsjöbaden. He had only been to Berger's house a few times. He supposed that was a sign of immaturity.

Exactly how her marriage with Greger Beckman functioned, he had no idea. He had known Berger since the early eighties. He planned to go on having a relationship with her until he was too old to get out of his wheelchair. They had broken it off in the late eighties when both he and Berger had met and married other people. The hiatus had lasted little more than a year.

In Blomkvist's case the consequence of his infidelity was a divorce. For Berger it led to Beckman's conceding that their long-term sexual passion was evidently so strong that it would be unreasonable to believe that mere convention could keep them apart. Nor did he propose to lose Berger the way that Blomkvist had lost his wife.

When Berger admitted having an affair, Beckman knocked on Blomkvist's door. Blomkvist had been dreading his visit, but instead of punching him in the face, Beckman had suggested they go out for a drink. They hit three bars in Södermalm before they were sufficiently tipsy to have a serious conversation, which took place on a park bench in Mariatorget around sunrise.

At first Blomkvist was sceptical, but Beckman eventually convinced him that if he tried to sabotage his marriage to Berger, he could expect to see Beckman come back sober with a baseball bat, but if it was simply physical desire and the soul's inability to rein itself in, that was OK as far as he was concerned.

So Blomkvist and Berger had taken up again, with Beckman's blessing and without trying to hide anything from him. All Berger had to do was pick up the telephone and tell him she was spending the night with Blomkvist when the spirit moved her, which it did with some regularity.

Beckman had never uttered a word of criticism against Blomkvist. On the contrary, he seemed to regard his relationship with his wife as beneficial; and his love for her was deepened because he knew he could never take her for granted.

Blomkvist, on the other hand, had never felt entirely at ease in Beckman's company—a dreary reminder that even liberated relationships had a price. Accordingly, he had been to Saltsjöbaden only on the few occasions when Berger had hosted parties where his absence would have been remarked on.

Now he stood at the door of their substantial villa. Despite his uneasiness about bringing bad news, he resolutely put his finger on the doorbell and held it there for about forty seconds until he heard footsteps. Beckman opened the door with a towel wrapped around his waist and his face full of bleary anger that changed to astonishment when he saw his wife's lover.

"Hi, Greger," Blomkvist said.

"Good morning, Blomkvist. What the hell time is it?"

Beckman was blond and thin. He had a lot of hair on his chest and hardly any on his head. He had a week's growth of beard and a prominent scar over his right eyebrow, the result of a sailing accident some years before.

"Just after 5:00," Blomkvist said. "Could you wake Erika? I have to talk to her."

Beckman took it that since Blomkvist had all of a sudden overcome his reluctance to visit Saltsjöbaden—and at that hour—something out of the ordinary must have happened. Besides, the man looked as if he badly needed a drink, or at least a bed so that he could sleep off whatever it was. Beckman held the door open and let him in.

"What happened?"

Before Blomkvist could reply, Berger appeared at the top of the stairs, tying the sash of a white terry-cloth bathrobe. She stopped halfway down when she saw Blomkvist in the hall.

"What?"

"Dag and Mia," Blomkvist said.

His face instantly revealed the news he had come to give her.

"No." She put a hand to her mouth.

"They were murdered last night. I just came from the police station."

"Murdered?" Berger and Beckman said at the same time.

"Somebody got into their apartment in Enskede and shot them. I was the one who found them."

Berger sat down on the stairs.

"I didn't want you to have to hear it on the morning news," Blomkvist said.

It was 6:59 a.m. on Maundy Thursday as Blomkvist and Berger let themselves into the *Millennium* offices. Berger had woken Malm and Eriksson with the news that Svensson and Johansson had been killed the night before. They lived much closer and had already arrived for the meeting. The coffeemaker was going in the kitchenette.

"What the hell is happening?" Malm wanted to know.

Eriksson shushed him and turned up the volume on the 7:00 a.m. news.

> Two people, a man and a woman, were shot dead late last night in an apartment in Enskede. The police say that it was a double homicide. Neither of the deceased was previously known to the police. The motive for the murders is still unknown. Our reporter Hanna Olofsson is at the scene.
>
> "It was just before midnight when the police received a report of shots fired in an apartment building on Björneborgsvägen here in Enskede. No suspect has yet been arrested. The police have cordoned off the apartment and a crime scene investigation is under way."

"That was pretty succinct," Eriksson said and turned the volume down. Then she started to cry. Berger put an arm around her shoulders.

"Jesus Christ," Malm said to no-one in particular.

"Sit down, everyone," Berger said in a firm voice. "Mikael . . ."

Blomkvist told them what he knew of what had happened. He spoke in a dull monotone and sounded like the radio reporter when he described how he had found Svensson and Johansson.

"Jesus Christ," Malm said again. "This is crazy."

Eriksson was once more overwhelmed by emotion. She began weeping again and made no attempt to hide her tears.

"I'm sorry," she said.

"I feel the same way," said Malm.

Blomkvist wondered why he could not cry. He felt only a huge emptiness, almost as if he were anesthetized.

"What we know this morning doesn't amount to very much," Berger said. "We have to discuss two things: first, we're three weeks from going to press with Dag's material; should we still publish it? Can we publish it? That's one thing. The other is a question that Mikael and I discussed on the way here."

"We don't know the motive for the murders," Blomkvist said. "It could be something to do with Dag and Mia's private life, or it could be a purely senseless act, but we can't rule out that it may have had something to do with what they were working on."

A long silence settled around the table.

At last Blomkvist cleared his throat. "As I said, we're about to publish a story in which we name people who are extremely anxious not to be identified in this connection. Dag started with the confrontations several weeks ago. I'm thinking that if one of them—"

"Wait," Eriksson said. "We're exposing three policemen, at least one of whom works for Säpo and another on the vice squad. Then there are several lawyers, one prosecutor, one judge, and a couple of dirty-old-men journalists. Could one of them have killed two people to prevent the publication?"

"Well, I don't know the answer to that," Blomkvist said. "They all have a hell of a lot to lose, but they're damn stupid if they thought they could quash a story like this by murdering a journalist. But we're also exposing a number of pimps, and even if we use fictitious names it wouldn't be hard to figure out who they are. Some of them already have records for violent crimes."

"OK," Malm said. "But you're making the murders out to be executions. If I'm reading Svensson's story correctly, we're not talking about very bright people. Are they up to pulling off a double murder and getting away with it?"

"How bright do you have to be to fire two shots?" Eriksson said.

"We're speculating here about something we know practically nothing about," Berger broke in. "But we do have to ask the question. If suppressing Dag's articles—or Mia's dissertation, for that matter—was the motive for the murders, then we have to beef up security here in the office."

"And a third question," Eriksson said. "Should we go to the police with the names? What did you tell the police last night, Mikael?"

"I told them what Dag was working on, but they didn't ask for details and I didn't give any names."

"We probably should," Berger said.

"It's not quite that simple," Blomkvist said. "We could give them a list of names, but what do we do if the police start asking questions about how we got hold of them? We can't reveal any source who wants to remain anonymous. And that's certainly true of several of the girls Mia talked to."

"What a fucking mess," Berger said. "We're back to the original question—should we publish?"

Blomkvist held up his hand. "Wait. We could take a vote on this, but I happen to be the publisher who's responsible, and for the first time I think I'll make a decision all on my own. The answer is no. We can't publish this material in the next issue. It's unreasonable for us simply to go ahead according to plan."

Silence descended over the table.

"I really want to publish, obviously, but we are going to have to rewrite quite a bit. It was Dag and Mia who had the documentation, and the story was based on the fact that Mia intended to file a police report against the people we were going to name. She had expert knowledge. Have we got any information on this?"

The front door slammed and Cortez stood in the doorway.

"Is it Dag and Mia?" he asked, out of breath.

They all nodded.

"Christ. This is crazy."

"How did you hear about it?" Blomkvist said.

"I was on my way home with my girlfriend when we heard it on a taxi radio. The police have been asking for information on fares going to their street. I didn't recognize the address. I had to come in."

Cortez looked so shaken that Berger got up and gave him a hug and asked him to join them at the table.

"I think Dag would want us to publish his story," she said.

"And I agree that we should. Definitely the book. But under the circumstances, we'll have to push back the publication date."

"So what do we do?" Eriksson said. "It's not just one article that has to be switched—it's a whole themed issue. The whole magazine has to be remade."

Berger was quiet for a moment, then gave her first tired smile of the day.

"Had you planned to take Easter off, Malin?" she said. "Well, forget it. This is what we'll do . . . Malin, you and I—and Christer—will sit down and plan a new issue without Dag's material. We'll have to see if we can pry loose a few articles that we'd planned for June. Mikael, how much material did you get from Dag?"

"I've got final versions of nine out of twelve chapters. I have drafts of chapters ten and eleven. Dag was going to email me the final versions—I'll check my inbox—but I only have an outline of chapter twelve. That's the summary and the conclusions."

"But you and Dag had talked through every one of the chapters, right?"

"Yes, and I know what he was planning to write in the last chapter, if that's what you mean."

"OK, you'll have to sit down with the manuscripts—both the book and the articles. I want to know how much is missing and whether we can write whatever Dag didn't manage to deliver. Could you do an objective assessment today?"

Blomkvist nodded.

"I also need you to think about what we're going to tell the police. What is within limits and at what point do we risk breaking our confidentiality agreement with our sources. Nobody at *Millennium* should say anything to anyone outside the magazine without your approval."

"That sounds good," Blomkvist said.

"How likely do you think it is that Dag's book was the motive for the murders?"

"Or Mia's dissertation . . . I don't know. But we can't rule it out."

"No, we can't. You'll have to keep it together."

"Keep what together?"

"The investigation."

"What investigation?"

"Our investigation, damn it." Berger suddenly raised her voice. "Dag was a journalist and he was working for *Millennium*. If he was killed because of his job, I want to know about it. So we—as an editorial team—are going to have to dig into what happened. You'll take care of that part, looking for a motive for the murders in all the material Dag gave us." She turned to Eriksson. "Malin, if you help me outline a new issue today, then Christer and I will do the draft layout. But you've worked a lot with Dag and on other articles in the themed issue. I want you to keep an eye on developments in the murder investigation alongside Mikael."

Eriksson nodded.

"Henry . . . can you work today?"

"Sure."

"Start by calling the rest of our staff and tell them what's going on. Then go to the police and find out what's happening. Ask them if there's going to be a press conference or anything. We have to stay on top of the news."

"I'll call everyone first. Then I'll run home and take a shower. I'll be back in forty-five minutes."

"Let's stay in touch all day."

"Right," Blomkvist said. "Are we finished? I have to make a call."

Harriet Vanger was having breakfast on the glass veranda of Henrik Vanger's house in Hedeby when her mobile rang. She answered without looking at the display.

"Good morning, Harriet," said Blomkvist.

"Good heavens. I thought you were one of those people who never gets up before eight."

"I don't, as long as I have a chance to go to bed. Which I didn't last night."

"Has something happened?"

"You didn't listen to the news?" Blomkvist gave her a report of the events of the night.

"That's terrible. How are you holding up?"

"Thanks for asking. I've felt better. But the reason I'm calling is that you're on *Millennium*'s board and should be informed. I'm guessing that some reporter will discover soon enough that I was the one who found Dag and Mia, and that will give rise to certain speculations, and when it leaks out that Dag was working on a massive exposé for *Millennium*, questions are going to be asked."

"And you think I ought to be prepared. So, what should I say?"

"Tell the truth. You've been told what happened. You're shocked about the murders, but you are not privy to the editorial work, so you cannot comment on any speculation. It's the police's job to investigate the murders, not *Millennium*'s."

"Thanks for the warning. Is there anything I can do?"

"Not right now. But if I think of something I'll let you know."

"Good. And Mikael . . . keep me informed, please."

CHAPTER 13

Maundy Thursday, March 24

The responsibility of leading the preliminary investigation into the double homicide in Enskede landed officially on Prosecutor Richard Ekström's desk at 7:00 on the morning of Maundy Thursday. The duty prosecutor of the night before, a relatively young and inexperienced lawyer, had realized that the Enskede murders could turn into a media sensation. He called and woke up the assistant county prosecutor, who in turn woke up the assistant county chief of police. Together they decided to pass the ball to a diligent and experienced prosecutor: Richard Ekström.

Ekström was a thin, vital man five feet six inches tall, forty-two years old, with thinning blond hair and a goatee. He was always impeccably dressed and he wore shoes with slightly raised heels. He had begun his career as the assistant prosecutor in Uppsala, until he was recruited as an investigator by the Ministry of Justice, where he worked on bringing Swedish law into accord with that of the EU, and he acquitted himself so well that for a time he was appointed division chief. He attracted attention with his report on organizational deficiencies within legal security, where he made a case for increased efficiency rather than complying with the requests for increased resources demanded by certain police authorities. After four years at the Ministry of Justice, he moved to the prosecutor's office in Stockholm, where he handled a number of cases involving high-profile robberies and violent crimes.

Within the administration he was taken for a Social Democrat, but in reality Ekström was uninterested in party politics. Even as he started to attract attention in the media, people in high places had begun to keep their eye on him. He was definitely a candidate for higher office, and thanks to his presumed party affiliation he had a broad network of contacts in political and police circles. Within the police force opinion was divided as to Ekström's ability. His investigations had not found support among those who were advocating that the best way to promote law and order was to recruit more police. On the other hand, he had excelled at not being afraid of getting his hands dirty when he drove a case to trial.

Ekström got a briefing from the criminal duty officer about the events in Enskede, and at once concluded that this was a case which would without a doubt create a stir in the media. The two victims were a criminologist and a journalist—the latter a calling Ekström either loved or hated, depending on the situation.

He had a rapid telephone conversation with the county chief of police. At 7:15 he picked up the phone again and woke Criminal Inspector Jan Bublanski, known to his colleagues as Officer Bubble. Bublanski was off duty over Easter week due to a mountain of overtime he had accumulated during the past year, but he was asked to interrupt his time off and come to police headquarters at once to run the investigation of the Enskede killings.

Bublanski was fifty-two and had been on the force since he was twenty-three. He had spent six years in patrol cars and served in both the weapons division and the burglary division before he took additional courses and advanced to the violent crimes division of the county criminal police. By all accounts, he had taken part in thirty-three murder or manslaughter investigations in the last ten years. He had been in charge of seventeen of these investigations, of which fourteen were solved and two were considered closed, which meant that the police knew who the killer was but there was insufficient evidence to bring the individual to trial. In the one remaining case, now six years old, Bublanski and his colleagues had failed. The case concerned a well-known alcoholic and troublemaker who was stabbed to death in his home in Bergshamra. The crime scene was a nightmare of fingerprints and DNA traces left over a period of years by several dozen people who had gotten drunk or been beat up in the apartment. Bublanski and his colleagues were convinced that the killer could be found among the man's prodigious network of fellow alcoholics and drug addicts, but despite their intensive work whoever it was had continued to elude the police.

Bublanski's statistics were good in terms of the number of cases he had solved, and he was held in high esteem by his colleagues. But they also considered him a bit odd, partly because he was Jewish. On certain high holy days he had been seen wearing a yarmulke in the corridors of police headquarters. This had occasioned a comment from a police commissioner, soon after retired, who was of the opinion that it was inappropriate to wear a yarmulke in police headquarters, in the same way he found it inappropriate for a policeman to wear a turban on duty. There was no further discussion about the matter. A journalist heard the comment and started asking questions, at which point the commissioner quickly repaired to his office.

Bublanski belonged to the Söder congregation and ate vegetarian food if kosher fare was unavailable. But he was not so Orthodox that he refused to work on the Sabbath. He immediately recognized that the killings in Enskede were not going to be a routine investigation. Ekström had taken him aside as soon as he appeared, just after 8:00.

"This seems to be a miserable story," Ekström said. "The two who were shot were a journalist and his partner, a criminologist. And that's not all. They were found by another journalist."

Bublanski nodded. That effectively guaranteed that the case would be closely watched by the media.

"And to add a pinch more salt to the wound, the journalist who found the couple was Mikael Blomkvist of *Millennium* magazine."

"Whoops," Bublanski said.

"Well known from the circus surrounding the Wennerström affair."

"What do we know about the motive?"

"So far, not a thing. Neither of the victims is known to us. They seem to have been a conscientious pair. The woman was going to get her doctorate in a few weeks. This case gets top priority."

For Bublanski, murder always had top priority.

"We're putting together a team. You'll have to work fast, and I'll ensure that you have all the resources you need. You've got Faste and Andersson. You'll have Holmberg. He's on the Rinkeby murder case, but it seems that the perp has skipped the country. You can also draw on the National Criminal Police as required."

"I want Sonja Modig."

"Isn't she a little young?"

Bublanski raised his eyebrows in surprise.

"She's thirty-nine, just about your age, and besides, she's exceedingly sharp."

"OK, you decide who you want on the team, but do it quickly. The brass are already after us."

Bublanski took that to be an exaggeration. At this hour, the brass would be at breakfast.

· · ·

The investigation formally began with a meeting just before 9:00, when Inspector Bublanski assembled his troops in a conference room at county police headquarters. He studied the group, not altogether happy with its composition.

Modig was the one he had the most confidence in. She had twelve years' experience, four of them in the violent crimes division, where she had been involved in several of the investigations led by Bublanski. She was exacting and methodical, but Bublanski had observed in her the trait he regarded as the most valuable in tricky investigations: she had imagination and the ability to make associations. In at least two complex cases, Modig had discovered peculiar and improbable connections that all the others had missed, and these had led to breakthroughs. She also had a fresh, intellectual humour that Bublanski appreciated.

He was pleased to have Jerker Holmberg on his team. Holmberg was fifty-five and originally from Ångermanland. He was a stocky, plain individual, who had none of Modig's imagination, but he was, in Bublanski's view, perhaps the best crime scene investigator in the entire Swedish police force. They had worked on numerous investigations together over the years, and Bublanski was convinced that if there was something worth finding at a crime scene, Holmberg would find it. His immediate task would be to take command of the work in the apartment in Enskede.

Bublanski hardly knew Curt Andersson. He was a laconic and solidly built officer with such a short stubble of blond hair that at a distance he looked completely bald. Andersson was thirty-eight and had only recently come to the division from Huddinge, where he had spent years dealing with gang crime. He had a reputation for being hot-tempered and tough, which was perhaps a euphemism for the fact that he employed methods that were not quite by the book. Ten years back he had been accused of brutality, but an enquiry cleared him on all counts.

In October 1999 he had driven with a colleague to Alby to pick up a hooligan for interrogation. This man was well known to the police, and for some years had terrorized the neighbours in his apartment building. Now, as the result of a tip, he was to be taken in for questioning in connection with the robbery of a video store in Norsborg. When confronted by Andersson and his colleague, the hooligan pulled a knife instead of coming along quietly. The other officer collected several wounds to his hands, and then his left thumb was sliced off before the thug directed his attention to Andersson, who for the first time in his career was obliged to use his service weapon. He fired three shots. The first was a warning shot, the second was deliberately aimed but missed the man—no easy matter since the distance was less than ten feet—and the third shot hit him in the middle of his chest, severing the aorta. The man bled to death in a matter of minutes. The inevitable enquiry had ultimately cleared Andersson of any wrongdoing, but only solidified his reputation.

Bublanski had had doubts about Andersson at first, but after six months he had encountered nothing to provoke his criticism or wrath. On the contrary, Bublanski was beginning to have some respect for Andersson's taciturn skill.

The last member of the team, Hans Faste, was forty-seven, a veteran of fifteen years in violent crimes, and the chief reason for Bublanski's not being totally satisfied. Faste had a plus side and also a minus side. On the plus side, he had extensive experience—and of complicated investigations too. On the minus side, he was egocentric and had a loudmouth sense of humour that especially bothered Bublanski. But when he was kept on a short leash he was a competent detective. Besides, he had become something of a mentor for Andersson, who did not seem to object to his personality.

Inspector Nyberg of the criminal division had been invited to the meeting to report on her interview with the journalist Blomkvist during the night. Superintendent Mårtensson was also present to report on what had happened at the crime scene. Both of them were worn out and eager to go home to bed, but Nyberg had already managed to get photographs of the apartment, and these she passed around to the team.

After half an hour they had the sequence of events clear. Bublanski said: "Bearing in mind that the forensic examination of the crime scene is still in progress, this is what we think happened . . . An unknown person entered the apartment in Enskede without the neighbours or any other witness noticing and killed the couple, Dag Svensson and Mia Johansson."

"We don't know yet," Nyberg said, "whether the gun that was found is the murder weapon, but it's at the National Forensics Laboratory, and it's top priority there. We've found a fragment of a bullet—the one that went into Svensson—relatively intact in the bedroom wall. But the bullet that struck Johansson is so fragmented that I doubt it will help much."

"Thanks for that information. A Colt Magnum is a damned cowboy pistol that ought to be banned outright. Have we got a serial number?"

"Not yet," Mårtensson said. "I sent the gun and bullet fragments to NFL by messenger direct from the crime scene. Better for them to take care of it than for me to start handling the weapon."

"That's good. I haven't had time to go to the crime scene yet, but the two of you have been there. What are your thoughts?"

Nyberg deferred to her older colleague to speak for them both.

"First of all, we think it was a lone gunman. Second, it was an execution, pure and simple. I get a feeling that someone had very good reason to kill Svensson and Johansson, and he did his job with precision."

"What do you base that on?" Faste said.

"The apartment was neat and tidy. It bore none of the hallmarks of a robbery or assault or anything like that. And only two shots were fired. Both hit their intended targets in the head. So it's someone who knows how to handle a gun."

"Makes sense to me."

"If we look at the sketch of the apartment . . . from what we could reconstruct, we think that the man, Svensson, was shot at close range—possibly point-blank. There are burn marks around the entry wound. We're guessing that he was shot first. He was thrown against the dining table. The gunman could have stood in the hall or just inside the doorway to the living room.

"According to witnesses, people who live on the same staircase, the shots were fired within a few seconds of each other. Mia Johansson was shot from a greater distance. She was probably standing in the entrance to the bedroom and tried to turn away. The bullet hit her below the left ear and exited just above the right eye. The impact threw her into the bedroom, where she was found. She hit the foot of the bed and slid to the floor."

"A single shot fired by someone used to handling guns," Faste said.

"More than that: there were no footprints to indicate that the killer went into the bedroom to check that she was dead. He knew he had hit his mark and he left the apartment. So, two shots, two bodies, and then out. We'll have to wait for forensics, but I'm guessing that the killer used hunting ammunition. Death would have been instantaneous. There were ghastly wounds in both victims."

The team considered this summary in silence. It was a debate that none of them needed to be reminded of. There are two types of ammunition: hard, full-metal-jacketed bullets that go straight through the body and cause comparatively modest damage, and soft ammunition that expands in the body on impact and does enormous damage. There is a vast difference between hitting a person with a bullet that's nine millimetres in diameter and a bullet that expands to a couple of centimetres or more in diameter. The latter type is called hunting ammunition, and its objective is to cause massive bleeding. It is considered more humane when hunting moose, since the aim is to put down the prey as quickly and painlessly as possible. But hunting ammunition is forbidden for use in war by international law, because a soldier hit by an expanding bullet almost always dies, no matter where the point of entry.

In its wisdom, however, the Swedish police had introduced hollow-body hunting ammunition to the police arsenal two years earlier. Exactly why was unclear, but it was quite clear that if, for example, the demonstrator Hannes Westberg, who was hit in the stomach during the World Trade Organization riots in Göteborg in 2001, had been shot with hunting ammo, he would not have survived.

"So the purpose, unquestionably, was to kill," Andersson said.

He was speaking of the murders in Enskede, but he was also voicing his opinion in the silent debate going on around the table.

Nyberg and Mårtensson agreed.

"Then we have this improbable time frame," Bublanski said.

"Exactly. Immediately after the fatal shots were fired, the killer leaves the apartment, goes down the stairs, drops the weapon, and vanishes into the night. Shortly thereafter—it can only have been a matter of seconds—Blomkvist and his sister drive up and park outside. One possibility is that the killer left through the basement. There's a side entrance he could have used—into the back courtyard and across a lawn to the street that runs parallel. But he would have had to have a key to the basement door."

"Is there any sign at all that the killer left that way?"

"No."

"So, no description to go on," Modig said. "But why did he ditch the weapon? If he had taken it with him—or if he had flung it away some distance from the building—we wouldn't have found it for a while."

It was a question that no-one could answer.

"What should we think about Blomkvist?" Faste said.

"No question he was in shock," Mårtensson said. "But he acted sensibly. He seemed clearheaded, and I thought he was trustworthy. His sister, a lawyer, confirmed the phone call and the drive there by car. I don't think he was involved."

"He's a celebrity journalist," Modig said.

"So this is going to turn into a media circus," Bublanski said. "All the more reason to wrap it up as fast as we can. OK . . . Jerker, you'll deal with the crime scene, of course, and the neighbours. Faste, you and Curt investigate the victims. Who were they, what were they working on, who was in their circle of friends, who might have had a motive to kill them? Sonja, you and I will go over the witness statements from that night. Then you'll make a schedule of what Svensson and Johansson were doing all day yesterday before they were killed. We'll meet here at 2:00 this afternoon."

Blomkvist began his working day at Svensson's desk. He sat quite still for a long while, as if he did not feel up to taking on the task.

Svensson had his own laptop and had initially worked mostly from home. He had usually spent two days a week in the office; more in the last weeks. At *Millennium* he had access to an older PowerMac G3, a computer that lived on his desk and could be used by any of the staff. Blomkvist turned on the G3 and found much of the material Svensson had been working on. He had primarily used the G3 to search the Net, but there were various folders that he had copied over from his laptop. He also had a complete backup on two disks that he kept locked in the desk drawer. Usually he had backed up new and updated material every day, but since he had not been in the office for a few days, the latest copy was from Sunday night. Three days were missing.

Blomkvist made a copy of the Zip disk and locked it in the safe in his office. Then he spent forty-five minutes going through the contents of the original disk. It contained around thirty folders and countless subfolders. Four years of Svensson's research on trafficking. He read the document names and looked for ones that might contain the most sensitive material— the names of sources that Svensson was protecting. He had clearly been very careful with his sources—all such material was in a folder labelled <Sources_confidential>. The folder contained 134 documents, most of them quite small. Blomkvist highlighted all the documents and deleted them. He dragged them to an icon for the Burn programme, which did not simply delete the documents but eradicated them byte by byte.

Then he tackled Svensson's email. He had been given his own email address at *Millennium*, which he used both at the office and on his laptop. He had his own password, but that did not present a problem, since Blomkvist had administrator rights and was able to access the entire mail server. He downloaded a copy of Svensson's email and burned it to a CD.

Finally he turned his attention to the mountain of paper made up of reference material, notes, press clippings, court judgments, and all the correspondence that Svensson had accumulated. He played it safe and made copies of everything that looked important. That came to two thousand pages and took him three hours.

He set to one side all the material that might in any way be connected to a confidential source. It was a stack of about forty pages, mainly notes from two A4 pads that Svensson had locked in his desk. Blomkvist put this material in an envelope and took it into his office. Then he carried all the other material that was part of Svensson's project to his desk.

When he was finished he took a deep breath and went down to the 7-Eleven, where he had a coffee and a slice of pizza. He mistakenly assumed that the police would arrive at any moment to go through Svensson's desk.

·   ·   ·

Bublanski had an unexpected breakthrough in the investigation just after 10:00 a.m., when he was called by Lennart Granlund of the National Forensics Laboratory in Linköping:

"It's about the killings in Enskede."

"So soon?"

"We received the weapon early this morning, and I'm not quite done with the analysis, but I have some information that might interest you."

"Good. Tell me what you've come up with," Bublanski said.

"The weapon is a Colt .45 Magnum, made in the USA in 1981. We have fingerprints and possible DNA—but that analysis will take a little time. We've also looked at the bullets that the couple were shot with. Not surprisingly, they appear to have been fired from that weapon. That's usually the case when we find a gun in the stairwell at a crime scene. The bullets are badly fragmented, but we have a piece to use for comparison. It's most likely that this is the murder weapon."

"An illegal weapon, I suppose. Do you have a serial number?"

"The weapon is quite legal. It belongs to a lawyer, Nils Erik Bjurman, and was bought in 1983. He's a member of the police shooting club. He lives on Upplandsgatan near Odenplan."

"What on earth are you saying?"

"We also found, as I mentioned, a number of prints on the weapon. Prints from at least two different people. We may expect that one set belongs to Bjurman, insofar as the weapon was not reported stolen or sold—but I have no information on that."

"Aha. In other words, we have a lead."

"We have a hit in the register for the second set. Prints from the right thumb and forefinger."

"Who is it?"

"A woman born on April 30, 1978. Arrested for an assault in Gamla Stan in 1995, when the prints were taken."

"Does she have a name?"

"Yes. Her name is Lisbeth Salander."

Bublanski wrote down the name and a social security number that Granlund gave him.

When Blomkvist returned to work after his late lunch, he went straight to his office and closed the door, making it clear that he did not want to be disturbed. He had not had time to deal with all the peripheral information in Svensson's email and notes. He would have to settle down and read through the book and the articles with completely new eyes, keeping in mind now that the author was dead and unable to answer any difficult questions that might need to be asked.

He had to decide whether the book could still be published. And he had to make up his mind whether there was anything in the material that might hint at a motive for murder. He switched on his computer and set to work.

Bublanski made a brief call to Ekström, to tell him what had developed at NFL. It was decided that Bublanski and Modig would pay a call on Advokat Bjurman. It could be for a talk, an interrogation, or even an arrest. Faste and Andersson would track down this Lisbeth Salander and ask her to explain how her fingerprints came to be on a murder weapon.

The search for Bjurman at first presented no difficulty. His address was listed in the tax records, the weapons registry, and the vehicle licencing database; it was even in the telephone book. Bublanski and Modig drove to Odenplan and managed to get into the building on Upplandsgatan when a young man came out just as they arrived.

After that it was trickier. When they rang Bjurman's doorbell, no-one answered. They drove to his office at St. Eriksplan, but got the same result there.

"Maybe he's in court," Modig said.

"Maybe he got on a plane to Brazil after shooting two people in Enskede," Bublanski said.

Modig glanced at her colleague. She enjoyed his company. She would not have had anything against flirting with him but for the fact that she was a mother of two and she and Bublanski were both happily married. From the brass nameplates on Bjurman's floor they noted that his nearest neighbours were a dentist, Dr. Norman, a company called N-Consulting, and Rune Håkansson, a lawyer.

They started with Håkansson.

"Hello, my name is Modig and this is Inspector Bublanski. We're from the police and have business with Nils Erik Bjurman, your colleague from next door. Do you know where we might find him?"

Håkansson shook his head. "I haven't seen much of him lately. He was seriously ill two years ago, and has more or less shut down his practice. I only see him about once every two months."

"Seriously ill?" Bublanski said.

"I'm not sure what with. He was always working flat out, and then he was taken ill. Cancer, I assumed. I hardly know him."

"Do you think or do you know that he got cancer?" Modig said.

"Well . . . No, I'm not sure. He had a secretary, Britt Karlsson, or Nilsson, something like that. An older woman. He let her go, and she was the one who told me that he was ill. That was in the spring of 2003. I didn't see him again until December of that year. He looked ten years older, gaunt and grey-haired. I drew my own conclusions."

They went back to the apartment. Still no answer. Bublanski took out his mobile and dialled Bjurman's mobile number. He got an automated message: *The subscriber you are calling cannot be reached at present. Please try again later.*

He tried the number at the apartment. On the landing they

could hear a faint ringing from the other side of the door before an answering machine clicked on and asked the caller to leave a message.

It was 1:00 p.m.

"Coffee?"

"I need a burger."

At Burger King on Odenplan, Modig had a Whopper and Bublanski a veggie burger. Then they returned to police headquarters.

Prosecutor Ekström called the meeting to order at the conference table in his office at 2:00. Bublanski and Modig took seats next to each other by the wall near the window. Andersson arrived two minutes later and sat down opposite them. Holmberg came in with a tray of coffee in paper cups. He had paid a brief visit to Enskede and intended to return later in the afternoon when the techs were finished.

"Where's Faste?" Ekström asked.

"He's with the social welfare agency. He called five minutes ago and said he'd be a little late," Andersson said.

"We'll get started anyway. What have we got?" Ekström began without ceremony. He pointed first to Bublanski.

"We've been looking for Nils Bjurman, the registered owner of what is probably the murder weapon. He isn't at home or at his office. According to another lawyer in the same building, he fell ill two years ago and has more or less shut down his practice."

Modig said: "Bjurman is fifty-five, not listed in the criminal register. He is mainly a business lawyer. I haven't had time to research his background beyond that."

"But he does own the gun that was used in Enskede."

"That's correct. He has a licence for it and he's a member of the police shooting club," Bublanski said. "I talked to Gunnarsson in weapons—he's the chairman of the club and knows

Bjurman well. He joined in 1978 and was treasurer from 1984 to 1992. Gunnarsson describes Bjurman as an excellent shot with a pistol, calm and collected, and no funny stuff."

"A gun freak?"

"Gunnarsson thinks Bjurman was more interested in club life than in the shooting itself. He liked to compete, but he didn't stand out, at least not as a gun fanatic. In 1983 he participated in the Swedish championships and came in thirteenth. For the past ten years he's cut back on shooting practice and just shows up for annual meetings and such."

"Does he own any other weapons?"

"He has had licences for four handguns since he joined the shooting club. In addition to the Colt, he's had a Beretta, a Smith & Wesson, and a competition pistol made by Rapid. The other three were sold within the club ten years ago, and the licences were transferred to other members."

"And we have no idea where he is."

"That's correct. But we've only been looking for him since 10:00 this morning. He may be out walking in Djurgården or in hospital or whatever."

At that moment Faste burst in. He seemed out of breath.

"Sorry I'm late. May I jump right in?"

Ekström motioned "be my guest."

"Lisbeth Salander is a very interesting character. I've spent the morning at the social welfare agency and the Guardianship Agency." He took off his leather jacket and hung it over the back of his chair before he sat down and opened a notebook.

"The Guardianship Agency?" Ekström said with a frown.

"This is one very disturbed lady," Faste said. "She was declared incompetent and put under guardianship. Guess who's her guardian." He paused for effect. "Nils Bjurman, the owner of the weapon that was used in Enskede."

This announcement certainly had the effect Faste had anticipated. It took him fifteen more minutes to brief the group on all he had learned about Salander.

THE GIRL WHO PLAYED WITH FIRE   249

"To sum up," Ekström said when Faste was finished, "we have fingerprints on the probable murder weapon from a woman who during her teens was in and out of psychiatric units, who is understood to make her living as a prostitute, who was declared incompetent by the district court, and who has been documented as having violent tendencies. We should be asking what the hell she's doing out on the streets at all."

"She's had violent tendencies since she was in elementary school," said Faste. "She seems to be a real psycho."

"But so far we have nothing to link her to the couple in Enskede." Ekström drummed his fingertips on the tabletop. "This double murder may not be so hard to solve after all. Have we got an address for Salander?"

"On Lundagatan in Södermalm. Tax records show that she declared periodic income from Milton Security."

"And what in God's name was she doing for them?"

"I don't know. It's a pretty modest annual income for several years. Maybe she's a cleaning woman or something."

"Hmm," Ekström said. "We'll have that checked out. Right now we have to find her."

"We'll have to work out the details gradually," Bublanski said. "But now we have a suspect. Hans, you and Curt go down to Lundagatan and pick up Salander. Be careful—we don't know if she has other weapons, and we don't really know how dangerous she may be."

"OK."

"Bubble," Ekström said, "the head of Milton Security is Dragan Armansky. I met him on a case a few years ago. He's reliable. Go to his office and have a private talk with him about Salander. You'd better get there before he leaves for the day."

Bublanski was visibly annoyed, partly because Ekström had used his nickname, partly because he had formulated his request as an order.

"Modig," Bublanski said, "keep looking for Bjurman. Knock

on all the neighbours' doors. I think it's just as important to find him."

"OK."

"We have to find the connection between Salander and the couple in Enskede. And we have to place Salander down in Enskede at the time of the murders. Jerker, get some pictures of her and check with everyone who lives in the apartment building. Knock on doors this evening. Get some uniforms to help you out."

Bublanski paused and scratched the back of his neck.

"Damn, with a little luck we could tie up this mess tonight—and I thought this was going to be a long, drawn-out affair."

"One more thing," Ekström said. "The media are obviously pressuring us. I've promised them a press conference at 3:00 p.m. I can handle it provided I get somebody from the press office to help out. I'm guessing that a number of journalists will call you directly as well. We'll say nothing at all about Salander and Bjurman for as long as need be."

Armansky had considered going home early. It was Maundy Thursday and he and his wife had planned to go to their summer cabin on Blidö over the Easter weekend. He had just closed his briefcase and put on his coat when the receptionist buzzed him and said that Criminal Inspector Jan Bublanski was looking for him. Armansky did not know Bublanski, but the fact that a senior police officer had come to the office was enough to make him hang his coat back on the coatrack. He did not feel like seeing anyone at all, but Milton Security could not afford to ignore the police. He met Bublanski by the elevator in the corridor.

"Thanks for taking the time to see me," Bublanski said. "My boss sends his greetings—Prosecutor Ekström."

They shook hands.

"Ekström—I've had dealings with him a few times. It's been several years. Would you like some coffee?"

Armansky stopped at the coffee machine and pressed the buttons for two cups before he invited Bublanski into his office and offered him the comfortable chair by the window.

"Armansky . . . Russian?" Bublanski said. "My name ends in -ski too."

"My family comes from Armenia. And yours?"

"Poland."

"How can I help you?"

Bublanski took out his notebook.

"I'm investigating the killings in Enskede. I assume you heard the news today."

Armansky gave a brisk nod.

"Ekström said that you're discreet."

"In my position it pays to cooperate with the police. I can keep a secret, if that's what you're wondering."

"Good. We're looking for an individual who worked for your company at one time. Lisbeth Salander. Do you know her?"

Armansky felt a lump of cement form in his stomach. His expression did not change.

"And why are you looking for Fröken Salander?"

"Let's say that we have reason to consider her a person of interest in the investigation."

The lump of cement in Armansky's stomach expanded. It almost caused him physical pain. Since the day he had first met Salander he had had a strong presentiment that her life was on a trajectory towards catastrophe. But he had always imagined her as a victim, not an offender. He still showed no emotion.

"So you suspect Lisbeth Salander of the killings in Enskede. Do I understand you correctly?"

Bublanski hesitated a moment, and then he nodded.

"What can you tell me about her?"

"What do you want to know?"

"First of all, how can we find her?"

"She lives on Lundagatan. I'll have to look up the exact address. I have a mobile telephone number for her."

"We have the address. The mobile number would be helpful."

Armansky went to his desk and read out the number, which Bublanski wrote down.

"She works for you?"

"She has her own business. I gave her freelance assignments now and then from 1998 until about a year and a half ago."

"What sort of jobs did she do?"

"Research."

Bublanski looked up from his notebook.

"Research?" he said.

"Personal investigations, to be more precise."

"Just a moment . . . are we talking about the same girl? The Lisbeth Salander we're looking for didn't finish school and was officially declared incompetent to manage her affairs."

"They don't say 'incompetent' nowadays," Armansky said calmly.

"I don't give a damn what they say nowadays. The girl we're looking for has a record which says she is a deeply disturbed and violence-prone individual. It says in her social welfare agency file that she was a prostitute in the late nineties. There is nothing anywhere in her records to indicate that she could hold down a white-collar job."

"Files are one thing. People are something else."

"You mean that she is qualified to do personal investigations for Milton Security?"

"Not only that. She is by far the best researcher I've ever had."

Bublanski put down his pen and frowned.

"It sounds as though you have . . . respect for her."

Armansky looked at his hands. The question marked a fork in the road. He had always feared that Salander would end up in hot water sooner or later, but he could not conceive of her being mixed up in a double murder in Enskede—as the killer or in any other way. But what did he know about her private life? Armansky thought of her recent visit to his office in which she had cryptically explained that she had enough money to get by and did not need a job.

The wisest thing to do at that moment would be to distance himself, and above all Milton Security, from all contact with Salander. But then Salander was probably the loneliest person he knew.

"I have respect for her skills. You won't find that in her school results or personal record."

"So you know about her background."

"The fact that she's under guardianship and that she had a pretty confused upbringing, yes."

"And yet you trusted her."

"That is precisely why I trusted her."

"Please explain."

"Her previous guardian, Holger Palmgren, was old J. F. Milton's lawyer. He took on her case when she was a teenager, and he persuaded me to give her a job. I employed her initially to sort the mail and look after the photocopier, things like that. But she turned out to have unbelievable talents. And you can forget any report that says she may have been a prostitute. That's nonsense. Lisbeth had a difficult period in her teens and was undoubtedly a bit wild—but that's not the same as breaking the law. Prostitution is probably the last thing in the world she would turn to."

"Her current guardian is a lawyer by the name of Nils Bjurman."

"I've never met him. Palmgren had a cerebral haemorrhage a couple of years ago. Lisbeth cut back on the work she did for me quite soon after that happened. The last job she did was in October a year and a half ago."

"Why did you stop employing her?"

"It wasn't my choice. She was the one who broke off contact and disappeared abroad. Without a word of explanation."

"Disappeared abroad?"

"She was gone for about a year."

"That can't be right. Bjurman sent in monthly reports on her for all of last year. We have copies up at Kungsholmen."

Armansky shrugged and smiled.

"When was the last time you saw her?"

"In early February. She popped up out of nowhere and paid me a social visit. She spent all of last year out of the country, travelling in Asia and the Caribbean."

"Forgive me, but I'm getting a little muddled here. I had the impression that this Lisbeth Salander was a mentally ill girl who hadn't even finished school and who was under guardianship. Now you tell me that you trusted her as an exceptional researcher, that she has her own business, and that she earned enough money to take a year off and travel around the world, all without her guardian sounding the alarm. Something doesn't add up here."

"There's quite a bit that doesn't add up regarding Fröken Salander."

"May I ask . . . what is your overall opinion of her?"

Armansky thought for a while. Finally he said: "She's one of the most irritating, inflexible people I've met in my whole life."

"Inflexible?"

"She won't do anything she doesn't want to do. She doesn't give a damn what other people think of her. She is tremendously skilled. And she is unlike anyone I've ever met."

"Is she unbalanced?"

"How do you define unbalanced?"

"Is she capable of murdering two people in cold blood?"

Armansky was quiet for a long time. "I'm sorry. I can't answer that question. I'm a cynic. I believe that everyone has it in them to kill another person. In desperation or hatred, or at least to defend themselves."

"You don't discount the possibility, at any rate."

"Lisbeth Salander will not do anything unless she has a good reason for it. If she murdered someone, then she must have felt that she had a very good reason to do so. On what grounds do you suspect her of being involved in these murders?"

Bublanski met Armansky's gaze.

"Can we keep this confidential?"

"Absolutely."

"The murder weapon belonged to her guardian. And her fingerprints were on it."

Armansky clenched his teeth. That was serious circumstantial evidence.

"I've only heard about the murders on the radio. What was it about? Drugs?"

"Is she mixed up with drugs?"

"Not that I know of. But, as I said, she went through a bad time in her teens, and she was arrested a few times for being drunk. Her record will tell you whether drugs were involved."

"We don't have a motive for the murders. They were a conscientious couple. She was a criminologist and was just about to get her doctorate. He was a journalist. Dag Svensson and Mia Johansson. Do those names ring any bells?"

Armansky shook his head.

"We're trying to find a connection between them and Lisbeth Salander."

"I've never heard of them."

Bublanski stood up. "Thanks for your time. It's been a fascinating conversation. I don't know how much the wiser I am for it, but I hope we can keep all of this between ourselves."

"Of course."

"I'll get back to you if necessary. And of course, if Salander should get in touch . . ."

"Certainly," Armansky said.

They shook hands. Bublanski was on his way out the door when he stopped.

"You don't happen to know anyone that Salander associates with, do you? Friends, acquaintances . . ."

Armansky shook his head.

"I don't know a single thing about her private life. Except
that her old guardian meant something to her. Holger Palmgren. He's in a nursing home in Ersta. She might have made
contact with him since she came back."

"She never had visitors when she was working here? Would
there be a record of that?"

"No. She worked from home mainly and came in only to
present her reports. With a few exceptions, she never even met
the clients. Possibly . . ." Armansky was struck by a thought.

"What?"

"There is just possibly one other person she may have got
in touch with, a journalist she knew a couple of years ago. He
was looking for her when she was out of the country."

"A journalist?"

"His name is Mikael Blomkvist. Do you remember the
Wennerström affair?"

Bublanski came slowly back into Armansky's office.

"It was Blomkvist who discovered the couple in Enskede.
You've just established a link between Salander and the murder
victims."

Armansky again felt the solid pain of the lump in his
stomach.

CHAPTER 14

Maundy Thursday, March 24

Modig tried three times in half an hour to reach Nils Bjurman on his mobile. Each time she got the message that the subscriber could not be reached.

At 3:30 p.m. she drove to Odenplan and rang his doorbell. Once more, no answer. She spent the next twenty minutes knocking on doors in the apartment building to see if any of Bjurman's neighbours knew where he might be.

In eleven of the nineteen apartments no-one was there. It was obviously the wrong time of day to be knocking on doors, and it would not get any better over the Easter weekend. In the eight apartments that were occupied, everyone was helpful. Five of them knew who Bjurman was—a polite, well-mannered gentleman on the fifth floor. No-one could provide any information as to his whereabouts. She managed to ascertain that Bjurman might be visiting one of his closest neighbours, a businessman named Sjöman. But nobody answered the door there either.

Frustrated, Modig took out her mobile and called Bjurman's answering machine once again. She gave her name, left her number, and asked him to please contact her as soon as he could.

She went back to Bjurman's door and wrote him a note asking him to call her. She got out a business card and dropped that through the mail slot as well. Just as she closed the flap, she heard a telephone ring inside the apartment. She leaned down and listened intently as it rang four times. She heard the answering machine click on, but she could not hear any message.

She closed the flap on the mail slot and stared at the door. Exactly what impulse made her reach out and touch the handle she could not have said, but to her great surprise the door was unlocked. She pushed it open and peered into the hall.

"Hello!" she called cautiously and listened. There was no sound.

She took a step into the hall and then hesitated. She had no warrant to search the premises and no right to be in the apartment, even if the door was unlocked. She looked to her left and got a glimpse of the living room. She had just decided to back out of the apartment when her glance fell on the hall table. She saw a box for a Colt Magnum pistol.

Modig suddenly had a strong sense of unease. She opened her jacket and drew her service weapon, which she had rarely done before.

She clicked off the safety catch and aimed the gun at the floor as she went to the living room and looked in. She saw nothing untoward, but her apprehension increased. She backed out and peered into the kitchen. Empty. She went down the corridor and pushed open the bedroom door.

Bjurman's naked body lay half stretched out on the bed. His knees were on the floor. It was as though he had knelt to say his prayers.

Even from the door Modig could tell that he was dead. Half of his forehead had been blown away by a shot to the back of his head.

Modig closed the apartment door behind her. She still had her service revolver in her hand as she flipped open her mobile and called Inspector Bublanski. She could not reach him. Next

THE GIRL WHO PLAYED WITH FIRE 259

she called Prosecutor Ekström. She made a note of the time. It was 4:18.

Faste looked at the entrance door to the building on Lunda-gatan. He looked at Andersson and then at his watch. 4:10.

After obtaining the entry code from the caretaker, they had already been inside the building and listened at the door with the nameplate SALANDER-WU. They had heard no sound from the apartment, and nobody had answered the bell. They returned to their car and parked where they could keep watch on the door.

From the car they had ascertained by phone that the person in Stockholm whose name had been recently added to the contract for the apartment on Lundagatan was Miriam Wu, born in 1974 and previously living at St. Eriksplan.

They had a passport photograph of Salander taped above the car radio. Faste muttered out loud that she looked like a bitch.

"Shit, the whores are looking worse all the time. You'd have to be pretty desperate to pick her up."

Andersson kept his mouth shut.

At 4:20 they were called by Bublanski, who told them he was on his way from Armansky's to the *Millennium* offices. He asked Faste and Andersson to maintain their watch at Lunda-gatan. Salander would have to be brought in for questioning, but they should be aware that the prosecutor did not think she could be linked to the killings in Enskede.

"All right," Faste said. "According to Bubble the prosecutor wants to have a confession before they arrest anybody."

Andersson said nothing. Listlessly they watched people moving through the neighbourhood.

At 4:40, Prosecutor Ekström called Faste's mobile.

"Things are happening. We found Bjurman shot in his apartment. He's been dead for at least twenty-four hours."

Faste sat up in his seat. "Got it. What should we do?"

"I'm going to issue an alert on Salander. She's being sought as a suspect in three murders. We'll send it out county-wide. We have to consider her dangerous and very possibly armed."

"Got it."

"I'm sending a van to Lundagatan. They'll go in and secure the apartment."

"Understood."

"Have you been in touch with Bublanski?"

"He's at *Millennium.*"

"And seems to have turned off his phone. Could you try to reach him and let him know?"

Faste and Andersson looked at each other.

"The question is, what do we do if she turns up?" Andersson said.

"If she's alone and things look good, we'll pick her up. This girl is as crazy as hell and obviously on a killing spree. There may be more weapons in the apartment."

Blomkvist was dead tired when he laid the pile of manuscript pages on Berger's desk and slumped into the chair by the window overlooking Götgatan. He had spent the whole afternoon trying to make up his mind what they ought to do with Svensson's unfinished book.

Svensson had been dead only a few hours, and already his publisher was debating what to do with the work he had left behind. An outsider might think it cynical and coldhearted, but Blomkvist did not see it that way. He felt as if he were in an almost weightless state. It was a sensation that every reporter or newspaper editor knew well, and it kicked in at moments of direst crisis.

When other people are grieving, the newspaperman turns efficient. And despite the numbing shock that afflicted the members of the *Millennium* team who were there that Maundy

Thursday morning, professionalism took over and was rigorously channelled into work.

For Blomkvist this went without saying. He and Svensson were two of a kind, and Svensson would have done the same himself if their roles had been reversed. He would have asked himself what he could do for Blomkvist. Svensson had left a legacy in the form of a manuscript with an explosive story. He had worked on it for four years; he had put his soul into a task which he would now never complete.

And he had chosen to work at *Millennium*.

The murders of Dag Svensson and Mia Johansson were not a national trauma on the scale of the murder of Olof Palme, and the investigation would not be minutely followed by a grieving nation. But for employees of *Millennium* the shock was perhaps greater—they were affected personally—and Svensson had a broad network of contacts in the media who were going to demand answers to their questions.

But now it was Blomkvist's and Berger's duty to finish Svensson's book, and to answer the questions Who killed them? And why?

"I can reconstruct the unfinished text," Blomkvist said. "Malin and I have to go through the unedited chapters line by line and see where more work still needs to be done. For most of it, all we have to do is follow Dag's notes, but we do have a problem in chapters four and five, which are largely based on Mia's interviews. Dag didn't fill in who the sources were, but with one or two exceptions I think we can use the references in her thesis as a primary source."

"What about the last chapter?"

"I have Dag's outline, and we talked it through so many times that I know more or less exactly what he wanted to say. I propose that we lift the summary and use it as an afterword, where I can also explain his reasoning."

"Fair enough, but I want to approve it. We can't be putting words in his mouth."

"No danger of that. I'll write the chapter as my personal reflection and sign it. I'll describe how he came to write and research the book and say what sort of person he was. I'll conclude by recapping what he said in at least a dozen conversations over the past few months. There's plenty in his draft that I can quote. I think I can make it sound dignified."

"I want this book published more than ever," Berger said.

Blomkvist understood exactly what she meant.

Berger put her reading glasses on the desk and shook her head. She got up and poured two cups of coffee from the thermos and sat down opposite Blomkvist.

"Christer and I have a layout for the replacement issue. We've taken two articles earmarked for the issue after this one and we're going to fill the gaps with freelance material. But it'll be a bit of this and a bit of that, an issue without any real focus."

They sat quietly for a moment.

"Have you listened to the news?" Berger asked.

"No. I know what they're going to say."

"It's the top story on every radio station. The second-place story is a political move by the Centre Party."

"Which means that absolutely nothing else is happening in the country."

"The police haven't released their names yet. They're being described as a 'conscientious couple.' No-one's mentioned that it was you who found them."

"I'll bet the police will do all they can to keep it quiet. At least that's to our advantage."

"Why would the police want to do that?"

"Because detectives basically hate a media circus. I would guess something will leak out sometime tonight or early tomorrow morning."

"So young and so cynical."

"We aren't that young anymore, Ricky. I thought about it while I was being questioned last night. The police inspector looked like she could still be at school."

Berger gave a weak laugh. She had had a few hours' sleep last night, but she was beginning to feel the strain. Still, in no time at all she would be editor in chief of one of the largest newspapers in Sweden. *And no—this was not the right time to reveal that news to Blomkvist.*

"Henry called a while ago. A preliminary investigation leader named Ekström held some sort of press conference this afternoon."

"Richard Ekström?"

"Yes. Do you know him?"

"Political flunky. Guaranteed media circus. This is going to get plenty of publicity."

"Well, he says that the police are already following up certain leads and hope to solve the case soon. Otherwise he pretty much said nothing. But apparently the place was jammed with reporters."

Blomkvist rubbed his eyes. "I can't get the image of Mia's body out of my mind. Damn, I was just getting to know them."

"Some crazy—"

"I don't know. I've been thinking about it all day."

"About what?"

"Mia was shot from the side. I saw the entry wound on the side of her neck and the exit wound in her forehead. Dag was shot from the front. The bullet went into his forehead, and came out the back of his head. Those looked to be the only two shots. It doesn't feel like the act of a lone nutcase."

Berger looked at her partner thoughtfully. "So what was it?"

"If it's not a random killing, then there has to be a motive. And the more I think about it, the more it feels as if this manuscript provides a damned good motive." Blomkvist gestured at the stack of paper on Berger's desk. She followed his eyes. Then they looked at each other. "Maybe it's not the book itself. Maybe they had done too much snooping and managed to . . . I don't know . . . maybe somebody felt threatened."

"And hired a hit man. Micke—that's the stuff of American movies. This book is about the exploiters, the users. It names police officers, politicians, journalists . . . So you think one of them murdered Dag and Mia?"

"I don't know, Ricky. But we're supposed to be going to press in three weeks with the toughest exposé of trafficking that's ever been published in Sweden."

At that moment Eriksson knocked and put her head round the door. An Inspector Bublanski wanted to speak with Blomkvist.

Bublanski shook hands with Berger and Blomkvist and sat down in the third chair at the table by the window. He studied Blomkvist and saw a hollow-eyed man with a day's growth of beard.

"Have there been any developments?" Blomkvist said.

"Maybe. I understand you were the one who found the couple in Enskede and called the police last night."

Blomkvist nodded wearily.

"I know that you told your story to the detective on duty last night, but I wonder if you could clarify a few details for me."

"What would you like to know?"

"How did you come to be driving over to see Svensson and Johansson so late at night?"

"That's not a detail, it's a whole novel," Blomkvist said with a tired smile. "I was at a dinner party at my sister's house—she lives in a new development in Stäket. Dag Svensson called me on my mobile and said that he wasn't going to have time to come to the office on Thursday—today, that is—as we had previously agreed. He was supposed to deliver some photographs to our art director. The reason he gave was that he and Mia had decided to drive up to her parents' house over the weekend, and they wanted to leave early in the morning. He asked if it would be OK if he messengered them to me last night instead. I said that since I lived so close, I could pick up the photographs on my way home from my sister's."

"So you drove to Enskede to pick up photographs."

"Yes."

"Can you think of any motive for the murders of Svensson and Johansson?"

Blomkvist and Berger glanced at each other. Neither said a word.

"What is it?" Bublanski wanted to know.

"We've discussed the matter today and we're having a bit of a disagreement. Well, actually not a disagreement—we're just not certain. We would rather not speculate."

"Tell me."

Blomkvist described to him the subject of Svensson's book, and how he and Berger had been discussing whether it might have some connection to the murders. Bublanski sat quietly for a moment, digesting the information.

"So Dag Svensson was about to expose police officers."

He did not at all like the turn the conversation had taken, and imagined how a "police trail" might wander back and forth in the media and give rise to all kinds of conspiracy theories.

"No," Blomkvist said. "He was about to expose criminals, a few of whom happen to be police officers. There are also one or two members of my own profession, namely journalists."

"And you're thinking of publishing this information now?"

Blomkvist turned to look at Berger.

"No," she said. "We've spent the day working on the next issue. In all probability we'll publish Svensson's book, but that won't happen until we know exactly what's going on. In light of what has happened, the book will have to be extensively reworked. We will do nothing to sabotage the investigation into the murder of our two friends, if that's what you're worried about."

"I'll have to take a look at Svensson's desk, but since these are the editorial offices of a magazine it might be a sensitive thing to put in hand a complete search."

"You'll find all Dag's material in his laptop," Berger said.

"I've gone through his desk," Blomkvist said. "I've taken

some documents that directly identify sources who want to remain anonymous. You are at liberty to examine everything else, and I've put a note on the desk to the effect that nothing may be touched or moved. The problem is that the contents of the book absolutely have to remain under wraps until it's printed. We badly need to avoid having the text passed around the police force, the more so since we're going to hang one or two policemen out to dry."

Shit, Bublanski thought. *Why didn't I come straight here this morning?* But he only nodded and changed tack.

"OK. We have a person we want to question in connection with the murders. I believe it's someone you know. I'd like to hear what you have to say about a woman named Lisbeth Salander."

For a second Blomkvist looked like a virtual question mark. Bublanski noted that Berger gave her colleague a sharp look.

"Now I don't understand."

"You know Lisbeth Salander?"

"Yes, I do know her."

"How do you know her?"

"Why do you ask?"

Bublanski was obviously irritated, but all he said was, "I'd like to interview her in connection with the murders. How do you know her?"

"But . . . that doesn't make sense. Lisbeth Salander has no connection whatsoever to Dag Svensson or Mia Johansson."

"That's something we'll establish in due course," Bublanski said patiently. "But my question remains. How do you know Lisbeth Salander?"

Blomkvist stroked the stubble on his chin and then rubbed his eyes as thoughts tumbled around in his head. At last he met Bublanski's gaze.

"I hired her about two years ago to do some research for me on a completely different project."

"What was that project?"

"I'm sorry, but now you'll have to take my word for it: it didn't have the slightest thing to do with Dag Svensson or Mia Johansson. And it's all over."

Bublanski did not like it when someone claimed there were matters that could not be discussed even in a murder investigation, but he chose to drop it for the time being.

"When was the last time you saw Salander?"

Blomkvist paused before he spoke.

"Here's how it is. During the autumn two years ago I was seeing her. The relationship ended around Christmas of that year. Then she disappeared from the city. I hadn't seen her for more than a year until a week ago."

Berger raised her eyebrows. Bublanski surmised that this was news to her.

"Tell me where you saw her."

Blomkvist took a deep breath and then gave a brisk account of the events on Lundagatan. Bublanski listened with gathering astonishment, unsure how much of the story Blomkvist was making up.

"So you didn't talk to her?"

"No, she disappeared on upper Lundagatan. I waited a long time, but she never came back. I wrote her a note and asked her to get in touch with me."

"And you're quite sure you know of no connection between her and the couple in Enskede."

"I am certain of it."

"Can you describe the man you say you saw attack her?"

"Not in detail. He attacked, and she defended herself and fled. I saw him from a distance of forty to forty-five yards. It was late at night and quite dark."

"Were you intoxicated?"

"I was a little under the influence, but I wasn't falling-down drunk. The man had lightish hair in a ponytail. He wore a dark waist-length jacket. He had a prominent belly. When I went up the stairs on Lundagatan I only saw him from behind, but he turned around when he clobbered me. I seem to remember that he had a thin face and blue eyes set close together."

"Why didn't you tell me this earlier?" Berger said.

Blomkvist shrugged. "There was a weekend in between, and you went to Göteborg to take part in that damned debate programme. You were gone Monday, and on Tuesday we only saw each other briefly. It didn't seem so important."

"But considering what has happened in Enskede . . . it's odd that you didn't mention this to the police," Bublanski said.

"Why would I mention it to the police? That's like saying I should have mentioned that I caught a pickpocket trying to rob me in the tunnelbana at T-Centralen a month ago. There is absolutely no imaginable connection between what happened on Lundagatan and what happened in Enskede."

"But you didn't report the attack to the police?"

"No." Blomkvist paused. "Lisbeth Salander is a very private person. I considered going to the police but decided it was up to her to do that if she wanted to. And I wanted to speak to her first."

"Which you haven't done?"

"I haven't spoken to her since the day after Christmas a year ago."

"Why did your—if *relationship* is the right word—why did it end?"

Blomkvist's eyes darkened.

"I don't know. She broke off contact with me—it happened practically overnight."

"Did something happen between you?"

"No, not if you mean an argument or anything like that. One day we were good friends. The next day she didn't answer her telephone. Then she melted into thin air and was gone from my life."

Bublanski contemplated Blomkvist's explanation. It sounded honest and was supported by the fact that Armansky had described her disappearance from Milton Security in similar terms. Something had apparently happened to Salander during the winter a year earlier. He turned to Berger.

"Do you know Salander too?"

"I met her once. Could you tell us why you're asking questions about her in connection with Enskede?" she said.

Bublanski shook his head. "She has been linked to the crime scene. That's all I can say. But I have to admit that the more I hear about Lisbeth Salander the more surprised I am. What is she like as a person?"

"In what respect?" Blomkvist said.

"How would you describe her?"

"Professionally—one of the best fact finders I have ever come across."

Berger glanced at Blomkvist and bit her lower lip. Bublanski was convinced that some piece of the puzzle was missing and that they knew something they were unwilling to tell him.

"And privately?"

Blomkvist paused for a long moment before he spoke.

"She is a very lonely and odd person," Blomkvist said. "Socially introverted. Doesn't like talking about herself. At the same time she's a person with a strong will. She has morals."

"Morals?"

"Yes. Her own particular moral standards. You can't talk her into doing anything against her will. In her world, things are either right or wrong, so to speak."

Again Blomkvist had described her in the same terms as Armansky had. Two men who knew her, and had the same evaluation.

"Do you know Dragan Armansky?"

"We've met a few times. I took him out for a beer once last year when I was trying to find out where Lisbeth had got to."

"And you say that she was a competent researcher?"

"The best," Blomkvist said.

Bublanski drummed his fingers on the table and looked down at the flow of people on Götgatan. He felt strangely torn.

The psychiatric reports that Faste had retrieved from the Guardianship Agency claimed that Salander was a deeply disturbed and possibly violent person who was for all intents and purposes mentally handicapped. What Armansky and Blomkvist had told him painted a very different picture from the one established by medical experts over several years of study. Both men conceded that Salander was an odd person, but both held her in high regard professionally.

Blomkvist had also said that he had been "seeing her" for a period—which indicated a sexual relationship. Bublanski wondered what rules applied for individuals who had been declared incompetent. Could Blomkvist have implicated himself in some form of abuse by exploiting a person in a position of dependency?

"And how did you perceive her social handicap?" he asked.

"What handicap?"

"The guardianship and her psychiatric problems."

"Guardianship?"

"What psychiatric problems?" Berger said.

Bublanski looked in astonishment from Blomkvist to Berger and back. *They didn't know. They really did not know.* Bublanski was suddenly angry at both Armansky and Blomkvist, and especially at Berger with her elegant clothes and her fashionable office looking down on Götgatan. *Here she sits, telling people what to think.* But he directed his annoyance at Blomkvist.

"I don't understand what's wrong with you and Armansky," he said.

"What the hell does that mean?"

"Lisbeth Salander has been in and out of psychiatric units since she was a teenager. A psychiatric assessment and a judgment in the district court determined that she was and still is unable to look after her own affairs. She was declared incompetent. She has a documented violent tendency and has been in trouble with the authorities all her life. And now she is a prime suspect in a murder investigation. And you and Arman-sky talk about her as though she were some sort of princess."

Blomkvist sat motionless, staring at Bublanski.

"I'll put it another way," Bublanski said. "We were looking for a connection between Salander and the couple in Enskede. It turns out that you not only discovered the victims, you are also the connection. Do you have anything to say to this?"

Blomkvist leaned back, closed his eyes, and tried to make heads or tails of the situation. Salander suspected of murder-ing Svensson and Johansson? *That can't be right. It doesn't make sense.* Was she capable of murder? Blomkvist suddenly saw in his mind's eye her expression from two years ago when she had gone after Martin Vanger with a golf club. *There was no shadow of doubt that she could have killed him. But she didn't, because she had to save my life.* He unconsciously reached for his neck, where Vanger's noose had been. But Svensson and Johans-son . . . *it doesn't make any logical sense whatsoever.*

He was aware that Bublanski was watching him closely. Like Armansky, Blomkvist had to make a choice. Sooner or later he would have to decide which corner of the ring he was going to be in if Salander was accused of murder. *Guilty or not guilty?*

Before he managed to say anything, the telephone on Berger's desk rang. She picked it up, listened, then handed the receiver to Bublanski.

"Somebody called Faste wants to speak to you."

Bublanski took the receiver and listened attentively. Blomkvist and Berger could see his expression change.

"When are they going in?"

Silence.

"What's the address again? Lundagatan. And the number? OK. I'm in the vicinity. I'll drive there."

Bublanski stood up.

"Excuse me, but I'll have to cut this conversation short. Salander's guardian has just been found shot dead. She's now being formally charged, in absentia, with three murders."

Berger's mouth dropped open. Blomkvist looked as if he had been struck by lightning.

The occupation of the apartment on Lundagatan was an uncomplicated procedure from a tactical perspective. Faste and Andersson leaned on the hood of their car keeping watch while the armed response team, supplied with backup weapons, occupied the stairwell and took control of the building and the rear courtyard.

The team swiftly confirmed what Faste and Andersson already knew. No-one opened the door when they rang the bell.

Faste looked down Lundagatan, which was blocked off from Zinkensdamm to Högalid Church, to the great annoyance of the passengers on the number 66 bus.

One bus had been stuck inside the barriers on the hill and could not go forward or back. Eventually Faste went over and ordered a patrolman to step aside and let the bus through. A large number of onlookers were watching the commotion from upper Lundagatan.

"There has to be a simpler way," Faste said.

"Simpler than what?" Andersson said.

"Simpler than sending in the storm troopers every time a stray hooligan has to be brought in."

Andersson refrained from commenting.

"After all, she's less than five feet tall and weighs about ninety pounds."

It had been decided that it was not necessary to break down the door with a sledgehammer. Bublanski joined them as they waited for a locksmith to drill out the lock, and then he stepped aside so that the troops could enter the apartment. It took about eight seconds to eyeball the 500 square feet and confirm that Salander was not hiding under the bed, in the bathroom, or in a wardrobe. Then Bublanski was given the all clear to come in.

The three detectives looked with curiosity around the impeccably kept and tastefully furnished apartment. The furniture was simple. The kitchen chairs were painted in different pastel colours. There were attractive black-and-white photographs in frames on the walls. In the hall was a shelf with a CD player and a large collection of CDs. Everything from hard rock to opera. It all looked arty. Elegant. Tasteful.

Andersson inspected the kitchen and found nothing out of the ordinary. He looked through a stack of newspapers and checked the countertop, the cupboards, and the freezer in the refrigerator.

Faste opened the wardrobes and the drawers of the chest in the bedroom. He whistled when he found handcuffs and a number of sex toys. In the wardrobe he found some latex clothing that his mother would have been embarrassed even to look at.

"There's been a party here," he said out loud, holding up a patent-leather outfit that according to the label was designed by Domino Fashion—whatever that was.

Bublanski looked in the desk in the hall, where he found a small pile of unopened letters addressed to Salander. He looked through the pile and saw that they were bills and bank statements, and one personal letter. It was from Mikael Blomkvist. So far, Blomkvist's story held up. Then he bent down and picked up the mail on the doormat, stained with footprints from the armed response team. It consisted of a magazine, *Thai Pro Boxing*, the free newspaper *Södermalm News*, and three envelopes addressed to Miriam Wu.

Bublanski was struck by an unpleasant suspicion. He went into the bathroom and opened the medicine cabinet. He found a box of paracetamol painkillers and a half-full tube of Citodon, paracetamol with codeine. Citodon was a prescription drug. The medicine was prescribed for Miriam Wu. There was one toothbrush in the medicine cabinet.

"Faste, why does it say SALANDER-WU on the door?" he said.

"No idea."

"OK, let me put it this way—why is there mail on the door-mat addressed to a Miriam Wu, and why is there a prescription tube of Citodon in the medicine cabinet made out to Miriam Wu? Why is there only one toothbrush? And why—when you consider that Lisbeth Salander is, according to our information, only one hand's breadth tall—do those leather pants you're holding up fit a person who is at least five foot eight?"

There was a brief, embarrassed silence in the apartment. It was broken by Andersson.

"Shit," he said.

CHAPTER 15

Maundy Thursday, March 24

Malm felt drained and miserable when he finally got home after the unplanned day at work. He smelled the aroma of something spicy from the kitchen and went in and hugged his boyfriend.

"How are you feeling?" Arnold Magnusson asked.

"Like a sack of shit."

"I've been hearing about it on the news all day long. They haven't released the names yet. But it sounds fucking awful."

"It *is* fucking awful. Dag worked for us. He was a friend and I liked him a lot. I didn't know his girlfriend, but both Micke and Erika did."

Malm looked around the kitchen. They had moved into the apartment on Allhelgonagatan only three months ago. Suddenly it felt like another world.

The telephone rang. They looked at each other and decided to ignore it. Then the answering machine switched on and they heard a familiar voice.

"Christer. Are you there? Pick up."

It was Berger calling to tell him that the police were now

looking for Blomkvist's former researcher, who was the prime suspect for the murders of Svensson and Johansson.

Malm received the news with a sense of unreality.

Cortez had missed the commotion on Lundagatan for the simple reason that he had been standing outside the police press office at Kungsholmen the whole time, from which no news had been released since the press conference earlier that afternoon.

He was tired, hungry, and annoyed at being ignored by the people he was trying to contact. Not until 6:00, when the raid at Salander's apartment was over, did he pick up a rumour that the police had a suspect in the investigation. The tip came from a colleague at an evening paper. But Cortez soon managed to find out Prosecutor Ekström's mobile phone number. He introduced himself and asked his questions about who, how, and why.

"What newspaper did you say you were from?" Ekström said.

"*Millennium* magazine. I knew one of the victims. I understand that the police are looking for a specific person. Can you confirm this?"

"I can't comment at present."

"Can you say when you will be able to provide some concrete information?"

"We may well call another press conference later this evening."

Ekström sounded evasive. Cortez tugged on the gold ring in his earlobe.

"Press conferences are for reporters who have immediate deadlines. I work for a monthly magazine, and we have a very special personal interest in knowing what progress is being made."

"I can't help you. You'll have to be patient like everyone else."

"According to my source it's a woman who is wanted for questioning. Who is she?"

"I can't comment just now."

"Can you confirm that you're searching for a woman?"

"I'm not going to confirm or deny anything at all. Goodbye."

Holmberg stood in the doorway of the bedroom and contemplated the huge pool of blood on the floor where Mia Johansson had been found. He turned and could see a similar pool of blood where Svensson had lain. He pondered the extensive blood loss. It was a lot more blood than he was used to finding at shootings; Supervisor Mårtensson had been correct in his assessment that the killer had used hunting ammo. The blood had coagulated in a black and rusty-brown mass that covered so much of the floor that the ambulance personnel and technical team had to walk through it, leaving footprints throughout the apartment. Holmberg was wearing gym shoes with blue plastic booties over them.

The real crime scene investigation began, in his view, now. The bodies of the victims had been removed. Holmberg was there by himself after the two remaining techs had said goodnight and left. They had photographed the victims and measured blood splatter on the walls and conferred about "splatter distribution areas" and "droplet velocity." Holmberg had not paid much attention to the technical examination. The crime scene techs' findings would be compiled in a report which would reveal in detail where the killer had stood in relation to his victims, and at what distance, in which order the shots had been fired, and which fingerprints might be of interest. But for Holmberg it was of no interest at all. The technical examination would not contain a syllable about who the killer was or what motive he or she—a woman was now the prime suspect—might have had for the murders. Those were the questions he now had to try to answer.

Holmberg went into the bedroom. He put a worn briefcase

on a chair and took out a Dictaphone, a digital camera, and a
notebook.

He began by going through the chest of drawers behind the
bedroom door. The top two drawers contained women's
underwear, sweaters, and a jewellery box. He arranged each
object on the bed and scrutinized the jewellery box. He did not
think it contained any pieces of great value. In the bottom
drawer he found two photograph albums and two folders containing household accounts. He turned on his tape recorder.

"Confiscation protocol for Björneborgsvägen 8B. Bedroom,
chest of drawers, bottom bureau drawer. Two bound photograph albums, size A4. One folder with black spine marked
HOUSEHOLD and one folder with blue spine marked FINANCIAL
DOCUMENTS containing information about a mortgage and
loans for the apartment. A small box containing handwritten
letters, postcards, and personal items."

He carried the objects to the hall and placed them in a suitcase. He continued with the drawers in the bedside tables on
each side of the double bed, finding nothing of interest. He
opened the wardrobes and sorted through clothes, feeling in
each pocket and in the shoes to check for any forgotten or hidden objects, and then turned his attention to the shelves at the
top of the wardrobes. He opened boxes and small storage containers. Every so often he found papers or items that he would
include for various reasons in the confiscation inventory.

There was a desk in one corner of the bedroom. It was a
very small home office with a desktop Compaq computer and
an old monitor. Under the desk was a two-drawer filing cabinet and on the floor next to the desk stood a low shelf unit.
Holmberg knew that it would be in this home office that he
would probably make the most important finds—to the extent
that there was anything to find—and so he saved the desk for
last. Instead he went into the living room and continued the
crime scene inspection. He opened the glass-fronted cabinet
and examined each bowl, each drawer, each shelf. Then he

turned his attention to the large bookcase along the outer wall and the wall of the bathroom. He took a chair and began at the top, checking whether anything was hidden on top of the bookcase. Then he went down it shelf by shelf, quickly picking out stacks of books and going through them, also checking whether anything was concealed behind them on the shelves. After forty-five minutes he put the last book back on the shelf. On the living-room table was a neat stack of books. He turned on the tape recorder.

"From the bookcase in the living room. A book by Mikael Blomkvist, *The Mafia's Banker*. A book in German entitled *Der Staat und die Autonomen*, a book in Swedish with the title *Revolutionary Terrorism*, and an English book *Islamic Jihad*."

He included the book by Blomkvist because its author had turned up in the preliminary investigation. The last three works were perhaps less obvious. Holmberg had no idea whether the murders were related to any form of political activity—or indeed whether Svensson or Johansson was politically involved—or whether the books were merely indicative of a general interest in politics as part of their academic or journalistic work. On the other hand, if two dead bodies were found in an apartment where there were books about terrorism, he was going to make note of the fact. He placed the books in the suitcase with the other items.

Then he looked through the drawers in an antique desk. On top of the desk was a CD player, and the drawers contained a great number of CDs. Holmberg spent half an hour opening every CD case and verifying that the contents matched the cover. He found about ten CDs that had no label, and were probably burned at home or were possibly pirated copies; he inserted the ones without labels into the CD player to check that they were not storing anything besides music. He examined the TV shelf nearest the bedroom door, where there was a large collection of videocassettes. He test-played several of them. They seemed to be everything from action movies to a hodgepodge of taped news programmes and reports from *Cold Facts, Insider,* and *Assignment Scrutiny.* He added thirty-six videocassettes to the inventory. Then he went to the kitchen, opened a thermos of coffee, and took a short break before he went on with his search.

From a shelf in a kitchen cupboard he gathered a number of jars and medicine bottles. They too were placed in a plastic bag and added to the confiscated material. He picked out food-stuffs from the pantry and refrigerator and opened every jar, coffee package, and recorked bottle. In a pot sitting on the win-dowsill he found 1,220 kronor plus some receipts. From the bathroom he took nothing, but he did observe that the laun-dry basket was overflowing. He went through all the clothing. He took coats out of a closet in the hall and searched in every pocket.

He found Svensson's wallet in the inner pocket of a sports jacket and added it to the inventory of confiscated items. Svens-son had a membership card to the Friskis & Svettis gym chain, a Handelsbanken ATM card, and just under 400 kronor in cash. He found Johansson's handbag and spent a few minutes going through its contents. She also had a card to Friskis & Svettis, an ATM card, a Konsum co-op loyalty card, and a membership card to something called Club Horizon, which had a globe as its logo. He found about 2,500 kronor in cash, a relatively large but not unreasonable sum, given that they were on their way out of Stockholm for the holiday weekend. That there was money in their wallets did reduce the likelihood of their deaths being robbery-related.

"From Johansson's handbag found on the shelf above the coatrack in the hall. One ProPlan pocket diary, a separate address book, and a leather-bound black notebook."

Holmberg took another break for coffee and noted that for a change he had so far found nothing embarrassing or intimate in the Svensson-Johansson couple's home—no hidden sex aids, no scandalous underwear, no drawer full of pornographic videos, no marijuana cigarettes or any sign at all of other illegal substances. They seemed to be a normal couple, possibly (from a police standpoint) somewhat duller than average.

Finally he returned to the bedroom and sat down at the desk. He opened the top drawer. He soon found that the desk and shelf unit next to it contained extensive source and reference materials for Johansson's doctoral thesis "From Russia with Love." The material was neatly arranged, exactly like a police report, and he lost himself for a while in certain sections of the text. *Mia Johansson was good enough to be on the force,* he told himself. One section of the bookshelf was only half full and seemed to contain material belonging to Svensson, mainly press clippings of his own articles and others on subjects that had interested him.

Holmberg spent a while going through the computer and found that it held almost five gigabytes, everything from software to letters and downloaded articles and PDF files. Certainly he was not going to be able to read through it in one evening. He added the computer and assorted CDs and a Zip drive with about thirty disks to the confiscated items.

Then he sat brooding for a while. The computer contained Johansson's work, as far as he could see. Svensson was a journalist, and a computer ought to be his most important tool, but he did not even get email on the desktop. So he must have had a computer somewhere else. Holmberg got up and went through the apartment, thinking. In the hall there was a black backpack with some notebooks that belonged to Svensson and an empty compartment for a computer. He could not find a laptop anywhere in the apartment. He took the keys and went down to the courtyard and searched Johansson's car and then the apartment's basement storage area. He found no computer there either.

The strange thing about the dog is that it did not bark, my dear Watson.

He made a note that at least one computer seemed to be missing.

. . .

Bublanski and Faste met Ekström in his office at 6:30 p.m., soon after they returned from Lundagatan. Andersson, after calling in, had been sent to Stockholm University to interview Johansson's tutor about her doctoral thesis. Holmberg was still in Enskede, and Modig was running the crime scene investigation at Odenplan. Ten hours had passed since Bublanski was appointed leader of the investigative team, and seven hours since the hunt for Salander had begun.

"And who is Miriam Wu?" Ekström said.

"We don't know much about her yet. She has no criminal record. It'll be Faste's task to start looking for her first thing tomorrow morning. But as far as we could see, there's no sign that Salander lives at Lundagatan. For one thing, all the clothes in the wardrobe were the wrong size for her."

"And they weren't your typical clothes, either," Faste said.

"Meaning what?" Ekström asked.

"Well, let's just say they weren't the type of clothes you'd buy for Mother's Day."

"We know nothing about the Wu woman at present," Bublanski said.

"How much do you have to know, for God's sake? She has a closet full of whore outfits."

"Whore outfits?" Ekström said.

"Black leather, patent leather, corsets, and fetishist whips and sex toys in a drawer. They didn't look like cheap stuff, either."

"Are you saying that Miriam Wu is a prostitute?"

"We know nothing about Fröken Wu at this stage," Bublanski said a little more sharply.

"One of Salander's social welfare reports indicated a few years ago that she was involved in prostitution," Ekström said.

"And social welfare usually knows what they're talking about," Faste said.

"The social welfare report was not supported by any police reports," Bublanski said. "There was an incident in Tantolunden when she was sixteen or seventeen; she was in the company of a considerably older man. Later the same year she was arrested for being drunk in public. Again with a considerably older man."

"You mean that we shouldn't draw conclusions too hastily," Ekström said. "OK. But it strikes me that Johansson's thesis having been on trafficking and prostitution, there's a possibility that in her work she made contact with Salander and this Wu and in some way provoked them, and that this might somehow constitute a motive for murder."

"Johansson might have got in touch with Salander's guardian and started the whole merry-go-round," Faste said.

"That's possible," Bublanski said. "But the investigation will have to document that. The important thing for now is to find Salander. She's obviously no longer living on Lundagatan. That means we also have to find Wu and discover how she came to live in that apartment and what her relationship with Salander is."

"And how do we find Salander?"

"She's out there somewhere. The problem is that the only address she ever had was on Lundagatan. No change of address was filed."

"You're forgetting that she was also admitted to St. Stefan's and lived with various different foster families."

"I'm not forgetting." Bublanski checked his papers. "She had three separate foster families when she was fifteen. It didn't go well. From just before she turned sixteen until she was eighteen, she lived with a couple in Hägersten. Fredrik and Monika Gullberg. Andersson is going out to see them this evening when he's finished at the university."

"How are we doing on the press conference?" Faste said.

. . .

The mood in Berger's office at 7:00 that evening was grim. Blomkvist had been sitting silent and almost immobile ever since Inspector Bublanski had left. Eriksson had cycled over to Lundagatan to watch what was going on there. She reported that no-one seemed to have been arrested and that traffic was flowing once again. Cortez had called in to tell them that the police were now looking for a second unnamed woman. Berger told him the name.

Berger and Eriksson had talked through what needed to be done, but the immediate situation was complicated by the fact that Blomkvist and Berger knew what role Salander had played in the denouement of the Wennerström affair—in her capacity as elite-level hacker she had been Blomkvist's secret source. Eriksson had no knowledge of this and had never even heard Salander's name mentioned. So the conversation occasionally lapsed into cryptic silences.

"I'm going home," Blomkvist said, getting up abruptly. "I'm so tired I can't think straight. I've got to get some sleep. Tomorrow being Good Friday, I plan to sleep and go through papers. Malin, can you work over Easter?"

"Do I have any choice?"

"No. We'll start at noon on Saturday. Could we work at my place rather than in the office?"

"That would be fine."

"I'm thinking of revamping the approach that we decided on this morning. Now it's no longer just a matter of trying to find out if Dag's exposé had something to do with the murders. It's about working out, from the material, who murdered Dag and Mia."

Eriksson wondered how they were going to go about doing any such thing, but she said nothing. Blomkvist waved goodbye to the two of them and left without another word.

· · ·

At 7:15 Inspector Bublanski reluctantly followed Prosecutor Ekström onto the podium in the police press centre. Bublanski had absolutely no interest in being in the spotlight in front of a dozen TV cameras. He was almost panic-stricken to be the focus of such attention. He would never get used to or begin to enjoy seeing himself on television.

Ekström, on the other hand, moved with ease, adjusted his glasses, and adopted a suitably serious expression. He let the photographers take their pictures before he raised his hands and asked for quiet.

"I'd like to welcome you all to this somewhat hastily arranged press conference regarding the murders in Enskede late last night. We have some more information to share with you. My name is Prosecutor Richard Ekström, and this is Criminal Inspector Jan Bublanski of the County Criminal Police Violent Crimes Division, who is leading the investigation. I have a statement to read, and then there will be an opportunity for you to ask questions."

Ekström looked at the assembled journalists. The murders in Enskede were big news, and getting bigger. He was pleased to note that *Aktuellt, Rapport,* and TV4 were all there, and he recognized reporters from the TT wire service and the evening and morning papers. There were also quite a few reporters he did not recognize.

"As you know, two people were murdered in Enskede last night. A weapon was found at the crime scene, a Colt .45 Magnum. Today the National Forensics Laboratory established that this gun was the murder weapon. The owner of the weapon was identified, and we went looking for him today."

Ekström paused for effect.

"At 4:15 this afternoon the owner of the weapon was found dead in his apartment in the vicinity of Odenplan. He had been shot. He is believed to have been dead at the time of the killings in Enskede. The police"—Ekström here gestured towards Bublanski—"have reason to believe that the same person was responsible for all three murders."

A murmur broke out among the reporters. Several of them began talking in low voices on their mobile telephones. "Have you got a suspect?" a reporter from Swedish Radio called out.

Ekström raised his voice. "If you would refrain from interrupting my statement, we'll get to that. This evening a person has been named whom the police want to question in connection with these three murders."

"Will you give us his name, please?"

"It's not a he, but a she. The police are looking for a twenty-six-year-old woman who has a connection to the owner of the weapon, and whom we know to have been at the scene of the murders in Enskede."

Bublanski frowned and then looked sullen. They had reached the point in the agenda over which he and Ekström had disagreed, namely the question of whether they should name their suspect.

Ekström had maintained that according to all available documentation, Salander was a mentally ill, potentially violent woman and that something had apparently triggered a murderous rage. There was no guarantee that the violence was at an end, and therefore it was in the public interest that she be named and apprehended as soon as possible.

Bublanski held that there was reason to wait at least for results of the technical examination of Bjurman's apartment before the investigative team committed itself unequivocally to one approach. But Ekström had prevailed.

Ekström held up a hand to interrupt the buzzing of the assembled reporters. The revelation that a woman was being sought for three murders would go off like a bomb. He passed the microphone to Bublanski, who cleared his throat twice, adjusted his glasses, and stared hard at the paper with the wording they had agreed on.

"The police are searching for a twenty-six-year-old woman by the name of Lisbeth Salander. A photograph from the passport office will be distributed. We do not know where she is at present, but we believe that she is in the greater Stockholm area. The police would like the public's assistance in finding this woman as soon as possible. Lisbeth Salander is four feet eleven inches tall, with a slim build."

He took a deep, nervous breath. He could feel the dampness under his arms.

"Lisbeth Salander has previously been in the care of a psychiatric clinic and is regarded as dangerous to herself and to the public. We would emphasize that we cannot say unequivocally that she is the killer, but circumstances dictate that we question her immediately to ascertain what knowledge she may have about the murders in Enskede and at Odenplan."

"You can't have it both ways," shouted a reporter from an evening paper. "Either she's a murder suspect or she isn't."

Bublanski gave Ekström a helpless look.

"The police are investigating on a broad front, and of course we're looking at various scenarios. But there is reason to suspect the woman we have named, and the police consider it extremely urgent that she is taken into custody. She is a suspect due to forensic evidence which emerged during the investigation of the crime scene."

"What sort of evidence?" someone in the crowded room immediately asked.

"We are not going to go into it."

Several reporters started talking at once. Ekström held up his hand and pointed to a reporter from *Dagens Eko.* He had dealt with him before and regarded him as objective.

"Inspector Bublanski said that Fröken Salander had been in a psychiatric clinic. Why was that?"

"This woman had a . . . a troubled upbringing and encountered over the years a number of problems. She is under guardianship, and the person who owned the weapon was her guardian."

"Who is he?"

"The individual who was shot in his apartment at Odenplan.

At present we are withholding his name until his next of kin are notified."

"What motive did she have for the murders?"

Bublanski took the microphone and said, "We will not speculate as to possible motives."

"Does she have a police record?"

"Yes."

Then came a question from a reporter with a deep, distinctive voice that could be heard over the crowd.

"Is she dangerous to the public?"

Ekström hesitated for a moment. Then he said: "We have reports which indicate that she could be considered prone to violence in stressful situations. We are issuing this statement because we want to get in touch with her as soon as possible."

Bublanski bit his lower lip.

Criminal Inspector Sonja Modig was still in Advokat Bjurman's apartment at 9:00 that evening. She had called home to explain the situation to her husband. After eleven years of marriage he had accepted that her job was never going to be nine to five. She was sitting at Bjurman's desk and reading through the papers that she had found in the drawers when she heard a knock on the door and turned to see Officer Bubble balancing two cups of coffee on his notebook, with a blue bag of cinnamon rolls from the local kiosk in his other hand. Wearily she waved him in.

"What don't you want me to touch?" Bublanski said.

"The techs have finished in here. They're working on the kitchen and the bedroom. The body's still in there."

Bublanski pulled up a chair and sat down. Modig opened the bag and took out a roll.

"Thanks. I was having such caffeine withdrawal I thought I'd die."

They munched quietly.

Modig licked her fingers and said, "I heard things didn't go so well at Lundagatan."

"There was nobody there. There were unopened letters for Salander, but someone called Miriam Wu lives there. We haven't found her yet either."

"Who is she?"

"Don't really know. Faste is working on her background. She was added to the contract about a month ago, but she just seems to be someone who lives in the apartment. I think Salander moved without filing a change of address."

"Maybe she planned all this."

"What? A triple murder?" Bublanski shook his head dejectedly. "What a mess this is turning into. Ekström insisted on holding a press conference, and now we're going to get it in the neck from the media. Have you found anything?"

"Apart from Bjurman's body in the bedroom, you mean? We found the empty box for the Magnum. It's being checked for prints. Bjurman has a file with copies of his monthly reports about Salander that he sent to the Guardianship Agency. If they are to be believed, Salander is a regular little angel, big time."

"Not him too," Bublanski said.

"Not him too what?"

"Another admirer of Fröken Salander."

Bublanski summed up what he had learned from Armansky and Blomkvist. Modig listened without interrupting. When he finished, she ran her fingers through her hair and rubbed her eyes.

"That sounds completely absurd," she said.

Bublanski tugged on his lower lip. Modig glanced at him and had to suppress a smile. He had a rough-chiselled face that looked almost brutal. But when he was confused or unsure of something, his expression turned sullen. It was in those moments that she thought of him as Officer Bubble. She had never used the nickname to his face and did not know who had coined it. But it suited him perfectly.

"How sure are *we*?"

"The prosecutor seems sure. An APB went out nationally for Salander this evening," Bublanski said. "She spent the past year abroad, and it's possible she could try to leave again."

"But how sure are we?"

He shrugged. "We've taken people in for a lot less."

"Her prints were on the murder weapon in Enskede. Her guardian was murdered. Without trying to get ahead of things, I'm guessing it's the same weapon that was used here. We'll know tomorrow—the techs found a fairly intact bullet fragment in the bed frame."

"Good."

"There are some rounds for the revolver in the bottom desk drawer. Bullets with uranium cores and gold tips."

"Very useful."

"We have lots of paperwork that says Salander is unstable. Bjurman was her guardian and he owned the gun."

"Mmm . . . ," Bublanski said glumly.

"We have a link between Salander and the couple in Enskede—Mikael Blomkvist."

"Mmm . . . ," he said again.

"You don't sound convinced."

"I can't get a clear line on Salander. The paperwork says one thing, but Armansky and Blomkvist say something else. According to the paperwork she is a developmentally disabled near-psychopath. According to the two men who have worked with her, she's a skilled researcher. That's a huge discrepancy. We have no motive for Bjurman and nothing to say that she knew the couple in Enskede."

"How much of a motive does a psychotic nutcase need?"

"I haven't been in the bedroom yet. How does it look?"

"I found the body prostrate against the bed. He was kneeling on the floor as if he were saying his prayers. He's naked. Shot in the back of the neck."

"One shot, just like in Enskede?"

"As far as I could see. It seems that Salander, if she's the one who did it, forced him onto his knees by the bed before she fired. The bullet went up through the back of his head and exited through his face."

"Like an execution, then."

"Precisely."

"I was thinking . . . somebody must have heard the shot."

"His bedroom overlooks the rear courtyard, and the neighbours above and below had left for the holiday. The window was closed. Besides, she used a pillow to muffle the sound."

"Smart thinking."

At that moment Gunnar Samuelsson from forensics stuck his head in the door.

"Hi, Bubble," he said, and then turned to his colleague. "Modig, we were thinking of removing the body, so we turned him over. There's something you ought to take a look at."

They all went into the bedroom. Bjurman's body had been placed on its back on a wheeled stretcher, the first stop on the way to the pathologist. There was no doubt about the cause of death. His forehead bore a wound four inches across, and a large part of his skull was hanging by a flap of skin. The blood splattered across the bed and the wall told the tale.

Bublanski pouted.

"What are we supposed to be looking at?" Modig asked.

Samuelsson lifted the plastic sheet which covered Bjurman's lower body. Bublanski put on his glasses when he and Modig stepped closer to read the text tattooed on Bjurman's abdomen. The letters were irregular and clumsy—obviously whoever wrote them was a novice tattoo artist—but the message could not have been clearer: I AM A SADISTIC PIG, A PERVERT, AND A RAPIST.

Modig and Bublanski looked at each other in astonishment.

"Are we possibly looking at a motive?" Modig said at last.

. . .

Blomkvist bought a pasta meal from the 7-Eleven on his way home and put the paper carton in the microwave as he undressed and stood under the shower for three minutes. He got a fork and ate standing up, right out of the carton. He was hungry, but he had no appetite for food; he just wanted to take it on board as fast as he could. When it was finished he opened a Vestfyn Pilsner beer and drank it straight from the bottle.

Without turning on a lamp he stood by the window overlooking Gamla Stan for more than twenty minutes, while he tried to stop thinking.

Twenty-four hours ago he had been at his sister's house when Svensson had called him on his mobile. He and Johansson had still been alive.

Blomkvist had not slept for thirty-six hours, and the days when he could skip a night's sleep with impunity were long gone. And he knew that he would not be able to sleep without thinking about what he had seen. The images from Enskede felt ingrained in his memory for all time.

Finally he turned off his mobile and crept under the covers. At 11:00 he was still awake. He got up and brewed some coffee. He put on the CD player and listened to Debbie Harry singing "Maria." He wrapped himself in a blanket and sat on the living-room sofa and drank coffee while he worried about Salander.

What did he actually know about her? Hardly anything.

She had a photographic memory and she was a hell of a hacker. He knew that she was a peculiar, introverted woman who didn't like to talk about herself, and that she had absolutely no trust in authority of any kind.

She could be viciously violent. He owed his life to that.

But he had had no idea that she had been declared incompetent or was under guardianship, or that she had spent any part of her teenage years in a psychiatric clinic.

He had to choose whose side he was on.

Sometime after midnight he decided that he couldn't accept the police's assumption that she had murdered Svensson and

Johansson. At the very least, he owed her a chance to explain herself before he passed judgment.

He had no idea when he nodded off, but at 4:30 a.m. he woke up on the sofa. He staggered into the bedroom and fell instantly back to sleep.

CHAPTER 16

Good Friday, March 25– Easter Saturday, March 26

Eriksson leaned back into Blomkvist's sofa. Without thinking, she put her feet up on the coffee table—exactly as she would have done at home—and quickly took them off again. Blomkvist gave her a smile.

"That's OK," he said. "Make yourself at home."

She grinned and put her feet up again.

On Good Friday Blomkvist had brought the copies of Svensson's papers from the *Millennium* offices to his apartment. He had laid out the material on the floor of the living room, and he and Eriksson had spent eight hours going through emails, notes, jottings in Svensson's notebook, and above all the manuscript of the book.

On Saturday morning Annika Giannini had come to see her brother. She brought the evening newspapers from the day before with their glaring headlines and a huge reproduction of Salander's passport photograph on the front page. One read:

WANTED FOR
TRIPLE MURDER

The other had opted for the more sensational headline:

POLICE HUNT
PSYCHOTIC MASS MURDERER

They talked for an hour, during which Blomkvist explained his relationship with Salander and why he couldn't believe that she was guilty. Finally he asked his sister whether she would consider representing Salander if or when she was caught.

"I've represented women in various cases of violence and abuse, but I'm not really a criminal defence lawyer," she said.

"You're the shrewdest lawyer I know, and Lisbeth is going to need somebody she can trust. I think in the end she would accept you."

Annika thought for a while before reluctantly agreeing to at least have a discussion with Salander if they ever got to that stage.

At 1:00 on Saturday afternoon, Inspector Modig called and asked if she could come over to pick up Salander's shoulder bag. The police had evidently opened and read the letter he sent to Salander's address on Lundagatan.

Modig arrived only twenty minutes later, and Blomkvist asked her to have a seat with Eriksson at the table in the living room. He went into the kitchen and took the bag down from the shelf next to the microwave. He hesitated a moment, then opened the bag and took out the hammer and the Mace canister. *Withholding evidence.* Mace was an illegal weapon and possession was a punishable offence. The hammer would only serve to support those who believed in Salander's violent tendencies. That wasn't necessary, Blomkvist thought.

He offered Modig some coffee.

"May I ask you some questions?" the inspector said.

"Please."

"In your letter to Salander which my colleagues found at

Lundagatan, you wrote that you are in her debt. What exactly did you mean by that?"

"Lisbeth Salander did me an enormous favour."

"What manner of favour was that?"

"It was a favour strictly between her and me, which I don't intend to discuss."

Modig looked at him intently. "This is a murder investigation we're carrying out here."

"And I hope that you will catch the bastard who killed Dag and Mia as soon as possible."

"You don't think Salander is that killer?"

"No, I do not."

"In that case, who do you think did shoot your friends?"

"I don't know. But Dag was intending to expose a large number of people who had a great deal to lose. One of them could be the killer."

"And why would such a person also shoot the lawyer, Nils Bjurman?"

"I don't know. At least not yet."

His gaze was steady with his own conviction. Modig suddenly smiled. She knew that he was nicknamed Kalle Blomkvist after the detective in Astrid Lindgren's books. Now she understood why.

"But you intend to find out?"

"If I can. You can tell that to Inspector Bublanski."

"I'll do that. And if Salander gets in touch, I hope you'll let us know."

"I don't expect her to contact me and confess that she's guilty of the murders, but if she does I'll do everything I can to persuade her to give herself up. In that case I would support her in any way I can—she's going to need a friend."

"And if she says she's not guilty?"

"Then I just hope she can shed some light on what happened."

"Herr Blomkvist, just between us and off the record, I hope

you realize that Lisbeth Salander has to be apprehended. Don't do anything stupid if she gets in touch with you. If you're wrong and she is responsible for these killings, it could be extremely dangerous for you."

Blomkvist nodded.

"I hope we won't have to put you under surveillance. You know, of course, that it is illegal to give help to a fugitive. Aiding and abetting anyone wanted for murder is a serious offence."

"For my part, I hope that you will devote some time to looking at the possibility that Salander had nothing to do with these killings."

"We will. Next question. Do you happen to know what sort of computer Dag Svensson worked on?"

"He had a secondhand Mac iBook 500, white, with a fourteen-inch screen. Just like mine but with a larger display." Blomkvist pointed to his machine on the table next to them.

"Do you have any idea where he kept it?"

"He usually carried it in a black bag. I assume it's in his apartment."

"It's not. Could it be at the office?"

"No. I've been through his desk and it definitely isn't there." They sat in silence for a moment.

"Do I take it that Dag's computer is missing?" Blomkvist said at last.

Blomkvist and Eriksson had made a list of the people who might theoretically have had a motive for killing Svensson. Each name had been written on large sheets of paper that Blomkvist taped up on his living-room wall. All of them were men, either johns or pimps, and they all appeared in the book. By 8:00 that night they had thirty-seven names, of which thirty were readily identified. Seven had been given pseudonyms in Svensson's text. Twenty-one of the men identified were johns who on various occasions had exploited one or another of the girls. The practical problem—from the point of view of whether they should publish the book—was that many of the claims were based on information that only Svensson or Johansson possessed. A writer who knew—inevitably—less about the subject would have to verify the information independently.

They estimated that about 80 percent of the existing text could be published without any great problems, but a good deal of legwork was going to have to be done before *Millennium* could risk publishing the remaining 20 percent. They didn't doubt the accuracy of the contents, but weren't sufficiently familiar with the detailed work behind the book's most explosive findings. If Svensson were still alive they would have been able to publish without question—he and Johansson could have easily dealt with and refuted any objections.

Blomkvist looked out the window. Night had fallen and it was raining. He asked if Eriksson wanted more coffee. She did not.

"We've got the manuscript under control," she said. "But we aren't any closer to pinpointing Dag and Mia's killer."

"It could be one of the names on the wall," Blomkvist said.

"It could be somebody who doesn't have anything whatsoever to do with the book. Or it could be your girlfriend."

"Lisbeth," Blomkvist said.

Eriksson stole a glance at him. She had worked at *Millennium* for eighteen months. She joined right in the middle of the chaos of the Wennerström affair. After years of temp jobs, *Millennium* was her first full-time position. She was doing splendidly. Working at *Millennium* was status. She had a close bond with Berger and the rest of the staff, but she had always felt a little uncomfortable in Blomkvist's company. There was no clear reason for it, but of all the people at *Millennium*, Blomkvist was the one she found the most reserved and unapproachable.

During the past year he had been coming in late and sitting in his office by himself a lot, or in Berger's office. He had often been away, and during her first few months at the magazine she seemed to see him more frequently on some sofa in a TV studio than in real life. He did not encourage small talk, and from the comments she heard from other staff members, he appeared to have changed. He was quieter and harder to talk to.

"If I'm going to work on trying to figure out why Dag and Mia were shot, I'll have to know more about Salander. I don't really know where to start, if . . ."

She left the sentence hanging. Blomkvist looked at her. Finally he sat down in the armchair at ninety degrees to her and put his feet up next to hers.

"Do you like working at *Millennium*?" he said, disconcertingly. "I mean, you've been working for us for a year and a half now, but I've been running around so much that we've never had a chance to get to know each other."

"I like working there a lot," she said. "Are you happy with me?"

"Erika and I have said over and over that we've never had such a valuable managing editor. We think you're a real find. And forgive me for not telling you as much before now."

Eriksson smiled contentedly. Praise from the great Blomkvist was extremely gratifying.

"But that's not what I was actually asking about," she said.

"You're wondering about Lisbeth Salander's links with *Millennium*."

"You've never said anything, and Erika is pretty tight-lipped about her."

Blomkvist met her gaze. He and Berger might have complete confidence in her, but there were things he just could not discuss.

"I agree with you," he said. "If we're going to dig into the murders, you're going to need more information. I'm a first-hand source, and also the link between Lisbeth and Dag and

Mia. Go ahead and ask me questions, and I'll answer them as best I can. And when I can't answer, I'll say so."

"Why all the secrecy? Who is Lisbeth Salander, and what does she have to do with *Millennium* in the first place?"

"This is how it is. Two years ago I hired her as a researcher for an extremely complicated job. That's the problem. I can't tell you what she worked on for me. Erika knows what it was, and she's bound by confidentiality."

"Two years ago . . . that was before you cracked Wennerström. Should I assume that she was doing research connected with that case?"

"No, you shouldn't assume that. I'm neither going to confirm or deny it. But I can tell you that I hired Lisbeth for an altogether different project and that she did an outstanding job."

"OK, that's when you were living like a hermit in Hedestad, as far as I've heard. And Hedestad didn't exactly go unnoticed on the media map that summer. Harriet Vanger resurfacing from the dead and all that. Strangely enough, we at *Millennium* haven't written a word about her resurrection."

"The reason we didn't write about Harriet is that she's on our board. We'll let the rest of the media scrutinize her. And as far as Salander is concerned, take my word for it when I tell you that what she did for me in the earlier project has absolutely no bearing on what happened in Enskede."

"I do take your word for it."

"Let me give you a piece of advice. Don't guess. Don't jump to conclusions. Just accept that she worked for me and that I cannot and will not discuss what it involved. She did something else for me. During that time she saved my life. Literally."

Eriksson looked up in surprise. She had not heard a word about that at *Millennium*.

"So that means you know her rather well."

"As well as anyone can know Lisbeth Salander, I suppose," Blomkvist said. "She is the most introverted person I've ever met."

He sprang to his feet and looked out into the darkness.

"I don't know if you want one, but I think I'll make myself a vodka and lime juice," he said at last.

"Sounds much better than another cup of coffee."

Armansky spent the Easter weekend at his cabin on the island of Blidö thinking about Salander. His children were grown up and had chosen not to spend the holiday with their parents. Ritva, his wife of twenty-five years, noticed that he seemed sometimes far away. He would subside into silent brooding and answered absentmindedly when she spoke to him. He drove every day to the nearest shop to buy the newspapers. He would sit by the window on the veranda and read about the hunt for Salander.

Armansky was disappointed that he had so terribly misjudged her. He had known for several years that she had mental problems. The idea that she could be violent and seriously injure someone who was threatening her did not surprise him. The idea that she had attacked her guardian—whom she would without a doubt perceive as someone who meddled in her affairs—was understandable. She viewed any attempt to control her life as provocative and possibly hostile.

On the other hand, he could not for the life of him understand what would have prompted her to murder two people who, according to all available information, were utterly unknown to her.

Armansky kept waiting for a link to be established between Salander and the couple in Enskede. But no such link was reported in the newspapers; instead there was speculation that the mentally ill woman must have had some sort of breakdown.

Twice he telephoned Inspector Bublanski and asked about developments, but not even the director of the investigation could give him a connection. Blomkvist knew both Salander and the couple, but there was nothing to suggest that Salander knew or had even heard of Svensson and Johansson. If the murder weapon had not had her fingerprints on it, and had there not been an unchallengable link to Bjurman, the police would have been fumbling in the dark.

"So let's sum up," Eriksson said. "The assignment is to find out whether Salander murdered Dag and Mia, as the police claim. Where to begin?"

"Look at it as an excavation job. We don't have to do our own police investigation. But we do have to stay on top of what the police uncover and worm out of them what they know. It'll be just like any other job, except that we don't necessarily have to publish everything we find out."

"But if Salander is the killer, there has to be a significant connection between her and Dag and Mia. And the only connection so far is you."

"And in fact I'm no connection at all. I haven't talked to Lisbeth in more than a year. How could she have known that—"

Blomkvist suddenly stopped. Lisbeth Salander: the world-class hacker. It dawned on him that his iBook was full of correspondence with Svensson, as well as various versions of the book and a file containing Johansson's thesis. He couldn't know if Salander was checking his computer. But what possible reason could she have to shoot Svensson and Johansson? What they were working on was a report about violence against women, and Salander should have encouraged them in every way. If Blomkvist knew her at all.

"You look like you've thought of something," Eriksson said.

He had no intention of telling her about Salander's talents with computers.

"No, I'm just tired and going a little off the rails," he said.

"Well, now, your Lisbeth is suspected of killing not only

Dag and Mia but also her guardian, and in that case the connection is crystal clear. What do you know about him?"

"Not a thing. I never heard his name; I didn't even know she had a guardian."

"But the likelihood of someone else having murdered all three of them is negligible. Even if someone killed Dag and Mia because of their story, there wouldn't be the slightest reason for whoever it was to kill Salander's guardian as well."

"I know, and I've worried myself sick over it. But I can imagine one scenario, at least, where an outside person might murder Dag and Mia as well as Lisbeth's guardian."

"And what's that?"

"Let's say that Dag and Mia were murdered because they were rooting around in the sex trade and Lisbeth had somehow gotten involved as a third party. If Bjurman was Lisbeth's guardian, then there's a chance that she confided in him and he thereby became a witness to or obtained knowledge of something that subsequently led to his murder."

"I see what you mean," Eriksson said. "But you don't have a grain of evidence for that theory."

"No, not one grain."

"So what do you think? Is she guilty or not?"

Blomkvist thought for a long time.

"You're asking me if she is capable of murder? The answer is yes. Salander has a violent streak. I've seen her in action when . . ."

"When she saved your life?"

Blomkvist looked at her, then said, "I can't tell you the circumstances. But there was a man who was going to kill me and he was just about to succeed. She stepped in and beat him senseless with a golf club."

"And you haven't told the police any of this?"

"Absolutely not. And this has to remain between you and me." He gave her a sharp look. "Malin, I have to be able to trust you on this."

"I won't tell anyone about anything we discuss. You're not just my boss—I like you too, and I don't want to do anything that would hurt you."

"I'm sorry."

"Stop apologizing."

He laughed and then turned serious again. "I'm convinced that if it had been necessary, she would have killed that man to protect me. But at the same time I believe she's quite rational. Peculiar, yes, but completely rational according to her own scheme of things. She used violence because she had to, not because she wanted to. To kill someone, she would have to be exceedingly threatened or provoked."

He thought for a while. Eriksson watched him patiently.

"I can't explain the lawyer. I don't know a thing about him. But I just can't imagine her being threatened or provoked—at all—by Dag and Mia. It's not possible."

They sat quietly for a long time. Eriksson looked at her watch and saw that it was 9:30.

"It's late. I have to be getting home."

"It's been a long day. We can go on sifting tomorrow. No, leave the dishes. I'll take care of it."

On the Saturday night before Easter, Armansky lay awake, listening to Ritva sleeping. He could not make sense of the drama. In the end he got up, put on his slippers and dressing gown, and went into the living room. The air was cool and he put a few pieces of wood in the soapstone stove, opened a beer, and sat looking out at the dark waters of the Furusund channel.

What do I know?

Salander was unpredictable. No doubt about that.

Something had happened in the winter of 2003, when she stopped working for him and disappeared on her year-long sabbatical abroad. Blomkvist was somehow mixed up in her sudden departure—but he didn't know what had happened to her either.

She came back and had come to see him. Claimed that she was "financially independent," which presumably meant that she had enough to get by for a while.

She had been regularly to see Palmgren. She had not been in touch with Blomkvist.

She had shot three people, two apparently unknown to her. *It doesn't make any sense.*

Armansky took a gulp of his beer and lit a cigarillo. He had a guilty conscience, and that contributed to his bad mood.

When Bublanski had been to see him, Armansky had unhesitatingly given him as much information as he could so that Salander could be caught. He had no doubt that she had to be caught—and the sooner the better. Armansky was a realist. If the police told him that a person was suspected of murder, the chances were that it was true. So Salander was guilty.

But the police weren't taking into account whether she might have felt that her actions were justified—or whether there might be some mitigating circumstance or a reasonable explanation for her having gone berserk. The police were required to catch her and prove that she had fired the shots, not dig into her psyche. They would be satisfied if they could find a motive, but failing that, they were ready to call it an act of insanity. He shook his head. He could not accept that she was an insane mass murderer. Salander never did anything against her will or without thinking through the consequences. *Peculiar—yes. Insane—no.*

So there had to be an explanation, no matter how obscure it might appear to anyone who did not know her.

At around 2:00 in the morning he made a decision.

CHAPTER 17

Easter Sunday,
March 27–
Tuesday, March 29

Armansky got up early on Sunday after hours of worrying. He padded downstairs without waking Ritva and made coffee and a sandwich. Then he opened his laptop.

He opened the report form that Milton Security used for personal investigations. He typed in as many facts as he could think of about Salander's personality.

At 9:00 Ritva came down and poured herself coffee. She wondered what he was doing. He gave a noncommittal answer and kept writing. He was going to be a lost cause all day.

Blomkvist turned out to be wrong, probably because it was Easter weekend and police headquarters was still relatively empty. It took until Sunday morning before the media discovered that he was the one who had found Svensson and Johansson. The first to call was a reporter from *Aftonbladet*, an old friend.

"Hello, Blomkvist. It's Nicklasson."

"Hello, Nicklasson."

"So you were the one who found the couple in Enskede."

Blomkvist confirmed that was true.

"My source tells me they worked for *Millennium*."

"Your source is part right and part wrong. Dag Svensson was doing a freelance report for *Millennium*. Mia Johansson wasn't working for us."

"Oh boy. This is a hell of a story, you've got to admit."

"I know," Blomkvist said wearily.

"Why haven't you released a statement?"

"Dag was a colleague and a friend. We thought it would be best at least to tell his and Mia's relatives what happened before we put out any story."

Blomkvist knew that he wouldn't be quoted on that point.

"That makes sense. What was Dag working on?"

"A story we commissioned."

"What about?"

"What sort of scoop are you planning at *Aftonbladet*?"

"So it was a scoop."

"Screw you, Nicklasson."

"Oh, come on, Blomman. You think the murders had anything to do with the story Dag Svensson was working on?"

"You call me Blomman one more time, and I'm hanging up and not talking to you for the rest of the year."

"All right, I'm sorry. Do you think Dag was murdered because of his work as an investigative journalist?"

"I have no idea why Dag was murdered."

"Did the story he was working on have anything to do with Lisbeth Salander?"

"No. Nothing whatsoever."

"Did Dag know that nutcase?"

"I have no idea."

"Dag wrote a bunch of articles on computer crime recently. Was that the type of story he was writing for *Millennium*?"

You just won't give up, will you? Blomkvist thought. He was about to tell Nicklasson to piss off when he sat bolt upright in bed. He had just had two great ideas. Nicklasson started to say something else.

"Hold on, Nicklasson. Don't move. I'll be right back."

Blomkvist got up and held his hand over the mouthpiece. He was suddenly on a completely different planet.

Ever since the murders, he had been racking his brains about how he could find a way to get in touch with Salander. There was a chance—a rather good chance—that she would read what he said to the newspapers, wherever she was. If he denied that he knew her, she might interpret that to mean that he had abandoned her or betrayed her. If he defended her, then other people would interpret it as meaning that he knew more about the murders than he had said. But if he made a statement in just the right way, it might give Salander an impulse to reach him.

"Sorry, I'm back. What did you say?"

"Was Dag writing about computer crime?"

"If you want a sound bite from me, I'll give you one."

"Go for it."

"Only if you quote me word for word."

"How else would I quote you?"

"I'd rather not answer that question."

"So what do you want to say?"

"I'll email it to you in fifteen minutes."

"What?"

"Check your email," Blomkvist said and hung up.

He went over to his desk and booted up his iBook. He opened Word and sat there concentrating for two minutes before he started writing.

Millennium's editor in chief, Erika Berger, is deeply shaken by the murder of freelance journalist and colleague Dag Svensson. She hopes that the murders will soon be solved.

It was *Millennium*'s publisher, Mikael Blomkvist, who discovered Dag Svensson and his girlfriend murdered last Wednesday night.

"Dag Svensson was a fantastically gifted journalist and a person I liked a lot. He had proposed several ideas for articles. Among other things, he was working on a major investigation into illegal computer hacking," Mikael Blomkvist tells *Aftonbladet.*

Neither Blomkvist nor Berger will speculate about who might be guilty of the murders, or what motive might lie behind them.

Blomkvist picked up the telephone and called Berger.

"Hi, Ricky. You've just been interviewed by *Aftonbladet.*"

"Do tell."

He read her the quote.

"How come?"

"Every word is true. Dag has worked freelance for ten years, and one of his specializations was computer security. I discussed it with him many times, and we were considering running an article by him on it when we finished the trafficking story. And do you know anyone else who is interested in hacking?"

Berger realized what he was trying to do.

"Smart, Micke. Damned smart. OK. Run it."

Nicklasson called back a minute after he got Blomkvist's email.

"That's not much of a sound bite."

"That's all you're getting, and it's more than any other paper will get. You run the whole quote or nothing."

Blomkvist went back to his iBook. He thought for a minute and then wrote:

Dear Lisbeth,

I'm writing this letter and leaving it on my hard drive knowing that sooner or later you'll read it. I remember

the way you took over Wennerström's hard drive two
years ago and suspect that you also made sure to hack
my machine. It's clear that you don't want to have anything to do with me now. I don't intend to ask why and
you don't have to explain.

The events of the past few days have linked us again,
whether you like it or not. The police are saying that
you murdered two people I was very fond of. I was the
one who discovered Dag and Mia minutes after they
were shot. I don't think it was you who shot them. I certainly hope it wasn't. The police claim you're a psychotic killer, but that would mean that I totally
misjudged you or that you've changed dramatically
over the past year. And if you're not the murderer, then
the police are chasing the wrong person.

In this situation I should probably urge you to turn yourself in to the police, but I suspect I'd be wasting my
breath. Sooner or later you're going to be found, and
when that happens you're going to need a friend. You
may not want to have anything to do with me, but I
have a sister called Annika Giannini and she's a lawyer.
The best. She's willing to represent you if you get in
touch with her. You can trust her.

As far as *Millennium* is concerned, we've begun our
own investigation into why Dag and Mia were murdered. What I'm doing right now is putting together a
list of the people who had reason to want to silence
Dag. I don't know if I'm on the right track, but I'm going
to check the list one person at a time.

One problem I have is that I don't understand how Nils
Bjurman fits into the picture. He isn't mentioned anywhere in Dag's material, and I can't fathom any connection between him and Dag and Mia.

Help me. Please. What's the connection?

Mikael.

P.S. You should get a new passport photo. That one doesn't do you justice.

He named the document [To Sally]. Then he created a folder that he named <Lisbeth Salander> and put an icon for it on the desktop of his iBook.

On Tuesday morning Armansky called a meeting in his office at Milton Security. He had brought in three people.

Johan Fräklund, a former criminal inspector with the Solna police, was the chief of Milton's operations unit. He had over-all responsibility for planning and analysis. Armansky had recruited him ten years earlier and had come to regard him, now in his early sixties, as one of the company's most valuable assets.

Armansky also called in Sonny Bohman and Niklas Hed-ström. Bohman too was a former policeman. He had received his training in the Norrmalm armed response squad in the eighties and then moved to the violent crimes division, where he had led a dozen dramatic investigations. During the ram-page of the "Laser Man" sniper in the early nineties, Bohman had been one of the key players, and in 1997 he had moved to Milton only after a great deal of persuasion and the offer of a significantly higher salary.

Niklas Hedström was regarded as a rookie. He had been trained at the police academy, but just before he was due to take his final exams he learned that he had a congenital heart defect. This not only required a major operation but also meant that his police career was already at an end.

Fräklund, who had been a contemporary of Hedström's father, had suggested to Armansky that they give him a chance.

Since there was a position free in the analysis unit, Armansky approved the recruitment, and he had never had cause to regret it. Hedström had worked for Milton for five years. He might lack field experience, but he stood out as a sharp-witted intellectual asset.

"Good morning, everyone. Take a seat and start reading," Armansky said. He handed out three folders with some fifty photocopied pages of press cuttings about the hunt for Salander, along with Armansky's three-page summary of her background. Hedström finished reading first and put the folder down. Armansky waited until Bohman and Fräklund were done.

"I presume none of you gentlemen has missed seeing the headlines in the papers over the weekend."

"Lisbeth Salander," Fräklund said in a gloomy voice.

Bohman shook his head.

Hedström stared into space with an inscrutable expression and the hint of a sad smile.

Armansky gave the trio a searching look.

"One of our employees," he said. "How well did you get to know her when she worked here?"

"I tried a little light banter with her once," Hedström said, again with a hint of a smile. "It didn't go so well. I thought she was going to bite my head off. She was a first-class sourpuss, and I hardly exchanged ten sentences with her."

"I found her seriously odd," Fräklund said.

Bohman shrugged. "She was a real pain to deal with. I knew she was weird, but not that she was this fucking crazy."

"She did things her own way," Armansky said. "She wasn't easy to handle. But I trusted her because she was the best researcher I've ever come across. She delivered results beyond expectation every time."

"I never understood that," Fräklund said. "I couldn't figure out how she could be so incredibly skilled and at the same time so hopeless socially."

"The explanation, of course, lies in her mental state," Armansky said, poking at one of the folders. "She was declared incompetent."

"I didn't have a clue about that," Hedström said. "I mean, she didn't wear a sign on her back. And you never said anything."

"No," Armansky said. "I didn't think she needed to be any more stigmatized than she already was. Everybody deserves a chance."

"And the result of that experiment is what we saw happen in Enskede," Bohman said.

"Could be," Armansky said.

He did not want to betray his weakness for Salander in front of these three professionals who were now watching him expectantly. They had adopted quite a neutral tone during the conversation, but Armansky knew that Salander was in fact detested by all three of them, as well as by the rest of the employees at Milton Security. He did not want to come across as soft or confused. It was important to present the matter in a way that created a measure of enthusiasm and professionalism.

"I've decided for the first time ever to utilize some of Milton's resources for a purely internal matter," he said. "It doesn't have to be a big expense in the budget, but I'm thinking of releasing you two, Bohman and Hedström, from your present duties. Your assignment, although I may be formulating it a bit vaguely, is to 'establish the truth' about Lisbeth Salander."

Both men gave Armansky a sceptical look.

"I want you, Fräklund, to lead and keep track of the investigation. I want to know what happened and what would have induced Salander to murder her guardian as well as the couple in Enskede. There has to be a rational explanation."

"Forgive my saying so, but this sounds like a job for the police," Fräklund said.

"No question," Armansky shot back. "But we have an advantage over the police. We knew Salander, and we have an insight into how she functions."

"Well, if you say so," Bohman said, sounding unsure. "I don't believe anyone here at the firm has any idea what went on in her little head."

"That doesn't matter," Armansky said. "Salander worked for Milton Security. In my view, we have a responsibility to establish the truth."

"Salander hasn't worked for us in . . . what is it, almost two years," Fräklund said. "I don't see us as responsible for what she may have done. And I don't think the police would appreciate it if we interfered in their investigation."

"On the contrary," Armansky said. This was his trump card, and he had to play it well.

"How's that?" Bohman wondered.

"Yesterday I had a couple of long conversations with the preliminary investigation leader, Prosecutor Ekström, and Criminal Inspector Bublanski, who's in charge of the investigation. Ekström is under pressure. This isn't some sort of showdown among gangsters; it's an event with enormous media potential in which a lawyer, a criminologist, and a journalist were all—it would appear—executed. I explained that since the prime suspect is a former employee of Milton Security, we have also decided to start an investigation of our own." Armansky paused to let this sink in before going on. "Ekström and I agree that the important thing right now is for Lisbeth Salander to be taken into custody as rapidly as possible—before she causes any more harm to herself or to others. Since we have more knowledge of her than the police do, we can contribute to the investigation. Ekström and I decided that you two"—he pointed at Bohman and Hedström—"will move over to Kungsholmen and be seconded to Bublanski's team."

All three of his employees looked astonished.

"Pardon me for asking a simple question . . . but we're only civilians," Bohman said. "Do the police really intend to let us into a murder investigation, just like that?"

"You'll be working under Bublanski, but you'll also report

to me. You will be given full access to the investigation. All the material we have and that you turn up will go to Bublanski. For the police, this means that his team will get free reinforcements. And none of you are 'only civilians.' You two, Fräklund and Bohman, worked for the police for longer than you've worked here, and even you, Hedström, went to the police academy."

"But it's against the principles—"

"Not at all. The police often bring civilian consultants into investigations, whether psychologists in sex crimes or inter-preters where foreigners are involved. You will simply partici-pate as civilian consultants with particular knowledge of the prime suspect."

Fräklund nodded slowly. "OK. Milton is joining the police investigation and trying to help catch Salander. Anything else?"

"Yes. Your principal assignment as far as Milton is con-cerned is to establish the truth. Nothing else. I want to know if Salander shot these three people—and if so, why."

"Is there any doubt about her guilt?" asked Hedström.

"The circumstantial evidence the police hold is very dam-aging to her. But I want to know whether there's another side to the story—whether there's some accomplice we don't know about, someone who may have been the one actually holding the gun, or whether there are any other as yet unknown cir-cumstances."

"It's going to be hard work to find mitigating circumstances in a triple murder," Fräklund said. "If that's what we're looking for, we'd have to suppose there's a possibility she's innocent. And I don't believe that."

"I don't either," Armansky said. "But your work will be to assist the police in every way and to help them take her into custody in the shortest time possible."

"Budget?" Fräklund said.

"Open. I want to be regularly updated on what this is cost-ing, and if it gets out of hand we'll shut it down. But assume that you'll be on this for a week at least, starting today. And since I'm the one here who knows Salander best, I should be one of the people you interview."

Modig hurtled down the corridor and made it into the con-ference room just as her colleagues had settled in their seats. She sat down next to Bublanski, who had gathered the whole investigative team for this meeting, including the preliminary investigation leader. Faste gave her an annoyed look and then took care of the introduction; he was the one who had asked for the meeting.

He had gone on burrowing through the years of confronta-tion between the social welfare bureaucracy and Salander—what he called the "psychopath trail"—and he had managed to assemble quite a body of material. He cleared his throat and turned to the man on his right.

"This is Dr. Peter Teleborian, head physician at St. Stefan's Psychiatric Clinic in Uppsala. He has been good enough to come down to Stockholm to assist in the investigation and to tell us what he knows about Lisbeth Salander."

Modig studied Dr. Teleborian. He was a short man with curly brown hair, steel-rimmed glasses, and a small goatee. He was casually dressed in a beige corduroy jacket, jeans, and a light-blue striped shirt buttoned at the neck. His features were sharp and his appearance boyish. Modig had come across Dr. Teleborian on several occasions but had never spoken to him. He had given a lecture on psychiatric disturbances when she was in her last term at the police academy, and on another occasion at a course he had spoken about psychopaths and psychopathic behaviour in young people. She had also attended the trial of a serial rapist when Teleborian was called as an expert witness. Dr. Teleborian was one of the best-known psychiatrists in Sweden. He had made a name for himself with his tough criticism of the cutbacks in psychiatric care that had resulted in the closure of mental hospitals. People who were obviously in need of care had been abandoned to the streets,

doomed to become homeless welfare cases. Since the assassination of Foreign Minister Anna Lindh,* Dr. Teleborian had
been a member of the government commission that reported
on the decline in psychiatric care.

Teleborian nodded to the group and poured mineral water
into his plastic cup.

"We'll have to see whether there's anything I can contribute," he began cautiously. "I hate being right in my predictions in situations like this."

"Your predictions?" Bublanski said.

"Yes. It's ironic. On the evening of the murders in Enskede,
I was on a TV panel discussing the time bomb that's ticking
almost everywhere in our society. It's terrible. I wasn't thinking
specifically of Lisbeth Salander just then, but I gave a number
of examples—with pseudonyms, of course—of patients who
quite simply ought to be in institutions rather than at liberty
on our streets. I would surmise that during this year alone the
police will have to solve half a dozen murder or manslaughter
cases where the killer is among this small group of patients."

"And you think that Lisbeth Salander is one of these
loonies?" Faste asked.

"*Loony* isn't a term we would use. Yet she is without doubt
one of these frayed individuals that I would not have let out
into society, were it up to me."

"Are you saying that she should have been locked up before
she committed a crime?" Modig asked. "That doesn't really accord
with the principles of a society governed by the rule of law."

Faste frowned and gave her a dirty look. Modig wondered
why Faste always seemed so hostile towards her.

*Anna Lindh was one of Sweden's most popular politicians, foreign min-
ister under Prime Minister Goran Persson from 1998 to 2003. She was assassinated in 2003 in a stabbing attack. Her alleged murderer confessed and was
sentenced to life in prison after a psychiatric evaluation. However, an appeals
court overturned the sentence in 2004, and the defendant was transferred from
prison to a closed psychiatric ward. Prosecutors reappealed to the Supreme
Court of Sweden, which has since reinstated the life sentence.

"You're perfectly right," Teleborian said, inadvertently coming to her rescue. "It's not compatible with a society based on the rule of law, at least not in its present form. It's a balancing act between respect for the individual and respect for the potential victims that a mentally ill person may leave in his wake. Every case is different, and each patient must be treated on an individual basis. It's inevitable that we in the psychiatric field also make mistakes and release people who shouldn't be out on the streets."

"Well, I don't think we need to go into social politics in great depth here," Bublanski said cautiously.

"Of course," Teleborian said. "We're dealing with a specific case. But let me just say that it's important for you all to understand that Lisbeth Salander is a sick person in need of care, just as any patient with a toothache or heart disease is in need of care. She can still get well, and she would have gotten well if she had received the care she needed when she was still treatable."

"So you weren't her doctor," Faste said.

"I'm one of many people who was involved with Lisbeth Salander's case. She was my patient in her early teens, and I was one of the doctors who evaluated her before it was decided to place her under guardianship when she turned eighteen."

"Could you give us a little background about her?" Bublanski asked. "What could have made her murder two people she didn't know, and what could have made her murder her guardian?"

Dr. Teleborian laughed.

"No, I can't tell you that. I haven't followed her development in several years, and I don't know what stage of psychosis she's in at present. But I can say without a shadow of a doubt that the couple in Enskede had to have been known to her."

"What makes you so sure?" Faste wanted to know.

"One of the failures in the treatment of Lisbeth Salander was that no complete diagnosis was ever established for her. That was because she was not receptive to treatment. She invariably refused to answer questions or participate in any form of therapy."

"So you don't actually know if she's sick or not," Modig said. "I mean, if there isn't any diagnosis."

"Look at it this way," Dr. Teleborian said. "I was given Lisbeth Salander just as she was about to turn thirteen. She was psychotic, showed obsessive behaviour, and was obviously suffering from paranoia. She was my patient for two years after she was committed to St. Stefan's. The reason for committing her was that throughout her childhood she had exhibited exceedingly violent behaviour towards schoolmates, teachers, and acquaintances. In repeated instances she was reported for assault. In every case that we know of, the violence was directed at people in her own circle, that is, against people she knew who said or did something that she perceived as an insult. There is no case of her ever having attacked a stranger. That's why I believe there must be a link between her and the couple in Enskede."

"Except for the attack in the tunnelbana when she was seventeen," Faste said.

"Well, on that occasion she was the one who was attacked and she was defending herself," Teleborian said. "Against, it should be said, a known sex offender. But it's also a good example of the way she behaves. She could have walked away or sought refuge among other passengers in the carriage. Instead she responded with aggravated assault. When she feels threatened she reacts with excessive violence."

"What's actually the matter with her?" Bublanski asked.

"As I said, we don't have a real diagnosis. I would say that she suffers from schizophrenia and is continually balancing on the brink of psychosis. She lacks empathy and in many respects can be described as a sociopath. It's surprising, frankly, that she has managed so well since she turned eighteen. She has been functioning in society, albeit under guardianship, for eight years without doing anything that led to a police report or arrest. But her prognosis—"

"Her prognosis?"

"During this entire time she has not received any treatment. My guess is that the illness we might have been able to treat and cure ten years ago is now a fixed part of her personality. I predict that when she is apprehended, she will not be given a prison sentence. She needs treatment."

"So why the hell did the district court decide to give her a free pass into society?" Faste asked.

"It should probably be viewed as a combination of things. She had a lawyer, an eloquent one, but it was also a manifestation of the current liberalization policies and cutbacks. It was a decision that I opposed when I was consulted by forensic medicine. But I had no say in the matter."

"But surely that kind of prognosis must be pretty much guesswork, don't you think?" Modig said. "You don't actually know what's been going on with her since she turned eighteen."

"It's more than a guess. It's based on my professional experience."

"Is she self-destructive?" Modig asked.

"You mean could I picture her committing suicide? No, I doubt that. She's more of an egomaniacal psychopath. It's all about her. Everyone else around her is unimportant."

"You said that she might react with excessive force," Faste said. "In other words, should we consider her to be dangerous?"

Dr. Teleborian looked at him for a long moment. Then he leaned forward and rubbed his forehead.

"You have no idea how difficult it is to say exactly how a person will react. I don't want Lisbeth Salander to be harmed when you apprehend her . . . but yes, in her case I would try to make sure the arrest is carried out with the utmost circumspection. If she is armed, there would be a very real risk that she will use the weapon."

CHAPTER 18

Tuesday, March 29– Wednesday, March 30

The three parallel investigations into the murders in Enskede churned on. Officer Bubble's investigation enjoyed the advantages of authority. On the surface, the solution seemed to lie within reach; they had a suspect and a murder weapon that was linked to the suspect. They had an ironclad connection to one victim and a possible connection via Blomkvist to the other two victims. For Bublanski it was now basically a matter of finding Salander and putting her in a cell in Kronoberg prison.

Armansky's investigation was formally subordinate to the police investigation, and he had his own agenda. His objective was somehow to watch out for Salander's interests—to discover the truth, preferably a truth in the form of a persuasively mitigating circumstance.

Millennium's investigation was the difficult one. The magazine lacked the resources of the police, obviously, and of Armansky's organization. Unlike the police, however, Blomkvist was not primarily interested in establishing a reasonable scenario for why Salander might have gone down to Enskede and murdered two of his friends. He had decided over the Easter weekend that he simply did not believe the story. If Salander was in some way involved in the murders, there had to be entirely different grounds from those the police were suggesting—someone else may have held the gun or something had happened that was beyond her control.

Hedström said nothing during the taxi journey from Slussen to Kungsholmen. He was in a daze from out of the blue ending up in a real police investigation. He glanced at Bohman, who was reading Armansky's presentation again.

Then all at once he smiled to himself. The assignment had given him an unexpected opportunity to realize an ambition that neither Armansky nor Bohman knew anything about. He was going to have a chance to get back at Salander. He hoped that he would be able to help catch her. He hoped above all that she would be sentenced to life in prison.

It was well known that Salander was not a popular person at Milton Security. Most of the staff who had ever had anything to do with her thought she was a pain. But no-one had any idea how profoundly Hedström loathed her.

Life had been unfair to Hedström. He was good-looking, he was young, and he was clever too. But he was forever denied the possibility of becoming what he had always wanted to be— a policeman. His Achilles heel was a microscopic hole in his pericardium that caused a heart murmur and meant that the wall of one chamber was compromised. He had had an operation and the problem was fixed, but having a heart condition meant that he was once and for all deprived of a place on the police force. He was relegated to second-class.

When he was given the chance to work for Milton Security he accepted, but without the slightest enthusiasm. Milton was a dump for has-beens—police officers who were too old and couldn't cut it anymore. He too had been turned down by the police—but in his case through no fault of his own.

When he started at Milton one of his first assignments had been to work with the operations unit on a personal protection analysis for a famous female singer. She had been frightened by an over-enthusiastic admirer, who also happened to be a mental patient on the run. The singer lived alone in a villa in Södertörn, and Milton had installed surveillance equipment and alarms and provided an on-site bodyguard.

Over a two-week period Hedström had regularly visited the villa in Södertörn along with other Milton employees. He thought the singer was a snobbish and standoffish old bitch. She gave him only a bewildered look when he turned on the charm, but she ought to have been grateful that any fan remembered her at all.

He hated the way Milton's staff sprang to do her bidding. But of course he didn't say a word about how he felt.

One afternoon, the singer and two of the Milton staff were by her pool while he was in the house taking photographs of windows and doors that might need reinforcing. He had gone from room to room, and when he came to her bedroom he could not resist the temptation to open her desk. He found a dozen photograph albums from when she was a big star in the seventies and eighties and had toured the world. He also found a box with some very private pictures of the singer. The pictures were relatively innocent, but with a little imagination they might be viewed as "erotic studies." *God, what a stupid cow she was.* He stole five of the most risqué images, which had obviously been taken by some lover.

He photographed the images there and then and put the originals back. He waited several months before he sold them to a British tabloid. He was paid 9,000 pounds for the photographs and they gave rise to sensational headlines.

He still did not know how Salander had managed it, but after the photographs were published, he had a visit from her. She knew that he was the one who had sold them. She was going to expose him to Armansky if he ever did anything like that again. She would have exposed him immediately if she could have proved it—but she obviously could not. From that day on he had felt her watching him. He had seen her little piggy eyes every time he turned around.

He felt stressed and frustrated. The only way to get back at her was to undermine her credibility by adding his contributions to the gossip about her in the canteen. But not even that had been very successful. He did not dare draw attention to himself, since for some unknown reason she was under Armansky's protection. He wondered what sort of hold she had over Milton's CEO, or if it was possible that the old bastard was fucking her in secret. But even though nobody at Milton was especially enamoured of Salander, the staff had great respect for Armansky and so they accepted her peculiar presence. It was a monumental relief to him when she began to play less of a role and finally stopped working at Milton altogether.

Now an opportunity had presented itself for him to get even. And it was risk-free. She could accuse him of anything she liked—nobody would believe her. Not even Armansky would take the word of a pathologically sick murderer.

Bublanski saw Faste coming out of the elevator with Bohman and Hedström from Milton. He had been sent down to bring these new colleagues through security. Bublanski was not entirely enchanted with the idea of giving outsiders access to a murder investigation, but the decision had been made way over his head and . . . what the hell, Bohman was a real police officer with a lot of miles on him. Hedström had graduated from the police academy and so could not be an outright idiot. Bublanski pointed towards the conference room.

The hunt for Salander was in its sixth day and it was time for a major evaluation. Prosecutor Ekström did not take part in the meeting. The group consisted of criminal inspectors Modig, Faste, Andersson, and Holmberg, reinforced by four officers from the search unit of the National Criminal Police. Bublanski began by introducing their new colleagues from Milton Security and asking if either of them wanted to say a few words. Bohman cleared his throat.

"It's been a while since I was last in this building, but some of you know me and know that I was a police officer for many years before I switched to the private sector. The reason we're here is that Salander worked for Milton over several years and we feel a measure of responsibility. Our job is to try and assist in her arrest. We can contribute some personal knowledge of her, but we're not here in any way to mess up the investigation or to try to trip you up."

"Tell us what she was like to work with," Faste said.

"She wasn't exactly a person you warmed to," Hedström said. He stopped when Bublanski held up his hand.

"We'll have a chance to talk in detail during the meeting. But let's take things one by one and get a grip on where we stand. After this meeting, you two will have to go to Prosecutor Ekström and sign a confidentiality statement. Let's begin with Sonja."

"It's frustrating. We had a breakthrough just a few hours after the murders and were able to identify Salander. We found where she lived—or at least where we thought she lived. After that, not a trace. We've received around thirty calls from people who think they've seen her, but so far they've all been false alarms. She seems to have gone up in smoke."

"That's a little hard to believe," Andersson said. "She looks unusual and has tattoos and shouldn't be that hard to find."

"The police in Uppsala went in with their weapons drawn yesterday after receiving a tip. They surrounded and scared the hell out of a fourteen-year-old boy who did look a lot like Salander. The parents were quite upset."

"It's a handicap that we're searching for someone who looks like a fourteen-year-old. She could melt into any crowd of teenagers."

"But with the attention she's been getting in the media, someone should have seen something," Andersson said. "They're running her picture on *Sweden's Most Wanted* this week, so maybe that will lead to something new."

"I doubt it, considering that she's already been on the front page of every newspaper in the country," Faste said.

"Which suggests that maybe we should change our approach," Bublanski said. "With accomplices, she could have slipped out of the country, but it's more probable that she's gone to ground."

Bohman held up his hand. Bublanski nodded to him.

"The profile we have of her is that she's self-destructive. On the other hand, she's a strategist who plans all her actions carefully. She does nothing without analysing the consequences. At least that's what Dragan Armansky thinks."

"That was the assessment her one-time psychiatrist gave as well. But let's hold off on the characterization for a while," Bublanski said. "Sooner or later she'll have to make a move. Jerker, what sort of resources does she have?"

"Now here's something you can sink your teeth into," Holmberg said. "She's had a bank account for several years at Handelsbanken. That's the income she declares. Or rather, the income that her guardian, Nils Bjurman, declared. A year ago the account held about 100,000 kronor. In the autumn of 2003 she withdrew the entire amount."

"She needed cash in the autumn of 2003. That was when she stopped working for Milton Security," Bohman said.

"Possibly. The account stood at zero for about two weeks. And then she put the same amount back into it."

"She thought she needed money for something, but she didn't spend it and put the money back?"

"Possibly. In December 2003 she used the account to pay a number of bills, including her rent for a year in advance. The account dropped to 70,000 kronor. After that the account wasn't touched for a year, except for a deposit of around 9,000 kronor. I've checked—it was an inheritance from her mother. In March this year she took out this sum—the exact amount was 9,312 kronor—and that's the only time she's touched the account."

"So what the hell does she live on?"

"Listen to this. In January of this year she opened a new account. This one at Svenska Enskilda Banken. She deposited two million kronor."

"Where did the money come from?" Modig asked.

"The money was transferred to her account from a bank in the Channel Islands."

Silence descended over the conference room.

"I don't understand any of this," Modig said after a moment.

"So this is money she hasn't declared?" Bublanski asked.

"No, but technically she doesn't have to until next year. What's interesting is that the sum is not recorded in Bjurman's report on her assets, and he filed a report every month."

"So—either he didn't know about it or else they were running a scam together. Jerker, where do we stand on forensics?"

"I had a report from the leader of the preliminary investigation yesterday evening. This is what we know. One: we can tie Salander to both crime scenes. We found her fingerprints on the murder weapon and on the shards of a broken coffee cup in Enskede. We're waiting for results from all the DNA samples we gathered, but there's no doubt that she was there in the apartment. Two: we have her prints on the box we found in Bjurman's apartment, the one the gun came in. Three: we finally have a witness who can place her at the site of the murders in Enskede. The owner of a corner shop telephoned to say that Salander was definitely in his shop on the night of the murders. She bought a pack of Marlboro Lights."

"And he comes out with this days after we asked the public for information?"

"He was away over the holidays, like everybody else. In any case"—Holmberg pointed at a map—"the corner shop is here, about two hundred yards from the crime scene. She came in just as he was closing at 10:00 p.m. He gave a perfect description of her."

"Tattoo on her neck?" Andersson said.

"He was a bit vague about that. He thought he saw a tattoo. But he definitely saw that she had a pierced eyebrow."

"What else?"

"Not that much in the way of technical evidence. But it should hold up."

"Faste—the apartment on Lundagatan?"

"We've got her prints, but we don't think she lives there. We've turned the place upside down, and it seems that a Miriam Wu is living there. Her name was added to the contract as recently as February this year."

"What do we know about Wu?"

"No police record. Known lesbian. She appears in shows at the Gay Pride Festival. Seems to be studying sociology and is part owner of Domino Fashion, a sex shop on Tegnérgatan."

"Sex shop?" Modig said with raised eyebrows.

On one occasion she had bought, to her husband's delight, some sexy lingerie at Domino Fashion. And she had absolutely no intention of revealing that to the men in the room.

"Yeah, they sell handcuffs and whore outfits and stuff like that. Need a whip?"

"It's not a sex shop. It's a fashion boutique for people who like sexy underwear."

"Same shit."

"Go on," Bublanski said angrily. "Is there any sign of Fröken Wu?"

"Not a trace."

"She could have gone away for Easter," Modig said.

"Or else Salander whacked her too," Faste said. "Maybe she wants to make a clean sweep of all her acquaintances."

"Wu is a lesbian. Should we conclude that she and Salander are a couple?"

"I think we can draw the conclusion that there's a sexual relationship," Andersson said. "First, we found Salander's prints on and around the bed in the apartment. We also found her prints on a pair of handcuffs."

"Then she'll appreciate the cuffs I've got ready for her," Faste said.

Modig groaned.

"Go on," Bublanski said to Andersson.

"We got a tip that Miriam Wu was seen at Kvarnen kissing a girl who matched Salander's description. That was about two weeks ago. The informant claimed that he knows who Salander is and has run into her there before, although he hadn't seen her in the past year. I haven't had time to double-check with the staff, but I'll do it this afternoon."

"In her casebook at social welfare it doesn't mention a thing about her being a lesbian. A number of times in her teens she ran away from her foster families and picked up men in bars. She was noticed by the police several times in the company of older men."

"Which doesn't mean shit if she was a whore," Faste said.

"What do we know about people she knows? Curt?"

"Hardly anything. She hasn't had a run-in with the police since she was eighteen. She knows Dragan Armansky and Mikael Blomkvist, we know that much. And she knows Miriam Wu, of course. The same source that tipped us off about her and Wu at Kvarnen says that she used to hang out with a bunch of girls there a while back. Some kind of girl band called Evil Fingers."

"Evil Fingers?" Bublanski repeated.

"Seems to be something occult."

"Don't tell me Salander is some damned Satanist too," Bublanski said. "The media are going to go nuts."

"Lesbian Satanists," Faste said helpfully.

"Hans, you've got a view of women from the Middle Ages," Modig said. "Even I've heard of Evil Fingers."

"You have?" Bublanski said.

"It was a girl rock band in the late nineties. No superstars, but they were pretty famous for a while."

"So, hard-rocking lesbian Satanists," Faste said.

"OK, enough goofing around," Bublanski said. "Hans, you and Curt check out who was in Evil Fingers and talk to them. Does Salander have any other friends?"

"Not many, other than her former guardian, Holger Palmgren. He's in long-term care now after a stroke and is apparently unwell. To be honest, I can't say that I found any circle of friends, though we haven't seen her address book. For that matter, we still don't know where she lives."

"Nobody can go around without leaving traces, like some kind of ghost. What do we think about Mikael Blomkvist?"

"We haven't had him under direct surveillance, but we've checked in with him off and on over the holiday," Faste said. "On the chance that Salander might pop up, that is. He went home after work on Thursday and doesn't seem to have left his apartment all weekend."

"I can't see him having anything to do with the murders," Modig said. "His story holds up, and he can account for every minute of that night."

"But he does know Salander. He's the link between her and the couple in Enskede. And besides, we have his statement that a man attacked Salander a week before the murders took place. What are we supposed to make of that?" Bublanski said.

"Other than the fact that Blomkvist was the only witness to the attack?" Faste said.

"You think Blomkvist is imagining things or lying?"

"Don't know. But it sounds to me like a bullshit story. How come a full-grown man couldn't take care of a tiny girl who weighs less than ninety pounds?"

"Why would Blomkvist lie?"

"To muddle our thinking about Salander?"

"But none of this really adds up. Blomkvist's hypothesis is that his friends were killed because of the book that Svensson was writing."

"Bullshit," Faste said. "It's Salander. Why would anybody murder their guardian to shut Dag Svensson up? And who else could it be . . . a policeman?"

"If Blomkvist goes public with his hypothesis, we're going to see a hell of a lot of police conspiracy theories," said Andersson.

Everyone at the table murmured agreement.

"All right," Modig said. "Why did she shoot Bjurman?"

"And what does the tattoo mean?" Bublanski said, pointing at a photograph of Bjurman's lower abdomen.

I AM A SADISTIC PIG, A PERVERT, AND A RAPIST.

"What does the pathologist's report say?" Bohman said.

"The tattoo is between one and three years old. That's measured by the extent of bleed-through in the skin," Modig said.

"I think we can rule out the likelihood of Bjurman actually having commissioned it."

"There are plenty of crazies around, but it can hardly be a standard motif among tattoo enthusiasts."

Modig waved her index finger. "The pathologist says that the tattoo has to have been done by a rank amateur. The needle penetrated to different depths, and it's a very large tattoo on a sensitive part of the body. All in all, it must have been a very painful procedure, comparable to aggravated assault."

"Except for the fact that Bjurman never filed a police report," Faste said.

"I wouldn't file a police report either, if somebody tattooed that on me," Andersson said.

"One more thing," Modig said. "And this might reinforce the confession, as it were, in the tattoo." She opened a folder of photographic printouts and passed them around. "I printed out some samples from a folder on Bjurman's hard drive. They're downloaded from the Internet. His computer contains about two thousand images of a similar nature."

Faste whistled and held up a photograph of a woman bound in a brutally uncomfortable position. "This may be something for Domino Fashion or Evil Fingers," he said.

Bublanski gestured in annoyance for Faste to shut up.

"What are we supposed to make of this?" Bohman said.

"Suppose the tattoo is about two years old," Bublanski said. "It would have been done around the time that Bjurman got sick. No medical records indicate that he had any illness, other than high blood pressure. So we can assume that there was a connection."

"Salander changed during that year," Bohman said. "She stopped working for Milton and without warning, I understand, went overseas."

"Should we assume that there's a connection there too? The message in the tattoo plainly says that Bjurman raped someone. Salander is a likely victim. And that would be a motive for murder."

"There are other ways to interpret this, of course," Faste said. "I can imagine a scenario where Salander and the Chinese girl are running some sort of escort service with S&M overtones. Bjurman could be one of those nuts who gets off on being whipped by small girls. He could have been in some sort of dependence relationship with Salander and things went wrong."

"But that doesn't explain what she was doing in Enskede."

"If Svensson and Johansson were about to expose the sex trade, they may have stumbled on Salander and Wu. That may be your motive for Salander to commit murder."

"So far this is mere speculation," said Modig.

The meeting went on for another hour, and also dealt with the fact that Svensson's laptop was missing. When they broke for lunch they were all frustrated. The investigation was fraught with more question marks than ever.

Berger called Magnus Borgsjö, CEO of *Svenska Morgon-Posten*, as soon as she reached the office on Tuesday morning.

"I'm interested," she said.

"I thought you would be."

"I meant to let you know right after the Easter holiday. But as you'll have heard, chaos has broken out here."

"The murder of Dag Svensson. I'm so sorry. A terrible thing."

"Then you'll understand that this is no time for me to announce my resignation."

He was silent for a moment.

"We have a problem," Borgsjö said. "The last time we spoke, we said that the job would start on August 1. But the thing is, our editor in chief, Håkan Morander, whom you would be replacing, is in very poor health. He has heart problems and has to cut back on work. He talked to his doctor a few days ago, and this weekend I learned that he's now planning to retire on July 1. The idea was that he would still be here until fall, and that you could work in tandem through August and September. But the way the situation looks now, we have a crisis. Erika—we're going to need you to start on May 1, and certainly no later than May 15."

"God. That's only weeks away."

"Are you still interested?"

"Yes, of course . . . but that means I have only a month to tidy things up here at *Millennium*."

"I know. I'm sorry to do it, Erika, but I have to rush you. A month should be enough time to straighten out affairs at a magazine with only half a dozen employees."

"But it means leaving in the midst of a crisis."

"You'd have to leave in any case. All we're doing is bringing forward your departure date by a few weeks."

"I do have some conditions."

"Let me hear them."

"I'll have to remain on *Millennium*'s board of directors."

"That might not be appropriate. *Millennium* is much smaller, of course, and a monthly magazine besides, but technically we're competitors."

"That can't be helped. I won't have anything to do with *Millennium*'s editorial work, but I won't sell my share of the business. So I have to stay on the board."

"OK, we can probably deal with that."

They agreed to meet with his board during the first week of April to iron out the details and draw up a contract.

Blomkvist had a feeling of déjà vu when he studied the list of suspects that he and Eriksson had put together over the weekend. Thirty-seven names, all people Dag Svensson was leaning on hard in his book, twenty-one of whom were johns he had identified.

It reminded Blomkvist of the gallery of suspects from when he had set out to track a murderer in Hedestad two years before.

At 10:00 on Tuesday morning he asked Eriksson to come into his office at *Millennium*. He closed the door behind her. They sat for a few moments, drinking their coffee. Then he passed her the list of names.

"What should we do?" Eriksson said.

"First we have to show the list to Erika—maybe in ten minutes. Then we have to check them off one by one. It's possible, it's even probable, that one of these people has a connection to the murders."

"And how do we check them off?"

"I'm thinking of focusing on the twenty-one johns. They have more to lose than the others. I'm thinking of following in Dag's footsteps, of going to see them one by one."

"And what do I do?"

"Two jobs. First, there are seven people here who aren't identified. Your assignment over the next couple of days is to try and identify them. Some of the names are in Mia's thesis; there may be ways of cross-referencing that would help you work out their real identities. Second, we know very little about

Nils Bjurman, Lisbeth's guardian. There was a brief CV in the papers, but my guess is that half of it is made up."

"So I should ferret out his background."

"Precisely. Everything you can find."

Harriet Vanger called Blomkvist at 5:00 in the afternoon.

"Can you talk?"

"For a minute."

"This girl the police are looking for . . . it's the same one who helped you track me down, isn't it?"

Harriet Vanger and Salander had never met.

"That's right," Blomkvist said. "I'm sorry I haven't had time to call and update you. But, yes, she's the one."

"What does it mean?"

"As far as you're concerned? Nothing, I hope."

"But she knows everything about me and what happened."

"Yes, she knows everything that happened."

Harriet was quiet on the other end of the line.

"Harriet, I don't think she did it. I'm working on the assumption that she's innocent of all these murders. I trust her."

"If I'm to believe what's in the newspapers, then—"

"But you shouldn't believe what's in the papers. And as far as it affects you, it's quite simple: she gave her word that she would keep her mouth shut. I believe she'll keep that promise for the rest of her life. Everything I know about her tells me that she is extremely principled."

"And if she didn't do it?"

"I don't know. Harriet, I'm doing everything in my power to discover what actually happened. Don't worry."

"I'm not worried, but I do want to be prepared for the worst. How are you holding up, Mikael?"

"So-so. We've been going nonstop."

"Mikael . . . I'm in Stockholm right now. I'm flying to Australia tomorrow—I'll be gone for a month."

"I see."

"I'm at the hotel."

"I don't know, Harriet. I feel spread really thin. I have to work tonight and I wouldn't be very good company."

"You don't have to be good company. Come over and relax for a while."

Mikael got home at one in the morning. He was tired and felt like saying the hell with everything and going to bed, but instead he booted up his iBook and checked his email. There was no new mail of any interest.

He opened the folder <Lisbeth Salander> and discovered a new document. It was named [To MikBlom], next to the document he had called [To Sally].

It was almost a physical shock to see the document on his computer. *She's here. Salander has been in my computer. Maybe she's even connected right now.* He double-clicked.

He was not sure what he had expected. A letter. An answer. A protestation of innocence. An explanation. Salander's reply was exasperatingly brief. The message consisted of one word, four letters.

Zala.

Mikael stared at the name.

Svensson had mentioned Zala in his last phone call, three hours before he was murdered.

What is she trying to say? Is Zala the link between Bjurman and Dag and Mia? How? Why? Who is he? And how did Salander know that? How is she involved?

He opened the document properties and saw that the text had been created not fifteen minutes before. Then he smiled. The document showed *Mikael Blomkvist* as its author. She had created the document in his computer with his own licenced Word programme. That was better than email and did not leave an IP address that could be traced, even though

Blomkvist was sure that Salander in any case would be impossible to trace through the Internet. And it proved beyond all doubt that Salander had done a hostile takeover—her term—of his computer.

He stood by the window and looked out at City Hall. He couldn't shake the feeling that he was being watched at that very moment by Salander, almost as if she were there in the room staring at him through the screen of his iBook. She could, of course, be anywhere in the world, but he suspected that she was close. Somewhere in Södermalm. Within a radius of a couple of miles from where he was.

He sat down and created a new Word document that he called [Sally-2] and placed it on the desktop. He wrote a pithy message.

> Lisbeth,
> You damn troublesome person. Who the hell is Zala? Is he the link? Do you know who murdered Dag & Mia? If so, tell me so we can solve this mess and go to sleep.
> Mikael.

She was inside Blomkvist's iBook now. The reply came within a minute. A new document appeared in the folder on his desktop, this time called [Kalle Blomkvist].

> You're the journalist. Find out.

Blomkvist frowned. She was teasing him and using the nickname she knew he loathed. And she gave him not the slightest help. He wrote the document [Sally-3] and put it on his desktop.

> Lisbeth,
> A journalist finds out things by asking questions of people who know. I'm asking you. Do you know

why Dag and Mia were murdered and who killed them?
If you do, please tell me. Give me something to go on.
Mikael.

For several hours he waited for another reply. At 4:00 a.m. he
gave up and went to bed.

CHAPTER 19

Wednesday, March 30–
Friday, April 1

Blomkvist spent Wednesday combing Svensson's material for every reference to Zala. Just as Salander had done earlier, he discovered the folder <Zala> on Svensson's computer and read the three documents [Irina P], [Sandström], and [Zala], and like Salander he discovered that Svensson had a police source by the name of Gulbrandsen. He traced him to the Criminal Police in Södertälje, but when he called he was told that Gulbrandsen was on a trip away from the office and would not be back until the following Monday.

He could see that Svensson had spent a great deal of time on Irina P. From the autopsy report he learned that the woman had been killed in a slow, cruel way. The murder had taken place at the end of February. The police had no leads as to who the killer might have been, but since she was a prostitute they assumed that it was one of her clients.

Blomkvist wondered why Svensson had put the [Irina P] document in the <Zala> folder. Evidently he had linked Zala to Irina P., but there were no such references in the text. Presumably he had made the connection late on.

The document [Zala] looked like rough working notes. Zala

(if indeed he existed) seemed almost like a phantom in the criminal world. He did not seem entirely credible, and the text lacked source references.

He closed the document and scratched his head. Solving the murders was going to be a considerably more difficult task than he had imagined. Nor could he avoid being assailed by doubt. Nothing told him unequivocally that Salander was innocent. All he had to go on was his instinct.

He knew that she was not short of funds. She had exploited her skills as a hacker to steal a sum of several billion kronor, but she didn't know that he knew this. Apart from when he had been forced to explain her computer talents to Berger, he had never betrayed her secrets to any outsider.

He didn't want to believe that Salander was guilty of the murders. He would never be able to repay his debt to her. She had not only saved his life, she had also salvaged his career and possibly *Millennium* magazine itself by delivering Hans-Erik Wennerström's head to them on a platter.

And he felt a great loyalty to her. Whether she was guilty or not, he was going to do everything he could to help her when she eventually was caught.

But there was so much that he didn't know about her. The psychiatric assessments, the fact that she had been committed to one of the country's most highly regarded institutions, and that she had even been declared incompetent, all tended to confirm that something was wrong with her. The chief of staff at St. Stefan's Psychiatric Clinic in Uppsala, Dr. Peter Teleborian, had been widely quoted in the press. As was appropriate, he had not made statements specifically about Salander but had commented on the national collapse of mental health care. Teleborian was renowned and respected not merely in Sweden but internationally as well. He had been thoroughly convincing and had managed to convey his sympathy for the murder victims and their families while making it known that he was most anxious about Salander's well-being.

Blomkvist wondered whether he ought to get in touch with Dr. Teleborian and whether he might be able to help in some way. But he refrained. The doctor would have plenty of time to help Salander once she was caught.

Finally he went to the kitchenette and poured coffee into a cup with the logo of the Moderate Unity Party and went in to see Berger.

"I have a long list of johns and pimps I have to interview," he said.

She looked at him with concern.

"It'll probably take a week or two to check off everyone on the list. They're dotted about from Strängnäs to Norrköping. I'll need a car."

She opened her handbag and took out the keys to her BMW.

"Is that really all right?"

"Of course it's all right. I drive to work as rarely as I drive out to Saltsjöbaden. And if need be I can take Greger's car."

"Thanks."

"There's one condition, though."

"What's that?"

"Some of these guys are serious thugs. If you're going out to accuse pimps of murdering Dag and Mia, I want you to take this with you and always keep it in the pocket of your jacket."

She put a canister of Mace on the desk.

"Where'd you get that?"

"I bought it in the States last year. I'll be damned if I'm going to run around alone at night without some sort of weapon."

"There'll be hell to pay if I get caught in possession of an illegal weapon."

"Better that than me having to write your obituary, Mikael . . . I'm not sure if you know this, but sometimes I really worry about you."

"I see."

"You take risks and you're so pigheaded that you can never back down from a stupid decision."

Blomkvist smiled and put the Mace on Erika's desk.

"Thanks for the concern. But I don't need it."

"Micke, I insist."

"That's fine. But I've already taken precautions."

He put his hand in his pocket and pulled out a canister. It was the Mace he had taken out of Salander's shoulder bag and had carried with him ever since.

Bublanski knocked on the open door of Modig's office and then sat down on the visitor's chair by her desk.

"Dag Svensson's computer," he said.

"I've been thinking about that too," she said. "I did a time-line of Svensson and Johansson's last day. There are still a few gaps, but Svensson never went to *Millennium*'s offices that day. On the other hand he did go into the centre of town, and at around 4:00 in the afternoon he ran into an old school friend. It was a chance meeting at a café on Drottninggatan. The friend says that Svensson definitely had his computer. He saw it and even made a comment about it."

"And by 11:00 that night—by the time the police arrived at his apartment—the computer was gone."

"Correct."

"What should we deduce from that?"

"He could have stopped somewhere else and for some reason left or forgotten his computer."

"How likely is that?"

"Not very likely. But he could have dropped it off for repair. Then there's the possibility that there was some other place he worked that we don't know about. For example, he once rented a desk at a freelancers' office near St. Eriksplan. Then, of course, there's the possibility that the killer took the computer with him."

"According to Armansky, Salander is very good with computers."

"Exactly," Modig said, nodding.

"Hmm. Blomkvist's theory is that Svensson and Johansson were murdered because of the research Svensson was doing. Which would all be on his computer."

"We're lagging a little behind. Three murder victims create so many loose ends that we can't really keep up, but we actually haven't done a proper search of Svensson's workplace at *Millennium* yet."

"I talked with Erika Berger this morning. She says they're surprised that we haven't been over to take a look at what he left there."

"We've been focusing too much on the hunt for Salander, and so far we don't have a clue about the motive. Could you . . . ?"

"I've made a rendezvous with Berger at *Millennium* for tomorrow."

"Thanks."

On Thursday Blomkvist was at his desk talking to Eriksson when a telephone rang somewhere else in the offices. Through the doorway he caught a glimpse of Cortez on his way to answer it. Then he registered somewhere in the back of his mind that it was the phone on Svensson's desk. He jumped to his feet.

"Stop—don't touch that phone!" he yelled.

Cortez had his hand on the receiver. Blomkvist hurried across the room. What the hell was the name of that phony company Svensson made up?

"Indigo Market Research, this is Mikael. May I help you?"

"Uh . . . hello, my name is Gunnar Björck. I got a letter saying I've won a mobile phone."

"Congratulations," Blomkvist said. "It's a Sony Ericsson, the latest model."

"And it's free?"

"That's right, it's free. To receive the gift you only have to be interviewed. We do market research studies and in-depth analyses for various companies. It'll take about an hour to answer the questions. After that your name will be entered in another drawing and you'll have the chance to win 100,000 kronor."

"I understand. Can we do it over the phone?"

"Unfortunately not. The questionnaire involves looking at company logos and identifying them. We will also be asking about what type of advertising images you like and we show you various alternatives. We have to send out one of our employees."

"I see . . . and how did I happen to be selected?"

"We do this type of study several times a year. Right now we're focusing on a number of successful men in your age group. We've drawn social security numbers at random within that demographic."

Björck finally agreed to a meeting. He told Blomkvist that he was on sick leave and was convalescing at a summer cabin up in Smådalarö. He gave directions on how to get there. They agreed to meet on Friday morning.

"YES!" Blomkvist cried when he hung up the phone. He punched the air with his fist. Eriksson and Cortez exchanged puzzled glances.

Paolo Roberto landed at Arlanda at 11:30 on Thursday morning. He had slept during much of the flight from New York, and for once did not have any jet lag.

He had spent a month in the United States talking boxing, watching exhibition fights, and looking for ideas for a production he was planning to sell to Strix Television. Sadly, he admitted to himself, he had left his own professional career on the shelf, partly because of gentle persuasion from his family, but also because he was simply feeling his age. It wasn't so much about keeping in shape, which he did with strenuous workouts at least once a week. He was still a name in the boxing world, and he expected to be working in the sport in some capacity for the rest of his life.

He collected his suitcase from the baggage carousel. At Customs he was stopped and about to be pulled aside when one of the Customs officers recognized him.

"Hello, Paolo. All you've got in your case is gloves, I presume?"

He was crossing the arrivals hall to the escalator down to the Arlanda Express when he stopped short, stunned by Salander's face on the headlines of the evening newspapers. He wondered if he was suffering from jet lag after all. Then he read the headline again.

HUNT FOR
LISBETH SALANDER

He looked at the other headline.

EXTRA!
PSYCHOPATH SOUGHT
FOR TRIPLE KILLING

He bought both the evening papers and the morning ones too and then went over to a cafeteria. He read the articles with growing astonishment.

When Blomkvist came home to Bellmansgatan at 11:00 on Thursday night he was tired and depressed. He had planned to make it an early night to catch up on his sleep, but he couldn't resist the temptation to switch on his iBook and check his email. Nothing of great interest there, but he opened the <Lisbeth Salander> folder. His pulse quickened when he discovered a new document entitled [MB2]. He double-clicked.

> Prosecutor E. is leaking information to the media. Ask him why he didn't leak the old police report.

Blomkvist pondered the message, baffled. What old police report? Why did she have to write every message like a riddle? He created a new document that he called [Cryptic].

> Hi, Sally. I'm tired as hell and I've been on the go nonstop since the murders. I don't feel like playing guessing games. Maybe you don't give a damn, but I want to know who killed my friends. M.

He waited at his desk. The reply [Cryptic 2] came a minute later.

> What would you do if it was me?

He replied with [Cryptic 3].

> Lisbeth, if it's true that you've really gone over the edge, then maybe you can ask Peter Teleborian to help you. But I don't believe you murdered Dag and Mia. I hope and pray that I'm right.
> Dag and Mia were going to publish their exposés of the sex trade. My theory is that could have been the reason for the murders. But I have nothing to go on.
> I don't know what went wrong between us, but you and I discussed friendship once. I said that friendship is built on two things—respect and trust. Even if you don't

like me, you can still depend on me and trust me. I've never shared your secrets with anyone. Not even what happened to Wennerström's billions. Trust me. I'm not your enemy. M.

Blomkvist had almost given up hope when, nearly fifty minutes later, the file [Cryptic 4] materialized.

I'll think about it.

Blomkvist sighed with relief. He felt a little ray of hope. The reply meant exactly what it said. She was going to think about it. It was the first time since, without a word of explanation, she had vanished from his life that she had held out the prospect of communicating with him at all. He wrote [Cryptic 5].

OK, I'll wait. But please don't take too long.

Inspector Faste got the call when he was on Långholmsgatan near Västerbron on his way to work on Friday morning. The police did not have the resources to put the apartment on Lundagatan under twenty-four-hour surveillance, so they had arranged for a neighbour, a retired policeman, to keep an eye on it.

"The Chinese girl just came in," the neighbour said.

Faste could hardly have been in a more convenient place. He made an illegal turn past the bus shelter on to Heleneborgsgatan just before Västerbron and drove down Högalidsgatan to Lundagatan. He was there less than two minutes after he got the call and jogged across the street and through to the back building.

Miriam Wu was still standing at the door of her apartment staring at the drilled-out lock and the police tape across the door when she heard footsteps on the stairs behind her. She turned and saw a powerfully built man looking intently at her. She felt he was hostile and dropped her bag on the floor and prepared to resort to Thai boxing if necessary.

"Are you Miriam Wu?" he said.

To her surprise he held up a police ID.

"Yes," she said. "What's going on here?"

"Where have you been staying the past week?"

"I've been away. What happened? Was there a break-in?"

"I'm going to have to ask you to come with me to Kungs-holmen," he said, putting a hand on her shoulder.

Bublanski and Modig watched as Miriam Wu was escorted by Faste into the interview room. She was plainly angry.

"Please have a seat. My name is Criminal Inspector Jan Bublanski, and this is my colleague Inspector Sonja Modig. I'm sorry we've had to bring you in like this, but we have a number of questions we need answered."

"OK. But why? That guy isn't very talkative." She jerked a thumb at Faste.

"We've been looking for you for some time. Can you tell us where you've been?"

"Yes, I can. But I don't feel like it, and as far as I'm concerned it's none of your business."

Bublanski raised his eyebrows.

"I come home to find my door broken open and police tape across it, and a guy pumped up on steroids drags me down here. Can I get an explanation?"

"Don't you like men?" Faste said.

Miriam Wu turned and stared at him, astonished. Bublanski gave him a furious look.

"You haven't read any newspapers in the past week? Have you been out of the country?"

"No, I haven't read any papers. I've been in Paris visiting my parents. For two weeks. I just came from Central Station."

"You took the train?"

"I don't like flying."

"And you didn't see any news headlines or Swedish papers today?"

"I got off the night train and took the tunnelbana home."

Bublanski thought for a moment. There hadn't been anything about Salander in the headlines this morning. He stood up and left the room. When he returned he was carrying *Aftonbladet*'s Easter edition with Salander's photograph on the front page.

Miriam Wu almost flipped.

Blomkvist followed the directions that Björck had given him to the cabin in Smådalarö. As he parked he saw that the "cabin" was a modern one-family home which looked to be habitable all year round. It had a view of the sea towards the Jungfrufjärden inlet. He walked up the gravel path and rang the bell. Björck was clearly recognizable from the passport photograph that Svensson had in his file.

"Good morning," Blomkvist said.

"Good, you found the place."

"Thanks to your directions."

"Come in. We can sit in the kitchen."

Björck appeared to be in good health, but he had a slight limp.

"I'm on sick leave," he said.

"Nothing serious, I hope."

"I'm waiting to have surgery on a slipped disk. Would you like coffee?"

"No thanks," Blomkvist said and sat at the kitchen table and opened his briefcase. He took out a folder. Björck sat down facing him.

"You look familiar. Have we met before?"

"I think not," Blomkvist said.

"I'm sure I've seen you somewhere."

"Maybe in the newspapers."

"What did you say your name was?"

"Mikael Blomkvist. I'm a journalist, I work at *Millennium* magazine."

Björck looked confused. Then the penny dropped. *Kalle Blomkvist. The Wennerström affair.* But still he did not understand the implications.

"*Millennium*? I didn't know you did market research."

"Once in a while. I'd like to begin by asking you to look at three photographs and tell me which one you like best."

Blomkvist put images of three girls on the table. One had been downloaded from a porn site on the Internet. The other two were blown-up passport photographs.

Björck turned pale as a corpse.

"I don't get it."

"No? This is Lidia Komarova, sixteen years old, from Minsk. Next to her is Myang So Chin, goes by the name of Jo-Jo, from Thailand. She's twenty-five. And lastly we have Yelena Barasova, nineteen, from Tallinn. You bought sex from all three of these women, and my question is: which one did you like best? Think of it as market research."

"To sum up, you claim that you have known Lisbeth Salander for about three years. Without expecting to be remunerated she signed over her apartment to you this spring and moved somewhere else. You have sex with her once in a while when she gets in touch, but you don't know where she lives, what kind of work she does, or how she supports herself. Do you expect me to believe that?"

Miriam Wu glowered at him. "I don't give a shit what you believe. I haven't done anything illegal, and how I choose to live my life and who I have sex with is none of your business or anyone else's."

Bublanski sighed. That morning, when he had received news of Miriam Wu's reappearance, he had felt a great sense of relief. *Finally a breakthrough.* But the information he was getting from her was anything but enlightening. It was most peculiar, in fact. And the problem was that he believed her. She gave clear, intelligible answers, without hesitation. She cited places and dates when she had met Salander, and she gave such a precise account of how it came about that she had moved to Lundagatan that Bublanski and Modig both strongly felt that such a bizarre story had to be true.

Faste had listened to the interview with mounting exasperation, but he managed to keep his mouth shut. He thought that Bublanski was too lenient by far with the Chinese girl, who was an arrogant bitch and used a lot of words to avoid answering the only question that mattered. Namely, where in burning hell was that fucking whore Salander hiding?

But Wu did not know where Salander was. She did not know what kind of work Salander did. She had never heard of Milton Security. She had never heard of Dag Svensson or Mia Johansson, and consequently she could not provide a single scrap of information of any interest. She had had no idea that Salander was under guardianship, or that in her teens she had been committed, or that she had copious psychiatric assessments on her CV.

On the other hand, she was willing to confirm that she and Salander had gone to Kvarnen and kissed and then gone home to Lundagatan and parted early the next morning. Days later Miriam Wu had taken the train to Paris and missed all the headlines in the Swedish papers. Apart from a quick visit to return her car keys, she had not seen Salander since that evening at Kvarnen.

"Car keys?" Bublanski asked. "Salander doesn't own a car."

Miriam Wu told him that she had a burgundy Honda which was parked outside the apartment building. Bublanski got up and looked at Modig.

"Can you take over the interview?" he said and left the room.

He had to find Holmberg and have him do a forensic

examination of a burgundy Honda parked on Lundagatan. And he needed to be alone to think.

Gunnar Björck, assistant chief of the immigration division of the Security Police, now on sick leave, sat ashen and ghostlike in the kitchen with its lovely view of Jungfrufjärden. Blomkvist watched him with a patient, neutral gaze. By now he was sure that Björck had had nothing to do with the murders. Since Svensson had never managed to confront him, Björck had no idea that he was about to be exposed, his name and photograph published in *Millennium* and in a book.

Björck did offer one valuable piece of information. He knew Nils Bjurman. They had met at the police shooting club, where Björck had been an active member for twenty-eight years. For a time he had even sat on the board along with Bjurman. They weren't close friends, but they had spent time together and occasionally had dinner.

No, he had not seen Bjurman in several months. The last time he ran into him was the previous summer, when they had been drinking in the same bar. He was sorry that Bjurman had been murdered—and by that psychopath—but he didn't plan to go to the funeral.

Blomkvist worried about the coincidence but gradually ran out of questions. Bjurman must have known hundreds of people in his professional and social life. The fact that he happened to know someone who turned up in Svensson's material was neither improbable nor statistically unusual. Blomkvist was himself casually acquainted with a journalist who also appeared in the book.

It was time to wind things up. Björck had gone through all the expected stages. First denial, then—when shown part of the documentation—anger, threats, attempted bribery, and, finally, pleading. Blomkvist had ignored all his outbursts.

"You'll ruin my life if you publish this stuff," said Björck.

THE GIRL WHO PLAYED WITH FIRE 353

"Yes."

"And you're going to do it."

"Absolutely."

"Why? Can't you give me a break? I'm not well."

"Interesting that you bring up human kindness as an argument."

"It doesn't cost a thing to be compassionate."

"You're right about that. While you moan about me destroying your life, you've enjoyed destroying the lives of young girls against whom you've committed crimes. We can prove three of them. God knows how many others there are. Where was your compassion then?"

He picked up his papers and stuffed them into his briefcase.

"I'll find my own way out."

As he reached the door, he turned back to Björck.

"Have you ever heard of a man named Zala?" he said.

Björck stared at him. He was still so agitated that he scarcely heard Blomkvist's question. Then his eyes widened.

Zala!

It's not possible.

Bjurman!

Could it be possible?

Blomkvist noticed the change and came back to the table.

"Why do you ask about Zala?" Björck said. He looked to be almost in shock.

"He interests me," Blomkvist said.

Blomkvist could almost see the wheels turning in Björck's head. After a while Björck grabbed a pack of cigarettes from the windowsill and lit one.

"If I do know something about Zala . . . what's it worth to you?"

"It depends on what you know."

Feelings and thoughts tumbled through Björck's head.

How the hell could Blomkvist know anything about Zalachenko?

"It's a name I haven't heard in a long time," Björck finally said.

"So you know who he is?"

"I didn't say that. What are you after?"

"He's one of the names on the list of people Svensson was investigating."

"What's it worth to you?" he said again.

"What's what worth?"

"If I can lead you to Zala . . . Would you leave me out of your report?"

Blomkvist sat down slowly. After Hedestad he had decided never again to bargain over a story. He did not intend to bargain with Björck either; no matter what happened he was going to hang him out to dry. But he realized he was unscrupulous enough to do a deal with Björck, then double-cross him. He felt no guilt. Björck was a policeman who had committed crimes. If he knew the name of a possible murderer, then it was his job to intervene—not to use the information to save his own skin. Blomkvist put his hand in his jacket pocket and switched on the tape recorder he had turned off when he got up from the table.

"Let's hear it," he said.

Modig was infuriated by Faste, but she did not allow her expression to reveal what she thought of him. The interview with Miriam Wu, which had continued after Bublanski left the room, was anything but by the book.

Modig was also surprised. She had never liked Faste and his macho style, but she had considered him a skilful police officer. That skill was glaringly absent today. It was obvious that Faste felt threatened by a beautiful, intelligent, and outspoken lesbian. It was equally obvious that Wu was aware of Faste's irritation and ruthlessly played to it.

"So you found the strap-on in my drawer. What did you fantasize about then?"

Miriam Wu gave a curious smirk. Faste looked like he was going to explode.

"Shut up and answer the question."

"You asked me if I ever fuck Lisbeth Salander with it. And my answer is that it's none of your fucking business."

Modig raised her hand: "The interview with Miriam Wu was interrupted for a break at 11:12 a.m."

She turned off the tape recorder.

"Would you stay here, please, Miriam? Faste, I'd like a word with you."

Miriam Wu smiled sweetly when Faste gave her a filthy look and slouched after Modig into the corridor. Modig spun around and looked Faste in the eye, her nose nearly touching his.

"Bublanski assigned me to take over the interview. Your help's not worth shit."

"Oh, come off it. That surly cunt is squirming like a snake."

"Could there be some sort of Freudian symbolism in your choice of similes?"

"What?"

"Forget it. Go and find Curt and challenge him to a game of tic-tac-toe, or go and shoot your pistol in the club room, or do whatever the hell you want. Just stay away from this interview."

"Why the hell are you acting this way, Modig?"

"Because you're sabotaging my interview."

"Are you so hot for her that you want to have her all to yourself?"

Before Modig could stop herself her hand shot out and slapped Faste across the face. She regretted it instantly, but it was too late. She glanced up and down the hall and saw that there were no witnesses, thank God.

At first Faste looked surprised. Then he sneered at her, tossed his jacket over his shoulder, and walked away. Modig almost called after him to apologize but decided against it. She waited a whole minute while she calmed down. Then she collected two cups of coffee from the vending machine and went back to Miriam Wu.

They sat in silence, drinking the coffee. At last Modig looked up.

"I'm sorry. This is probably one of the worst interviews ever conducted in police headquarters."

"He seems like a great guy to work with. Let me guess: he's heterosexual, divorced, and in charge of cracking gay jokes during coffee breaks."

"He's . . . a relic of something. That's all I can say."

"And you aren't?"

"At least I'm not homophobic."

"I'll buy that."

"Miriam, I . . . we, all of us, have been working around the clock for ten days now. We're tired and pissed off. We're trying to get to the bottom of a horrible double murder in Enskede and an equally horrible murder near Odenplan. Your friend Lisbeth Salander has been linked to the sites of both crimes. We have forensic evidence. A nationwide alert has been put out for her. Please understand that, whatever the cost, we have to apprehend her before she does harm to someone else or maybe to herself."

"I know Lisbeth Salander. I can't believe she murdered anyone."

"You can't believe it or you don't want to? Miriam, we don't put out a nationwide alert for someone without a damn good reason. But I can tell you this much: my boss, Criminal Inspector Bublanski, isn't convinced that she's guilty. We're discussing the possibility that she had an accomplice, or that she was somehow drawn into all this against her will. But we have to find her. You believe she's innocent, Miriam, but what happens if you're wrong? You say yourself that you don't know that much about her."

"I don't know what to believe."

"Then help us figure out the truth."

"Am I being arrested for anything?"

"No."

"Can I leave here when I want?"

"Technically, yes."

"And untechnically?"

"You'll remain a question mark in our eyes."

Miriam Wu weighed Modig's words. "Fire away. If your questions piss me off I won't answer."

Modig turned on the tape recorder again.

CHAPTER 20

Friday, April 1–Sunday, April 3

Miriam Wu spent one more hour with Modig. Towards the end of the interview, Bublanski came into the room and sat down and listened without saying a word. Miriam Wu acknowledged him politely, but she carried on talking only to Modig.

Finally Modig looked at Bublanski and asked whether he had any more questions. Bublanski shook his head.

"I declare the interview with Miriam Wu concluded. The time is 1:09 p.m." She turned off the tape recorder.

"I understand there was a little problem with Criminal Inspector Faste," Bublanski said.

"He had difficulty concentrating," said Modig neutrally.

"He's an idiot," said Miriam Wu.

"Criminal Inspector Faste actually does have many good points, but he may not be the best choice to interview a young woman," said Bublanski, looking Miriam Wu in the eye. "I shouldn't have entrusted him with the task. I apologize."

Miriam Wu looked surprised. "Apology accepted. I was quite unfriendly to you at first too."

Bublanski waved it off.

"May I ask you a few more things? With the tape recorder off?"

"Go ahead."

"The more I hear about Lisbeth Salander, the more puzzled I become. The picture I get from the people who know her is inconsistent with the documentation from the social welfare and psychiatric agencies."

"So?"

"Please give me some straight answers."

"All right."

"The psychiatric evaluation that was done when Salander was eighteen concludes that she is mentally retarded."

"Nonsense. Lisbeth is probably smarter than anyone I know."

"She never graduated from school and doesn't even have a certificate that says she can read and write."

"Lisbeth reads and writes a whole lot better than I do. Sometimes she sits and scribbles mathematical formulas. Pure algebra. I have no clue about that sort of math."

"Mathematics?"

"It's a hobby she's taken up."

"A hobby?" asked Bublanski after a moment.

"Some sort of equations. I don't even know what the symbols mean."

Bublanski sighed.

"Social services wrote a report after she was brought in one time from Tantolunden when she was seventeen. It indicated that she was supporting herself as a prostitute."

"Lisbeth a whore? Bullshit. I don't know what sort of work she does, but I'm not the least bit surprised that she had a job at that security company."

"How does she make a living?"

"I don't know."

"Is she a lesbian?"

"No. Lisbeth has sex with me, but that isn't the same thing as being a dyke. I don't think she knows herself what sort of sexual identity she has. I'd guess she's bisexual."

"What about the fact that you two use handcuffs and that

sort of thing? Is Salander sadistically inclined, or how would you describe her?"

"You misunderstood all those sex toys. We may use handcuffs sometimes for role-playing, but it has nothing to do with sadism or violence. It's a game."

"Has she ever been violent towards you?"

"No. I'm usually the dominant one in our games."

Miriam Wu smiled sweetly.

The afternoon meeting at 3:00 resulted in the first serious disagreement of the investigation. Bublanski gave an update and then explained that he felt they should be widening their scope.

"From day one we've been focusing all our energies on finding Lisbeth Salander. She is definitely a top suspect—this is based on evidence—but our picture of her is meeting resistance from everyone who knows her. Armansky, Blomkvist, and Miriam Wu don't hold with the picture of her as a psychotic killer. Therefore I want us to expand our thinking a bit, to consider alternative killers and the possibility that Salander herself may have had an accomplice or merely have been present when the shots were fired."

Bublanski's comments triggered a vigorous debate, in which he encountered strong opposition from Faste as well as Bohman from Milton Security. Bohman reminded the team that the simplest explanation was most often the right one.

"It's possible, of course, that Salander didn't act alone, but we have no forensic trace of any accomplice."

"We could always follow up on Blomkvist's leads within the police," Faste said acidly.

In the discussion, Bublanski was backed up only by Modig. Andersson and Holmberg were content with making isolated comments. Hedström from Milton was as quiet as a mouse during the whole discussion. Finally Prosecutor Ekström raised a hand.

"Bublanski—as I understand it, you don't want to elimi-nate Salander from the investigation."

"No, of course not. We have her fingerprints. But so far we have no motive. I want us to start thinking along different lines. Could several people have been involved? Could it still be related to that book about the sex trade that Svensson was writing? Blomkvist is certainly right that several people named in the book have a motive for murder."

"How do you want to proceed?" Ekström said.

"I want two people to start looking at alternative killers. Sonja and Niklas can work together."

"Me?" said Hedström in astonishment.

Bublanski had chosen him because he was the youngest person in the room and the one who was most likely to think outside the box.

"You'll work with Modig. Go through everything we know so far and try to find anything we might have missed. Faste, you, Andersson, and Bohman keep on the hunt for Salander. That's our number one priority."

"What should I do?" asked Holmberg.

"Focus on Advokat Bjurman. Do a fresh examination of his apartment in case we missed anything. Questions?"

Nobody had any.

"OK. We'll keep it quiet that Miriam Wu has turned up. She might have more to tell us, and I don't want the media jump-ing all over her."

Ekström agreed that they should proceed according to Bublanski's plan.

"Right," Hedström said, looking at Modig. "You're the detec-tive, you tell me what we're going to do."

They were in the corridor outside the conference room.

"I think we should have another talk with Mikael Blomkvist," she said. "But first I have to discuss one or two things with Bublanski. I have tomorrow and Sunday off. That means we won't get started until Monday morning. Spend the weekend going through the case material."

They said goodbye to each other. Modig walked into Bublanski's office as Ekström was leaving.

"Do you have a minute?" she said.

"Sit down."

"I got so angry with Faste that I lost my temper."

"He mentioned that you really laid into him."

"He said that I obviously wanted to be alone with Wu because I was turned on by her."

"That qualifies as sexual harassment. Would you like to file a complaint?"

"I slapped his face. That was enough."

"You were extremely provoked."

"I was."

"Faste has problems with strong women."

"I've noticed that."

"You're a strong woman and a very good cop."

"Thanks."

"But I'd appreciate it if you didn't beat up the staff."

"It won't happen again. I didn't even get a chance to go through Svensson's desk at *Millennium* today."

"Go home and take it easy over the weekend. We'll get started with the new approach on Monday."

Hedström stopped off at Central Station and had a coffee at George Café. He felt depressed. All week he had been waiting for the news that Salander had been caught. If she had resisted arrest, with a little luck some right-minded cop might have shot her.

And that was an appealing fantasy.

But Salander was still at liberty. Not only that, but Bublanski was floating the idea that she might not be the murderer. Not a positive development.

Being subordinate to Bohman was bad enough—the man was one of the most boring and least imaginative people at Milton—but now he had been put under Inspector Modig, and she was the most sceptical of the Salander lead. She was probably the one who had put doubts in Bublanski's mind. He wondered whether the famous Officer Bubble had something going on with that bitch. It wouldn't surprise him. He seemed thoroughly pussy-whipped by her. Of all the officers in the investigation, only Faste had enough balls to say what he thought.

Hedström was thinking hard. That morning he and Bohman had had a brief meeting at Milton with Armansky and Fräklund. A week of investigating had turned up nothing, and Armansky was frustrated that nobody had found any explanation for the murders. Fräklund had suggested that Milton Security should rethink its involvement—there were other more pressing tasks for Bohman and Hedström than to work as unpaid labour for the police.

Armansky decided that Bohman and Hedström should stay on for one more week. If by then there was no result, the assignment would be called off.

In other words, Hedström had only a week before the door to his involvement in the investigation would slam shut. He wasn't sure what he was going to do.

After a while he took out his mobile and called Tony Scala, a freelance journalist who made a living writing drivel for men's magazines. Hedström had met him a few times. He told Scala that he had one or two bits of information about the investigation into the murders in Enskede. He explained how he had ended up right in the middle of the hottest police investigation in years. Scala took the bait at once: it might turn into a scoop for a major magazine. They agreed to meet for a coffee an hour later at the Aveny on Kungsgatan.

Scala was fat. Seriously fat.

"If you want information from me there are two preconditions," Hedström said.

"Shoot."

"First, no mention of Milton Security in the article. Our role is as consultants only."

"Although it *is* newsworthy given that Salander worked at Milton."

"Cleaning and stuff like that," Hedström said, brushing him off. "That's no news."

"If you say so."

"Second, you have to slant the article so it sounds as though a woman leaked the information."

"How come?"

"To divert suspicion from me."

"All right. So what have you got?"

"Salander's lesbian girlfriend just showed up."

"OK, excellent! The chick she signed over the Lundagatan apartment to? The one who disappeared?"

"Miriam Wu. Is that worth anything to you?"

"You'd better believe it. Where was she?"

"Out of the country. She claims she hadn't even heard about the murders."

"Is she a suspect at all?"

"No. Not yet anyway. She was interviewed today and released three hours ago."

"I see. Do you believe her story?"

"I think she's lying through her teeth. She knows something."

"Great stuff, Niklas."

"But check her out. We're talking about a girl who goes in for S&M with Salander."

"You know this for a fact?"

"She admitted to it during the interview. We found handcuffs, leather outfits, whips, and the whole shebang when we searched the place."

The stuff about the whips was an exaggeration. All right, it was a total lie, but surely that Chinese cunt played with whips too.

"Are you kidding?" Scala said.

Paolo Roberto was one of the last to leave the library. He had spent the afternoon reading every line that had been written about the hunt for Salander.

He came out on Sveavägen feeling depressed and confused. And hungry. He went into McDonald's, ordered a burger, and sat down at a corner table.

Lisbeth Salander a triple murderer. He could hardly believe it. Not that skinny little fucking freaky chick. But should he do something about it? And if so, what?

Miriam Wu took a cab back to Lundagatan and slowly took in the devastation of her newly decorated apartment. Cupboards, wardrobes, storage boxes, and desk drawers had been emptied out. There was fingerprint powder on every surface. Her highly private sex toys were heaped on the bed. But as far as she could tell, nothing had been taken.

She put on the coffeemaker and shook her head. *Lisbeth, Lisbeth, what the fuck have you got yourself mixed up in?*

She took out her mobile and called Salander's number, but got the message that the subscriber could not be reached. She sat for a long time at her kitchen table and tried to work out what was real and what wasn't. The Salander she knew was no psychotic killer, but on the other hand she didn't know her very well. Salander was hot in bed, sure, but she could be a very cold fish if her mood changed.

She promised herself not to make up her mind before she saw Salander and got her own explanation. She felt like crying and spent two hours cleaning up.

By 7:00 p.m. the apartment was more or less habitable again. She took a shower and was in the kitchen dressed in a black-and-gold Oriental silk robe when the doorbell rang. At the door was an unshaven, exceptionally fat man.

"Hi, Miriam, my name is Tony Scala. I'm a journalist. Can I ask you a few questions?"

Standing next to him was a photographer who took a flash picture right in her face.

Miriam Wu contemplated a dropkick and an elbow to his nose, but she had the presence of mind to realize that it would only give them more photo ops.

"Have you been out of the country with Lisbeth Salander? Do you know where she is?"

Miriam Wu shut the door in their faces and locked it with the newly installed dead bolt. Scala pushed open the mail slot.

"Miriam, sooner or later you'll have to talk to the press. I can help you."

She balled up her fist and smashed it down on Scala's fingers. She heard a wail of pain. Then she closed the inner door and lay on the bed, closing her eyes. *Lisbeth, I'm going to wring your neck when I find you.*

After his trip to Smådalarö, Blomkvist spent the afternoon visiting another of the men that Svensson had planned to name. So far that week he had crossed off six of the thirty-seven names. The latest one was a retired judge living in Tumba; he had presided over several cases involving prostitution.

Refreshingly, the wretched man did not attempt denials, threats, or pleas for mercy. On the contrary, he cheerfully conceded that he had screwed whores from the East. No, he did not feel a grain of remorse. Prostitution was an honourable profession and he considered he was doing the girls a favour by being their customer.

Blomkvist was driving through Liljeholmen around 10:00 p.m. when Eriksson called him.

"Hi," she said. "Did you read the online edition of the *Morgon-Posten*?"

"No, what've they got?"

"Salander's girlfriend came home today."

"What? Who?"

"That dyke Miriam Wu who lives in her apartment on Lundagatan."

Wu, Blomkvist thought. SALANDER-WU on the nameplate.

"Thanks. I'm on my way."

Wu had unplugged the phone in her apartment and turned off her mobile. By 7:30 that evening news of her homecoming had appeared on the website of one of the morning papers. Soon after that *Aftonbladet* called, and three minutes later *Expressen*. *Aktuellt* ran the story without naming her, but by 9:00 no fewer than sixteen reporters from various media had tried to get a comment out of her.

Twice the doorbell had rung. She had not opened the door, and she turned off all the lights in the apartment. She felt like breaking the nose of the next reporter who hassled her. In the end she turned on her mobile and called a girlfriend who lived within walking distance down by Hornstull and asked if she could spend the night there.

She slipped out the entrance door on Lundagatan less than five minutes before Blomkvist rang her doorbell.

Bublanski called Modig just after 10:00 on Saturday morning. She had slept until 9:00 and then played with the children before her husband took them out for a Saturday treat.

"Have you read the papers today?"

"No, not yet. I've only been up an hour, and busy with the kids. Did something happen?"

"Somebody on our team is leaking stuff to the press."

"We've known that all along. Someone leaked Salander's psychiatric report several days ago."

"That was Ekström."

"It was?" Modig said.

"Of course, though he'll never admit it. He's trying to generate interest because it's to his advantage. But not this. A freelancer called Tony Scala talked to someone who told him all kinds of stuff about Miriam Wu. Among other things, details from what was said in the interview yesterday. That was something we wanted to keep quiet, and Ekström has gone through the roof."

"Damn it."

"The reporter didn't name anyone. The source was described as a person with a 'central position in the investigation.' "

"Shit," Modig said.

"The article describes the source as a 'she.' "

Modig said nothing for ten seconds. She was the only woman on the investigative team.

"Bublanski . . . I haven't said one word to a single journalist. I haven't discussed the investigation with anyone outside our corridor. Not even with my husband."

"I don't for a second believe that you would leak information. But unfortunately Prosecutor Ekström does. And Faste, who's on weekend duty, is brimming with insinuations."

Modig felt quite weary. "So what happens now?"

"Ekström is insisting that you be taken off the investigation while the charge is checked out."

"What charge? This is absurd. How am I supposed to prove—"

"You don't have to prove a thing. The person making the accusation has to come up with the proof."

"I know, but . . . damn it all. How long is this going to take?"

"It's already over."

"What?"

"I've just asked you. You said that you hadn't leaked any information. So the investigation is done and I write a report. I'll see you at 9:00 on Monday in Ekström's office, and I'll handle the questions."

"Thank you, Bublanski."

"My pleasure."

"There is one problem."

"I know."

"Since I didn't leak anything, somebody else on the team must have."

"Any suggestions?"

"My first guess would be Faste, but I don't really think he could be the one."

"I'm inclined to agree with you. He can be a total prick, but he was genuinely outraged at the leak."

Bublanski liked his walks, depending on the weather and how much time he had. It was exercise he enjoyed. He lived on Katarina Bangata in Södermalm, not so far from *Millennium*'s offices, or from Milton Security for that matter, where Salander had worked, and Lundagatan, where she had lived. It was also within walking distance of the synagogue on St. Paulsgatan. On Saturday afternoon he walked to all of these places.

His wife Agnes accompanied him for the first part of the walk. They had been married for twenty-three years, and in all that time he had never strayed.

They stopped at the synagogue for a while and talked to the rabbi. Bublanski was a Polish Jew, while Agnes' family—the few who had survived Auschwitz—were originally from Hungary.

After visiting the synagogue they parted—Agnes to go shopping, Bublanski to keep walking. He needed to be alone, to think about the investigation. He went back over the measures he had taken since the job had landed on his desk on the morning of Maundy Thursday, and he could identify only a couple of mistakes.

One was that he hadn't immediately sent someone to go through Svensson's desk at *Millennium*. When eventually he remembered to do it—and he had done it himself—Blomkvist had already cleaned out God knows what.

Another mistake was missing the fact that Salander had bought a car. But Holmberg had reported that the car contained nothing of interest.

Apart from these two errors, the investigation had been as thorough as could have been expected.

He stopped at a kiosk near Zinkensdamm and stared at a newspaper headline. The passport photograph of Salander had been cropped to a small but easily recognizable size and the focus had shifted to a more sensational line of news:

POLICE TRACKING
LESBIAN SATANIST CULT

He bought a copy and found the spread, which was dominated by a photograph of five girls in their late teens dressed in black leather jackets with rivets, torn black jeans, and tight T-shirts. One of the girls was holding up a flag with a pentagram and another was making a sign with her index and little fingers. The caption read: *Lisbeth Salander hung out with a death-metal band that played in small clubs. In 1996 the group paid homage to the Church of Satan and had a hit with "Etiquette of Evil."*

The name Evil Fingers was not mentioned, and the newspaper had blacked out their eyes, but friends of the rock group would certainly recognize the girls.

The story was mainly about Miriam Wu and was illustrated with a picture taken from a show at Bern's in which she had performed. She was topless and wearing a Russian army officer's cap. Her eyes were blacked out too.

SALANDER'S GIRLFRIEND WROTE ABOUT LESBIAN S&M SEX

The 31-year-old woman is well known in Stockholm's trendy nightspots. She makes no secret that she picks up women and likes to dominate her partner.

The reporter had even found a girl he called Sara who, according to her own testimony, had been the object of the woman's pickup attempts. Her boyfriend had been "disturbed" by the incident. The article went on to say that the band was an obscure and elitist feminist variant on the fringes of the gay movement, and that it had acquired a certain fame for hosting a "bondage workshop" at the Gay Pride Festival. The rest of the article was based on a deliberately provocative piece Wu had written six years earlier for a feminist fanzine. Bublanski scanned the text and then tossed the paper into a trash can.

He brooded over Faste and Modig, both competent detectives. But Faste was a problem; he got on people's nerves. He would have to have a talk with the man, but he didn't think he was the source of the leaks.

When Bublanski got his bearings again he was standing on Lundagatan staring at the front door of Salander's building. It had not been a conscious decision to walk there.

He walked up the steps to upper Lundagatan, where he stood for a long time thinking about Blomkvist's story of Salander's attack. That didn't lead anywhere either. There was no police report, no names of persons involved, and not even an adequate description of the attacker. Blomkvist had claimed that he could not read the licence plate of the van that drove away from the scene.

Assuming any of it had happened at all.

Another dead end.

Bublanski looked down Lundagatan at the burgundy Honda that was still parked in the street, and at that moment Blomkvist walked up to the front door.

Miriam Wu awoke late in the day, tangled in the sheets. She sat up and looked around at the unfamiliar room.

She had used the torrent of media attention as an excuse to call a girlfriend. But she had also left the apartment, she realized, because she was afraid that Salander might knock on her door. Her interview with the police and the newspaper coverage had affected her profoundly, and even though she had resolved not to make up her mind one way or the other until Salander had a chance to explain what had happened, she had started to suspect that her friend might actually be guilty.

She glanced down at Viktoria Viktorsson—known as Double-V and 100 percent dyke. She was lying on her stomach and mumbling in her sleep. Miriam slipped out of bed and took a shower. Then she went out to buy rolls for breakfast. It was not until she was standing at the cash register of the shop next to Café Cinnamon on Verkstadsgatan that she saw the headlines. She fled back to Double-V's apartment.

Blomkvist punched in the entry code and went inside. He was gone for two minutes before he reappeared. Nobody home. He looked up and down the street, apparently undecided. Bublanski watched him intently.

What bothered Bublanski was that if Blomkvist had lied about the attack on Lundagatan then he was playing some kind of game, which in the worst case could mean that he was involved in the murders. But if he was telling the truth there was still a hidden element in the drama; there were more players than those who were visible, and the murders could be considerably more complex than an attack of insanity in a pathologically disturbed girl.

As Blomkvist moved towards Zinkensdamm, Bublanski called after him. Blomkvist stopped, saw the detective, and walked over to him. They met at the foot of the steps.

"Hello, Blomkvist. Looking for Lisbeth Salander?"

"As a matter of fact, no. I'm looking for Miriam Wu."

"She isn't home. Somebody leaked the news to the press that she had resurfaced."

"What did she have to say?"

Bublanski gave Blomkvist a searching look. *Kalle Blomkvist.*

"Walk with me," Bublanski said. "I need a cup of coffee."

They passed Högalid Church in silence. Bublanski took him to Café Lillasyster, near to where Liljeholmsbron crosses the Norrström to the southern suburb of Liljeholmen. Bublanski ordered a double espresso with a teaspoonful of cold milk and Blomkvist a caffè latte. They sat in the smoking section.

"It's been a long time since I've had such a frustrating case," Bublanski said. "How much can I discuss with you without having to read it in *Expressen* tomorrow morning?"

"I don't work for *Expressen.*"

"You know what I mean."

"Bublanski—I don't believe Lisbeth is guilty."

"And now you're doing your own private investigation? Is that why they call you Kalle Blomkvist?"

Blomkvist smiled. "They tell me you're called Officer Bubble."

Bublanski gave him a stiff smile. "Why do you think Salander is innocent?"

"I don't know a thing about her guardian, but she had no reason whatsoever to murder Dag and Mia. Especially not Mia. Lisbeth loathes men who hate women, and Mia was in the process of putting the screws to a whole bunch of prostitutes' clients. What Mia was doing was completely in line with what Lisbeth herself would have done. She is a very moral creature."

"I can't seem to piece together a coherent picture of her. A retarded psycho case or a skilled researcher?"

"Lisbeth is just different. She's abnormally antisocial, but there is definitely nothing wrong with her intelligence. On the contrary, she's probably smarter than you or me."

Bublanski sighed. Blomkvist was giving him the same story that Miriam Wu had.

"She has to be caught, come what may. I can't go into the details, but she was at the murder scene, and she has been linked to the murder weapon."

"I suppose that means you found her fingerprints on it. That doesn't prove she fired the shots."

Bublanski nodded. "Dragan Armansky doesn't believe it either. He's too cautious to say it straight out, but he's also looking for proof that she's innocent."

"And you? What do you think?"

"I'm a detective. I arrest people and question them. Right now things look dismal for Fröken Salander. We've put away murderers on considerably weaker circumstantial evidence."

"You didn't answer my question."

"I don't know. If she did turn out to be innocent . . . Who do you think would have a motive for killing both her guardian and your two friends?"

Blomkvist took out a pack of cigarettes and offered it to Bublanski, who shook his head. He did not want to lie to the police. He ought to say something about the man known as Zala. He should also tell Bublanski about Superintendent Gunnar Björck of the Security Police.

But Bublanski and his colleagues had access to Svensson's material, which contained the same <Zala> folder. All they had to do was read it. Instead they were charging along like a steamroller and feeding salacious details about Salander to the press.

He had an idea, but didn't know where it would lead. He didn't want to name Björck before he was sure. *Zalachenko.* That was the link between Bjurman and Dag and Mia. The problem was that Björck so far hadn't told him anything.

"Let me dig a little deeper, then I'll give you an alternative theory."

"No police traces, I hope."

"Not yet. What did Miriam Wu say?"

"Just about the same as you. They had a relationship."

"None of my business," Blomkvist said.

"She and Salander have known each other for three years. She says she knows nothing about Salander's background and didn't even know where she worked. It's hard to believe, but I think she's telling the truth."

"Lisbeth is obsessively private," Blomkvist said. "Do you have Miriam Wu's phone number?"

"Yes."

"Can I have it?"

"No."

"Why not?"

"Mikael, this is police business. We don't need private investigators with wild theories."

"I don't have *any* theories yet. On the other hand, I think the answer lies somewhere in Svensson's material."

"You could get in touch with Wu if you made an effort."

"Probably, but the simplest way is to ask somebody who already has the number."

Bublanski sighed.

Blomkvist was suddenly very annoyed with him. "Are policemen more talented than normal people, the ones you call private investigators?"

"No, I don't think that. But the police have the training and it's their job to solve crimes."

"Ordinary people have training too," Blomkvist said slowly. "And sometimes a private investigator is better at working things out than a real detective."

"So you believe."

"I know it. Take the Rahman case.* A bunch of policemen sat on their backsides with their eyes closed for five years while Rahman was locked up, innocent of the murder of an old lady. He would still be locked up today if a schoolteacher hadn't devoted several years to a serious investigation. She did it without the resources you have at your disposal. Not only did she prove that he was innocent, but she also identified the person who in all probability was the real killer."

"We did lose face in the Rahman case. The prosecutor refused to listen to the facts."

"Bublanski . . . I'm going to tell you something. At this very moment you're losing face in the Salander case as well. I'm damn sure that she did not kill Dag and Mia, and I'm going to prove it. I'm going to produce another killer for you, and when that happens I am also going to write an article that you and your colleagues are going to find painful reading."

On his way home to Katarina Bangata, Bublanski felt an urge to talk with God about the case, but instead of going to the synagogue he went to the Catholic church on Folkungagatan. He sat in one of the pews at the back and did not move for over an hour. As a Jew he had no business being in a church, but it was a peaceful place that he regularly visited when he felt the need to sort out his thoughts, and he knew that God did not mind. There was a difference, besides, between Catholicism

*Joy Rahman was sentenced to life in prison in 1994 for the murder of a seventy-two-year-old woman. He was granted a retrial in 2002, exonerated by the Stockholm Court of Appeal, and received 10.2 million kronor in damages, the largest damages claim ever awarded in Sweden.

and Judaism. He went to the synagogue when he needed company and fellowship with other people. Catholics went to church to seek peace in the presence of God. The church invited silence and visitors would always be left to themselves.

He brooded about Salander and Wu. And he wondered what Berger and Blomkvist might be withholding from him—certainly they knew something about Salander that they hadn't told him. What sort of research had Salander done for Blomkvist? For a moment Bublanski considered whether she might have worked on the Wennerström exposé, but then dismissed that possibility. Salander couldn't have contributed anything of value there, no matter how good she was at personal investigations.

Bublanski was worried: he did not like Blomkvist's cocksure certainty that Salander was innocent. It was one thing for him as a detective to be beset by doubt—doubting was his job. It was quite another thing for Blomkvist to deliver an ultimatum as a private investigator.

He didn't care for private investigators because they often produced conspiracy theories, which prompted headlines in the newspapers but also created a lot of unnecessary extra work for the police.

This had developed into the most exasperating murder investigation he had ever been involved in. Somehow he had lost his focus. There had to be a chain of logical consequences.

If a teenager is found stabbed to death on Mariatorget, it's a matter of tracking down which skinhead gang or other mob was rampaging through Söder station an hour earlier. There are friends, acquaintances, and witnesses, and very soon there are suspects.

If a man is killed with three bullets in a bar in Skärholmen and it turns out he was a heavy in the Yugoslav mafia, then it's a matter of finding out which thugs are trying to take control of cigarette smuggling.

If a young woman with a decent background and normal

lifestyle is found strangled in her apartment, it's a matter of finding out who her boyfriend was, or who was the last person she talked to at the bar the night before.

Bublanski had run so many investigations like these that he could do them in his sleep.

The current investigation had started off so well. After only a few hours they had found a prime suspect. Salander was practically designed for the role—an obvious psycho case, known to have suffered from violent, uncontrollable outbursts her whole life. It was simply a matter of picking her up and getting a confession or, depending on the circumstances, putting her into psychiatric care.

But after the promising beginning everything had gone to hell. Salander did not live at her address. She had friends like Armansky and Blomkvist. She had a relationship with a lesbian who liked sex with handcuffs, and that put the media in a new frenzy. She had 2.5 million kronor in the bank and no known employer. Then Blomkvist shows up with theories about trafficking and conspiracies—and as a celebrity journalist he has the political clout to create utter chaos in the investigation with a single article.

Above all, the prime suspect had proven to be impossible to locate, despite the fact that she was no taller than a hand's breadth and had tattoos all over her body. It had been almost two weeks since the murders and there wasn't so much as a whisper as to where she might be hiding.

Björck had had a wretched day since Blomkvist stepped across his threshold. He had a continuous dull ache in his back, but he paced back and forth in his borrowed house, incapable either of relaxing or of taking any initiative. He couldn't make any sense of the story. The pieces of the puzzle would not fall into place.

When he'd first heard the news about Bjurman's murder,

he was aghast. But he hadn't been surprised when Salander was almost immediately identified as the prime suspect and then the hue and cry for her began. He had followed every report on TV, and he bought all the daily papers he could get hold of and read every word written about the case.

He didn't doubt for a second that Salander was mentally ill and capable of killing. He had no reason to question her guilt or the assumptions of the police—on the contrary, everything he knew about Salander told him that she really was a psychotic madwoman. He had been just about to call in and offer his advice to the investigation, or at least check that the case was being handled properly, but then he realized that it actually no longer concerned him. Besides, a call from him might attract the sort of attention that he wanted to avoid. Instead he kept following the breaking news developments with absentminded interest.

Blomkvist's visit had turned his peace and quiet upside down. Björck never had any inkling that Salander's orgy of murder might involve him personally—that one of her victims had been a media swine who was about to expose him to the whole of Sweden.

He had even less of an idea that the name Zala would crop up in the story like a hand grenade with its pin pulled, and least of all that the name would be known to a journalist like Blomkvist. It defied all common sense.

The day after Blomkvist's visit, Björck telephoned his former boss, who was seventy-eight years old and living in Laholm. He had to try to worm out the context without letting on that he was calling for any reason other than pure curiosity and professional concern. It was a relatively short conversation.

"This is Björck. I assume you've read the papers."

"I have. She's popped up again."

"And she doesn't seem to have changed much."

"It's no longer our concern."

"You don't think that—"

"No, I don't. All that is dead and buried. There's no connection."

"But Bjurman, of all people. I presume it wasn't by chance that he became her guardian."

There were several seconds of silence on the line.

"No, it was no accident. It seemed like a good idea two years ago. Who could have predicted this?"

"How much did Bjurman know?"

His former boss chuckled. "You know quite well what Bjurman was like. Not the most talented actor."

"I mean . . . did he know about the connection? Could there be something among his papers or personal effects that would lead anyone to—"

"No, of course not. I understand what you're getting at, but don't worry. Salander has always been the loose cannon in this story. We arranged it so that Bjurman got the assignment, but that was only so we'd have someone we could check up on. Better that than an unknown quantity. If she had started blabbing, he would have come to us. Now this will all work out for the best."

"What do you mean?"

"Well, after this, Salander is going to be sitting in a psychiatric ward for a long, long time."

"That makes sense."

"Don't worry. Go and enjoy your sick leave in peace and quiet."

But that was exactly what Björck was unable to do. Blomkvist had seen to that. He sat at the kitchen table and looked out over Jungfrufjärden as he tried to sum up his own situation. He was being threatened from two flanks.

Blomkvist was going to hang him out to dry as a john. There was a serious risk that he would end his police career by being convicted of breaking the sex-trade law.

But even more serious was the fact that Blomkvist was trying to track down Zalachenko. Somehow he was mixed up in the story too. And Zala would lead him back to Björck's front door.

His former boss had apparently been assured that there was nothing among Bjurman's personal effects that could provide a further lead. But there was. The report from 1991. And Bjurman had gotten it from Björck.

He tried to visualize the meeting with Bjurman more than three months earlier. They had met in Gamla Stan. Bjurman had called him one afternoon at work and suggested they have a beer. They talked about the shooting club and everything under the sun, but Bjurman had sought him out for a particular reason. He needed a favour. He had asked about Zalachenko . . .

Björck got up and stood by the kitchen window. He had been a little tipsy at the meeting. In fact he was quite drunk. What had Bjurman asked him?

"Speaking of which . . . I'm in the middle of doing something for an old acquaintance who's popped up . . ."

"Oh yeah, who's that?"

"Alexander Zalachenko. Do you remember him?"

"Are you kidding? He's not an easy man to forget."

"Whatever happened to him?"

Technically, it was none of Bjurman's business. In fact there was good reason to put Bjurman under the microscope just for having asked . . . but he was Salander's guardian. He said he needed the old report. *And I gave it to him.*

Björck had made a serious mistake. He had assumed that Bjurman had already been informed—anything else would have seemed unthinkable. And Bjurman had presented the matter as though he was only trying to take a shortcut through the plodding bureaucratic procedure in which everything was stamped "confidential" and hush-hush and could drag on for months. In particular anything that had to do with Zalachenko.

I gave him the report. It was still stamped "confidential," but it was for a good and understandable reason, and Bjurman was not someone who would spill the beans. He was stupid, but he had never been a gossip. What could it hurt? It was so many years ago.

Bjurman had made a fool of him. The more Björck thought about it, the more convinced he was that Bjurman had chosen his words deliberately, very cautiously.

But what the fuck was Bjurman after? And why would Salander have murdered him?

Blomkvist went to the apartment in Lundagatan four more times on Saturday in the hope of finding Miriam Wu, but she was never there.

He spent a good part of the day at the Kaffebar on Hornsgatan with his iBook, rereading the emails that Svensson had received at his *Millennium* address and the contents of the folder named <Zala>. In the weeks before he was murdered, Svensson had spent more and more time researching Zala.

Blomkvist wished he could phone Svensson and ask him why the document about Irina P. was in the <Zala> folder. The only reasonable conclusion was that Svensson had suspected Zala of murdering her.

At 5:00 p.m. Bublanski called and gave him Miriam Wu's phone number. He didn't know what had made the detective change his mind, but now that he had the number he tried it about once every half hour. Not until 11:00 p.m. did she answer. It was a short conversation.

"Hello, Miriam. My name is Mikael Blomkvist."

"And who the hell are you?"

"I'm a journalist and I work at a magazine called *Millennium.*"

Miriam Wu expressed her feelings in a pithy way. "Ah yes. That Blomkvist. Go to hell, journalist creep."

She broke off the connection before Blomkvist had a chance to explain what he wanted. He directed some bad thoughts at Tony Scala and tried to call back. She did not answer. In the end he sent a text message.

Please call me. It's important.

She never called.

Late that night Blomkvist shut down his computer, undressed, and crawled into bed. He wished he had Berger to keep him company.

PART 4

Terminator Mode

A root of an equation is a number which substituted into the equation instead of an unknown converts the equation into an identity. The root is said to satisfy the equation. Solving an equation implies finding all of its roots. An equation that is always satisfied, no matter the choice of values for its unknowns, is called an identity.

$$(a + b)^2 = a^2 + 2ab + b^2$$

CHAPTER 21

Maundy Thursday, March 24– Monday, April 4

Salander spent the first week of the police hunt far from the drama. She remained in peace and quiet in her apartment on Fiskargatan. Her mobile was turned off and the SIM card taken out. She did not intend to use that phone again. Her eyes grew wide with astonishment as she followed the stories in the online editions of the newspapers and on the TV news programmes.

She was irritated by the passport photograph that appeared everywhere. She looked stupid.

Despite her years of striving for anonymity, she had been transformed overnight into one of the most notorious and talked-about individuals in Sweden. She began to realize that a nationwide alert for a short girl suspected of three murders was one of the year's biggest news stories. She followed the commentary and speculation in the media with amazement, fascinated that confidential documents about her medical history seemed to be accessible to any newsroom that wanted to publish them. One headline in particular awakened buried memories:

ARRESTED FOR
ASSAULT IN GAMLA STAN

A court reporter at TT wire service had scooped his competitors by digging up a medical report that had been written when Salander was arrested for kicking a passenger in the face at Gamla Stan tunnelbana station.

She had been at Odenplan and was on her way back to her foster home in Hägersten. At Rådmansgatan an apparently sober stranger got on the train and immediately focused his attention on her. Later she discovered that he was Karl Evert Norgren, an unemployed former athlete from Gävle. Despite the fact that the carriage was half empty, he sat down next to her and began to bother her. He put his hand on her knee and tried to start a conversation along the lines of "I'll give you two hundred if you come home with me." When she ignored him he got pushy and called her a sour old cunt. The fact that she refused to talk to him and had changed seats at T-Centralen had no effect.

As they were approaching Gamla Stan he put his arms around her from behind and pushed them up inside her sweater, whispering in her ear that she was a whore. She replied with an elbow to his eye and then grabbed one of the upright poles, lifted herself up, and kicked him with both heels across the bridge of his nose, which prompted heavy bleeding.

She was dressed as a punk and had blue-dyed hair, so she had little chance to melt into the crowd when the train stopped at the platform. A friend of law and order had grappled with her and held her down on the ground until the police arrived.

She cursed her gender. Nobody would have dared attack her if she had been a man.

She hardly made any attempt to explain why she had kicked Karl Evert Norgren in the face. She didn't think it was worth trying to explain anything to uniformed authorities. She refused on principle to respond when psychiatrists tried to determine her mental state. As luck would have it, several other passengers had observed the whole course of events, including a persistent woman from Härnösand who happened to be a member of parliament for the Centre Party. The woman testified that Norgren had assaulted Salander before the violence broke out. When it later turned out that Norgren had been convicted for sexual offences twice before, the prosecutor decided to drop the case. But that did not mean that the social welfare report on Salander was set aside. Not long afterwards the district court declared her incompetent, and she ended up under the guardianship of Holger Palmgren, and later Nils Bjurman.

Now all of these intimate and confidential details were on the Net for public consumption. Her personal record was supplemented with colourful descriptions of how she had come into conflict with people around her since elementary school, and how she spent her early teens in a children's psychiatric clinic.

The diagnoses of Salander in the press varied depending on which edition and which newspaper was doing the reporting. Sometimes she was described as psychotic and sometimes as schizophrenic or paranoid. All the papers subscribed to the view that she was mentally handicapped—after all, she hadn't been able to finish school. The public should have no doubt that she was unbalanced and inclined to violence.

When it was discovered that Salander was friends with the lesbian Miriam Wu, a frenzy broke out in certain papers. Wu had appeared in Benita Costa's show at the Gay Pride Festival, a provocative performance in which she was photographed topless wearing leather chaps with suspenders and high-heeled patent-leather boots. She had also written articles for a gay newspaper that were widely quoted, as were the interviews she had given in connection with her appearance in various shows.

The combination of mass murder and titillating S&M sex was evidently doing wonders for circulation figures.

Since Wu hadn't surfaced during that first dramatic week, there was speculation that she too might have fallen victim to Salander's violence or that she could have been an accomplice. These speculations, however, were restricted for the most part to the unsophisticated Internet chat room "Exile." On the other hand, several newspapers floated the theory that since Mia Johansson's thesis dealt with the sex trade, this might be Salander's motive for the murders, on the grounds that—according to the social welfare agency—she was a prostitute.

At the end of the week the media discovered that Salander also had connections to a group of young women who flirted with Satanism. They called themselves Evil Fingers, and this caused an older male cultural columnist to write about the rootlessness of youth and the dangers that lurk in everything from skinhead culture to hip-hop.

When all the media assertions were put together, the police appeared to be hunting for a psychotic lesbian who had joined a cult of Satanists that propagandized for S&M sex and hated society in general and men in particular. Because Salander had been abroad for the past year, there might be international connections too.

In only one case did Salander react with any great emotion to the media uproar:

"WE WERE SCARED OF HER"
She threatened to kill us,
say teacher and schoolmates

The person making this statement was a former teacher, now a textile artist, named Birgitta Miåås.

Salander had been eleven on the occasion in question. She remembered Miåås as an unpleasant substitute math teacher who time after time had tried to get her to answer a question that she'd already answered correctly, even though the answer key in the textbook said she was wrong. In fact, the textbook was wrong, and as far as Salander was concerned that should have been obvious to everyone. But Miåås had grown more and more obstinate, and Salander became less and less willing to discuss the matter. She sat there pouting until Miåås, out of sheer frustration, grabbed her by the shoulder and shook her to get her attention. Lisbeth responded by throwing the textbook at Miåås' head, which started a big hullabaloo. She spat and hissed and kicked when her classmates tried to hold on to her.

The article ran as a feature in an evening paper, and allowed space for a sidebar with some quotes and a photograph of a former classmate posing in front of the entrance to her old school. This was David Gustavsson, who now called himself a financial assistant. He claimed that the students were afraid of Salander because "she threatened to kill somebody once." Salander remembered Gustavsson as one of the biggest bullies in school, a powerful brute with the IQ of a stump, who seldom passed up an opportunity to dish out insults and punches in the hallway. Once he had attacked her behind the gym during lunch break, and as usual she had fought back. From a purely physical standpoint she didn't have a chance, but her attitude was that death was better than capitulation. The incident deteriorated when a large number of her schoolmates gathered in a circle to watch Gustavsson knock her to the ground over and over again. It had been amusing up to a point, but the stupid girl did not seem to understand what was good for her and refused to back down. She didn't even cry or beg for mercy. Finally he gave Salander two serious punches that split her lip and knocked the wind out of her. Her schoolmates left her in a miserable heap behind the gym and ran away laughing.

Salander had gone home and licked her wounds. Two days later she came back carrying a bat. In the middle of the playground she slugged Gustavsson in the ear. As he lay there in shock she bent down, pressed the bat to his throat, and whispered in his ear that if he ever touched her again she would kill him. When the teachers discovered what had happened, Gustavsson was taken to the school nurse while Salander was sent to the head teacher for punishment, further comments in her record, and more social welfare reports.

Salander had not thought about either Miåås or Gustavsson for at least fifteen years. She made a mental note to check out what they were up to these days when she had some spare time.

The result of all this press attention was that Salander had become both famous and infamous to the entire Swedish population. Her background was charted, scrutinized, and published down to the most minute detail, from her outbursts in elementary school to her being committed to St. Stefan's Psychiatric Clinic for Children, outside Uppsala, where she spent more than two years.

She pricked up her ears when chief of staff Dr. Peter Teleborian was interviewed on TV. Salander had last seen him eight years earlier, in connection with the district court hearing regarding her declaration of incompetence. His brow was deeply furrowed and he scratched at a thin beard when he turned to the studio reporter with concern and explained that he was bound by confidentiality and thus could not discuss an individual patient. All he could say was that Salander's was an extremely complex case, that she required expert care, and that the district court, against his recommendation, had decided to place her under guardianship in society rather than give her the institutional care she needed. It was a scandal, Teleborian claimed. He regretted that three people had now paid with their lives as a result of this misjudgment, and he made sure to get in a few jabs at the cutbacks in psychiatric care that the government had forced through in recent decades.

Salander noted that no newspaper revealed that the most common form of care in the secure ward of the children's psychiatric hospital, for which Dr. Teleborian was responsible, was to place "unruly and unmanageable patients" in a room that was "free of stimuli." The room contained only a bed with a restraining belt. The textbook explanation was that unruly children could not receive any "stimuli" that might trigger an outburst.

When she grew older she discovered that there was another term for the same thing. *Sensory deprivation*. According to the Geneva Conventions, subjecting prisoners to sensory deprivation was classified as inhumane. It was a commonly used element in experiments with brainwashing conducted by various dictatorial regimes, and there was evidence that the political prisoners who confessed to all sorts of crimes during the Moscow trials in the 1930s had been subjected to such treatment.

As Salander watched Teleborian's face on TV, her heart became a little lump of ice. She wondered whether he still used the same disgusting aftershave. He had been responsible for what was defined as her care. Salander had rapidly come to the realization that an "unruly and unmanageable patient" was equivalent to one who questioned Teleborian's reasoning and expertise.

She had spent about half of her time at St. Stefan's strapped to the bed in the "stimulus-free" room.

Teleborian had never touched her sexually. He had never touched her at all, other than in the most innocent situations. On one occasion he had placed a hand on her shoulder as a warning when she lay strapped down in isolation.

She wondered if her teeth marks were still visible on the knuckle of his little finger.

The whole thing had developed into a vicious game, in

which Teleborian held all the cards. Her defence had been to ignore him completely whenever he was in the room.

She was twelve when she was transported by two police-women to St. Stefan's. It was a few weeks after "All The Evil" had occurred. She remembered every detail. First she had thought that everything would work out somehow. She had tried to explain her version to police officers, social workers, hospital personnel, nurses, doctors, psychiatrists, and even a pastor, who wanted her to pray with him. As she sat in the backseat of the police car and they passed the Wenner-Gren Centre on the way north to Uppsala, she still did not know where they were heading. Nobody told her. That was when she began to sense that nothing would ever work out.

She had tried to explain to Teleborian.

The result of her efforts was that on the night she turned thirteen, she lay strapped to the bed.

Teleborian was the most loathsome and disgusting sadist Salander had ever met in her life, bar none. He outclassed Bjur-man by a mile. Bjurman had been unspeakably brutal, but she could handle him. Teleborian, on the other hand, was shielded behind a curtain of documents, assessments, academic hon-ours, and psychiatric mumbo jumbo. Not a single one of his actions could ever be reported or criticized.

He had a state-endorsed mandate to tie down disobedient little girls with leather straps.

And every time Salander lay shackled on her back and he tightened the straps and she met his gaze, she could read his excitement. She knew. And he knew that she knew.

The night she turned thirteen she decided never again to exchange a word with Teleborian or any other psychiatrist or shrink. That was her birthday present to herself. And she had kept her promise. She knew that it infuriated Teleborian and perhaps contributed more than anything else to her being strapped down so tightly night after night. But that was a price she was willing to pay.

She taught herself everything about self-control. She had no more outbursts, nor did she throw things on the days she was released from isolation.

But she refused to talk to doctors.

On the other hand, she spoke politely to the nurses, the kitchen staff, and the cleaning women. This was noted. A friendly nurse whose name was Carolina, and whom Salander trusted up to a point, asked her one day why she acted the way she did. Salander gave her a quizzical look.

Why won't you talk to the doctors?

Because they don't listen to what I say.

She was aware that all such comments were entered into her record, documenting that her silence was a completely rational decision.

During her last year at St. Stefan's, Salander was placed in the isolation cell less often. When it did happen it was always because she had irritated Dr. Teleborian in some way, which she seemed to do as soon as he laid eyes on her. He tried over and over again to break through her obstinate silence and force her to acknowledge his existence.

For a time he prescribed Salander a type of psychiatric drug that made it hard for her to breathe or think, which in turn brought on anxiety. From then on she refused to take her medicine, and this resulted in the decision to force-feed her three tablets a day.

Her resistance was so strong that the staff had to hold her down, pry open her mouth, and then force her to swallow. The first time, Salander immediately stuck her fingers down her throat and vomited her lunch onto the nearest orderly. After that she was given the tablets when she was strapped down, so she learned to throw up without having to stick her fingers down her throat. Her obstinate resistance and the extra work this made for the staff led to a suspension of the medication.

She had just turned fifteen when she was without warning moved back to Stockholm to live once more with a foster family. The change came as a shock to her. At that time Teleborian was not yet running St. Stefan's. Salander was sure that this was the only reason she had been released. If Teleborian had been given responsibility for the decision, she would still be strapped to the bed in the isolation cell.

Now she was watching him on TV. She wondered if he fantasized about her ending up in his care again, or if she was now too old to arouse him. His reference to the district court's decision not to institutionalize her provoked the indignation of the interviewer, although apparently he had no idea what questions to ask. There was nobody to contradict Teleborian. The former chief of staff at St. Stefan's had since died. The district court judge who had presided over Salander's case, and who now had in part to accept the role as the villain in the drama, had retired and was refusing to comment to the press.

Salander found one of the most astonishing articles in the online edition of a newspaper published in central Sweden. She read it three times before she turned off her computer and lit a cigarette. She sat on her IKEA pillow in the window seat and dejectedly watched the lights outside.

"SHE'S BISEXUAL,"
SAYS CHILDHOOD FRIEND

The 26-year-old woman sought in connection with three murders is described as an introverted eccentric who had great difficulties adjusting to school. Despite many attempts to include her in the group, she remained an outsider.

"She obviously had problems with her sexual identity," recalls Johanna, one of her few close friends at school.

"It was clear early on that she was different and that she was bisexual. We were very concerned about her."

The article went on to describe some episodes that this Johanna remembered. Salander frowned. She could remember neither the episodes nor that she'd had a close friend named Johanna. In fact, she could not recall ever knowing anyone who could be described as a close friend or who tried to draw her into a group at school.

The article did not specify when these episodes were supposed to have taken place, but she had left school when she was twelve. This meant that her concerned childhood friend must have discovered Salander's bisexuality when she was ten, maybe eleven.

Among the flood of ridiculous articles over the past week, the one quoting Johanna hit her hardest. It was so obviously fabricated. Either the reporter had run across a mythomaniac or he had made up the story himself. She memorized the reporter's name and added him to the list of subjects for future research.

Not even the more positive reports, ones that criticized society with headlines such as SOCIETY FAILS or SHE NEVER GOT THE HELP SHE NEEDED, could dilute her standing as public enemy number one—a mass murderer who in one fit of insanity had executed three honourable citizens.

Salander read these interpretations of her life with a certain fascination and noted an obvious hole in the public knowledge. Despite apparently unlimited access to the most classified details of her life, the media had completely missed "All The Evil," which had happened just before her thirteenth birthday. The published information ranged from kindergarten to the age of eleven, and was taken up again when, at the age of fifteen, she was released from the psychiatric clinic.

Somebody within the police investigation must be providing the media with information, but for reasons unknown to
Salander, the source had decided to cover up "All The Evil."
This surprised her. If the police wanted to emphasize her pen-
chant for vicious behaviour, then that report in her file would
have been the most damning by far. It was the very reason that
she was sent to St. Stefan's.

On Easter Sunday Salander began to follow the police investigation more closely. From what she culled from the media she
built a picture of its participants. Prosecutor Richard Ekström
was the leader of the preliminary investigation and usually the
spokesman at press conferences. The actual investigation was
headed by Criminal Inspector Jan Bublanski, a somewhat overweight man in an ill-fitting suit who flanked Ekström when
they were speaking to the press.

After a few days she had identified Sonja Modig as the
team's only female detective and the person who had found
Bjurman. She noted the names Hans Faste and Curt Andersson, but she missed Jerker Holmberg altogether, as his name
was not mentioned in any of the articles. She created a file on
her computer for each person on the team and began to fill
them with information.

Naturally, information about how the police investigation
was proceeding was kept on the computers used by the investigating detectives, and their databases were stored on the
server at police headquarters. Salander knew that it would be
exceptionally hard to hack into the police intranet, but it was
by no means impossible. She had done it before.

When working on an assignment for Armansky several
years earlier, she had plotted the structure of the police intranet
and assessed the possibility of hacking into the criminal register to make her own entries. She had failed miserably in her
attempts to hack in from outside—the police firewalls were too

sophisticated and mined with all sorts of traps that might result in unwelcome attention.

The internal police network was a state-of-the-art design with its own cabling, shielded from external connections and the Internet itself. In other words, what she needed was either a police officer who had authorization to access the network or the next best thing—to make the police intranet believe that she was an authorized person. In this respect, fortunately, the police security experts had left a gaping hole. Police stations all around the country had uplinks to the network, and several of them were small local units that were unstaffed at night and often had no burglar alarms or security patrols. The police station in Långvik outside Västerås was one of these. It occupied about 1,400 square feet in the same building that housed the public library and the regional social security office, and it was manned in the daytime by three officers.

At the time Salander had failed in her efforts to hack into the network for the research she was working on, but she had decided it might be worthwhile to spend a little time and energy acquiring access for future research. She had thought over the possibilities and then applied for a summer job at the library in Långvik. In a break from her cleaning duties, it took her about ten minutes to get detailed blueprints of the whole building. She had keys to the building but, understandably, not to the police offices. She had discovered, however, that without much difficulty she could climb through a bathroom window on the third floor that was left open at night in the summer heat. The police station was patrolled by a freelance security firm, and the officer on duty made rounds only once a night. Ridiculous.

It took her about five minutes to find the username and password underneath the police chief's desk blotter, and one night of experimenting to understand the structure of the network and identify what sort of access he had and what access had been classified as beyond the realm of the local authorities.

As a bonus she also got the usernames and passwords of the two local police officers. One of them was thirty-two-year-old Maria Ottosson, and in her computer Salander found out that she had recently applied and been accepted for service as a detective in the fraud division of the Stockholm police. Salander got full administrator rights for Ottosson, who also had left her Dell PC laptop in an unlocked desk drawer. Brilliant. Salander booted up the machine and inserted her CD with the programme Asphyxia 1.0, the very first version of her spyware. She downloaded the software in two locations, as an active, integrated part of Microsoft Internet Explorer and as backup in Ottosson's address book. Salander figured that even if Ottosson bought a new computer, she would copy over her address book, and chances were that she would transfer it to the computer at the fraud division in Stockholm when she reported for duty a few weeks later.

Salander also placed software in the officers' desktop computers, making it possible for her to gather data from outside and, by simply stealing their identities, to make adjustments to the criminal register. However, she had to proceed with the utmost caution. The police security division had an automatic alarm if any local officer logged on to the network outside working hours or if the number of modifications increased too dramatically. If she fished for information from investigations in which the local police would not normally be involved, it would trigger the alarm.

Over the past year she had worked together with her hacker associate Plague to take control of the police IT network. This proved to be fraught with such difficulty that eventually they gave up the project, but in the process they had accumulated almost a hundred existing police identities that they could borrow at will.

Plague had a breakthrough when he succeeded in hacking into the home computer of the head of the police data security division. He was a civil service economist with no in-depth IT knowledge but with a wealth of information on his laptop. Salander and Plague thereafter had the opportunity, if not to hack into, at least to devastatingly disrupt the police intranet with viruses of various types—an activity in which neither of them had the slightest interest. They were hackers, not saboteurs. They wanted access to functioning networks, not to destroy them.

Salander now checked her list and saw that none of the individuals whose identity she had stolen was working on the investigation into the three murders—that would have been too much to hope for. But she was able to get in without much trouble and read details of the nationwide alert, including updated APBs on herself. She discovered that she had been sighted and pursued in Uppsala, Norrköping, Göteborg, Malmö, Hässleholm, and Kalmar, and that a classified computer image giving a better idea of what she looked like had been circulated.

One of Salander's few advantages in all the media attention was that not many photographs of her existed. Apart from a four-year-old passport photograph, which was also used on her driver's licence, and a police mug shot taken when she was eighteen (which did not look anything like her today), there were only pictures from old school yearbooks and photographs taken by a teacher on a field trip to the Nacka nature reserve when she was twelve. The pictures from the field trip showed a blurry figure sitting a little apart from the others.

The passport photograph showed her with staring eyes, her mouth compressed to a thin line, and her head leaning a bit forward. It fitted the image of a retarded, asocial killer, and the media published millions of copies of it. But she now looked so different that very few people would recognize her from it.

. . .

She read with interest the profiles of the three murder victims. On Tuesday the media began to tread water, and with the lack of any new or dramatic revelations in the hunt for Salander, interest focused on the victims. Dag Svensson, Mia Johansson, and Nils Bjurman were portrayed in a long article in one of the evening papers.

Nils Bjurman came across as a respected and socially involved lawyer who belonged to Greenpeace and had a "commitment to young people." A column was devoted to his close friend and colleague Jan Håkansson, who had an office in the same building. Håkansson confirmed the image of Bjurman as a man who fought for the rights of the little people. A civil servant at the Guardianship Agency described him as genuinely committed to his ward.

Salander smiled her first lopsided smile of the day.

Johansson, the female victim in the drama, elicited great interest in the media. She was described as a sweet and enormously intelligent young woman with an already impressive record of achievement and a brilliant career ahead of her. Shocked friends, colleagues at the university, and a tutor had given comments, and the question they had all asked was "why?" Pictures showed flowers and lighted candles outside the door of the apartment building in Enskede.

By comparison, very little space was devoted to Svensson. He was described as a sharp, fearless reporter. But the main interest was in his partner.

Salander noted with mild surprise that it took till Easter Sunday before anyone seemed to realize that Svensson had been working on a big report for *Millennium* magazine. And even then, there was no mention in the articles about what specifically he was working on.

She never read the quote Blomkvist had sent to *Aftonbladet*. It was not until late Tuesday, when it was mentioned on the TV news, that she realized Blomkvist was purposely putting out misleading information. He claimed that Svensson had been involved in writing a report on computer security and illegal hacking.

Salander frowned. She knew that was false, and wondered what game *Millennium* was playing. Then she understood the message and smiled her second lopsided smile of the day. She connected to the server in Holland and double-clicked on the *MikBlom/laptop* icon. She found the folder <Lisbeth Salander> and the document [To Sally] prominently displayed in the middle of the desktop. She double-clicked and read it.

Then she sat for a long time staring at Blomkvist's letter. She wrestled with contradictory feelings. Up until then it had been her against the rest of Sweden, which in its simplicity was quite an elegant and lucid equation. Now suddenly she had an ally, or at least a potential ally, who claimed to believe she was innocent. And of course it would be the only man in Sweden that she never wanted to see again under any circumstances. She sighed. Blomkvist was, as always, a naive do-gooder. Salander hadn't been innocent since the age of ten.

There are no innocents. There are, however, different degrees of responsibility.

Bjurman was dead because he had chosen not to play according to the rules she had stipulated. He had had every chance, but still he had hired some fucking alpha male to do her harm. That was not her responsibility.

But Kalle Blomkvist's involvement should not be underrated. He could be useful.

He was good at riddles and he was unmatchably stubborn. She had found that out in Hedestad. When he sank his teeth into something he simply would not let go. He really was naive. But he could move in places where she couldn't. He might be useful until she could get safely out of the country. Which was what she assumed she would soon be forced to do.

Unfortunately, Blomkvist could not be controlled. He needed a reason of his own to act. And he needed a moral excuse as well.

In other words, he was quite predictable. She thought for a while and then created a new document called [To MikBlom] and wrote a single word.

Zala.

That would give him something to think about.

She was still sitting there thinking when she noticed that Blomkvist had booted up his computer. His reply came shortly after he read her message:

Lisbeth,
You damn troublesome person. Who the hell is Zala? Is he the link? Do you know who murdered Dag & Mia? If so, tell me so we can solve this mess and go to sleep.
Mikael.

OK. Time to hook him.

She created another document and called it [Kalle Blomkvist]. She knew that would upset him. Then she wrote a brief message:

You're the journalist. Find out.

As expected, he replied at once with an appeal for her to listen to reason, and he tried to play on her feelings. She smiled and closed her connection to his hard drive.

Now that she had started snooping around, she moved on and opened Armansky's hard drive. She read the report about herself that he had written the day after Easter. It was not clear to whom the report was addressed, but she assumed that the only reasonable explanation was that Armansky was working with the police to help bring her in.

She spent a while going through Armansky's email, but found nothing of interest. Just as she was about to disconnect, she lit upon a message to the technical chief at Milton Security with instructions for the installation of a hidden surveillance camera in his office.

Bingo.

She looked at the date and saw that the message was sent about an hour after her social call in February.

That meant she would have to adjust certain routines in the automatic surveillance system before she paid another visit to Armansky's office.

CHAPTER 22

Tuesday, March 29– Sunday, April 3

On Tuesday morning Salander accessed the police criminal register and looked up Alexander Zalachenko. He was not listed, which was not surprising, since as far as she knew he had never been convicted of a crime in Sweden and was not even in the national database.

When she had accessed the criminal register she used the identity of Superintendent Douglas Skiöld of the Malmö police. She got a mild shock when her computer suddenly pinged and an icon in the menu toolbar started blinking to signal that someone was looking for her in the ICQ chat programme.

Her first impulse was to pull the plug and shut down. Then she thought about it. Skiöld had not had the ICQ programme on his machine. Very few older people did.

Which meant that someone was looking for *her*. And there were not many alternatives to choose from. She clicked on ICQ and typed the words:

```
<What do you want Plague?>
<Wasp. You're hard to find. Don't you ever
check your mail?>
```

```
<How'd you find me?>
<Skiöld. I've got the same list. I
assumed you'd be using one of the
identities with the highest
authorization.>
<What do you want?>
<Who is this Zalachenko you did the
search on?>
<MYOB.>
<?>
<Mind Your Own Business.>
<What's happening?>
<FO, Plague>
<I thought I had a social handicap, as
you call it. If I believed the papers,
I'd seem totally normal compared to you.>
<🖐>
<Fuck you too. Need help?>
```

Salander hesitated. First Blomkvist and now Plague. Was there
no end to all the people coming to her rescue? The problem
with Plague was that he was a 350-pound recluse who com-
municated almost exclusively via the Internet and made Salander look like a miracle of social skills. When she didn't answer,
Plague typed another line:

```
<Still there? Do you need help getting
out of the country?>
<No.>
<Why did you shoot them?>
<Piss off.>
<Do you intend to shoot more people, and
if so do I have to worry? I'm probably
the only one who can track you.>
<Mind your own business and you don't
have to worry.>
```

```
<I'm not worried. Look for me on hotmail
if you need anything. Weapon? New
passport?>
<You're a sociopath.>
<Compared to you you mean?>
```

Lisbeth disconnected from ICQ and sat down on the sofa to think. Ten minutes later she sent an email to Plague's hotmail address.

Prosecutor Richard Ekström, leader of the preliminary investigation, lives in Täby. He's married with two children and has a broadband connection to his house. I need access to his laptop or home computer. I need to read him in real time. Hostile takeover with mirrored hard drive.

She knew that Plague himself seldom left his apartment in Sundbyberg, so she hoped he had cultivated some pimply teenager to do the field work. There was no need to sign the message. She got an answer fifteen minutes later.

How much are you paying?

10,000 to your account + expenses and 5,000 to your assistant.

I'll be in touch.

On Thursday morning she had one email from Plague containing an FTP address. Salander was amazed. She had not expected a result for at least two weeks. Doing a hostile takeover, even with Plague's brilliant programme and his specially designed hardware, was a laborious process that required slipping bits of information into a computer one kilobyte at a time until a simple piece of software had been created. How rapidly it could be done depended on how often Ekström used his computer, and then it should normally take another few days to transfer all the data to a mirrored hard drive. Forty-eight hours was not merely exceptional, it was theoretically impossible. Salander was impressed. She pinged his ICQ:

```
<How'd you do that?>
<Four computers in his household. Can you
imagine?—they have no firewall. Security
zero. All I had to do was plug in the
cable and upload. My expenses are 6,000
kronor. Can you handle it?>
<Yep. Plus a bonus for the quick work.>
```

She thought for a moment and then transferred 30,000 kronor to Plague's account via the Internet. She did not want to frighten him off with excessive amounts. Then she made herself comfortable on her Verksam IKEA chair and opened Ekström's laptop.

Within an hour she had read all the reports that Inspector Bublanski had sent to Ekström. Salander suspected that, technically, reports like these were not allowed to leave police headquarters. It proved once again the theory that no security system is a match for a stupid employee. Through Ekström's computer she gleaned several important pieces of information.

First, she discovered that Armansky had assigned two of his staff to join Bublanski's investigative team without remuneration, which in practice meant that Milton Security was sponsoring the police hunt for her. Their assignment was to assist in the arrest of Salander by all possible means. *Thanks a lot, Armansky. I'll remember that.* She frowned when she discovered which employees they were. Bohman she had taken for a straight arrow, and he had been perfectly decent in his behaviour towards her. Hedström was a corrupt nobody who had

exploited his position at Milton Security to swindle one of the
company's clients.

Salander had a selective morality. She had nothing at all
against swindling the company's clients herself—provided they
deserved it—but if she had accepted a job with a confidentiality agreement in it, she would never have broken it.

Salander soon discovered that the person who had leaked the
information to the media was Ekström himself. This was evi-
dent from an email in which he answered follow-up questions
about both Salander's psychiatric report and the connection
between her and Miriam Wu.

The third significant piece of information was the insight
that Bublanski's team did not have a single lead as to where
they should look for Salander. She read with interest a report
on what measures had been taken and which addresses had
been put under sporadic surveillance. It was a short list. Lundagatan, obviously, but also Blomkvist's address, Miriam's old
address at St. Eriksplan, and Kvarnen, where they had been
seen together. *Fuck, why did I have to involve Mimmi? What a
mistake that was.*

On Friday Ekström's researchers had also found the link to
Evil Fingers. She guessed that would mean more addresses
being visited. She frowned. So the girls in the group would vanish from her circle of friends too, even though she had had no
contact with them since her return to Sweden.

The more she thought about all this, the more confused she
became. Ekström was leaking all kinds of bullshit to the media.
His objective was clear. He was building publicity and doing
the groundwork for the day when he would issue a charge
against her.

But why hadn't he leaked the police report from 1991, which
had led her to be locked up at St. Stefan's? Why keep that story
hidden?

She went into Ekström's computer again and pored over his documents. When she was finished she lit a cigarette. She had not found a single reference to the events of 1991 on his computer. It was strange, but the only explanation was that he didn't know about the police report.

For a moment she was at a loss. Then she glanced at her PowerBook. This was precisely the kind of thing that Kalle Fucking Blomkvist could sink his teeth into. She rebooted her computer to access his hard drive and created the document [MB2].

> Prosecutor E. is leaking information to the media. Ask
> him why he didn't leak the old police report.

That should be enough to get him going. She sat patiently and waited two hours for Blomkvist to get online. He read his email and it took fifteen minutes before he noticed her document and another five minutes before he replied with the document [Cryptic]. He didn't bite. Instead he insisted that he wanted to know who murdered his friends.

That was an argument that Salander could understand. She softened a bit and answered with [Cryptic 2].

> What would you do if it was me?

Which was intended as a personal question. He replied with [Cryptic 3]. It shook her.

> Lisbeth, if it's true that you've really gone over the
> edge, then maybe you can ask Peter Teleborian to help
> you. But I don't believe you murdered Dag and Mia. I
> hope and pray that I'm right.
>   Dag and Mia were going to publish their exposés of
> the sex trade. My theory is that could have been the
> reason for the murders. But I have nothing to go on.

I don't know what went wrong between us, but you and I discussed friendship once. I said that friendship is built on two things—respect and trust. Even if you don't like me, you can still depend on me and trust me. I've never shared your secrets with anyone. Not even what happened to Wennerström's billions. Trust me. I'm not your enemy. M.

Blomkvist's reference to Teleborian at first made her furious. Then she realized that he was not trying to start a fight. He had no idea who Teleborian was and had probably only seen him on TV, where he came across as a responsible, internationally respected expert.

But what really shook her was the reference to Wennerström's billions. She had no idea how he had wormed out that information. She was absolutely certain that she had made no mistakes and that nobody in the world could know what she had done.

She read the letter over several times.

The reference to friendship made her uncomfortable. She didn't know how to respond to it.

A short time later she created [Cryptic 4].

I'll think about it.

She disconnected and went to her window seat.

Salander had exhausted her supply of Billy's Pan Pizza as well as the last crumb of bread and rind of cheese. For the last three days she had survived on a packet of instant oats that she had bought on impulse with the vague idea that she ought to eat more nourishing food. She discovered that half a cup of oats with a few raisins and a cup of water turned into an edible portion of hot cereal after a minute in the microwave.

It was not only the lack of food that got her on the move. She had someone to look after. Unfortunately that was not something she could do while holed up in her apartment. She went to her wardrobe and took out the blond wig and Irene Nesser's Norwegian passport.

Fröken Nesser did exist in real life. She was similar in appearance to Salander and she had lost her passport three years earlier. It came to be in Salander's hands thanks to Plague, and she had used Nesser's identity when necessary for almost eighteen months.

Salander took the ring out of her eyebrow and put on makeup at the bathroom mirror. She dressed in dark jeans, a warm brown sweater with yellow trim, and walking boots with heels. She took out a Mace canister from her small supply. She also found her Taser, which she hadn't touched in a year, and plugged it in to charge. She put a change of clothes in a shoulder bag. And at 11:00 on Friday night, nine days after the murders, Salander left her apartment in Mosebacke.

She walked to McDonald's on Hornsgatan. It was less likely that any of her former colleagues from Milton Security would run into her there than at the one near Slussen or at Medborgarplatsen. She ate a Big Mac and drank a large Coke.

Then she took the number 4 bus across Västerbron to St. Eriksplan. She walked to Odenplan and found herself outside Bjurman's apartment building on Upplandsgatan just after midnight. She did not expect the apartment to be under surveillance, but she saw a light in the window of an apartment on the same floor, so she walked on towards Vanadisplan. The light was off when she came back an hour later.

She went up the stairs on tiptoe without turning on the light in the stairwell. With the aid of a Stanley knife she cut the police tape that sealed the apartment. She opened the door without a sound.

She turned on the hall lamp, which she knew could not be seen from the outside, and switched on a pen torch to light her way to the bedroom. The venetian blinds were closed. She played the beam of light over the bloodstained bed. She recalled that she had been very close to dying in that bed and suddenly had a feeling of deep satisfaction that Bjurman was forever out of her life.

The reason for her visit to the crime scene was to get two pieces of information. First, she didn't understand the connection between Bjurman and Zala. She was convinced there had to be one, but she hadn't been able to find it from anything she found in Bjurman's computer.

Second was an inconsistency that kept gnawing at her. During her nighttime visit a few weeks earlier she noticed that Bjurman had taken documentation about her out of the file box where he kept all his guardianship material. The pages that were missing were part of his brief from the agency which summarized Salander's psychological state in the most concise terms. Bjurman no longer had any need of these pages, and it was possible that he had cleared out the file and thrown them away. On the other hand, lawyers never throw away documents relating to an unfinished case. And yet these papers had once been in the file box relating to her, and she had not found them in his desk or anywhere near it.

She saw that the police had removed the files that dealt with her case, as well as some others. She spent more than two hours searching every inch of the apartment in case the police had missed anything, but eventually she came to the conclusion that they had not.

In the kitchen she found a drawer which contained various keys: car keys, as well as a general key to the building and a padlock key. She quietly went up to the attic floor, where she tried all the padlocks until she found Bjurman's storage unit. In it was some furniture, as well as a wardrobe full of old clothes, skis, a car battery, cardboard boxes of books, and some other junk. She discovered nothing of interest, so she went back downstairs and used the general key to get into the garage. She

THE GIRL WHO PLAYED WITH FIRE   415

worked out which was his Mercedes, but a brief search turned
up nothing of value there either.

She did not bother to go to his office. She had been there
only a few weeks earlier, around the time of her previous visit
to his apartment, and she knew that for the past two years he
had hardly used it.

Salander returned to Bjurman's apartment and sat on his
living-room sofa to think. After a few minutes she got up and
went back to the key drawer in the kitchen. She studied the
keys one by one. One set belonged to front-door and dead-bolt
locks, but another key was rusty and old-fashioned. She
frowned. Then she raised her eyes to a shelf above the kitchen
counter, where Bjurman had put about twenty seed packets,
seeds for an herb garden.

*He has a summer cabin. Or an allotment somewhere. That's
what I missed.*

It took her three minutes to locate a receipt, six years old, in
Bjurman's account book showing that he had paid for work on
his driveway, and it took another minute to find an insurance
policy for a property near Stallarholmen outside Mariefred.

At 5:00 in the morning she stopped at the twenty-four-hour
7-Eleven at the top of Hantverkargatan up by Fridhemsplan.
She bought an armful of Billy's Pan Pizzas, some milk, bread,
cheese, and other staples. She also bought a morning paper
with a headline that fascinated her.

Wanted woman fled country?

This particular paper did not, for some reason, name her. She
was referred to instead as the "26-year-old woman." The article
stated that a source within the police claimed that she might
have escaped abroad and could now be in Berlin. The police

had apparently received a tip that she had been seen in Kreuzberg at an "anarcho-feminist club" described as a hang-out for young people associated with everything from terrorism to antiglobalization and Satanism.

She took the number 4 bus back to Södermalm, where she got off at Rosenlundsgatan and walked home to Mose-backe. She made coffee and had a sandwich before she went to bed.

She slept until late in the afternoon. When she woke she took stock and decided that it was high time she changed the sheets. She spent the evening cleaning her apartment. She took out the trash and collected newspapers in two plastic bags and put them in a closet in the stairwell. She washed a load of under-wear and T-shirts and then a load of jeans. She filled the dish-washer and turned it on. Then she vacuumed and mopped the floor.

It was 9:00 p.m. and she was drenched with sweat. She turned on the faucet in the tub and poured in plenty of bubble bath. She lay back and closed her eyes and brooded. When she woke up, it was midnight and the water was cold. She got out, dried off, and went back to bed. She fell asleep almost imme-diately.

On Sunday morning Salander was filled with rage when she booted up her PowerBook and read all the stupid things that had been written about Miriam Wu. She felt miserable and guilty. Wu's only crime was that she was Salander's . . . acquain-tance? Friend? Lover?

She didn't quite know which word would describe her rela-tionship with Mimmi, but she realized that whichever one she chose, it was probably over. She would have to cross one more name off her already short list of acquaintances. After all the shit written in the press, she could not imagine that her friend would want to have anything to do with that psychotic Salander woman ever again.

It made her furious.

She committed to memory the name of Tony Scala, the journalist who had started it all. She also resolved one day to confront a nasty columnist pictured in a checked jacket whose article had made repeated jocular references to Mimmi as an "S&M dyke."

The number of people Salander was going to have to deal with was growing. But first she had to find Zala.

What would happen when she found him she didn't know.

Blomkvist was woken by the telephone at 7:30 on Sunday morning. He stretched out his hand and answered it sleepily.

"Good morning," Berger said.

"Mmm," said Mikael.

"Are you alone?"

"Unfortunately."

"Then I suggest you take a shower and put on some coffee. You'll have a visitor in fifteen minutes."

"I will?"

"Paolo Roberto."

"The boxer? The king of kings?"

"He called me and we talked for half an hour."

"How come?"

"How come he called me? Well, we know each other well enough to say hello. I did an interview with him when he was in Hildebrand's film, and we've run into each other a few times over the years."

"I didn't know that. But my question was why is he visiting me?"

"Because . . . well, I think it's better if he explains that himself."

. . .

Blomkvist had only just showered and put on his pants when the doorbell rang. He opened the door and asked the boxer to take a seat at the table while he found a clean shirt and made two double espressos, which he served with a teaspoon of milk. Paolo Roberto inspected the coffee, impressed.

"You wanted to talk to me?" Blomkvist said.

"It was Erika Berger's suggestion."

"I see. Talk away."

"I know Lisbeth Salander."

Blomkvist raised his eyebrows. "You do?"

"I was a little surprised when Erika told me that you knew her too."

"I think perhaps it would be better if you started at the beginning."

"OK. Here's the deal. I came home the day before yesterday after a month in New York and found Lisbeth's face on every fucking newspaper in town. The papers are writing a load of fucking crap about her. And not one of those fuckers seems to have a good word to say."

"You got three *fucks* into that outburst."

Paolo Roberto laughed. "Sorry. But I'm really pissed off. In fact, I called Erika because I needed to talk and didn't really know who else to call. Since that journalist in Enskede worked for *Millennium* and since I happen to know Erika, I called her."

"So?"

"Even if Salander went completely off her rocker and did everything the police are claiming she did, she has to be given a sporting chance. We do happen to have the rule of law in this country, and nobody should be condemned without their day in court."

"I believe that too."

"That's what I understood from Erika. When I called her I thought that you guys at *Millennium* were after her scalp too, considering that the Svensson guy was writing for you. But Erika said you thought she was innocent."

"I know Lisbeth. I can't see her as a deranged killer."

Paolo Roberto laughed out loud. "She's one fucking freaky chick . . . but she's one of the good ones. I like her."

"How do you know her?"

"I've boxed with Salander since she was seventeen."

Blomkvist closed his eyes for ten seconds before he opened them and looked at the boxing champ. Salander was, as always, full of surprises.

"Of course. Lisbeth Salander boxes with Paolo Roberto. You're in the same division."

"I'm not joking."

"I believe you. She told me once that she used to spar with the boys at some boxing club."

"Let me tell you how it happened. Ten years ago I took a job as a trainer for juniors who wanted to start boxing down at the Zinken club. I was already established, and the club's junior leader thought I'd be a big draw, so I'd come in afternoons and spar with the guys. As it turned out, I stayed the whole summer and part of the autumn too. They ran a campaign and put up posters and all that, trying to lure the local kids. And it did attract a lot of fifteen- and sixteen-year-olds and some a few years older too. Quite a few immigrant kids. Boxing is a great alternative to running around town and raising hell. Ask me. I know."

"I believe you."

"Then one day in the middle of summer this skinny girl turns up out of nowhere. You know how she looks, right? She came into the club and said she wanted to learn to box."

"I can picture the scene."

"There was a roar of laughter from half a dozen guys who weighed about twice as much as she did and were obviously a whole lot bigger. I laughed too. It was nothing serious, but we teased her a little. We have a girls' section too, and I said something stupid about the fact that little chicks were only allowed to box on Thursdays or something like that."

"She didn't laugh, I bet."

"No. She didn't laugh. She looked at me with those black eyes of hers. Then she reached for a pair of boxing gloves that somebody had left lying around. They weren't tied up or anything and they were way too big for her. But we weren't laughing any more. You know what I mean?"

"This doesn't sound good."

Paolo Roberto laughed again. "Since I was the instructor I went up and pretended to jab at her, you know, for make-believe."

"Uh-oh . . ."

"Right. All of a sudden she whipped out a punch that caught me smack above my mouth. I was just clowning with her and was totally unprepared. She got in two or three punches before I even began to block them. Anyway, she had no muscle strength and it was like being walloped by a feather. But when I started blocking she changed tactics. She boxed instinctively and landed a few more smacks. Then I started blocking seriously and found out that she was quicker than a fucking lizard. If she had been bigger and stronger I would have had a match on my hands."

"I'm not surprised."

"And then she switched tactics again and whacked me a good one right in the balls. I felt that one."

Blomkvist winced.

"Then I jabbed back and got her in the face. I mean, it wasn't a hard punch or anything, just a pop. Then she kicked me in the shin. Anyway, it was totally freaky. I was three times bigger and heavier and she didn't have a chance, but she bashed at me as if her life was at stake."

"You made her angry."

"I realized that later. And I was ashamed. I mean . . . we had put up posters and tried to draw in young people, and here she came and asked quite seriously to learn to box, and ran up against a gang of guys who just stood there and made fun of her. I would have lost it, too, if anyone had treated me that way."

"But you might have thought twice about having a crack at Paolo Roberto!"

"Well, Salander's problem was that her punches were worthless. So I started training with her. We had her in the girls' section for a couple of weeks, and she lost several matches because sooner or later somebody would always get a punch in, and then we had to sort of stop and carry her into the locker room because she was so mad and started kicking and biting and slugging us."

"That sounds like Lisbeth."

"She never gave up. But finally she had pissed off so many girls that their trainer kicked her out."

"And then?"

"It was completely impossible to box with her. She only had one style, which we called Terminator Mode. She would try to nail her opponent, and it didn't matter if it was just a warm-up or friendly sparring. And girls kept going home all scraped up because she had kicked them. That was when I had an idea. I had problems with a guy called Samir. He was seventeen and from Syria. He was a good boxer, powerfully built and with a good jab . . . but he couldn't move. He stood still the whole time. So I asked Salander to come to the club one afternoon when I was going to train him. She changed and I put her in the ring with him, headgear and mouthpiece and everything. At first Samir refused to spar with her because she was 'just a fuck-ing chick,' all the usual macho crap. So I told him, loud so everyone could hear, that this was no sparring match, and I put up 500 kronor that said she would nail him. To Salander I said that this was no training session and that Samir would pound her in bloody earnest. She looked at me with mistrust. Samir was still standing there babbling when the bell went off. Lisbeth went at him for king and country and thumped him one in the face so he went down on his ass. By then I'd been training her for a whole summer and she was starting to get some muscles and a little power in her punch."

"I bet your Syrian boy was happy."

"Well, they talked about that match for months afterwards. Samir took a licking. She won on points. If she'd had more body strength she really could have hurt him. After a while Samir was so frustrated that he started slugging away full force. I was dead afraid he might actually land a punch and we'd have to call an ambulance. She took some bruises when she blocked with her shoulders a few times, and he managed to get her on the ropes because she couldn't stand up to the force of his blows. But he was nowhere near hitting her for real."

"I wish I'd seen that."

"That day the guys in the club began to respect Salander. Especially Samir. So I started putting her in the ring to spar with considerably bigger and heavier guys. She was my secret weapon and it was great training. We arranged sessions so that Lisbeth's goal was to land five punches on various parts of the body—jaw, forehead, stomach, and so on. And the guys she boxed with had to defend themselves and protect those areas. It turned into sort of a prestige thing to have boxed with Salander. It was like scrapping with a hornet. We actually called her 'the Wasp,' and she became like the mascot of the club. I think she even liked it, because one day she came to the club with a wasp tattooed on her neck."

Blomkvist smiled. He remembered the wasp well. And it was part of the police description of her.

"How long did all this go on?"

"One evening a week for about three years. I was there full-time during that summer and then sporadically after that. The guy who kept up the training with Salander was our junior trainer, Putte Karlsson. Then Salander started working and didn't have time to come as often, but up until last year she'd be there at least once a month. I saw her a few times a year and did sparring sessions with her. It was good training, and we were sweaty afterwards. She hardly ever talked to anyone. When there was no sparring she would work the heavy bag intensely for two hours, as if it were her mortal enemy."

CHAPTER 23

Sunday, April 3– Monday, April 4

Blomkvist made two more espressos. He apologized when he lit a cigarette. Paolo Roberto shrugged.

He had the public reputation of being a cocky type who would say exactly what he thought. Blomkvist quickly saw that he was just as cocky in private, but that he was an intelligent and modest human being. He reminded himself that Paolo Roberto had also made a bid for a political career as a Social Democrat candidate for parliament. He definitely had something between his ears. Blomkvist found he was beginning to like him.

"Why are you coming to me with this story?"

"That girl's really in the soup, right? I don't know what to do, but she probably could use a friend in her corner."

"I agree."

"Why do you think she's innocent?"

"It's hard to explain. Lisbeth is an uncompromising person, but I just don't believe the story that she could have shot Dag and Mia. Especially not Mia. For one thing, she had no motive—"

"At least none that we know of."

"Fair enough. Lisbeth would have no problem using violence against somebody who deserved it. But I don't know. I've decided to challenge Bublanski, the detective in charge of the investigation. I think there's a reason why Dag and Mia were murdered. And I think the reason is somewhere in the story Dag was working on."

"If you're right, Salander will need more than a hand to hold when she's arrested—she'll need a whole other kind of support."

"I know."

Paolo Roberto had a dangerous glint in his eye. "If she's innocent she's been subjected to one of the worst fucking legal scandals in history. She's been painted as a murderer by the media and the police, and after all the shit that's been written . . ."

"I know."

"What can we do? Can I help out somehow?"

"The best help we could offer would be to find an alternative suspect. That's what I'm working on. The next best thing would be to get to her before some police thug shoots her dead. Lisbeth isn't the type of person who would give herself up voluntarily."

"So how do we find her?"

"I don't know. But there is one thing you could do. Something practical, if you have the time and energy."

"My girlfriend is away all week. So I do have the time and the energy."

"Well, I was thinking that since you're a boxer . . ."

"Yes?"

"Lisbeth has a girlfriend, Miriam Wu. You've probably read about her."

"Better known as the S&M dyke . . . Yeah, I've read about her."

"I have her mobile number and I've been trying to get hold of her. She hangs up as soon as she hears it's a reporter."

"I don't blame her."

"I don't really have time to chase after Fröken Wu. But I read somewhere that she trains in kickboxing. I was thinking that if a famous boxer wanted to get in touch with her . . ."

"I'm with you. And you're hoping that she might provide a lead to Salander."

"When the police interviewed her she said she had no idea where Lisbeth was staying. But it's worth a try."

"Give me her number. I'll talk to her."

Blomkvist gave him the number and the address on Lundagatan.

Björck had spent the weekend analysing his situation. His prospects, he decided, were hanging by a fraying thread, and he would have to make the most of the hand he'd been dealt.

Blomkvist was a fucking swine. The only question was whether he could be persuaded to keep his mouth shut about . . . about the fact that Björck had hired the services of those bitches. It was a chargeable offence, and he would be fired if it were made public. The press would rip him to shreds. A member of the Security Police who exploited teenage prostitutes . . . If only those fucking cunts hadn't been so young.

Sitting here doing nothing would certainly seal his fate. Björck was smart enough not to have said anything to Blomkvist. He had read his expression. The man was in agony. He wanted information. But he was going to be forced to pay for it, and the price was his silence.

Zala brought a whole new dimension to the murder investigation.

Svensson had been hunting Zala.

Bjurman had been hunting Zala.

And Superintendent Björck was the only one who knew that there was a link between Zala and Bjurman, which meant that Zala was a clue to the murders at Enskede and Odenplan.

This created another serious problem for Björck's future well-being. He was the one who had given Bjurman the information about Zalachenko—as a friendly gesture and in spite of the fact that the file was still top secret. That was a detail, but it meant that he had committed another chargeable offence.

Furthermore, since Blomkvist's visit on Friday he had involved himself in yet one more crime. As a police officer, if he had information in a murder investigation it was his duty to inform his colleagues immediately. But if he gave the information to Bublanski or Ekström, he would implicate himself. It would all eventually come out. Not just the whores, but the whole Zalachenko affair.

On Saturday he had gone to his office at the Security Police on Kungsholmen. He had picked out all the old documents about Zalachenko and read through them. He was the one who had written the reports, but it was many years ago. The oldest of the documents were almost thirty years old. The most recent was ten years old.

Zalachenko.

A slippery fucker.

Zala.

Björck himself had called him that in his report, although he could not remember ever having used the name.

But the connection was crystal clear. To Enskede. To Bjurman. And to Salander.

Björck still did not understand how all the pieces of the puzzle fit together, but he thought he knew why Salander had been in Enskede. He could also easily imagine her flying into a rage and killing Svensson and Johansson, either because they had refused to cooperate or because they had provoked her. She had a motive, known only to Björck and perhaps two or three other people in the whole country.

She is completely insane. I hope to God that some officer shoots her dead when she's apprehended. She knows. She could break the whole story wide open if she talked.

No matter how Björck looked at his situation, Blomkvist was his only possible way out. And that was the one thing that mattered to him. He felt a growing desperation. Blomkvist had to be persuaded to treat him as a confidential source and to keep quiet about his . . . foolish escapades with those fucking whores. *Damn, if only Salander would blow Blomkvist's head off too.*

He looked at Zalachenko's phone number and weighed the pros and cons of contacting him. He was incapable of making up his mind.

Blomkvist had made a point, at every stage, of summing up his thinking on the investigation. When Paolo Roberto left, he spent an hour on the task. It had turned into a journal in which he let his thoughts run free while at the same time he meticulously wrote up every conversation and every meeting, as well as all the research he was doing. He encrypted the document using PGP and emailed copies to Berger and Eriksson, so that his colleagues were kept up to date.

Svensson had concentrated on Zala in the last weeks of his life. The name had cropped up in his final telephone conversation with Blomkvist three hours before he was killed. Björck claimed to know something about Zala.

Blomkvist ran through everything he had unearthed about Björck, which was not very much.

Gunnar Björck was sixty-two years old, unmarried, born in Falun. Had been in the police force since he was twenty-one. Began as a patrol officer, but studied law and ended up in Säpo, the Security Police, when he was twenty-six or twenty-seven. That was in 1969 or 1970, just at the end of Per Gunnar Vinge's time as chief there.

Vinge was dismissed after making the claim in a conversation with Ragnar Lassinanti, the governor of Norrbotten County, that Olof Palme was spying for the Russians. Then came the Internal Bureau affair, and Holmér, and the Letter Carrier, and the Palme assassination, and one scandal after another.

Björck's career between 1970 and 1985 was largely undocumented, which was not so odd, since anything that had to do with Säpo activities was confidential. He could have been sharpening pencils in the stationery department or he could have been a secret agent in China.

In October 1985 Björck moved to the Swedish Embassy in Washington for two years. In 1988, back with Säpo in Stockholm. In 1996 he became a public figure: appointed deputy bureau chief of the immigration division (whatever that entailed). After 1996 he made various statements to the media, in connection with the deportation of suspect Arabs, and drew particular attention in 1998 when several Iraqi diplomats were expelled.

What does any of this have to do with Salander and the murders of Svensson and Johansson? Maybe nothing.

But Björck knows about Zala.

There has to be a connection.

Berger told no-one, not even her husband, from whom she rarely kept secrets, that she was going to *Svenska Morgon-Posten*. She had about a month left at *Millennium*. The anxiety was getting to her. The days would rush by and suddenly she would be facing her last day there.

She was also growing uneasy about Blomkvist. She had read his latest email with a sinking feeling. She recognized the signs. It was the same stubbornness that made him stick it out in Hedestad two years ago, the same obsessive determination with which he had gone after Wennerström. Since Maundy Thursday, nothing had existed for him but to find out who had murdered his friends and somehow to establish Salander's innocence.

She fully sympathized with his objectives—Dag and Mia had been her friends too—but there was a side to Blomkvist that made her uncomfortable. He could become ruthless when he smelled blood.

From the moment he had called her the day before and told her how he had challenged Bublanski and begun sizing him up like some fucking macho cowboy, she knew that the hunt for Salander would keep Blomkvist busy for the foreseeable future. She knew from experience that he would be impossible to deal with until he solved the problem. He would vacillate between self-absorption and depression. And somewhere in the equation he would also take risks that were probably utterly unnecessary.

And Salander. Berger had met her only once, and she didn't know enough about that strange girl to share Blomkvist's certainty that she was innocent. What if Bublanski was right? What if she *was* guilty? What if Blomkvist did manage to track her down and she turned out to be a lunatic armed with a gun?

Nor had Paolo Roberto's astonishing conversation earlier that morning been reassuring. It was good, of course, that Blomkvist was not the only one on Salander's side, but Paolo was a cowboy too.

And where was she going to find someone to replace her at *Millennium*? It was now becoming urgent. She thought of discussing the matter with Malm, but she couldn't tell him and still keep the news from Blomkvist.

Blomkvist was a brilliant reporter, but he would be a disaster as editor in chief. She and Malm were much more alike, but she was not at all sure that he would accept the offer. Eriksson was too young, not confident enough yet. Nilsson was too self-absorbed. Cortez was a good reporter, but he was way too inexperienced. Lotta Karim was too flaky. And Berger could not be sure that Malm or Blomkvist would be happy with someone recruited from the outside.

It was a hell of a mess. Not at all the way she wanted to end her tenure at *Millennium*.

. . .

On Sunday evening Salander opened Asphyxia 1.3 and went into the mirrored hard drive of *MikBlom/laptop*. He was not online and she read through the material that had been added in the past two days.

She read Blomkvist's research journal and wondered whether he might be writing it in such detail for her sake, and if so, what that could mean. He knew that she was accessing his computer, so it was natural to conclude that he wanted her to read what he wrote. The real question, however, was what he was not writing. Since he knew she was accessing his machine, he could manipulate the flow of information. She noted in passing that he apparently hadn't gotten much further with Bublanski than challenging him to some sort of a duel over her innocence. This annoyed her. Blomkvist was basing his conclusions on emotion rather than on facts. *What a naive idiot.*

But he had also zeroed in on Zala. *Good thinking, Kalle Blomkvist.*

Then she noticed with mild surprise that Paolo Roberto had popped up on the scene. That was good news. She smiled. She liked that cocky fucker. He was macho to his fingertips. He used to give her a pretty good drubbing when they met in the ring. The few times he managed to connect, that is.

Then she sat up in her chair when she decrypted and read Blomkvist's most recent email to Berger.

Gunnar Björck. Säpo. Knows about Zala.

Björck knows Bjurman.

Salander's eyes went blurry as she sketched a triangle in her mind. *Zala. Bjurman. Björck. Yes, that makes sense.* She had never looked at the problem from that perspective before. Maybe Blomkvist wasn't so dumb after all. But of course he had not worked out the connection. She had not even done that herself, even though she had a lot more insight into what had happened. She thought for a while about Bjurman and

realized that the fact that he knew Björck turned him into a
bigger roadblock than she had previously imagined.

She also realized that she would probably have to pay a visit
to Smådalarö.

Then she went into Blomkvist's hard drive and created a
new document in the folder <Lisbeth Salander> which she
called [Ring corner]. He would see it the next time he switched
on his iBook.

1. Keep away from Teleborian. He's evil.
2. Miriam Wu has absolutely nothing to do with this.
3. You're right to focus on Zala. He's the key. But you're
not going to find him in any public records.
4. There's a connection between Bjurman and Zala. I
don't know what it is, but I'm working on it. Björck?
5. Important. There's a damaging police report on me
from March 1991. I don't know the file number and can't
find it. Why hasn't Ekström given it to the media?
Answer: It's not on his computer. Conclusion: He doesn't
know about it. How can that be possible?

She thought for a moment and then added a P.S.:

P.S. Mikael, I'm not innocent. But I didn't kill Dag and
Mia—I have nothing to do with their murders. I saw
them that evening—before the murders occurred—but I
left them before it happened. Thanks for believing in
me. Say hello to Paolo Roberto and tell him he has a
wimpy left hook.

P.P.S. How did you know about the Wennerström thing?

Blomkvist found Salander's document some three hours later.
He read the message line by line at least five times. For the first
time she had clearly stated that she did not murder Svensson

and Johansson. He believed her and felt enormous relief. And finally she was talking to him, although as cryptically as ever.

He also noted that she denied murdering Dag and Mia, but she said nothing about Bjurman. Which Blomkvist assumed was because he had mentioned only the two of them in his message. He thought for a while and then created [Ring corner 2].

> Hi Sally.
> Thanks for finally telling me you're innocent. I believed in you, but even I have been affected by the media noise and felt some doubt. Forgive me. It feels good to hear it straight from your keyboard. All that's left is to uncover the real killer. You and I have done that before. It would help if you weren't so cagey. I assume you're reading my research journal. Then you know about as much as I do and how I'm thinking. I think Björck knows something and I'll have another talk with him in the next few days. Am I on the wrong track, checking off the girls' clients?
>   This thing with the police report surprises me. I'll get my colleague Malin Eriksson to dig into it. You were how old then, twelve or thirteen? What was the report about?
>   Your attitude towards Teleborian is duly noted.
>   M.
>
> P.S. You made a mistake in the Wennerström coup. I knew what you'd done—in Sandhamn over Christmas— but didn't ask since you didn't mention it. And I have no intention of telling you what the mistake was unless you meet me for a coffee.

The reply, when it came, said:

> You can forget about the johns. Zala's the one who's of interest. And a blond giant. But the police report is

interesting since somebody seems to want to hide it.
That can't be an accident.

Prosecutor Ekström was in a foul mood when Bublanski's team
gathered for the morning meeting on Monday. More than a
week's searching for a named suspect with a distinctive appearance had produced no result. Ekström's mood did not improve
when Andersson, who had been on duty over the weekend, told
him of the latest development.

"A break-in?" Ekström said with undisguised amazement.

"The neighbour called on Sunday evening to say that the
police tape on Bjurman's door had been cut. I checked on it."

"And?"

"The tape was cut in three places. Probably a razor blade or
a Stanley knife. A slick job. It was hard to see."

"A burglary? There are hooligans who specialize in dead
people's apartments—"

"Not a burglary. I went through the apartment. All the valuables, DVD player and such, were still there. But Bjurman's car
key was lying on the kitchen table."

"Car key?"

"Jerker was in the apartment on Wednesday to check if we'd
missed something. He also checked the car. He swears there
wasn't a car key on the kitchen table when he left the apartment and put the tape back up."

"Could he have forgotten and left it out? Nobody's perfect."

"Jerker never used that key. He used the one on Bjurman's
key ring, which we had already confiscated."

Bublanski stroked his chin. "So, not a normal break-in
then."

"Someone got into Bjurman's apartment and sniffed
around. It must have happened between Wednesday and Sunday evening, when the neighbour telephoned."

"Somebody was looking for something. What? Jerker?"

"There's nothing of any interest left in there, nothing that we didn't already confiscate."

"Nothing that we know of, at least. The motive for the murder is still unclear. We assume that Salander is a psychopath, but even psychopaths need motives."

"What do you suggest?"

"I don't know. Someone searched Bjurman's apartment. First question: Who? Second question: Why? What was it we missed?"

"Jerker?"

Holmberg gave a resigned sigh. "OK. I'll go through the apartment. This time with tweezers."

Salander woke up at 11:00 on Monday morning. She lay dozing for about half an hour before she got up, put on coffee, and took a shower. Then she made herself some breakfast and sat down at her PowerBook for an update on what was happening in Prosecutor Ekström's computer and to read the online editions of the papers. Interest in the Enskede murders had evidently declined. Then she opened Svensson's research folder and read through his notes from his meeting with the journalist Per-Åke Sandström, the john who ran errands for the sex mafia and who knew something about Zala. When she was finished, she poured herself more coffee and sat in her window seat to think.

By 4:00 she had thought enough.

She needed cash. She had three credit cards. One of them was in her own name and so for all practical purposes useless. One was issued to Irene Nesser, but she wanted to avoid using it since identifying herself with Irene Nesser's passport would be risky. One was issued to Wasp Enterprises and was linked to an account that held about three million kronor and could be replenished with transfers via the Internet. Anyone could use the card, but they would have to identify themselves.

She went into the kitchen, opened a biscuit tin, and took out a wad of banknotes. She had 950 kronor in cash, not a whole lot. Fortunately she also had 1,800 American dollars that had been lying around since she returned from her travels; she could exchange them without ID at a Forex currency window. That improved the situation.

She put on Irene Nesser's wig, dressed up, and put a change of clothes and a box of theatre makeup in a backpack. Then she set off on her second expedition from Mosebacke. She walked to Folkungagatan and then down to Erstagatan, and got to the Watski shop just before closing time. She bought electrical tape and a block and tackle with eight yards of cotton rope.

She took the number 66 bus back. At Medborgarplatsen she saw a woman waiting for the bus. She did not recognize her at first, but an alarm went off in the back of her mind, and when she looked again she realized that the woman was Irene Flemström, the salaries clerk at Milton Security. She had a new, trendier hairdo. Salander slipped off the bus as Flemström got on. She looked around carefully, searching as always for faces that might be familiar. She walked past the semicircular Bofills Båge apartment building to Södra station and took the local train north.

Inspector Modig shook hands with Berger, who immediately offered her some coffee. She noticed that all the mugs in the kitchenette had logos and ads for political parties and professional organizations.

"They're mostly from election-night parties and interviews," Berger explained, handing her a Liberal Youth Party mug.

Modig worked at Svensson's old desk. Eriksson offered to help, both in explaining what Svensson's book and article were about and in navigating the research material. Modig was impressed by the scope of it. It had been an irritation for the investigative team that Svensson's computer was missing and that his work seemed inaccessible. But in fact backups had been made of most of it and had been available all along at the *Millennium* offices.

Blomkvist was not in the office, but Berger gave Modig a list of the material he had taken from Svensson's desk, which dealt exclusively with the identity of sources. Modig called Bublanski and explained the situation. They decided that all the material on Svensson's desk, including *Millennium*'s computer, would have to be confiscated and that Bublanski would return with a warrant if necessary to requisition the material that Blomkvist had already removed. Modig then drew up a confiscation inventory, and Cortez helped her carry the cardboard boxes down to her car.

On Monday evening Blomkvist was feeling deeply frustrated. He had now checked off ten of the names Svensson had intended to expose. In each instance he had encountered worried, excitable, and shocked men. He estimated their average income at around 400,000 kronor a year. They were a group of pathetic, frightened individuals.

He had not felt, however, that any of them had anything to hide with respect to the murders.

Blomkvist opened his iBook to check whether he had a new message from Salander. He did not. In her previous note she had said that the johns were of no interest and that he was wasting his time with them. He cursed her with a string of expletives. He was hungry, but he did not feel like making himself supper. Besides, he hadn't been shopping for two weeks, except to buy milk from the corner store. He put on his jacket and went down to the Greek taverna on Hornsgatan and ordered the grilled lamb.

.   .   .

Salander first took a look at the stairwell and at dusk made two cautious circuits of the adjacent buildings. They were low-frame buildings that she suspected were not soundproof and hardly ideal for her purposes. The journalist Sandström lived in a corner apartment on the fourth floor, the highest. Then the stairwell continued up to an attic door. It would have to do.

The problem was that there was no light in any of the apartment's windows.

She walked to a pizzeria a few streets away, where she ordered a Hawaiian and sat in a corner to read the evening papers. Just before 9:00 she bought a caffè latte at the Pressbyrå kiosk and returned to the building. The apartment was still in darkness. She entered the stairwell and sat on the steps to the attic. From there she had a view of Sandström's door half a flight down. She drank her latte while she waited.

Inspector Faste finally tracked down Cilla Norén, lead singer of the Satanist group Evil Fingers, at the studio of Recent Trash Records in an industrial building in Älvsjö. It was a cultural collision of about the same magnitude as the Spanish first encountering the Carib Indians.

After several futile attempts at Norén's parents' house, Faste had succeeded at the studio, where according to her sister she was "helping out" with the production of a CD by the band Cold Wax from Borlänge. Faste had never heard of the band, which seemed to consist of guys in their twenties. As soon as he entered the corridor outside the studio he was met by a wall of sound that took his breath away. He watched Cold Wax through a window and waited until there was a pause in the cacophony.

Norén had raven black hair with red and green braids and black eye makeup. She was on the chubby side and wore a short skirt and top which revealed a pierced belly button. She had a belt full of rivets around her hips and looked like something out of a French horror movie.

Faste held up his police ID and said he needed to talk to her. She went on chewing gum and gave him a sceptical look. She pointed to a door and led him into a sort of canteen, where he tripped and almost fell over a bag of trash that had been dumped right by the door. Norén ran water into an empty plastic bottle, drank about half of it, and then sat down at a table and lit a cigarette. She fixed Faste with her clear blue eyes.

"What is Recent Trash Records?"

She seemed bored out of her skull.

"It's a record company that produces new bands."

"What's your role here?"

"I'm the sound engineer."

Faste gave her a hard look. "Are you trained to do that?"

"Nope. I taught myself."

"Can you make a living from it?"

"Why do you ask?"

"I'm just curious. I assume you've read about Lisbeth Salander in the papers lately."

She nodded.

"We believe that you know her. Is that correct?"

"Could be."

"Is it correct or not correct?"

"It depends what you're looking for."

"I'm looking for an insane woman who committed a triple murder. I want information about Lisbeth Salander."

"I haven't heard from Lisbeth since last year."

"When was the last time you saw her?"

"Sometime in the fall two years ago. At Kvarnen. She used to hang out there, but then she stopped coming."

"Have you tried to get in touch with her?"

"I've called her mobile a few times. The number's been disconnected."

"And you don't know how to get hold of her otherwise?"

"No."

"What is Evil Fingers?"

Norén looked amused. "Don't you read the papers?"

"What does that mean?"

"They say we're a Satanist band."

"Are you?"

"Do I look like a Satanist?"

"What does a Satanist look like?"

"Well, I don't know who's dumber—the police or the newspapers."

"Listen here, young lady, this is a very serious matter."

"Whether we're Satanists or not?"

"Stop screwing around and answer the question."

"And what was the question?"

Faste closed his eyes for a second and thought about a visit he had paid to the police in Greece when he was on vacation some years earlier. The Greek police, despite all their problems, had one big advantage compared to the Swedish police. If this young woman had taken the same attitude over there he would have been able to bend her over and give her three whacks with a baton. He looked at her.

"Was Lisbeth Salander a member of Evil Fingers?"

"I wouldn't think so."

"What is that supposed to mean?"

"Lisbeth is probably the most tone-deaf person I've ever met."

"Tone-deaf?"

"She can tell the difference between trumpet and drums, but that's about as far as her musical talent stretches."

"I mean, was she in the group Evil Fingers?"

"And I just answered your question. What the hell do you think Evil Fingers is?"

"You tell me."

"You're running a police investigation by reading idiotic newspaper articles."

"Answer the question."

"Evil Fingers was a rock band. We were a bunch of girls in the mid-nineties who liked hard rock and played for fun. We promoted ourselves with a pentagram and a little 'Sympathy for the Devil.' Then the band broke up, and I'm the only one who's still working in music."

"And Lisbeth Salander was not, you say, a member of the band?"

"Like I said."

"So why do our sources claim that Salander was in the band?"

"Because your sources are about as stupid as the news-papers."

"Explain."

"There were five of us girls in the band, and we still get together now and then. In the old days we used to meet once a week at Kvarnen. Now it's about once a month. But we stay in touch."

"And what do you do when you get together?"

"What do you think people do at Kvarnen?"

Faste sighed. "So you get together to drink."

"We usually drink beer. And we gossip. What do you do when you get together with your friends?"

"And how does Salander come into the picture?"

"I met her at KomVux several years ago. She used to show up from time to time at Kvarnen and have a beer with us."

"So Evil Fingers can't be regarded as an organization?"

Norén looked at him as if he were from another planet.

"Are you dykes?"

"Would you like a punch in the mouth?"

"Answer the question."

"It's none of your business what we are."

"Take it easy. You can't provoke me."

"Hello? The police are claiming that Lisbeth murdered three people and you come here to ask me about my sexual preferences. You can go to hell."

"You know, I could take you in."

"For what? By the way, I forgot to tell you that I've been

studying law for three years and my father is Ulf Norén of Norén & Knape, the law firm. See you in court."

"I thought you worked in the music business."

"I do this because it's fun. You think I make a living doing this?"

"I have no idea how you make a living."

"I don't make a living as a lesbian Satanist, if that's what you think. And if that's the basis of the police search for Lisbeth, then I can see why you haven't found her."

"Do you know where she is?"

Norén began rocking her upper body back and forth and let her hands glide up in front of her.

"I can feel that she's close . . . Wait a minute, I'll check my telepathic powers."

"Cut it out."

"I've already told you I haven't heard from her for almost two years. I have no idea where she is. So now, if there isn't anything else . . ."

Modig hooked up Svensson's computer and spent the evening cataloguing the contents of his hard drive and the disks. She sat there until 11:00 reading his book.

She came to two realizations. First, that Svensson was a brilliant writer who described the business of the sex trade with compelling objectivity. She wished he could have lectured at the police academy—his knowledge would have been a valuable addition to the curriculum. Faste, for example, could have benefited from Svensson's insights.

The second realization was that Blomkvist's theory about Svensson's research providing a motive for murder was completely valid. Svensson's planned exposure of prostitutes' clients would have done more than merely hurt a number of men. It was a brutal revelation. Some of the prominent players, several of whom had handed down verdicts in sex-crime trials or participated in the public debate, would be annihilated.

The problem was that even if a john who risked being exposed had decided to murder Svensson, there was, as yet, no prospect of such a link to Nils Bjurman. He did not feature in Svensson's material, and that fact not only diminished the strength of Blomkvist's argument but also reinforced the likelihood of Salander's being the only possible suspect.

Even if a motive for the murders of Svensson and Johansson was still unclear, Salander had been at the crime scene and her fingerprints were on the murder weapon.

The weapon was also directly linked to the murder of Bjurman. There was a personal connection and a possible motive—the decoration on Bjurman's abdomen raised the possibility of some form of sexual assault or a sadomasochistic relationship between the two. It was impossible to imagine Bjurman having voluntarily submitted to such a bizarre and painful tattoo. Either he had found pleasure in the humiliation or Salander—if she was the one who had done the tattooing—had first made him powerless. How it had actually happened was not something Modig wanted to speculate about.

On the other hand, Teleborian had confirmed that Salander's violence was directed at people whom she regarded as a threat or who had offended her.

He had seemed genuinely protective, as if he did not want his former patient to come to any harm. All the same, the investigation had been based largely on his analysis of her—as a sociopath on the border of psychosis.

But Blomkvist's theory was attractive.

She chewed her lower lip as she tried to visualize some alternative scenario to Salander the killer, working alone. Finally she wrote a line in her notebook.

Two completely separate motives? Two murderers? One murder weapon?

She had a fleeting thought that she could not quite pin down, but it was something she intended to ask Bublanski at the morning meeting. She could not explain why she suddenly felt so uncomfortable with the theory of Salander as a killer working alone.

Then she called it a night, resolutely shut down her computer, and locked the disks in her desk drawer. She put on her jacket, turned off the desk lamp, and was just about to lock the door to her office when she heard a sound further down the corridor. She frowned. She had thought she was alone in the department. She walked down the corridor to Faste's office. His door was ajar and she heard him talking on the phone.

"It undeniably links things together," she heard him say.

She stood undecided for a moment before she took a deep breath and knocked on the doorjamb. Faste looked up in surprise. She waved.

"Modig is still in the building," Faste said into the phone. He listened and nodded without releasing her from his gaze. "OK, I'll tell her." He hung up. "Bubble," he said in explanation. "What do you want?"

"What is it that links things together?" she asked.

He gave her a searching look. "Were you eavesdropping?"

"No, but your door was open and I heard you say that just as I knocked."

Faste shrugged. "I called Bubble to tell him that the NFL have finally come up with something useful."

"What's that?"

"Svensson had a mobile with a Comviq cash card. They've produced a list of calls which confirms the conversation with Mikael Blomkvist at 7:30 p.m. That's when Blomkvist was at dinner at his sister's house."

"Good. But I don't think Blomkvist has anything to do with the murders."

"Me neither. But Svensson made another call that night. At 9:34. The call lasted three minutes."

"And?"

"He called Nils Bjurman's home phone. In other words, there's a link between the two murders."

Modig sank down into Faste's visitor's chair.

"Sure. Have a seat, be my guest."

She ignored him.

"OK. What does the time frame look like? At 7:30 Svensson calls Blomkvist and sets up a meeting for later that evening. At 9:30 Svensson calls Bjurman. Just before closing time at 10:00 Salander buys cigarettes at the corner shop in Enskede. Soon after 11:00 Blomkvist and his sister arrive in Enskede and at 11:11 he calls the police."

"That seems to be correct, Miss Marple."

"But it isn't correct at all. According to the pathologist, Bjurman was shot between 10:00 and 11:00 that night. By which time Salander was in Enskede. We've been working on the assumption that Salander shot Bjurman first and then the couple in Enskede."

"That doesn't mean a thing. I talked with the pathologist again. We didn't find Bjurman until the night after, almost twenty-four hours later. The pathologist says that the time of death could be plus or minus an hour."

"But Bjurman must have been the first victim, since we found the murder weapon in Enskede. That would mean that she shot Bjurman some time after 9:34 and then drove to Enskede, where she bought her cigarettes. Was there enough time to get from Odenplan to Enskede?"

"Yes, there was. She didn't take public transportation as we assumed earlier. She had a car. Sonny Bohman and I test-drove the route and we had plenty of time."

"But then she waits for an hour before she shoots Svensson and Johansson? What was she doing all that time?"

"She had coffee with them. We have her prints on the cup."

He gave her a triumphant look. Modig sighed and sat silently for a minute.

"Hans, you're looking at this like it's some sort of prestige thing. You can be a fucking shithead and you drive people crazy sometimes, but I actually knocked on your door to ask you to forgive me for slapping you. I was out of line."

He looked at her for a long moment. "Modig, you might think I'm a shithead. But I think you're unprofessional and don't have any business being a police officer. At least not at this level."

Modig weighed various replies, but in the end she just shrugged and stood up.

"Well, now we know where we stand."

"We know where we stand. And believe me, you're not going to last long here."

Modig closed the door behind her harder than she meant to. *Don't let that fucking asshole get to you.* She went down to the garage.

Faste smiled contentedly at the closed door.

Blomkvist had just gotten home when his mobile rang.

"Hi. It's Malin. Can you talk?"

"Sure."

"Something struck me yesterday."

"Tell me."

"I was going through all the clippings we have here on the hunt for Salander, and I found that spread on her time at the psychiatric clinic. What I'm wondering is why there's such a big gap in her biography."

"What gap?"

"There's plenty of stuff about the trouble she was mixed up in at school. Trouble with teachers and classmates and so on."

"I remember that. There was even a teacher who said she was afraid of Lisbeth when she was eleven."

"Birgitta Miåås."

"That's the one."

"And there are details about Lisbeth at the psychiatric clinic. Plus a lot of stuff about her with foster families during her teens and about the assault in Gamla Stan."

"So what are you thinking?"

"She was taken into the clinic just before her thirteenth birthday."

"Yes?"

"And there isn't a word about *why* she was committed. Obviously if a twelve-year-old is committed, something has to have happened. And in Lisbeth's case it was most likely some huge outburst that should have shown up in her biography. But there's nothing there."

Blomkvist frowned. "Malin, I have it from a source I trust that there's a police report on Lisbeth dated March 1991, when she was twelve. It's not in the file. I was at the point of asking you to dig around for it."

"If there's a report then it would have to be a part of her file. It would be breaking the law not to have it there. Have you really checked?"

"No, but my source says that it's not in the file."

Eriksson paused for a second. "And how reliable is your source?"

"Very."

Eriksson and Blomkvist had arrived at the same conclusion simultaneously.

"Säpo," Eriksson said.

"Björck," Blomkvist said.

CHAPTER 24

Monday, April 4–
Tuesday, April 5

Per-Åke Sandström, a freelance journalist in his late forties, came home just after midnight. He was a little drunk and felt a lump of panic lurking in his stomach. He had spent the day doing nothing. He was, quite simply, terrified.

It was almost two weeks since Svensson had been killed. Sandström had watched the TV news that night in shock. He had felt a wave of relief and hope—Svensson was dead, so maybe the book about trafficking, in which Sandström would be exposed, was history.

He hated Svensson. He had begged and pleaded, he had *crawled* for that fucking pig.

It was not until the day after that that he began to consider his situation. The police would find Svensson's text and start digging into his little escapade. Jesus . . . he could even be a murder suspect.

His panic had subsided when Salander's face was slapped on every front page in the country. *Who the hell was this Salander?* He had never heard her name before. But the police clearly considered her a serious suspect, and according to the prosecutor's statement, the murders might soon be solved. It was possible that no-one would show any interest in him at all. But from his own experience he knew that journalists always saved documentation and notes. *Millennium. A piece-of-shit magazine with an undeserved reputation. They were like all the rest. Poking around and whining and damaging people.*

He had no way of knowing how long the research had been going on. There was nobody he could ask. He felt as if he was in a vacuum.

He vacillated between panic and intoxication. Apparently the police were not looking for him. Maybe—if he was lucky— he would get away scot-free. But if he was not lucky, his working life would be over.

He stuck the key in his front door and turned the lock. When he opened the door he suddenly heard a rustling sound behind him and before he could turn he felt a paralyzing pain in the small of his back.

Björck had not yet gone to bed when the telephone rang. He was in his pajamas and dressing gown, but he was still sitting in the kitchen in the dark, gnawing on his dilemma. In his whole long career he had never found himself even close to being in such a fix.

He had not intended to pick up the phone. It was after midnight. But it kept ringing. After the tenth ring he could resist no longer.

"It's Mikael Blomkvist," said a voice on the other end.

Shit.

"I was in bed."

"I thought you might be interested in hearing what I have to say."

"What do you want?"

"Tomorrow at 10:00 a.m. I'm giving a press conference on the murders of Dag Svensson and Mia Johansson."

Björck swallowed hard.

"I'm going to give an account of the details in the book about the sex trade that Svensson had all but finished. The only john I'll be naming is you."

"You promised to give me some time . . ." He heard the fear in his voice and stopped.

"It's been several days. You said you'd call me after the weekend. Tomorrow is Tuesday. Either you tell me now or I'm holding that press conference in the morning."

"If you hold that press conference you'll never find out a damn thing about Zala."

"That's possible. But then it won't be my problem anymore either. You'll have to do your talking to the police investigation instead. And to the rest of the media, of course."

There was no room for negotiation.

Björck agreed to meet Blomkvist, but he succeeded in putting the meeting off until Wednesday. A short reprieve. But he was ready.

It was sink or swim.

He woke up on the floor of his living room. He did not know how long he had been unconscious. His body hurt all over and he couldn't move. It took him a while to realize that his hands were tied behind his back with electrical tape and his feet were bound. He had a piece of tape over his mouth. The lamps in the room were lit and the blinds were closed. He couldn't understand what had happened.

He was aware of sounds that seemed to be coming from his office. He lay still and listened and heard a drawer being opened and closed. *A robbery?* He heard the sound of paper and someone rummaging through the drawers.

It seemed like an eternity before he heard footsteps behind him. He tried turning his head, but he couldn't see anyone. He told himself to stay calm.

Suddenly a loop of thick cotton rope was slipped over his

head. A noose was tightened around his neck. The panic almost made him shit himself. He looked up and saw the rope run up to a block that was fastened to a hook where the ceiling lamp usually hung. Then the person who had assaulted him came into view. The first thing he saw was a pair of black boots.

The shock could not have been greater when he raised his eyes. He did not at first recognize the psychopath whose passport photograph had been plastered outside every Press-byrå kiosk since Easter. She had short black hair and did not look that much like the picture in the papers. She was dressed all in black—jeans, midlength cotton jacket, T-shirt, gloves.

But what terrified him the most was her face. It was painted. She wore black lipstick, eyeliner, and dramatically prominent greenish-black eye shadow. The rest of her face was covered in white makeup. She had painted a red stripe from the left side of her forehead across her nose and down to the right side of her chin.

It was a grotesque mask. She looked out of her fucking mind.

His brain resisted. It seemed unreal.

Salander grasped the end of the rope and pulled. He felt the rope cut into his neck and for a few seconds he couldn't breathe. Then he fought to get his feet under himself. With a block and tackle she hardly had to exert herself to pull him to his feet. When he was upright she stopped pulling and looped the rope a few times around a radiator pipe. She tied it with a clove hitch.

Then she vanished from his field of vision. She was gone for more than fifteen minutes. When she came back she pulled up a chair and sat in front of him. He tried to avoid looking at her painted face, but he could not help it. She laid a pistol on the living-room table. *His pistol. She had found it in the shoebox in the wardrobe.* A Colt 1911 Government. An illegal weapon he had had for several years. He had bought it from a friend but never even fired it. Right before his eyes she took out the magazine and filled it with rounds. She shoved it back in and cocked the weapon. Sandström was about to faint. He forced himself to meet her gaze.

"I don't understand why men always have to document their perversions," she said.

She had a soft but ice-cold voice. She held up a photograph. She must have printed it from his hard drive, for God's sake.

"I assume that this is Ines Hammujärvi, Estonian, seventeen years old, from Riepalu near Narva. Did you have fun with her?"

The question was rhetorical. Sandström had no way of answering. His mouth was taped shut and his brain was incapable of formulating a response. The photograph showed . . . *Good God, why did I save those pictures?*

"You know who I am? Nod."

Sandström nodded.

"You're a sadistic pig, a pervert, and a rapist."

He made no move.

"Nod."

He nodded. Suddenly he had tears in his eyes.

"Let's get the rules of engagement 100 percent clear," Salander said. "As far as I'm concerned, you should be put to death at once. Whether you survive the night or not makes no difference to me at all. Understand?"

He nodded.

"It has probably not escaped your attention that I'm a madwoman who likes killing people. Especially men."

She pointed at the recent newspapers that he had collected on the living-room table.

"I'm going to remove the tape from your mouth. If you scream or raise your voice I will zap you with this." She held up a Taser. "This horrific device puts out 50,000 volts. About 40,000 volts next time, since I've used it once and haven't recharged it. Understand?"

He looked doubtful.

"That means that your muscles will stop functioning. That was what you experienced at the door when you came staggering home." She smiled at him. "And it means that your legs will not hold you up and you'll end up hanging yourself. After I've zapped you, all I have to do is get up and leave the apartment."

He nodded. *Good God, she's a fucking crazy killer.* He could not help it: the tears flowed uncontrollably down his cheeks. He sniffled.

She got up and pulled off the tape. Her grotesque face was only an inch from his.

"Don't say a word," she said. "If you talk without permission, I'll zap you."

She waited until he stopped snuffling and met her eyes.

"You have one chance to survive the night," she said. "One chance—not two. I'm going to ask you a number of questions. If you answer them, I'll let you live. Nod if you understand."

He nodded.

"If you refuse to answer a question I'll have to zap you. Understand?"

He nodded.

"If you lie to me or give an evasive answer I'll zap you."

He nodded.

"I'm not going to bargain with you. There will be no second chance. You answer my questions immediately or you die. If you answer satisfactorily, then you'll survive. It's that simple."

He nodded. He believed her. He had no choice.

"Please," he said. "I don't want to die . . ."

"It's up to you whether you live or die. But you just broke my first rule: you do not talk without my permission."

He pressed his lips together. *God, she's completely insane.*

Blomkvist was too frustrated and restless to know what to do. Finally he put on his jacket and scarf and walked aimlessly to Södra station, past Bofills Båge, before he ended up at the

Millennium offices on Götgatan. It was perfectly quiet. He did not turn on any lights, but he did put on the coffeemaker and then stood at the window looking down at Götgatan. He tried to put his thoughts in order. The murder investigation was like a broken mosaic in which he could make out some pieces while others were simply missing. Somewhere there was a pattern. He could sense it, but he could not figure it out. Too many pieces were missing.

He was assailed by doubt. *She is not a deranged killer,* he reminded himself. She had written to tell him that she had not shot his friends. He believed her. But in some unfathomable way she was still intimately involved in the murders.

Slowly he began to reevaluate the theory he had clung to since he walked into the apartment in Enskede. He had immediately assumed that Svensson's investigative reporting about sex trafficking was the only plausible motive for the murders. Now he was coming to accept Bublanski's assertion that this couldn't explain Bjurman's murder.

Salander had told him in her message that he should forget about the johns and focus on Zala instead. *Why?* The damn pest. Why couldn't she tell him anything that made sense?

Blomkvist poured coffee into a Young Left mug. He sat on one of the sofas in the middle of the office, put his feet up on the coffee table, and lit a forbidden cigarette.

Björck was on the list of johns. Bjurman had been Salander's guardian. It could not be an accident that Bjurman and Björck had both worked at Säpo. A police report about Salander had disappeared.

Could there be more than one motive?

Could Lisbeth Salander be the motive?

Blomkvist sat there with an idea that he couldn't put into words. There was something still unexplored, but he couldn't explain exactly what he meant by the idea that Salander herself could be a motive for murder. He experienced a fleeting sense of discovery.

Then he realized that he was too tired and poured out his coffee, rinsed the machine, and went home to bed. Lying in the dark, he took up the thread again and for two hours tried to understand what it was he wanted to articulate.

Salander smoked a cigarette, comfortably leaning back in the chair in front of him. She crossed her right leg over her left and fixed him with her gaze. Sandström had never seen such an intense look before. When she spoke her voice was still soft.

"In January 2003 you visited Ines Hammujärvi for the first time at her apartment in Norsborg. She had just turned sixteen. Why did you visit her?"

Sandström did not know how to answer. He could hardly make sense of it himself, how it had begun or why he . . . She raised the Taser.

"I . . . I don't know. I wanted her. She was so beautiful."

"Beautiful?"

"Yes. She was beautiful."

"And you thought that you had the right to tie her to the bed and fuck her."

"She went along with it. I swear. She went along with it."

"You paid her?"

Sandström bit his tongue. "No."

"Why not? She was a whore. Whores get paid."

"She was a . . . she was a present."

"*A present?*" Her voice had taken on a dangerous tone.

"It was in return for a favour I did someone."

"Per-Åke," Salander said in a reasonable tone, "you wouldn't be trying to avoid answering my question, would you?"

"I swear. I'll answer anything you ask. I won't lie."

"Good. What favour and who was it for?"

"I'd smuggled in some anabolic steroids. I was on a business trip to Estonia and I brought the pills back in my car. The guy

I went with was called Harry Ranta. Although he didn't come with me in the car."

"How did you meet Harry Ranta?"

"I've known him for years. Since the eighties, in fact. He's a friend. We used to go to bars together."

"And it was Harry Ranta who offered you Ines Hammu-järvi as . . . a present?"

"Yes . . . no, I'm sorry, that was later, here in Stockholm. It was his brother, Atho Ranta."

"So you're saying that Atho Ranta knocked on your door and asked if you wanted to drive to Norsborg and fuck Ines?"

"No . . . I was at . . . we had a party in . . . damn, I can't remember where we were . . ."

He was suddenly shaking uncontrollably and felt his knees begin to give way. He needed to brace his legs against something to stand upright.

"Answer calmly," Salander said. "I'm not going to hang you because you need time to collect your thoughts. But the minute I get the idea you're trying to dodge a question, then . . . *pow!*"

She raised her eyebrows and to his astonishment looked angelic. As angelic as anyone could look behind such a hideous mask.

Sandström swallowed. His mouth was dry as a bone, and he could feel the rope tightening around his neck.

"Where you went drinking isn't important. How come Atho Ranta offered you Ines?"

"We were talking about . . . we . . . I told him that I wanted . . ." He realized he was crying.

"You said that you wanted to have one of his whores."

He nodded. "I was drunk. He said that she needed . . . needed . . ."

"What was it she needed?"

"Atho said that she needed punishment. She was difficult. She didn't do what he wanted."

"And what did he want her to do?"

"Whore for him. He offered me . . . I was drunk and didn't know what I was doing. I didn't mean . . . Forgive me."

He snuffled.

"It's not me you need to ask for forgiveness. So you offered to help Atho punish Ines and the two of you drove over to her place."

"That's not how it was."

"Tell me how it was. Why did you go with Atho to her place?"

She balanced the Taser on her knee. He was shaking again.

"I went because I wanted to have her. She was there and she was available. Ines lived with a girlfriend of Harry Ranta's. I don't think I ever knew her name. Atho tied Ines to the bed and I . . . I had sex with her. Atho watched."

"No . . . you didn't have sex with her. You raped her."

He said nothing.

"Or what?"

He nodded.

"What did Ines say?"

"She didn't say anything."

"Did she protest?"

He shook his head.

"So she thought it was cool that a middle-aged dickwad tied her up and fucked her."

"She was drunk. She didn't care."

Salander sighed in resignation.

"OK. And then you kept on going to visit Ines."

"She was so . . . She wanted me."

"Bullshit."

He looked at Salander in despair. Then he nodded.

"I . . . I raped her. Harry and Atho had given permission. They wanted her to be . . . to be trained."

"Did you pay them?"

He nodded.

"How much?"

"It was a friendly deal. I helped out with the smuggling."

"How much?"

"A few grand altogether."

"In one of your pictures Ines is here in the apartment."

"Harry brought her here."

He snuffled again.

"So for a few thousand you got a girl you could do with as you pleased. How many times did you rape her?"

"I don't know . . . several times."

"OK. Who runs this gang?"

"They're going to kill me if I rat on them."

"I don't give a shit. Right now I'm a much bigger problem for you than the Ranta brothers." She held up the Taser.

"Atho. He's the older one. Harry is the fixer."

"How many more are there in the gang?"

"I only know Harry and Atho. Atho's girl is in it too. And a guy called . . . I don't know. Pelle something. He's Swedish. I don't know who he is. He's a junkie who runs errands for them."

"Atho's girl?"

"Silvia. She's a whore."

Salander sat for a moment, thinking. Then she raised her eyes.

"Who is Zala?"

Sandström turned pale. *The same question that Svensson had hounded him about.* He said nothing for so long that he noticed the girl was getting pissed off.

"I don't know," he said. "I don't know who he is."

Salander's expression darkened.

"You've been doing fine up to now. Don't throw away your only chance," she said.

"I swear to God, honest. I don't know who he is. The journalist you shot . . ."

He stopped. It might not be a good idea to bring up her massacre in Enskede.

"Yes?"

"He asked me the same thing. I don't know. If I knew I'd tell you. I swear. He's somebody Atho knows."

"You've talked to him?"

"Just for a minute once on the phone. I talked to someone who said his name was Zala. Or rather, he talked to me."

"Why?"

Sandström blinked. Drops of sweat were running into his eyes and he could feel snot running down his chin.

"I . . . they wanted me to do them another favour."

"The story is getting annoyingly slow," Salander said.

"They wanted me to take another trip to Tallinn and bring back a car that was prepared already. Amphetamines. I didn't want to do it."

"Why not?"

"It was too much. They were such gangsters. I wanted out. I had a job to get on with."

"So you think you were just a gangster in your free time."

"I'm not really like that."

"Oh, right." Her voice contained such contempt that Sandström closed his eyes.

"Keep going. How did Zala come into the picture?"

"It was a nightmare."

The tears were running again. He bit his lip so hard that it began to bleed.

"Boring," Salander said.

"Atho kept after me about it. Harry warned me and said that Atho was getting angry and that he didn't know how it would pan out. Finally I agreed to meet Atho. That was in August of last year. I drove to Norsborg with Harry . . ."

His mouth kept moving but the words disappeared. Salander's eyes narrowed. He found his voice again.

"Atho was a nutcase. He's very brutal. You have no idea how brutal he can be. He said that it was too late for me to pull out and that if I didn't do as he said I wouldn't be allowed to live. He was going to give me a demonstration."

"Oh yeah?"

"They forced me to go with them. We drove towards Södertälje. Atho told me to put on a hood. It was a bag that he tied over my eyes. I was scared to death."

"So you were in a car with a bag over your head. Then what happened?"

"The car stopped. I didn't know where I was."

"Where did they put the bag on you?"

"Just before Södertälje."

"And how long did it take you to get there?"

"Maybe . . . half an hour. They got me out of the car. It was some sort of warehouse."

"What happened?"

"Harry and Atho led me inside. There were lights on. The first thing I saw was some poor guy lying on a cement floor. He was tied up. He'd been beaten really badly."

"Who was it?"

"His name was Kenneth Gustafsson. But I didn't find that out until later."

"What happened?"

"There was a man there. He was the biggest man I've ever seen. Enormous. Nothing but muscle."

"What did he look like?"

"He looked like the Devil himself. Blond."

"Name?"

"He never said his name."

"OK. A big blond guy. Who else?"

"There was another man. He looked stressed. Hair in a ponytail."

Magge Lundin.

"More?"

"Plus me and Harry and Atho."

"Keep going."

"The huge guy . . . he set out a chair for me. He didn't say a word. It was Atho who did the talking. He said that the guy on the floor was a snitch. He wanted me to know what happened to people who made trouble." Sandström was blubbering unrestrainedly.

"The big guy lifted the other guy off the floor and put him on another chair facing me. We were sitting a yard or so apart. I looked him in the eyes. Then the giant stood behind him and put his hands around his neck . . . He . . . he . . ."

"Strangled him?"

"Yeah . . . no . . . he squeezed him to death. I think he broke his neck with his bare hands. I heard the guy's neck snap and he died right in front of me."

Sandström was swaying on the rope. Tears were streaming down his face. He had never told anyone this before. Salander gave him a minute to collect himself.

"And then?"

"The other man—the one with the ponytail—started up a chain saw and sawed off the guy's head and then his hands. After that the giant came up to me. He put his hands around my neck. I tried to pull his hands away. I pulled as hard as I could, but I couldn't budge him an inch. But he didn't squeeze—he just held his hands there for a long time. Meanwhile Atho took out his mobile and made a call in Russian. Then he said that Zala wanted to talk to me and held the phone to my ear."

"What did Zala say?"

"He just asked whether I still wanted to pull out. I promised to go to Tallinn and get the car with the amphetamines. What else could I do?"

Salander sat without speaking for a long time. She contemplated the snuffling journalist on the rope and seemed to be thinking about something.

"Describe his voice."

"It . . . sounded normal."

"Deep voice, high voice?"

"Deep. Ordinary. Gruff."

"What language did he speak?"

"Swedish."

"Accent?"

"Yeah, maybe a little. But good Swedish. He and Atho spoke Russian."

"Do you understand Russian?"

"A little. Not fluent. Just a little."

"What did Atho say to him?"

"He just said that the demonstration was over."

"Have you told anyone else about this?"

"No."

"Svensson?"

"No . . . no."

"Svensson visited you."

Sandström nodded.

"I can't hear you."

"Yes."

"How come?"

"He knew that I had . . . the whores."

"What did he ask?"

"He wanted to know . . . about Zala. He asked about Zala. That was the second visit."

"The second visit?"

"He got in touch two weeks before he died. That was the first visit. Then he came back two days before you . . . he . . . "

"Before I shot him?"

"Yes."

"And he asked about Zala then?"

"Yeah."

"What did you tell him?"

"Nothing. I couldn't tell him anything. I admitted that I'd spoken to him on the phone. That was all. I didn't say anything about the blond monster or what they did to Gustafsson."

"OK. Tell me exactly what Svensson asked."

"I . . . he just wanted to know what I knew about Zala. That was all."

"And you didn't tell him anything?"

"Nothing of any use. I don't know anything."

She bit her lower lip pensively. *There was something he wasn't saying.*

"Who did you tell about Svensson's visit?"

Sandström seemed to shiver.

Salander waved the Taser.

"I called Harry."

"When?"

He swallowed. "The night Svensson visited me the first time."

She kept on for another half hour, but he was just repeating himself, adding details here and there. She stood up and put a hand on the rope.

"You must be one of the sorriest perverts I've ever met," Salander said. "What you did to Ines deserves the death penalty. But I told you that you would live if you answered my questions. I keep my promises."

She loosened the knot. Sandström collapsed in a slobbering heap on the floor. He saw her put a stool on his coffee table and climb up and unhook the block and tackle. She coiled the rope and stuffed it in a backpack. She went into the bathroom. He heard the water running. When she came back she had washed off the makeup.

Her face looked scrubbed and naked.

"You can cut yourself free."

She dropped a kitchen knife beside him.

He heard her out in the hall for a long time. It sounded as though she was changing clothes. Then he heard the front door open and close. It took him half an hour to cut off the tape. He first sank down on the sofa, then staggered to his feet and searched the apartment. She had taken his Colt 1911 Government.

· · ·

Salander arrived home at 4:55 a.m. She took off the Irene Nesser wig and went straight to bed without turning on her computer to see whether Blomkvist had solved the mystery of the missing police report.

She was awake at 9:00 and spent all of Tuesday digging up information about the Ranta brothers.

Atho Ranta had an extensive record in the police criminal files. He was a Finnish citizen from an Estonian family. He came to Sweden in 1971. From 1972 to 1978 he worked as a carpenter for Skånska Concrete Pouring. He was dismissed after being caught stealing from a building site and sentenced to seven months in prison. Between 1980 and 1982 he worked for a smaller builder. He was kicked out after turning up drunk at work several times. For the remainder of the eighties he made a living as a bouncer, a technician at a company that serviced oil-fired boilers, a dishwasher, and a janitor at a school. He was fired from all these jobs for drunkenness or for getting into fights. His janitorial job lasted only a few months: a teacher reported him for sexual harassment and threatening behaviour.

In 1987 he was fined and sentenced to a month in prison for car theft, driving without insurance, and receiving stolen property. The following year he was fined for possession of an illegal weapon. In 1990 he was convicted of a sexual offence that wasn't specified in his criminal record. In 1991 he was charged with intimidation but acquitted. The same year he was fined and put on probation for smuggling alcohol. He served three months in 1992 for beating up his girlfriend and making threats against her sister. He managed to stay out of trouble until 1997, when he was convicted of handling stolen goods and aggravated assault. This time he got ten months in prison.

Harry, his younger brother, followed him to Sweden in 1982 and worked in a warehouse for a long time. His criminal record showed three convictions: in 1990 for insurance fraud, in 1992 with a sentence of two years—for aggravated assault, receiving stolen property, theft, and rape. He was deported to Finland but in 1996 returned to Sweden, when he was once more sentenced to ten months in prison for aggravated assault and rape. The verdict was appealed and the appeals court acquitted him on the rape charge. But the conviction for assault was upheld, and he served six months. In 2000 he was charged again, this time for intimidation and rape. The charges were later dropped and the case dismissed.

Salander traced their last-known addresses: Atho's was in Norsborg, Harry's in Alby.

Paolo Roberto got Miriam Wu's answering machine for the fifteenth time. He'd been to the address on Lundagatan several times already that day. No-one answered when he rang her doorbell.

It was past 8:00 on Tuesday evening. She had to come home sometime, damn it. He understood that Wu would want to stay out of sight, but the worst of the media blitz had subsided. He might as well sit outside the door of her building in case she turned up, even if it was only for a change of clothing. He filled a thermos with coffee and made himself some sandwiches. Before he left his apartment he made the sign of the cross in front of the crucifix and the Madonna.

He parked about a hundred feet from the entrance on Lundagatan and pushed back the seat to make more room for his legs. He played the radio at a low volume. He taped up a photograph of Wu that he'd cut out of a newspaper. She looked great, he thought. He patiently watched the few people walking past. Miriam Wu was not one of them.

Every ten minutes he dialled her number. He gave up trying to call at around 9:00 when his mobile told him that the battery was almost dead.

. . .

Sandström spent Tuesday in a state approaching apathy. He had slept the night on the sofa in the living room, incapable of going to bed and unable to stop the sobbing fits that regularly overcame him. On Tuesday morning he went down to Systembolaget in Solna and bought a bottle of Skåne Aquavit. Then he went back to his sofa and drank half of it.

Not until later did he come to a clear understanding of his situation and begin to consider what he could do about it. He wished that he had never heard of the Ranta brothers and their whores. He could not believe that he had been so stupid as to let himself be enticed to the apartment in Norsborg where Atho had tied the heavily drugged Ines Hammujärvi to a bed with her legs spread, then challenged him about who had the bigger rod. They had taken turns, and he had won the contest for the greater number of sexual feats performed that night.

The girl woke up once and tried to resist. Atho spent half an hour alternating between slapping her and filling her with drink, after which she was pacified and he invited Sandström to continue the sport.

Fucking whore.

How *could* he have been so stupid?

He could hardly expect any mercy from *Millennium.* They made their living with that type of scandal.

He was scared to death of the madwoman Salander.

Not to mention that blond monster.

Obviously he couldn't go to the police.

He wasn't going to be able to manage on his own, and the problem wasn't going to go away by itself.

There was only one slim possibility open to him, one place where he could expect an ounce of sympathy and maybe a solution of sorts. He was clutching at straws, but it was his only option.

That afternoon he gathered his courage and called Harry Ranta's mobile. There was no answer. He kept trying until 10:00 that night. After thinking about the matter for a long time (and fortifying himself with the rest of the aquavit) he called Atho Ranta. It was Atho's girlfriend Silvia who answered. She told him that the Ranta brothers were on vacation in Tallinn. No, she did not know how to reach them. No, she had no idea when they would be back. They would be in Estonia for quite a while. She sounded glad of that.

Sandström wasn't sure if he was depressed or relieved. It meant that he didn't have to explain things to Atho. But the underlying message, that the Ranta brothers had decided to take a breather in Tallinn for the foreseeable future, did not do much to calm Sandström's nerves.

CHAPTER 25

Tuesday, April 5–
Wednesday, April 6

Paolo Roberto had not gone to sleep, but he was so deeply immersed in his thoughts that it was a moment before he noticed the woman walking down from Högalid Church after 11:00 p.m. He saw her in his rearview mirror. Not until she passed under a streetlight about seventy yards behind him did he snap his head around and at once recognize that it was Miriam Wu.

He sat up in his seat. His immediate thought was to get out of the car, but he might scare her off. It was better to wait until she reached the front door.

As he watched her approach, he saw a dark-coloured van pull up next to her. Paolo Roberto looked on, horrified, as a man—a devilishly huge beast—hopped out from the sliding doors and grabbed Wu. She was taken completely by surprise. She tried to wriggle away by backing up, but the man held her wrists in a viselike grip.

Paolo Roberto's mouth dropped open when he saw Wu's leg come up in a fast arc. *She's a kickboxer!* She landed a blow on the man's head but it didn't seem to faze him in the least. Instead the man raised his hand and slapped Wu on the side of her head. Paolo Roberto heard the blow from where he was sitting. Wu hit the deck as if struck by lightning. The man bent down, picked her up with one hand, and simply tossed her into the van. That was when Paolo Roberto closed his mouth and came to life. He threw open the car door and sprinted towards the van.

After only a few steps he realized how fruitless it was. The van that Miriam Wu had been thrown into like a sack of potatoes had made a U-turn and was already moving down the street before he reached full speed. It was headed towards Högalid Church. Paolo Roberto spun around and raced back to his car. He too made a U-turn. The van had vanished when he came to the corner. He braked, looked down Högalidsgatan, and then took a chance and turned left towards Hornsgatan.

When he reached Hornsgatan he came up against a red light, but there was no traffic, so he eased into the intersection and looked around. The only taillights he could see were turning left up towards Liljeholmsbron at Långholmsgatan. He could not see if it was the van, but it was the only vehicle in sight. He accelerated in pursuit but was stopped by the lights at Långholmsgatan and had to let the traffic from Kungsholmen pass as the seconds ticked away. When the traffic cleared, he accelerated hard, ignoring another red light.

He drove as fast as he dared across Liljeholmsbron and faster as he passed through Liljeholmen. He still didn't know if it was the van whose taillights he had seen, and he didn't know whether it had turned off to Gröndal or Årsta. He decided to go straight and floored it again. He was doing more than ninety miles an hour and blew past the sluggish, law-abiding traffic, assuming some driver or other would take down his licence plate number.

When he reached Bredäng he spotted the vehicle again. He closed in until he was only fifty yards behind and was sure it was the van. He slowed to about fifty miles an hour and fell back to two hundred yards. Only then did he start breathing normally.

. . .

Miriam Wu felt the blood running down her neck as she landed on the floor of the van. Her nose was bleeding. He had split her lower lip and probably broken her nose. The attack had come like a bolt out of the blue. Her resistance had been quashed in less than a second. She felt the van start up as soon as her attacker slid the doors shut. For a moment, as the driver turned the van, the blond giant lost his balance.

She twisted around and braced her hips against the floor. When the man turned towards her she lashed out with a kick, striking him on the side of his head. She even saw that her heel left a mark. It was a kick that should have hurt.

He looked at her in surprise. Then he smiled.

Jesus, what kind of a fucking monster is this?

She kicked again, but he caught her leg and twisted her foot so hard that she shrieked in pain and had to roll over onto her stomach.

Then he leaned over her and slapped her again. He hit the side of her head. Wu saw stars. It felt like being struck by a sledgehammer. He sat on her back. She tried to lift him, but she could not move him an inch. He twisted her arms behind her back and locked them in handcuffs. She was helpless. Suddenly she felt a paralyzing fear.

Blomkvist was passing the Globe Arena on his way home from Tyresö. He had spent the afternoon and evening visiting three people on Svensson's list. Not a thing had come of it. He had encountered panic-stricken men who had already been confronted by Svensson and were just waiting for the sky to fall. They had begged and pleaded with him. He crossed all of them off his private list of murder suspects.

He took out his mobile as he drove across Skanstullsbron and called Berger. She didn't answer. He tried Eriksson. No

answer there either. Damn. It was late. He wanted to talk about
this with somebody.

He wondered whether Paolo Roberto had had any success
with Miriam Wu and dialled his number. It rang five times
before he got an answer.

"Paolo."

"Hi. It's Blomkvist. I'm wondering how it went—"

"Blomkvist, I'm on *skrrritch skrrritch* a van with Miriam."

"I can't hear you."

"*Skrp skrrrraaap skrraaaap.*"

"You're breaking up. I can't hear you."

Then the connection broke off.

Paolo Roberto swore. His battery died just as he went through
Fittja. He pushed the ON button and brought the phone back
to life. He dialled the number for emergency services, but as
soon as they answered his mobile went dead again.

Shit.

He had a battery charger that worked in the cigarette
lighter. But the charger was in the hall at home. He tossed the
mobile onto the passenger seat and concentrated on keeping
the taillights of the van in sight. He was driving a BMW with
a full tank, and there wasn't a chance in hell that the van would
be able to outrun him. But he didn't want to attract attention,
so he increased the distance to several hundred yards.

*A giant on steroids beats up a girl right in front of me. Just
wait till I get my hands on that fucker.*

If Erika Berger had been there she would have called him a
macho cowboy. Paolo Roberto called it being pissed off.

Blomkvist drove down Lundagatan. Miriam Wu's apartment
was in darkness. He tried calling Paolo Roberto again, but got
the message that the subscriber could not be reached. He swore

to himself and then drove home and made coffee and a sandwich.

The drive took longer than Paolo Roberto had anticipated. The van went as far as Södertälje before it headed west on the E20 towards Strängnäs. Just past Nykvarn, it turned off to the left onto smaller roads through the countryside of Sörmland.

The smaller the roads, the greater the risk that he would be noticed by the men in the van. He eased off the accelerator and fell back even more.

He was unsure of his geography out here, but as far as he could tell they were passing to the west of Lake Yngern. He lost the van from view and went faster. He came out on a long straightaway.

The van had disappeared. There were small roads on both sides. He had lost them.

Miriam Wu felt pain in her neck and face, but she had overcome her panic at being helpless. He had not hit her again. She had managed to sit up and was leaning against the back of the driver's seat. Her hands were cuffed behind her back and there was a strip of duct tape over her mouth. One nostril was clogged with blood and she was having difficulty breathing.

She looked at her assailant. Since he had taped her mouth he hadn't said a word. She looked at the mark where she had kicked him. It was a blow that should have caused serious damage. He seemed hardly to have noticed it.

He was massively built, and on a huge scale. He had muscles that spoke of long hours spent in a gym. But he was not a bodybuilder. His muscles looked completely natural. His hands were as big as frying pans.

The van was bumping along a road full of potholes. She thought they had taken the E4 south for a long time before they turned off onto country roads.

She knew that even if her hands were free she wouldn't stand a chance against this giant.

Eriksson called Blomkvist a little before midnight.

"I'm sorry for calling so late. I've been trying to reach you for hours, but you didn't answer your mobile."

"I had it turned off all day while I was dealing with some of the johns."

"I came up with something that could be of interest," Eriksson said.

"Tell me."

"Bjurman. You asked me to look into his background."

"What did you find?"

"He was born in 1950, and began studying law in 1970. He took his law degree in 1976, started working at Klang and Reine in 1978, and opened his own practice in 1989. One of his side jobs was as a clerk at a district court for a few weeks in 1976. Right after he got his degree in 1976 he worked for two years, from 1976 to 1978, as a lawyer at National Police headquarters."

"Interesting."

"I checked out what sort of work he did there. It wasn't easy to dig up. But he was, for one thing, in charge of legal matters for the Security Police. He worked on immigration."

"Which tells us?"

"That he worked there with your man Björck."

"That bastard. He didn't say a word about having actually worked with Bjurman."

The van had to be somewhere in the vicinity.

Paolo Roberto had glimpsed it only a minute before he lost it. He reversed onto the grass verge and turned back. He drove slowly, looking for side roads.

After only a hundred and fifty yards he spotted a light glinting through a narrow gap in the curtain of trees. He saw a

forest track on the opposite side of the road and drove up it
about fifty feet, turned, and parked facing out, not bothering
to lock the car. Then he jogged back across the road and
hopped over a ditch. He wished he had a flashlight as he wound
his way forward through the undergrowth and low branches.

Very soon he came out onto a sandy gravel area and could
see some low, dark buildings. As he walked towards them the
light above a loading bay came on.

He dropped to his knees and stayed motionless. A second
later the lights went on inside the building. It appeared to be a
warehouse about a hundred feet long with a row of narrow windows high on one side. The yard was full of containers, and to
his right was parked a yellow front-end loader. Next to it was a
white Volvo. In the glow of the outdoor light he suddenly saw
the van, parked only twenty-five yards from where he crouched.

Then a door opened in the loading bay right in front of
him. A man with mousy hair and a beer belly came out of the
warehouse and lit a cigarette. Paolo Roberto saw, against the
light from the door, that he had a ponytail.

He kept stock-still. He was in full view less than twenty
yards from the man, but the flame from his cigarette lighter
had knocked out his night vision. Then he and the man with
the ponytail both heard a half-choked howl from the van. As
Ponytail moved towards the van, Paolo Roberto eased himself
down flat on the ground.

He heard a rattle as the sliding doors of the van opened and
saw the huge blond man get out, reach back inside, and haul
out Miriam Wu. He took her under one arm and held her in an
easy grip as she struggled. The two men exchanged some
words, but Paolo Roberto could not hear what they said. Then
Ponytail opened the door on the driver's side and hopped in.
He started up the van and made a tight turn in the yard. The
beams of the headlights swung past only a few yards from
Paolo Roberto. The van disappeared down an access road and
the noise of its engine faded into the distance.

The giant carried Miriam Wu through the door in the loading bay. Paolo Roberto could see a shadow through the windows high on the wall. It seemed as if the shadow was moving towards the far end of the building.

He got up cautiously. His clothes felt sticky. He was relieved and uneasy. He was relieved because he had managed to track the van and had Miriam Wu within reach. But he was in awe of the giant who had plucked her out of the van as if she were a bag of groceries.

The sane thing to do would be to retreat and call the police. But his battery was dead, and he had only a vague idea of where he was. He certainly couldn't give directions to anyone else as to how to get there. And he had no clue what was happening to the girl inside the building.

He made a slow circuit and discovered that there was only one entrance. After two minutes he was back near the door and had to make a decision. No question that the giant was a bad guy. He had kidnapped Miriam Wu. Paolo Roberto did not feel particularly afraid—he had great self-confidence and knew that he could give as good as he got if it came to a fight. The question was whether the man inside the warehouse was armed and whether there were other people with him. He hesitated. There shouldn't be any others besides the girl and the blond giant.

The loading bay was wide enough for a front-end loader to drive through it, and there was a normal-sized door fitted into the gate. Paolo Roberto walked over and pressed down the handle to open it. He entered a big warehouse bathed in light, filled with assorted building materials, crushed boxes, and trash.

Miriam Wu felt tears running down her cheeks. She was crying not so much from pain as from helplessness. During the journey the giant had handled her as if she weighed nothing at all.

He ripped the tape off her mouth when the van stopped. He lifted her and carried her inside without the least effort and dumped her on the cement floor, paying no heed to her protests. When he looked at her his eyes were ice cold.

Miriam Wu knew that she was going to die in this warehouse.

He turned his back on her and walked to a table, where he opened a bottle of mineral water, drinking from it in long gulps. He had not taped her legs together, and she attempted to stand up.

He turned to her and smiled. He was closer to the door than she was. She would have no chance of making it past him. Resigned, she sank to her knees, furious at herself. *I'll be damned if I give up without a fight.* She got up again and clenched her teeth. *Come on, you fucking tub of lard.*

She felt clumsy and off balance with her hands cuffed behind her, but when he came towards her she backed, circling away, watching for an opening. She lashed out with a lightning kick to his ribs, wheeled around and kicked again at his crotch. She hit his hip, backed off a few feet, and switched legs for the next kick. With her hands manacled she did not have the balance to kick at his face, but she delivered a swift kick to his breastbone.

He reached out a hand and grabbed her by the shoulder, spun her around and gave her a single blow with his fist, not very hard, to the kidneys. Miriam Wu shrieked like a madwoman as a paralyzing pain sliced through her midsection. She sank to her knees again. He gave her one more slap to the side of her head, and she tumbled to the floor. Then he kicked her in the torso. She gasped for breath as she heard a rib crack.

Paolo Roberto saw nothing of the beating, but he did hear Miriam Wu wail in pain, a sharp, shrill scream that was immediately cut off. He looked in the direction of the sound and clenched his teeth. There was a room beyond a dividing wall.

He moved silently through the warehouse and peered through the doorway just as the man rolled the girl onto her back. The giant vanished from his field of view for a few seconds and came back with a chain saw, which he set on the floor in front of her. Paolo Roberto slipped off his jacket.

"I want the answer to a simple question."

He had a high-pitched voice, almost as if it had never broken, and an accent.

"Where is Lisbeth Salander?"

"I don't know," Miriam Wu said, obviously in pain.

"That's the wrong answer. You'll have one more chance before I start this thing."

He squatted down and patted the chain saw.

"Where is Lisbeth Salander hiding?"

Wu shook her head.

When the man reached for the chain saw, Paolo Roberto took three determined strides into the room and threw a hard right hook at his kidneys.

Paolo Roberto had not become a world-famous boxer by being tentative in the ring. He had fought thirty-three bouts in his professional career and won twenty-eight of them. When he punched someone as hard as he could he expected to see his opponent feel pain. But this time he felt as if he had smashed his hand into a concrete wall. He had never experienced anything like it in all the years he'd spent as a boxer. He looked in astonishment at the colossus in front of him.

The man turned and looked with equal astonishment at the boxer.

"What do you say we find you somebody in your own weight class?" said Paolo Roberto.

He got off a string of right-left-right punches to the body and put some muscle behind them. They were heavy blows. The only effect was that the giant took half a step back, more from surprise than from the effect of the punches. Then he smiled.

"You're Paolo Roberto," he said.

Paolo Roberto stopped, amazed. He had just landed four punches that should have put the giant on the deck while the referee counted to ten. But his blows seemed not to have had the slightest effect.

Good God. This isn't normal.

Then he saw as if in slow motion the man's right hook come flying towards him. He was slow and telegraphed the punch in advance. Paolo Roberto had time to move, but the blow glanced off his shoulder. It felt as if he had been hit by a steel bar.

Paolo Roberto backed up two steps, filled with new respect for his opponent.

There's something wrong with him. Nobody can hit this hard.

He automatically blocked a left hook with his forearm and felt at once a sharp pain. He did not manage to block the right hook that came out of nowhere and landed on his forehead.

Paolo Roberto tumbled backwards out the door. He landed against a mound of wooden pallets and shook his head. He felt blood streaming down his face. *He cut my eyebrow. It'll have to be sewn up. Again.*

In the next moment the giant came into view and Paolo Roberto instinctively twisted to the side. He escaped by a hairsbreadth another clublike blow from those enormous fists. He quickly backed up, three, four shuffles, and got his arms up in a defensive position. He was shaken.

The man regarded him with eyes that were curious and almost amused. Then he assumed the same defensive position. *This guy is a boxer.* They began to circle each other slowly.

The hundred and eighty seconds that followed became the most bizarre match that Paolo Roberto had ever fought. There were no coaches, no referee. There was no bell to call a halt to the round and send the fighters to their corners. No pause for water and smelling salts and a towel to wipe the blood from his eyes.

Paolo Roberto knew now that he was fighting for his life. All his training, all the years of hammering on punching bags, all the sparring, and all the experience from all the bouts he had fought came together as the adrenaline pumped in a way he had never before experienced.

They went at each other in an exchange into which Paolo Roberto put all his power and all his fury. Left, right, left, left again, and a jab with the right to the face, duck the left hook, back up a step, attack with the right. Every punch landed with solid force.

He was in the biggest battle of his life. He was hitting with his brain as much as with his fists. He managed to avoid every punch his opponent threw at him.

He landed a right hook clear as a bell to the jaw that felt like he had broken a bone in his hand and that should have made his opponent collapse in a heap. He glanced at his knuckles and saw that they were bloody. He could see bruises and a swollen area on the giant's face. But his opponent seemed not even to feel the blows.

Paolo Roberto backed up, breathed as steadily as he could, and took stock. *He's no boxer. He moves like a boxer, but he can't box for shit. He's only pretending. He can't block. He telegraphs his punches. And he's as slow as a tortoise.*

In the next instant the giant got in a left hook to the side of Paolo Roberto's rib cage. That was the second time he had connected well. Paolo Roberto felt pain shoot through his body as a rib cracked. Again he backed away, but he tripped over a pile of scaffolding and fell on his back. He saw the giant towering over him, but he flung himself into a roll to the side and staggered to his feet.

He squared up, trying to gather his strength, but the man was on him again. He ducked, ducked again, and backed away, feeling terrible pain each time he parried a blow with his shoulder.

Then came the moment that every boxer has experienced

with dread. The feeling that could turn up any time in the middle of a bout. The feeling of just not being good enough. The realization that you are *about to lose.*

That's the crux of almost every fight, the moment when the strength drains out of you and the adrenaline pumps so hard that it becomes a burden and surrender appears like a ghost at ringside. That's the moment that separates the pros from the amateurs and the winner from the loser. Few boxers who find themselves at the edge of that abyss manage to turn the match around, turn certain defeat into victory.

Paolo Roberto was struck by this insight. He felt a roaring in his head that made him dizzy and he experienced the moment as if he were watching the scene from outside, peering at this giant through a camera lens. This was the moment when it was a matter of winning or disappearing for good.

He backed in a wide semicircle to collect his strength and buy time. The man followed him steadily but slowly, precisely as though he knew that the outcome was decided but he wanted to draw the round out. *He boxes, but he can't really box. He knows who I am. He's a rank amateur. But he has a devastating power in his punch and he seems insensitive to all punishment.*

These thoughts rattled around in Paolo Roberto's head as he tried to decide what to do.

Suddenly he was reliving the night in Mariehamn two years before when his career as a professional boxer had ended in the most brutal way. He had met the Argentine Sebastián Luján, or rather, Sebastián Luján met him. Paolo Roberto had walked into the first knockout of his life and had been unconscious for fifteen seconds.

He often thought about what had gone wrong. He was in tip-top shape. He was focused. But the Argentine had landed a solid punch and the round had been transformed into a raging sea.

Watching the video afterwards, he saw how he had staggered around the ring, as defenceless as Donald Duck. The knockout came twenty-three seconds later.

Sebastián Luján hadn't been any better, or better trained than he was. The margins of error being so small, the bout could have gone either way.

The only difference he could detect later was that Luján had been hungrier. When Paolo Roberto went into that ring in Mariehamn he was set on winning, but he wasn't dying to box. It did not mean life or death any more. A loss was not a catastrophe.

A year and a half later he was still a boxer. But he was no longer a pro, and he took on only friendly sparring matches. He went on training, and he had not put on weight or gone soft in the gut. He was not as well-tuned an instrument as before a title bout for which his body had been drilled for months, but he was Paolo Roberto and not some nobody. And unlike Mariehamn, the bout in the warehouse south of Nykvarn literally meant life or death.

He made a decision. He stopped short and let the giant come in close. He feinted with his left and put everything he had behind a right hook. He lashed out with a punch that hit the man across the mouth and nose. His attack was totally unexpected since he had been in retreat for the past few moments. He heard something give way. He followed up with a left-right-left and landed all three in the man's face.

The man was boxing in slow motion. He struck back with his right. Paolo Roberto saw the punch coming far in advance and ducked under the huge fist. He saw the giant shift his body weight and knew that he was going to follow up with a left. Instead of blocking, Paolo Roberto leaned back and let the left hook pass in front of his nose. He replied with a massive blow to the body, just below the ribs. When the man turned to meet the attack, Paolo Roberto's left hook came up and hit him across the nose again.

He suddenly felt that everything he was doing was utterly right and that he was in control of the bout. The giant backed away. His nose was bleeding. He was not smiling now.

Then the giant kicked him.

His foot shot up and took Paolo Roberto by surprise. He had not been expecting a kick. It felt as if a sledgehammer had hit his thigh just above the knee, and pain ran right through his leg. No. He took a step back and his right leg gave way. He was on his back.

The giant looked down at him. For a second their eyes met. The message was unmistakable. *The fight was over.*

Then the giant's eyes widened as Miriam Wu kicked him in the crotch from behind.

Every muscle in Miriam Wu's body was aching, but somehow she had managed to slip her bound hands underneath her and then—agonizingly—over her feet so that she got her arms in front of her body.

She had pain in her ribs, neck, back, and kidneys, and only with difficulty did she get to her feet. Finally she wobbled to the door and looked on wide-eyed as Paolo Roberto—*where did he come from?*—hit the giant with a right hook and then a combination to the face before he was kicked to the ground.

Miriam Wu realized that she could not care less how or why Paolo Roberto had shown up. He was one of the good guys. But for the first time in her life she felt a murderous desire to damage another human being. She took a few quick steps forward, mobilizing every bit of energy and all the muscles she had intact. She came up to the giant from behind and landed a kick in his balls. It may not have been elegant Thai boxing, but the kick had the desired effect.

Miriam Wu nodded to herself. Men could be as big as a house and made of granite, but they all had balls in the same place. For the first time the man looked shaken. He gave a moan, grabbed at his crotch, and went down on one knee.

Wu stood indecisive until she realized that she had to do more to try to end this. She was going to kick him in the face, but to her amazement he lifted an arm. It should have been impossible for him to recover so fast. And it had felt like kicking a tree trunk. He grabbed her foot, dragged her down, and began to haul her in. She saw him raise a fist and she twisted desperately, kicking with her free leg. She hit him above the ear at the same instant his blow struck her on the temple. She saw lightning and blackness alternating before her eyes.

The giant began to scramble to his feet.

That was when Paolo Roberto swung a plank into the back of his head. The man fell forward and landed with a crash.

Paolo Roberto looked around as if in a dream. The giant was writhing on the floor. The girl had a glassy look and seemed to be totally drained. Their combined efforts had bought them only a brief respite.

Paolo Roberto could barely support himself on his injured leg, and he was afraid that a muscle had torn just above his knee. He limped over to Miriam Wu and pulled her to her feet. She began to move again, but her eyes could not seem to focus. Without a word he slung her over his shoulder and started hobbling towards the door. The pain in his right knee was acute.

It was exhilarating to come out into the dark, cold air. But he had no time to pause. He navigated across the yard and into the curtain of woods, the same way he had come. He was no sooner in the trees than he tripped over a root and tumbled to the ground. Miriam Wu moaned and he heard the door of the warehouse slam open with a crash.

The giant was a monumental silhouette in the bright rectangle of the doorway. Paolo Roberto put a hand over the girl's mouth. He bent down and whispered in her ear to be utterly still and quiet.

Then he groped among the roots of a fallen tree and found

a stone that was bigger than his fist. He made the sign of the cross. For the first time in his sinful life he was ready to kill another human being, if it proved necessary. He was so shattered that he knew he would not be able to go another round. But nobody, not even a freak of nature, could go on fighting with a crushed skull. He squeezed the rock and felt that it was oval-shaped with a sharp edge.

The man went unsteadily to the corner of the building and then made a long sweep across the yard. He stopped less than ten paces from where Paolo Roberto was holding his breath. He listened and peered around—but he could only guess which way they had disappeared into the night. After a few minutes he seemed to realize that the search was futile. He went back into the building with quick determination and was gone for a minute or so. He turned off the lights and then came out with a bag and walked over to the Volvo. He drove off down the access road. Paolo Roberto listened until he could no longer hear the sound of the engine. When he looked down he saw a pair of eyes gleaming in the dark.

"Hi, Miriam," he said. "My name is Paolo—you don't have to be afraid of me."

"I know."

Her voice was weak. He slumped exhausted against the fallen tree and felt his adrenaline dropping to zero.

"I don't know how I'm going to get up," he said. "But I have a car on the other side of the main road."

The blond giant was shaken and dazed and had a strange feeling in his head. He braked and turned into a side road east of Nykvarn.

For the first time in his life he had been beaten in a fight. And the one who had dished out the punishment was Paolo Roberto . . . the boxer. It felt like an absurd dream, the kind he might have on a restless night. He could not understand where the boxer had come from. Out of the blue he was just there, standing inside the warehouse.

It made no sense.

He had not even felt the punches. That did not surprise him. But he *had* felt the kick in the balls. And that terrific thump on the head had made him black out. Gingerly he explored the back of his neck and touched an enormous lump. He pressed with his fingers but he sensed no pain. And yet he felt groggy. He had lost a tooth on the left side of his upper jaw. His mouth was full of the taste of blood. He held his nose between his thumb and forefinger and bent it experimentally upwards. He heard a snapping sound inside his head and could tell that his nose was broken.

He had done the right thing in taking his bag and leaving the warehouse before the police could get there. But he had made a colossal mistake. On the Discovery Channel he had seen how crime scene investigators could find any amount of forensic evidence. Blood. Hair. DNA.

He didn't have the slightest desire to return to the warehouse, but he had no choice. He had to clean up. He made a U-turn and started back. Just before Nykvarn he passed a car coming the other way, but he thought no more about it.

The trip back to Stockholm was a nightmare. Paolo Roberto had blood in his eyes and was so beaten up that his whole body hurt. He was driving like a drunk, weaving all over the road. He wiped his eyes with one hand and tentatively felt his nose. It really hurt, and he had to breathe through his mouth. He kept looking out for a white Volvo and thought he saw one pass going the other way near Nykvarn.

When he got on the E20 the driving was a little easier. He thought about stopping in Södertälje, but he had no idea where to go. He glanced back at the girl, still in handcuffs, lying on the backseat without a seat belt. He had had to carry her to the car, and as soon as she landed on the seat she went out like a light. He didn't know if she had fainted from her wounds or shut down out of sheer exhaustion.

He hesitated, then turned onto the E4 and headed for Stockholm.

Blomkvist had slept only an hour before the telephone started ringing. He squinted at the clock and saw that it was just past 4:00 a.m. He reached groggily for the receiver. It was Berger, and at first he could not understand what she was saying.

"Paolo Roberto is where?"

"At the hospital in Söder with the Wu girl. He tried to reach you, but you weren't answering."

"I turned my mobile off. What the hell is he doing in the hospital?"

Berger's voice sounded patient but determined.

"Mikael, get a taxi over there right away and find out. He sounded totally confused and was talking about a chain saw and some building out in the woods and a monster who couldn't box."

Blomkvist blinked himself awake. Then he shook his head and made for the shower.

Paolo Roberto looked miserable lying there in his shorts on the hospital bed. Blomkvist had waited an hour to be allowed to see him. His nose was hidden beneath a bandage. His left eye was covered too and one eyebrow had surgical tape over five stitches. He had a bandage wrapped round his chest, and cuts and bruises all over his body. His right knee was in a brace.

Blomkvist offered him a coffee from the machine in the hall and inspected his face critically.

"You look like a car crash," he said. "Tell me what happened."

Paolo Roberto shook his head and met Blomkvist's gaze. "A fucking monster happened," he said.

He shook his head again and inspected his fists. His knuckles were so swollen that he could scarcely hold the cup. His right hand and wrist were in a splint. His girlfriend already had a lukewarm attitude towards boxing—now she was going to be furious.

"I'm a boxer," he said. "I mean, when I was active I wasn't afraid to step into the ring with anybody. I've taken a punch or two, but I know how to dish them out too. When I punch somebody they're supposed to sit down and hurt."

"But this one didn't do that."

Paolo Roberto shook his head for the third time. Then he told Blomkvist what had happened during the night.

"I hit him at least thirty times. Fourteen or fifteen times to the head. I hit him on the jaw four times. At first I was holding back a bit—I didn't want to kill him, just protect myself. But in the end I gave it everything I had. One of my punches should have broken his jaw. But that fucking monster just shook his head a little and kept on coming. That is not a normal human being, I swear to God."

"What did he look like?"

"He was built like a tank. I'm not exaggerating. He was over six foot six and weighed at least 300 pounds. All muscle and armour plating. A fucking giant who doesn't know what pain is."

"You've never seen him before?"

"Never. He had no idea how to box. I could feint and throw him off his guard and he didn't have a clue how to move to avoid being hit. He was out of it. But at the same time he tried to move like a boxer. He held his arms up the right way and he kept recovering to a starting stance. Maybe he'd trained in boxing but hadn't heard a word of what the trainer said. What saved my life—and the girl's—was that he moved so slowly. He would throw roundhouse swings that he telegraphed a month in advance, and I could duck or parry them. He got in two good punches on me—one to the face, and you see what that did, then one to the body, where he cracked a rib. But neither of them was full power. If he'd landed them properly he would have knocked my head off."

Paolo Roberto laughed, a bubbling sort of laugh.

"What's funny?"

"I won. That moron tried to kill me and I won. I actually decked him. But I had to use a fucking plank to get him down for the count."

He turned serious again. "If Miriam Wu hadn't kicked him in the balls at just the right moment, I don't want to think about how the hell it would have ended."

"Paolo—I'm really, really glad you won. Miriam is going to say the same thing when she wakes up. Have you heard how she's doing?"

"She looks about the same as I do. She has a concussion, several cracked ribs, a broken nose, and damage to her kidneys."

Blomkvist bent forward and put his hand on Paolo Roberto's good knee. "If you ever need me to do anything . . ." he said.

Paolo Roberto smiled. "Blomkvist—if *you* ever need a favour again . . ."

"Yes?"

". . . ask Sebastián Luján to do it for you."

CHAPTER 26

Wednesday, April 6

Inspector Bublanski was in a dismal mood when he met Modig in the parking lot outside the hospital just before 7:00. Blomkvist had woken him up, and he in turn called Modig and woke her up. They met Blomkvist by the entrance and went with him to Paolo Roberto's room.

Bublanski could hardly grasp the bewildering details, but what was eventually clear was that Wu had been kidnapped and that the boxer had beaten up the kidnapper. Except that to judge by his face, it was far from obvious who had beaten up whom. As far as Bublanski was concerned, the night's events had lifted the investigation of Lisbeth Salander to a whole new level of complication. Nothing in this infernal case seemed to be normal.

How had Paolo Roberto even gotten involved in the affair?

"I'm a good friend of Lisbeth Salander's," he told them.

Bublanski and Modig looked at each other, surprised and sceptical.

"She sparred with me at the gym."

Bublanski fixed his gaze somewhere on the wall behind Paolo Roberto. Modig could not help laughing out loud. After a while they had written down all the details he could give them.

"I'd like to make a few points," Blomkvist said dryly.

They turned to him.

"First of all, Paolo's description of the man who drove away from the warehouse in the van matches the one I gave of the person who attacked Salander at the same spot on Lundagatan. A tall guy with a light brown ponytail and a beer belly. OK?"

Bublanski nodded.

"Second, the point of the kidnapping was to force Miriam Wu to reveal where Lisbeth Salander is hiding. So these two thugs have been looking for Salander since at least a week before the murders. Agreed?"

Modig murmured a "yes."

"Third, it looks less likely that Salander is the lone nutcase she has been portrayed as. And neither of these maniacs seems, on the face of it, to be a member of a lesbian Satanist gang."

Neither Bublanski nor Modig said a word.

"And finally, number four. I think this story has something to do with a man called Zala. Dag Svensson did a lot of work on him in his last two weeks. All the relevant information is in his computer. Dag linked him to the murder of a prostitute named Irina Petrova in Södertälje. The autopsy recorded that she was very severely beaten. So severely that any one of three of the worst blows would have been fatal on its own. Her injuries sound very like the ones that Miriam Wu and Paolo Roberto have been subjected to. In both cases the instruments of this extraordinary violence could be the hands of a gigantic thug."

"And Bjurman?" Bublanski said. "Let's suppose that some-one had a reason to silence Svensson. Who would have had a motive to murder Salander's guardian?"

"All the pieces of the puzzle aren't in place yet, but there's a connection between Bjurman and Zala. That's the only credible solution. Could you agree to start thinking along new lines? I think that these crimes have something to do with the sex trade. And Salander would sooner die than be involved in something like that. I told you she's a damned moralist."

"So what was her role? What was she doing at Svensson and Johansson's apartment?"

"I don't know. Witness? Opponent? Maybe she was there to warn Dag and Mia that their lives were in danger."

Bublanski set the wheels in motion. He called the Södertälje police and gave them Paolo Roberto's directions to a dilapidated warehouse southwest of Lake Yngern. Then he called Holmberg—he lived in Flemingsberg and was closest of the team to Södertälje—and asked him to join up with the Södertälje police as soon as he possibly could to assist with the crime scene investigation.

Holmberg called back an hour later. He had arrived at the crime scene. The Södertälje police had had no difficulty finding the warehouse. Along with two smaller storage sheds it had burned to the ground, and the fire department was there now, mopping up. There were two discarded gasoline cans in the yard.

Bublanski felt a sense of frustration approaching fury.

What the hell was going on? Who were these thugs? Who was this Salander person really? And why was it impossible to find her?

The situation did not improve when Ekström joined the fray at the 9:00 meeting. Bublanski told him about the morning's dramatic developments and proposed that the search be reprioritized in light of the mysterious events that had taken place, which cast doubt on the scenario that the team had been working on.

Paolo Roberto's story reinforced Blomkvist's account of the attack on Salander on Lundagatan. The hypothesis that all three murders were committed by one mentally ill woman no longer seemed valid. The suspicions regarding Salander could not altogether be discarded—they needed an explanation for her fingerprints being on the murder weapon—but it did mean that the investigation had to work on the possibility of a different killer. There was only one theory at present— Blomkvist's belief that the murders had to do with Svensson's imminent exposé of the sex trade. Bublanski identified three significant points.

The prime task was to find and identify the abnormally large man and his associate with the ponytail who had kidnapped and assaulted Miriam Wu. The giant should be relatively easy to find.

Andersson reminded them that Salander also had an unusual appearance, and that after three weeks of searching, the police still had no idea where she was.

The second task was to add to the investigative team a group that would actively focus on the list of prostitutes' clients in Svensson's computer. There was a logistical problem associated with this. The team had Svensson's computer from *Millennium* and the Zip disks that held the backup of his missing laptop, but they contained several years' worth of collected research and thousands of pages. It would take time to catalogue and study them. The team needed reinforcements, and Bublanski detailed Modig to head that unit.

The third task was to focus on a person who went by the name of Zala. The team would enlist the assistance of the National Criminal Investigation Department, since they apparently had come across the name. He assigned that task to Faste.

Finally, Andersson was to coordinate the continued search for Salander.

Bublanski's report took six minutes, but it touched off an hour-long dispute. Faste was vociferous in his resistance to Bublanski's proposals, and he made no attempt to conceal this. His opinion was that the investigation, regardless of the new— peripheral, he called it—information, had to stay focused on

Salander. The chain of evidence was so strong that it was unreasonable to divide the effort into different channels.

"This is all bullshit. We have a violence-prone nutcase who has grown worse and worse over the years. Do you actually believe that all the psychiatric reports and results from forensics are a joke? She's tied to the crime scene. We know she's a hooker, and there's a large sum of money unaccounted for in her bank account."

"I'm aware of all that."

"She's also a member of some sort of lesbian sex cult. And I'll be damned if that dyke Cilla Norén doesn't know more than she's letting on."

Bublanski raised his voice. "Faste. Stop it. You're totally obsessed with this gay angle. It's way past professional."

He at once regretted speaking out in front of the whole group. A private talk with Faste would have been more productive. Finally Ekström interrupted the raised voices to approve Bublanski's plan of action.

Bublanski glanced at Bohman and Hedström.

"As I understand it, we only have you for three more days, so let's make the best of the situation. Bohman, can you help Andersson track down Salander? Hedström, you'll stay with Modig."

Ekström raised his hand as they were about to break up.

"One last thing. We're keeping the part about Paolo Roberto under our hats. The media will go ballistic if one more celebrity springs to light in this investigation. So not a word about it outside this room."

After the meeting Modig took Bublanski aside.

"It was unprofessional of me to lose patience with Faste," Bublanski said.

"I know how it feels," she said with a smile. "I started on Svensson's computer last Monday."

"I know. How far did you get?"

"He had a dozen versions of the manuscript and a huge amount of research material, and I don't know yet what's important and what's safe to ignore. Just cataloguing it with meaningful names and looking through all the documents will take several days."

"What about Hedström?"

Modig hesitated. Then she turned and closed Bublanski's door.

"To tell you the truth . . . I don't want to trash him, but he isn't much help."

Bublanski frowned. "Out with it."

"I don't know, he's obviously not a real policeman like Bohman. He talks a lot of drivel. He has about the same attitude towards Miriam Wu as Faste does, and he's totally uninterested in the assignment. And—although I can't put my finger on it—he has some kind of problem with Salander."

"How so?"

"I've got a feeling there's some bad blood between them."

Bublanski nodded slowly. "That's a shame. Bohman's OK, but I don't really like having outsiders involved in this investigation."

"So what shall we do?"

"You'll have to put up with him for the rest of the week. Armansky said they'll break it off if they don't get results. Keep digging and count on having to do the whole job yourself."

Modig was interrupted after only forty-five minutes. She was called to Ekström's office. Bublanski was with him. Both men were red in the face. Tony Scala, the freelance journalist, had just released a scoop with the news that Paolo Roberto had rescued the S&M dyke Miriam Wu from an unknown kidnapper. The article contained several details that could only be known to someone inside the investigation. It was written in such a way as to suggest that the police were considering filing charges against Paolo Roberto for assault.

Ekström had already received several phone calls from other papers that wanted news about the boxer's role. He was livid. He accused Modig of having leaked the story. Modig vigorously objected to the accusation, but in vain. Ekström wanted her off the investigation.

"Sonja says she didn't leak anything," Bublanski said. "That's good enough for me. It's insane to remove an experienced detective who's familiar with every detail of the case."

Ekström refused to budge.

"Modig, I can't prove that you leaked the information, but I have no confidence in you with regard to this investigation. You are relieved from the team, effective immediately. Take the rest of the week off. You'll be given other assignments on Monday."

Modig nodded and headed for the door. Bublanski stopped her.

"Sonja. For the record: I don't believe one word of this, and you have my full confidence. But I'm not the one who decides. See me in my office before you go home, please."

Bublanski's face had taken on a dangerous hue. Ekström looked furious.

Modig went back to her office, where she and Hedström had been working on Svensson's computer. She was angry and close to tears. Hedström could tell that something was wrong, but he said nothing and she ignored him. She sat at her desk and stared into space. There was an oppressive silence in the room.

After a while Hedström excused himself and said he had to get a cup of coffee. He asked if he could bring her one. She shook her head.

When he had left she got up and put on her jacket. She took her shoulder bag and went to Bublanski's office. He pointed to the visitor's chair.

"Sonja, I don't intend to yield in this matter unless Ekström removes me from the investigation too. I won't accept it and I'm thinking of filing a complaint. Until you hear otherwise from me, you'll remain on the team. At my direction. Understand?"

She nodded.

"You will not take the rest of the week off as Ekström said. I want you to go to *Millennium*'s offices and have another talk with Blomkvist. Ask him for help in guiding you through Dag Svensson's hard drive. They have a copy there. We can save a lot of time if we have somebody who's already familiar with the material picking out the things that might be important."

Modig breathed more easily.

"I didn't say anything to Hedström."

"I'll take care of him. He can help Andersson. Have you seen Faste?"

"No. He left right after the meeting."

Bublanski sighed.

Blomkvist had arrived home from the hospital at 8:00 a.m. He had had too little sleep and he had to be at his best for an afternoon meeting with Björck in Smådalarö. He undressed, set the alarm for 10:30, and got two more hours of much-needed sleep. He shaved, showered, and put on a clean shirt. As he was driving past Gullmarsplan, Modig called his mobile. Blomkvist explained that he would not be able to meet her. She told him what she needed, and he referred her to Berger.

When she arrived at *Millennium*'s offices, Modig found that she liked the self-confident and slightly domineering woman with the dimples and shock of short blond hair. She vaguely wondered whether Berger was a dyke too, since all the women in this investigation, according to Faste, seemed to have that inclination. But then she remembered that she had read somewhere that Berger was married to the artist Greger Beckman.

"There's a problem here," Berger said, after listening to her request.

"What's that?"

"It's not that we don't want to solve the murders or help the police. Besides, you already have all the material in the computer you took from here. The dilemma is an ethical one. The media and the police don't work very well together."

"Believe me, I found that out this morning," Modig said with a smile.

"How so?"

"Nothing. Just a personal reflection."

"OK. To maintain their credibility, the media have to keep a clear distance from the authorities. Journalists who run to the police station and cooperate with police investigations will end up being errand boys for the police."

"I've met some of those," Modig said. "But the opposite can also be true. And the police end up running errands for certain newspapers."

Berger laughed. "That's right. I'm afraid to say that at *Millennium* we simply can't afford to be associated with that sort of mercenary journalism. This isn't about you wanting to question any of *Millennium*'s staff—which we would allow without hesitation—but about a formal request for us to assist actively in a police investigation by placing our journalistic material at your disposal."

Modig nodded.

"There are two points of view on that," Berger said. "First, one of our journalists has been murdered. So we will help out all we can. But the second point is that there are some things we cannot and will not give to the police. And that has to do with our sources."

"I can be flexible. I can pledge to protect your sources."

"It's not a matter of your intent or our trust in you. It is that we never reveal a source, no matter what the circumstances."

"Understood."

"Then there's the fact that at *Millennium* we're conducting our own investigation into the murders, which should be viewed as a journalistic assignment. In this case I'm prepared to hand over information to the police when we have something finished that we are ready to publish—but not before." Berger frowned as she paused to think. "I also have to be able to live with myself. Let's do this . . . You can work with Malin Eriksson. She's familiar with the material and competent to decide where the boundaries lie. She'll guide you through Dag's book—with the objective of compiling a list of all those who might be suspects."

As she caught the shuttle train from Södra station to Södertälje, Irene Nesser was unaware of the drama that had occurred the night before. She was wearing a midlength black leather jacket, dark pants, and a neat red sweater. She wore glasses that she had pushed up on her forehead.

In Södertälje she walked to the Strängnäs bus and bought a ticket to Stallarholmen. She got off the bus a little south of Stallarholmen just after 11:00 a.m. There were no buildings in sight. She visualized the map in her head. Lake Mälaren was a few miles to the northeast. It was summer-cabin country, with a scattering of year-round residences. Bjurman's property was about two miles from the bus stop. She took a swallow of water from her bottle and started walking. She got there about forty-five minutes later.

She began by making a tour of the area and studying the neighbouring houses. About a hundred and fifty yards to the right, she saw the next cabin. Nobody was at home. To the left was a ravine. She passed two summer houses before she reached a group of cabins where she noticed signs of life: an open window and the sound of a radio. But that was three hundred yards from Bjurman's cabin. She could work undisturbed.

She had taken the keys from his apartment. Once inside,

she first unscrewed a window shutter at the back of the house, giving her an escape route in case any unpleasantness should occur at the front. The unpleasantness she was prepared for was that some cop might get the idea to show up at the cabin.

Bjurman's was one of the older buildings, with one main room, one bedroom, and a small kitchen with running water. The toilet was a compost outhouse in the backyard. She spent twenty minutes looking through the closets, wardrobes, and dressers. She did not find so much as one scrap of paper that could have anything to do with Lisbeth Salander or Zala.

Then she went and searched the outhouse and woodshed. She found nothing of interest, and no paperwork at all. The journey had apparently been in vain.

She sat on the porch and drank some water and ate an apple.

When she went to close the shutter, she stopped short in the hallway as she caught sight of an aluminium stepladder three feet high. She went into the main room again and examined the clapboard ceiling. The opening to the attic was almost invisible between two roof beams. She got the stepladder, opened the trapdoor, and immediately found two A4 file boxes, each containing several folders and various other documents.

Things had gone all wrong. One disaster had followed another. The blond giant was worried.

Sandström had gotten hold of the Rantas. They said he sounded terrified and reported that the journalist Svensson had been planning an exposé about his whoring activities and about the Rantas. So far it hadn't been a big deal. If the media exposed Sandström it was none of his business, and the Ranta brothers could lie low for as long as they needed to. They had taken the *Baltic Star* to Estonia for a vacation. It was unlikely that the whole mess would lead to a court case, but if the worst should happen they had done time before. It was part of the job description.

More troublesome was that Salander had managed to elude Magge Lundin. This was incredible, since Salander was a rag doll compared to Lundin. All he had to do was stuff her in a car and take her to the warehouse south of Nykvarn.

Then Sandström had received another visit, and this time Svensson was after Zala. That put everything in a whole new light. Between Bjurman's panic and Svensson's continued snooping, a potentially dangerous situation had arisen.

An amateur is a gangster who is not prepared to take the consequences. Bjurman was a rank amateur. The giant had advised Zala not to have anything to do with Bjurman, but for Zala the name Lisbeth Salander had been irresistible. He loathed Salander. It was a reflex, like pressing a button.

It was pure chance that he had been at Bjurman's place the night Svensson called. The same fucking journalist who had already caused problems for Sandström and the Rantas. He had gone to Bjurman's to calm him down or to threaten him, as needed, after the abortive attempt to kidnap Salander. Svensson's call had triggered a wild panic in Bjurman, a reaction of unreasonable stupidity. All of a sudden he wanted out.

To top it off, Bjurman had fetched his cowboy pistol to threaten him. The giant had just looked at Bjurman in surprise and had taken the gun from him. He was already wearing gloves, so fingerprints weren't a problem. He had no choice. Bjurman had obviously flipped out.

Bjurman knew about Zala, of course. That was why he was a liability. The giant couldn't really explain why he made Bjurman take off his clothes, except that he hated the lawyer and wanted to make that clear to him. He had almost lost it when he saw the tattoo on Bjurman's abdomen: I AM A SADISTIC PIG, A PERVERT, AND A RAPIST.

For a moment he almost felt sorry for the man. He was such

a total idiot. But he was in a business where such feelings could not be allowed to interfere with what they had to do. So he had led Bjurman into the bedroom, forced him to his knees, and used a pillow as a silencer.

He had spent five minutes searching through Bjurman's apartment for the slightest connection to Zala. The only thing he found was his own mobile number. To be on the safe side he took Bjurman's mobile with him.

Svensson was the next problem. When Bjurman was found dead, Svensson would inevitably call the police and tell them about his call to the lawyer to ask about Zala. Zala would then become the object of police interest.

The blond giant considered himself smart, but he had an enormous respect for Zala's almost uncanny strategic gifts. They had been working together for nearly twelve years. It had been a successful decade, and he looked up to Zala with reverence. He could listen for hours as Zala explained human nature and its weaknesses and how one could profit from them.

But quite unexpectedly their business dealings were in trouble.

He had driven straight from Bjurman's to Enskede and parked the white Volvo two streets away. As luck would have it, the front door of the building was not locked. He went up and rang the doorbell with the nameplate SVENSSON-JOHANSSON.

He had fired two shots—there was a woman in the apartment too. He didn't search the apartment or take any of their papers with him. He did take a computer that was on the table in the living room. He turned on his heel, went down the stairs, and out to his car. His only mistake had been dropping the revolver on the stairs while he was trying to balance the laptop and at the same time fish out his car keys. He stopped for a second, but the gun had skittered down the stairs to the basement, and he decided it would take too much time to go down and get it. He knew he was someone people would not forget having seen, so the important thing was to get out of there before anyone laid eyes on him.

The dropped revolver had been at first a source of criticism until Zala realized its implications. They were astonished when the police began a search for Salander. His mistake had turned into an incredible stroke of luck.

It also created a new problem. Salander became the only remaining weak link. She had known Bjurman and she knew Zala. She could put two and two together. When he and Zala conferred about the matter they were in agreement. They had to find Salander and bury her somewhere. It would be ideal if she were never found. Then the murder investigation would eventually be shelved.

They had taken a chance that Miriam Wu could lead them to Salander. And then everything had gone wrong again. *Paolo Roberto.* Of all people. Out of nowhere. And according to the newspapers he was also friends with Salander.

The giant was dumbfounded.

After Nykvarn he had gone to Lundin's house in Svavelsjö, only a hundred yards from Svavelsjö MC's headquarters. Not an ideal hiding place, but he didn't have many options. He had to find somewhere to lie low until the bruises on his face began to fade and he could make himself scarce. He fingered his broken nose and felt the lump on his neck. The swelling had begun to subside.

It had been a good move to go back and burn down the whole fucking place.

Then, suddenly, he went ice cold.

Bjurman. He had met Bjurman once at his summer cabin. In early February—when Zala had accepted the job of taking care of Salander. Bjurman had had a file about Salander that he had leafed through. How could he have forgotten that? It could lead to Zala.

He went down to the kitchen and told Lundin to get himself to Stallarholmen as fast as he could and start another fire.

. . .

Bublanski spent his lunch break trying to put in order the investigation he knew was about to collapse. He spent time with Andersson and Bohman, who brought him up to date on the hunt for Salander. Tips had come in from Göteborg and Norrköping. Göteborg they ruled out right away, but the Norrköping sighting had potential. They informed their colleagues, and a cautious stakeout was put on an address where a girl who looked a little like Salander had been seen.

He tried to find Faste, but he was not in the building and did not answer his mobile. After the stormy meeting, Faste had vanished.

Bublanski then went to see Ekström to try to defuse the problem with Modig. He set out all his reasons for thinking the decision to take her off the case was foolhardy. Ekström would not listen, and Bublanski decided to file a complaint after the weekend. It was an idiotic situation.

Just after 3:00 he stepped into the corridor and saw Hedström coming out of Modig's office, where he was still supposed to be combing through Svensson's hard drive. Bublanski thought it was now a meaningless exercise, since no real detective was looking over his shoulder to check what he might have missed. He decided that Hedström should be with Andersson for the rest of the week.

Before he had a chance to say anything, Hedström disappeared into the toilet at the far end of the corridor. Bublanski went over to Modig's empty office to wait for him to return.

Then his eye fell on Hedström's mobile, which lay forgotten on the shelf behind his desk.

Bublanski glanced at the door to the toilet, still closed. On pure impulse he stepped into the office, stuffed Hedström's mobile into his pocket, walked rapidly back to his own office, and closed the door. He clicked up the list of calls.

At 9:57, five minutes after the morning meeting was over,

Hedström had called a number with an 070 area code. Bublan-ski lifted the receiver of his desk telephone and dialled the number. Tony Scala answered.

He hung up and stared at Hedström's mobile. Then he got up with an expression like a thundercloud. He had taken two steps towards the door when his telephone rang. He went back to pick it up and shouted his name into the receiver.

"It's Jerker. I'm back at the warehouse outside Nykvarn."

"What did you find?"

"The fire is out. We've been busy the last two hours. The Södertälje police brought a corpse-sniffing dog to check the area in case there was someone in the wreckage."

"Was there?"

"There was not. But we took a break so the dog could rest his nose for a while. The handler says it's necessary since the smells at an arson site are really strong."

"Get to the point, Jerker. I'm a bit pressed here."

"Well, he took a walk and let the dog loose away from the site of the fire. The dog signalled a spot about seventy-five yards into the woods behind the warehouse. We started dig-ging. Ten minutes ago we found a human leg with a shoe. It seems to be a man's shoe. It was buried fairly shallow."

"Oh shit. Jerker, you've got to—"

"I've already taken command of the site and put a stop to the digging. I want to get forensics out here and proper techs before we proceed."

"Very well done."

"But that's not all. Five minutes ago the dog marked another spot some eighty yards from the first."

Salander had made coffee on Bjurman's stove and eaten another apple. She spent two hours reading through Bjurman's notes on her, page by page. She was actually impressed. He had put quite a lot of effort into the task and systematized the information. He had found material about her that she didn't even know existed.

She read Palmgren's journal with mixed feelings. It took up two black notebooks. He had started keeping a diary about her when she was fifteen. She had just run away from her third set of foster parents, an elderly couple in Sigtuna; he was a sociologist and she was an author of children's books. Salander had stayed with them for twelve days and could tell that they were tremendously proud of making a social contribution by taking her in, and that they expected her constantly to express gratitude. She had finally had enough when her foster mother, boasting to a neighbour, started expounding about how important it was that someone took care of young people who had obvious problems. *I'm not a fucking social project*, she wanted to scream. On the twelfth day she stole 100 kronor from their food money and took the bus to Upplands-Väsby and the shuttle train to Stockholm Central. The police found her six weeks later in the house of a sixty-seven-year-old man in Haninge.

He had been an OK guy. He provided her with food and a place to live. She did not have to do much in return. He wanted to look at her when she was naked. He never touched her. She knew he would be considered a pedophile, but she had never felt the least threat from him. She thought him an introverted and socially handicapped person. She even came to experience a feeling of kinship when she thought about him. They were both outsiders.

Someone had finally spotted her and called the police. A social worker did her best to persuade her to report the man for sexual assault. She had obstinately refused to say that anything untoward had occurred, and in any case she was fifteen and legal. Fuck you. Then Palmgren had intervened and signed for her. He started a diary in what appeared to be a frustrated attempt to allay and resolve his own doubts. The first entries were written in December 1993:

L. increasingly appears to be the most unmanageable young person I've ever had to deal with. The question is whether I'm doing the right thing when I oppose her return to St. Stefan's. She has now run away from three foster families in three months and obviously risks coming to some harm during her excursions. I have to decide soon whether I should give up the assignment and request that she be put under the care of real experts. I don't know what's right and what's wrong. Today I had a serious talk with her.

Salander remembered every word of that serious talk. It was the day before Christmas Eve. Palmgren had taken her to his place and installed her in his spare room. He made spaghetti with meat sauce for supper and then put her on the living-room sofa and sat in an armchair across from her. She remembered wondering if Palmgren too wanted to see her naked. Instead he spoke to her as if she were a grown-up.

In fact it had been a two-hour monologue. She had hardly uttered a word. He had spelled out the realities, which were in effect that now she had to decide between going back to St. Stefan's and living with a foster family. He would do what he could to find a family acceptable to her, and he insisted that she go with his choice. He had decided that she should spend the Christmas holidays with him so she would have time to think about her future. It was up to her, but on the day after Christmas he wanted a clear answer and a promise from her that if she had problems she would turn to him instead of running away. Then he had sent her to bed and apparently sat down to write the first lines in his diary.

The threat of being transported back to St. Stefan's frightened her more than Holger Palmgren could know. She spent an unhappy Christmas suspiciously watching every move he made. The next day he still had not attempted to paw her, nor did he show any sign of wanting to sneak a look at her in the bath. On the contrary, he got really angry when she tried to provoke him by marching naked from his spare room to the bathroom. He had slammed the bathroom door hard. Later she had made him the promises he demanded. She had kept her word. Well, more or less.

In his journal Palmgren commented methodically on every meeting he had with her. Sometimes it was three lines, sometimes he filled several pages with his thoughts. Every so often she was surprised. Palmgren had been more insightful than she had imagined, and occasionally commented on incidents when she had tried to fool him but he had seen through her.

Then she opened the police report from 1991.

And the pieces of the puzzle fell into place. She felt as if the ground had started to shake.

She read the medical report written by a Dr. Jesper H. Löderman, in which Dr. Peter Teleborian figured prominently. Löderman had been the prosecutor's trump card when he tried to get her institutionalized at the hearing when she was eighteen.

Then she found an envelope containing correspondence between Teleborian and some policeman called Gunnar Björck. The letters were all dated 1991, just after "All The Evil" happened.

Nothing was said straight out in the correspondence, but suddenly a trapdoor opened beneath Salander. It took her several minutes to grasp the implications. Björck referred to some conversation they must have had. His wording was irreproachable, but between the lines he was saying that it would be all right with him if Salander were locked up in an asylum for the rest of her life.

> It is important for the child to get some distance from the context. I cannot evaluate her psychological condition or what sort of care she needs, but the longer she can be kept institutionalized, the less risk there is

that she would unintentionally create problems regarding the current matter.

Regarding the current matter. Salander rolled the phrase around in her mind for a while.

Teleborian was responsible for her care at St. Stefan's. It had been no accident. The tone of the correspondence led her to understand that these letters were never intended to see the light of day.

Teleborian had known Björck.

Salander bit her lower lip as she pondered. She had never done any research on Teleborian, but he had started out in forensic medicine, and even the Security Police occasionally needed to consult a forensic medical expert or psychiatrist for their investigations. If she started digging, she would surely find a connection. At some point during his career, Teleborian and Björck's paths had crossed. When Björck needed someone who could bury Salander, he had turned to Teleborian.

That was how it had happened. What previously looked like chance now took on a whole new dimension.

She sat still for a long time staring into space. Nobody was innocent. There were only varying degrees of responsibility. And somebody was responsible for Salander. She would definitely have to pay a visit to Smådalarö. She assumed that no-one in the shipwreck that was the state justice system would have any desire to discuss the subject with her, and in the absence of anyone else, a talk with Gunnar Björck would have to do.

She looked forward to that talk.

She did not need to take all the folders with her. As she read them they became forever imprinted on her photographic memory. She took along Palmgren's notebooks, Björck's police report from 1991, the medical report from 1996 when she was declared incompetent, and the correspondence between Teleborian and Björck. That was enough to fill her backpack.

She closed the door, but before she had time to lock it she heard the sound of motorcycles behind her. She looked around. It was too late to try to hide, and she didn't have the slightest chance of outrunning two bikers on Harley-Davidsons. She stepped down warily from the porch and met them in the driveway.

Bublanski marched furiously down the corridor and saw that Hedström had not yet returned to Modig's office. But the toilet was vacant. He continued down the corridor and found him holding a plastic cup from the coffee vending machine, talking to Andersson and Bohman.

Bublanski turned unseen at the doorway and walked up one flight to Ekström's office. He shoved the door open without knocking, interrupting Ekström in the middle of a phone conversation.

"Come with me," he said.

"I beg your pardon?" Ekström said.

"Put the telephone down and come with me."

Bublanski's expression was such that Ekström did as he was told. In this situation it was easy to understand why Bublanski had been given the nickname Officer Bubble. His face looked like a bright red antiaircraft balloon. They went downstairs. Bublanski marched up to Hedström, took a firm grip on his hair, and turned him to Ekström.

"Hey, what the hell are you doing? Are you crazy?"

"Bublanski!" Ekström shouted, startled.

Hedström looked nervous. Bohman's mouth dropped open.

"Is this yours?" Bublanski asked, holding out the Sony Ericsson mobile.

"Let me go!"

"IS THIS YOUR MOBILE?"

"Yeah, damn it. Let me go."

"Not yet. You're under arrest."

"I'm *what?*"

"You're under arrest for breach of secrecy and for interfering with a police investigation. Or else give us a reasonable explanation for why, according to your list of calls, you called a journalist who answers to the name of Tony Scala at 9:57 this morning, right after the meeting and just before Scala went public with the very information we had decided to keep secret."

After getting instructions to go to Stallarholmen and set a fire, Lundin had wandered over to the clubhouse in the abandoned printing factory on the outskirts of Svavelsjö and taken Nieminen with him. It was perfect weather to roll out the hogs for the first time since winter. He had been given detailed directions and had studied a map. They put on their leathers and covered the distance from Svavelsjö to Stallarholmen in no time.

Lundin did not believe his eyes when he saw Lisbeth Salander in the driveway in front of Bjurman's summer cabin. It was a bonus that would blow the giant's fucking mind. He was sure it was her, although she looked different. Was that a wig? She was just standing there, waiting for them.

They rode up and parked six feet away on each side of her. When they switched off their motors it was utterly silent in the woods. Lundin didn't quite know what to say. At last he managed to speak.

"Well, how about that? We've been looking for you for a while, Salander. Sonny, meet Fröken Salander."

He smiled. Salander regarded Lundin with expressionless eyes. She noticed that he still had a bright red, newly healed welt on his cheek and jaw where she had cut him with her keys. She raised her eyes and looked at the treetops behind him. Then she lowered them again. Her eyes were disconcertingly coal black.

"I've had a fucking miserable week and I'm in a fucking bad mood," she said. "You know what the worst thing is? Every time I turn around there's some fucking pile of shit with a beer belly in my way acting tough. Now I'd like to leave. So move your ass."

Lundin's mouth was hanging open. He thought he had heard wrong. Then he started laughing involuntarily. The situation was ridiculous. There stood a skinny girl who could fit into his breast pocket getting cheeky with two fully grown men with leather vests that showed they belonged to Svavelsjö MC, which meant they were the most dangerous of bikers and would soon be members of Hell's Angels. They could tear her apart and stuff her in their saddlebags.

Even if the girl was as nutty as a fruitcake—which she obviously was, according to the newspapers and what he had just seen of her here—their emblem still ought to command respect. And she didn't show the smallest sign of that. This sort of behaviour could not be tolerated, no matter how ridiculous the situation. He glanced at Nieminen.

"I think the dyke needs some cock, Sonny," he said, climbing off the Harley and setting his kickstand. He took two slow steps towards Salander and looked down at her. She did not shift an inch. Lundin shook his head and sighed. Then he lashed out a backhand with the same considerable power with which he had struck Blomkvist on Lundagatan.

He met nothing but thin air. At the instant his hand should have hit her face, she took one step back and stood there just out of his reach.

Nieminen was leaning on the handlebars of his Harley and watching his fellow club member with amusement. Lundin was red in the face and took another couple of swings at her. She backed up again. Lundin swung faster.

Salander stopped abruptly and emptied half the contents of a Mace canister in his face. His eyes burned like fire. The toe of her boot shot up with full force and was transformed into kinetic energy in his crotch with a pressure of about 1,700 pounds per square inch. Lundin dropped gasping to his knees and stayed there at a more comfortable height for Salander. She kicked him in the face, deliberately, as if she were taking a penalty in soccer. There was an ugly crunching sound before Lundin toppled over like a sack of potatoes.

It took a few seconds for Nieminen to realize that something unbelievable had happened before his eyes. He tried to set the kickstand of his Harley, missed, and had to look down. Then he decided to play it safe and started groping for the pistol he had in his vest's inside pocket. As he was pulling down the zipper he caught a movement out of the corner of his eye.

When he looked up he saw Salander coming at him like a cannonball. She jumped with both feet and kicked him full force in the hip, which didn't injure him but was hard enough to knock over both him and his motorcycle. He narrowly missed having his leg pinned under the bike and stumbled a few paces backwards before he regained his balance.

When he had her in view again he saw her arm move, and a stone as big as his fist flew through the air. He ducked and it missed his head by about an inch.

He finally got out his pistol and tried to flick off the safety, but when he looked up again Salander was upon him. He saw evil in her eyes and felt for the first time a shocked terror.

"Goodnight," Salander said.

She shoved the Taser into his crotch and fired off 50,000 volts, holding the electrodes against him for at least twenty seconds. Nieminen was transformed into a vegetable.

Salander heard a noise behind her and spun around to see Lundin laboriously getting to his knees. She looked at him with raised eyebrows. He was fumbling blindly through the burning fog of the Mace.

"I'm going to kill you!" he roared.

He was groping around, trying to locate Salander. She watched him circumspectly. Then he said:

"Fucking whore."

Salander bent down and picked up Nieminen's pistol, noticing that it was a Polish P-83 Wanad.

She opened the magazine and checked that it was loaded with the correct 9 mm Makarov. She cocked it. She stepped over Nieminen and went across to Lundin, took aim with both hands, and shot him in the foot. He shrieked in shock and collapsed again.

She wondered if she should bother asking about the identity of the hulk she had seen him with at Blomberg's Café. According to Sandström, the man had murdered someone in a warehouse with Lundin's help. Hmm. She should have waited to fire the pistol until she had asked her questions.

Lundin did not seem to be in any condition now to carry on a lucid conversation, and there was the possibility that someone had heard the shot. So she ought to leave the area right away. She could always find Lundin at some later date and ask him the question under less stressful circumstances. She secured the weapon's safety, zipped it into her jacket pocket, and picked up her backpack.

She had gone about ten yards down the road when she stopped and turned around. She walked back slowly and studied Lundin's motorcycle.

"Harley-Davidson," she said. "Sweet."

CHAPTER 27

Wednesday, April 6

It was a beautiful spring day as Blomkvist drove Berger's car south towards Nynäsvägen. Already there was a hint of green in the black fields, and there was real warmth in the air. It was perfect weather to forget all his problems and drive out for a few days to be at peace in his cabin in Sandhamn.

He had agreed with Björck that he would be there at 1:00, but he arrived early and stopped in Dalarö to have coffee and read the papers. He did not prepare for the meeting. Björck had something to tell him, and Blomkvist was determined that this time he would come away from Smådalarö with concrete information about Zala.

Björck met him in the driveway. He looked more self-assured, more pleased with himself than he had two days before. *What sort of move are you planning?* Blomkvist did not shake hands with him.

"I can give you information about Zala," Björck said, "but I have certain conditions."

"Let's hear them."

"I won't be named in *Millennium*'s exposé."

"Agreed."

Björck looked surprised. Blomkvist had accepted straight off, without argument, the point about which Björck was expecting to have a long negotiation. That was his only card. Information about the murders in exchange for anonymity. Blomkvist had agreed, and given up the chance of a strong headline in the magazine.

"I'm serious," Björck said. "And I want it in writing."

"You can have it in writing, but a document like that wouldn't be of any use to you. You've committed a crime that I know about and which I'm bound to report to the police. But you know things, and you're using your position to buy my silence. I've thought about the matter and I accept. I won't mention your name in *Millennium*. Either you take my word for it or you don't."

While Björck thought about it, Blomkvist said: "I have some conditions too. The price of my silence is that you tell me everything you know. If I discover that you're hiding something, our agreement is void, and I'll hang your name out to dry on every single news headline in Sweden, just as I did with Wennerström."

Björck shuddered at the memory.

"OK," he said. "I don't have a choice. I'll tell you who Zala is. But I'm going to need absolute confidentiality."

He reached out his hand. Blomkvist grasped it. He had just promised to assist in covering up a crime, but it didn't trouble him for a moment. All he had promised was that he himself and *Millennium* magazine would not write about Björck. Svensson had already written the whole story in his book. And the book would be published.

The call came through to the police in Strängnäs at 3:18 p.m. It came directly to the switchboard and not through the emergency services. A man named Öberg, owner of a summer cabin just east of Stallarholmen, reported that he had heard what sounded like a shot and went to see what was going on. He had found two severely wounded men. Well, one of the men may not have been so severely wounded, but he was in a lot of pain. And the cabin they were lying in front of was owned by Nils Bjurman, a lawyer. The late Nils Bjurman, that is—the man there was so much about in the papers.

The Strängnäs police had already had an eventful day with an extensive traffic check in the community. During the course of the morning the traffic assignment had been interrupted when a call came in that a middle-aged woman had been killed by her boyfriend at the house they shared in Finninge. At almost the same time a fire had spread from an outhouse into a property in Storgärdet. One body was found in the wreckage. And to top it all off, two cars had collided head-on on the Enköping highway. Accordingly, the Strängnäs police force was busy, almost to a man.

The duty officer, however, had been following the developments in Nykvarn that morning, and she deduced that this new commotion must have something to do with that Lisbeth Salander everyone was talking about. Not least since Nils Bjurman was a part of the investigation. She took action on three fronts. She requisitioned the only remaining police van and drove directly to Stallarholmen. She called her colleagues in Södertälje and asked for assistance. The Södertälje force was also spread thin since part of their manpower had been sent to dig up bodies around a burned-out warehouse south of Nykvarn, but the possible connection between Nykvarn and Stallarholmen prompted another duty officer in Södertälje to dispatch two cruisers to Stallarholmen to assist. In the end the duty officer from Strängnäs called Inspector Bublanski in Stockholm. She reached him on his mobile.

Bublanski was at Milton Security in a meeting with its CEO, Armansky, and two of his staff, Fräklund and Bohman. Hedström was conspicuous by his absence.

Bublanski immediately sent Andersson out to Bjurman's

summer cabin and told him to take Faste if he could get hold of him. After thinking for a moment, Bublanski also called Holmberg, who was near Nykvarn and therefore considerably closer to Stallarholmen.

Holmberg had some news for him too. "We've identified the body in the pit."

"That's impossible. How so fast?"

"Everything's simple when the corpse considerately has himself buried with his wallet and laminated ID."

"Who is it?"

"A bit of a celebrity. Kenneth Gustafsson, known as the Vagabond. Does it ring a bell?"

"Are you kidding? Downtown hooligan, pusher, petty thief, and addict? He's lying in a hole in Nykvarn?"

"Yes, that's the man. At least that's the ID in the wallet. Identification will have to be confirmed by forensics, and it's going to be like putting a puzzle together. The Vagabond was chopped into five or six pieces."

"Interesting. Paolo Roberto said that the super heavyweight he was fighting threatened Miriam Wu with a chain saw."

"Could very well have been a chain saw, but I haven't looked that closely. We've just started digging up the second site. They're busy setting up the tent."

"That's good. Jerker—it's been a long day, I know, but can you stay on this evening?"

"Sure, OK. I'll let them get on with it here and head on to Stallarholmen."

Bublanski disconnected and rubbed his eyes.

The armed response team hastily assembled from Strängnäs arrived at Bjurman's summer cabin at 3:44 p.m. On the access road they literally collided with a man on a Harley-Davidson, who was wobbling along until he steered right into the oncoming van. It was not a serious collision. The police climbed out and identified Sonny Nieminen, thirty-seven years old and a known killer from the mid-nineties. Nieminen seemed to be in bad shape. When they put the cuffs on him, they were surprised to find that the back of his vest was slashed. A piece of leather about eight inches square was missing. It looked peculiar. Nieminen was unwilling to discuss the matter.

They locked him in the van and drove on two hundred yards to the cabin. They found a retired harbour worker by the name of Öberg putting a splint on the foot of one Carl-Magnus Lundin, thirty-six years old and president of the gang that called itself Svavelsjö MC.

The leader of the police team was Inspector Nils-Henrik Johansson. He climbed out, straightened his shoulder belt, and looked at the sorry creature on the ground.

Öberg stopped bandaging Lundin's foot and gave Johansson a wry look.

"I'm the one who called."

"You reported shots being fired."

"I reported that I heard a single shot and came over to investigate and found these guys. This one has been shot in the foot and beaten up pretty badly. I think he needs an ambulance."

Öberg glanced towards the police van.

"I see you got the other guy. He was out cold when I arrived, but he didn't seem to be wounded. He came to after a while, but he didn't stick around to help his buddy."

Holmberg arrived at the same time as the police from Södertälje, just as the ambulance was driving away. He was given a brief rundown of the team's observations. Neither Lundin nor Nieminen had been willing to explain how he came to be there. Lundin was hardly in any condition to talk at all.

"So—two bikers in leathers, one Harley-Davidson, one gunshot victim, and no weapon. Have I got it right?" Holmberg said.

Johansson nodded.

"Should we discount that one of these macho heroes rode bitch?"

"I think that would be considered unmanly in their circles," Johansson said.

"In that case, we're missing one motorcycle. Since the weapon is missing too, we may conclude that a third party has left the scene with one motorcycle and one weapon."

"Sounds reasonable."

"And it creates a conundrum. If these two gentlemen from Svavelsjö came on motorcycles, we're also missing the vehicle in which the third party arrived. The third party couldn't have taken both his own vehicle and the bike. And it's a pretty long walk from the Strängnäs highway."

"Unless the third party was living in the cabin."

"Hmm," Holmberg said. "But the cabin is owned by the deceased Advokat Bjurman, and he definitely no longer lives here."

"Maybe there was a fourth party who left in a car."

"Then why wouldn't the two have gone in the car together? I'm assuming that this story isn't about the theft of a Harley, no matter how desirable they are."

He thought for a moment and then asked the team to assign two uniforms to look for an abandoned vehicle on the forest roads nearby and to knock on doors in the area to ask if anyone had seen anything unusual.

"There aren't that many cabins inhabited at this time of year," the team leader said, but he promised to do his best.

Holmberg opened the unlocked door to the cabin. He straightaway found the box of files on the kitchen table with Bjurman's reports about Salander. He sat down and began paging through them, his astonishment growing.

Holmberg's team was in luck. Just half an hour after they began knocking on doors among the intermittently populated cabins, they found Anna Viktoria Hansson. She had spent the spring morning clearing up a garden near the access road to the summer-cabin area. Yes indeed, she might be seventy-two, but she had good eyesight. Yes indeed, she had seen a short girl in a dark jacket walk past around lunchtime. At three in the afternoon two men on motorcycles had driven by. They made an appalling racket. And shortly after that, the girl had gone back the other way on one of the motorcycles, or maybe on a different one altogether. Well, it looked like the girl, but in the helmet she could not be 100 percent certain. And then the police cars started arriving.

Just as Holmberg was getting this statement, Andersson arrived at the cabin.

"What's happening here?" he said.

Holmberg looked glumly at his colleague. "I don't quite know how to explain this to you," he said.

"Jerker, are you trying to tell me that Salander turned up at Bjurman's cabin and all by herself beat the shit out of the top echelon of the Svavelsjö MC?" Bublanski sounded tense.

"Well, she was trained by Paolo Roberto."

"Jerker, please. Give me a break."

"OK, listen to this. Magnus Lundin has a bullet wound in his foot. Which is going to do him permanent damage. The bullet went out the back of his heel, blew his boot to kingdom come."

"At least she didn't shoot him in the head."

"Apparently that wasn't necessary. According to the local team, Lundin has serious injuries to his face: a broken jaw and two teeth knocked out. The medics suspected a concussion. Besides the gunshot wound to his foot, he also has a massive pain in his abdomen."

"How's Nieminen doing?"

"He seems unhurt. But according to the old man who called

in, he was unconscious when he arrived. Nieminen came to after a while and was trying to leave just as the Strängnäs team got there."

Bublanski was speechless.

"There's one mysterious detail," Holmberg said.

"Another one?"

"Nieminen's leather vest . . . He came here on his bike."

"Yes?"

"It was ripped."

"What do you mean, ripped?"

"There's a chunk missing. About eight by eight inches cut out of the back of it. Just where Svavelsjö MC has its insignia."

Bublanski raised his eyebrows. "Why would Salander cut a square out of his vest? For a trophy? For revenge? But revenge for what?"

"No idea. But I thought of one other thing," Holmberg said. "Magnus Lundin is a hefty guy with a ponytail. One of the guys who kidnapped Salander's girlfriend had a beer belly and a ponytail."

Salander had not had such a rush since she visited Gröna Lund amusement park several years before and rode on the Freefall. She went on it three times and could have gone another three if she had had the money.

It was one thing to ride a 125cc lightweight Kawasaki, which was really no more than a heavily souped-up moped, but it was something else entirely to maintain control of a 1450cc Harley-Davidson. Her first three hundred yards on Bjurman's badly maintained forest track was a regular roller coaster, and she felt like a living gyro. Twice she almost rode into the woods before at the last second she managed to regain control of the hog.

The helmet kept slipping down and masking her vision, even though she had put in some extra stuffing using a piece of leather she'd cut out of Nieminen's padded vest.

She did not dare stop to adjust the helmet for fear she would not be able to manage the bike's weight. She was too short to reach the ground with both feet and was afraid the Harley would tip over. If that happened, she would never be able to get it upright again.

Things went more smoothly once she got on the wider gravel road leading to the summer-cabin area. When she turned onto the Strängnäs highway a few minutes later, she risked taking one hand off the handlebars to set the helmet right. Then she gave the bike some gas. She covered the distance to Södertälje in record time, smiling in delight the whole way. Just before she reached Södertälje, two blue-and-yellow police Volvos with their sirens on flew by in the other direction.

The sensible course would be to dump the Harley in Södertälje and let Irene Nesser take the shuttle train into Stockholm, but Salander couldn't resist the temptation. She turned onto the E4 and accelerated. She did not go over the speed limit—well, not much anyway—but it still felt as though she were in freefall. Not until she reached Älvsjö did she turn off and find her way to the fairground, where she managed to park the beast without tipping it over. She was very sad to leave the bike behind, along with the helmet and the piece of leather from Nieminen's vest. She walked to the shuttle train. She was seriously chilled. She rode the one stop to Södra station, then walked home to Mosebacke and ran herself a hot bath.

"His name is Alexander Zalachenko," Björck said. "But officially he doesn't exist. You won't find him on the national register."

Zala. Alexander Zalachenko. Finally a name.

"Who is he and how can I find him?"

"He's not someone you'd want to find."

"Tell me anyway."

"What I'm going to tell you is top secret information. If it came out that I told you this, I'd be sent to prison. It's one of the most deeply buried secrets we have within the Swedish defence system. You have to understand why it's so important that you guarantee my anonymity."

"I've already done that," Blomkvist said impatiently.

"Alexander Zalachenko was born in 1940 in Stalingrad. When he was a year old, the German offensive on the eastern front began. Both of Zalachenko's parents died in the war. At least that's what Zalachenko thinks. He doesn't really know what happened during the war. His earliest memories are of an orphanage in the Ural Mountains."

Blomkvist made swift notes.

"The orphanage was in a garrison town and was, as it were, sponsored by the Red Army. You might say that Zalachenko got a military education very early. Since the end of the Soviet Union, documents have emerged which show there were experiments to create a cadre of particularly athletic, elite soldiers among the orphans who were being raised by the state. Zalachenko was one of them. To make a long story short, when he was five he was put in an army school. It turned out that he was talented. When he was fifteen, in 1955, he was sent to a military school in Novosibirsk, where together with two thousand other pupils he underwent training similar to Spetsnaz, the Russian elite troops."

"OK, let's get to the adult stuff."

"In 1958, when he was eighteen, he was moved to Minsk, to specialist training with the GRU—*Glavnoye razvedyvatelnoye upravlenie,* the military intelligence service that is directly subordinate to the army high command, not to be confused with the KGB, the civil secret police. The GRU usually took care of espionage and foreign operations. When he was twenty, Zalachenko was sent to Cuba. It was a training period and he was still only the equivalent of a second lieutenant. But he was there for two years, during the Cuban missile crisis and the invasion at the Bay of Pigs. In 1963 he went back to Minsk for further training. Thereafter he was stationed first in Bulgaria and then in Hungary. In 1965 he was promoted to lieutenant and got his first posting to Western Europe, in Rome, where he served for a year. That was his first undercover assignment. He was a civilian with a fake passport, obviously, and with no contact with the embassy."

Blomkvist nodded as he wrote. Against his will he was starting to get interested.

"In 1967 he was moved to London. There he organized the execution of a defected KGB agent. Over the next ten years he became one of the GRU's top agents. He belonged to the real elite of devoted political soldiers. He speaks six languages fluently. He's worked as a journalist, a photographer, in advertising, as a sailor—you name it. He's a survival artist, an expert in disguise and deception. He commanded his own agents and organized or carried out his own operations. Several of these operations were contracts for hits, and a large number of them took place in the third world, but he was also involved in extortion, intimidation, and all kinds of other assignments that his superiors needed him to perform. In 1969 he was promoted to captain, in 1972 to major, and in 1975 to lieutenant colonel."

"Why did he come to Sweden?"

"I'm getting to that. Over the years he became corrupt, and he squirrelled away a little money here and there. He drank too much and did too much womanizing. All this was noted by his superiors, but he was still a favourite and they could overlook the small stuff. In 1976 he was sent to Spain on a mission. We don't need to go into the details, but he made a fool of himself. The mission failed and all of a sudden he was in disgrace and called back to Russia. He chose to ignore the order and thereby ended up in an even worse situation. The GRU ordered a military attaché at the embassy in Madrid to find him and talk some sense into him. Something went wrong, and Zalachenko killed the man. Now he had no choice. He had burned his bridges and rashly decided to defect. He laid a trail that seemed to lead from Spain to Portugal and possibly to a boating accident. He also left clues indicating he intended to flee to the United States. He chose in fact to defect to the most improbable country in Europe. He came to Sweden, where he contacted the Security Police, Säpo, and sought asylum. This was well thought out, because the probability that a death squad from the KGB or the GRU would look for him here was almost zero."

Björck fell silent.

"And?"

"What's the government supposed to do if one of the Soviet Union's top spies defects and seeks asylum in Sweden? A conservative government was coming into power. As a matter of fact, it was one of the very first matters we had to take to the newly appointed foreign minister. Those political cowards tried to get rid of him like a hot potato, of course, but they couldn't just send him back to the Soviets—that would have been a scandal of unmatched proportions if it ever came out. Instead they tried to send him to the States or to England. Zalachenko refused. He didn't like America and he knew that England was one of those countries where the Soviets had agents at the highest levels within military intelligence. He didn't want to go to Israel, because he didn't like Jews. So he decided to make his home in Sweden."

The whole thing sounded so improbable that it occurred to Blomkvist that Björck might be pulling his leg.

"So he stayed in Sweden?"

"Exactly. For many years it was one of the country's best-kept military secrets. The thing was, we got plenty of good information out of Zalachenko. For a time during the late seventies and early eighties, he was the jewel in the crown among defectors, the most senior from one of the GRU's elite commands."

"So he could sell information?"

"Precisely. He played his cards well and doled out information when it suited him best. We were able to identify an agent at NATO headquarters in Brussels. An agent in Rome. A contact for a whole ring of spies in Berlin. The identity of hit men he'd used in Ankara and Athens. He didn't know that much about Sweden, but the information he did have we could pass on in return for favours. He was a gold mine."

"So you started cooperating with him."

"We gave him a new identity, a passport, a little money, and he took care of himself. That was what he was trained to do."

Blomkvist sat for a while in silence, digesting this information. Then he looked up at Björck.

"You lied to me the last time I was here."

"I did?"

"You said that you met Bjurman at your police shooting club in the eighties. But you met him long before that."

"It was an automatic reaction. It's confidential, and I had no reason to go into how Bjurman and I met. It wasn't until you asked about Zala that I made the connection."

"Tell me what happened."

"I was thirty-three and had been working at Säpo for three years. Bjurman was a good deal younger and had just finished his degree. He was handling certain legal matters at Säpo. It was a kind of trainee job. Bjurman was from Karlskrona, and his father worked in military intelligence."

"And?"

"Neither Bjurman nor I was remotely qualified to handle someone like Zalachenko, but he made contact on election day in 1976. There was hardly a soul in police headquarters— everyone was either off that day or working on stakeouts and the like. Zalachenko chose that moment to walk into Norrmalm police station and declare that he was seeking political asylum and wanted to talk to somebody in the Security Police. He didn't give his name. I was on duty and thought it was a straightforward refugee case, so I took Bjurman with me as legal advisor."

Björck rubbed his eyes.

"There he sat and told us calmly and matter-of-factly who he was, and what he had worked on. Bjurman took notes. After a while I realized what I was dealing with. I stopped the conversation and got Zalachenko and Bjurman the hell out of that police station. I didn't know what to do, so I booked a room at the Hotel Continental right across from Central Station and stowed him there. I told Bjurman to babysit him while I went downstairs and called my superior." He laughed. "I've often thought that we behaved like total amateurs. But that's how it happened."

"Who was your boss?"

"That's not relevant. I'm not going to name anyone else."

Blomkvist shrugged and let the matter drop.

"He made it very clear that this was a matter that required the greatest possible discretion and that we should get as few people involved as possible. Bjurman should never have had anything to do with it—it was way above his level—but since he already knew what was going on it was better to keep him on rather than bring in somebody new. I assume that the same reasoning applied to a junior officer like myself. There came to be a total of seven people associated with the Security Police who knew of Zalachenko's existence."

"How many others know this story?"

"From 1976 up to the beginning of 1990 . . . all in all about twenty people in the government, military high command, and within Säpo."

"And after the beginning of 1990?"

Björck shrugged. "The moment the Soviet Union collapsed he became uninteresting."

"But what happened after Zalachenko came to Sweden?"

Björck said nothing for so long that Blomkvist began to get restless.

"To be honest . . . Zalachenko was a big success, and those of us who were involved built our careers on it. Don't misunderstand me, it was also a full-time job. I was assigned to be

Zalachenko's mentor in Sweden, and over the first ten years we met at least a couple of times a week. This was all during the important years when he was full of fresh information. But it was just as much about keeping him under control."

"In what sense?"

"Zalachenko was a sly devil. He could be incredibly charming, but he could also be paranoid and crazy. He would go on drinking binges and then turn violent. More than once I had to go out at night and sort out some mess he'd gotten himself into."

"For instance . . ."

"For instance, the time he went to a bar and got into an argument and beat the living daylights out of two bouncers who tried to calm him down. He was quite a small man, but exceptionally skilled at close combat, which regrettably he chose to demonstrate on various occasions. Once I had to pick him up at a police station."

"He risked attracting serious attention to himself. That doesn't sound very professional."

"That was the way he was. He hadn't committed any crime in Sweden and was never arrested. We had provided him with a Swedish name, a Swedish passport and ID. And he had a house that the Security Police paid for. He received a salary from Säpo just to keep him available. But we couldn't prevent him from going to bars or from womanizing. All we could do was clean up after him. That was my job until 1985, when I got a new post and my successor took over as Zalachenko's handler."

"And Bjurman's role?"

"To be honest, Bjurman was deadweight. He wasn't particularly clever. In fact he was the wrong man in the wrong job. It was pure chance that he was part of the whole Zalachenko business at all, and he was only involved in the very early days and on the occasions when we needed him to deal with legal formalities. My superior solved the problem with Bjurman."

"How?"

"The easiest possible way. He was given a job outside the police force at a law firm that had, as you might say, close ties to us."

"Klang and Reine."

Björck gave Mikael a sharp look.

"Yes. Over the years he always had assignments, minor investigations, from Säpo. So in a way he too built his career on Zalachenko."

"Where is Zalachenko today?"

"I really don't know. My contact with him dried up after 1985, and I haven't seen him in over twelve years. The last I heard, he left Sweden in 1992."

"Apparently he's back. He's cropped up in connection with weapons, drugs, and sex trafficking."

"I wouldn't be surprised," Björck said. "But we can't know for sure if it's the Zala you're looking for or somebody else."

"The likelihood of two separate Zalachenkos appearing in this story must be microscopic. What was his Swedish name?"

"I'm not going to reveal that."

"Now you're being evasive."

"You wanted to know who Zala was. I've told you. But I won't give you the last piece of the puzzle before I know you've kept your side of the bargain."

"Zala has probably committed three murders and the police are looking for the wrong person. If you think I'll be satisfied without his name, you're mistaken."

"What makes you think Lisbeth Salander isn't the murderer?"

"I know."

Björck smiled at Blomkvist. He suddenly felt much safer.

"I think Zala is the killer," Blomkvist said.

"Wrong. Zala hasn't shot anyone."

"How do you know that?"

"Because Zala is sixty-plus years old now and severely

disabled. He's had a foot amputated and doesn't do much walking. So he hasn't been running around Odenplan and Enskede shooting people. If he was going to murder somebody, he'd have to call the disabled transport service."

Eriksson smiled politely at Modig. "You'll have to ask Mikael about that."

"OK, I will."

"I can't discuss his research with you."

"And if this Zala is a potential suspect . . ."

"You'll have to discuss that with Mikael," Eriksson said. "I can help you with what Dag was working on, but I can't tell you about our own research."

Modig sighed. "What can you tell me about the people on this list?"

"Only what Dag wrote, nothing about the sources. But I can say that Mikael has crossed about a dozen people off this list so far. That might help."

No, that won't help. The police will have to do their own formal interviews. A judge. Two lawyers. Several politicians and journalists . . . and police colleagues. A real merry-go-round. Modig knew that they should have started doing this the day after the murders.

Her eyes lighted on one name on the list. Gunnar Björck.

"There's no address for this man."

"No."

"Why not?"

"He works for the Security Police. His address is unlisted. Actually he's on sick leave. Dag was never able to track him down."

"And have you?" Modig said with a smile.

"Ask Mikael."

Modig stared at the wall above Svensson's desk. She was thinking. "May I ask a personal question?"

"Go right ahead."

"Who do *you* think murdered your friends and the lawyer?"

Eriksson wished Blomkvist were here to handle these questions. It was uncomfortable to be quizzed by a police officer. It was even more unpleasant not to be able to explain exactly what conclusions *Millennium* had reached. Then she heard Berger's voice behind her back.

"Our theory is that the murders were committed to prevent some part of Dag's exposé from reaching the light of day. But we don't know who the killer was. Mikael is focusing on someone who goes by the name of Zala."

Modig turned to look at *Millennium*'s editor in chief. Berger held out two mugs of coffee. They were decorated with the logos of the civil service union HTF and the Christian Democratic Party, respectively. Berger smiled sweetly and went back to her office.

She came out again three minutes later.

"Inspector Modig, your boss has just called. Your mobile is off. He wants you to call him."

An APB was sent out to say that Lisbeth Salander had at last surfaced. The bulletin indicated that she was probably riding a Harley-Davidson and contained the warning that she was armed and had shot someone at a summer cabin in the vicinity of Stallarholmen.

The police set up roadblocks on routes into Strängnäs, Mariefred, and Södertälje. Every commuter train between Södertälje and Stockholm was searched that evening. But no-one answering to Salander's description was found.

At around 7:00 p.m. a police patrol found the Harley-Davidson outside the fairground in Älvsjö, and that shifted the focus of the search from Södertälje to Stockholm. The report from Älvsjö said that part of a leather jacket with the insignia of Svavelsjö MC had also been found. News of the find made Inspector Bublanski push his glasses up on his head and peer glumly at the darkness outside his office on Kungsholmen.

The day's developments had led to nothing but bafflement. The kidnapping of Salander's girlfriend, the inexplicable involvement of the boxer Paolo Roberto, the arson near Södertälje, and bodies buried in the woods there. And finally this bizarre business in Stallarholmen.

Bublanski went out to the main office and looked at the map of Stockholm and its environs. He found Stallarholmen, Nykvarn, Svavelsjö, and finally Älvsjö, the four places that for apparently different reasons were of current interest. He moved his gaze to Enskede and sighed. He had the unpleasant feeling that the police investigation was many miles behind the unfolding events. Whatever the Enskede murders had been about, it was much more complicated than they had supposed.

Blomkvist was unaware of the drama at Stallarholmen. He left Smådalarö around 3:00 in the afternoon. He stopped at a gas station and had some coffee as he tried to make sense of what he had discovered.

He was surprised that Björck had given him so many details, but the man had absolutely refused to give him the last piece of the puzzle: Zalachenko's Swedish identity.

"We had a deal," Blomkvist said.

"And I've fulfilled my part of it. I've told you who Zalachenko is. If you want more than that we'll have to make a new agreement. I'll need guarantees that my name will be taken out of all your research material. And I'll need guarantees that you won't write about me at all in connection with the Zalachenko story."

Blomkvist was willing to go so far as to treat Björck as an anonymous source in connection with the background story, but he could not guarantee that Björck would not be identified by anyone else—the police, for example.

"I'm not worried about the police," Björck said.

They agreed in the end to think about everything for a day or so before resuming their conversation.

As Blomkvist sat drinking his coffee, he felt that there was something right in front of his nose that he wasn't seeing. He was so close that he could sense shapes, but he couldn't bring the picture into focus. Then it came to him that there was another person who might be able to shed some light on the story. He was quite close to the rehabilitation home in Ersta. He checked his watch. He would go to see Holger Palmgren.

After the meeting Björck was exhausted. His back hurt worse than ever. He took three painkillers and had to stretch out on the sofa in the living room. Thoughts were churning around in his head. After about an hour he got up and boiled some water and took out a Lipton's tea bag. He sat at the kitchen table and brooded.

Could he trust Blomkvist? He was now at the man's mercy. But he had held back the crucial information: Zala's identity and his role in the whole drama.

How the hell had he landed in this mess? All he did was pay some whores. He was a bachelor. That sixteen-year-old bitch hadn't even pretended that she liked him. He had felt her disgust.

Fucking cunt. If she hadn't been so young. If she'd been at least twenty it wouldn't have looked so bad. Blomkvist detested him too, and made no effort to hide it.

Zalachenko.

A pimp. What irony. He had fucked Zalachenko's whores. But Zalachenko had been smart enough to stay in the background.

Bjurman and Salander.

And Blomkvist.

A way out.

After an hour of worrying he went to his study and found the piece of paper with the telephone number he had retrieved from his office earlier in the week. It wasn't the only thing he'd kept from Blomkvist. He knew exactly where Zalachenko was, though he hadn't spoken to him in more than twelve years. Nor had he any desire to do so ever again.

But Zalachenko was a sly devil. He would understand the problem. He would be able to vanish from the face of the earth. Go abroad and retire. The real catastrophe would be if he were actually caught. Then everything would come crashing down.

He hesitated a long time before he dialled the number.

"Hello. It's Sven Jansson," he said. A name that he had not used in a very long time. Zalachenko remembered instantly who he was.

CHAPTER 28

Wednesday, April 6

Bublanski met Modig for coffee and a bite to eat at Wayne's on Vasagatan at 8:00 in the evening. She had never seen her boss so downcast before. He told her everything that had happened that day. Finally she reached out and put her hand over his. It was the first time she had ever touched Bublanski, and there was no other reason than companionship. He smiled sadly and patted her hand in an equally friendly way.

"Maybe I should retire," he said.

She smiled at him indulgently.

"This investigation is falling apart," he went on. "It's already in pieces. I informed Ekström of everything that occurred today, and he just said, 'Do what you think is best.' He seems incapable of action."

"I don't want to bad-mouth a superior, but as far as I'm concerned, Ekström can go jump in the lake."

Bublanski nodded. "You're officially back on the case, but don't expect he'll come up with an apology. Also, Faste stormed out this morning and has had his mobile switched off all day. If he doesn't turn up tomorrow I'm going to have to get somebody to look for him."

STIEG LARSSON

"Faste can stay out of it too. What's happening with Hed-ström?"

"Nothing. I wanted to have him charged, but Ekström doesn't dare. We kicked him out and I had a serious talk with Armansky. We broke off working with Milton, which unfortunately means that we've lost Sonny Bohman too. Which is a shame. He was a talented detective."

"How did Armansky take it?"

"He was crushed. The curious thing is that . . ."

"What?"

"He said that Salander never liked Hedström. He remembered she told him a couple of years ago that Hedström should be fired. She said he was a shithead, but apparently wouldn't explain why. Armansky of course didn't do as she suggested."

"Interesting."

"Curt is still down in Södertälje. They're about to do a search of Carl-Magnus Lundin's place. Jerker is fully occupied digging up bits of Kenneth 'the Vagabond' Gustafsson. And just before I got here he called to say that there's another body in the second grave. From the clothes it's probably a woman. Seems to have been there quite a while."

"A woodland cemetery. Jan, I assume Salander is not a suspect in the murders at Nykvarn."

Bublanski smiled for the first time in hours. "No. She had to be crossed off that one. But she's definitely carrying a weapon and she did shoot Lundin."

"Mind you, she shot him in the foot, not in the head. In Lundin's case there's probably not much difference, but don't forget that whoever committed the murders in Enskede is an excellent shot."

"Sonja . . . this is totally absurd. Magge Lundin and Sonny Nieminen are two hooligans with long police records. Lundin may have put on a pound or two and he may not be in top form, but he's still dangerous. And Nieminen is a brutal bastard that even the tough guys are afraid of. I simply can't imagine how a skinny little creature like Salander could beat the shit out of them like that. Not that he doesn't deserve a beating, don't get me wrong. It's just that I don't understand how it could have happened."

"We'll have to ask her when we find her. She has been documented as violent, after all."

"Even Curt would have thought twice about taking those guys on. And Curt isn't exactly a pansy."

"The question is whether she had some reason to attack Lundin and Nieminen."

"One little girl with two psychopaths in a deserted summer cabin? I can think of a reason or two," Bublanski said.

"Could she have had help from someone? Could there have been other people involved?"

"There's nothing in the report to indicate that. Salander was inside the cabin. There was a coffee cup on the table. And besides, we have a statement from Anna Viktoria Hansson, who keeps an eye on everyone's movements. She swears that the only people who passed her were Salander and our two heroes from Svavelsjö."

"How did Salander get into the cabin?"

"With a key. I'm guessing she took it from Bjurman's apartment. You remember—"

"The cut police tape. She's been busy."

Modig drummed her fingertips on the table and then took a new approach.

"Has it been confirmed that it was Lundin who had a part in the kidnapping of Miriam Wu?"

"Paolo Roberto looked through mug shots of three dozen bikers. He picked him out right away, no shadow of a doubt that was the man he saw at the warehouse in Nykvarn."

"And Blomkvist?"

"I haven't gotten hold of him yet. He's not answering his mobile."

"But Lundin matches his description of Salander's attacker

on Lundagatan. So we can assume that Svavelsjö MC has been hunting Salander for a while. Why?"

Bublanski threw up his hands.

Modig asked, "Was Salander living in Bjurman's summer cabin all the time we were looking for her?"

"I thought of that too. But Jerker doesn't think so. The cabin doesn't look as if it's been lived in recently, and we have a witness who says she arrived on foot earlier today."

"Why did she go there? I don't suppose she'd set up a meeting with Lundin."

"Hardly. She must have been looking for something. And the only thing we found was a bunch of files that seem to contain Bjurman's own investigation of Salander. It's all the material about her from social welfare, the Guardianship Agency, and old school reports. But it seems that some of the folders are missing. They were numbered. We have folders 1, 4, and 5."

"So 2 and 3 are missing."

"And maybe more with higher numbers."

"Which raises a question. Why would Salander be looking for information about herself?" Modig said.

"I can think of two reasons. Either she wants to hide something that she knew Bjurman had written about her, or else she wants to find out something. But there's another question too."

"What's that?"

"Why would Bjurman compile an extensive report on her and then hide it in his summer cabin? Salander seems to have found the material in the attic. He was her guardian and was assigned to handle her finances and other matters. But the material there gives the impression that he was almost obsessed with charting her life."

"Bjurman is looking more and more like a disreputable character. I was thinking about that today when I went through the list of johns at *Millennium*. I suddenly expected his name to turn up there too."

"Good thinking. Remember the violent porn you found on his computer. Did you find anything at *Millennium*?"

"I don't really know. Blomkvist is busy checking off the names on their list, but according to Malin Eriksson, one of the editors there, he hasn't turned up anything of interest. Jan . . . I have to say one thing."

"What?"

"I don't think Salander did any of this. Enskede and Odenplan, I mean. I was just as persuaded as all the others when we started, but I don't believe it now. And I can't really explain why."

Bublanski realized that he agreed with Modig.

The giant paced back and forth in Lundin's house in Svavelsjö. He stopped by the kitchen window and looked down the road. They should have been back by now. He had a sinking feeling in his stomach. Something was wrong.

He didn't like being alone in this house. He didn't feel at home here. There was a draft in his room upstairs, and there were always strange noises. He tried to shake off his uneasiness. It was foolish, he knew, but he had never liked being alone. He was not in the least afraid of flesh-and-blood people, but empty houses out in the country he thought were indescribably horrible. The noises got his imagination working. He couldn't shed the sense that something dark and evil was watching him through the crack in the door. Something he believed he could hear breathing.

When he was younger he'd been troubled by a fear of the dark. That is, he'd been troubled until he had aggressively told off his friends, his own age and sometimes a lot older, who were amused by such weaknesses. He was good at telling people off.

But it was embarrassing. He hated darkness and being alone. He hated the creatures that inhabited darkness and solitude. He wished Lundin would come home. Lundin's presence would restore the balance, even if they didn't exchange a word or weren't even in the same room. He would hear real sounds and he would know that there were people nearby.

He tried to ward off his anxiety by playing CDs on the stereo, and restlessly he tried to find something he wanted to read on Lundin's shelves. Lundin's taste in books left much to be desired, and he had to settle for a collection of motorcycle magazines, men's magazines, and paperback thrillers of the type that had never interested him. The solitude became more and more claustrophobic. He cleaned and oiled the pistol he kept in his bag, and for a while that had a calming effect.

Eventually he had to get out of the house. He walked around the garden to get some fresh air. He stayed out of sight of the neighbouring houses, but stopped so that he could watch the lighted windows where there were people. If he stood quite still he could hear the sound of music in the distance.

When he felt he had to go back inside Lundin's wooden shack he stood for a long time on the steps before shaking off the oppressive feeling and resolutely going in.

At 7:00 he watched the news on TV4. He listened with horror to the headlines and then to a report on the shoot-out at the summer cabin in Stallarholmen.

He ran up the stairs to his room on the top floor and stuffed his belongings into a bag. Two minutes later he was driving away in his white Volvo.

He had made his escape in the nick of time. Just two miles outside Svavelsjö two police cars with their blue lights flashing passed him, on their way into the village.

After a great deal of patient negotiation Blomkvist was allowed to see Holger Palmgren. He was so insistent that the nurse in charge called Dr. Sivarnandan, who apparently lived nearby. Sivarnandan arrived fifteen minutes later and assumed responsibility for dealing with the stubborn journalist. At first he was not at all sympathetic. Over the past two weeks several reporters had found out where Palmgren was and had used all sorts of strategies to get a statement. Palmgren himself had refused on any account to receive such visitors, and the staff had instructions to let no-one in to see him.

Dr. Sivarnandan had been following the case with much distress. He was shocked at the headlines that Salander had generated in the press. Palmgren had fallen into a deep depression which, Sivarnandan suspected, was a result of his inability to help Salander in any way. Palmgren had broken off his rehabilitation therapy and now spent the days reading newspapers and following the hunt for the girl on TV. Otherwise he sat in his room and brooded.

Blomkvist remained standing at Sivarnandan's desk and explained that of course he had no wish to subject Palmgren to any unpleasantness. He didn't want a statement from him. He was a good friend of Salander, he was persuaded of her innocence, and he was desperately searching for information that might shed some light on certain aspects of her past.

Dr. Sivarnandan was hard to convince. Blomkvist had to explain in detail his own role in the drama. Not until half an hour of discussion had passed did Sivarnandan give his consent. He asked Blomkvist to wait while he went up to ask Palmgren whether he would see him.

Sivarnandan returned after ten minutes.

"He's agreed to see you. If he doesn't like you then he'll put you out on your ear. You are not to interview him or write anything in the press about the visit."

"I won't write a line about this."

Palmgren had a small room containing a bed, a bureau, a table, and a couple of chairs. He was white-haired and thin as a scarecrow. He evidently had trouble with his balance, but he stood up anyway when Blomkvist was shown into the room. He did not hold out his hand, but motioned to one of the chairs by the table. Blomkvist sat down. Dr. Sivarnandan remained in the room. Blomkvist had difficulty at first understanding Palmgren's slurred speech.

"Who are you, claiming to be Lisbeth's friend, and what do you want?"

"You don't have to say anything to me. But I ask you to listen to what I have to say before you throw me out."

Palmgren nodded curtly and shuffled over to the chair opposite Blomkvist.

"I met Lisbeth Salander for the first time two years ago. I hired her to do some research for me. She visited me in another town where I was living at the time, and we worked together for several weeks."

He wondered how much he had to explain to Palmgren. He decided to stay as close to the truth as possible.

"During that time two important things happened. One was that Lisbeth saved my life. The other was that we became very good friends. I came to know her well and I think very highly of her."

Without going into detail, Blomkvist told Palmgren how his relationship with her had suddenly ended after the Christmas holiday a year ago, when Salander left the country.

Then he told Palmgren about his work at *Millennium* and about how Svensson and Johansson were murdered and how he had been drawn into the hunt for the killer.

"I've heard that you've been bothered by reporters lately, and certainly the papers have published one idiotic story after the other. All I can do now is to assure you that I'm not here to gather material for yet another article. I'm here because of Lisbeth, as her friend. I'm probably one of the few people in the country right now who unhesitatingly, and without an ulterior motive, is on her side. I believe her to be innocent. I believe that a man named Zalachenko is behind the murders."

Blomkvist paused. Something had glimmered in Palmgren's eyes when he said the name Zalachenko.

THE GIRL WHO PLAYED WITH FIRE 543

"If you can contribute anything that would shed some light on Lisbeth's past, this is the time to do it. If you don't want to help her, then I'm wasting my time and yours and I'll know where you stand."

Palmgren had not said a word during this monologue. As Blomkvist finished, his eyes flashed again. But he was smiling. He spoke as clearly as he could.

"You really want to help her."

Blomkvist nodded.

Palmgren leaned forward. "Describe the sofa in her living room."

"On the occasions I visited her she had a worn-out, extremely ugly piece of furniture with a certain curiosity value. I would guess it's from the early fifties. It has two shapeless cushions covered in brown cloth with a yellow pattern of sorts on it. The cloth is torn in several places and the stuffing was coming out when I last saw it."

All of a sudden Palmgren laughed. It sounded more like he was clearing his throat. He looked at Dr. Sivarnandan.

"He's been to her apartment at least. Does the doctor think it would be possible to offer my guest a cup of coffee?"

"Certainly." Dr. Sivarnandan got up to leave. He paused in the doorway to nod at Blomkvist.

"Alexander Zalachenko," Palmgren said as soon as the door was closed.

"So you know that name?"

"Lisbeth told me the name. And I think it's important that I tell this story to someone . . . should I happen to drop dead, which is all too possible."

"Lisbeth? How would she know anything about his existence?"

"He is Lisbeth's father."

At first Blomkvist could not make out what Palmgren was saying. Then the words sank in.

"What the hell are you saying?"

"Zalachenko was some sort of a political refugee—I've never gotten the story quite straight, and Lisbeth was always tight-lipped about it. It was something she absolutely did not want to talk about."

Her birth certificate. Father unknown.

"Zalachenko is Lisbeth's father," Blomkvist repeated aloud.

"On only one occasion in all the years I've known her did she tell me what happened. Here's how I understood it—Zalachenko came here in the mid-seventies. He met Lisbeth's mother in 1977, they had a relationship, and the result was two children."

"Two?"

"Lisbeth and her twin sister Camilla."

"Good God—there are two of her?"

"They're very different. But that's another story. Lisbeth's mother's name was in fact Agneta Sofia Sjölander. She was seventeen when she met Zalachenko. I don't know anything else about how they met, but I gather she was quite a dependent young girl and easy prey for an older, more experienced man. She was impressed by him and probably head over heels in love with him. Zalachenko turned out to be anything but nice. I assume he was just after a willing woman and not much else. Naturally she fantasized about a secure future with him, but he wasn't the least bit interested in marriage. They never did marry, but in 1979 she changed her name from Sjölander to Salander. That was, I suppose, her way of showing that they belonged together."

"How do you mean?"

"Zala. *Salander.*"

"Jesus," Blomkvist said.

"I started looking into the whole matter just before I fell ill. She had the right to take the name because her mother, Lisbeth's grandmother, was actually named Salander. Then what happened was that Zalachenko proved himself to be a psychopath on a grand scale. He drank and savagely abused

Agneta. As far as I know, this abuse went on throughout the girls' childhood. As long as Lisbeth can remember, Zalachenko would turn up from time to time. Sometimes he would be gone for long periods, but then he was suddenly there again in the apartment on Lundagatan. And every time it was the same old story. He came there to have sex and to get drunk, and it ended with him abusing Lisbeth's mother in various ways. Lisbeth told me things that indicated it was more than physical abuse. He carried a gun and was threatening, and there were elements of sadism and psychological terrorizing. I gather it only got worse as the years went on. Lisbeth's mother spent a great part of the eighties living in fear."

"Did he hit the children too?"

"No. Apparently he was totally uninterested in his daughters. He hardly even said hello to them. Their mother used to send them to their room when Zalachenko turned up, and they weren't allowed to come out without permission. On one occasion he may have spanked Lisbeth or her sister, but that was mostly because they were irritating him or were somehow in the way. All the violence was directed towards their mother."

"Jesus Christ. Poor Lisbeth."

Palmgren nodded. "Lisbeth told me all this about a month before I had my stroke. It was the first time she had spoken openly about what had happened. I'd just decided that it was time to put an end to the absurd declaration of incompetence. Lisbeth is as smart as anyone I know, and I was prepared to take up her case again with the district court. Then I had the stroke . . . and when I woke up I was here."

He waved at his confined quarters. A nurse knocked at the door and brought in coffee. Palmgren sat in silence until she left.

"There are some aspects of Lisbeth's story that I don't understand," he said. "Agneta had been forced to go to the hospital dozens of times. I read her medical record. It was perfectly obvious that she was the victim of aggravated assault, and social welfare should have intervened. But nothing happened. Lisbeth and Camilla had to stay at the social emergency service whenever she sought care, but as soon as she was discharged she would go back home and it would start all over again. I can only interpret this as the collapse of the whole social safety net, and Agneta was too terrified to do anything but wait for her torturer. Then something happened. Lisbeth calls it 'All The Evil.' "

"What was it?"

"Zalachenko had been gone for several months. Lisbeth had turned twelve. She had apparently begun to think that he was gone for good. But he wasn't, of course. One day he came back. First Agneta locked Lisbeth and her sister in their room. Then she and Zalachenko went to bed. And then he started hitting her. He enjoyed beating people. But this time it wasn't two helpless little girls who were locked up . . . The twins reacted quite differently. Camilla was panic-stricken that someone would find out what was going on in their apartment. She repressed everything and made out that her mother was never beaten. When the abuse was over, Camilla would go in and hug her father and pretend that everything was fine."

"Her way of protecting herself, no doubt."

"Right. But Lisbeth was a whole different story. This time she interrupted the beating. She went into the kitchen and got a knife and stabbed Zalachenko in the shoulder. She stabbed him five times before he managed to take the knife away and punch her in the face. They weren't deep wounds, it seems, but he was bleeding like a stuck pig and he ran off."

"That sounds like Lisbeth."

Palmgren laughed. "Yes, it does. Don't ever fight with Lisbeth Salander. Her attitude towards the rest of the world is that if someone threatens her with a gun, she'll get a bigger gun. That's what frightens me about what's going on right now."

"So that was 'All The Evil'?"

"No, no. Then two things happened. I can't understand it.

Zalachenko was wounded so badly that he had to go to the hospital. There should have been a police report."

"But?"

"But as far as I could discover, there were absolutely no repercussions. Lisbeth remembers that a man came and talked with Agneta. She didn't know what was said or who he was. And then her mother told her that Zalachenko had forgiven her everything."

"Forgiven?"

"That was the expression she used."

And suddenly Blomkvist understood.

Björck. Or one of Björck's colleagues. It was about cleaning up after Zalachenko. Those fucking pigs. He closed his eyes.

"What is it?" Palmgren said.

"I think I know what happened. And someone is going to pay for this. But go on with the story."

"Zalachenko was gone for several months. Lisbeth waited for him and made her preparations. She had played truant from school every single day to watch out for her mother. She was scared to death that Zalachenko would really hurt her. She was twelve and felt responsible for her mother, who did not dare to go to the police and couldn't break it off with Zalachenko, or who perhaps did not understand the seriousness of the situation. But on the day Zalachenko finally turned up, Lisbeth was at school. She came home just as he was leaving the apartment. He didn't say a word. He just laughed at her. Lisbeth went in and found her mother unconscious on the kitchen floor."

"But Zalachenko didn't touch Lisbeth?"

"No. She caught up with him just as he was getting into his car. He rolled down the window, possibly to say something. Lisbeth was ready. She threw a milk carton she had filled with gasoline into the car. Then she threw in a burning match."

"Good God."

"She tried to kill her father twice. This time there were

consequences. A man sitting in a car on Lundagatan burning like a beacon could hardly go unnoticed."

"But he survived."

"He suffered horribly. One of his feet had to be amputated. His face and other parts of his body suffered serious burns. And Lisbeth ended up at St. Stefan's Psychiatric Clinic for Children."

Despite the fact that she already knew every word by heart, Salander once again read through the material about herself that she had found in Bjurman's files. She sat in the window seat and opened the cigarette case Miriam Wu had given her. She lit a cigarette and looked out towards Djurgården. She had discovered some things about her life that she had never known before.

In fact so much fell into place that she turned quite cold. Above all she was interested in the report filed by Björck in March 1991. She wasn't certain which one of the many grown-ups who had talked to her was Björck, but she thought she knew. He had introduced himself with another name. Sven Jansson. She remembered every feature of his face, every word he said, and every gesture he made on the three occasions she had encountered him.

The whole thing was a disaster.

Zalachenko had burned like fury inside the car. He had managed to push open the door and roll out onto the pavement, but his leg got caught inside by the seat belt. People had come rushing up to smother the flames. A fire engine arrived and put out the fire. An ambulance arrived and Lisbeth had tried to get the medics to ignore Zalachenko and come and see to her mother. They had shoved her aside. The police arrived, and there were witnesses who pointed to her. She tried to explain what had happened, but it felt as if nobody was listening to her, and suddenly she was sitting in the backseat of a police car and it took minutes and minutes and minutes and finally almost an hour before the police went into the apartment and found her mother.

Agneta Sofia Salander was unconscious. She had brain damage. The first in a long series of small cerebral haemorrhages had been triggered by the beating. She would never recover.

Salander now understood why nobody had read the police report, why Palmgren had failed in his attempt to have it released, and why even today Prosecutor Ekström, who was leading the search for her, did not have access to it. It had not been written by the regular police. It had been put together by some creep in the Security Police. It had rubber stamps on it saying that the report was classified as top secret according to the law of national security.

Zalachenko had worked for Säpo.

It was no report. It was a cover-up. Zalachenko was more important than Agneta Salander. He could not be identified or exposed. Zalachenko did not exist.

It was not Zalachenko who was the problem—it was Lisbeth Salander, the crazy kid who threatened to crack one of the country's most crucial secrets wide open.

A secret that she had not known anything about. She brooded. Zalachenko had met her mother very soon after he had arrived in Sweden. He had introduced himself using his real name. Perhaps at that time he had not yet been given a cover name or a Swedish identity, or he was not using it for her. She only knew his real name. But he had been given a new name by the Swedish government. That explained why Lisbeth had never found his name in any public records in all these years.

She got the point. If Zalachenko were accused of aggravated assault, Agneta Salander's lawyer would start looking into his past. *Where do you work, Herr Zalachenko? What's your real name? Where do you come from?*

If Salander ended up with social services maybe somebody would start digging around. She was too young to be charged, but if the gasoline-bomb attack were investigated in too much detail, the same thing would happen. She could imagine the headlines in the papers. The investigation would have to be conducted by a trusted person. And then stamped top secret and buried so deep that nobody would find it. And Salander would have to be buried so deep that nobody would find her either.

Gunnar Björck.

St. Stefan's.

Peter Teleborian.

The explanation was driving her wild.

Dear Government . . . I'm going to have a serious talk with you if I ever find anyone to talk to.

She wondered fleetingly what the minister of health and social welfare would think about getting a Molotov cocktail tossed through the front doors of his department. But in the absence of anyone else who could be held responsible, Teleborian was a good substitute. She made a mental note to deal with him in earnest as soon as she had tidied up the rest of this mess.

But she still didn't understand the whole picture. Zalachenko had suddenly sprung to life again after all these years. He was in danger of being exposed by Svensson. *Two shots. Svensson and Johansson.* A gun with her fingerprints on it . . .

Zalachenko or whomever he sent to carry out the executions could not have known that she had found the revolver in the box in Bjurman's desk drawer and handled it. It had been pure chance, but for her it had already been clear from the start that there had to be a connection between Bjurman and Zala.

Yet the story still did not add up. She mulled it over, trying out the pieces of the puzzle one by one.

There was only one reasonable answer.

Bjurman.

Bjurman had done his investigation into her life. He had discovered the connection. He had turned to Zalachenko.

She had the video of Bjurman raping her. That was her sword over his neck. Perhaps he dreamed that Zalachenko would force her into giving it up.

She hopped down from the window seat, opened her desk drawer, and took out the DVD with BJURMAN written on it in marker pen. She had not even put it in a plastic sleeve. She had not looked at it since she had given Bjurman his very own screening two years ago. She weighed it in her hand and put it back in the drawer.

Bjurman was a fool. If he'd only kept his distance she would have released him as soon as he'd managed to get her declaration of incompetence rescinded. He would have been transformed forever into Zalachenko's lapdog, and that would have been a fair punishment.

Zalachenko's network. Some of the tentacles went all the way to Svavelsjö MC.

The blond giant.

He was her key.

She had to find him and force him to tell her where Zalachenko was.

She lit another cigarette and looked out at the citadel next to Skeppsholmen. She looked across to the roller coaster at Gröna Lund. She was talking to herself. And in a voice she had heard once in a film, she said:

Daaaaddyyyyy, I'm coming to get yoooou.

At 7:30 she turned on the TV to catch up on the latest developments in the hunt for Lisbeth Salander. She was stunned by what she saw.

Bublanski finally got hold of Faste on his mobile just after 8:00 in the evening. No pleasantries were exchanged. He did not ask what Faste had been up to, but coolly gave him his instructions.

Faste had had more than he could bear of the circus at

headquarters that morning and had done something he had never done before on duty. He went out on the town. He turned off his mobile and sat in the bar at Central Station and drank two beers while he boiled with rage.

Then he went home, took a shower, and went to bed.

He needed to catch up on his sleep.

He woke up in time for *Rapport* and his eyes almost popped out of his head when he heard the top stories. Bodies dug up in Nykvarn. Salander had shot a leader of Svavelsjö MC. Police hunt through the southern suburbs. The net was tightening.

He turned on his mobile.

Almost immediately that fucker Bublanski called. He said that the investigation was now redirecting its focus to identifying an alternative killer, and that Faste was to relieve Holmberg at the crime scene in Nykvarn. During the wrapping up of the Salander investigation Faste was supposed to be collecting cigarette butts in the woods. Other people would be hunting Salander.

What the hell did Svavelsjö MC have to do with all this?

Suppose there *was* something to the reasoning of that fucking dyke Modig.

It wasn't possible.

It had to be Salander.

He wanted to be the one who caught her. He wanted to catch her so badly that it almost made his hands hurt as he held his mobile.

Palmgren calmly watched Blomkvist pace back and forth in front of the window in the small room. It was getting on towards 7:30 in the evening, and they had been talking non-stop for almost an hour. At last Palmgren tapped on the table-top to get Blomkvist's attention.

"Sit down before you wear out your shoes," he said.

Blomkvist sat down.

"All these secrets," Palmgren said. "I never understood the connection until you explained Zalachenko's background. All I've seen are the assessments of Lisbeth claiming that she's mentally disturbed."

"Peter Teleborian."

"He must have some sort of deal with Björck. They have to have been working together somehow."

Blomkvist nodded pensively. Whatever happened, Teleborian was going to be the object of journalistic scrutiny.

"Lisbeth said that I should stay away from him. That he was evil."

Palmgren looked at him sharply. "When did she say that?"

Blomkvist said nothing for some moments. Then he smiled and looked at Palmgren.

"More secrets, damn it. I've been in touch with her while she's been in hiding. By computer. Only short, cryptic messages on her part, but she has always led me in the right direction."

Palmgren sighed. "And of course you didn't tell the police."

"No. Not exactly."

"Then you haven't told me either. She's quite good with computers."

You have no idea how good.

"I have a great belief in her ability to land on her feet. She may be hard up, but she's a survivor."

Not that hard up. She stole almost three billion kronor. She's not going to starve. She has a bag full of gold, just like Pippi Longstocking.

"What I don't quite understand," Blomkvist said, "is why you didn't take up her case in all those years."

Palmgren sighed again. He felt infinitely sad.

"I failed her," he said. "When I became her trustee she was only one in a series of difficult young people with problems. I've dealt with dozens of others. I was given the assignment by Stefan Brådhensjö when he was minister of welfare. By then she was already at St. Stefan's, and I didn't even see her that first year. I talked to Teleborian a couple of times and he explained that she was psychotic and that she was getting the best possible care. I believed him—and why not? But I also talked to Jonas Beringer, who was senior clinician at that time. I don't think he had anything to do with her case. He made an assessment at my request, and we agreed to try and get her back into society again by way of a foster family. That was when she was fifteen."

"And you backed her up over the years."

"Not enough. I took her side after the episode in the tunnelbana. By then I had gotten to know her and I liked her a lot. She was feisty. I stopped them from putting her back in an institution. The price of that was that she was declared incompetent and I became her guardian."

"Presumably Björck wasn't running around telling the court what to decide. It would have attracted attention. He wanted her locked up, and he counted on painting a bleak picture of her through psychiatric assessments from Teleborian and others, assuming that the court would come to the logical conclusion. But instead they followed your recommendation."

"I've never thought that she ought to be under guardianship. But to be honest, I didn't do much to get the ruling reversed. I should have acted sooner and more forcefully. But I was quite enchanted by Lisbeth and . . . I always put it off. I had too many irons in the fire. And then I got sick."

"I don't think you should blame yourself. No-one else looked after her interests better over the years."

"The problem was always that I didn't know enough. Lisbeth was my client, but she never uttered a word about Zalachenko. When she got out of St. Stefan's it was years before she manifested the slightest trust in me. It was only after the hearing that I sensed she was very slowly starting to communicate with me beyond the necessary formalities."

"How did she happen to start telling you about Zalachenko?"

"I suppose that in spite of everything she had begun to trust me. Besides, on a number of occasions I'd raised the subject of having the incompetency declaration rescinded. Apparently, she thought it over and then one day she called and wanted to meet. And she told me the whole story about Zalachenko and how she viewed what had happened. You'll probably appreciate that it was a lot for me to take in. But I started digging around in the story straightaway. I couldn't find a Zalachenko in any database in all of Sweden. I did sometimes wonder whether she might be imagining the whole thing."

"After you had your stroke, Bjurman became her guardian. That couldn't have been an accident."

"No. I don't know if we'll ever be able to prove it, but I've been thinking that if we tried hard enough we would find . . . whoever it is that took over after Björck and is in charge of the cleanup of the Zalachenko affair."

"I don't wonder at Lisbeth's absolute refusal to talk to psychiatrists or the authorities," Blomkvist said. "Every time she did, it only made matters worse. She tried to explain what had happened and no-one listened. She, a child all by herself, tried to save her mother's life and defend her against a psychopath. In the end she did the only thing she felt she could do. And instead of saying 'well done' and 'good girl,' they locked her up in an asylum."

"It's not that straightforward. I hope you understand that there really is something wrong with Lisbeth," Palmgren said sharply.

"How do you mean?"

"You're aware that she had a lot of trouble when she was growing up and problems in school and all that."

"It's been in every daily paper. And I would have had trouble in school myself if I'd had the childhood she had."

"Her problems go way beyond the problems she had at home. I've read all the psychiatric assessments, and there isn't even a diagnosis. I think we can agree that Lisbeth Salander isn't like normal people. Have you ever played chess with her?"

"No."

"She has a photographic memory."

"I know. I realized that when I was working with her."

"She loves puzzles. One time when she came over for Christmas dinner I enticed her into solving some problems from a Mensa intelligence test. It was the kind where they show you five similar symbols and you have to decide what the sixth one will look like. I'd tried myself and got about half of them right. And I plodded away at it for two evenings. She took one look at the paper and answered every question correctly."

"Lisbeth is a very special girl."

"She has an extremely hard time relating to other people. I thought she had Asperger's syndrome or something like it. If you read the clinical descriptions of patients diagnosed with Asperger's, there are things that seem to fit Lisbeth very well, but there are just as many symptoms that don't apply at all. Mind you, she's not the least bit dangerous to people who leave her in peace and treat her with respect. But she is violent, without a doubt," said Palmgren in a low voice. "If she's provoked or threatened, she can strike back with appalling violence."

Blomkvist nodded.

"The question is, what do we do now?" Palmgren said.

"We find Zalachenko," Blomkvist said.

At that moment Dr. Sivarnandan knocked and came in.

"I hope I'm not disturbing you. But if you're interested in Lisbeth Salander, you might want to turn on the TV and watch the news."

CHAPTER 29

Wednesday, April 6– Thursday, April 7

Salander was shaking with rage. That morning she had gone to Bjurman's summer cabin in peace and quiet. She hadn't opened her computer since the night before, and during the day she had been too busy to listen to the news. She was half expecting the incident in Stallarholmen to get a mention, but she was completely unprepared for the storm that she now encountered on the TV news.

Miriam Wu was in Söder hospital, attacked and badly wounded by a gigantic assailant who had kidnapped her outside the apartment building on Lundagatan. Her condition was described as serious.

She'd been rescued by the former professional boxer Paolo Roberto. How he had come to be in a warehouse in Nykvarn was not explained. He was mobbed by reporters when he came out of the hospital, but he didn't want to make any comments. His face looked as if he had gone ten rounds with his hands tied behind his back.

Two bodies had been found buried in the woods close to where Miriam Wu had been assaulted. It was reported that the police had designated a third site to be excavated as well, and that this might not be the last of it.

And then there was the search for the fugitive Lisbeth Salander.

The net, so they said, was tightening. That day the police had surrounded the neighbourhood of Stallarholmen. She was armed and dangerous. She had shot and wounded a Hell's Angels biker, possibly two. The shoot-out had taken place at the summer cabin of the murdered lawyer Nils Bjurman. By evening the police were ready to concede that she might have managed to elude the cordon.

Ekström had called a press conference. His responses were evasive. No, he could not say whether Salander had dealings with the Hell's Angels. No, he could not confirm the rumour that Salander had been seen at the warehouse in Nykvarn. No, there was nothing to indicate that this was an underworld gang war. No, it could not be confirmed that Salander alone was responsible for the Enskede murders. They were now searching for her solely to question her about the circumstances of the murders.

Salander frowned. Something had shifted within the police investigation.

She went online and first read the newspapers' reports, then accessed the hard drives of Ekström, Armansky, and Blomkvist, one by one.

Ekström's email contained several messages of interest, in particular a memo sent by Jan Bublanski at 5:22 p.m. The email was brisk and devastatingly critical of Ekström's management of the preliminary investigation. It ended with what was effectively an ultimatum. He demanded (a) that Inspector Modig be reinstated, effective immediately; (b) that the focus of the investigation be redirected so as to explore alternative solutions to the Enskede murders; and (c) that research be started without delay on the figure known only as Zala.

The accusations against Salander are based on a
single direct piece of evidence—her fingerprints on the
murder weapon. Which, I remind you, is proof that she
handled the weapon but no proof that she fired it, and
even less that she fired it at the murder victims.

We now know there are other players involved. The
Södertälje police have found (so far) two bodies in shallow graves close to a warehouse owned by a cousin of
Carl-Magnus Lundin. It should be obvious that Salander,
however violent and whatever her psychological profile,
had nothing to do with those deaths.

Bublanski finished by saying that if his demands were not met
he would leave the investigative team, which he did not intend
to do quietly. Ekström had replied that Bublanski should do
what he thought was best.

Salander obtained even more surprising information from
Armansky's hard drive. A brief exchange of emails with Milton's payroll office established that Niklas Hedström had left
the company, effective immediately. He would get vacation pay
and three months' severance. An email to the manager on duty
stated that if Hedström came back to the building he could be
escorted to his desk to remove personal effects and then
escorted from the premises. An email to the technical department advised them that Hedström's card key was to be deval-
idated.

But most interesting was an exchange between Armansky
and Milton Security's lawyer, Frank Alenius. Armansky asked
how Salander could best be represented in the event that she
was taken into custody. Alenius replied that there was no reason for Milton to become concerned with a former employee
who had committed murder—it would not reflect well upon
Milton Security were the company to be so involved. Armansky replied brusquely that Salander's involvement in any
murder was still an open question, and that his concern was to

provide support for a former employee whom he considered innocent.

Blomkvist had not, Salander discovered, been on his computer since early the previous day. So no news.

Bohman laid the folder on the table in Armansky's office. He sat down heavily. Fräklund opened it and began to read. Armansky stood by the window looking out at Gamla Stan.

"This is the last report I can deliver. I've been kicked off the investigation," Bohman said.

"Not your fault," Fräklund said.

"No, not your fault," Armansky said and sat down. He had collected all the material that Bohman had provided over the course of two weeks in a pile on the conference table.

"I talked to Bublanski. You've done a good job, Sonny. He is sorry to lose you, but he had no choice because of Hedström."

"That's OK. I discovered that I get along much better here at Milton than down at Kungsholmen."

"Can you give us a summary?"

"Well, if the objective was to find Lisbeth Salander, then obviously we failed. It was a very messy investigation with a number of competing personalities, and Bublanski may not have had ultimate control over the search."

"Hans Faste—"

"Faste is a real fuckup. But the problem is not just Faste and a sloppy investigation. Bublanski saw to it that all the leads were followed as far as they could be. The fact is, Salander has been damn good at covering her tracks."

"But your job wasn't only to pin down Salander," Armansky said.

"No, and I'm thankful that we didn't tell Hedström about my other assignment to act as your mole and see to it that Salander wasn't falsely accused."

"And what do you think today?"

"When we started I was positive that she was guilty. Today I'm not sure one way or the other. So many things don't fit . . ."

"Yes?"

"Well, I would no longer consider her the prime suspect. I'm leaning more and more towards thinking there's something to Mikael Blomkvist's reasoning."

"Which means that we have to identify and find the killers. Shall we take the investigation from the beginning?" Armansky said, pouring coffee.

Salander had one of the worst evenings of her life. She was thinking about when she had thrown the firebomb into Zalachenko's car. In that instant the nightmares stopped and she had felt a great inner peace. She had had other problems, but they had always been about her, and she could handle them. Now it was about Mimmi.

Mimmi had been beaten up and was in the hospital. She was innocent. She'd had nothing to do with any of this. Her only crime was that she knew Salander.

She cursed herself. She was riddled with feelings of guilt. The blame was all hers. *Her* address was secret; *she* was safe. And then she had persuaded Mimmi to live in her apartment, at the address that anyone could find.

How could she have been so thoughtless? She might as well have beaten her up herself.

She felt so wretched that tears came to her eyes. But Salander never cried. She wiped them away.

At 10:30 she was so restless that she could not stay in the apartment. She put on her coat and boots and set off into the night. She walked down side streets until she reached Ringvägen and stood at the end of the driveway to Söder hospital. She wanted to go to Mimmi's room and wake her up and tell her that everything was going to be all right. Then she saw blue lights from a police car near Zinken and stepped into an alleyway to avoid being seen.

She was home again just after midnight. She was freezing, so she undressed and crawled into bed. She could not sleep. At 1:00 a.m. she was up again, walking naked through the unlit apartment. She went into the guest bedroom, where there was a bed and a desk. She had never set foot in it before. She sat on the floor with her back to the wall and stared into the night.

Lisbeth Salander has a guest bedroom. What a joke.

She sat there until after 2:00, and by then she was so cold that she was shivering. Then she started to cry again.

Some time before dawn, Salander took a shower and dressed. She put on the coffeemaker and made breakfast and turned on her computer. She went into Blomkvist's hard drive. She was surprised to discover that he had not updated his research journal, and instead she opened the folder <Lisbeth Salander>. There was a new document titled [Lisbeth-IMPORTANT]. She looked at the document properties. It had been created at 12:52 a.m. She double-clicked.

> Lisbeth, contact me right away. This story is worse than I could have dreamed. I know who Zalachenko is and I think I know what happened. I've talked to Holger Palmgren. I understand Teleborian's role and why they locked you up at the clinic. I think I know who murdered Dag and Mia. I also think I know why, but I'm missing some crucial pieces of information. I don't understand Bjurman's role. CALL ME. CONTACT ME AT ONCE. WE CAN SOLVE THIS. Mikael

Salander read the document slowly again. Kalle Blomkvist had been busy. Practical Pig. *Practical Fucking Pig.* He still thought there was something to solve.

He meant well. He wanted to help.

He didn't understand that whatever happened, her life was over.

It had ended before she even turned thirteen.

There was only one solution.

She created a new document and tried to write a reply, but the thoughts were whirling around in her head and there were so many things she wanted to say to him.

Salander in love. What a fucking joke.

He would never find out. She would never give him the satisfaction.

She deleted the document and stared at the empty screen. But no answer at all was less than he deserved. He had stood faithfully in her corner like a steadfast tin soldier. She created a new document and wrote:

Thanks for being my friend.

First she had a number of logistical decisions to take. She needed a means of transport. Using the burgundy Honda, still on Lundagatan, was tempting but out of the question. There was nothing in Prosecutor Ekström's laptop to indicate that anyone in the police investigation had discovered that she had bought a car, which might be because she had not yet managed to send in the registration documents and insurance papers. But Mimmi might have talked about the car when she was questioned by the police, and obviously Lundagatan was under sporadic surveillance.

The police knew that she had a motorcycle, and it would be even more obtrusive to take it out of storage from the apartment building on Lundagatan. Besides, after a number of summer-like days, a change in the weather was forecast, and she had no great desire to venture out on a bike on rain-slick highways.

One alternative, of course, would be to rent a car in Irene Nesser's name, but there were risks involved with that too. Someone might recognize her, and the fake identity would then be lost to her. That would be a catastrophe; it was her escape route out of the country.

Then she gave a lopsided smile. There was one other possibility. She booted up her computer, logged on to Milton Security's network and navigated to the car pool, which was
administered by a secretary in Milton's reception area. Milton
Security had close to forty cars at its disposal, some of which
carried the company logo and were used on business trips. The
majority were unmarked surveillance cars, and these were kept
in the garage at Milton's HQ near Slussen. Practically around
the corner.

She studied the personnel files and chose employee Marcus Collander, who had just gone on vacation for two weeks.
He had left the telephone number of a hotel in the Canary
Islands. She changed the hotel name and scrambled the digits
of the phone number where he could be reached. Then she
entered a note that Collander's last action while on duty had
been to drop off one of the cars for servicing. She picked a Toyota Corolla automatic, which she had driven before, and
recorded that it would be back a week later.

Finally she went into the surveillance system and repro-
grammed the cameras she would have to walk past. Between
4:30 and 5:00 a.m. they would show a repeat of the previous
half hour, but with an altered time code.

At 4:15 she packed her backpack. She had two changes of
clothes, two Mace canisters, and the fully charged Taser. She
looked at the two guns she had acquired. She rejected
Sandström's Colt 1911 Government and chose Nieminen's Polish P-83 Wanad, which had one round missing from the
magazine. It was slimmer and fit her hand better. She put it
into her jacket pocket.

Salander closed the lid of her PowerBook but left the computer
on the desk. She had transferred the contents of her hard drive
to an encrypted backup on the Net and then erased her whole
hard drive with a programme she had written herself, which

THE GIRL WHO PLAYED WITH FIRE   565

guaranteed that not even she could reconstruct the contents. She did not want to rely on her PowerBook, which would just be cumbersome to drag around. Instead she took her Palm Tungsten PDA with her.

She looked around her office. She had a feeling that she would not be coming back to the apartment in Mosebacke and knew that she was leaving secrets behind that she should probably destroy. But glancing at her watch she realized that she did not have much time. She turned off the desk lamp.

She walked to Milton Security, went into the garage, and took the elevator up to the administrative offices. She met no-one in the empty corridors and taking the car keys out of the unlocked cabinet in reception presented no difficulty.

She was in the garage thirty seconds later, and blipped open the door lock on the Corolla. She dumped her backpack in the passenger seat and adjusted the driver's seat and the rearview mirror. She used her old card key to open the garage door.

Just before 5:00 she turned up from Söder Mälarstrand at Västerbron. It was starting to get light.

Blomkvist woke up at 6:30. He had not set his alarm clock and had slept for only three hours. He got up and switched on his iBook and opened the folder <Lisbeth Salander> to look for her reply.

Thanks for being my friend.

Blomkvist felt a chill run down his spine. Hardly the answer he had hoped for. It felt like a farewell letter. *Salander alone against the world.* He went to the kitchen and started the coffeemaker and then had a shower. He put on a pair of worn jeans and realized that he had not had time to do laundry for weeks. He had no clean shirts. He put on a wine-red sweatshirt under his grey jacket.

As he made breakfast in the kitchen, a glint of metal on the counter behind the microwave caught his eye. With a fork he fished out a key ring.

Salander's keys. He had found them after the attack on Lundagatan and put them on top of the microwave with her shoulder bag. He had forgotten to give them to Inspector-Modig with the bag, and they must have fallen down in back.

He stared at the bunch of keys. Three large ones and three small. The three large keys were presumably to an entrance door, an apartment, and a dead bolt. *Her apartment.* Obviously not the apartment on Lundagatan. So where the hell did she live?

He examined the three small keys more closely. One was probably for her Kawasaki. One looked like it was for a safety-deposit box or storage cabinet. He held up the third key. The number 24914 was stamped on it. The realization hit him.

A P.O. box. Lisbeth Salander has a P.O. box.

He looked up the post offices in Södermalm in the phone book. She had lived on Lundagatan. Ringvägen was too far away. Maybe Hornsgatan. Or Rosenlundsgatan.

He turned off the coffeemaker, abandoned his break-fast, and drove Berger's BMW to Rosenlundsgatan. The key did not fit. He drove on to Hornsgatan. The key fit perfectly in box 24914. He opened it and found twenty-two items of post, which he stuffed into the outside pocket of his laptop case.

He drove on to Hornsgatan, parked by the Kvarter cinema, and had breakfast at Copacabana on Bergsundsstrand. As he waited for his caffè latte he examined the letters one by one. All were addressed to Wasp Enterprises. Nine letters had been sent from Switzerland, eight from the Cayman Islands, one from the Channel Islands, and four from Gibraltar. With no pang of conscience he slit open the envelopes. The first twenty-one contained bank statements and reports on various accounts and funds. Salander was as rich as a troll.

The twenty-second letter was thicker. The address was handwritten. The envelope had a printed logo and the return address of Buchanan House, Queensway Quay, Gibraltar. The enclosed letter was on the stationery of a Jeremy S. MacMillan, Solicitor. He had neat handwriting.

> *Dear Ms. Salander,*
> *This is to confirm that the final payment on your property was concluded as of January 20. As agreed, I am enclosing copies of all documentation, but I will keep the original set. I trust this will meet with your satisfaction.*
> *Let me add that I hope everything is well with you. I very much enjoyed your surprise visit of last summer, and must tell you that I found your company refreshing. I look forward to being of further service as necessary.*
> *Yours sincerely,*
> *J.S.M.*

The letter was dated January 24. Salander apparently did not pick up her mail very often. Blomkvist looked at the attached documentation for the purchase of an apartment in a building at Fiskargatan 9 in Mosebacke.

Then he almost choked on his coffee. The price paid was twenty-five million kronor, and the deal was concluded with two payments a year apart.

Salander watched a solid, dark-haired man unlock the side door of Auto-Expert in Eskilstuna. It was a garage, a repair shop, and a car rental agency. A typical franchise. It was 6:50, and according to a handwritten sign on the front door, the shop did not open until 7:30. She went across the street and followed the man through the side door into the shop. The man heard her and turned round.

"Refik Alba?" she said.

"Yes. Who are you? I'm not open yet."

She raised Nieminen's P-83 Wanad and held the weapon with two hands aimed at his face.

"I don't want to haggle with you. I just want to see your list of cars rented out. I want to see it now. You have ten seconds to produce it."

Refik Alba was forty-two years old, a Kurd born in Diyarbakir, and he had seen his fill of guns. He stood as if paralyzed. Then he concluded that if this crazy woman came into his garage with a pistol in her hand, there was not going to be much to discuss.

"It's on the computer," he said.

"Turn it on."

He did as she told him.

"What's behind that door?" she asked as the computer booted up and the screen began to flicker.

"It's just a closet."

"Open it."

It contained some overalls.

"OK. Go into the closet, stay calm, and I won't have to hurt you."

He obeyed her without protest.

"Take out your mobile, put it on the floor, and kick it over to me."

He did as she said.

"Good. Now close the door behind you."

It was an antique PC with Windows 95 and a 280 MB hard drive. It took an eternity to open the Excel document with the car rental listing. The white Volvo had been rented on two occasions. First for two weeks in January, and then from March 1. It had not yet been returned. He was paying a weekly fee for a long-term rental.

The name was Ronald Niedermann.

She looked through the folders on the shelf above the computer. One of them had the label IDENTIFICATION printed neatly on it. She took the folder down and paged through to Ronald Niedermann. When he rented the car in January he had given his passport as ID, and Refik Alba had made a photocopy. She recognized the blond hulk at once. According to the passport he was German, thirty-five years old, born in Hamburg. The fact that Alba had made a copy from the passport showed that Niedermann was just a customer, not a friend.

At the bottom of the page Alba had written a mobile number and a P.O. box address in Göteborg.

Salander replaced the folder and turned off the computer. She looked around and found a rubber doorstop next to the front door. She picked it up and went back to the closet and knocked on the door with the barrel of her gun.

"Can you hear me in there?"

"Yes."

"Do you know who I am?"

Silence.

He'd have to be blind not to recognize me.

"OK. You know who I am. Are you afraid of me?"

"Yes."

"Don't be afraid of me, Herr Alba. I'm not going to hurt you. I'm almost finished here. I'm sorry for putting you to this trouble."

"Uh . . . OK."

"Have you got enough air to breathe in there?"

"Yes . . . what do you want, anyway?"

"I wanted to see whether a certain woman had hired a car from you two years ago," she lied. "I didn't find what I wanted, but it's not your fault. I'll be leaving in a few minutes. I'm going to put the doorstop under the closet door here. The door is thin enough for you to break your way out, but it will take a while. You don't have to call the police. You'll never see me

again, and you can open up as usual today and pretend that
this never happened."

The chances of him not calling the police were pretty
remote, but it did not hurt to give him the option to think
about. She left the garage and walked to the Toyota Corolla
around the corner, where she swiftly changed into Irene Nesser.

She was annoyed not to have found a street address for
Ronald Niedermann in the Stockholm area, just a P.O. box
address on the other side of Sweden. But it was the only lead
she had. *So, to Göteborg.*

She made for the E20 and turned west towards Arboga. She
turned on the radio, but she had just missed the news and got
some commercial station. She listened to David Bowie singing
"putting out fire with gasoline." She didn't know the name of
the song, but she took the words as prophetic.

CHAPTER 30

Thursday, April 7

Blomkvist looked at the entrance door of Fiskargatan 9. It was one of Stockholm's most exclusive addresses. He put the key in the lock and it turned perfectly. The list of residents in the lobby was no help. Blomkvist assumed it would be mostly corporate apartments, but there seemed to be one or two private residences among them. It hardly surprised him that Salander's name was not listed, yet it still seemed unlikely that this would be her hideout.

He walked up floor by floor, reading the nameplates on the doors. None of them rang a bell. Then he got to the top floor and read V. KULLA.

Blomkvist slapped his forehead. He had to smile. The choice of name may not have been intended to make fun of him personally; it was more likely some private ironic reflection of Salander's—but where else should Kalle Blomkvist, nicknamed for an Astrid Lindgren character, look for her than at Pippi Longstocking's Villa Villekulla?

He rang the doorbell and waited a minute. Then he took out the keys and unfastened the dead bolt and the bottom lock.

The instant he opened the door, the burglar alarm device was activated.

Salander's mobile began beeping. She was near Glanshammar just outside Örebro. She braked and pulled onto the shoulder. She took her Palm from her jacket pocket and plugged it into her phone.

Fifteen seconds earlier someone had opened the door to her apartment. The alarm was not connected to any security company. Its only purpose was to alert her that someone had broken in or had opened the door in some other way. After thirty seconds an alarm bell would go off and the uninvited visitor would get an unpleasant surprise in the form of a paint bomb hidden in a fake fuse box next to the door. She smiled in anticipation and counted down the seconds.

Blomkvist stared in frustration at the alarm display by the door. For some reason he hadn't even thought that the apartment might have an alarm. He watched the digital clock counting down. *Millennium*'s alarm was triggered if someone failed to key in the correct four-digit code within thirty seconds, and shortly thereafter a couple of muscular guys from a security company would come through the door.

His first impulse was to close the door and make a quick exit from the building. But he just stood there, frozen to the spot.

Four digits. Impossible to guess the code at random.

25–24–23–22 . . .

Damned Pippi Long . . .

19–18 . . .

What code would you use?

15–14–13 . . .

He felt his panic growing.

10–9–8 . . .

Then he raised his hand and desperately punched in the only number he could think of: 9277. The numbers that corresponded to the letters *W-A-S-P* on the keypad.

To his astonishment the countdown stopped with six seconds to go. Then the alarm beeped one last time before the display was reset to zero and a green light came on.

Salander opened her eyes wide. She thought she had to be seeing things and actually shook her PDA, which she realized was irrational. The countdown had stopped six seconds before the paint bomb was supposed to explode. And a second later the display reset to zero.

Impossible.

No other person in the world knew the code.

How could it be possible? The police? No. Zala? Inconceivable.

She dialled a number on her mobile and waited for the surveillance camera to connect and begin to send low-resolution images through. The camera was hidden in what looked like a smoke detector in the hall ceiling, and it took a low-res photograph every second. She played back the sequence from zero, the moment the door was opened and the alarm activated. Then a lopsided smile spread across her face as she looked down at Mikael Blomkvist, who for half a minute acted out a jerky pantomime before he finally punched in the code and then leaned on the doorjamb looking as though he had just avoided having a heart attack.

Kalle Fucking Blomkvist had tracked her down.

He had the keys she had dropped on Lundagatan. He was smart enough to remember that *Wasp* was her handle on the Net. And if he had found the apartment, then he had probably also worked out that it was owned by Wasp Enterprises. As she watched he began to move jerkily down the hall and disappeared from the camera's view.

Shit. How could I have been so predictable? And why did I drop those keys? . . . Now her every secret lay open to Blomkvist's prying eyes.

After thinking about it for a couple of minutes she decided that it no longer made any difference. She had erased the hard drive. That was the important thing. It could even be to her advantage that he was the one to have found her hideout. He already knew more of her secrets than anyone else did. Practical Pig would do the right thing. He would not sell her out. She hoped. She put the car in drive and pressed on, deep in thought, towards Göteborg.

Eriksson ran into Paolo Roberto in the stairwell to *Millennium*'s offices when she arrived at 8:30. She recognized him at once, introduced herself, and let him in. He had a bad limp. She smelled coffee and knew that Berger was already there.

"Hello, Erika. Thanks for agreeing to see me at such short notice," the boxer said.

Berger studied the impressive collection of bruises and lumps on his face before she leaned forward and gave him a kiss on the cheek.

"You look like shit," she said.

"I've broken my nose before. Where are you keeping Blomkvist?"

"He's out somewhere playing detective, looking for leads. As usual it's impossible to get hold of him. Except for a strange email last night I haven't heard from him since yesterday morning. Thank you for . . . well, thanks."

She pointed to his face.

Paolo Roberto laughed.

"Would you like coffee? You said you had something to tell me. Malin, join us."

They sat in the comfortable chairs in Berger's office.

"It's that big blond fucker I had the fight with. I told Mikael that his boxing wasn't worth a rotten lingonberry. But the funny thing was, he kept assuming the defensive position with his fists and circled around as if he *were* a boxer. It seemed as if he had actually had some sort of training."

"Mikael mentioned that on the phone yesterday," Eriksson said.

"I couldn't stop thinking about it, so yesterday when I got home I sat down and sent out emails to boxing clubs all over Europe. I described what had happened and gave as detailed a description as I could of the guy."

"Did you have any luck?"

"I think I got a nibble."

He put a faxed photograph on the table in front of Berger and Eriksson. It looked to have been taken during a training session at a boxing club. Two boxers were standing listening to instructions from a heavyset older man in a narrow-brimmed leather hat and tracksuit. Half a dozen people were hanging around the ring listening. In the background stood a large man who looked like a skinhead. A circle had been drawn around him with a marker pen.

"The picture is seventeen years old. The guy in the background is Ronald Niedermann. He was eighteen when the picture was taken, so he should be about thirty-five now. That fits with the giant that kidnapped Miriam Wu. I can't say with 100 percent certainty that it's him. The picture is a little too old and it's poor quality. But I can say that he looks quite similar."

"Where did you get the picture?"

"I got an answer from Hans Münster, a veteran trainer at Dynamic in Hamburg. Ronald Niedermann boxed for them for a year in the late eighties. Or rather, he tried to box for them. I got the email first thing this morning and called Münster before I came here. To sum up what Münster said: Niedermann is from Hamburg and hung out with a skinhead gang in the eighties. He has a brother a few years older, a very talented boxer, and it was through him that he joined the club.

Niedermann had fearsome strength and a physique that was almost unparalleled. Münster said that he'd never seen anyone hit so hard, not even among the elite. They measured the weight of his punch one time and he went right off the scale."

"It sounds as though he could have made a career in the ring," Berger said.

Paolo Roberto shook his head. "According to Münster he was impossible, for several reasons. First, he couldn't learn to box. He would stand still throwing haymakers. He was phenomenally clumsy—that fits the guy I fought in Nykvarn—but what was worse, he didn't understand his own strength. Now and then he'd land a punch that would cause a horrible injury during sparring practice. There were broken noses and jaws—a whole series of unnecessary injuries. They just couldn't keep him around."

"So he could box, but not really. Is that it?" Eriksson said.

"Exactly. But the reason for him stopping was medical."

"How do you mean?"

"He was apparently invulnerable. It didn't matter how many punches he took, he just shook them off and kept fighting. It turned out that he suffers from a very rare condition called congenital analgesia. I looked it up. It's an inherited genetic defect that means the transmitter substance in his nerve synapses doesn't function properly. Or in lay terms, he can't feel pain."

"That sounds like a gold mine for a boxer."

Paolo Roberto shook his head once more. "On the contrary. It can be a life-threatening disorder. Most people with congenital analgesia die relatively young, between twenty and twenty-five. Pain is the body's warning system that something's wrong. If you put your hand on a red-hot burner, it hurts and you snatch it away. But if you have this disease you don't do anything until you start smelling burned flesh."

Eriksson and Berger looked at each other.

"Are you serious?" Berger said.

"Absolutely. Niedermann can't feel a thing, and he goes around as if he's had a massive dose of local anaesthesia twenty-four hours a day. He's managed to deal with it because he has another genetic feature that compensates for it. He has an extraordinary build with an extremely strong skeleton, which makes him almost invulnerable. His raw strength is damn near unique. And above all, he must heal easily."

"I'm beginning to understand what an interesting boxing match it must have been."

"It certainly was that. I wouldn't want to do it again. The only thing that made an impression on him was when Miriam Wu kicked him in the balls. He actually fell to his knees for a second . . . which must be because there's some sort of physical reaction connected to a blow of that type, since he doesn't feel any pain. And believe me—even I would have collapsed if she had kicked me like that."

"So how did you end up beating him?"

"People with this disease can in fact be injured just like anyone else. Forget that Niedermann seems to have bones of concrete. But when I whacked him with a plank on the back of his head he dropped like a rock. He was probably concussed."

Berger looked at Eriksson.

"I'll call Mikael," Eriksson said.

Blomkvist heard his mobile go off, but he was so stunned that he did not answer until the fifth ring.

"Hi, it's Malin. Paolo Roberto thinks he's identified the giant."

"That's good," Blomkvist said absentmindedly.

"Where are you?"

"That's hard to say."

"You sound funny."

"Sorry. What did you say?"

Eriksson summed up Paolo Roberto's story.

"Follow up on it," Blomkvist said, "and see if you can find him in some database. I think it's urgent. Call me on my mobile."

To Eriksson's surprise, he disconnected without even saying goodbye.

Blomkvist was standing at that moment by a window, looking out at a magnificent view that stretched far from Gamla Stan towards Saltsjön. He felt numb. There was a kitchen off the hall to the right of the front door. Then there was a living room, an office, a bedroom, and even a small guest room that seemed not to have been used. The mattress was still in its plastic wrapper and there were no sheets. All the furniture was brand-new, straight from IKEA.

What floored Blomkvist was that Salander had bought the pied-à-terre that had belonged to Percy Barnevik, a captain of industry. The apartment was about 3,800 square feet and worth twenty-five million kronor.

Blomkvist wandered through deserted, almost eerily empty corridors and rooms with patterned parquet floors of different kinds of wood, and Tricia Guild wallpaper of the type that Berger had at one time coveted. At the centre of the apartment was a wonderfully bright living room with an open fireplace, but Salander seemed never to have had a fire. There was an enormous balcony with a fantastic view. There was a laundry room, a sauna, a gym, storage rooms, and a bathroom with a king-size bath. There was even a wine cellar, which was empty except for an unopened bottle of Quinta do Noval port—*Nacional!*—from 1976. Blomkvist struggled to imagine Salander with a glass of port in her hand. An elegant card indicated that it had been a moving-in present from the estate agent.

The kitchen contained all manner of equipment, with a shiny French gourmet stove with a gas oven as the focus. Blomkvist had never before set eyes on a La Cornue Château 120. Salander probably used it for boiling tea water.

On the other hand he admired with awe the espresso machine on its own separate table. She had a Jura Impressa X7 with an attached milk cooler. The machine looked barely used and had probably been in the kitchen when she bought the apartment. Blomkvist knew that a Jura was the espresso equivalent of a Rolls-Royce—a professional machine for domestic use that cost in the neighbourhood of 70,000 kronor. He had an espresso machine that he had bought at John Wall, which had cost around 3,500 kronor—one of the few extravagances he had allowed himself for his own household, and a fraction of the grandeur of Salander's machine.

The refrigerator contained an open milk carton, some cheese, butter, caviar, and a half-empty jar of pickled gherkins. The kitchen cupboard contained four half-empty jars of vitamins, tea bags, coffee for an ordinary coffeemaker, two loaves of bread, and a packet of crispbreads. On the kitchen table was a bowl of apples. There were three ham pies and a fish casserole in the freezer. That was all the food he found in the apartment. In the trash under the counter next to the stove he saw several empty packages for Billy's Pan Pizza.

The arrangement was all out of proportion. Salander had stolen several billion kronor and bought herself an apartment with space for an entire court. But she only needed the three rooms she had furnished. The other eighteen rooms were empty.

Blomkvist ended his tour in her office. There were no flowers anywhere. There were no paintings or even posters on the walls. There were no rugs or wall hangings. He could not see a single decorative bowl, candlestick, or even a knickknack that had been saved for sentimental reasons.

Blomkvist felt as if someone were squeezing his heart. He felt that he had to find Salander and hold her close.

She would probably bite him if he tried.

Fucking Zalachenko.

Then he sat down at her desk and opened the folder with

Björck's report from 1991. He did not read it all, but skimmed through it, trying to absorb the essentials.

He booted up her PowerBook with the 17-inch screen, 200 GB hard drive, and 1,000 MB of RAM. It was empty. She had wiped it. That was ominous.

He opened her desk drawer and found a 9 mm Colt 1911 Government single-action with a fully loaded magazine, seven rounds. It was the pistol Salander had taken from the journalist Sandström, though Blomkvist knew nothing about that. He had not yet reached the letter *S* on the list of johns.

Then he found a DVD marked BJURMAN.

He stuck it into his iBook and watched its contents with horror. He sat in stunned silence as he saw Salander beaten up, raped, almost murdered. The film seemed to have been made with a hidden camera. He did not watch it all but skipped from one section to the next, each worse than the last.

Bjurman.

Salander's guardian had raped her, and she had documented the event to the final detail. A digital date showed that the film had been recorded two years earlier. That was before he met her. Pieces of the puzzle were falling into place.

Björck and Bjurman together with Zalachenko in the seventies.

Zalachenko and Salander and a Molotov cocktail made from a milk carton in the early nineties.

Then Bjurman again, now her guardian, having replaced Palmgren. The circle had been closed. Bjurman had attacked his ward. He had treated her as a mentally ill, defenceless girl, but Salander was anything but defenceless. She was the girl who at the age of twelve had gone to war with a hit man who had defected from the GRU, and she had crippled him for life.

Salander was the woman who hated men who hate women.

He thought back to the time when he had come to know her in Hedestad. It must have been a matter of months after the rape. He could not recall that she had hinted by so much as a single word that any such thing had happened to her. She had not revealed much at all about herself. Blomkvist could not guess what she had done to Bjurman—but she had not killed him. *Oddly enough.* Otherwise Bjurman would have been dead two years ago. She must have been controlling him in some way and for some purpose that he could not begin to understand. Then he realized that he had the means of her control right there on the desk. The DVD. As long as she had that, Bjurman was her helpless slave. And Bjurman had turned to the man he supposed was an ally. Zalachenko. Her worst enemy. Her father.

Then a whole chain of events. Bjurman had been shot first, then Svensson and Johansson.

But how? What could have made Svensson such a threat?

And suddenly he knew what *must* have happened in Enskede.

Blomkvist found a piece of paper on the floor beneath the window. Salander had printed out a page, crumpled it into a ball, and tossed it away. He smoothed it out. It was from *Aftonbladet*'s online edition about the kidnapping of Miriam Wu.

He did not know what role Wu had played in the drama— if any—but she had been one of Salander's very few friends. Maybe her only friend. Salander had given her old apartment to her. Now she was lying in the hospital, badly beaten.

Niedermann and Zalachenko.

First her mother. Then Miriam Wu. Salander must be crazy with hatred.

This was one provocation too many.

And now she was on the hunt.

At lunchtime Armansky received a call from the rehabilitation home in Ersta. He had expected to hear from Palmgren much earlier and had avoided making contact with him. He'd been afraid that he would have to report that Salander was guilty beyond all doubt. Now at least he could tell him that there was in fact reasonable doubt of her guilt.

"How far did you get?" Palmgren said without beating about the bush.

"With what?"

"With your investigation of Salander."

"And what makes you think I'm doing any such investigation?"

"Don't waste my time, Dragan."

Armansky sighed. "You're right."

"I want you to come and see me," Palmgren said.

"I can come this weekend."

"Not good enough. I want you to come tonight. We have a great deal to discuss."

Blomkvist had made himself coffee and a sandwich in Salander's kitchen. He half hoped to hear her keys in the door. But he was not optimistic. The empty hard drive in her PowerBook told him that she had already left her hideout for good. He had found her apartment too late.

At 2:30 in the afternoon he was still sitting at Salander's desk. He had read Björck's "non-report" three times. It had been formulated as a memo to an unnamed superior. The recommendation was simple: get a pliable psychiatrist who would admit Salander to the children's psychiatric clinic. The girl was disturbed, as was clearly demonstrated by her behaviour.

Blomkvist was going to devote very particular attention to Björck and Teleborian in the coming days. He was looking forward to it. His mobile rang and interrupted his train of thought.

"Hi again. It's Malin. I think I've got something."

"What?"

"There's no Ronald Niedermann in the social security records in Sweden. He's not in any telephone book or tax records or on the vehicle licencing database, or anywhere else. But listen to this. In 1998 a corporation was registered with the Patent Office. It's called KAB Import AB and has a P.O. box address in Göteborg. The company imports electronics. The chairman of the board is Karl Axel Bodin, hence KAB, born in 1941."

"It doesn't ring a bell."

"Not for me either. There's also an accountant on the board who's registered at a couple of dozen other companies. He seems to be one of those nominal finance directors that small companies need. The company has been more or less dormant since it was set up. But then the third member of the board is an R. Niedermann. He doesn't have a social security number in Sweden. He was born on January 18, 1970, and is listed as the company's representative in the German market."

"Good work, Malin. Very good. Do we have an address apart from the P.O. box?"

"No, but I've tracked down Karl Axel Bodin. He's registered in West Sweden and lives at the address for P.O. box 612 in Gosseberga. I looked it up; it seems to be a property in the country not far from Nossebro, northeast of Göteborg."

"What do we know about him?"

"He declared an income of 260,000 kronor two years ago. According to our friend on the police force, he has no criminal record. He has a licence for a moose rifle and a shotgun. He has two cars, a Ford and a Saab, both older models. No points on his licence. He's unmarried and calls himself a farmer."

"A man about whom we know nothing, who has no police record." Blomkvist thought for a few moments. He had to make a decision.

"One more thing. Dragan Armansky called several times looking for you."

"Thanks, Malin. I'll call you later."

"Mikael . . . is everything OK with you?"

"No, everything isn't OK, but I'll be in touch."

As a good citizen he ought to call Bublanski. If he did, he would either have to tell him the truth about Salander or end up in a muddled situation of half-truths and withheld facts. But that was not the real problem.

Salander was out looking for Niedermann and Zalachenko. He had no idea how far she had gotten, but if he and Eriksson could find an address for P.O. box 612 in Gosseberga, there was no doubt that Salander could too. It was very likely that she was heading to Gosseberga. That was the natural next step.

If he called the police and told them where Niedermann was hiding, he'd have to tell them that Salander was probably on her way there. She was being sought for three murders and the shooting in Stallarholmen, which would mean that the national armed response team or some equivalent would be tasked with taking her in.

And Salander would no doubt put up a violent resistance.

Blomkvist got a pen and paper and made a list of things he could not or would not want to tell the police.

First *the address in Mosebacke.*

Salander had gone to a great deal of trouble to ensure the privacy of her apartment. This was where she had her life and her secrets. He was not going to give her away.

Then he wrote *Bjurman* and added a question mark after the name.

He glanced at the DVD on the desk. Bjurman had raped Salander. He had nearly killed her. He had outrageously abused his position as her guardian. He should be exposed for the swine he was. But there was an ethical dilemma here. Salander had not told the police. Did she want to be exposed in the media by a police investigation in which the most harrowing, intimate details would be leaked in a matter of hours? The DVD was proof, and stills from it would probably end up in the evening papers.

It was up to Salander to decide how she wanted to proceed.

But if he had been able to track down her apartment, sooner or later the police would do so too. He put the DVD in his bag.

Then he wrote *Björck's report*. In 1991 it had been stamped top secret. It shed light on everything that had happened. It named Zalachenko and made clear Björck's role, and together with the list of johns from Svensson's computer it would give Björck some anxious hours facing Bublanski. And in light of the correspondence, Teleborian would find himself in deep shit too.

The documents would lead the police to Gosseberga, but at least he would have a head start.

He started Word and wrote in outline form the key facts he had discovered during the past twenty-four hours from his conversations with Björck and Palmgren, and from the material he had found at Salander's place. It took him about an hour. He burned the document onto a CD along with his own research.

He wondered whether he ought to check in with Armansky, but thought the hell with it. He had enough balls to juggle already.

Blomkvist walked into *Millennium* and went straight to Berger's office.

"His name is Zalachenko," he said without even saying hello. "He's a former Soviet hit man from one of the intelligence services. He defected in 1976 and was granted asylum in Sweden and given a salary by Säpo. After the end of the Soviet Union he became, like many others, a full-time gangster. Now he's involved in sex trafficking and smuggling weapons and drugs."

Berger put down her pen. "Why am I not surprised that the KGB is popping up in the action?"

"It's not the KGB. It's the GRU. The military intelligence service."

"So it's serious."

Blomkvist nodded.

"You mean he's the one who murdered Dag and Mia?"

"It wasn't him, no. He sent someone. Ronald Niedermann, the monster that Malin has been finding out about."

"Can you prove this?"

"More or less. Some of it is guesswork. But Bjurman was murdered because he asked Zalachenko for help in dealing with Lisbeth."

Blomkvist told her about the DVD Salander had left in her desk.

"Zalachenko is her father. Bjurman worked formally for Säpo in the mid-seventies and was one of those who made Zalachenko officially welcome when he defected. Later Bjurman became a lawyer with his own practice and a full-time crook, doing jobs for an elite group within the Security Police. I would think there's an inner circle that meets now and then in the men's sauna to control the world and keep the secret about Zalachenko. I'm guessing that the rest of Säpo has never even heard of the bastard. Lisbeth threatened to crack the secret wide open. So they locked her up in a children's psychiatric unit."

"That can't be true."

"Oh, but it is," Blomkvist said. "Lisbeth wasn't especially manageable then, nor is she now . . . but since she was twelve years old she's been a threat to national security."

He gave her a summary of the story.

"This is quite a bit to digest," Berger said. "And Dag and Mia . . ."

"Were murdered because Dag discovered the link between Bjurman and Zalachenko."

"So what happens now? We have to tell the police, don't we?"

"Parts of it, but not all. I've copied the significant information onto this disk as backup, just in case. Lisbeth is looking for Zalachenko. I'm going to try to find her. Nothing of this must be shared with anybody."

"Mikael . . . I don't like this. We can't withhold information in a murder investigation."

"And we're not going to. I intend to call Bublanski. But my guess is that Lisbeth is on her way to Gosseberga. She's still being sought for three murders, and if we call the police they'll unleash their armed response team and backup weapons with hunting ammunition, and there's a real risk that she would resist arrest. And then anything could happen." He stopped and smiled grimly. "If nothing else, we ought to keep the police out of it so that the armed response team doesn't come to a sticky end. I have to find her first."

Berger looked dubious.

"I don't intend to reveal Lisbeth's secrets. Bublanski will have to figure those out for himself. I want you to do me a favour. This folder contains Björck's report from 1991 and some correspondence between Björck and Teleborian. I want you to make a copy and offer it to Bublanski or Modig. I'm leaving for Göteborg in twenty minutes."

"Mikael . . ."

"I know. But I'm on Lisbeth's side through it all."

Berger pressed her lips together and said nothing. Then she nodded.

"Be careful," she said, but he had already left.

I should go with him, she thought. That was the only decent thing to do. But she still hadn't told him that she was going to leave *Millennium* and that it was all over, no matter what happened. She took the folder and headed for the photocopier.

The box was in a post office in a shopping centre. Salander didn't know Göteborg, nor where in the city she was, but she found the post office and positioned herself in a café where she could keep watch on the box through a gap in a window where there was a poster advertising the Svensk Kassatjänst, the improved Swedish postal system.

Irene Nesser wore more discreet makeup than Lisbeth

Salander. She had some silly necklaces on and was reading *Crime and Punishment,* which she had found in a bookshop one street away. She took her time, occasionally turning a page. She'd begun her surveillance at lunchtime and had no idea whether anyone came regularly to pick up the mail, whether it might be daily or every other week, whether it had already been collected earlier in the day, or whether anyone ever turned up at all. But it was her only lead, and she drank a caffè latte while she waited.

She was about to doze off when she suddenly saw the door to the box being opened. She glanced at the clock. A quarter to two. *Lucky as shit.*

She got up quickly and walked over to the window, where she spotted someone in a black leather jacket leaving the area where the boxes were. She caught up with him on the street outside. He was a thin young man in his twenties. He walked round the corner to a Renault and unlocked the door. Salander memorized the licence plate number and ran back to her Corolla, which was parked only a hundred yards away on the same street. She caught up with the car as it turned onto Linné-gatan. She followed him down Avenyn and up towards Nordstan.

Blomkvist arrived at Central Station in time to catch the X2000 train at 5:10 p.m. He bought a ticket on board with his credit card, took a seat in the restaurant car, and ordered a late lunch.

He felt a gnawing uneasiness in the pit of his stomach and was afraid he had set off too late. He prayed that Salander would call him, but he knew that she wouldn't.

She had done her best to kill Zalachenko in 1991. Now, after all these years, he had struck back.

Palmgren had delivered a prescient analysis. Salander had experienced personally that it was no use talking to the authorities.

Blomkvist glanced at his laptop bag. He had brought along the Colt that he'd found in her desk. He wasn't sure why he had taken the gun, but he'd felt instinctively that he must not leave it in her apartment. He knew that wasn't much of a logical argument.

As the train rolled across Årstabron he flipped open his mobile and called Bublanski.

"What do you want?" Bublanski said, obviously annoyed.

"To tie up loose ends," Blomkvist said.

"Loose ends of what?"

"This whole mess. Do you want to know who murdered Svensson, Johansson, and Bjurman?"

"If you have information I'd like to hear it."

"The murderer's name is Ronald Niedermann. That's the giant who boxed with Paolo Roberto. He's a German citizen, thirty-five years old, and he works for a scumbag named Alexander Zalachenko, also known as Zala."

Bublanski said nothing for a long time, and then Blomkvist heard him sigh, turn over a sheet of paper, and click his ball-point.

"And you're sure about this?"

"Yes."

"OK. So where are Niedermann and this Zalachenko?"

"I don't know yet. But as soon as I work it out I'll let you know. In a little while Erika Berger will deliver to you a police report from 1991. In it you'll find all sorts of information about Zalachenko and Salander."

"Like what?"

"That Zalachenko is Lisbeth's father, for example. That he's a hit man who defected from the Soviet Union during the Cold War."

"A Russian hit man?" Bublanski echoed.

"A faction within Säpo has been supporting him and concealing his criminal dealings."

Blomkvist heard Bublanski pull up a chair and sit down.

"I think it would be best if you came in and made a formal statement."

"I don't have time for that. I'm sorry."

"Excuse me?"

"I'm not in Stockholm at the moment. But I'll send word as soon as I find Zalachenko."

"Blomkvist . . . You don't have to prove anything. I have doubts about Salander's guilt too."

"But I'm just a simple private investigator who doesn't know the first thing about police work."

It was childish, he knew, but he disconnected without waiting for Bublanski's reply. Instead he called Annika Giannini.

"Hi, Sis."

"Hi. Anything new?"

"I might be needing a good lawyer tomorrow."

"What have you done?"

"Nothing too serious yet, but I might be arrested for obstructing a police investigation. But that's not why I called. You couldn't represent me anyway."

"Why not?"

"Because I want you to take on the defence of Lisbeth Salander, and you can't look after both of us."

Blomkvist gave her a rapid rundown of the story. Giannini was ominously silent. Finally she said, "And you have documentation of all this . . ."

"I do."

"I'd have to think it over. Lisbeth really needs a criminal lawyer."

"You'd be perfect."

"Micke . . ."

"Listen, you were the one who was furious with me because I didn't ask for help when I needed it."

When they'd finished their conversation, Blomkvist sat thinking. Then he picked up his mobile and called Holger Palmgren. He didn't have any particular reason for doing so, but he wanted to tell him that he was following up one or two leads, and that he hoped the whole story would be resolved within the next few hours.

The problem was that Salander had leads too.

Salander reached for an apple in her backpack without taking her eyes off the farm. She lay stretched out at the edge of the woods with a floor mat from the Corolla as a groundsheet. She had taken off her wig and changed into green tracksuit pants with pockets, a thick sweater, and a midlength windbreaker with a thermal lining.

Gosseberga Farm lay about four hundred yards from the road. There were four buildings. The main building was about a hundred and twenty yards in front of her, an ordinary white-frame house on two floors, with a shed and a barn seventy yards beyond the farmhouse. Through the barn door she could see the front of a white car. She thought it was a Volvo, but it was too far away for her to be sure.

Between her and the main building there was a muddy field that extended to the right about two hundred yards down towards a pond. The driveway cut through the field and disappeared into a small stand of trees towards the road. Next to the road there was another farmhouse that looked to be abandoned; the windows were covered with plastic sheeting. Beyond the main building was a grove of trees that served to block the view of the nearest neighbour, a clump of buildings almost six hundred yards away. So the farm in front of her was relatively isolated.

She was close to Lake Anten in an area of rounded glacial moraines where fields alternated with small communities and dense woodland. The road map gave no detail, but she had followed the black Renault from Göteborg along the E20 and turned west towards Sollebrunn in Alingsås district. After about forty minutes the car made a sharp turn onto a forest road at a sign that said GOSSEBERGA. She had driven on and parked behind a barn in a clump of trees about a hundred yards north of the access road, then returned on foot.

She had never heard of Gosseberga, but as far as she could tell the name referred to the house and barn in front of her. She had passed the mailbox on the road. Painted on it was P.O. BOX 192—K. A. BODIN. The name meant nothing to her.

She had made a wide circuit of the buildings and finally selected her lookout spot. She had the afternoon sun at her back. Since she'd gotten into position at around 3:30, only one thing had happened. At 4:00 the driver of the Renault came out of the house. He exchanged some words in the doorway with someone she could not see. Then he drove away and did not come back. Otherwise she had seen no movement at the farm. She waited patiently and watched the building through a pair of Minolta 8x binoculars.

Blomkvist drummed his fingers in annoyance on the tabletop in the restaurant car. The X2000 had stopped in Katrineholm and had been standing there for almost an hour. There was some malfunction in one of the carriages that had to be fixed. An announcement apologized for the delay.

He sighed in frustration and ordered more coffee. At last, fifteen minutes later, the train started up with a jerk. He looked at his watch. 8:00 p.m.

He should have taken a plane or rented a car.

He was now even more troubled by the feeling that he had started too late.

At around 6:00 p.m. someone had turned on a lamp in a room on the ground floor, and shortly after that an oil lamp was lit. Salander glimpsed shadows in what she imagined was the kitchen, to the right of the front door, but she could not make out any faces.

Then the front door opened and the giant named Ronald Niedermann came out. He wore dark trousers and a tight T-shirt that emphasized his muscles. She had been right. She saw once more that Niedermann really was massive. But he was flesh and blood like everyone else, no matter what Paolo Roberto and Miriam Wu had been through. Niedermann walked around the house and went into the barn where the car was parked. He came out with a small bag and went back inside the house.

After only a few minutes he appeared again. He was accompanied by a short, thin older man who was using a crutch. It was too dark for Salander to make out his features, but she felt an icy chill creep along the back of her neck.

Daaaddyyy, I'm heeeere . . .

She watched Zalachenko and Niedermann as they walked up the road. They stopped at the shed, where Niedermann collected some firewood. Then they went back to the house and closed the door.

Salander lay still for several minutes. Then she lowered her binoculars and retreated until she was completely concealed among the trees. She opened her backpack, took out a thermos, and poured some coffee. She put a lump of sugar in her mouth and began to suck on it. She ate a cheese sandwich she had bought earlier in the day on the way to Göteborg. As she ate she thought about the situation.

After she had finished she took out Nieminen's Polish P-83 Wanad. She ejected the magazine and checked that nothing was blocking the bolt or the bore. She did a blind fire. She had six rounds of 9 mm Makarov. That should be enough. She shoved the magazine back in place and chambered a round. She put the safety catch on and slipped the weapon into her right-hand jacket pocket.

Salander began her advance towards the house, moving in a circle through the woods. She had gone about a hundred and fifty yards when suddenly she stopped in mid-stride.

In the margin of his copy of *Arithmetica,* Pierre de Fermat had jotted the words *I have a truly marvellous demonstration of this proposition which this margin is too narrow to contain.*

The square had been converted to a cube, $(x^3 + y^3 = z^3)$, and mathematicians had spent centuries looking for the answer to Fermat's riddle. By the time Andrew Wiles solved the puzzle in the 1990s, he had been at it for ten years using the world's most advanced computer programme.

And all of a sudden she understood. The answer was so disarmingly simple. A game with numbers that lined up and then fell into place in a simple formula that was most similar to a rebus.

Fermat had no computer, of course, and Wiles' solution was based on mathematics that had not been invented when Fermat formulated his theorem. Fermat would never have been able to produce the proof that Wiles had presented. Fermat's solution was quite different.

She was so stunned that she had to sit down on a tree stump. She gazed straight ahead as she checked the equation.

So that's what he meant. No wonder mathematicians were tearing out their hair.

Then she giggled.

A philosopher would have had a better chance of solving this riddle.

She wished she could have known Fermat.

He was a cocky devil.

After a while she stood up and continued her approach through the trees. She kept the barn between her and the house.

CHAPTER 31

Thursday, April 7

Salander got into the barn through the outside hatch to an old manure drain. There were no livestock. She saw that the barn contained three cars—the white Volvo from Auto-Expert, an old Ford, and a somewhat newer Saab. Further in was a rusty harrow and other tools from the days when this had been a working farm.

She lingered in the darkness of the barn and watched the house. It was dusk and the lights were on in all the rooms on the ground floor. She couldn't see any movement, but she thought she saw the flickering glow of a television set. She glanced at her watch. 7:30. Time for *Rapport*.

She was surprised that Zalachenko would have chosen to live in such an isolated place. It was not like the man she remembered. She would never have expected to find him out in the country in a little white farmhouse. In some anonymous villa community, maybe, or in a vacation spot abroad. He must have made more enemies even than Salander herself. She was troubled that the place looked so undefended. But she had no doubt that he had weapons in the house.

After lingering for a long time, she slipped out of the barn into the twilight. She hurried across the yard, keeping her step light and her back to the facade of the house. Then she heard the faint sound of music. She walked noiselessly around the house and tried to peer through the windows, but they were too high.

Salander was instinctively uneasy. For the first half of her life she had lived in fear of the man inside that house. During the second half, ever since she had failed in her attempt to kill him, she had waited for the moment when he would come back into her life. This time she wasn't going to make any mistakes.

Zalachenko might be an old cripple, but he was a trained assassin who had survived on more than one field of battle. Besides, there was Ronald Niedermann to take into account. She would have much preferred to surprise Zalachenko outdoors, where he would be unprotected. She had no wish to talk to him and would have been satisfied with a rifle and a telescopic lens. But she had no rifle, and it was unlikely that he'd be taking an evening stroll. If she wanted to wait for a better opportunity, she would have to withdraw and spend the night in the woods. She had no sleeping bag, and even though the evening was mild, the night would be cold. Now that she had him within reach, she didn't want to risk letting him slip away again. She thought about Miriam Wu and about her mother.

She would have to get inside the house, but that was the worst possible scenario. Sure, she could knock on the door and fire her gun as soon as the door opened, and then go in to find the other bastard. But whoever was left would be alerted, and he would probably be armed. Time for a risk assessment. *What were the options?*

She caught sight of Niedermann's profile as he walked past a window only a few yards from her. He was saying something over his shoulder to someone.

Both of them were in the room to the left of the front door. Salander made up her mind. She took the pistol out of her jacket pocket, clicked off the safety, and moved silently onto the porch. She held the gun in her left hand as she pressed the front door handle down with excruciating caution. It was unlocked. She frowned and hesitated. The door had double dead bolts.

Zalachenko should not have left the door unlocked. It was giving her goose bumps on the back of her neck.

It felt wrong.

The hallway was black as pitch. To the right she glimpsed the stairs to the upper floor. There were two doors straight ahead and one to the left. Light was seeping through a crack above the door. She stood still and listened. Then she heard a voice and the scraping of a chair in the room to the left.

She took two swift steps and threw open the door and aimed her gun at . . . *the room was empty.*

She heard the rustle of clothing behind her and spun around like a lizard. As she tried to raise the gun to firing position, one of Niedermann's enormous hands closed like an iron vise around her neck and the other clamped around her gun hand. He held her by the neck and lifted her straight up in the air as if she were a doll.

For a moment she kicked her feet in midair. Then she twisted around and kicked at Niedermann's crotch. She hit his hip instead. It felt like kicking a tree trunk. Her vision was going black as he squeezed her neck and she felt herself drop the gun.

Fuckers.

Then Niedermann threw her across the room. She landed on a sofa with a crash and slid to the floor. She felt blood rushing to her head and staggered to her feet. She saw a heavy glass ashtray on a table and grabbed it and tried to fling it backhand. Niedermann caught her arm in mid-swing. She reached into her left pants pocket with her free hand and pulled out the Taser, twisting around to shove it into Niedermann's crotch.

She felt a hefty jolt from the electric shock come through the arm Niedermann was holding her with. She had expected him to collapse in pain. Instead he looked down at her with a surprised expression. Salander's eyes widened in alarm. He seemed to experience some unpleasantness, but if he felt any pain he ignored it. *This man is not normal.*

Niedermann bent and took the Taser from her and examined it with a puzzled look. Then he slapped her across the head. It was like being hit with a club. She tumbled to the floor next to the sofa. She looked up and saw that Niedermann was watching her curiously, as if wondering what her next move would be. Like a cat getting ready to play with its prey.

Then she sensed a movement in the doorway. She turned her head.

He came slowly into the light.

He was leaning on a forearm crutch and she could see a prosthesis sticking out from his pants leg. There were two fingers missing from his left hand.

She raised her eyes to his face. The left half was a patchwork of scar tissue. His ear was a little stump and he had no eyebrows. He was bald. She remembered him as a virile and athletic man with wavy black hair. Now he was about five foot four, and emaciated.

"Hello, Pappa," she said tonelessly.

Alexander Zalachenko regarded his daughter without expression.

Niedermann turned on the ceiling light. He checked that she had no more weapons by running his hands over her clothes and then clicked the safety on the P-83 Wanad and released the magazine. Zalachenko shuffled past them, sat in an armchair, and picked up a remote control.

Salander's eyes fell on the TV behind him. Zalachenko pressed the remote, and she saw a green flickering image of the area behind the barn and part of the driveway to the house. *Infrared camera. They had known she was coming.*

"I was beginning to think that you wouldn't dare to make an approach," Zalachenko said. "We've been watching you since 4:00. You tripped just about every alarm around the farm."

"Motion detectors," Salander said.

"Two by the road and four in the clearing on the other side of the field. You set up your observation post on precisely the spot where we'd positioned alarms. It's the best view of the farm. Usually it's moose or deer, and sometimes berry-pickers who come too close. But we don't often get to see somebody sneak up to the front door with a gun in their hand." He paused for a moment. "Did you really think Zalachenko would sit in his little house in the country completely unprotected?"

Salander massaged the back of her neck and began to get up.

"Stay there on the floor," Zalachenko said.

Niedermann stopped fiddling with the gun and watched her quietly. He raised an eyebrow and smiled at her. Salander remembered Paolo Roberto's battered face on TV and decided it would be a good idea to stay on the floor. She breathed out and leaned back against the sofa.

Zalachenko held out his intact right hand. Niedermann pulled a weapon out of his waistband, cocked it, and gave it to him. Salander noticed that it was a Sig Sauer, standard police issue. Zalachenko nodded, and Niedermann turned away and put on a jacket. He left the room and Salander heard the front door open and close.

"In case you get any stupid ideas, if you even try to get up I'll shoot you right in the gut."

Salander relaxed. He might manage to get off two, maybe three shots before she could reach him, and he was probably using ammo that would make her bleed to death in a few minutes.

"You look like shit," Zalachenko said. "Like a fucking whore. But you've got my eyes."

"Does it hurt?" she asked, nodding at his prosthesis.

Zalachenko looked at her for a long time. "No. Not anymore."

Salander stared at him.

"You'd really like to kill me, wouldn't you?" he said.

She said nothing. He laughed.

"I've thought about you over the years. In fact almost every time I look in the mirror."

"You should have left my mother alone."

"Your mother was a whore."

Salander's eyes turned black as coal. "She was no whore. She worked as a cashier in a supermarket and tried to make ends meet."

Zalachenko laughed again. "You can have whatever fantasies you want about her. But I know that she was a whore. And she made sure to get pregnant right away and then tried to get me to marry her. As if I'd marry a whore."

Salander looked down the barrel of the gun and hoped he would relax his concentration for an instant.

"The firebomb was sneaky. I hated you for that. But in time it didn't matter. You weren't worth the energy. If you'd only let things be."

"Bullshit. Bjurman asked you to fix me."

"That was another thing entirely. He needed a film that you have, so I made a little business deal."

"And you thought I'd give the film to you."

"Yes, my dear daughter. I'm convinced that you would have. You have no idea how cooperative people can be when Ronald asks for something. And especially when he starts up a chain saw and saws off one of your feet. In this case it would have been appropriate compensation—a foot for a foot."

Salander thought about Miriam at the hands of Niedermann in the warehouse. Zalachenko misinterpreted her expression.

"You don't have to worry. We don't intend to cut you up. But tell me: did Bjurman rape you?"

She said nothing.

"Damn, what appalling taste he must have had. I read in the paper that you're some sort of fucking dyke. That's no surprise. There can't be a man who'd want you."

Salander still said nothing.

"Maybe I should ask Niedermann to screw you. You look as if you need it." He thought about it. "Although Ronald doesn't have sex with girls. He's not a fairy. He just doesn't have sex."

"Then maybe you should screw me," Salander said to provoke him.

Come closer. Make a mistake.

"No, thanks all the same. That would be perverse."

They were silent for a moment.

"What are we waiting for?" Salander asked.

"My companion is coming right back. He just had to move his car and run a little errand. Where's your sister?"

Salander shrugged.

"Answer me."

"I don't know and I honestly don't give a shit."

He laughed again. "Sisterly love, eh? Camilla was always the one with the brains—you were just worthless filth. But I have to admit it's quite satisfying to see you again up close."

"Zalachenko," she said, "you're a tiresome fuck. Was it Niedermann who shot Bjurman?"

"Naturally. Ronald is the perfect soldier. He not only obeys orders, he also takes his own initiative when necessary."

"Where did you dig him up?"

Zalachenko gave his daughter a peculiar look. He opened his mouth as if to say something, but decided against it. He glanced at the front door and then smiled at Salander.

"You mean you haven't worked it out yet?" he said. "According to Bjurman you're supposed to be a good researcher." Then Zalachenko roared with laughter. "We used to hang out together in Spain in the early nineties when I was convalescing from your little firebomb. He was twenty-two and became my arms and legs. He isn't an employee . . . it's a partnership. We have a flourishing business."

"Sex trafficking."

"You could say that we've diversified and deal with many different goods and services. Our business model is to stay in the background and never be seen. But you must have worked out who Ronald is."

Salander did not know what he was getting at.

"He's your brother," Zalachenko said.

"No," Salander said, breathless.

Zalachenko laughed again. But the barrel of the pistol was still pointed unnervingly at her.

"Well, I should say he's your half brother," Zalachenko said. "The result of a brief diversion during an assignment I had in Germany in 1969."

"You've turned your son into a murderer."

"Oh no, I've only helped him realize his potential. He had the ability to kill long before I took over his training. And he's going to run the family business long after I'm gone."

"Does he know that we're half siblings?"

"Of course. But if you think you can appeal to his brotherly love, forget it. I'm his family. You're just a buzz on the horizon. And he isn't your only sibling. You have at least four more brothers and three sisters in various countries. One of your other brothers is an idiot, but another actually has potential. He runs the Tallinn arm of the business. But Ronald is the only one who really lives up to the Zalachenko genes."

"I don't suppose my sisters will get a role in the family business."

Zalachenko looked startled at the suggestion.

"Zalachenko . . . you're just an ordinary asshole who hates women. Why did you kill Bjurman?"

"Bjurman was a moron. He couldn't believe it when he learned you were my daughter. He was one of the few people in this country who knew about my background. I have to admit that it made me nervous when he contacted me out of the blue, but then everything turned out for the best. He died and you got the blame."

"But why shoot him?"

"Well, it wasn't really planned. It's always useful to have a back door into Säpo. Even if I haven't needed one for years. And even if he's a moron. But that journalist in Enskede had somehow found a connection between him and me and called him just as Ronald was at his apartment. Bjurman panicked, went berserk. Ronald had to make a decision on the spot. He acted quite correctly."

Salander's heart sank like a stone when her father confirmed what she had already suspected. Svensson had found a connection. She had talked to Svensson and Johansson for more than an hour. She'd liked the woman immediately but was a little cooler towards the journalist. He reminded her too much of Blomkvist—an insufferable do-gooder who thought he could change everything with a book. But she had recognized his honest intentions.

It turned out that her visit had been a waste of time. They couldn't point her to Zalachenko. Svensson had found his name and started digging, but he wasn't able to identify him.

Instead, she had made a devastating mistake. She knew that there had to be a connection between Bjurman and Zalachenko, and she asked questions about Bjurman in an attempt to ascertain whether Svensson had come across his name. He hadn't, but his suspicions were instantly aroused. He zeroed right in on Bjurman and plied her with questions.

She gave him very little, but he had understood that Salander was a player in the drama. He also realized that he had information she wanted. They had agreed to meet again for further discussions after Easter. Then Salander had gone home to bed. When she woke up the next morning, she was greeted by the news that two people had been murdered in an apartment in Enskede.

She had given Svensson only one piece of usable information: the name Nils Bjurman. He must have called Bjurman the minute she left the apartment.

And she was the link. If she hadn't visited Svensson, he and Johansson would still be alive.

Zalachenko said: "You have no idea how surprised we were when the police started hunting you for the murders."

Salander bit her lip.

Zalachenko scrutinized her. "How did you find me?" he said.

She shrugged.

"Lisbeth . . . Ronald is coming back soon. I can tell him to break the bones in your body one by one until you answer. Save us the trouble."

"The P.O. box. I traced Niedermann's car from the rental agency and waited until that pimply shit showed up and emptied the box."

"Aha. So simple. Thanks. I'll remember that."

The muzzle of the pistol was still pointing at her chest.

"Do you really think this is going to blow over?" Salander said. "You've made too many mistakes. The police are going to identify you."

"I know. Björck called yesterday and told me that a journalist from *Millennium* has been sniffing around and that it was just a matter of time. It's possible that we'll have to do something about that."

"It'll be a long list," Salander said. "Mikael Blomkvist and Erika Berger, the editor in chief, the managing editor, and half a dozen others at Millennium alone. And then you have Dragan Armansky and some of his staff at Milton Security. And Detective Inspector Bublanski and everyone involved in the investigation. How many people would you have to kill to cover this up? No, they're going to get to you."

Zalachenko gave her a horrible twisted smile.

"So what? I haven't shot anybody, and there isn't one shred of forensic evidence against me. They can identify whoever the hell they want. Believe me . . . they can search this house from top to bottom and they won't find so much as a speck of dust that could connect me to any criminal activity. It was Säpo who locked you up in the asylum, not me, and it won't take much for them to put all the papers on the table."

"Niedermann," Lisbeth reminded him.

"Early tomorrow morning Ronald is going on vacation abroad for a while and he'll wait out whatever develops."

Zalachenko gave Salander a triumphant look.

"You're still going to be the prime suspect. So it's best if you just disappear."

It was almost an hour before Niedermann returned. He was wearing boots.

Salander glanced at the man who according to her father was her half brother. She couldn't see the slightest resemblance. In fact, he was her diametrical opposite. But she felt very strongly that there was something wrong with Niedermann. His build, the weak face, and the voice that hadn't really broken—they all seemed like genetic defects of some sort. He had evidently been insensitive to the Taser, and his hands were enormous. Nothing about Ronald Niedermann seemed quite normal.

There are all sorts of genetic defects in the Zalachenko family, she thought bitterly.

"Ready?" Zalachenko asked.

Niedermann nodded. He held out his hand for the Sig Sauer.

"I'll come with you," Zalachenko said.

Niedermann hesitated. "It's quite a walk."

"I'll come anyway. Get my jacket."

Niedermann shrugged and did as he was told. Zalachenko

put on his jacket and vanished into the next room for a while. Salander watched as Niedermann screwed what appeared to be a homemade silencer onto the gun.

"All right, let's go," Zalachenko said from the door.

Niedermann bent and pulled Salander to her feet. She looked him in the eye.

"I'm going to kill you too," she said.

"You're very sure of yourself. I'll say that for you," her father said.

Niedermann smiled mildly and then pushed her towards the front door and out into the yard. He kept a firm grip on the back of her neck. His fingers could reach almost all the way around it. He steered her towards the woods beyond the barn.

They moved slowly and Niedermann stopped occasionally to let Zalachenko catch up. They both had powerful flashlights. When they reached the edge of the woods Niedermann let go of Salander's neck. He kept the pistol trained on her back.

They followed a difficult path for about four hundred yards. Salander stumbled twice, but each time was lifted to her feet.

"Turn right here," Niedermann said.

After about fifty feet they came into a clearing. Lisbeth saw a hole in the ground. In the beam of Niedermann's flashlight she saw a spade stuck in a mound of soil. Then she understood Niedermann's assignment. He pushed her towards the hole and she tripped and went down on all fours with her hands buried deep in the sandy earth. She got up and gave him an expressionless look. Zalachenko was taking his time, and Niedermann waited patiently. The muzzle of the pistol was unswervingly aimed at her chest.

Zalachenko was out of breath. It was more than a minute before he could speak.

"I ought to say something, but I don't think I have anything to say to you," he said.

"That's fine by me," Salander said. "I don't have much to say to you either." She gave him a lopsided smile.

"Let's get it over with," Zalachenko said.

"I'm glad that my very last act was to have you locked away forever," Salander said. "The police will be here tonight."

"Bullshit. I was expecting you to try a bluff. You came here to kill me and nothing else. You didn't say anything to anybody."

Salander's smile broadened. She suddenly looked malevolent.

"May I show you something, Pappa?"

Slowly she reached into her left-hand pants pocket and took out a rectangular object. Niedermann watched her every move.

"Every word you've said in the past hour has been broadcast over Internet radio."

She held up her Palm Tungsten T3 computer.

Zalachenko's brow furrowed where his eyebrows should have been.

"Let's see that," he said, holding out his good hand.

Salander lobbed the PDA to him. He caught it in midair.

"Bullshit," Zalachenko said. "This is an ordinary Palm."

As Niedermann bent to look at her computer, Salander flung a fistful of sand right into his eyes. He was blinded, but instinctively fired a round from his pistol. Salander had already moved two steps to one side and the bullet only tore a hole through the air where she had been standing. She grabbed the spade and swung it at his gun hand. She hit him with the sharp edge full force across the knuckles and saw his Sig Sauer fly in a wide arc away from them and into some bushes. Blood spurted from a gash above his index finger.

He should be screaming with pain.

Niedermann fumbled with his wounded hand as he desperately tried to rub his eyes with the other. Her only chance to win this fight was to cause him massive damage, and as quickly as possible. If it came down to a physical contest she was hopelessly lost. She needed five seconds to make it into the woods. She swung the spade back over her shoulder and tried to twist the handle so that the edge would hit first, but she was in the wrong position. The flat side of the spade smacked into Niedermann's face.

Niedermann grunted as his nose broke for the second time in a matter of days. He was still blinded by the sand, but he swung his right arm and managed to shove Salander away from him. She stumbled over a tree root. For a second she was down on the ground but sprang instantly to her feet. Niedermann was briefly out of action.

I'm going to make it.

She took two steps towards the undergrowth when out of the corner of her eye—*click*—she saw Zalachenko raise his arm.

The fucking old man has a gun too.

The realization cracked like a whip through her mind.

She changed direction in the same instant the shot was fired. The bullet struck the outside of her hip and made her spin off balance.

She felt no pain.

The second bullet hit her in the back and stopped against her left shoulder blade. A paralyzing pain sliced through her body.

She went down on her knees. For a few seconds she could not move. She was conscious that Zalachenko was behind her, about twenty feet away. With one last surge of energy she stubbornly hurled herself to her feet and took a wobbly step towards the cover of the bushes.

Zalachenko had time to aim.

The third bullet caught her about an inch below the top of her left ear. It penetrated her skull and caused a spiderweb of radial cracks in her cranium. The lead came to rest in the grey matter about two inches beneath the cerebral cortex, by the cerebrum.

For Salander the medical detail was academic. The bullet caused immediate massive trauma. Her last sensation was a glowing red shock that turned into a white light.

Then darkness.

Click.

Zalachenko tried to fire one more round, but his hands were shaking so hard that he couldn't aim. *She almost got away.* And then he realized that she was dead and he lowered his weapon, shivering as the adrenaline flowed through his body. He looked down at his gun. He had considered leaving it behind, but had gone to get it and put it in his jacket pocket as though he needed a mascot. *A monster.* They were two fully grown men, and one of them was Ronald Niedermann, who had been armed with his Sig Sauer. *And that fucking whore almost got away.*

He glanced at his daughter's body. In the beam from his flashlight she looked like a bloody rag doll. He clicked the safety catch on and stuffed the pistol into his jacket pocket and went over to Niedermann, who was standing helpless, tears running from his dirt-filled eyes and blood from his hand and nose. "I think I broke my nose again," he said.

"Idiot," Zalachenko said. "She almost got away."

Niedermann kept rubbing his eyes. They didn't hurt, but the tears were flowing and he could scarcely see.

"Stand up straight, damn it." Zalachenko shook his head in contempt. "What the hell would you do without me?"

Niedermann blinked in despair. Zalachenko limped over to his daughter's body and grabbed her jacket by the collar. He dragged her to the grave that was only a hole in the ground, too small even for Salander to lie stretched out. He lifted the body so that her feet were over the opening and let her tumble in. She landed facedown in a fetal position, her legs bent under her.

"Fill it in so we can go home," Zalachenko commanded.

It took the half-blind Niedermann a while to shovel the soil in around her. What was left over he spread out around the clearing with powerful jabs of the spade.

Zalachenko smoked a cigarette as he watched Niedermann work. He was still shivering, but the adrenaline had begun to subside. He felt a sudden relief that she was gone. He could still picture her eyes as she threw the firebomb all those many years ago.

It was 9:30 when Zalachenko shone his flashlight around and declared himself satisfied. It took a while longer to find the Sig Sauer in the undergrowth. Then they went back to the house. Zalachenko was feeling wonderfully gratified. He tended to Niedermann's hand. The spade had cut deep and he had to find a needle and thread to sew up the wound—a skill he had learned in military school in Novosibirsk as a fifteen-year-old. At least he didn't need to administer an anaesthetic. But it was possible that the wound was sufficiently serious for Niedermann to have to go to the hospital. He put a splint on the finger and bandaged it. They would decide in the morning.

When he was finished he got himself a beer as Niedermann rinsed his eyes over and over in the bathroom.

CHAPTER 32

Thursday, April 7

Blomkvist arrived at Göteborg Central Station just after 9:00 p.m. The X2000 had made up some time, but it was still late. He had spent the last hour of the journey calling car rental companies. He'd first thought of finding a car in Alingsås and getting off there, but the office was closed already. Ultimately he managed to order a Volkswagen through a hotel booking agency in the city. He could pick up the car at Järntorget. He decided not to try to navigate Göteborg's confusing local traffic and incomprehensible ticket system and took a cab to the lot.

When he got to the car there was no map in the glove compartment. He bought one in a gas station, along with a flashlight, a bottle of mineral water, and a cup of coffee, which he put in the holder on the dashboard. It was 10:30 before he drove out of the city on the road to Alingsås.

A fox stopped and looked about restlessly. He knew that something was buried there. But from somewhere nearby came the rustle of an unwary night animal and the fox was instantly on the alert for easier prey. He took a cautious step. But before he continued his hunt he lifted his hind leg and pissed on the spot to mark his territory.

Bublanski did not normally call his colleagues late in the evening, but this time he couldn't resist. He picked up the phone and dialled Modig's number.

"Pardon me for calling so late. Are you up?"

"No problem."

"I've just finished going through Björck's report."

"I'm sure you had as much trouble putting it down as I did."

"Sonja . . . how do you make sense of what's going on?"

"It seems to me that Gunnar Björck, a prominent name on the list of johns, if you remember, had Lisbeth Salander put in an asylum after she tried to protect herself and her mother from a lunatic sadist who was working for Säpo. He was abetted in this by Dr. Teleborian, among others, on whose testimony we in part based our own evaluation of her mental state."

"This changes the entire picture we have of her."

"It explains a great deal."

"Sonja, can you pick me up in the morning at 8:00?"

"Of course."

"We're going to go down to Smådalarö to have a talk with Gunnar Björck. I made some enquiries. He's on sick leave."

"I'm looking forward to it already."

Beckman looked at his wife as she stood by the window in the living room, staring out at the water. She had her mobile in her hand, and he knew that she was waiting for a call from Blomkvist. She looked so unhappy that he went over and put his arm around her.

"Blomkvist is a grown man," he said. "But if you're really so worried you should call that policeman."

Berger sighed. "I should have done that hours ago. But that's not why I'm unhappy."

"Is it something I should know about?"

"I've been hiding something from you. And from Mikael. And from everyone else at the magazine."

"Hiding? Hiding what?"

She turned to her husband and told him that she had been offered the job of editor in chief at *Svenska Morgon-Posten.* Beckman raised his eyebrows.

"But I don't understand why you didn't tell me," he said. "That's a huge coup. Congratulations."

"It's just that I feel like a traitor."

"Mikael will understand. Everyone has to move on when it's time. And right now it's time for you."

"I know."

"Have you already made up your mind?"

"Yes. I've made up my mind. But I haven't had the guts to tell anybody. And it feels as if I'm leaving in the midst of a huge disaster."

Beckman took his wife in his arms.

Armansky rubbed his eyes and looked out into the darkness.

"We ought to call Bublanski," he said.

"No," Palmgren said. "Neither Bublanski nor any other authority figure has ever lifted a finger to help her. Let her take care of her own affairs."

Armansky looked at Salander's former guardian. He was still amazed by the improvement in Palmgren's condition compared with when he last saw him over Christmas. He still slurred his words, but he had a new vitality in his eyes. There was also a fury about the man that Armansky had never seen before. Palmgren told him the whole story that Blomkvist had pieced together. Armansky was shocked.

"She's going to try to kill her father."

"That's possible," Palmgren said calmly.

"Or else Zalachenko might try to kill her."

"That's also possible."

"So we're just supposed to wait?"

"Dragan . . . you're a good person. But what Lisbeth Salander does or doesn't do, whether she survives or whether she dies, is not your responsibility."

Palmgren threw out his arms. All of a sudden he had rediscovered a coordination that he hadn't had in a long time. It was as though the drama of the past few weeks had revived his dulled senses.

"I've never been sympathetic towards people who take the law into their own hands. But I've never heard of anyone who had such a good reason to do so. At the risk of sounding like a cynic, what happens tonight will happen, no matter what you or I think. It's been written in the stars since she was born. And all that remains is for us to decide how we're going to behave towards Lisbeth if she makes it back."

Armansky sighed and looked grimly at the old lawyer.

"And if she spends the next ten years in prison, at least she was the one who chose that path. I'll still be her friend," Palmgren said.

"I had no idea you had such a libertarian view of humanity."

"Neither did I," he said.

Miriam Wu stared at the ceiling. She had the nightlight on and the radio was playing "On a Slow Boat to China" at a low volume.

The day before she had woken to find herself in the hospital where Paolo Roberto had brought her. She slept and woke restlessly and went to sleep again with no real grasp of passing time. The doctors told her that she had a concussion. In any case she needed to rest. She had a broken nose, three broken ribs, and bruises all over her body. Her left eyebrow was so swollen that her eye was merely a slit. It hurt whenever she tried to change position. It hurt when she breathed in. Her neck was painful and she was wearing a brace, just to be on the safe side. But the doctors had assured her that she would make a complete recovery.

When she awoke towards evening, Paolo Roberto was sitting next to her bed. He grinned and asked how she felt. She wondered if she looked as awful as he did.

She asked questions and he answered them. For some reason it didn't seem at all odd that he was a good friend of Salander's. He was a cocky devil. Lisbeth liked cocky devils, just as she detested pompous jerks. There was only a subtle difference, but Paolo Roberto belonged to the former category.

She now had an explanation for why he had suddenly sprung out of nowhere into the warehouse, but she was surprised that he'd decided so stubbornly to pursue the van. And she was frightened by the news that the police were digging up bodies in the woods around the warehouse.

"Thank you," she said. "You saved my life."

He shook his head and sat quietly for a while.

"I tried to explain it to Blomkvist. He didn't really get it. But I think you might understand since you box yourself."

She knew what he meant. No-one who hadn't been there would ever know what it was to fight a monster who couldn't feel pain. She thought about how helpless she'd been.

After that she had just held his bandaged hand. They didn't speak for a long time. There was nothing more to say. When she woke up, he was gone. She wished that Lisbeth would get in touch. She was the one Niedermann had been after.

Miriam was afraid that he would catch her.

Salander couldn't breathe. She had no sense of time, but she knew that she had been shot, and she realized—more by instinct than by rational thought—that she was buried underground. Her left arm was unusable, she couldn't move a muscle without waves of pain shooting through her shoulder, and she was floating in and out of a foggy consciousness. *I have to get air.* Her head was bursting with a throbbing pain the likes of which she had never felt before.

Her right hand had ended up underneath her face, and she began instinctively to nudge the earth away from her nose and mouth. It was sandy and relatively dry. She managed to create a space the size of her fist in front of her face.

How long she had been lying there buried she had no idea. But finally she formulated a lucid thought and it gripped her with panic. *He buried me alive.* She couldn't breathe. She couldn't move. A vast weight of soil held her bound to the primal rock.

She tried to move a leg, but she could scarcely tense her muscles. Then she made the mistake of trying to get up. She pressed down with her head to try to raise herself and the pain flew like an electric charge through her temples. *I can't throw up.* She sank back into muddled consciousness.

When she could think again, she felt carefully to determine which parts of her body were functional. The only limb she could move an inch or two was her right hand, the one in front of her face. *I have to get air.* The air was above her, above the grave.

Salander began to scratch. She pressed down on her elbow and managed to make a little room to manoeuvre. With the back of her hand she enlarged the area in front of her face by pressing the dirt away from her. *I need to dig.*

She discovered that she had a cavity within her fetal position, between her elbows and her knees. That was where most of the air that was keeping her alive had been trapped. She began desperately twisting her upper body back and forth and felt how the soil ran into the space beneath her. The pressure on her chest lifted a little. She could move her arm.

Minute by minute she worked in a semiconscious state. She

scratched sandy earth from her face and pressed handful after handful into the cavity beneath her. Gradually she managed to free her arm so that she could shift the soil away from the top of her head. Inch by inch she enlarged the space around her head. She felt something hard and was suddenly holding a small root or stick in her hand. She scratched upwards. The soil was still full of air and not very compact.

The fox paused by Salander's grave on the way back to his den. He had found two field mice and was feeling satisfied when suddenly he sensed another presence. He froze and pricked up his ears. His whiskers and nose were quivering.

Salander's fingers emerged like something dead from beneath the earth. Had there been any human watching, he would probably have reacted like the fox. He was gone like a shot.

Salander felt cool air stream down her arm. She could breathe again.

It took her half an hour more to free herself from the grave. She found it odd that she couldn't use her left hand, but mechanically went on scratching at the dirt and sand with her right.

She needed something else to dig with. She pulled her arm down into the hole, got to her breast pocket and worked the cigarette case free. She opened it and used it as a scoop. She scraped soil loose and flicked it away. And then at last she could move her right shoulder and managed to press it upwards through the earth above her. Then she scraped more sand and dirt and eventually was able to straighten her head. She now had her right arm and head above the ground. When she had released part of her upper body she could start squirming upwards an inch at a time until the ground suddenly released its grip on her legs.

She crawled from the grave with her eyes closed and didn't

stop until her shoulder hit a tree trunk. Slowly she turned her
body so that she had the tree to lean on and wiped the dirt
from her eyes with the back of her hand before she opened
them. It was pitch-black around her and the air was icy cold.
She was sweating. She felt a dull pain in her head, in her left
shoulder, and in her hip, but didn't spend any energy wondering why. She sat still for ten minutes, breathing. Then it came
to her that she couldn't stay there.

She struggled to her feet as the world swirled around her.

She felt instantly sick and bent over to vomit.

Then she started to walk. She had no idea which direction
she was going. The pain in her left hip was excruciating and
she kept stumbling to her knees. Each time an even greater
pain shot through her head.

She didn't know how long she'd been walking when she saw
a light out of the corner of her eye. She changed direction. It
was only when she was standing by the woodshed in the yard
that she realized she had walked straight back to Zalachenko's
farmhouse. She swayed like a drunk.

*Photo cells on the driveway and in the clearing. She had come
from the other direction. They would not have noticed her.*

She was confused. She knew that she was in no condition to
take on Niedermann and Zalachenko. She looked at the white
farmhouse.

Click. Wood. Click. Fire.

She fantasized about a gasoline can and a match.

With enormous effort she turned towards the shed and
staggered over to a door that was secured with a crossbar. She
managed to lift it by putting her right shoulder under it. She
heard the noise when the crossbar fell to the ground and hit
the side of the door with a bang. She took a step into the darkness and looked around.

It was a woodshed. There was no gasoline.

. . .

At the kitchen table Zalachenko looked up when he heard the sound of the falling crossbar. He pulled the curtain aside and peered out into the darkness. It was a few seconds before his eyes adjusted. The wind was blowing harder now. The weather forecast had predicted a stormy weekend. Then he saw that the door to the woodshed was ajar.

He and Niedermann had brought in wood earlier that afternoon. It had been unnecessary, but its purpose was to provide Salander with confirmation that she had come to the right place and to draw her out.

Niedermann had obviously not set the crossbar in place properly. He could be so phenomenally clumsy. Zalachenko glanced towards the door of the living room, where Niedermann had dozed off on the sofa. He thought of waking him, but decided not to.

To find gasoline Salander would have to go to the barn, where the cars were parked. She leaned against a chopping block, breathing hard. She had to rest. She sat there for about a minute before she heard the halting steps of Zalachenko's prosthesis.

In the dark Blomkvist took a wrong turn at Mellby, north of Sollebrunn. Instead of getting off at Nossebro he had continued north. He realized his mistake just before he got to Trökörna. He stopped and looked at the map.

He cursed and turned back towards Nossebro.

With her right hand Salander grabbed the axe from the chopping block a second before Zalachenko came into the woodshed. She didn't have the strength to lift it over her shoulder, but she swung it with one hand in an upward arc, putting her weight on her uninjured hip and turning her body in a semi-circle.

At the same moment that Zalachenko turned on the light switch, the blade of the axe struck him across the right side of his face, smashing his cheekbone and penetrating into his fore-head. He didn't know what had happened, but in the next second his brain registered the pain and he howled as if possessed.

Niedermann woke with a start and sat up, bewildered. He heard a screaming that at first he couldn't believe was human. It was coming from outside. Then he realized it was Zalachenko. He got swiftly to his feet.

Salander planted her feet and swung the axe again, but her body was not obeying orders. Her aim was to bury the axe in her father's head, but she had exhausted all her strength and struck him far from the intended target, just below his kneecap. But the weight of the axe head buried it so deep that it stuck and was pulled out of her hands when Zalachenko pitched forward into the shed. He was screaming incessantly.

She bent again to grasp the axe. The earth shook as lightning flashed inside her head. She had to sit down. She reached out her hand and felt his jacket pockets. He still had the gun, and she focused her gaze as the ground swayed.

A Browning .22 calibre.

A fucking Boy Scout pistol.

That was why she was still alive. If she'd been hit with a bullet from Niedermann's Sig Sauer or from a revolver with heavier ammo, she would have a gigantic hole through her skull.

At that moment she heard the stumbling approach of Niedermann, who then filled the doorway of the shed. He stopped short and registered the scene before him with uncomprehending and staring eyes. Zalachenko was wailing like a man possessed. His face was a bloody mask. He had an axe wedged in his knee. A bloody and filthy Salander was sitting on the floor next to him. She looked like something from a horror movie, and far too many of those had already played out in Niedermann's mind.

He, who could feel no pain and was built like a tank, had never liked the dark.

With his own eyes he had seen creatures in the dark, and an indeterminate terror was always lurking, waiting for him. And now the terror had materialized.

The girl on the floor was dead. There was no doubt about that.

He had buried her himself.

Consequently, the creature on the floor was no girl, but a being from the other side of the grave who couldn't be conquered with human strength or weapons known to man.

The transformation from human being to corpse had already begun. Her skin had changed into a lizardlike armour. Her bared teeth were piercing spikes for ripping chunks of meat from her prey. Her reptilian tongue shot out and licked around her mouth. Her bloody hands had razor-sharp claws four inches long. He could see her eyes glowing. He could hear her growling low and saw her tense her muscles to pounce at his throat.

He saw clearly that she had a tail that curled and ominously began to whip the floor.

Then she raised the pistol and fired. The bullet passed so close to Niedermann's ear that he could feel the lash of the wind. He saw her mouth spout flames at him.

That was too much.

He stopped thinking.

He spun around and ran for his life. She fired another shot that missed him but that seemed to give him wings. He hopped over a fence and was swallowed up by the darkness of the field as he sprinted towards the main road.

Salander watched in astonishment as he disappeared from view.

She shuffled to the doorway and gazed into the darkness, but she couldn't see him. After a while Zalachenko stopped screaming, but he lay moaning in shock. She opened the pistol, checked that she had one round left, and considered shooting him in the head. Then she remembered that Niedermann was still there, out in the dark, and she had better save it. She would need more than one .22 bullet for him. But it was better than nothing.

It took her five minutes to put the crossbar in place. She staggered across the yard and into the house and found the telephone on a sideboard in the kitchen. She dialled a number she hadn't used in two years. The answering machine clicked in.

Hi. This is Mikael Blomkvist. I can't answer right now, but please leave your name and number and I'll call you as soon as I can.

Beep.

"Mir-g-kral," she said, and heard that her voice sounded like mush. She swallowed. "Mikael. It's Salander."

Then she did not know what to say.

She hung up the receiver.

Niedermann's Sig Sauer lay disassembled for cleaning on the kitchen table in front of her, and next to it Sonny Nieminen's P-83 Wanad. She dropped Zalachenko's Browning on the floor and lurched over to pick up the Wanad and check the magazine. She also found her Palm PDA and dropped it in her pocket. Then she hobbled to the sink and filled an unwashed cup with cold water. She drank four cups. When she looked up she saw her face in an old shaving mirror on the wall. She almost fired a shot out of sheer fright. What she saw reminded her more of an animal than a human being. She was a mad-woman with a distorted face and a gaping mouth. She was plastered with dirt. Her face and neck were a coagulated gruel of blood and soil. Now she had an idea what Niedermann had encountered in the woodshed.

She went closer to the mirror and was suddenly aware that her left leg was dragging behind her. She had a sharp pain in her hip where Zalachenko's first bullet had hit her. His second bullet had struck her shoulder and paralyzed her left arm. It hurt.

But the pain in her head was so sharp it made her stagger. Slowly she raised her right hand and fumbled across the back of her head. With her fingers she could feel the crater of the entry wound.

As she fingered the hole in her skull she realized with sudden horror that she was touching her own brain, that she was so seriously wounded she was dying or maybe should already be dead. She couldn't comprehend how she could still be on her feet.

She was suddenly overcome by a numbing weariness. She wasn't sure if she was about to faint or fall asleep, but she made her way to the kitchen bench, where she stretched out and laid the unwounded right side of her head on a cushion.

She had to regain her strength, but she knew that she couldn't risk sleeping while Niedermann was still at large. Sooner or later he would come back. Sooner or later Zalachenko would manage to get out of the woodshed and drag himself to the house. But she no longer had the energy to stay upright. She was freezing. She clicked off the safety on the pistol.

Niedermann stood, undecided, on the road from Sollebrunn to Nossebro. He was alone. It was dark. He had begun to think rationally again and was ashamed that he had run away. He didn't understand how it could have happened, but he came to the logical conclusion that she must have survived. *Somehow she must have managed to dig herself out.*

Zalachenko needed him. He ought to go back to the house and wring her neck.

At the same time he had a powerful feeling that everything was over. He had had that feeling for a long time. Things had started to go wrong and kept going wrong from the moment Bjurman had contacted them. Zalachenko had changed beyond recognition when he heard the name Lisbeth Salander. All the rules about caution and moderation he had preached for so many years had been blown away.

Niedermann hesitated.

Zalachenko needed to be looked after.

If she hadn't already killed him.

That meant there would be questions.

He bit his lower lip.

He had been his father's partner for many years. They had been good years. He had money put away and he also knew where Zalachenko had hidden his own fortune. He had the resources and the skill required to drive the business forward. The sensible thing would be to walk away from all this and not look back. If there was one thing that Zalachenko had drummed into him, it was always to retain the ability to walk away, without sentimentality, from a situation that felt unmanageable. That was a basic rule for survival. *Don't lift a finger for a lost cause.*

She wasn't supernatural. But she was bad news. She was his half sister.

He had underestimated her.

Niedermann was torn. Part of him wanted to go back and wring her neck. Part of him wanted to keep running through the night.

He had his passport and wallet in his pocket. He didn't want to go back. There was nothing at the farm he needed.

Except perhaps a car.

He was still hesitating when he saw the gleam of headlights approaching from the other side of the hill. He turned his head. All he needed was a car to get him to Göteborg.

For the first time in her life—at least since she had been a little girl—Salander was unable to take command of her situation. Over the years she had been mixed up in fights, subjected to abuse, been the object of both official and private injustices. She had taken many more punches to both body and soul than anyone should ever have to endure.

But she had been able to rebel every time. She had refused to answer Teleborian's questions, and when she was subjected to any kind of physical violence, she had been able to slink away and retreat.

A broken nose she could live with.

But she couldn't live with a hole in her skull.

This time she couldn't drag herself home to bed, pull the covers over her head, sleep for two days and then get up and go back to her daily routine as if nothing had happened.

She was so seriously injured that she couldn't cope with the situation by herself. She was so exhausted that her body refused to listen to her commands.

I have to sleep for a while, she thought. And suddenly she realized that if she closed her eyes and let go there was a good chance she would never wake up again. She analyzed this conclusion and gradually came to understand that she didn't care. On the contrary. She felt almost attracted by the thought. *To rest. To not wake up.*

Her last thoughts were of Miriam Wu.

Forgive me, Mimmi.

She was still holding Nieminen's pistol, with the safety off, when she closed her eyes.

. . .

Blomkvist saw Niedermann in the beam of his headlights from a long way off and recognized him at once. It was hard to mistake a blond behemoth built like an armor-piercing robot. Niedermann was running in his direction, waving his arms. Blomkvist slowed down. He slipped his hand into the outer pocket of his laptop case and took out the Colt 1911 Government he had found on Salander's desk. He stopped about five yards away from Niedermann and turned off the engine before opening the car door and stepping out.

"Thanks for stopping," Niedermann said, out of breath. "I had a . . . car accident. Can you give me a lift to town?"

He had a surprisingly high-pitched voice.

"Of course. I can see that you get to town," Blomkvist said. He pointed the gun at Niedermann. "Lie down on the ground."

There was no end to the tribulations Niedermann was having to suffer that night. He stared in puzzlement at Blomkvist.

Niedermann was not the least bit afraid of either the pistol or the man holding it. On the other hand, he had respect for weapons. He had lived with violence all his life. He assumed that if somebody pointed a gun at him, that person was prepared to use it. He squinted and tried to take stock of the man behind the pistol, but the headlights turned him into a shadowy figure. *Police? He didn't sound like a cop. Cops usually identified themselves. At least that's what they did in the movies.*

He weighed his chances. He knew that if he charged the man he could take away the gun. But the man sounded cold and was standing behind the car door. He would be hit by at least one, maybe two bullets. If he moved fast the man might miss, or at least not hit a vital organ, but even if he survived, the bullets would make it difficult and perhaps impossible for him to escape. It would be better to wait for a more suitable opportunity.

"LIE DOWN NOW!" Blomkvist yelled.

He moved the muzzle an inch and fired a round into the ditch.

"The next one hits your kneecap," Blomkvist said in a loud, clear voice of command.

Niedermann got down on his knees, blinded by the headlights.

"Who are you?" he said.

Blomkvist reached his other hand into the pocket in the car door and took out the flashlight he had bought at the gas station. He shone the beam into Niedermann's face.

"Hands behind your back," Blomkvist commanded. "And spread your legs."

He waited until Niedermann reluctantly obeyed the orders.

"I know who you are. If you even begin to do anything stupid I'll shoot you without warning. I'm aiming at your lung below your shoulder blade. You might be able to take me . . . but it'll cost you."

He put the flashlight on the ground and took off his belt and made a noose with it, exactly as he'd learned two decades earlier as a rifleman in Kiruna when he did his military service. He stood between the giant's legs, looped the noose around his arms and pulled it tight above the elbows. The mighty Niedermann was for all practical purposes helpless.

And then what? Blomkvist looked around. They were completely alone on a road in the dark. Paolo Roberto hadn't been exaggerating when he described Niedermann. The man was huge. The question was only why such a massive guy had come running in the middle of the night as if he were being chased by the Devil himself.

"I'm looking for Lisbeth Salander. I assume you met her."

Niedermann did not answer.

"Where is Lisbeth Salander?"

Niedermann gave him a peculiar look. He didn't understand what was happening to him on this strange night when everything seemed to be going wrong.

Blomkvist shrugged. He went back to the car, opened the trunk, and found a neatly coiled rope. He couldn't leave

Niedermann tied up in the middle of the road, so he looked around. Thirty yards further along the road he saw a traffic sign in the headlights. CAUTION: MOOSE CROSSING.

"Get up."

He put the muzzle of the gun against Niedermann's neck, led him to the sign, and forced him into the ditch. He told Niedermann to sit with his back against the pole. Niedermann hesitated.

"This is all quite simple," Blomkvist said. "You killed Dag Svensson and Mia Johansson. They were my friends. I'm not going to let you loose on the road, so either you sit here while I tie you or I'll shoot you in the kneecap. Your choice."

Niedermann sat. Blomkvist ran the tow rope around his neck and tied his head securely to the pole. Then he used fifty feet of rope to bind the giant fast around the torso and waist. He saved a length to tie his forearms to the pole, and finished off his handiwork with some real sailor's knots.

When he was finished, he asked again where Salander was. He got no reply, so he shrugged and left Niedermann there. It wasn't until he was back in the car that he felt the adrenaline flowing and realized what he had just done. The image of Johansson's face flickered before his eyes.

Blomkvist lit a cigarette and drank some water out of the bottle. He looked at the figure in the dark beneath the moose sign. Then he looked at the map and saw that he had about half a mile before the turnoff to Karl Axel Bodin's farm. He started the engine and drove past Niedermann.

He drove slowly past the turnoff with the sign to Gosseberga and parked next to a barn on a forest road a hundred yards further north. He took his pistol and turned his flashlight on. He found fresh tire tracks in the mud and decided that another car had been parked in that same place earlier, but he didn't stop to consider what that might mean. He walked back to the turnoff and shone light on the mailbox. P.O. BOX 192—K. A. BODIN. He continued along the road.

It was almost midnight when he saw the lights from Bodin's farmhouse. He stood still for several minutes but heard nothing other than the usual nighttime sounds. Instead of taking the road straight to the farm, he walked along the edge of the field and approached the building from the barn, stopping in the yard about a hundred feet from the house. His every nerve was on edge. The fact that Niedermann had been running away was reason enough to believe that some catastrophe had occurred here.

Suddenly he heard a sound. He spun around and dropped to one knee with his gun raised. It took him a few seconds to identify the source: one of the outbuildings. Somebody moaning. He moved quickly across the grass and stopped by the shed. Peering round the corner he could see a light inside.

He listened. Someone was moving around. Holding the pistol in front of him, he lifted the crossbar with his left hand, pulled open the door, and was confronted by a pair of terrified eyes in a blood-streaked face. He saw the axe on the floor.

"Holy shit," he said.

Then he saw the prosthesis.

Zalachenko.

Salander had definitely paid him a visit, but Blomkvist couldn't imagine what must have happened. He closed the door and replaced the crossbar.

With Zalachenko in the woodshed and Niedermann bound hand and foot beside the road to Sollebrunn, Blomkvist hurried across the courtyard to the farmhouse. It was possible that there was a third person who might yet be a danger, but the house seemed unoccupied, almost abandoned. Pointing his gun at the ground, he eased open the front door. He came into a dark hall and saw a rectangle of light from the kitchen. The

only sound was the ticking of a wall clock. When he reached
the door he saw Salander lying on the kitchen bench.

For a moment he stood as if petrified, staring at her
mangled body. He noticed that she was holding a pistol in her
hand, which hung loosely off the edge of the bench. He went
to her side and sank to his knees. He thought about how he
had found Svensson and Johansson and thought that she was
dead too. Then he saw a slight movement in her chest and
heard a feeble, wheezing breath.

He reached out his hand and carefully loosened the gun
from her grip. Suddenly her fist tightened around its butt. She
opened her eyes to two narrow slits and stared at him for many
long seconds. Her eyes were unfocused. Then he heard her
mutter in such a low voice that he could only with difficulty
catch the words.

Kalle Fucking Blomkvist.

She closed her eyes and let go of the gun. He put it on the
floor, took out his mobile, and dialled the number for emergency services.

AN EXCERPT FROM THE FORTHCOMING

The Girl Who Kicked the Hornet's Nest

by Stieg Larsson

Available from Alfred A. Knopf
Summer 2010

CHAPTER 1

Friday, April 8

Dr. Jonasson was woken by a nurse five minutes before the helicopter was expected to land. It was just before 1:30 in the morning.

"What?" he said, confused.

"Rescue Service helicopter coming in. Two patients. An injured man and a younger woman. The woman has a gunshot wound."

"All right," Jonasson said wearily.

Although he had slept for only half an hour, he felt groggy. He was on the night shift in the ER at Sahlgrenska hospital in Göteborg. It had been a strenuous evening.

By 12:30 the steady flow of emergency cases had eased off. He had made a round to check on the state of his patients and then gone back to the staff bedroom to try to rest for a while. He was on duty until 6:00, and seldom got the chance to sleep even if no emergency patients came in. But this time he had fallen asleep almost as soon as he turned out the light.

Jonasson saw lightning out over the sea. He knew that the helicopter was coming in in the nick of time. All of a sudden a heavy downpour lashed at the window. The storm had moved in over Göteborg.

He heard the sound of the chopper and watched as it banked through the storm squalls down toward the helipad. For a second he held his breath when the pilot seemed to have difficulty controlling the aircraft. Then it vanished from his field of vision and he heard the engine slowing to land. He took a hasty swallow of his tea and set down the cup.

Jonasson met the emergency team in the admissions area. The other doctor on duty took on the first patient who was wheeled in—an elderly man with his head bandaged, apparently with a serious wound to the face. Jonasson was left with the second patient, the woman who had been shot. He did a quick visual examination: it looked like she was a teenager, very dirty and bloody, and severely wounded. He lifted the blanket that the Rescue Service had wrapped around her body and saw that the wounds to her hip and shoulder were bandaged with duct tape, which he considered a pretty clever idea. The tape kept bacteria out and blood in. One bullet had entered her hip and gone straight through the muscle tissue. He gently raised her shoulder and located the entry wound in her back. There was no exit wound: the round was still inside her shoulder. He hoped it had not penetrated her lung, and since he did not see any blood in the woman's mouth he concluded that probably it had not.

"Radiology," he told the nurse in attendance. That was all he needed to say.

Then he cut away the bandage that the emergency team had wrapped around her skull. He froze when he saw another entry wound. The woman had been shot in the head, and there was no exit wound there either.

Dr. Jonasson paused for a second, looking down at the girl. He felt dejected. He often described his job as being like that of a goalkeeper. Every day people came to his place of work in varying conditions but with one objective: to get help.

Jonasson was the goalkeeper who stood between the patient

and Fonus Funeral Service. His job was to decide what to do. If he made the wrong decision, the patient might die or perhaps wake up disabled for life. Most often he made the right decision, because the vast majority of injured people had an obvious and specific problem. A stab wound to the lung or a crushing injury after a car crash were both particular and recognizable problems that could be dealt with. The survival of the patient depended on the extent of the damage and on Dr. Jonasson's skill.

There were two kinds of injury that he hated. One was a serious burn case, because no matter what measures he took the burns would almost inevitably result in a lifetime of suffering. The second was an injury to the brain.

The girl on the gurney could live with a piece of lead in her hip and a piece of lead in her shoulder. But a piece of lead inside her brain was a trauma of a whole different magnitude. He was suddenly aware of the nurse saying something.

"Sorry. I wasn't listening."

"It's her."

"What do you mean?"

"It's Lisbeth Salander. The girl they've been hunting for the past few weeks, for the triple murder in Stockholm."

Jonasson looked again at the unconscious patient's face. He realized at once that the nurse was right. He and the whole of Sweden had seen Salander's passport photograph on billboards outside every newspaper kiosk for weeks. And now the murderer herself had been shot, which was surely poetic justice of a sort.

But that was not his concern. His job was to save his patient's life, irrespective of whether she was a triple murderer or a Nobel Prize winner. Or both.

Then the efficient chaos, the same in every ER the world over, erupted. The staff on Jonasson's shift set about their appointed

tasks. Salander's clothes were cut away. A nurse reported on
her blood pressure—100/70—while the doctor put his stetho-
scope to her chest and listened to her heartbeat. It was surprisingly regular, but her breathing was not quite normal.

Jonasson did not hesitate to classify Salander's condition as
critical. The wounds in her shoulder and hip could wait until
later with a compress on each, or even with the duct tape that
some inspired soul had applied. What mattered was her head.
Jonasson ordered tomography with the new and improved CT
scanner that the hospital had lately acquired.

Dr. Jonasson had a view of medicine that was at times
unorthodox. He thought doctors often drew conclusions that
they could not substantiate. This meant that they gave up far
too easily; alternatively they spent too much time at the acute
stage trying to work out exactly what was wrong with the
patient so as to decide on the right treatment. This was correct
procedure, of course. The problem was that the patient was in
danger of dying while the doctor was still doing his thinking.

But Jonasson had never before had a patient with a bullet
in her skull. Most likely he would need a brain surgeon. He had
all the theoretical knowledge required to make an incursion
into the brain, but he did not by any means consider himself a
brain surgeon. He felt inadequate, but all of a sudden he realized that he might be luckier than he deserved. Before he
scrubbed up and put on his operating clothes he sent for the
nurse.

"There's an American professor from Boston working at
the Karolinska hospital in Stockholm. He happens to be in
Göteborg tonight, staying at the Radisson on Avenyn. He just
gave a lecture on brain research. He's a good friend of mine.
Could you get the number?"

While Jonasson was still waiting for the X-rays, the nurse
came back with the number of the Radisson. Jonasson picked
up the phone. The night porter at the Radisson was very reluctant to wake a guest at that time of night and Jonasson had to

come up with a few choice phrases about the critical nature of the situation before his call was put through.

"Good morning, Frank," Jonasson said when the call was finally answered. "It's Anders. Do you feel like coming over to Sahlgrenska to help out in a brain op?"

"Are you bullshitting me?" Dr. Frank Ellis had lived in Sweden for many years and was fluent in Swedish—albeit with an American accent—but when Jonasson spoke to him in Swedish, Ellis always replied in his mother tongue.

"The patient is in her mid-twenties. Entry wound, no exit."

"And she's alive?"

"Weak but regular pulse, less regular breathing, blood pressure one hundred over seventy. She also has a bullet wound in her shoulder and another in her hip. But I know how to handle those two."

"Sounds promising," Ellis said.

"Promising?"

"If somebody has a bullet in their head and they're still alive, that points to hopeful."

"I understand. . . . Frank, can you help me out?"

"I spent the evening in the company of good friends, Anders. I got to bed at 1:00 and no doubt I have an impressive blood alcohol content."

"I'll make the decisions and do the surgery. But I need somebody to tell me if I'm doing anything stupid. Even a falling-down drunk Professor Ellis is several classes better than I could ever be when it comes to assessing brain damage."

"OK, I'll come. But you're going to owe me one."

"I'll have a taxi waiting outside by the time you get down to the lobby. The driver will know where to drop you, and a nurse will be there to meet you and get you scrubbed in."

· · ·

Mikael Blomkvist looked up at the clock and saw that it was just after 3:00 in the morning. He was handcuffed and increasingly uncomfortable. He closed his eyes for a moment. He was dead tired but running on adrenaline. He opened them again and gave the policeman an angry glare. Inspector Thomas Paulsson had a shocked expression on his face. They were sitting at a kitchen table in a white farmhouse called Gosseberga, somewhere near Nossebro. Blomkvist had heard of the place for the first time less than twelve hours earlier.

There was no denying the disaster that had occurred.

"Imbecile," Blomkvist said.

"Now, you listen here—"

"Imbecile," Blomkvist said again. "I warned you he was dangerous, for Christ's sake. I told you that you would have to handle him like a live grenade. He's murdered at least three people with his bare hands and he's built like a tank. And you send a couple of village policemen to arrest him as if he were some Saturday-night drunk."

Blomkvist shut his eyes again, wondering what else could go wrong that night.

He had found Lisbeth Salander just after midnight. She was very badly wounded. He had sent for the police and the Rescue Service.

The only thing that had gone right was that he had persuaded them to send a helicopter to take the girl to Sahlgrenska hospital. He had given them a clear description of her injuries and the bullet wound in her head, and some bright spark at the Rescue Service got the message.

Even so, it had taken over half an hour for the Puma from the helicopter unit in Säve to arrive at the farmhouse. Blomkvist had gotten two cars out of the barn. He switched on their headlights to illuminate a landing area in the field in front of the house.

The helicopter crew and two paramedics had proceeded in a routine and professional manner. One of the medics tended to Salander while the other took care of Alexander Zalachenko, known locally as Karl Axel Bodin. Zalachenko was Salander's father and her worst enemy. He had tried to kill her, but he had failed. Blomkvist had found him in the woodshed at the farm with a nasty-looking gash—probably from an axe—in his face and some shattering damage to one of his legs which Blomkvist did not bother to investigate.

While he waited for the helicopter, he did what he could for Salander. He took a clean sheet from a linen cupboard and cut it up to make bandages. The blood had coagulated at the entry wound in her head, and he did not know whether he dared to put a bandage on it or not. In the end he fixed the fabric very loosely around her head, mostly so that the wound would not be exposed to bacteria or dirt. But he had stopped the bleeding from the wounds in her hip and shoulder in the simplest possible way. He had found a roll of duct tape and had used it to close the wounds. The medics remarked that this, in their experience, was a brand-new form of bandage. He had also bathed Salander's face with a wet towel and done his best to wipe off the dirt.

He had not gone back to the woodshed to tend to Zalachenko. He honestly did not give a damn about the man. But he did call Erika Berger, editor in chief of *Millennium* magazine, on his cell phone and told her the situation.

"Are you all right?" Berger asked him.

"I'm OK," Blomkvist said. "Lisbeth is the one who's in real danger."

"That poor girl," Berger said. "I read Björck's Säpo report this evening. How should I deal with it?"

"I don't have the energy to think that through right now," Blomkvist said. Security Police matters were going to have to wait until the next day, even if the report could help vindicate Lisbeth.

As he talked to Berger, he sat on the floor next to the bench and kept a watchful eye on Salander. He had taken off her shoes and her pants so that he could bandage the wound to her hip, and now his hand rested on the pants, which he had dropped on the floor next to the bench. There was something in one of the pockets. He pulled out a Palm Tungsten T3.

He frowned and looked long and hard at the hand-held computer. When he heard the approaching helicopter he stuffed it into the inside pocket of his jacket and then went through all her other pockets. He found another set of keys to the apartment in Mosebacke and a passport in the name of Irene Nesser. He put these swiftly into a side pocket of his laptop case.

The first patrol car from the station in Trollhättan arrived a few minutes after the helicopter landed. Next to arrive was Inspector Paulsson, who took charge immediately. Blomkvist began to explain what had happened. He very soon realized that Paulsson was a pompous, rigid drill-sergeant type. He did not seem to take in anything that Blomkvist said. It was when Paulsson arrived that things really started to go awry.

The only thing he seemed capable of grasping was that the badly damaged girl being cared for by the medics on the floor next to the kitchen bench was the triple murderer Lisbeth Salander. And above all, it was important that he make the arrest. Three times Paulsson had asked the urgently occupied medical orderly whether the girl could be arrested on the spot. In the end the orderly stood up and shouted at Paulsson to keep the hell out of his way.

Paulsson had then turned his attention to the wounded man in the woodshed, and Blomkvist heard the inspector report over his radio that Salander had evidently attempted to kill yet another person.

By now Blomkvist was so infuriated with Paulsson, who had obviously not paid attention to a word he had said, that he yelled at him to call Inspector Bublanski in Stockholm without delay. Blomkvist had even taken out his cell phone and offered to dial the number for him, but Paulsson was not interested.

Blomkvist then made two mistakes.

First, he patiently but firmly explained that the man who had committed the murders in Stockholm was Ronald Niedermann, who was built like a heavily armoured robot and suffered from a disease called congenital analgesia, and who at that moment was sitting in a ditch on the road to Nossebro tied to a traffic sign. Blomkvist told Paulsson exactly where Niedermann was to be found, and urged him to send a platoon armed with automatic weapons to pick him up. Paulsson finally asked how Niedermann had come to be in that ditch, and Blomkvist freely admitted that he himself had put him there, and had managed only by holding a gun on him the whole time.

"Assault with a deadly weapon," was Paulsson's immediate response.

At this point Blomkvist should have realized that Paulsson was dangerously stupid. He should have called Bublanski himself and asked him to intervene, to bring some clarity to the fog in which Paulsson was apparently enveloped. Instead he made his second mistake: he offered to hand over the weapon he had in his jacket pocket—the Colt .45 1911 Government model that he had found earlier that day at Salander's apartment in Stockholm. It was the weapon he had used to disarm and disable Niedermann—not a straightforward matter with that giant of a man.

After which Paulsson swiftly arrested Blomkvist for possession of an illegal weapon. He then ordered his two officers to drive over to the Nossebro road. They were to find out if there was any truth to Blomkvist's story that a man was sitting in a ditch there, tied to a MOOSE CROSSING sign. If this was the case, the officers were to handcuff the person in question and bring him to the farm in Gosseberga.

Blomkvist had objected at once, pointing out that Niedermann was not a man who could be arrested and handcuffed just like that: he was a maniacal killer, for God's sake. When Blomkvist's objections were ignored by Paulsson, the exhaustion of the day made him reckless. He told Paulsson he was an incompetent fool and yelled at him that the officers should fucking forget about untying Niedermann until they had called for backup. As a result of this outburst, he was hand-cuffed and pushed into the back seat of Paulsson's car. Cursing, he watched as the policemen drove off in their patrol car. The only glimmer of light in the darkness was that Salander had been carried to the helicopter, which was even now disappear-ing over the treetops in the direction of Göteborg. Blomkvist felt utterly helpless: he could only hope that she would be given the very best care. She was going to need it, or she would die.

The hugely anticipated final
installment of the trilogy by

Stieg Larsson

The Girl Who Kicked
the Hornet's Nest

Once upon a time,
she was a victim.

Now, Lisbeth Salander
is ready to fight back.

Now available in hardcover from Knopf
$27.95 • 576 pages • 978-0-307-26999-7

Please visit www.stieglarsson.net

ALSO BY STIEG LARSSON

*"Wildly suspenseful . . . an intelligent, ingeniously plotted,
utterly engrossing thriller."*
—The Washington Post

THE GIRL WITH THE DRAGON TATTOO

An international publishing sensation, *The Girl with the
Dragon Tattoo* combines murder mystery, family saga,
love story, and financial intrigue into one satisfyingly complex and entertainingly atmospheric novel. Harriet Vanger,
a scion of one of Sweden's wealthiest families disappeared
over forty years ago. All these years later, her aged uncle
continues to seek the truth. He hires Mikael Blomkvist, a
crusading journalist recently trapped by a libel conviction,
to investigate. He is aided by the pierced and tattooed punk
prodigy Lisbeth Salander. Together they tap into a vein of
unfathomable iniquity and astonishing corruption.

Crime Fiction/978-0-307-47347-9 (mass market)
978-0-307-45454-6 (trade paperback)

VINTAGE CRIME/BLACK LIZARD
Available at your local bookstore, or visit
www.randomhouse.com

Meet with Interesting People
Enjoy Stimulating Conversation
Discover Wonderful Books